MEMO FROM DAVID O. SELZNICK

MEMO
from
DAVID O. SELZNICK

———————————•———————————

SELECTED AND EDITED BY RUDY BEHLMER

With an Introduction by S. N. Behrman

The Viking Press / *New York*

MEMO FROM DAVID O. SELZNICK, edited by Rudy Behlmer
Copyright © 1972 by Selznick Properties, Ltd.
All rights reserved
First published in 1972 by The Viking Press, Inc.
625 Madison Avenue, New York, N.Y. 10022
Published simultaneously in Canada by
The Macmillan Company of Canada Limited
SBN 670–46766–9
Library of Congress catalog card number: 72–75743
Printed in U.S.A. by The Haddon Craftsmen, Inc.

ACKNOWLEDGMENTS

Leslie Frewin Publishers Limited, London: From *Light of A Star*
by Gwen Robyns. Reprinted by permission.
Hamish Hamilton Ltd.: From *Vivien Leigh: A Bouquet*, Copyright © 1969
by Alan Dent (Hamish Hamilton, London).

Acknowledgments

For their various courtesies and generous cooperation,
the editor wishes to thank the following individuals
and organizations (in alphabetical order).

Academy of Motion Picture Arts and Sciences Library:
   Mildred Simpson and Staff
Bekins Business Records Center: Jim Boston
Lenora Cole
Merian C. Cooper
George Cukor
Shirley Harden Diaz
Margaret Hodgson
Sally Hope
David Impastato
Arthur P. Jacobs
Max Lamb
Marjorie MacDougall
Clifford McCarty
Metro-Goldwyn-Mayer:
   James T. Aubrey, Jr.
   Roger L. Mayer
   Florence Warner
Daniel T. O'Shea
RKO Radio Pictures: Vernon Harbin
Irene Mayer Selznick
Robert Whitehead
John Hay Whitney
And particular thanks to Daniel Selznick, who virtually made this
project possible, and who proved in all ways to be an enthusiastic and
supportive mentor.

Most of the photographs reproduced in this book are from the Selznick
files, or were acquired through the courtesy of members of the Selznick
family. Other still pictures came from the following sources:

Gunnard Nelson
Kenneth G. Lawrence
Bennett's Book Store
Ray Stuart

Grateful acknowledgment is given to the following companies
for permission to use stills from their films:

Metro-Goldwyn-Mayer
Paramount Pictures
Republic Pictures
RKO Radio Pictures
Twentieth Century-Fox
Warner Bros.

Contents

Illustrations follow pages 38, 134, and 326.

Introduction

DAVID O. SELZNICK IN PERSON

by S. N. Behrman

One day in the winter of 1947, my agent, Harold Freedman, called me
to say that David Selznick wanted me to work on the filmscript of
Robert Nathan's novel *Portrait of Jennie*. Freedman asked me to read
the novel, as Selznick was going to call me to discuss it.

I read the book at once. It is gracefully written and I appreciated
the style, but it encountered at once an almost congenital prejudice
of my own: it was a fantasy, a literary form I have never cared for. (I
think this prejudice started when I was a boy in Worcester, Massachusetts, and ushering in the Worcester Theatre. During a performance
of *Peter Pan*, the ineffable Maude Adams rushed to the footlights and
implored me to believe in fairies. I believed in Maude Adams, but
somehow, I resisted the larger assignment.) Also, I kept stumbling on
discrepancies in the *Jennie* narrative.

Selznick's call came late that night. My notes were ready. I brought
up various points. Selznick managed to defend some of the discrepancies, but several stumped him. "Why don't you ask the author?" I said.
"He's out there in California." "I did," said David, "but he didn't
know." Finally David said, "Let's make a deal. I'm coming to New
York. We'll argue it out. If you persuade me, I won't make the film.
If I persuade you, you'll write it." This seemed eminently fair—I
agreed.

Selznick arrived several days later, with two secretaries. He was
preparing a memorandum to meet my queries. We made a date to
meet at ten o'clock that night in his suite at the Sherry-Netherland

Hotel. A wan and exhausted secretary made her exit just as I came in. She had been working since early morning.

David was in wonderful form. To read his critical memos does not altogether convey the essence of his personality. Even though he drove the directors who worked for him crazy, in person he was genial, affectionate, and warm.

We got to talking about the story. The stubborn discrepancies remained; David could not dissipate them. I did not think it necessary to tell him that I could not go to work on it with these jagged points unresolved. Nor did I remind him of his promise not to make the film if he could not persuade me. The discussion went on and on. It got to be 3 a.m. David, I knew, often worked all night on problems in his films, but I said I had to go to bed. I headed for a closet where I had left my hat and coat. David shouted a warning.

"Don't go in there," he cried. "There's a dead secretary in there!" The conference ended in laughter. Many conferences with David ended in laughter.

The whole Selznick family had limitless energy. The Selznick boys, Myron and David, had sniffed the smell of celluloid from infancy. Their father, Lewis J. Selznick, was one of the pioneer film producers who, at his apogee, could call himself a film magnate. Myron was a maverick character who refused to be swamped by the elegancies of upper-class Hollywood. When he became a leading agent, he set his own disreputable style and was the pet of many writers, even among those who were not his clients.

David's lifelong ambition was to produce on his own. There is a moving letter here to his father-in-law, Louis B. Mayer, asking to be released from his MGM contract. David had been placed in a high-salaried position at Metro after he married Mayer's daughter, Irene. The marriage was a happy one for many years, but David's sensitivity to the charges of nepotism was acute. These charges were rife; they gave birth to the mocking phrase, "the son-in-law also rises." David finally left Metro and his $4000 a week job and raised the capital to start Selznick International Films.

With all that has been written about Hollywood, I don't know where you can get the play-by-play account of what is actually involved in producing a major film that you can get from this book. The chapter on *Gone With the Wind,* perhaps the most popular picture ever made, is a manual of vicissitude and hazard: the casting problems, the script problems, the directorial problems. Myriad insolubilities seem increasingly impossible until the final result is achieved.

In a memorial film prepared after Selznick's death, Alfred Hitchcock recalls, with affectionate humor, the impact on him of the first memorandum he ever received from David. He had begun to read it when he went to work on *Rebecca* in 1939 but, he confesses with a happy grin, he hasn't quite got through it yet.

It occurred to me, while reading this book, that for Selznick, for a creative producer, all the memos, letters, telegrams he employed served the same purpose that notebooks serve for a creative writer. From day to day, from hour to hour, the minutiae of the creative process are recorded—and revealed—here. All his inner thoughts, his convictions, his vacillations, his aspirations are expressed in these memoranda. They *are* his notebooks.

There is a series of letters in this compilation from David to his staff, imploring them to find a name for Phylis Walker. The result of this mass concentration, to which David contributed, was Jennifer Jones. That name satisfied David: it was democratic and yet it had piquancy. He began to have an obsessive concern about every aspect—clothes, lighting, script changes—of Jennifer's films, even those he didn't produce. "It's a Pygmalion relationship," people said, classifying it with other instances of Selznick's interest in a budding film career Ingrid Bergman, for example. Whatever relationship David had with anybody, providing he or she was in the film business, was a Pygmalion relationship.

David and I never got together on *Portrait of Jennie,* but I had already done two films for him: *A Tale of Two Cities* with Ronald Colman, and *Anna Karenina* with Greta Garbo. He knew these two books, it would appear, by heart. He couldn't bear to leave out a felicitous phrase. He would be after me, every minute, to somehow get it in. (It will be apparent that he did as much for Margaret Mitchell and Daphne du Maurier as he did for Dickens and Tolstoi.)

The most venerated of the producers in Hollywood at that time was Irving Thalberg, a veneration in which Selznick shared. I was working for Thalberg just before he died. He was charming, gifted, and reserved—but I never got the kick from him that I got from David Selznick. David was not reserved; he was outgoing. He was tremendously courageous, farsighted, and unsparing of himself when it came to pursuing the inner dictate of his own vision. It was his film: he could allow nothing, no one, to take it away from him. He was the sole guardian of his own standards.

Editor's Foreword

"The difference between myself and other producers," David O. Selznick told Art Buchwald in 1957, "is I am interested in the thousands and thousands of details that go into the making of a film. It is the sum total of all these things that either makes a great picture or destroys it. The way I see it, my function is to be responsible for everything."

That dictum permeates the thirty-six years of memorandums, letters, teletypes, and telegrams published here. Selznick loved the actual process of making movies and was fascinated by all the details inherent in that unique combination of art, craft, and industry.

Although the making of professional motion pictures is necessarily a collaborative process, one man frequently dominates the conception and/or the execution of a film. The major force behind films in Hollywood's heyday, however, was generally the character of each motion-picture studio: connoisseurs had little trouble in differentiating the product of, say, Metro-Goldwyn-Mayer, Warner Bros., and Twentieth Century-Fox. The style of each company was based on front-office attitudes regarding the kind of material it was felt would have the best commercial potential, how much money was behind the company, the type of players under contract, formulas proven successful in the past, and the resulting chemistry brought about by the interaction of key people. Independent producers functioned, as they do today, in various ways: as entrepreneurs, guiding hands, promoters, packagers, or, as in the case of David O. Selznick, by "being responsible for everything."

Before he founded his own company, Selznick International, Selznick had been through the studio systems of the time in different capacities. He was completely familiar with what it was like to start one film every Monday and ship another film every Friday for the

Paramount assembly line; he went through the rigors of being in charge of the entire feature output of the relatively modest RKO Radio Studios for a short time during the Depression in the early 1930s, and he knew the luxury and security of operating his own unit at opulent Metro-Goldwyn-Mayer.

Long before Selznick produced *Gone With the Wind,* the most popular and profitable film to date, his over-all record was quite remarkable. Most commercial films of bygone eras today seem dated, but many of Selznick's personally produced pictures remain exceptional examples of time-defying film-making.

In 1935, Merian C. Cooper—himself a tough and difficult executive, producer, and director—wrote to financier Frank Vanderlip about a rumored reorganization of the production end of Paramount Pictures:

> . . . In working with Selznick, his ability to size up a situation quickly and accurately and, once having arrived at a decision, his unshakeable courage in carrying it through, aroused my admiration. As to his character: I have watched him for years steer a clean course through the trickeries of a not too rigidly correct business. His business word is unimpeachable.
>
> Certainly Selznick has his faults. He is somewhat egotistical; he is occasionally very quick-tempered; and sometimes is carried too far with his ideas by the natural enthusiasm of youth. But, believe me, I can say with all sincerity that if I had to back a picture company with my personal money, he is the one man out here of whom I would feel confident.

William Cameron Menzies, the eminent production designer and art director who worked under Selznick on *Gone With the Wind* and three other films, once told him that his greatest gift was an ability to make people transcend themselves. Many of his employees were intensely loyal and stayed with him for years despite his reputation for being an extraordinarily difficult person to work for. Even directors George Cukor and King Vidor remained good friends with Selznick after disagreements culminating in their leaving *Gone With the Wind* and *Duel in the Sun,* respectively, during production.

Selznick was loyal to those who served him well. He also was scrupulous about giving credit—on the screen and otherwise—to those individuals who contributed strongly to his enterprises. Such distinguished writers, for example, as Robert E. Sherwood, S. N. Behrman, Dorothy Parker, Sidney Howard, Ben Hecht, Hugh Walpole, and Gene Fowler, among others, worked on Selznick's finest adaptations and originals for the screen. A wide range of directors who were known as the dominant force behind their own films worked for and with Selznick: Alfred Hitchcock, King Vidor, George Cukor, William Wellman, Clarence Brown, and others. For Selznick's idea of collaboration was to hire first-rate talent, extract certain attributes from that talent, and mold them to suit his vision.

Not surprisingly, Selznick has been described as overbearing, egocentric, aggressive, exhausting, and impossible. Correspondent Lloyd Shearer once wrote that Selznick gave the impression that he stormed through life demanding to see the manager—and that, when the manager appeared, Selznick would hand him a twenty-page memo announcing his instant banishment to Elba.

Val Lewton, Selznick's long-time West Coast Story Editor, told him in 1940 that employing a writer for the adaptation of a book was money thrown down the drain, inasmuch as Selznick did, possibly without realizing it, eighty per cent of the work himself, and the writer, however good he is, became merely a super-secretary.

As the years went by, Selznick became more and more dominant in all phases of the shaping of his films—particularly in the areas of writing and direction. Although he was always a strong collaborator on his scripts, in the 1940s he began to do all of the writing on many of his films himself. In earlier years, he would discuss in advance with the director the interpretation and physical approach to the shooting of a scene, but he would not be constantly hovering about the set as he did later in the 1940s and 1950s. Director Charles Vidor, during the filming of *A Farewell to Arms* in 1957, became exasperated with Selznick in this respect and wrote him at the time, "It is remarkable how you blame everybody but yourself for the snail's pace progress of this picture. . . . Your constant nagging about the photography in general . . . your eternal criticism . . . interfering in the middle of lighting about shadows and lights . . . you don't realize that after all these years you've been in the business, you are still not a cameraman. . . . Your last-minute changes and interferences with preparation cannot but affect my speed."

Selznick told the press in 1957, "My conception of the producer's role is that it is similar to being the conductor of an orchestra. The conductor oversees every detail and interprets as he sees fit. I am a perfectionist. My sights are set high. But I've found that most people have to be forced into raising their sights."

As he states in the introductory section on memorandum-writing compiled for this book, Selznick dictated his legendary memos for various reasons. The often lengthy communications were usually given at night, and sometimes until dawn—often in a hoarse voice (which stopped speaking only long enough to light cigarettes)—to secretaries who worked in shifts; they were typed on yellow paper and carried the inscription, "Dictated but not read by David O. Selznick." Many of them dealt with routine, day-to-day matters and would have little or no interest to anyone now save the most ardent of film scholars, but that still leaves a good number that are exceptionally absorbing. The breadth and range of the memos make it clear that Selznick had an uncanny ability to concentrate on a multitude of details pertaining to various concurrent projects.

Many of Selznick's elongated dictations have been pruned—in some instances considerably—for this volume. Selznick rarely exercised the task of rewriting (which presumably would involve cutting); he dictated in a stream-of-consciousness style, and consequently his memos are often redundant. Also, minor subjects and incidental matters often were included in a memo devoted to a major topic. Still, the lengthy discourses work to advantage in certain instances, and here and there have been let alone.

At times the memos included in this collection were not sent, and are so noted. Selznick did have second thoughts, and often when he and Irene Mayer were married, she would convince him to halt the delivery of an outraged memorandum and urge him to reconsider it in the morning light. Also, his chief aide, Daniel T. O'Shea, would frequently stall the sending of a memo for an indefinite period after Selznick had shown it to him for counsel.

I asked Selznick about his memos one evening in 1963 while preparing a magazine article about him, and he replied that he had a carbon copy in his files of every memo he had ever written—a somewhat exaggerated declaration, as I was to discover later. He was considering putting some of them into a book to be called *Memo Strikes Back*, and inquired whether I would be interested in working on such a compilation in the indefinite future. I told him I would indeed be interested. And that was that.

At the time of his death two years later, I wondered about all those memos and what, if anything, was happening with them.

Four and a half more years were to go by before the subject came up again. The occasion was a luncheon with Selznick's younger son, Daniel, whom I was meeting for the first time at Universal Studios. Danny had remembered the article I had written about his father, and much to my astonishment, he later asked me if I would be interested in creating a book from his father's memos.

After expressing interest, I'll never forget walking into the building in which the files are stored for the first time and being confronted by approximately two thousand file boxes! There were three factors preventing me from exiting gracefully at that moment: one, the material was reasonably well organized; two, I had coincidentally just finished taking a speed-reading course; and three, an overwhelming curiosity about the contents of each one of those two thousand boxes superseded everything else.

So, I started carting boxes home containing correspondence on *Rebecca, A Star Is Born,* and *The Prisoner of Zenda* as a starter, "to see how things would work out." Within a week, I was hopelessly hooked; and within two months, I took a deep breath, steeled myself, and plunged into the copious *Gone With the Wind* papers. For the next two and a half years, life became a montage of memos.

The resulting book reduced the contents of those two thousand file boxes to the equivalent of one or two boxes at the most.

Danny Selznick proved to have some of his father's passion for perfection by insisting on exhausting all possibilities (as well as the editor). His editorial participation was invaluable.

It could be argued that this compilation presents a rather one-sided case, with no opportunity for the several victims of Selznick's unhappiness or, in some instances, wrath, to offer rebuttals or countercharges. Also, since the papers selected represent only a small fraction of the total number in the files, one might say that the selection and editing are loaded and pro-Selznick, with unflattering glimpses left on the cutting-room floor (or, in this case, the business-records storage floor). I have tried, while selecting from the large collection, to show all sides of the man's professional approach. Selznick certainly made his share of mistakes—such as turning down the opportunity to make *Stagecoach* with John Ford directing, and, on another occasion, not signing Gregory Peck on the basis of an early screen test. Selznick was at times pontificating and overly fussy; but he was also brilliant, knowledgeable, tasteful, painstaking, and possessed by what he was doing.

My aim was to include representative written samplings dealing with a good many of Selznick's films, but there were great gaps in the files—particularly in the important RKO and MGM period (1931–1935). These studios were kind enough to let me check what they had, but records dating so far back are spotty or no longer there. In other instances, the Selznick files on a specific film or person were available in the vaults, but they contained nothing beyond communications of routine, ephemeral interest.

There are no extensive files for films produced by Selznick prior to 1936—just occasional, stray correspondence. Finding just one memo on some early and important films proved to be a major undertaking, which more often than not yielded little or nothing.

Beginning with the formation of Selznick International in late 1935, the files are reasonably complete, and of course this is reflected in the book. The papers of Selznick's older brother, Myron—who died in 1944—were destroyed several years ago. Certainly these records would have contained some interesting correspondence between the two brothers.

Many times, pertinent matters relating to one film would crop up in the files of other films. I have included whichever memo, in my opinion, presented the situation better, thereby letting the films selected speak for all. There were a few instances in which communications, presumably classified as highly confidential, were no longer—if they ever were—in the files. Lastly, work was often discussed in conferences, screening and editing rooms, on the telephone, etc., but not committed to paper. So if you miss a memo, for example, on the initial testing of Katharine Hepburn at RKO, or one on behind-the-scenes activity during the evolution of *King Kong, Viva Villa!, Nothing Sacred,* or something regarding Miklos Rozsa's fine score for *Spellbound* —so do I.

The story of the creation of each of Selznick's films could fill its own book, but I have chosen to let Selznick's magnum opus, *Gone With the Wind*, serve as the in-depth example.

Although Selznick did not produce *Tender Is the Night*, which is dealt with extensively toward the close of this book, he originated the project and worked on the script before selling the package to Twentieth Century-Fox. Since he did not live to produce another picture, his involvement with this, in effect, his last film, is significant. He had an intense love for the F. Scott Fitzgerald novel and nurtured the project over the years. Unable to personally produce the film for various reasons, his outpouring of memos to various executives and creative people at Fox distills his cumulative convictions of what the functions of the creative producer really are.

Since Selznick rarely proofread his dictated memos, I have corrected occasional misspellings and typographical errors. The word "stop," sometimes used to indicate a period in early telegrams, has been deleted, and some punctuation marks have been added to all teletyped material to aid in readability.

I decided, in the cases of *Gone With the Wind, Rebecca,* and *Intermezzo,* among others, to let Selznick's interest in a given project develop from beginning to end, rather than adhere to the over-all chronology used elsewhere.

A Cast of Characters at the conclusion of the book provides information on the principal persons mentioned in the text, who are more briefly identified throughout in footnotes and brackets.

In addition to presenting insights into the professional life of one of the major figures in the history of motion pictures, the memos reveal the creative development of some of the most highly regarded films of their time, and they show relatively unknown performers becoming stars. The memos take us behind the scenes and allow us to be privy to the inspirations, doubts, decisions, and turmoils that accompany the making of a film, while reflecting the varying conditions and evolution of the film industry as a whole, as well as the differences between operations at several of the studios.

Anyone interested in the making of films can only be glad that Selznick saved his carbons, for it is one thing to read or listen to reminiscences of someone noted in his field selectively recalling what happened many years before—with all the attendant inaccuracies and imbalances—but it is quite another when one is able to assess film history recorded at the time the events occurred, with the drama of the moment intact.

—RUDY BEHLMER

February, 1972

Selznick on
the Writing of Memos

(A blending by the editor of various notes dictated on the subject through the years by Selznick.)

My memo-writing probably had its beginning through my working with my father,[1] who was terribly impatient of interviews with people. I remember hearing him complain many times that most people took fifteen minutes to say what they should say in ten seconds. As a result of his phobia on this subject he did an enormous amount of dictation himself.

Even when I worked with and for him, I had a dread of wasting his time by taking too long to say something about business; and I also found that between his impatience, and the interruptions of telephone calls, executives coming in and out of his office, etc., it was easier for me to say exactly what I wanted to say to him on paper. Furthermore, I then fancied myself as an embryonic writer, and loved nothing so much as writing.

My father had given me a typewriter when I was still in grammar school, on which I had taught myself to type out all my homework. I found, when I got along in school and at the Columbia University extension courses, that I was much more critical of writing if it was in cold type. Somehow I was much more tolerant of my own work when it was written by hand than when it was typed. Furthermore—and I honestly think this is true of most people—I found that there was a

[1] Lewis J. Selznick, pioneer film producer, who left his native Russia at the age of twelve and came to the United States via England. A successful jeweler, he eventually entered films, appointing himself General Manager of Universal Pictures (1912). He later coorganized World Films, founded Lewis J. Selznick Enterprises Inc., Select Pictures Corporation, and Selznick Pictures Corporation, all during the silent era.

tendency not to read back things that I had written in hand, and therefore not to do as much rewriting as was indicated when the same pieces were put into cold type. . . . The fact that I wrote things out by hand first meant that it necessarily went through one rewrite as I started to type it.

From the habit of writing memos to my father, a natural development was writing memos to other people in the office. There was also another factor: I was very young when I held important executive jobs with my father. While I was still at school at the age of seventeen, I was supervising a large advertising and publicity department after school hours. I was self-conscious about my youth and in giving orders and expressing myself verbally, but dictating permitted me to hide behind the front of what I liked to think were impressive memos.

When I went to work for Harry Rapf[2] at MGM in 1926, it was impossible for me to have as much contact with the executives of that big plant as I wanted to have in order to make an impression. Furthermore, I had already learned that I could sell an idea much better in written form than I could verbally—or at least so I thought—although subsequently I have been accused of being a great salesman verbally. Accordingly, an easy answer was the flooding of the MGM executives with probably the first memos that they had ever received from anybody working for them in the executive department. I honestly don't remember in all the time I was working at MGM—or for that matter, in most of the time I worked in most other studios (except Paramount) —seeing a single memo written from one executive to another when these executives were in offices anywhere near. Even when the executives were three thousand miles apart, they resorted to the telephone. Secretaries were mostly receptionists and guardswomen placed to keep people away.

When I went to Paramount I found, to my joy, a memo paradise. Ben Schulberg,[3] for reasons unknown to me, simply doted on memos. Every day every associate producer and other executives in the studio were deluged with notes from him. Naturally I seized the opportunity to impress him by replying in kind, and by making my suggestions in memo form. I say Ben doted on memos, but I think I finally cured him to an extent, because he finally screamed "Uncle!" and asked me if there weren't a lot of things I wrote him about that I couldn't take up with him personally. Even this had its benefits, as it secured time for

[2]MGM Associate Producer.
[3]General Manager of Paramount's West Coast production.

me with him beyond what was granted to other executives, and this gave me the chance to sell many of my ideas that led to my rapid rise at Paramount. Of course, by this time the memo habit was so firmly formed in me that I don't suppose I'll ever lose it.

Incidentally, I dictate easily; the memos flow right along. However, I don't read them after I dictate them, and it's possible things that would sound all right verbally sound tough in print.

I dictate as much as I do for other reasons besides those mentioned. To begin with, I find that I can think a thing through to its conclusion more clearly if I can express my views completely without interruptions and without argument. Two, I like to have my views a matter of record and reference. Three, I find that when a man receives written instructions he is much more likely to follow them, and certainly much more likely to follow them exactly, than if he receives them verbally. Particularly, it eliminates dependence on his memory and argument as to what was said *exactly*. Furthermore, it is an advantage in arguments to be able to refer to the written communications instead of depending on the memory of two people. I believe in this so much that I often send memos to people who are going to see me half an hour later, which I also find is an advantage from *their* standpoint, because it gives them the opportunity to thoroughly digest my viewpoint, and to think up their answers and counterarguments before they see me, instead of after they see me. Among other things this saves additional conferences.

I can tell you pretty well the punctuating habits of the writers that I read as a child. As a result of this study of punctuation, I still find myself actually reading the punctuation marks to this day, and as a further result, I continually insult my secretaries by dictating punctuation. Similarly, Dickens, who was above all writers my childhood god, so impressed me with his torturous sentences and his long-windedness that the sentences in my memos are probably two or three times as long as they should be for these modern times. (Maybe that also accounts in some way for the length of my pictures! But if this latter point is true, I'm not sorry because I think some of the quality people have found in my pictures is due to my insistence on detail, and in taking the time and footage to fully develop scenes of both dialogue and of characterizations and of plot alike.)

An anecdote in connection with the fact that I am undoubtedly a suppressed writer is the offer Ben Hecht made to me. Ben did two scripts for me at $5000 weekly. When the job was finished, he offered me $5000 weekly to collaborate with him on plays. Robert Sherwood, the Pulitzer Prize winner, has told everybody in New York that I did the script of *Rebecca* for which he was so widely acclaimed.

The only thing I have ever had in print was a verse in *Good Housekeeping* for which I got $5.00.[4]

---

[4]The verse appeared in the June 1941 issue. It was written by Selznick to commemorate the birth of his first son nine years earlier.

> So we are three:
>   My darling, and my darling's darling,
>   And, humbly, me. . . .
> And where, before,
> We thought there were no more
> To add to Happiness,
> 'Tis only now we know
> What Life . . . and Love . . . are for.

Editor's Note

The autobiographical introductions at the beginning of each section of the book have been spliced together from portions of memos or letters Selznick wrote over the years—mostly to writers who were working on articles about him. For example, Selznick sent reminiscences on paper to Quentin Reynolds to help him compose a two-part piece called "The Amazing Selznicks" for *Collier's* in 1938. Again, in 1942, when Alva Johnston was writing "The Great Dictater" (a marvelous title) about Selznick for *The Saturday Evening Post,* it inspired letters from Selznick to Johnston and a number of memos to Whitney Bolton, Selznick's Director of Advertising and Publicity, bringing up biographical points to pass on to Johnston. Other bridging sentences or paragraphs were taken from memos having primarily to do with something else, but which, in order to emphasize a point, included a parallel with an incident from the past. Parts of a *Collier's* piece by Selznick, "Discovering the New Ones" (1941), were extracted; and portions of text were blended from an article written by Selznick for the *Los Angeles Times,* December 1, 1957, titled "Why I Started Making Movies Again." A good deal of the introductory material was lifted from notes and transcripts sent by Selznick to Henry Hart and myself in connection with our Selznick career article for the June-July 1963 issue of *Films in Review.*

The only insertions I have made in the autobiographical introductory sections are dates, full names or titles of people, companies, institutions, or films—to serve as a frame of reference—and an occasional word or very short phrase of connective tissue when absolutely necessary. These minor inserts have not been bracketed in order to preserve a readable flow.

THE EARLY YEARS
MGM (1926–1928)

I HAVE NO MIDDLE NAME. I briefly used my mother's maiden name, Sachs. I had an uncle, whom I greatly disliked, who was also named David Selznick, so in order to avoid the growing confusion between the two of us, I decided to take a middle initial and went through the alphabet to find one that seemed to me to give the best punctuation, and decided on "O."

My father gave lectures, as far back as I can remember, on the wonders of Dickens, Tolstoi, etc. When most people were reading Frank Merriwell—which, believe it or not, I never read—I was reading David Copperfield and Anna Karenina. And if most adults found it slow going on the classics, imagine how slow it would be for a child trying to absorb them so he could discuss them intelligently with his father.

On top of this, my father was very proud of my "compositions," even when I was extremely young, and this encouraged me to try to improve my vocabulary. So I found myself night after night with a dictionary by my side, laboriously looking up all the words in the classics that I couldn't understand. This process was so slow that naturally the scenes engraved themselves indelibly on my mind. I found myself going over them three or four times; and from this came, I like to believe, an understanding and appreciation of style. I can to this day tell the exact details of scenes from books that I read when I must have been somewhere between ten and twelve years old.

All this naturally limited the amount of my reading, but I found that I developed a certain pride in what I read, and a certain intimate acquaintance with the characters in the comparatively small number of books that I read.

I went to public schools in Brooklyn and Manhattan, and in the seventh grade I started a school paper for which I was the sole editor and printer—by means of my typewriter. Each evening when I had finished my homework I would write out enough news to fill a full page, type it out, headlines and all, and illustrate it carefully with little sketches and pictures that I would clip out of magazines. The paper was tacked up on the bulletin board.

It is my pride and joy, though not exactly any sign of my erudition, that I graduated second in a class that must have numbered at least one hundred and fifty or two hundred; and I might also add that anything I ever learned in school, I learned in the public schools of New York City.

I spent two and a half years at the Hamilton Institute for Boys, with just the kind of life I wanted, for the school let out at two-thirty, and by three o'clock I was in either my father's office or at his studio in Fort Lee. The days I was in the office I would ride home regularly every night with my father, discussing the picture business, and learning a great deal that was useful to me later on.

I was trained by my father in motion-picture distribution and finance and advertising, his idea being that my older brother, Myron, would take care of the producing end and I would take care of the other things. The experience I gained in those areas served me mightily. It is unfortunately true that there are very few producers in the picture business who know what they ought to know about domestic and foreign distribution, merchandising and advertising, and finance. I don't think there is any branch or any phase of the picture business in which I have not worked, except as a cutter.

I was, after school hours, in charge of a monumental publicity and advertising department: my father was the industry's biggest advertiser; in fact, the first big advertiser of the business. He was the first man to advertise in national magazines. He had at one time eight huge electric signs on Broadway. I was in charge of the department, personally designing a great deal of the advertising and most of the posters. I took care of all the accessories, created trailers and things of that sort.

Then I became the editor of the Selznick Newsreel, *still after school hours. This was a twice-a-week newsreel. I had a very tiny budget and I had to get out the newsreel with a staff of only five cameramen. To fill in on footage that I needed, I conceived the idea of having approximately one minute a week of captions carrying Will Rogers's comments on the national scene, as I had heard him speak them at the Ziegfeld Follies. I sold Rogers the idea of what great publicity this would be for him—as indeed it turned out to be—for it was the beginning of him on the national scene, and his comments were subsequently syndicated, leading to his becoming a national figure. My arrangement with Rogers did not call for any monetary payment in view of the publicity value to him, until one day he demanded $100 weekly. Since this was still cheaper than any other footage I could get, I agreed to it.*

Then I was put into sales, and no exhibition contract was considered approved without my signature, so I had to sign thousands of exhibition contracts, on which my father would cross-examine me at night, so I had to know what I was reading.

I used to be embarrassed when I would think of the way my father used to drag Myron or myself or both of us to the most important kind of business meetings when we were kids in short trousers. As I grew older, it was one of my fondest memories of him, and, I think, one of the most touching of his many demonstrations of overwhelming devotion to and pride in us. I remember at the age of ten or eleven being dragged down to a big Long Island estate where I sat on the porch while my father organized the World Film Company—with my father occasionally directing questions at me. As far as he was concerned, we were more able to run a picture company when we were fifteen than other people who were in it. It's a great pity in a way that he had this much confidence in us, because if he'd dragged out executives instead of us two kids, he'd have unquestionably been better off. Adolph Zukor[1] said to me years later, "If your father had you two boys as you are today when he was running a picture company, or if you two boys had him today, you would own the whole business." We may have inherited some of his traits, but neither of us has his vision or genius for big-scale operations.

While working for my father I prepared for Yale, which I never got to, even though I took most of the entrance examinations and studied over a period of years off and on. I took all sorts of extension courses at Columbia University, primarily in literature and philosophy and history. Columbia permitted me to keep on with my education but never for a day leave the picture business. I was at Columbia on and off for about six years.

*What had been my continuing dreams of going to Yale, which I had clung to for many years, were smashed when my father went broke in 1923. Everything we owned personally was taken away from us, and we went out to make a living. Ironically, the two most successful pictures my brother, Myron, produced—*Rupert of Hentzau *and one of the very first of the remakes, a new production of* The Common Law—*were released after the enterprises were taken away from my father.*

My mother wasn't disturbed in the least bit by my father's defeat. We had a seventeen-room apartment at 270 Park Avenue, with an enormous staff of servants, a flock of Rolls-Royces, etc. Two weeks after the crash, we were living in a three-room flat, and my

[1]President and later Chairman of the Board of Paramount Pictures.

mother was doing all the housework and cooking.

I organized what was to be a new publishing company with Arthur Brentano, Jr., called Selznick-Brentano, with a view to doing some publishing and revolutionizing distribution of books throughout the country. I was just a kid then, but Brentano and myself finally jointly decided not to go forward with it, because we had very little capital, and instead I went down to Florida to try to make my fortune during the land boom. Of course, you know what happened to the Florida land boom!

Since I had been trained to ambitious dreams, and since the family needed money desperately, I decided that I could not afford to take a job, and spent weeks promoting a bankroll for a new picture enterprise. I promoted Will He Conquer Dempsey? *[1923], a two-reeler with the prizefighter Luis Firpo, made at a total cost of $2,000—of which $1,000 went to Firpo. Firpo's agreement was to perform for $1,000 a day. As I look back on it, I must have been out of my mind to tell him at the end of the first day that the picture was finished. I spent $875 of the remaining $1,000 making the picture. We ran Firpo's tail ragged around Central Park, and wore the big bull out boxing on roofs and in other places where I didn't have to pay any rentals or pay for any lights. The film made a profit for me and my partners.*

Rudolph Valentino had been off the screen as a result of a fight with Paramount, and the public was clamoring to see him. I didn't sell him the idea of judging a beauty contest; the Mineralava[2] people did that. What I did was to sell the Mineralava people on the value of having a motion picture on the finals of the beauty contest; and by convincing them of the advertising value of this, I didn't have to give them anything. Accordingly, I had a two-reel Valentino picture for the cost of the film plus the lights in Madison Square Garden. I made $15,000 on it.

I promoted and made for $17,000 a little picture called Roulette *[1924], which had an all-star cast including some stars that I engaged for one hour! As I recall, it didn't lose any money, but didn't make any worth mentioning.*

Myron had gone to California and urged me to go out. My father was then the head of Associated Exhibitors, and I went to California in the summer of 1926 with the hope of promoting some independent pictures for Associated Exhibitors, which was a distributing company in need of product. I lined up some quickies for their release, but they

[2]The company sponsoring the event.

folded before anything could happen, leaving me without a salary for the weeks I'd tried, and without work. I didn't know what to do, and it was my brother who insisted I should try to get a job at MGM.

A few years before, when my father was broke, he had heard about the deal on Ben-Hur [1925], which called for MGM to pay fifty per cent of the gross of the film to Klaw and Erlanger (owners of the theatrical rights). This deal had been inherited by MGM when they took over the old Goldwyn Company. Aware that MGM had spent millions producing the film and could not afford to go through with this deal, my father conceived the idea of buying up the Klaw and Erlanger half. He got a man by the name of Pat Powers to agree to back him up to a million dollars, with the profits to be divided fifty-fifty between Powers and my father. When MGM heard about it, they were frantic. Nick Schenck[3] asked my father to come to see him, and my father took me along. My father said, "Let's go up and see Nick, I think we'll have some fun."

Nick stated that MGM could not afford to let the interest go to anybody else; they would have to pay whatever was necessary to get it, and all my father could succeed in doing was to cost Nick money. My father said, "That's all well and good, Nick. But when you did everything possible to break me, and refused to help me since, I see no reason why I should do you a favor." The atmosphere was getting rather thick: Nick insisted that my father had no place in the whole deal and no right to inject himself into it. My father finally said, "I'll put it up to David. Anything he says, I'll do." Needless to say, I was frightened and flabbergasted. Nick turned to me and said, "Well, Davie, my boy, what's it to be?" I said, "I think you ought to drop out of it, Pop." My father said, "That's it, Nick." We rose to leave. Nick said if there was ever anything he could do for me to call on him. My father never said another word to me about it.

When I tried to get a job at MGM, Harry Rapf was one of the heads of the studio. He had been Myron's assistant at Fort Lee, and Myron arranged the appointment. Harry didn't see quite what I could do, but I asked him for a job to prove that I could contribute to the picture program. After a couple of conferences, I persuaded him to let me have a two-week trial at $75 a week. I was told to report for work the next day. When I arrived, Harry told me that he was sorry, but Louis B. Mayer had said that he would not have any Selznick in the studio.

[3]Nicholas M. Schenck, President of Metro-Goldwyn-Mayer and Loew's, Inc., the parent company.

(Mayer had been my father's New England branch manager and had had a row with him after one month.)

I had read that Nick Schenck was in town, staying at the Ambassador, and I waited for him outside the barbershop. After I introduced myself, he remembered me, and I reminded him of the Ben-Hur incident and his promise. For once, a Schenck remembered, and he asked what he could do. I told him I wanted him to invest $150 in me on the basis of a two-week job at $75 per week, and assured him that he wouldn't ever hear of me after that if the studio didn't keep me, despite Louis Mayer's antagonism.

So, in October of 1926, I got a job as a reader for Harry Rapf at MGM, and from then on I rose very quickly.

Myron and I struck up a close friendship with director Lewis Milestone, who had had a fight with Warners and couldn't get a job. As long as I was getting my weekly pay check at MGM, the three of us took a couple of rooms together at a lousy Hollywood apartment and we all three lived grandly—on my salary. I got up at eight and took the bus to Culver City, while Myron (who had lost his job at United Artists by then) and Milly got up at noon and took our rented Chrysler over to the Athletic Club, where they played handball all afternoon.

After stuffing the suggestion box daily for two weeks while working for $75.00 per week, I became manager of the Writer's Department at MGM, then head of the Writer's Department, then assistant story editor, then associate story editor, then assistant stooge to Harry Rapf, then assistant producer under him, and then finally was given my chance to make a Tim McCoy Western simply because the man who had been producing these pictures was sick of them. They needed somebody else, and I pleaded for a chance to show what I could do even with a Western. After getting this opportunity, I sat down and tried to figure out how in God's name anybody could make a reputation producing Westerns.

The quality of the MGM Westerns had always been excellent, and clearly I could not improve on them. I had to do something startling to attract attention. After studying the previous Tim McCoy films, I decided they all seemed to fit a pattern and that it would be just as easy to make two of them at a time as one.[4] I sent out a director— Woody Van Dyke [W. S. Van Dyke II]—with two scripts and two leading ladies. We did all our action material for both of them at the same

---

[4] *Spoilers of the West* (1927) and *Wyoming* (1928).

time, and made two of them for the price of about one and one-eighth.
The pictures came off very well. Maybe the idea was not new with me.
It certainly must have been done before I did it, at the quickie studios;
but the idea was certainly a shocking and a new one for MGM.

At that time all pictures at Metro were made under the over-all
management of Louis B. Mayer, but under the production guidance
of Irving Thalberg. Although Thalberg was the executive producer on
all of the pictures, he made some of the pictures personally, as I
subsequently did at RKO, and he was a really great, farsighted pro-
ducer for an extremely young man. (At that time, it was a young man's
business. Louis B. Mayer was regarded at forty as an old man!) He also
was directly concerned with the principal decisions on the pictures
made by the other producers. There were three producers only there
at that time in addition to Thalberg: Hunt Stromberg, Bernard Hy-
man, and Harry Rapf. I became the fifth, with the Westerns, which
had previously been made by Hyman.

:: :: :: :: :: :: :: :: :: :: :: ::

To: Mr. Harry Rapf   October 15, 1926

It was my privilege a few months ago to be present at two private
screenings of what is unquestionably one of the greatest motion pictures ever made, *The Armored Cruiser Potemkin*, made in Russia
under the supervision of the Soviet Government.

I shall not here discuss the commercial or political aspects of the
picture, but simply say that regardless of what they may be, the film
is a superb piece of craftsmanship. It possesses a technique entirely
new to the screen, and I therefore suggest that it might be very
advantageous to have the organization view it in the same way that
a group of artists might view and study a Rubens or a Raphael.

The picture has no characters in an individual sense; it has not one
studio set; yet it is gripping beyond words—its vivid and realistic
reproduction of a bit of history being far more interesting than could
any film of fiction, and this simply because of the genius of its production and direction. (The firm might well consider securing the man
responsible for it, a young Russian director named [Sergei] Eisenstein.)
Notable, incidentally, are its types and their lack of make-up, and the

exquisite pieces of photography that alternate with the starkly realistic dramatic scenes.

Could and would you secure a print of it?[5]

David O. Selznick

To: Mr. Irving Thalberg   November 19, 1926

In furtherance of my verbal suggestions to you regarding a story of life at Yale, I should like to say that this would appear to be an almost sure-fire follow-up to *Brown of Harvard* [1926]. I should think that the very name of Yale would have high value in connection with a starring vehicle for William Haines on the 1927–28 program.

There is no question but that *Brown of Harvard* would have been a much better picture even than it was, and that much criticism would have been avoided, if the firm had been able to secure the cooperation of the Harvard authorities. . . .

I suggest that we offer a substantial prize for the best and most typical story of life at Yale. The contest should be open only to Yale undergraduates and alumni; the judges to include representatives of MGM, the Yale faculty, and perhaps the student body or college press; and the finished picture to be filmed partly in New Haven, with the aid and encouragement of the University administrators, to the end that an honest romance of college life may be shown the world.

The value to the firm and to the star, in publicity and prestige, incident to this contest and picture, should be immense; and, in addition, we would undoubtedly secure a really fine college picture.

David O. Selznick

To: Mr. Mayer   May 17, 1927

You wished to be reminded to discuss with Mr. Thalberg and with Mr. Feist[6] and the other sales executives the possibility of adding twelve one-reel[7] or two-reel dramas to the 1927–28 program. Mr. Rapf is already heartily in favor of the plan. . . .

It would seem reasonable to suppose that a theater that was running any . . . feature comedies would prefer to balance its program with a two-reel drama rather than with a two-reel comedy.

[5]This is one of the first memos written by Selznick at MGM.
[6]Felix Feist, in Charge of Sales, MGM.
[7]Approximately eleven minutes each.

In searching for stories we have found hundreds of incidents and plays that would have been simply gems if there had been any way of producing them in one or two reels, but which were not feature subjects, either commercially or pictorially. One of the few ways in which we, or the industry generally, can hope to make artistic strides forward, is through testing the public on short subjects once it is in the theater to see the feature attraction. I should think that men like Mr. Hays[8] and yourself, and indeed the entire newly formed Society of Arts and Sciences,[9] would get very strongly behind a project of this kind.

We are not equipped to make short comedies, but we are most decidedly equipped to make short dramas. Sets that are standing could be used without any change whatever; there are always sufficient members of the staff under salary that are idle for a long enough period to make a two-reeler; the services of well-known staff players could be also used, and we could offer theaters big feature names in short subjects.

I do not suggest that we use our stars in these subjects, but that we star our feature players; people like Lionel Barrymore, Renée Adorée, Conrad Nagel, etc. We could also star new players whom we hope to make stars a year or two hence.

I am sure that our directors would enter into the thing with a spirit of enthusiasm, for almost every creator in the picture business has some ideas that he would like to put over in a short subject. But personally, I would be in favor of using the short subjects as a training school for directors rather than as a side issue with the directors we already have. I am thoroughly convinced, as I think yourself and the supervisors are, that there are many men among our scenario writers, editors, and assistant directors, who would make extremely able directors if they were given the opportunity; but we cannot afford to give them this opportunity on a feature subject. A series of short subjects would be worth a fortune to us if only because they could give us in a year's time four or six new directors at very low salaries. I think that it is up to firms like ourselves to introduce new men into the creative departments of our organization, or we will be ever more and more at the mercy of the oldtimers, and salaries will continue to increase.

The argument may be advanced that such a unit might hold up the

[8]Will H. Hays, President of the Motion Picture Producers and Distributors of America, Inc.
[9]The Academy of Motion Picture Arts and Sciences.

staff in the performance of its feature functions; such an argument could only be construed as a confession of a lack of organization. If one man is responsible for these subjects (and I respectfully nominate myself as that one man), there is no reason why any of the other executives should be bothered even to the extent of knowing that a short subject is being made until it is screened for them complete.[10]

David O. Selznick

[10]Not until some years later did MGM begin to make short dramas (series titles: *The Passing Parade, Crime Does Not Pay, Miniatures,* etc.). Various important writers, directors, actors etc., served their apprenticeship working on these successful shorts during the 1930s and 1940s.

PART

PARAMOUNT
(1928–1931)

WHILE STILL AT MGM, I was assigned to act as Hunt Stromberg's assistant, which, even though it was going from producer to assistant producer, was in the nature of a big advancement because Stromberg was making big pictures. I was madly in love with White Shadows in the South Seas, *Frederick O'Brien's book on the destruction of the Polynesian race by the white man. I recommended for the direction of it my director on the Westerns, W. S. Van Dyke, who had never done anything but Westerns, but whom I thought capable of much better things, which subsequently proved to be the case. I then was delighted to be told that I was to produce the picture, which had been in the hands of Stromberg, who at one time had been publicity direc-tor for my father. I met with Stromberg to talk over the picture. He told me his ideas about it, with many of which I disagreed.*

I was a very idealistic young man and I was particularly shocked by Stromberg's statements to me that the only reason he was making the picture was because it presented an opportunity to show women's breasts—only in more graphic language! I disagreed entirely with his concepts of the proposed picture. Also, he told me the picture was to be codirected by Robert Flaherty and Van Dyke. Flaherty was one of my closest friends, and I had been the sponsor of Van Dyke. I said that either man could do the picture very well, but I knew, from my close personal relationship with them, that the idea of their codirecting was absurd. The argument became heated. To my astonishment Strom-berg made clear that he was still to be the producer of the picture, and that I was to be his associate in the South Seas. *I was to have the job of reconciling Flaherty and Van Dyke. So I went to see Thalberg and had a very acrimonious discussion, in which Thalberg agreed with Stromberg. I told Thalberg in the rather strong language of youth that he didn't know what he was talking about, and I was fired. He gave me a chance to apologize for having disagreed with him, which I refused to do, and I was out of a job.*

After leaving MGM, I was sent for in early 1928 by Paramount's B. (Ben) P. Schulberg, who hated MGM and was jealous of its success. He was anxious to tell me and the rest of Hollywood that Paramount had more respect for independent opinion than did MGM. He had heard about me from the director Bill Wellman, with whom I had struck up a personal friendship, and who had had many difficulties with the producers to whom he had been assigned. Schulberg told Wellman that he didn't believe he could work with any producer, and Wellman suggested that he could work with me. Three other friends—Paul Bern,[1] B. P. Fineman,[2] and Bennie Zeidman[3]—brought pressure on Schulberg.

However, there was to be a snag: Schulberg's then assistant kept me waiting an entire afternoon, following my first interview with Schulberg, to tell me that I would have to work for less money than I had received at MGM, and that he wasn't sure they wanted me anyway. I demanded more money and walked out in a huff. It took some time for my pals at Paramount to persuade Schulberg to see me again, and when I did, he told me that my reputation for arrogance was apparently well founded; and he inquired as to how long it would take me to make good. I told Schulberg that I never wanted more than two weeks any place, and once again I was put on with a challenge from Schulberg that I would have to make awfully good in those two weeks to stay on.

During these two weeks I did all sorts of things: I deluged him with my famous or notorious memoranda; I got the studio to accept about five or six story ideas; I named about ten of their pictures for which they were looking for new titles. (They provided in my contract, later, that I would no longer get the $100 bonus that was offered for new titles!) I gave them script critiques and preview critiques; I devised a whole new control system of the work of the producers and writers.

At the end of two weeks, Schulberg raised my salary and made me his assistant. I was also given charge of the Story Department and the writers. Then, a few months later, he made me his executive assistant. They kept raising my salary and finally put me under contract.

George Cukor had never been in pictures when my association with him began. He had been a New York stage director, and the whole Paramount studio was hipped at the time on the idea that pictures should be directed by stage directors because of their greater experience in directing dialogue. (Some of them have come through with flying colors; more of them disappeared because they didn't master the screen technique.) Cukor arrived at the studio, I recall, in midsummer, wearing a black overcoat and a black fedora hat, which he persisted in wearing for the first several weeks in Hollywood. He worked as dialogue director, assisting one or two screen directors without

---

[1]MGM Production Executive.
[2]Paramount Production Supervisor.
[3]Paramount Production Supervisor.

making much of an impression and failing in his pleas for an assignment. Lewis Milestone was just doing All Quiet on the Western Front. *I sold Milestone, who had never had any association with the theater, on using Cukor as the dialogue director on this picture. I sold Schulberg (Cukor was under contract to Paramount, of course) on the great value to Cukor of learning screen technique from as great a silent director as Milestone.*

Through this period I became very friendly with Cukor, despite the fact that we were always mistaken for each other. It's curious because, although probably we bear some facial resemblance to each other, George is about six inches shorter than I am. In this connection, my mother once protested violently in Cukor's presence, when the subject came up, that we didn't look like each other at all. George replied, "It's all right, Mrs. Selznick. My mother doesn't like it either."

There were many headaches during the transition from silent pictures to sound: the outstanding thing that occurs to me is the awe in which the technician at Paramount in charge of sound was held. He was the only man at the plant at that time who knew anything about sound and had been in charge of the trick effects previously. He had gone East to study the new sound process, and when he came back he was treated as a thing apart. He allowed no one on the sound stage, presumably lest the secret leak out; he relaxed this rule only for short periods. He insisted on handling everything himself, which included the direction of the scene. He was as much qualified to direct as directors were qualified to head the trick department.

It reached the point where one day I told him that we had cast a certain actor in the next sound picture, and he told me curtly that the sooner we executives realized that there would be no casting in sound pictures without his approval, the better off we would be. We all were terrified, particularly we who were not in charge. But after a period of a few months it became apparent that other studios were making sound pictures and maybe there were other gods that could be obtained. Schulberg contacted the Western Electric authorities. They sent out their technicians, who had no ambitions whatsoever other than to do a good technical job; and the new king was toppled from his throne. Within a few weeks everyone in the studio knew all they needed to know about sound, and in an amazingly short space of time the transition was made and we were making sound pictures along the same assembly-line methods that were employed for the silent pictures.

One heartbreaking episode occurred during this time at Paramount. You must realize that the stages used for making silent pictures

*were not soundproof and it was impossible to make talking pictures
on them. Paramount executives had allotted a huge amount of money
to build a tremendous sound stage, and the studio had to go on making
silent pictures until the sound stage was completed. Everyone in the
studio eagerly counted the days until this stage should be ready. About
one week before the first sound picture was scheduled to start, we all
received a telephone call that the studio was on fire. We all rushed to
the studio to find that it wasn't the whole studio, but something almost
equally tragic—the new sound stage! It seems that the fire had gotten
well under way before the firemen had arrived. The Hollywood and
Los Angeles fire departments did valiant service, but to no avail. The
stage was gone.*

*With the courage and organization ability that always characterized
him, Schulberg called a group of us into his office that very night. He
told us that we would not be stopped from making sound pictures; that
we could not be behind the parade, and that he had an idea on which
he wanted the cooperation of the entire studio. He appealed to us as
executives to sell this idea to the directors, to the actors, the technicians, and the rest of the studio. His idea was that we should immediately put into work all the sound pictures we had prepared, shooting
them at night! (The interference of outside sound was, of course, at a
minimum at night.) We were inspired by his talk, and within a week
his plan was in effect and we had pictures started. The whole first
group of Paramount's sound pictures was made at night, with a staff
of policemen through the streets of the studio to keep them silent
when the whistle blew. And they were enormously successful. (The
first experimental pictures made by Paramount were made on a very
tiny experimental sound stage, one obviously impractical except for
the first very few pictures that were released.) As a result of this,
Paramount was on the market with sound pictures many, many
months ahead of its principal competitor, MGM, which was waiting for
its sound stages to be completed. Eventually, of course, Paramount
completed new sound stages.*

*Schulberg was the most efficient general manager of a studio I have
ever known. There has never been, to my knowledge, in the history
of the business, any studio to compete with Paramount at that time for
sheer efficiency. There was never such a thing as a writer or director
without an assignment for a specific picture that was planned to be
made. People were cut off the payroll as soon as their usefulness was
ended. Their daily work was checked. No loafing was tolerated. There
were committees that functioned regularly on every phase of the
studio's activities; budgets were strictly adhered to and a meeting*

called the minute a budget was exceeded, and an attempt made, usually successful, to make up the overage. Associate producers felt the responsibility of going below the budget on their next production to make up for the overage on their last. The total budget of the program was a sacred thing. Release dates were never missed, and pictures were turned out once a week. There were regular meetings of all executives promptly at nine o'clock every Friday morning, and every man knew if he'd committed any errors during the week, they had to be thrashed out at this meeting in the presence of all his confreres.

Schulberg was a really great mill foreman—which was both his strength and his weakness: his strength was in the days when people had the movie-going habit, when pictures were sold en masse, and when a difference in quality made extremely little difference in the gross on the picture. But as the industry changed, and as the public became more selective, and as the method of selling pictures changed, the assembly-line method of making pictures obviously became out-dated and destroyed its adherents.

:: :: :: :: :: :: :: :: :: :: :: ::

To: Mr. Henry Herzbrun[4]   May 9, 1928

Listed below are those of my main title suggestions which have either been accepted or which are under consideration. It is my understanding that I will receive $100 for each of these as and when they are used.

THREE SINNERS	DIRIGIBLE
(For which I have been paid)	
THE FIRST KISS	THE SAWDUST PARADISE
THE MAN I LOVE	SOPHOMORE
HIGH SOCIETY	THE WOLF OF WALL STREET
HOT NEWS	SOUBRETTE
THREE WEEKENDS	THE WHITE LIE
THE GAY DEBUTANTE	YOUNG LOVERS
THE WOMAN FROM MOSCOW	GOOD LITTLE CHORUS GIRLS
HIGH SEAS	FLIGHT
SUBMARINE	RED BLOOD

[4]Resident attorney, West Coast Studios, Paramount Publix Corporation.

LOVE AMONG THE CO-EDS   SHOW-GIRL
ANNAPOLIS   YOUNG LOVE
CAMPUS NIGHTS   BELOVED
THE SCHOOL FOR PETTING   TAHITI
CARESS   LOVE AMONG THE RICH
MANDARIN   PETTING PARTIES
CHILDREN OF MOSCOW   DIAMOND JIM
THE BIG KILLING   BLACK SHEEP
   (For which I have been paid)

There are many others which have been rejected for the time being; and if any of these are used, I will undertake to convince Mr. Schulberg of their submission by me prior to the signing of my new contract.[5]

David O. Selznick

MR. B. P. SCHULBERG   JULY 2, 1928
DRAWING-ROOM A,
CAR 431
CENTURY LIMITED FROM
CHICAGO, ILLINOIS

THE MORE WE WORK ON "DIRIGIBLE"[6] THE MORE CONVINCED WE ARE THAT THE COOPERATION OF THE NAVY DEPARTMENT IS WITHOUT VALUE TO US AND IS INDEED A DETRIMENT INSTEAD. THE NAVY DEPARTMENT DEMANDS A STORY DEMONSTRATING THE SAFETY OF DIRIGIBLES WHEN IT IS APPARENT THAT OUR STORY DEPENDS FOR ITS MELODRAMATIC VALUES UPON THE DANGER OF DIRIGIBLES. EVEN IF WE STRUGGLE WITH THE NAVY'S DEMANDS AND SATISFY THEM ON EVERY STORY POINT, I DO NOT SEE WHAT THEY CAN GIVE US. THEY CERTAINLY WILL NOT ENDANGER A NAVY DIRIGIBLE, AND ANY SCENES OF VALUE WILL HAVE TO BE TRICKED IN ANY EVENT. . . . WE HEAR THAT HOWARD

[5]Paramount used the following titles: *Three Sinners* (1928), *The First Kiss* (1928), *The Man I Love* (1929), *Hot News* (1928), *Three Weekends* (1928), *The Woman from Moscow* (1928), *The Big Killing* (1928), *The Sawdust Paradise* (1928) and *The Wolf of Wall Street* (1929). Three titles were sold to Columbia Pictures: *Submarine* (1928), *Flight* (1929), and *Dirigible* (1931). Pathé made *Annapolis* (1928) and *Sophomore* (1929); Universal eventually produced *Beloved* (1934) and *Diamond Jim* (1935); Fox released *Black Sheep* in 1935; *High Society* was used twice, but not until the mid-1950s. Rayart had already used the *Show-Girl* title the year before this memo was written, and First National used it again for a film released several months following the memo.

[6]*Dirigible* was planned as a follow-up to the highly successful *Wings* (1927), but for reasons unknown was not produced at Paramount.

HUGHES[7] HAS OBTAINED UNBELIEVABLY MAGNIFICENT DIRIGIBLE
SCENES WITH THE USE OF A TWENTY-FIVE FOOT MINIATURE
DIRIGIBLE [FOR *Hell's Angels* (1930)]. HAVE HAD DISCUSSION WITH
[O. W.] ROBERTS OF EFFECT DEPARTMENT WHO IS CONFIDENT HE
CAN GIVE US EVERYTHING WE NEED WITH DIRIGIBLES AFLIGHT, IN
DANGER AT NIGHT, EXPLODING, ETC., WHICH WE SURELY CANNOT
GET WITH REAL DIRIGIBLE. . . .

DAVID O. SELZNICK

MR. ERNEST B. SCHOEDSACK[8]　　　　　　　　　APRIL 2, 1929
HOTEL SHELTON
NEW YORK CITY, N.Y.

DEAR MONTY:[9] . . . THE PREVIEW OF "FOUR FEATHERS"[10] IN ITS
NEW FORM WITH THE BATTLE AT THE END WENT OVER EVEN
BETTER THAN WE HAD HOPED FOR. THERE IS NO QUESTION
WHATEVER IN OUR MINDS NOW THAT THIS IS THE IDEAL FORM
FOR THE PICTURE. THE PICTURE GRIPPED THE AUDIENCE ALL THE
WAY THROUGH AND THERE WAS NO LETDOWN IN THE MIDDLE AS
AT OUR FIRST PREVIEW. . . . PLEASE TAKE MY WORD ABOUT THE
AUDIENCE REACTION. THE HIPPOPOTAMUS SCENES GOT GASPS AS
NOW CUT INSTEAD OF LAUGHS AS PREVIOUSLY, AND WE ARE SURE
THAT THIS IS TRACEABLE TO THE RECUTTING OF THE SEQUENCE
AND ALSO TO ITS NEW PLACE IN THE STORY CONTINUITY. THIS FOR
YOUR INFORMATION IN CASE YOU ARE TEMPTED TO DO ANY
RECUTTING. ALL THOSE WHO WERE SKEPTICAL ABOUT THE
PICTURE NOW BELIEVE IN IT WHOLEHEARTEDLY AND ARE CERTAIN
OF ITS SUCCESS ONLY WITH THE SOLITARY FEAR THAT IT MAY NOT
DO AS WELL AS IT WOULD HAVE A YEAR AGO BECAUSE OF THE
TALKING-PICTURE SITUATION.[11] HOWEVER, THERE IS NO QUESTION
THAT THIS IS ONE STORY WHICH SHOULD BE BETTER WITH MUSIC
AND SOUND EFFECTS THAN WITH MID-VICTORIAN DIALOGUE.
PREVIEW CARDS WERE UNANIMOUSLY ENTHUSIASTIC. . . . I FEEL

[7]President of the Hughes Tool Company and the Caddo Company, motion-picture producers.
[8]Codirector of *The Four Feathers* (1929) and cocinematographer of the African location footage.
[9]Schoedsack's nickname.
[10]Not to be confused with the British production of *The Four Feathers* produced ten years later.
[11]*The Four Feathers* was made as a silent picture (with synchronized music score and sound effects) during the transition period to sound.

CONFIDENT THAT YOU AND COOPER[12] WILL BOTH AGREE THAT
THE RE-EDITING HAS REALLY BEEN A TREMENDOUS GAME[13] AND
THAT YOU WILL CONGRATULATE US AS I NOW CONGRATULATE
YOU. . . . PASS THIS WIRE ALONG TO MERIAN. . . . CORDIALLY AND
SINCERELY

DAVID

[Writer] Bartlett Cormack   August 13, 1929
Paramount Office
New York, N.Y.

Dear Bart:

Answering your letter, we are in need mostly of stories for Nancy
Carroll and for Dick Arlen. Carroll's vehicles should be rather on the
emotional side, with a little comedy of the precious type, if possible.
We have found that Nancy is at her best in her dramatic and wistful
moments. Her work in *The Shopworn Angel* and *Burlesque* [*The
Dance of Life*, 1929)] is typical; although we very definitely and positively want to steer clear of the theater background in our pictures
with her in the future.

The Arlen budget is very limited, so that while Dick falls most
naturally into the soldier-of-fortune and the man-who-came-back formulas, we cannot go in for big production values, or have anything
that would take a great deal of shooting time, such as an abundance
of exteriors. We shall very likely be forced into the George M. Cohan
type of romantic melodrama, in which we should do very well, and
which should increase his popularity.

I think that Carroll and Arlen are our most serious needs in that we
have only one story ahead for Nancy, and none for Dick. However, we
also need material for [actor George] Bancroft beyond the submarine
story which [writer] Jules Furthman is now working on. . . .

We are in splendid shape on William Powell, and fairly well off on
Clara Bow, Evelyn Brent, Ruth Chatterton, and Gary Cooper. We
have two stories ahead for Buddy Rogers, but could use a couple more
very nicely.

I do hope that this gives you what you want. . . .

Cordially yours,

[12]Merian C. Cooper, Codirector of *The Four Feathers* and Cocinematographer of the
African location footage.
[13]This could have been intended to read "gain."

To: Mr. A. A. Kaufman[14]   August 13, 1929

Dear Al:

May I suggest for the Revue [*Paramount on Parade* (1930)] that we might do something very amusing on the contrast of silent pictures and talking pictures? As an initial idea along these lines, we might have a very romantic love scene played without the voices being heard, first advising the audience to put their own interpretation on the dialogue, which they cannot hear; and then playing the exact same scene with ridiculous and amusing dialogue, completely contrary to what the audience has thought it to be.[15]

An idea something along these lines was used in the *Music Box Revue* in New York some years ago, when a very melodramatic scene was played with nonsensical dialogue. We have an excuse for such a scene, which they did not have.

You know from experience that often in silent pictures very romantic love scenes were played with the actors talking about a party the night before, or some other totally irrelevant subject.

David O. Selznick

To: Mr. A. A. Kaufman   August 13, 1929

Dear Al:

. . . I wonder if it would not be entertaining to have a little burlesque in the Revue [*Paramount on Parade* (1930)] of Philo Vance (William Powell), and Sherlock Holmes (Clive Brook), in pursuit of Fu Manchu (Warner Oland).[16] There have been several magazine articles, theatrical numbers, and even books based upon similar ideas—i.e., Arsène Lupin versus Sherlock Holmes; and a skit about these three celebrated characters of fiction, and of Paramount pictures, might be intriguing and diverting. . . .[17]

David O. Selznick

[14]Albert A. Kaufman, Executive Assistant to Jesse L. Lasky (Vice-President of Paramount).
[15]The idea was not used.
[16]Paramount's films based on these characters were extremely popular.
[17]A skit based on this idea was used.

MISS IRENE MAYER[18]   NEW YORK, N.Y.
625 OCEAN FRONT   JAN 19, 1930
SANTA MONICA, CALIF.

DEAR MISS MAYER: YOUR MANUSCRIPT IS THE MOST MAGNIFICENT I
HAVE EVER RECEIVED.[19] CANNOT COMMENT TOO HIGHLY ON YOUR
HUMOR, ORIGINALITY, SINCERITY, AND SHEER WRITING ABILITY.
BECAUSE OF THE FINE PROMISE SHOWN BY EVERYTHING YOU HAVE
DONE TO DATE, YOU MAY CONSIDER YOURSELF ENGAGED ON YOUR
OWN TERMS.

                                             D. O. SELZNICK

Miss Irene Mayer   January 30, 1930
625 Ocean Front
Santa Monica

Darling,

I am at the moment a glorified wreck: a wreck because seemingly
I am no longer the young man of Manhattan, and the New Yorker's
thrill that might make this pace tenable is lacking. . . .[20]

Today I spent at Nyack with Ben Hecht. I found him ninety per cent
of my conception of him these several years since we have met. And
thus he is the only one of all my Eastern figures that has not been
shattered. We had a delightful afternoon walking through the snows
over bleak roads along the Hudson. He has bought a house a century
and a half old and added to it an incongruous, amazing assortment of
things, including swimming pools indoors and out; a gymnasium, odd
little reading rooms. . . . The house sounds romantic, but is not, but
rather like a junk shop for incompleted dreams. Hecht is less jovial but
more picturesque when without his present affluence.

I went over my publishing ideas with him, which he seemed to find
confusing: a halfhearted compromise between an adolescent dream
and the movies.[21] He was pleased at my retention of the dream however; and eventually impressed with my plans. He is to meet me
tomorrow with [Pascal] Covici and [Donald] Friede, two publishers he
wants me to know with a possible view to their joining me, maybe
getting it underway until I am ready to go in (if ever) with both feet.

[18]Louis B. Mayer's daughter and Selznick's fiancée.
[19]Referring to a personal letter she had written to Selznick.
[20]Selznick was in New York on business.
[21]Selznick had plans to go into publishing with new methods for distribution and
chain book-selling, etc.

However, details concerning the publishing progress must await my return. This much I should like to promise you (note the quibbling): either I will have gotten something started by the time I leave, or I shall try to forget the books and forgive the films. . . .[22]

As to my vacation, tomorrow is typical: the morning, without sleep, to the office for conference with Walter[23] on the plays I have seen, and other things. . . . At eleven to Guinzburg[24] of The Viking Press, to whom [screenwriter] Oliver Garrett has kindly sent me, to discuss publishing. Later with Hecht to Covici. Lunch with [playwright and stage director] George Abbott at the Harvard Club. (Hecht, incidentally, pleaded with me today to go into play producing. What the hell!)

David

March 26, 1930

Dear Henry [Herzbrun]:

All kidding aside, I hope you remember our talk at the time my contract was signed about my salary on my wedding trip; and I hope also that Ben [Schulberg] remembers he promised Irene and myself we could have this. As to the number of weeks please remember that while I was entitled to two weeks vacation each year, I have never taken it; and as I am in my third year here, the firm owes me six weeks on this alone. Also, I was supposed to get a vacation trip when Ben came back, but as you know, this deteriorated into a series of jobs in New York. So, all in all, I honestly think I am entitled to a couple of months. Also, I am sure the firm would like to see me get off to the right start. Think of all the extra work they are going to get out of me by my being a married man![25]

David O. Selznick

To: Mr. B. P. Schulberg   July 18, 1930

We have an opportunity to secure Dashiell Hammett to do one story for us before he goes abroad in about three months.

Hammett has recently created quite a stir in literary circles by his creation of two books for Knopf, *The Maltese Falcon* and *Red Harvest*.

[22]Selznick's publishing plans did not materialize.
[23]Walter Wanger, Paramount General Manager of Production.
[24]Harold Guinzburg, President of The Viking Press.
[25]Selznick and Irene Mayer were married on April 29, 1930.

I believe that he is another Van Dine[26]—indeed, that he possesses more originality than Van Dine, and might very well prove to be the creator of something new and startlingly original for us.

I would recommend having him do a police story for Bancroft. . . . Hammett was a Pinkerton man for a good many years before becoming a writer. . . .

Hammett is unspoiled as to money, but on the other hand anxious not to tie himself up with a long-term contract. I was in hopes that we could get him for about $400 weekly, but he claims that this is only about half of his present earning capacity between books and magazine stories, and I am inclined to believe him inasmuch as his vogue is on the rise.

So far, I have tentatively discussed some such arrangement as the following: . . .

Four weeks at $300 weekly;

An option for eight weeks at the same salary;

And a bonus of $5000 for an original. . . .[27]

David O. Selznick

To: Mr. B. P. Schulberg   October 8, 1930

I have just finished reading the Eisenstein[28] adaptation of *An American Tragedy*. It was for me a memorable experience; the most moving script I have ever read. It was so effective, that it was positively torturing. When I had finished it, I was so depressed that I wanted to reach for the bourbon bottle. As entertainment, I don't think it has one chance in a hundred.

. . . Is it too late to try to persuade the enthusiasts of the picture from making it? Even if the dialogue rights have been purchased, even if Dreiser's services have been arranged for, I think it an inexcusable gamble on the part of this department to put into a subject as depressing as is this one, anything like the cost that an Eisenstein production must necessarily entail.

If we want to make *An American Tragedy* as a glorious experiment, and purely for the advancement of the art (which I certainly do not

[26]Mystery-story writer S. S. Van Dine, whose real name was Willard Huntington Wright.

[27]Hammett was put under contract.

[28]Sergei Eisenstein, the famous Russian director, had been brought to America by Jesse L. Lasky and put under contract for six months. At the suggestion of Paramount, Eisenstein and his associates prepared a script based upon the novel by Theodore Dreiser. The film was to be directed by Eisenstein.

think is the business of this organization), then let's do it with a [John] Cromwell directing, and chop three or four hundred thousand dollars off the loss. If the cry of "Courage!" be raised against this protest, I should like to suggest that we have the courage not to make the picture, but to take whatever rap is coming to us for not supporting Eisenstein the artist (as he proves himself to be with this script), with a million or more of the stockholders' cash.

Let's try new things, by all means. But let's keep these gambles within the bounds of those that would be indulged in by rational businessmen; and let's not put more money than we have into any one picture for years into a subject that will appeal to our vanity through the critical acclaim that must necessarily attach to its production, but that cannot possibly offer anything but a most miserable two hours to millions of happy-minded young Americans.[29]

David O. Selznick

To: Mr. Schulberg   November 1, 1930

. . . *Dishonored* will, I am sure, prove to be another magnificent [director Josef] von Sternberg picture. Joe has been his usual obnoxious, brilliant self; refusing to concede the merit of suggestions and then acting upon them; making changes that would be aggravating in any other director that turn out all right. As with all his pictures, he makes silly things look great, and I am confident that we will have another knockout from him. . . .

To: Mr. B. P. Schulberg   November 17, 1930

It occurs to me that we sometimes arrive too quickly at decisions at our Friday Executive Meetings. Options involving hundreds of thousands of dollars are decided upon affirmatively or negatively literally within a few seconds after the names come up. That this is wrong, that quick decisions are sometimes arrived at that we soon regret, has several times been proven of late by our desire to settle commitments soon after they are entered into.

To correct this situation, I should like to suggest that each member of the Executive Committee be given a list of matters to be discussed several days in advance of the respective committee meetings. It might even be advisable to prepare this list a full week in advance, to

---

[29]The Eisenstein version was not produced.

be distributed one meeting ahead. This would enable each of us to give study and careful consideration, first, to the record of each man involved; and second, to his possible use during the optional period (or the first period, if he is a new employee).

Speaking only for myself, I should like to have time to go over each writer's work just before his name comes up, and be prepared to make recommendations as to how he might be used in the future. The same goes for directors. It might even be possible to submit alternate names, men that could be substituted at smaller salaries. In the case of stock actors, we would have an opportunity to figure out how much the actor had cost us per picture. And so on down the line.

David O. Selznick

To: Mr. Schulberg   February 2, 1931

Dear Mr. Schulberg:

I am quite disappointed by the Sternberg-Hoffenstein first script, dated January 30, of *An American Tragedy;*[30] and more especially by the first half, or whatever section it is that leads up to the trial. . . .

Before I go into criticisms of the script itself, I should like to add one or two more qualms to the long list of those that have attended every step of the consideration and planning of this production. In the first place, seeing the thing in actual script form renews for me all of our old worries concerning its entertainment values. . . .

I couldn't help feeling . . . that even if we do do it, we are better off to let Joe make a sure-fire success for us while some other director handles the *Tragedy,* for in this way, we are sure of one more successful Sternberg picture that we lose if Joe does the *Tragedy.*

This feeling is strengthened by a growing conviction on my part that, all other considerations aside, Sternberg is the wrong man for this job. I don't think he has the basic honesty of approach this subject absolutely requires, that he has the sympathy, the tolerance, the understanding that the story cries for. Joe's series of triumphs have all been those of good theater, in each case dealing with completely fake people in wholly fake situations. He has forced audiences to swallow things that their intelligence would normally reject, by means of a series of brilliant tricks. The *Tragedy* is different: unless people understand the boy's psychology every step of the way, believe implicitly in

[30] After the Eisenstein script was rejected, the poet and humorist Samuel Hoffenstein collaborated with Sternberg on a new version.

the reality of the story, and are convinced that they are watching a page from life, there is nothing. Nothing whatever in Joe's past work indicates that it is possible for him to approach the subject in this manner. And the first script, in my opinion, reinforces this fear: we don't know the boy, we don't like or tolerate or even understand him. The other characters, and certain scenes through the picture, are phony to a degree—certainly to an infinitely lesser degree than any of Joe's other pictures, but then, granted Dreiser's book as a basis, not even Joe could be one hundred per cent phony. . . .

Mr. B. P. Schulberg   February 2, 1931
Paramount Publix Corp.
Hollywood, California

Dear Mr. Schulberg:

As my current year with the company draws near an end, I should like to bring your attention to the matter of my salary, which I respectively submit is out of proportion with the executive and creative work I am doing. This statement is based upon salaries within the industry for similar work, and within the company for other editorial executives, and others doing similar work.

Granted, for the sake of discussion, that we are in a period of unusually high salaries, I do not think it fair that I should be alone not benefiting during this period.

As is undoubtedly known to all of you, salaries of gentlemen of the type of Harry Rapf and Hunt Stromberg are considerably greater than my own, even though in each of the many cases that might be mentioned these gentlemen are doing only a portion of the work in their respective studios, corresponding to what I am handling at Paramount.

My salary is $1500 weekly; the company's option on my services for the coming year is at the same figure. . . .

We have repeatedly bemoaned the fact that the largest percentage of the best brains in the industry are drawn to direction and writing, rather than to executive work. This is not difficult to understand when, despite the fact that a great portion of a writer's and director's time is his own between assignments, and that even when working, his hours and work are not nearly so trying as those of an executive in a position like my own, we find writers and directors of even undistinguished talents receiving $2000 weekly, $2500 weekly, and upward.

During the coming year, we will make at this studio, probably sixty-five pictures. Mr. [E. Lloyd] Sheldon, judging by past experience, will supervise a maximum of ten; Mr. [Louis D.] Lighton, from what we know of his capabilities, cannot handle more than eight. You, with a minimum of assistance from myself, will probably look after six of our most important productions. This means that there are about forty pictures on which I must act virtually as supervisor, in addition to keeping, as I have in the past, contact with the remaining twenty-five pictures, attempting to contribute to all of them in the matter of assignments; main titles; stories; editorial and casting suggestions; etc.

In addition to this, there is the not inconsiderable amount of routine work as your assistant, which includes the management of the Writers' Department, the supervision of securing new material, participation in most executive decisions, etc. I am the first to say that this situation is almost impossible. I am certain that it exists in no other major studio. At that of our outstanding contemporary, Metro-Goldwyn-Mayer, the equivalent of my work is handled by no less than six high-salaried executives. Allowing that Mr. Thalberg corresponds to Mr. Schulberg, Mr. Rapf and Mr. Stromberg to Mr. Sheldon and Mr. Lighton, we find that, making fifteen or twenty pictures less than we do, they have Mr. [Paul] Bern, Mr. [Bernard] Hyman, Mr. [Albert] Lewin, Mr. [B. P.] Fineman, Mr. [Lawrence] Weingarten, and to a minor degree, Mr. [E. J.] Mannix.

I do not say that ours is the better situation. Even allowing that you handle two or three times the amount of work that Mr. Thalberg does (which I know to be a fact), I still do not claim that I can do anything like the quality of work that can be done by the various men mentioned above combined. I should like to see the situation remedied; but I see no hope for relief, for there is absolutely no good manpower available. But so long as it does exist, I should like to be adequately compensated. Otherwise, I am not at all certain that I am being fair to myself in continuing to carry the burden.

I should be grateful for the opportunity to go over everything I have done in the past several years for the company. I should be happy to prepare a list of my contributions and opinions during any period of my employ by Paramount, and to have weighed against these the list of my mistakes. . . .

I know, as I am sure you will concede, that the best of our writers, Oliver Garrett, Vincent Lawrence, and Zoë Akins, are with us because I fought for their retention against the advice of the rest of the Executive Departments; and that I fought for opportunities for Cromwell and Cukor, and . . . that I pleaded for [director A. Edward] Sutherland

and for [director Leo] McCarey and [director] Richard Jones, and the latter two cases in vain; . . . that Paul Lukas is not in Hungary today, because I insisted on retaining him against the advice of the entire Executive Committee during your absence in Europe; . . . that every single part of importance that Kay Francis played was due to my forcing her (in the case of the first important part, *Street of Chance,* after a bitter struggle against John Cromwell); that William Powell was made an important star by two stories on which I was actually collaborator, and the development of which I suggested and planned and supervised, namely *Street of Chance* and *For the Defense;* . . . that I started and planned in its entirety *Honey,* despite abuse; that I started, and am responsible for, the remaking of *Manslaughter;* that I fought for [writer] Joe Mankiewicz, and gave him his opportunity; that I have personally contributed dozens of main titles in the last three years; that I originated the Censorship Department . . . and am responsible for the first organized handling of main titles; . . . that I suggested and planned the first organized consideration of new material, the Weekly Story Bulletin, and the reporting on same; that I handled the entire Production Department, with a very minimum of assistance, considerably less than you have ever had, during the periods that you were away in Europe and in New York; . . . that I personally supervised, during the past three years, more pictures than any three other executives in the studio combined; that I have originated several times more story ideas that saw production than any other single individual in the studio, whether executive or writer or director, and regardless of his salary; . . . that I fought against *No Limit* as no story to make with Clara Bow at a time in her career when only a great picture would save her; . . . that I fought strenuously against the making of *Fighting Caravans* under any circumstances right up to the week of its making, and then reopened the matter time and again; that I fought against the making of *Monte Carlo* without a greater picture personality than Jeanette MacDonald or Jack Buchanan; . . . that I developed Mitzi Green by putting her in *Honey;* . . . that when the entire studio had failed to find a "Sooky" for *Skippy,* I suggested Bobby Coogan; that for two years, I have been suggesting the signing of Herbert Marshall; . . . that I went far toward giving us another potential star, when I kept insisting on Carole Lombard for *Ladies Man,* when everybody else was saying that only a great New York stage actress could play the part; that I suggested Samuel Hoffenstein as the ideal man for von Sternberg; that I first suggested, long ago, [actor] Phillips Holmes for *An American Tragedy;* that I brought in [writer and director Edmund] Goulding, under contract, and his story *The Devil's Holiday;* that over a period of years, I repeatedly fought to bring in Milestone under contract, several times when we could have had him for a fraction of what he is now getting, and was the very first in the industry to hail him as one of our greatest directors, if not actually our greatest; that I have suggested many of the best Clara Bow title ideas, starting from *Three Weekends,* through *The Wild Party;* . . . that I have maintained our Writers' Department at very low cost, and have been very largely responsible for keeping our important writers' salaries at a lower level than those of any other major studio; that I was the first to see Jack Oakie as a possible star, and to work on his stories and pictures accordingly; . . . that I am responsible for Skeets Gallagher's being brought from New York, and first suggested teaming him with Oakie; that I first suggested the *Fu Manchu* stories; . . . that I have personally suggested from a half to three-fourths of all of our writing and directorial assignments, and that this line alone could be amplified to fill many pages.

I have gone over with you the matter of the many offers I have received. The latest of these is to take full charge of one of the smaller studios, the first salary mentioned to me in this connection being $3000 a week, with an indication that they would go higher; I have reason to believe that I will shortly be made other offers of a similar nature.

I have a contract; but I should like to remind Mr. Lasky that when I was reluctant to sign it, he told me any time I was unhappy, I could consider it torn up.[31]

Respectfully yours,

B. P. SCHULBERG   FEBRUARY 25, 1931
SANTA FE CHIEF
EASTBOUND

PLEASE WIRE INSTRUCTIONS CONCERNING LAURENCE OLIVIER AND JILL ESMOND.[32] OPINION HERE DIVIDED, WITH MAJORITY BELIEVING ESMOND MORE DESIRABLE FOR STOCK THAN OLIVIER. HOWEVER, FELIX YOUNG[33] AND MYSELF ARE ONLY TWO THAT HAVE SEEN OLIVIER APART FROM TEST, AND WE BOTH CONSIDER HIM EXCELLENT POSSIBILITY. MY OWN FEELING IS THAT, IN SPITE

[31]Selznick received a raise in salary.
[32]Olivier's wife at the time.
[33]Production executive.

OF THEIR UNQUESTIONED MERIT, THEIR SALARY IS WAY OUT OF
LINE FOR BEGINNERS, ESPECIALLY AS WE HAVE NO PARTS IN SIGHT
FOR EITHER. WOULD RECOMMEND HAVING NEW YORK TRY TO USE
THEM. . . .[34]

To: Mr. B. P. Schulberg   April 15, 1931
                                                           NOT SENT

I wish you would give another minute's thought to my suggestion
that we do *Dr. Jekyll and Mr. Hyde* with [Emil] Jannings.

Granted that Jannings is not the Englishman of the book, and
granted also that he has not the beautiful physical appearance of Dr.
Jekyll, there is certainly nobody else in the world that could give the
magnificent dual performance that could be counted upon from Jannings. Any script of *Dr. Jekyll and Mr. Hyde* would almost certainly
be a pretty free adaptation—and certainly the character could be
molded to fit the versatile Jannings. When one thinks of the variety of
roles he has played so sensationally, from the kindly professor to the
lascivious Nero, from Louis XV to the trapeze artist of *Variety*, one
realizes that he is an artist without nationality and without limitation.
I am certain that he could overcome even the limitations of dialect.
For purposes of a horror picture no one, I am certain, would criticize
us for having the artist Jannings play a Teutonic Dr. Jekyll.

Granted that on most pictures, the name of Jannings is today no
draw, the combination of his name with that of the celebrated story
seems like a "natural." Just as we would not be interested in Dolores
Del Rio, and yet seize the chance to use her as *The Rose of the Rancho*,
so, in my opinion, we are passing up an opportunity to have the most
important horror attraction that could be conceived: Emil Jannings in
Dr. Jekyll and Mr. Hyde.[35]

David O. Selznick

To: Mr. B. P. Schulberg   June 3, 1931

As we have all long known, a good showman trick is the combination
of one or more players of importance or even of moderate importance
with one or more players on the downgrade, to give an effect of an
all-star cast. Thus putting Clive Brook and Richard Arlen with Buddy

[34]Neither was signed by Paramount.
[35]Fredric March played the role in the 1932 production.

Rogers, Fay Wray, and Jean Arthur in *The Lawyer's Secret,* probably gives the picture an appearance of importance, to exhibitors and public alike, way beyond its real strength if carefully analyzed. I feel that the picture is benefiting materially from this, and that it is helping get the public in to see a new Buddy Rogers.

I wonder if we could not do the same for Bow by the use of such a trick, as we have done for Rogers. As an example, George Bancroft and Clara Bow in *The Miracle Man.* (Maybe the story is wrong, although I think it merits discussion; but the choice of story is not material to this argument.) At one time, when Bancroft and Bow were strong, we discussed costarring this pair; but you felt that we would be losing a picture by it, and that subsequent pictures starring these players individually would suffer through a seeming comparative weakness after a costarring picture. But now, with Bow on her way out, and with Bancroft certainly not as strong as he was a year ago, I think that a Bancroft-Bow picture would assume real importance; that we would be extracting the last ounce of value out of Bow before letting her go; and that we might find that we would be taking the first important step toward saving Bow. . . .[36]

David O. Selznick

Mr. B. P. Schulberg   June 15, 1931
Paramount Studios
Hollywood, Calif.

Dear Mr. Schulberg:

You have asked each of us to individually decide on the proposed executive salary cut, in accordance with the dictates of our respective convictions—to which, aware of all inferences concerning the future, I should like to add the dictates of our courage.

My own decision is this: I cannot consider accepting any cut whatever in my salary.

I think I have the correct perspective on my abilities and the value of my services; and, judging even by present low salary standards, I do not think that I am being overpaid.

I do not feel that I am responsible in any way for the current depression in the firm's business. On the contrary, I think that the average of my contributions has been substantially profit-making. For the major mistakes of others, I feel in no way obligated to pay.

---

[36]Bow and Bancroft did not costar in a film.

I think that to single out six or eight executives to take salary cuts as a method of bringing down cost is as unwise as it is unfair. The company recognizes the impossibility of executing a cut in the salaries of contract players, writers, and directors—a cut which would, of course, aggregate an important saving. In the face of this impossibility, to ask those few of us who have most conscientiously strived to decrease and keep down cost, and in whose hands the future reform of costs almost completely rests, seems a shortsighted step that will save a few thousand dollars, and greatly weaken the very foundation of the studio organization. . . .

I regard as superficial the statement that as we have been partners in good times, we must be partners in bad times also. Certainly we did not share in the gigantic salaries, bonuses, and stock profits of the boom days. . . .

In refusing the cut, I am fully aware of the possible critical reaction of those responsible for the move, and completely willing to accept any consequences to my future with the company that may result. If the company wishes to measure my value to it in these terms, I can only say that it climaxes a growing discontent with my work and my post. The present production policies of the company are such as to tie the hands of all who might save it from a continuance of bad times. In these unsatisfactory circumstances, I will gladly attempt to relieve the company of its obligation to me as soon as I can conveniently arrange to do so. (My contract has more than ten months to run at $2000 weekly.) Please advise me whether I may proceed accordingly.

At this time permit me to reiterate my appreciation of your consideration and favors in times past. I like to think that I have repaid this consideration and these favors with conscientious, loyal, and able service.

Very sincerely yours,

To: Mr. B. P. Schulberg
June 27, 1931
NOT SENT

I have as yet received no reply to that section of my letter to you of the 15th, that suggests the cancellation of my contract with the company. . . .

Increasingly, I am of the conviction that our present policies are wrong; that our troubles are very much more deep-rooted than the very minor steps that the company is taking to cure them would seem to indicate; that machines such as ours are doomed, if quality is to increase and cost is to decrease. In the face of these convictions, my continuance in an important post in this machine seems to me completely hypocritical; my acceptance of a large salary cowardly.

In addition to my feelings concerning the fallacy of the general production system now in vogue, I have many misgivings concerning our own individual policies as a studio.

Production is being influenced to what I consider as being an extremely unfortunate degree by men who are, to my mind, and to the minds of some of the best creative brains in the studio, completely unqualified. A small personal group is known throughout the studio to have more influence on executive decisions than the directors and writers of respective pictures, men who have concentrated for months on individualized production problems.

Nor can I consider as wise the policy whereby any studio head, whoever he may be, carries in his mind (necessarily superficially, human limitations being what they are), the plans of seventy pictures yearly, plus the enormous amount of material from which these seventy are selected, plus the executive work involved in the management of a large studio. There must, of course, be an executive head to a studio, but I cannot believe that he should function in the manner to which we are now accustomed—with stories on which months have been spent rewritten in ten minutes, with casts and decisions which have been the result of sleepless nights upset in a moment over the dictograph.

I see no hope for changing this system; but, on the other hand, feeling as I do, I see no reason why I should subscribe to it. We have the players, the directors, the writers—a staff comprised of people of enormous talent and great ambition, however thwarted, cynical, and indifferent they may at the moment be. The system that turns these people into automatons is obviously what is wrong.

I am not the first to make this discovery; it is known throughout Hollywood, and decried wherever pictures are discussed—not merely by the disgruntled few, not merely by the failures with imaginary grievances, but by the successful, the beneficiaries of the system, the brains acknowledged by executives and artists alike to be the best in the industry.

I am not the first to discover this, but it is possible that I am the first executive holding a position of some importance to voice it while still holding that position. I do not claim that there is anything heroic in this attitude—merely honesty, candor, and whatever courage there may be in the preservation of one's self-respect, regardless of personal loss.

Concerning this latter phase, the element of personal loss, I should like the company to know that in tendering my resignation, I have not sought or received any other offers (beyond those which were tendered me some six months ago); that I have no other job lined up or in prospect; and that my only ambition at the moment is to attempt the organization of an independent unit—for I believe most strongly the best way out of the pit of bad and costly pictures in which we are now sunk is through breaking up production, in whole or in part, into smaller units that, however they may be controlled, will achieve a degree of independence from overhead and accumulations, from formulas, prejudices, and unsound influences.

I recognize the difficulties at this time of my starting anything of my own, the industry condition being what it is, and the money situation being what it is. In spite of this, I am anxious to take my chances, rather than longer take part in anything in which I have lost enthusiasm, faith, confidence, and even interest. I feel that in leaving, the most I can lose is money.

I feel that in view of all of the above, you will agree that the only possible course is the termination of my contract with the company, and would sincerely appreciate your giving this your immediate attention.

Young David Selznick (circa 1913; he was about eleven years old).

Lewis J. Selznick, father of David O. Selznick (circa 1908).

David O. Selznick (left), Lewis J. Selznick, and Myron Selznick (circa 1920).

Myron Selznick, silent-film actress Elaine Hammerstein, and David O. Selznick on location for *One Week of Love*, which Myron Selznick produced for his father's company in 1922.

The Four Feathers; Selznick was Associate Producer while at Paramount (1929).

Left to right, bottom row: Irving Thalberg, Norma Shearer, Selznick, Irene Mayer, B. P. Fineman. Back row: Edith Mayer, Zion Myers, Bennie Zeidman (circa 1929).

Irene Mayer and Selznick (circa 1930).

At the wedding of Irene Mayer and Selznick (April 29, 1930). Left to right: Myron Selznick, B. P. Schulberg, Selznick, Paul Bern, William Goetz, Oliver H. P. Garrett.

Constance Bennett, Lowell Sherman, and Gregory Ratoff (right) in *What Price Hollywood?* (1932).

John Barrymore and Katharine Hepburn in *A Bill of Divorcement* (1932).

Selznick with his wife, mother, father, and first child—Lewis Jeffrey (1932).

Wallace Beery and Jean Harlow in *Dinner at Eight* (1933).

On the set during the making of *Dinner at Eight*. Left to right, sitting: Madge Evans, Louise Closser Hale, Billie Burke, Marie Dressler, Karen Morley, Grant Mitchell. Standing: Edmund Lowe, Director George Cukor, Lionel Barrymore, Jean Harlow, Phillips Holmes.

Fred Astaire and Joan Crawford in *Dancing Lady* (1933).

Wallace Beery and Leo Carrillo in *Viva Villa!* (1934).

W. C. Fields and Freddie Bartholomew in *David Copperfield* (1935).

On the set of *Anna Karenina* (1935). Behind the camera: Director of Photography William Daniels. Sitting: Director Clarence Brown. In the carriage: Greta Garbo and Basil Rathbone.

Garbo and Fredric March in *Anna Karenina*.

Garbo and Basil Rathbone in *Anna Karenina*.

Ronald Colman (right) and Isabel Jewell in *A Tale of Two Cities* (1935).

David and Irene Selznick at the opening of *A Tale of Two Cities*.

Irving Thalberg and Selznick (circa 1935).

Merian C. Cooper, John Hay Whitney, and Selznick announcing
the formation of Selznick International (1935).

Selznick with the key New York executives of Selznick International: John Hay Whitney,
John Wharton, and Katharine Brown (1935).

On the set of *Little Lord Fauntleroy* (1936). Actors C. Aubrey Smith and Freddie Bartholomew. Seated at right with pipe: Director John Cromwell.

Selznick International signs to distribute through United Artists (1935). Left to right: Douglas Fairbanks, Jr., Charles Chaplin, Samuel Goldwyn, John Hay Whitney, Selznick, Walter Wanger, Jesse L. Lasky, Douglas Fairbanks, Sr., Roy Disney. Seated: Mary Pickford.

Filming *The Garden of Allah* (1936). Left to right: W. Howard Greene, Technicolor Cameraman (beside camera, with hat); Director Richard Boleslawski (with pipe), Director of Photography Harold Rosson, Charles Boyer, C. Aubrey Smith, Joseph Schildkraut, Marlene Dietrich.

Marlene Dietrich on location near Yuma, Arizona, during the filming of *The Garden of Allah*.

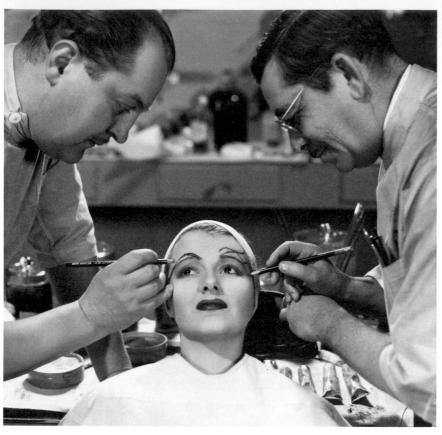

Janet Gaynor in *A Star Is Born* (1937). Applying makeup are Eddie Voight (left) and Paul Stanhope (right).

Director William Wellman and Selznick on the set of *A Star Is Born*.

PART

RKO
(1931–1933)

WHEN SCHULBERG WENT TO EUROPE in 1929, I was put in charge of the studio for a few months. A year or so later, Jesse L. Lasky sent for me and told me they were thinking of putting me permanently in charge of the studio, replacing Schulberg. In response to my question as to what would happen to Schulberg, he said, in effect, that they would be kicking him upstairs. I went to see Schulberg and asked him how he felt about it.. He was very angry, and I said that in that case, he should forget it, since I would not consider taking the job of the man who had brought me in; and I so notified Lasky. Schulberg, from that point on, would not even see me and wouldn't talk to me.

One of my rows with Paramount, leading to the demand that they cancel my contract, was my insistence that no one man could possibly personally *produce* more than a few pictures a year. I visualized the pictures being broken into individual units. The term "associate producer" was used long before this; my thought was to change the supervising or associate producer into an actual producer, and it was I who actually got the producers started in this business as such, both as to authority and as to credit. Up to the time I insisted upon it, no producer other than the head of the studio ever had vital authority or ever had his name on the screen. Indeed, until I returned to Metro in 1933 no one had ever been credited at that studio.

Paramount was actually headed for trouble at this time. They were making strictly formula pictures and were way behind time in material and the treatment of it. All sorts of things were still taboo there. I remember one instance: I had made Street of Chance the picture that made William Powell a star. I was told by the Paramount executives that the so-called "tragic ending," the death of the gambler, had cost them hundreds of thousands of dollars in gross. I asked them to believe that this was utterly ridiculous. The picture would have been nothing without this ending, and in fact, the entire story was built in terms of the gambler suffering for his own code: he had killed a man for violating this code and was himself killed when he violated it. Any other ending would have completely destroyed the picture. With Schulberg's increasingly antagonistic attitude toward me, and with his increasing use of his veto power over me, I encountered this sort of thing on everything I did. And it was this approach *to pictures generally that within the space of a few years took Paramount disastrously downhill.*

After my resignation from Paramount in June of 1931, I decided to follow up on what I had long believed: that the whole system of assembly-line-production picture studios was absurd, and that the business had to be broken into small producing units. I made a handshake deal with Lewis Milestone, who was then in gigantic demand by all the studios, having made All Quiet on the Western Front *and* The Front Page. *We formed a partnership. I made tentative arrangements that if I was able to finance and promote them, my next two units were to be with the directors Ernst Lubitsch and King Vidor.*

I went East in the summer of 1931 to promote the Selznick-Milestone unit, only to find myself up against a complete stone wall. At that time it was extremely difficult to get a release.[1] You could not get a release unless you had the money, and you could not get the money unless you had the release. Also, and as I learned subsequently, Louis B. Mayer, who was by then my father-in-law (I had married Irene while I was at Paramount—I met her at a New Year's Eve party in 1926), had called a meeting of all the companies to say that I must not be given a release, because if I were, the studios would break up and every producer and director would want his own independent unit.[2] So I spent three months in fruitless efforts at promotion. I was offered many jobs during the interim, which I refused.

Finally I decided that there was only one man that was outside the group and that was David Sarnoff, so I went to see him and told him my story and my convictions. (General Sarnoff was, of course, President of RCA, which at that time owned RKO Radio and RKO Pathé.) General Sarnoff instructed Hiram Brown, President of RKO, to make a deal with Milestone and myself for RKO to finance and distribute seven pictures a year for our unit. However, the others got to Milestone and he was offered a job, which I had refused, in charge of production for United Artists, and he accepted. So I had to go back to Sarnoff and tell him that I could not deliver under the deal. General Sarnoff was most sympathetic and asked me what I was going to do. I said I needed a job, so after many discussions, I sold him the idea of putting me in charge not only of production at RKO, but

---

[1] Theatrical distribution arrangement for a completed film.

[2] Prior to this, Selznick had been promised a release for his independent pictures by Jesse L. Lasky of Paramount.

*also of his own rival production unit, Pathé. In October of 1931 I signed
a contract to take over both studios and to merge them.*

I had wanted to do A Bill of Divorcement *for many years but could
never sell it to my bosses, because of the insanity angle which was
supposed to be taboo for pictures. But when I became my own boss,
it was practically the first story I bought. I went through one of those
searches for a new girl that drive everybody crazy, because we needed
new stars at RKO, and because I was convinced that the story would
be more moving and believable if it was played by a girl that hadn't
previously been identified with other parts. Furthermore, the role had
made great stars on the stage, such as Katharine Cornell.*

*After a long series of tests, George Cukor and I decided on Katha-
rine Hepburn,*[3] *who had recently made a favorable impression in a
New York play. Everybody was shocked silly. The world knows that
startling Hepburn face now, but when she first appeared on the RKO
lot there was consternation. "Ye gods, that horse face!" they cried, and
when the first rushes were shown, the gloom around the studio was
so heavy you could cut it with a knife. Not until the preview was the
staff convinced we had a great screen personality. During the first few
feet you could feel the audience's bewilderment at this completely
new type, and also feel that they weren't quite used to this kind of a
face. But very early in the picture there was a scene in which Hepburn
just walked across the room, stretched her arms, and then lay out on
the floor before the fireplace. It sounds very simple, but you could
almost feel, and you could definitely hear, the excitement in the audience. It was one of the greatest experiences I've ever had. In those few
simple feet of film a new star was born. Immediately after the preview
I decided to do* Little Women *with her, and started making production plans for it, although I left RKO to go back to MGM just before
the actual filming began, and never had the pleasure of personally
carrying out my plans.*

*Most casting successes are a matter of common sense. Myrna Loy
had been playing Oriental sirens for years, which was always a joke
with people who knew her. She is a beautiful girl, but in real life
she is no more a siren than I am. It was considered a revolutionary
thing to put her into a polite comedy such as* The Animal Kingdom, *but when this casting was suggested to me by Ned [Edward
H.] Griffith, the director, I leaped at the idea. Curiously, nobody
objected very much, probably because they knew Myrna person-*

[3]Selznick agreed to use Hepburn in the role after being strongly persuaded by Cukor.

ally—but it's strange that she was so long in reaching her natural field. We followed it up by casting her in a straight comedy role, the lead opposite John Barrymore in Topaze

It is hard to draw the line at RKO as to which pictures I personally produced and those on which I was the executive producer. In fact I originated the title of executive producer, which had not previously been used in the business. We had a very small total budget for a very large number of films, so what I decided to do was to make the smaller pictures even smaller in order to save money on those for a few big films, and I naturally devoted myself more to the bigger films than to the smaller ones. On my personal productions there, I was certainly the producer, even though I had associate producers (so-called) on them, such as Pandro Berman, who was my assistant and to whom I gave the title of associate producer on some of the pictures. I would say that I personally produced A Bill of Divorcement, The Animal Kingdom, Bird of Paradise, Topaze, *even though on that Kenneth Macgowan received associate producer credit, and a few others.*

As to King Kong, *I would say I was simply executive producer. RKO, when I took it over, had a big investment in an animation process of Willis O'Brien's. I brought back into the business as my Executive Assistant Merian C. Cooper, with whom I had been associated at Paramount on* The Four Feathers, *and assigned to him as one of his jobs a study of this animation process, and Cooper conceived the King Kong character idea.[4] I had signed up and sent for Edgar Wallace and brought him to California, where unfortunately he died in consequence of getting pneumonia and refusing to have a doctor since he was a Christian Scientist. But while he was in California, I assigned him to work with Cooper on* King Kong. *I have never believed that Wallace contributed much to* King Kong, *but the circumstances of his death complicated the writing credits. The picture was really made primarily by Cooper and Ernest Schoedsack, under my guidance; and one of the biggest gambles I took at RKO was to squeeze money out of the budgets of other pictures for this venture.*

I stayed at RKO until my contract expired in early 1933. My new contract, in which I had terms unprecedented in the business, was about to be signed when "Deac" [Merlin Hall] Aylesworth became head of the company, succeeding Hiram Brown. Aylesworth insisted

[4]Cooper actually had conceived the Kong character in late 1929, but not until December 1931, after studying O'Brien's animation process at Selznick's request, did he decide that *King Kong* could be produced utilizing that method combined with various special effects. Cooper then elicited Selznick's enthusiasm and support.

upon the new but still unsigned contract being changed to the extent of giving him approval of everything connected with production. I refused to accept this.

:: :: :: :: :: :: :: :: :: :: :: ::

TELETYPE TO RKO IN NEW YORK   MARCH 4, 1932

SUGGEST SENSATIONAL COMEBACK FOR CLARA BOW IN A HOLLYWOOD PICTURE TITLED "THE TRUTH ABOUT HOLLYWOOD." . . . FEEL VERY STRONGLY ANY OBJECTIONS TO HOLLYWOOD STORY AS SUCH HAVE NO BASIS WHATEVER. AM SURE THIS WILL BE PROVEN BY OTHER STUDIOS RUSHING PICTURES OF THIS TYPE. . . . ADELA ROGERS'S STORY IS IN EXCELLENT SHAPE . . . REASON WHY WE ARE AT TAIL END OF CYCLES IS OBJECTION TO DEPARTURES SUCH AS HOLLYWOOD STORY, WHICH STORY GIVES US OPPORTUNITY TO LEAD FIELD.[5]. . .

TELETYPE TO RKO IN NEW YORK   MARCH 26, 1932

PLEASE ADVISE REACTION TO IDEA OF [Merian C.] COOPER'S, WHICH I THINK HAS GREAT MERIT, OF ADVENTURE JUNGLE PICTURE ON NEXT YEAR'S PROGRAM, TO BE MADE IN WHAT I UNDERSTAND FROM COOPER, WHO HAS SEEN IT, IS SENSATIONAL NEW SECRET THREE COLOR-PROCESS [three-color Technicolor], WHICH WILL BE READY FOR PRODUCTION IN FOUR TO EIGHT MONTHS AND WHICH ELIMINATES MOST OF THE PHONY THINGS ABOUT PREVIOUS COLOR PROCESSES. . . . IF PROCESS IS AS SUPERB AS HE SAYS, MY PREVIOUS OBJECTIONS TO COLOR PICTURE WOULD BE REMOVED, AS I FEEL THAT IT ISN'T THAT PUBLIC DOESN'T WANT COLOR SO MUCH AS IT DOESN'T WANT THE ILLUSION-DESTROYING BAD COLORS WHICH HAVE BEEN FOISTED UPON IT. COOPER BRINGS OUT THAT WE COULD BUILD ARTIFICIAL JUNGLE SPLASHED WITH BRILLIANT COLORS SUCH AS USUAL ARTIST'S CONCEPTION, AND THAT SELECTION OF ANIMALS SUCH AS TIGERS, LEOPARDS, WHITE MONKEYS, ETC., WOULD ALL LEND

[5]The New York office replied that past experience proved "Hollywood stories did unfavorable business." Selznick persevered, and the project evolved into *What Price Hollywood?* (1932) with Constance Bennett. The picture did reasonably well and was a fororunnor of Selznick's *A Star Is Born* (1937).

THEMSELVES TO SENSATIONAL RESULTS IN PICTURE THAT MIGHT
BE AS INTERESTING AND SENSATIONAL AS FIRST JUNGLE PICTURE
WITH SOUND, "AFRICA SPEAKS."[6]

ROUGH DRAFT OF A LETTER INTENDED FOR ONE OF THE
RKO EXECUTIVES IN THE NEW YORK OFFICE, BUT APPARENTLY
NOT SENT
August 22, 1932

I have been greatly disturbed by the fact that it is apparent you do
not believe we are operating efficiently and economically. For this
reason, I respectfully request that you do not accept anyone's opinion,
not even my own, but examine and have checked the actual figures
of schedules, which I will forward.

When I took charge of the production of this company and saw the
chaotic studio condition which existed, with an unbalanced staff and
foolish expensive commitments, I definitely and repeatedly stated that
it would take six months at least to bring about a semblance of order,
and that the pictures I would have to make to complete the 1931–1932
program would cost ridiculously high prices. I also stated that when
these were completed that I could and would make better product,
more efficiently and far more economically. First, however, it was
necessary to clean up the studio, put it in working order, and get a
competent staff operating. To accomplish this, I have put into effect the
following reforms:

(1) Against decided opposition, I insisted on combining the production operations of Radio and Pathé under one staff, and in one studio.

(2) I put into effect as rapidly as possible, an entirely new, flexible
system of commitments. Whereas formerly the studio was loaded down
with long-term, expensive commitments, I have reduced these to an
average of four months' commitments, with many people on a week-to-
week basis. Also, in making new commitments, I have made them,
whenever possible, on greatly reduced terms. This flexible system
automatically protects the company in case of any change in policy.

(3) I have had each and every department rigidly checked, and have
made reductions in personnel and costs all along the line, which is

[6]The New York office turned down the proposal because they did not want to experiment with "anything so uncertain at this time." The first three-color Technicolor picture for theatrical release was a Walt Disney "Silly Symphony" short-subject cartoon,
Flowers and Trees, released in late 1932. The first feature production photographed in
the new Technicolor process was *Becky Sharp* (1935).

being, and will be, reflected in the entire 1932–1933 program.

(4) I have established a technical committee, which has instituted a number of reforms which show a very real reduction in production costs, and in increased mechanical efficiency of the plant.

(5) I have done away with the expensive producer system, and with only two assistants,[7] have taken over all production work.

(6) I have established a rigid economy policy in making capital expenditures. . . .

What has been the results of these reforms?

(1) Radio and Pathé together last year made forty-two features, six Westerns, and sixty-five shorts, at a cost of $16,021,538.17.

This year we are making forty-one features, six Westerns and thirty shorts at a budgeted cost of $10,221,000.00. . . . This saving of approximately $5,000,000.00 is being done despite the fact that we are making better product and using better directors, players, and writers.

. . . It is hampering and discouraging to me to be constantly criticized on costs. I believe, in this space of time, no studio in the business has ever had such great reduction in costs, considering quality. I can only believe that you have either been misinformed, or never properly informed, of the actual conditions.

To: Mr. O'Shea[8]   September 9, 1932

I hear rumors that Miss Hepburn[9] is under twenty-one, which we should take immediate steps to confirm, to find out whether it is necessary to get the approval of the courts. I understand she is prone to exaggerate her age and likes to be thought much older than she is.[10]

DOS

Mr. Louis B. Mayer   November 12, 1932
Metro-Goldwyn-Mayer Corp.   CONFIDENTIAL
Culver City, California

Dear Dad:

I have decided that under no circumstances would it be right for me to go with MGM.[11]

[7]Merian C. Cooper and Pandro S. Berman.
[8]Daniel T. O'Shea, Resident Counsel, RKO Studios.
[9]Katharine Hepburn had just completed *A Bill of Divorcement.*
[10]Selznick was advised that Miss Hepburn was over twenty-one.
[11]Selznick had been Executive Vice-President in Charge of Production at RKO for fourteen months at the time this letter was written.

Believe me, I am appreciative of the kindness of yourself and the others in the matter. The figures mentioned are flattering, and I cannot believe they are dictated by other than a sincere desire to have me for what you regard as my ability. That I am wanted for such a job by the most successful producing company in the business is a very high compliment indeed. But my reasons for not accepting the proposal seem to me to be separately and collectively much too important to disregard.

That you may know my reasons are sincere, I want you to know that at the time I am writing this note, I have not yet had a single word with the top RKO and RCA executives concerning my future. I do not know whether I shall be able to get together with them, and I have, as yet, not done a single thing to get myself an alternate position elsewhere. It is, accordingly, possible that I will be without a suitable proposition for myself. I do not fear this, but I say it is possible; and I point it out that you may know my decision is arrived at independently of any equal or better proposition elsewhere than the one I might possibly have with you.

My reasons follow:

1. Should RKO wish to continue with me on terms that are mutually agreeable, I feel that I owe them my allegiance. They gambled, and gambled heavily on me. They have permitted me to spend many millions of dollars entirely as I have seen fit. I think I have learned a great deal, and that they, as well as I, are entitled to the benefit of this learning. That they did not take any legal options on me is, in my opinion, beside the point; and I feel that there are certain moral obligations on my part, particularly in the face of their generosity about my bonus, etc.

2. I have taken on a certain spirit—call it collegiate or patriotic, or what you will—of trying to put the company over in the face of obstacles and handicaps. I know it is difficult, but this is part of the fun; and I discount the attitude of many people that it is impossible, just as I discounted a year ago the statements that the company could not survive a month and could not borrow a quarter of a million dollars.

3. I have had a great deal of satisfaction out of feeling that in a comparatively short space of time, I have advanced my career appreciably; on my own efforts. This sense of accomplishment would be seriously impaired, and much of the fun of life and work gone, if I took my place in an organization in which I would be a relative—an inlaw, what's worse!—of the company's head. I share the opinion of the world about the generality of relatives in business, even conceding that there

are exceptions. I know what is thought of them in business generally; what is thought of them within the industry; and, yes, even what is thought of them at MGM. It is not that I care so much what other people say or think as that these opinions must inevitably have a result on the advancement of my career. One doesn't get ahead in business without the esteem of his fellow workers. And, even more than this, I cannot face the prospect of being a relative in business without cringing and without an inevitable subsequent loss of self-respect. I would never know whether I had gotten ahead on my own or through the help of someone—whether I had been helped in my successes and protected in my failures—and I am not alone willing but, believe me, anxious to take the rap whenever I am wrong: it helps me grow. Moreover, I believe there is a hazard to my life with Irene, which might lose a great deal of its balance were I an employee of her father. This is too personal a matter to do much writing about, but I may say, in passing, that Irene shares my opinion. I think, among other things, that she would lose her pride in me, which I may say I enjoy.

4. I have the most enormous respect for Irving Thalberg. I regard him as the greatest producer the industry has yet developed. I intend to try goddam hard to equal his achievements, and I hope one day to surpass them. I cannot do this at MGM for two reasons: first, if I did succeed, it would be with the assets and the facilities that he has been so largely responsible for developing. (And, incidentally, I would have to be pretty conceited to think I could do better with these assets and these facilities than he has done.) I want to continue to develop my own people and my own stars and my own facilities from the scratch line where I started a year ago. Then truly, if I put it over, I will have done something—and that is the best reward! Secondly, I could not help but be subordinate to Irving— and much as I respect him, I do not want, in my own field, to be subordinate to anybody. I have passed that stage, and I hope I will not have to retrogress. Irving could give me all the assurances in the world that I would be independent, and I would still be subordinate; working for MGM, I would expect to be. His record is too excellent for me not to regard him as the master of that particular situation; and I should think very little indeed of his organization if they did not regard him as their master.

5. Certainly it would be a whole lot easier—by a thousand per cent —to make good pictures at MGM than at RKO. I have no tools to speak of; I have only a fraction of the money to spend; and while I believe I have the generous sympathy and faith of the men at the top of the company, still it is true that they, as yet, have not a full understanding

of the problems and of the wise things to do, at least as I see them, in the conduct of production. I would have a great deal of grief at RKO that I would never know at MGM. But this doesn't faze me; I am too young to worry about it, and it is good for me, in the bargain, which I well know when I am not emotionally disturbed and upset. But in spite of this, or perhaps because of it, I would enjoy more putting the thing over in spite of every handicap, than treading a comparative bed of roses. I suppose it is something akin to the fellows who would rather plan and dig roads through mountains than drive over the boulevards in a Lincoln.

There is an excellent chance that the time will come, a year or a month or, perhaps, even a week from now, when you will be able to say, "If he had not been so headstrong, he would not be having that trouble now." But I have taken that chance before, and if it comes, I will face it. I will know, at least, that I acted in accordance with the dictates of what I conceived to be the best thing for my character, if not for my eventual monetary reward.

I beg that you should not consider me ungrateful, or lacking in family spirit, and I should be very sad about it if you do. I hope you will consider me affectionately, and certainly you cannot consider me other than,

Most sincerely yours,

[P.S.] RKO had an amazing faith in me at a time when my previous employers did everything to run me down, and when very few other companies in the business had even an appreciable respect for my ability. Notably, MGM did not change in its disrespect for these abilities from the time I left its employ about six years ago, up until a few months ago. Faith, I feel, should be returned with faith.

To: Mr. Brock[12]   January 13, 1933
cc: Mr. Sandrich[13]

I think you might reconcile yourself to the unquestionable fact that it would be utterly impossible for us to buy a name that is worth a damn, within the limits of your budget on the picture which Sandrich is to direct [probably *Melody Cruise* (1933)]. . . .

I am tremendously enthused about the suggestion New York has made of using Fred Astaire. If he photographs (I have ordered a test),

[12]Louis Brock, RKO Associate Producer.
[13]Mark Sandrich, RKO Director.

he may prove to be a really sensational bet. . . . Astaire is one of the great artists of the day: a magnificent performer, a man conceded to be perhaps, next to Leslie Howard, the most charming in the American theater, and unquestionably the outstanding young leader of American musical comedy. He would be, in my opinion, good enough to use in the lead in a million-dollar Lubitsch picture—provided only that he photographs, which I hope is the case. I trust you and Mr. Sandrich will keep confidential the fact that we are considering and negotiating with him, since I am certain that as soon as it becomes generally known that he is at last considering pictures, there will be a wild scramble on the part of all studios to test him.

DOS

To: Mr. Siff[14]   January 26, 1933

Please arrange for the executives, including Brock, to see the test of Fred Astaire. I am a little uncertain about the man, but I feel, in spite of his enormous ears and bad chin line, that his charm is so tremendous that it comes through even in this wretched test, and I would be perfectly willing to go ahead with him for the lead in the Brock musical. I should like to have Brock's opinion; but even if he is opposed to Astaire, I would be in favor of signing him for this part if some of the other studio executives have any enthusiasm for the man.[15]

DOS

To: Mr. Kahane[16]   January 27, 1933

Dear Ben:

Apparently you misunderstood my query concerning story approval. I did not mean whether *we* had the final word, but whether *I* had the final word in story purchase and assignment, as well as in all other production matters.

While recognizing you as the head of the company in matters of finance and policy, I could not consider accepting the possibility of any veto power on the part of anybody on stories which I might select. This

[14]Philip Siff, assistant to Selznick.

[15]Astaire was signed. When Selznick moved to MGM in 1933, he introduced Astaire in *Dancing Lady*. Astaire's first RKO picture was *Flying Down to Rio* (1933).

[16]Benjamin B. Kahane, President of RKO Radio Studios and RKO Pathé Studios; Vice-President of the parent corporation, Radio-Keith-Orpheum.

is in all due respect to you, but is a matter of policy under any change from which I do not think it possible for a production head to function properly.

As you know, I have been completely in charge not merely of costs but also of everything that went into the making of a picture. I have been given to understand that this has not been made clear in New York. I am perfectly willing to stand on my record on both costs and quality, and I insist upon standing upon my record in the future in both respects, which I can do only if I continue to have final authority —and by final, I mean final: somebody has to have the last word in every studio organization, and I see no reason why this should be that of any other man but the production head, simply because that other man happens to carry the title of President. Certainly Irving Thalberg has never been subject to the word or approval of Nicholas Schenck; on the other hand, Ben Schulberg was responsible to New York executives, and you have seen the result; and poor Bill Le Baron[17] met his undoing in the unjustifiable necessity of President Schnitzer's[18] approvals. . . .

DOS

To: Mr. B. B. Kahane   February 3, 1933
                                                        NEVER SENT

Dear Ben:

After our talk last night, I should like to clarify the reasons for my leaving.

Following our chat of the other day, about the matter of your authority, I was convinced that I had nothing to fear from your direction. As you so truly pointed out, your authority had never been obtrusive; we had gotten along in complete harmony; there was no reason to fear that there would be any trouble in the future between us; and I was satisfied that the corporate structure required the President to have the final word, should its exercise for any reason become necessary. I was perfectly willing, as I expressed myself to you, to accept your authority.

But an authority in addition to your own on production matters, that of New York—was something else again. I consider that it would be completely impossible for any production head to operate if he had to

---

[17]William Le Baron, ex-Vice-President in Charge of Production at RKO Radio Pictures.
[18]Joseph I. Schnitzer, ex-President of RKO Radio Pictures.

submit himself to what Mr. Aylesworth demanded—the approval by himself of every script and budget. . . .

But more important than the matter of authority is that the company, after months of changing . . . the terms of my contract, finally agreed on terms; authorized you to close with me; and seduced me into operating not merely on pictures to be made immediately but on the future program, with the wired assurance, which I still have on file, from Mr. Sarnoff, that any representation made by you was official from the company. It is not surprising to me that Mr. Aylesworth should again prove himself undependable in his dealings with me; but when Mr. Sarnoff, whom I completely depended upon as a man of his word, a man whose assurances I could take literally, a man who never failed to give me a reply when I asked him for one, a man who told me, as recently as last week, that the contract would be approved immediately you and I got together—when this man, too, let me down, and tried to change a basic part of the deal, I lost all hope of ever knowing where I stood, of ever being able to feel that I had the support of the New York executives, and could count on them to deal with me dependably.

To leave the realm of business relationships, honor among coworkers, etc. (about which I am apparently still a little naïve), and become practical, a simple investigation of the figures shows that the new proposition submitted, increasing (on our present standard of distribution cost) the percentage charge to me for distribution probably five per cent—until that mythical future date when distribution costs would be reduced—would rob me of all hope of profit.

I should like to say, finally, that in all your dealings with me, I believe you to have been completely frank and honest and appreciative. I believe that you alone, of the principal executives of the company, know the job that I have done, in the face of every conceivable handicap, on costs and quality, and the extent to which I have guarded every penny of the company's money. It has been a great pleasure to know you, and I hope your friendship will continue unabated for a long time.

Very sincerely yours,

PART

MGM
(1933–1935)

AFTER REFUSING THE NEW CONDITIONS AT RKO, *I accepted an offer in early 1933 to become a vice-president of MGM, in charge of my own unit—the first departure from the traditional setup at MGM. My first picture for MGM was an all-star adaptation of the stage success,* Dinner at Eight. *Later came* Viva Villa! *with Wallace Beery—one of my favorites.*

I still had the pleasure of introducing Fred Astaire to the screen by borrowing him from my former studio, which was uncertain as to what it had bought, and introducing him in Dancing Lady *at MGM, a picture which also introduced Nelson Eddy, and which rescued Joan Crawford from the threatened oblivion caused by a series of flops including* Rain. Dancing Lady *was the most successful picture Joan Crawford and Clark Gable had made, and for years was rated by MGM as the hundred-per-cent commercial picture by which all other pictures were measured. In spite of the fact that this venture on my part into the musical field was a sensation, I don't like making musical comedies.*

Manhattan Melodrama *brought William Powell to Metro against the protests of some of the executives, who thought I was making a serious mistake in engaging a "washed-up" star instead of using one of their stock players. Powell worked with Myrna Loy for the first time in this picture. Also,* Manhattan Melodrama *was "the film that caught Dillinger." This was the picture he couldn't resist seeing because it was about a gangster who went to the electric chair. The FBI caught him in the theater. The picture was quite successful.*

Of course I made some flops. To give you some outstanding ones of earlier days: there was an awful attempt at a melodrama at Paramount called Chinatown Nights *[1929] with Wally Beery. I thought that a picture about a tong war would be exciting, but somehow it didn't come off. There was at MGM in 1933 a horror that I produced called* Meet the Baron, *starring Jack Pearl. MGM had decided to capitalize on the popularity of radio stars, and at the suggestion of Harry Rapf, signed Ed Wynn and Jack Pearl. I have never been a devotee of radio comics. I had never heard either Wynn or Pearl on the radio. You will recall that Rapf had been my benefactor in the early days at Metro, and so, when he appealed to me to take one of them over (because he had initiated both, had felt responsibility for both, and felt he could only handle one at a time), I agreed and he gave me Pearl. I made the picture with a loathing for it, and it was a terrible flop. I learned then what I should have learned long before: never to tackle a picture for which I had no enthusiasm, never to tackle a subject for which I had not a personal liking, and for which I lacked confidence in my ability to translate to the screen effectively.*

One of my most difficult experiences while at MGM was casting David Copperfield. *Nobody else liked even the idea of making* David Copperfield, *and when the months went by without our finding a boy for the part, the enthusiasm didn't increase. The studio tried to put pressure on me to use Jackie Cooper, but although I was a great enthusiast for Jackie in other roles, I thought him completely unsuited to play David; and furthermore, I felt very strongly that we needed an English boy, and one of the most infinite charm and of the greatest dramatic talent.*

When we were in England on the David Copperfield *search for locations, second-unit[1] shots, casting, research, etc., I lugged with me every place we went the old-fashioned red leather copy of* Copperfield *which my father had given me, with its tiny type on bad paper and its heavy binding. Half sentimentally, half superstitiously, on most of the classics that I have purchased from the books he first suggested I read, I used the very volumes that he gave me.*

I am sure that the opposition to filming David Copperfield *was based largely upon the fact that both classics and costume pictures had been taboo in the industry for a long time. I had encountered the same sort of opposition when, shortly before, I had decided to make* Little Women. *The executives and sales heads of RKO had suggested that I "modernize" the story, but I can't say there was anyone at MGM who was silly enough to suggest this on* Copperfield. *I think it was simply that it very obviously couldn't be a star vehicle, that it was a very expensive picture to make and would violate all the rules of showmanship that were then considered sacred and inviolable.*

The opposition lasted all through the picture, and the entire studio thought I was going to go on my nose. Even at the preview, the executives still didn't realize what we had and pressed me with their consoling opinion that "it might do well in England." Hollywood trade papers suggested that the second half be thrown away and the picture

---

[1]Another director, cameraman, and crew usually assembled to film specialized material (not always involving the leading players). E. g., action sequences, atmospheric shots, special effects, animal sequences, location material, etc.

end when the story of the children ends.[2] *Not until its sensational success at the Capitol Theatre in New York did the company realize that it had one of the outstanding successes of all time. And even then, it was thought that perhaps it would not repeat its success throughout the country—that there might have been just enough lovers of Dickens in New York to support the run at the Capitol.*

It's true that other classics have been attempted with unhappy results. This was, I'm sure, due to two factors: some of the classics produced have been selected from those that are no longer read or loved. The others were very badly made with attempts to make them conform to the scenario formulas of that time.

:: :: :: :: :: :: :: :: :: :: :: ::

To: Mr. Siff   March 1, 1933

In arranging for the stars for *Dinner at Eight*, we are simply to notify Mr. Mayer and Mr. Thau[3] of whom we decide to use, and they will make all arrangements. Accordingly, please advise Thau now to make necessary arrangements for Wallace Beery, Jean Harlow, Clark Gable, Marie Dressler, Lionel Barrymore, Lee Tracy, Louise Closser Hale. We will discuss, upon completion of the script, whether or not to attempt to have Joan Crawford play the girl. We will, also, discuss the possibility of signing John Barrymore for the part of the actor, after the other deal with Barrymore is closed. Please follow up Cukor on the tests of Alice Brady and Billie Burke for the part of the wife. Also, discuss with Cukor the possibility of using Burke as the doctor's wife, and Alice Brady as Oliver's wife.[4] . . .

We should keep confidential our work on *Garden of Allah* until the dialogue rights are closed. As soon as these rights are closed, remind

[2]This is not entirely accurate. *Variety* thought that "the first half . . . is almost without flaw, but in the latter half there is some floundering and digression which may be cured by considerable cutting of the preview footage." *The Hollywood Reporter* thought that "the first half is as brilliant a piece of screen entertainment as has been shown . . . but the picture, as a whole, is way over length." The uncredited reviewer suggested that the film be released in two separate versions; that is, divided into two parts.

[3]Benjamin Thau, assistant to Louis B. Mayer.

[4]Clark Gable presumably was going to play the role eventually assigned to Edmund Lowe; Madge Evans—not Joan Crawford—played the girl; Billie Burke was the wife, and Karen Morley the doctor's wife. Alice Brady did not appear in the production. The other performers mentioned were cast.

me to try to close with Sidney Howard to do the script. I am planning on this for Garbo. Keep in close touch with the availability of Herbert Marshall to play opposite Garbo in this subject.[5]

The Beverly Wilshire
Beverly Hills, California
March 16, 1933

Darling,[6]

The promise to Morpheus has gone the way of most things: after substituting a nap last night for my accustomed protracted coma, here I am at three a.m.

I've just left Myron, pickled as aye, after sitting with him for hours at the Zanuck[7] party; Oomkins[8] somnambulistically interested in Romance or Argument, but too sleepy to pursue either. Someone—Bill [Powell], I think—said he looked tonight like Lionel Barrymore's father. . . .

I'm no more settled mentally, I regret to report—unless a further resignation to High-Salaried Defeat be termed progress. I'm regretfully arriving at the conclusion that I am "hoist on my own petard." I suppose, accordingly, that I've no alternative to sticking it a while and making the best.

(Here I collapsed)

I hate like the devil to have to tell you that I'm just as upset . . . I've gone through every possible mood—except the good ones. Most of the time, I feel like some form of commercial pimp, and my conviction that I'm about four times as valuable as most of the incompetents around here [MGM] helps only momentarily. Incidentally, I've been pretty good about the press attacks, but their persistence commences to be annoying. You should see the anti-Selznick issue of Beaton's[9] sheet this week!

Enough of whining . . . I've only the hope left in the mess I've made of seven years of progress, and that's that I'll have character enough

---

[5]Selznick did not make *The Garden of Allah* until 1936, at which time he produced it for his own company—Selznick International—with Marlene Dietrich and Charles Boyer.

[6]Irene Selznick, who was in New York briefly.

[7]Darryl F. Zanuck, Head of Production, in association with Jack L. Warner, at Warner Bros.–First National.

[8]A pet name for Myron Selznick.

[9] *The Hollywood Spectator*, a publication edited and published by Welford Beaton. The issue referred to contained an editorial that was extremely critical of Louis B. Mayer's hiring his son-in-law at a reported salary of $4000 per week.

not to subject you to a repetition of suspicion even that I blame you.[10] I'm abject in humiliation over that. Believe me, darling.

I wanted to write you a love letter; I felt like writing you one. There's no use trying now: the obligato of discontent is much too strong.

Forgive me, sweetheart. . . .

David O.

Mr. Nicholas M. Schenck   May 16, 1933
Metro-Goldwyn-Mayer
New York City

Dear Nick:

. . . As I told you on the telephone, I think the present setup is working out nicely and I believe it to be a decided improvement in the studio organization.[11] . . .

However, I have not changed my conviction that (although like any other studio plan it has its disadvantages) a single centralized production head, operating under a company head such as L. B. [Mayer], and having a dictatorship over all the production and editorial activities of the studio, is the soundest plan of operation. No compromise oligarchy or system of dual or triple control can, in my opinion, be very effective in the elimination of waste and the meeting of the company's commercial problems.

. . . We have a magnificent stock company that, perhaps, should be weeded somewhat and certainly should be supplemented by a few more people for development into stars a year, two years, or three years hence. Notably we are lacking in leading men. We have a group of superb staff directors: [Clarence] Brown, [Robert Z.] Leonard, [Sidney] Franklin, Van Dyke, Cukor; and others who are extremely valuable, such as [Jack] Conway and [Sam] Wood— who, indeed, it is possible deserve rating with the others. I believe we should augment this list with the permanent addition of men like Vidor, Fleming, and Borzage[12]—for I think we should be a lot better off with fewer supervisors and more producing directors, in-

[10]Selznick had gone to MGM on the advice of his father just before his death (January 25, 1933), not at the urging of his wife.

[11]When Selznick joined MGM in February of 1933, he headed one of five separate producing units, each responsible for a group of films each year.

[12]King Vidor, Victor Fleming, and Frank Borzage. Vidor did not join MGM until 1938, Fleming was signed the same year this memo was written, and Borzage joined in 1937.

creasing our chances of getting an even greater number of out-standing pictures. I believe it the destiny of MGM to acquire top talent whenever it develops, with the other companies serving as minor leagues developing this talent, and with MGM prepared to pay for the best talent. In the production of the type of pictures that we want, it is the mediocre talent in quantity that swells cost and reduces quality.

But even as we are today, we are in splendid shape from the directorial standpoint; it is in the writing staff that we are woefully weak. We would be much better situated with twenty men, each getting, if necessary, very high salaries, writing the bulk of our program (with others to be engaged by the picture when required), than we are with a staff of seventy-five, probably not ten of whom are worth their salt (and of this ten, there is a much smaller number who, in addition to being able, are sincere, conscientious workers). I should like to see a reduced writing staff augmented with brains of the type of Ben Hecht, [playwright] Sidney Howard, and [playwright] Philip Barry[13]—and we could let out half a dozen incompetents for each of these men we engaged.

With a staff that comprised eighty per cent of the ranking writing and directing brains of the world, we would not alone need fewer producers, but they would get in the way, for their creative ability is not comparable. With such a setup and a centralized production head, we could have all the advantages of the Zanuck system,[14] plus the quality of the better Thalberg pictures.

I think we are today quite well off on story material and on completed scripts—certainly much better off than the studio has ever been before, if I am to accept what I hear about the past.

. . . I am trying to make a selection from *The Forsyte Saga* by Galsworthy for the remaining picture we have with John Barrymore. I also plan on using Lionel Barrymore in this picture and at the right time may submit for your consideration something that I fear will offhand have opposition from you—the thought of again using Ethel Barrymore. I think we could get an extremely important picture by having the three Barrymores as members of a single family, and assure

[13]Hecht was to be employed by MGM occasionally, Sidney Howard worked on only one assignment, and Philip Barry by his own choice never went to MGM (or any studio).

[14]Zanuck had just resigned his position at Warner Bros.-First National, where the emphasis was on original story ideas and scripts executed in a collective, cost-conscious manner. At MGM the emphasis was on adapted works, high-priced talent, and opulent production.

you we will not have the grief of *Rasputin*,[15] because it will be a finished script and Ethel, if we decide to use her and have the right part for her, can take the part or leave it. Also, Cukor, who is very enthusiastic about the idea, has handled the Barrymores on many occasions, without the slightest difficulty—perhaps the only director of which this can be said. In any case, this is not until next September, when John Barrymore returns from his trip; and I expect to have the script ready for consideration sufficiently long enough before his return to give every consideration to the idea.[16]

Most cordially and sincerely yours,

Mr. Louis B. Mayer   June 14, 1933
Metro-Goldwyn-Mayer Corp.
Culver City, California

Dear Dad:

You have repeatedly told both Irene and myself that your principal interest is for my happiness. Believing in the sincerity of your statements, I take courage to tell you what otherwise I might feel would be too much of a bombshell.

I write you instead of telling you verbally because I have learned that I write much better than I talk; because I want to be sure I tell you exactly how I feel, and by reading the letter myself before sending it to you, I know I am saying what I want to say; and because you might like to transmit the contents to Nick [Schenck].

I want to get out of MGM, and the quicker the better. I would not want to leave the company in a hole on anything it depends on getting from me, and would, consequently, gladly finish the pictures I have been planning, even though they took me several months; but the most desirable thing in my life, at the moment, would be to know and have it definitely understood and announced, that I shall be leaving at a date in the future, to be fixed—or at once, if that is preferable to the company.

You may recall that Nick told you about a letter that I read to him,

---

[15] *Rasputin and the Empress* (1932), featuring the three Barrymores, was a problem picture from many standpoints. The grief commenced when the filming started before a satisfactory script was ready; this was necessary because Ethel Barrymore had only a limited time available prior to a theatrical commitment in New York. The script was rewritten during production. Then, there was a change in director; dissatisfactions with the character interpretations; and, as a climax, expensive libel suits.

[16] A film derived from *The Forsyte Saga* was not made by MGM until 1949. The three Barrymores did not appear in another film together.

which I did not send because, subsequent to my reading of it to Nick, Irene implored me not to, saying that I did not know the extent of your feelings and that you might interpret my attitude incorrectly. I am sorry now that I did not send this letter, because it might have avoided a lot of trouble for both of us. . . .[17]

The letter is useful to me in establishing one thing: never again will I take a major step on anyone's opinion but my own. This may sound vain, but it is true: I have been wrong hundreds of times in minor business and production matters; but the first time in my business career that I have taken the wrong major step was coming to MGM; and in this step my convictions were right, but I was weak and felt that the advice of my immediate family should be heeded.

On top of this, the decision to be made unfortunately coincided with my father's death, and I was under a unique emotional strain: I felt I should let the family tie influence my decision; and, above everything, I was mindful of the last advice my father gave me, which was to go to MGM. It is easy for me to see how he could have thought this best for me, just as it is easy for me to understand your advice to the same effect, and the very sincere devotion behind which I do not doubt— but neither of you were aware of the psychology of the matter, either my own or that of the industry. This is largely my fault: if I had sent you the letter as I originally intended, you would have known it.

Certainly I have no blame for anyone in any of the guidance they offered me on this or on earlier matters, for surely my family, including you, tried to influence me properly and in what they conceived to be my best interests. Like my father, you went far, far out of your way to give me the benefit of experience and position and influence, and you were guided by a devotion more that of a father than a father-in-law. But my father, the memory of whom is the basis of one of the finest emotions of my life, and to whom I owe everything, and who formerly was proven right in all his advice to me, was, in this case, guided by his heart alone—and so were you. I have no hesitancy in guessing that if you will look back on your own career, you will find that more often than not other people, even those very close to you, gave you advice that was as wrong as it was sincere and mature and affectionate, and that, if followed, would have stunted your development into the man you are today. . . .

I was told what a mistake it was to argue with Irving [Thalberg]

[17]Selznick wrote preliminary drafts of letters dealing with his desire to leave MGM quite frequently during this period.

some six or seven years ago and to quit MGM rather than agree with him. I was told I was wrong when I tore up my Paramount contract rather than subscribe to the Schulberg policies that I knew would tear us all down, and you yourself urged me to go back to Paramount and attempt to compromise my difficulties with them. I was told I was wrong when I tried desperately to put over some independent units on the very basis which those who opposed and stopped me are now supporting in the cases of Zanuck, Lasky, and others. I was told I was wrong not to accept the United Artists job which Milestone later undertook and which, to his undoing, proved so thin an opportunity, what with Jolson,[18] *Rain* [1932], lack of finances, etc. I was told I was wrong to accept the RKO job in preference to that at United Artists, that the company could not last three months, and that it would be a black eye for me. I was told the following year that the profits on the RKO deal which were offered me some months back for renewal of my contract would prove to be imaginary, when in fact Cooper's[19] profits are proving that my income from these profits would have been fabulous compared to any executive salary—although do not for an instant get the idea that I feel that $4000 weekly is anything but an extremely high, and even quite possibly too high, salary, for I believe in shares in profits rather than such salaries. And finally, I was dissuaded a second time from organizing a company to operate on the exact lines that Twentieth Century is now operating, the product of which proposed enterprise you may not know Joe Schenck[20] was willing to release, with Nick also saying that he thought he would be willing to violate MGM custom, and distribute.

I had more capital lined up, ready and anxious to back me, than Zanuck could possibly have available to him; I urged the theory of a company operating outside the Producer Agreement;[21] and I had stars lined up and ready to sign with me that might have given me very close to a major company virtually overnight. I feel very keenly that the dissuasion from these plans cost me the opportunity of my life; possibly, over a period of years, millions of dollars; and, most important, fulfillment of my long-cherished dreams. If I get out of MGM, it

[18]A reference to an Al Jolson failure, *Hallelujah, I'm a Bum* (1933).
[19]Merian C. Cooper had taken over Selznick's position at RKO.
[20]Joseph M. Schenck (the brother of Nicholas M. Schenck), President of United Artists; Schenck was also President of Twentieth Century Pictures (prior to the merger of Twentieth Century with Fox Films).
[21]Motion Picture Producers and Distributors Association Agreement, a voluntary code of regulation and self-censorship agreed to by substantially all the principal motion picture theatrical producers in the United States.

may be that I shall want to try to resurrect these plans. . . .

I am today regarded, not merely by a few sheets[22] . . . but by the industry at large, as the outstanding example of a nepotism that I must, unfortunately, agree is the curse of the business. Were I on the outside, and someone else in my place, I would share the opinion that others have of me today. All past accomplishment is wiped out, because this is a business that forgets yesterday at dawn today; and any appreciation of future accomplishment is impossible because I am not an executive here, as I believe I am, by right of six or seven years of struggle, but a relative here by right of marriage. The studio is split in two: on the one side the workers; and on the other side . . . twenty or thirty others,[23] and, leading the parade, David Selznick. I am more objectionable than any of them in ratio to our respective salaries. Ask anyone for an honest comment on what damage I have done to the morale of your plant.

And even if this were all not true, and is pure imagination on my part, it does not matter. The important thing is that I believe it to be true. You have said you are glad to have been able to save me from what you considered to be the heartaches of RKO; I assure you that I was deliriously happy at RKO by comparison with the heartache I suffer here and have suffered since the first day I started.

And on top of this, I find myself fighting to overcome an enormous prejudice throughout the studio against me, not merely because I am a relative, but because of the wretched way in which the company handled the announcement of my coming here, a mishandling due to a desire to protect Thalberg's feelings rather than my position. This is history, but I bring it up now because it contributed largely to my terrible position here. You have said repeatedly that I have made tremendous progress in overcoming this prejudice, and I believe you. But why should I fight? I am all worn out and feeling run-down physically; to make good pictures takes just about everything one has, without having to win a political fight as well. And I am in no state of mind to fight an issue that has nothing to do with success or failure, an issue that would certainly be recurrent and that would never, so far as I am concerned, be obviated. . . .

I have hesitated for some weeks to send you this letter because you extended yourself so much to get me in here, and there hangs over me the feeling of obligation on my part, despite your kind assurances,

[22]Industry publications.
[23]Relatives of high-ranking executives at MGM.

and those of Nick, that my coming in was such a help to the company. But, on the other hand, I have had to take a lot more abuse as a result of it than you have had; and you are in a position where you can take it, where I cannot, your career and position being established and secure beyond any damage that could be done to it by me.

This is not to say that I am not deeply appreciative of all the faith and encouragement you have given me since I have come here, because I am: and I know you have tried repeatedly to give me every possible break with the hope that my success would reflect credit on you as well as on myself, and justify the judgment that you made against opposition. But each aid that you rendered me only served to accentuate the position I was in and to make me feel that any success I won here I could not regard as my own. You have sometimes indicated (although you may not even have known that you have done so) that you regarded my obvious disinclination to accept your favors and your aid as ungracious, and my reception of your recent help as perhaps unappreciative, and as certainly undemonstrative—although undemonstrative I have always been and always will be. I hope fervently that one day you will know me as not ungrateful, but ungrasping; that I may have the chance to prove my affection without monetary or commercial reward; and that I can demonstrate that proper family relationships need have no commercial ties, but are, in fact, more secure without them.

My grief started from the first hour I came here, and has continued unabated up to this writing. I feel slightly better, at this moment, for merely having written this letter, than I have for months. This is the first unhappy year of my entire life. No doubt the loss of my father had a large part in this, but I have a conviction that my moroseness has been aggravated enormously by my false commercial position. I have had other periods when things did not go so well, in fact a whole period of years from the time that the family went broke along with the Selznick Company, and literally no one of us had a dollar to our names, up to the time that I first began to feel that I was achieving something at Paramount—but those were days of ambition with a drive to make good. Never was there a moment of depression, and certainly none of the mercurial moods of indifference and depression that have made me almost impossible to live with, and that have colored every side of my life. The salary I am making is futile in the face of my definite and unshakeable philosophy that money may abet happiness, but that under no circumstances can it be the source of it. I have no illusion that if I get out of here I can make anything like the money I am making today—certainly not for a few years at least. But I could enjoy Columbia [Pictures Corporation] if I'd made it; and I couldn't enjoy MGM if it were dropped in my lap.

I say I have hesitated for weeks in sending you this, but I send it now because I have very carefully considered all the angles and feel that a little foresight will show it to be the kindest and best thing for all of us. I know that if I am anchored here for years, I shall never feel differently and will slowly, but surely, decay: already I am completely without incentive or interest and, for the first time in my life, have to force myself to work.

Regarding the time element, I believe, even though you may not, that there is certain to be a clash with Irving when he returns,[24] if not with you over me, then certainly with me: he would have to be a far bigger character than would be human not to be affected by the attitude of his staff, the resentment in the air. Then too, there will be a lot of things that, as a partner, he will not like, ranging all the way from little things such as whether certain players he will want for his pictures should be in my pictures, and whether I am, in his sincere opinion, affecting adversely properties which he considers his, to major differences in matters of policy. Believing that this clash is sooner or later certain, even though his generosity and our mutual diplomacy might postpone it a while, when it comes he will either step out of the company, in which case I shall be linked forever to the institution that you have had the thrill of building, and forever be denied the only pleasure of commercial life, that of building my own; or I shall step out with an even worse black eye than I am prepared to receive if I step out today—because I shall then, in the industry's eyes, have been put out. Thus my request—nay, a great deal more: my urgent plea—that you permit my resignation to be known before Irving's return. Maybe I am running away, but discretion is the better part of valor; and I cannot refuse the joint urgings of my heart and my head. I have taken a beating in coming here; I shall take another beating in leaving—but the worst beating would be to leave later. I should like to preserve enough face to start again; and I have enough confidence to believe that in a year or two, I can beat back to where I was a year ago, at least to my own former estimation of myself, at any spot in the wide, wide world except this acreage in Culver City.

You may accuse me of selfishness in my attitude. But I was not selfish when I came here, for your arguments that you wanted me to help you

[24]Thalberg was on an extended leave of absence.

had no small part in my decision. And I do not think I am selfish in leaving, because though you may suffer some slight hurt through it, I shall suffer a great deal more. And I cannot believe that I will be any help to you, feeling as I do. In fact, I am much more likely to harm you through being unable to live up to your expectations— and particularly to the expectations of Nick [Schenck]. I feel tremendous regret at having to take this attitude, not merely because of you but also because of Nick, who has shown me a kindness and an appreciation completely unique in my business experience. My gratitude to him equals my respect for him. I can never expect to be associated with anyone else who will treat me as you have and as he has. . . .

If you are momentarily annoyed or disappointed, I believe that you will eventually agree that I am doing the right thing in facing the matter squarely. Suffering in silence any longer is not going to do either of us any good; and what is worse, and this will undoubtedly distress you as it has me, even the clause in the letter [presumably of November 12, 1932] about my coming with MGM affecting my life with Irene, is coming true. Try as I have these months to keep from taking it out on her, it has crept through. I will not go into this any further except to tell you that Irene and I have sat up until dawn many nights torturing ourselves with my acute discontent. If I am completely honest with myself, it is possible—indeed, it is likely—that my state of mind has contributed to her bad health. And Irene in all the world knows that my spirit, my pride, my ambition are gone. You may call it false pride, lack of family feeling, oversensitiveness, youthful arrogance, insanity, or whatever else you like. Call it by whatever name, my happiness rests on it.

I have yet to ask you, since I have been married to Irene or before, a solitary favor. I ask now my first: please, please release me from my contract.[25]

Affectionately, sincerely, and passionately yours,

To: Mr. Mannix[26]   June 23, 1933

If we are successful in purchasing *The Paradine Case*, I think the announcement book should be changed, so that instead of having "one John Barrymore starring vehicle" we have the much more important

[25]Selznick was not released from his contract.
[26]Edgar J. Mannix, MGM Vice-President.

setup of "John Barrymore, Lionel Barrymore, and Diana Wynyard in *The Paradine Case*."

However, the matter should be kept confidential until we succeed in closing for the story.[27]

                                                          DOS

To: Mr. Mayer   September 6, 1933

I have arranged with Ben Hecht to do the final script of *Viva Villa!* My arrangements with Mr. Hecht . . . are as follows:

He is to receive $10,000 for the job, plus a $5000 bonus if it is completed to my entire satisfaction within fifteen days.

I expressly included the time element because this is, at the moment, as important to us as the quality of the work, since we plan on having Howard Hawks[28] leave for Mexico in two weeks, and I want to be sure the company is on the ground and working on [Wallace] Beery's return from Europe. On the quality we are protected not merely by Hecht's ability but by the clause that the work must be to my satisfaction. It may seem like a short space of time for a man to do a complete new script, but Hecht is famous for his speed, and did the entire job on *Scarface* in eleven days. I do not think we should take into consideration the fact that we are paying him a seemingly large sum of money for two weeks' work, because this would merely be penalizing him for doing in two weeks what it would take a lesser man to do, with certainly infinitely poorer results, in six or eight weeks.

                                                          DOS

Mr. M. Lincoln Schuster   January 8, 1934
Simon & Schuster, Publishers
New York City, New York

Dear Mr. Schuster:

I hear that you have had great success with Laurence Stallings's *The First World War* and, seemingly, another collection of photographs called *The American Procession* is also having a fair sale. This prompts

---

[27]MGM purchased *The Paradine Case*, but did not produce it. Years later Selznick bought it from MGM for his own production company; the resulting film was released in 1948.
[28]The director, who was replaced during filming by Jack Conway.

me to inquire whether you would be interested in a pictorial history of the movies for publication in a similar form. If so, I should like to try my hand at getting together such a collection, which I think I would be in a better position to do than most people.

I am aware that you have had no luck with Terry Ramsaye's excellent history of the movies [*A Million and One Nights* (1926)], but if I may say so, I think this was largely because of price; and, even more important, because there are very few people interested in the financial and mechanical development of the film industry, by comparison with the many millions who are seemingly fascinated by any publication dealing with the pictorial and player angles.

The book I have in mind would have stills from the very first movies, such as *The Great Train Robbery,* all the way through the first *Quo Vadis, Cabiria,* early Mary Pickford films in which she was known only as "the girl with the curls" (the use of her name being expressly forbidden by contract), up through the stage of *The Birth of a Nation* and all the films of the [director D. W.] Griffith imitators, etc. . . .

I should appreciate hearing from you.

With cordial regards to Mr. Simon and yourself, I am,

Very sincerely yours,

To: Mrs. Corbaley[29]   March 3, 1934
cc: Mr. Mayer

I have been mad about *Beau Geste* [1926, silent] for years—in fact, *Beau Geste* and *The Merry Widow* [1925, silent] are still my favorite pictures of all time.

If we can buy *Beau Geste*, by all means let's do so. I am sure we could make it in such a way that it would not be offensive to the French Government, as the first picture was. To me, the strength of the story is in the relationship of the brothers before they meet their death, not in the cruelty of the sergeant, played in the original picture by Noah Beery.

I wish you would discuss with Mr. Mayer immediately how to handle this with Paramount.[30]

DOS

[29]Kate Corbaley, MGM Assistant Story Editor.
[30]MGM decided against purchasing *Beau Geste* from Paramount. However, it was remade by Paramount in 1939, and the sadistic sergeant was changed from French to Russian.

To: Mr. Marx,[31] Mrs. Corbaley   March 19, 1934

Tender Is the Night.[32] I cannot get anything out of this synopsis, but I am such a Scott Fitzgerald fan that I hope to be able to read the book. If you hear of any company being about to close, I wish you would advise me. . . .

DOS

David Copperfield

MR. ARTHUR LOEW[33]   MARCH 17, 1934
METRO-GOLDWYN-MAYER CORP.
1540 BROADWAY
NEW YORK, N.Y.

DEAR ARTHUR: . . . WE WOULD LIKE YOUR REACTION TO THOUGHT OF PRODUCING "DAVID COPPERFIELD" IN ENGLAND. PLAN WOULD BE FOR MYSELF AND CUKOR TO PREPARE SCRIPT COMPLETELY HERE AND THEN CAST AND SHOOT IT ENTIRELY IN ENGLAND. MESSRS. MAYER AND MANNIX SHARE MY BELIEF THAT IT SHOULD ADD HUNDREDS OF THOUSANDS OF DOLLARS TO BRITISH EMPIRE GROSS WHILE STILL GIVING US PICTURE THAT WOULD BE AS GOOD FOR THIS COUNTRY, AND AT THE SAME TIME DO WONDERS FOR ENTIRE STANDING OF OUR BRITISH COMPANY. WOULD TRY ALSO TO FIND ANOTHER STORY TO PRODUCE IN ENGLAND AT SAME TIME, POSSIBLY "CLIVE OF INDIA" IF COULD GET COOPERATION OF BRITISH GOVERNMENT, OR POSSIBLY "BEAU BRUMMEL" WITH BOB MONTGOMERY. WOULD APPRECIATE IMMEDIATE REPLY SINCE MY ENTIRE PRODUCTION PROGRAM FOR NEXT SEVERAL MONTHS DEPENDS UPON THIS DECISION. MR. MAYER IS PARTICULARLY ENTHUSIASTIC ABOUT IDEA AND I AM UNDER IMPRESSION MR. [Nick] SCHENCK IS ALSO FAVORABLY DISPOSED.[34] . . .

DAVID SELZNICK

[31]Samuel Marx, MGM Story Editor.
[32]The first book-publishing date of *Tender Is the Night* was approximately three weeks after this memo.
[33]First Vice-President of Loew's, Inc. (son of the founder, Marcus Loew).
[34]*David Copperfield* eventually was made on the MGM lot in Culver City.

TO: E. J. MANNIX   APRIL 24, 1934

. . . IN DISCUSSION WITH NICK [Schenck] TODAY TOLD HIM THAT
COULD MAKE TWO PICTURES OUT OF "DAVID COPPERFIELD" FOR
PROBABLY HUNDRED THOUSAND DOLLARS MORE THAN ONE
PICTURE AND PRODUCE THEM SO THAT EACH PICTURE WOULD BE
COMPLETE IN ITSELF. POSSIBLY RELEASING SECOND SEVERAL
MONTHS AFTER FIRST, OR POSSIBLY RELEASING THEM TOGETHER
FOR EXHIBITION DURING SUCCEEDING WEEKS. NICK SURPRISED ME
BY SAYING THAT PLAN WAS EXCELLENT ONE AND WE SHOULD BY
ALL MEANS PROCEED WITH IT.[35] . . .

                                                       DAVID

TO: L. B. MAYER   MAY 17, 1934
                                                       LONDON

. . . MUST KNOW WHAT CHANCE CHARLES LAUGHTON FOR ROLE OF
MICAWBER. FEEL MORE THAN EVER VITAL IMPORTANCE OF
BENDING EVERY EFFORT TO SECURE HIM, BUT MUST KNOW WITHIN
FEW DAYS SO CAN DECIDE WHETHER TO SIGN ANOTHER
MICAWBER. IF LAUGHTON UNAVAILABLE FOR MICAWBER, MIGHT
LIKE W. C. FIELDS. CAN WE GET HIM? TO AVOID NECESSITY OF
TRYING PARAMOUNT, THINK WE SHOULD GET WORD TO FIELDS
DIRECT, WHO WOULD PROBABLY GIVE EYE TOOTH TO PLAY
MICAWBER. . . . CORDIALLY

                                                       DAVID

SOL ROSENBLATT[36]   AUGUST 17, 1934
THE BALSAMS
DIXVILLE HOTEL
NEW HAMPSHIRE

DEAR SOL: FREDDIE BARTHOLOMEW, ENGLISH CHILD,
ACCOMPANIED BY HIS GUARDIAN, ARRIVED IN HOLLYWOOD,
HAVING COME HERE WITH HOPES GETTING TITLE ROLE "DAVID
COPPERFIELD," FOR WHICH WE THOUGHT HIM STRONG
POSSIBILITY. HOWEVER, HIS FATHER GAVE OUT INTERVIEWS TO
ENGLISH PRESS THAT WE HAD ENGAGED HIM BEFORE HE LEFT,
FALSELY PUTTING US IN POSITION OF TRYING TO VIOLATE ENGLISH

---

[35] *David Copperfield* eventually was released as one film.
[36] Attorney and Deputy NRA Government Administrator.

LAW AGAINST IMPORTATION OF CHILDREN FOR LABOR. SINCE WE
OBVIOUSLY COULD NOT AFFORD TO EVEN APPEAR IN POSITION OF
VIOLATING LAW, WE NATURALLY WOULD NOT EMPLOY CHILD
WITHOUT PERMISSION OF BRITISH GOVERNMENT, EVEN THOUGH
THIS COSTING US A THOUSAND DOLLARS DAILY BECAUSE REST OF
STAFF AND CAST ENGAGED. WE HAVE SPENT FORTUNE TRYING TO
FIND ANOTHER CHILD WITHOUT ANY SUCCESS, AND SEEMS TO US
BRITISH GOVERNMENT WOULD GIVE US THIS PERMISSION IF
MATTER PROPERLY PRESENTED TO THEM. CHILD'S ENTIRE FUTURE
WILL BE BENEFITED THROUGH HAVING MONEY FOR EDUCATION.
HIS SCHOOLING WILL NOT BE AFFECTED. ENGLISH PUBLIC WOULD
CERTAINLY RESENT SEEING AMERICAN CHILD AS DAVID
COPPERFIELD. PLEASE KEEP ME ADVISED. REGARDS,

DAVID

ECKMAN[37]
METROFILMS
LONDON

RELEASING FOLLOWING STORY TO PRESS: QUOTE . . . FREDDIE
BARTHOLOMEW HAS BEEN SELECTED TO PLAY THE PART OF DAVID
COPPERFIELD AS A BOY IN MGM'S PICTURIZATION OF THE FAMOUS
CHARLES DICKENS NOVEL. . . . FEW DAYS AGO IT APPEARED HE
HAD LOST ROLE TO LITTLE DAVID JACK HOLT, BUT FREDDIE'S
STAGE EXPERIENCE PLUS CHARMING PERSONALITY AND
DISTINCTLY ENGLISH MANNER OF SPEECH SWAYED OPINION IN HIS
FAVOR. HIS SELECTION CLIMAXES EIGHT MONTHS OF ALMOST
CONTINUOUS SEARCH IN ENGLAND, AMERICA, AND CANADA.
UNQUOTE. REGARDS

DAVID O. SELZNICK

J. ROBERT RUBIN[38]   SEPTEMBER 27, 1934
1540 BROADWAY
NEW YORK, N.Y.

CONFIDENTIALLY, ENTIRELY POSSIBLE WE WILL NOT, IN SPITE OF
EVERYTHING WE WENT THROUGH, BE ABLE USE CHARLES
LAUGHTON IN "COPPERFIELD" BECAUSE HIS ILLNESS HAS DELAYED

---

[37]Sam Eckman, Jr., Managing Director of MGM Pictures, Ltd., London.
[38]MGM Vice-President and Secretary, and a Director of Loew's, Inc.

HIS PARAMOUNT PICTURE AND IF WE WAITED UNTIL HE FINISHED
THAT, COST WOULD BE IMPOSSIBLE. ALSO WE ARE HAVING
CERTAIN DIFFICULTIES WITH HIM. WHAT I WOULD LIKE TO KNOW
IMMEDIATELY IS WHETHER IF IT COMES TO ISSUE, HOW MUCH
DIFFERENCE COMMERCIALLY WOULD THERE BE HAVING
W. C. FIELDS INSTEAD OF LAUGHTON? IT OF COURSE NOT CERTAIN
WHETHER WE CAN OBTAIN FIELDS, BUT AM RAISING QUESTION IN
HOPE WE COULD. FIELDS WOULD PROBABLY MAKE BETTER
MICAWBER, BUT WE'VE ALWAYS FELT WE REQUIRED THE ONE
IMPORTANT NAME IN CAST IN LAUGHTON. WOULD YOU CHECK THIS
IMMEDIATELY WITH FOREIGN AND DOMESTIC SALES DEPARTMENTS
AND ADVISE ME.[39] REGARDS

DAVID SELZNICK

Anna Karenina

Miss Greta Garbo   January 7, 1935
La Quinta, California

Dear Miss Garbo:

I was extremely sorry to hear this morning that you had left for Palm
Springs, because we must arrive at an immediate decision, which, I
think, will have a telling effect on your entire career.

As I told you the other day, we have lost our enthusiasm for a
production of *Anna Karenina* as your next picture. I personally feel
that audiences are waiting to see you in a smart, modern picture and
that to do a heavy Russian drama on the heels of so many ponderous,
similar films, in which they have seen you and other stars recently,
would prove to be a mistake. I still think *Karenina* can be a magnificent film and I would be willing to make it with you later, but to do
it now, following the disappointment of *Queen Christina* and *The
Painted Veil*, is something I dislike contemplating very greatly.

Mr. Cukor shares my feeling and it seems a pity that we must start
our first joint venture with you with such a lack of enthusiasm and such
an instinct of dread for the outcome. If we make the picture, Mr.

[39]Rubin's reply was that the consensus of opinion indicated Fields was far more
valuable commercially in America, although Laughton would probably be more valuable commercially in England. A month later, after two days of shooting, Laughton felt
he could not do justice to the role and asked to be relieved of the assignment. Four days
later Fields replaced him.

Cukor and I will put our very best efforts into it and I am sure we could make a fine film, hopefully one excellent enough to dissipate the obvious pitfalls of the subject from the viewpoint of your millions of admirers. But I do hope you will not force us to proceed.

We have spent some time in searching for a comedy and although several have been brought to me, there are none I feel sufficiently important enough to justify the jump into comedy; to say nothing of the difficulty of preparing a comedy in the limited time left to us.[40]

Therefore, since you feel that you must leave the end of May and cannot give us additional time, we have been faced with the task of finding a subject that could be prepared in time and which might inspire us with a feeling that we could make a picture comparable to your former sensations and one that would, at the same time, meet my very strong feeling that you should do a modern subject at this particular moment in your career. The odds against our finding such a subject were very remote and I was very distressed and felt there was no alternative left to us but to proceed with *Karenina*. Now, however, I find that if I act very quickly, I can purchase *Dark Victory*, the owners of which have resisted offers from several companies for many months. The play is at the top of the list at several studios and if we do not purchase it, the likelihood is that it will be purchased at once for Katharine Hepburn.[41] The owner of the play, Jock Whitney, is leaving for New York tomorrow and it would be a pity if we were delayed in receiving your decision concerning it. . . . Therefore, I have asked [writer] Salka [Viertel] to see you and to bring you this letter and to tell you the story—which I consider the best modern woman's vehicle, potentially, I've read since *A Bill of Divorcement* and which I think has the makings of a strikingly fine film. Mr. Cukor and many others share this opinion. . . .

Fredric March will only do *Anna Karenina* if he is forced to by his employers, Twentieth Century Pictures. He has told me repeatedly that he is fed up on doing costume pictures; that he thinks it a mistake to do another; that he knows he is much better in modern subjects and that all these reasons are aggravated by the fact that *Anna Karenina* would come close on the heels of the [actress] Anna Sten-[director Rouben] Mamoulian-[producer Samuel] Goldwyn picture, *We Live Again*, from *Resurrection*, a picture which has been a failure and in which March appeared in a role similar to that in *Karenina*. Mr. March

[40]Garbo's first comedy was not produced until 1939 *(Ninotchka)*.
[41]Warner Bros. eventually purchased *Dark Victory* (1939) for Bette Davis.

is most anxious to do a modern picture and I consider his judgment about himself very sound.[42] We are doubly fortunate in finding in *Dark Victory* that the male lead is also strikingly well suited to Mr. March.

For all these reasons, I request and most earnestly urge you to permit us to switch from *Anna Karenina* to *Dark Victory* and you will have a most enthusiastic producer and director, respectively, in the persons of myself and Mr. Cukor.

I have asked Salka to telephone me as soon as she has discussed the matter thoroughly with you, and I can say no more than that I will be very disappointed, indeed, if you do not agree with our conclusions.

Most cordially and sincerely yours,

J. ROBERT RUBIN   JANUARY 10, 1935
METRO-GOLDWYN-MAYER
NEW YORK

DEAR BOB: I KNOW IT WILL DISAPPOINT YOU TO HEAR WE HAVE DECIDED TO DO "DARK VICTORY" WITH GARBO IF WE CAN GET PHILIP BARRY TO WRITE IT AND IF CAN PURCHASE PLAY AT REASONABLE FIGURE. . . . IF, HOWEVER, CANNOT GET BARRY WILL THEN GO AHEAD WITH "KARENINA," MOST REGRETFULLY I ASSURE YOU. . . .

DAVID SELZNICK

J. ROBERT RUBIN   JANUARY 19, 1935
METRO-GOLDWYN-MAYER
NEW YORK

DEAR BOB: AS YOU UNDOUBTEDLY KNOW WE HAVE BEEN ADVISED TO PROCEED WITH "KARENINA.". . . AS YOU KNOW, HAVE FOR YEARS WANTED PHILIP BARRY AND THINK WE CAN TAKE ADVANTAGE OF INTEREST THAT HAS BEEN CREATED IN HAVING HIM COME OUT FOR GARBO SCRIPT TO MAKE DEAL WITH HIM FOR SOME OTHER JOB. THERE ARE VERY FEW PICTURES I HAVE I WOULDN'T LOVE HAVE BARRY ON. . . . REGARDS

DAVID

[42]Fredric March eventually did play Vronsky in *Anna Karenina*.

CLEMENCE DANE[43]   JANUARY 19, 1935
CURTIS BROWN
18 EAST 48TH STREET
NEW YORK

DEAR WINIFRED: WE ARE UNDOUBTEDLY PROCEEDING WITH
"KARENINA," BUT THERE IS VERY GOOD CHANCE WE WILL CHANGE
DIRECTORS AND ASSIGN SOMEONE MORE ENTHUSIASTIC THAN
GEORGE [Cukor].[44] DO NOT WANT TO BRING YOU OUT UNTIL
DIRECTOR ASSIGNED AS THINK FINAL DRAFT SHOULD BE DONE IN
CONSULTATION WITH DIRECTOR. . . . REGARDS

                                                     DAVID

SELZNICK'S NOTES ON ANNA KARENINA[45]

September 1935

The trend to the classics on the screen made a new production of
Anna Karenina almost inevitable. Having just gone through the difficulties of adapting *David Copperfield,* the prospect of compressing
Tolstoi's work without too great a loss of values did not faze us; having
to find a vehicle for Greta Garbo, it became apparent that here of all
the actresses in the world was the ideal Anna; so the remaining problem was that of meeting censorship questions.

This problem was complicated by the fact that we undertook the
production of the story at a time when the Legion of Decency's[46]
outcry was the loudest—that period when producers who attempted
worthy pictures began to suffer for the sins of those who had stooped
to a tasteless commercialism. It was further complicated by the new
code that was drawn up by the producers, which had a blanket prohibition against stories dealing with adultery. Although it was conceded
by authorities that there might be exceptions, yet it was made perfectly clear that the lesson always to be taught was that "adultery
doesn't pay."

I sent for Clemence Dane, whose brilliant play *A Bill of Divorcement* it had been my pleasure to produce on the screen, to do the

---

[43]English authoress and playwright whose real name was Winifred Ashton.
[44]Clarence Brown was finally assigned.
[45]From the booklet *A Guide to the Study of the Screen Version of Tolstoy's "Anna
Karenina,"* ed. William Lavin, Educational and Recreational Guides, Inc., 1935.
[46]A body made up of Catholic churchmen and lay members.

initial adaptation of the work because of her celebrated ability at portraying the dramatic lives of women and because of her skill at editing. When Miss Dane arrived in Hollywood, she was aghast that there could be any circumstances or series of circumstances that would permit a classification of so splendid a classic as *Anna Karenina* with the cheap sex dramas which had caused the outcry from many quarters, much less force a distortion of the work. We finally persuaded Miss Dane to work with us and with the collaborator we assigned her, the very competent Salka Viertel, and attempt to preserve as many values as possible and still come within the bounds of good taste and prescribed rules.[47]

Our first blow was a flat refusal by the Hays office to permit the entire section of the story dealing with Anna's illegitimate child. This decision was so heartrending, especially as it meant the elimination of the marvelous bedside scenes between Anna, her husband and her lover, that we were sorely tempted to abandon the whole project— but even what remained of the personal story of Anna seemed so far superior to such inventions of writers of today as could be considered possibilities for Miss Garbo, that we went on with the job.

There is no point in detailing the censorship problems beyond this. We had to eliminate everything that could even remotely be classified as a passionate love scene; and we had to make it perfectly clear that not merely did Anna suffer but that Vronsky suffered. But enough about censorship.

Our next step in the adaptation was to decide which of the several stories that are told in the book we could tell on the screen without diverting the audience's interest from one line to another. This meant the minimizing of the story of Levin, including that magnificent scene, the death of Levin's brother.

We retained only such of the story of Kitty and Levin as crossed the story of Anna and Vronsky. We naturally eliminated most of the discussions about the agricultural and economic problems of Russia of the day, considering these of little interest to the large part of our audience who came to see Greta Garbo as Anna Karenina and Fredric March as Vronsky.

From this point on, it became a matter of the careful selection and editing of Tolstoi's scenes, with a surprising little amount of original writing necessary. . . . I like to think that we retained the literary quality and the greater part of the poignant story of a woman torn

[47]S. N. Behrman later did some rewriting on the script.

between two equal loves and doomed to tragedy whichever one she chose. We tried to sound Anna's doom very early in the picture so that the tragedy was inevitable and so that the audience would feel it coming with each scene and not be overwhelmed by an unexpected and unhappy ending. A good deal of what original writing we did had to do with the scenes between Anna and her son, who was portrayed in the picture by Freddie Bartholomew. . . .

The direction of Clarence Brown is, in my opinion as a producer, masterly, and whatever fine qualities the picture has are largely attributable to his work.

:: :: :: :: :: :: :: :: :: :: :: ::

Mr. M. Lincoln Schuster   February 16, 1935
396 Fourth Avenue
New York, N.Y.

Dear Mr. Schuster:

I was glad to hear of your renewed interest in the pictorial history of the movies.

As I recall our correspondence on the subject, we abandoned the idea because you would not say definitely whether you would or would not go ahead with the publication of the book if I got it together. There is an enormous amount of labor involved in this, and, frankly, I would not care to undertake this without a specific commitment from you. I would most certainly not be going into this for the financial reward, but rather as a labor of love. And to spend all the time it would take, and to bother the thousands of people I know from whom I would have to secure the stills, would not be justified merely by the hope of having the book published. On the other hand, since the idea originated with me, I do not think you should turn it over to anyone else.

May I hear from you as to whether you would like definitely to go ahead with me on this?[48]

Cordially yours,

[48]The project was dropped by Selznick and publisher Schuster. During the following year, the first pictorial survey of significant films, *Movie Parade*—by Paul Rotha—was published jointly in London and New York. Simon and Schuster's *A Pictorial History of the Movies*, by Deems Taylor, Marcelene Peterson, and Bryant Hale was first published in 1943. Since then there have been several histories of the film made up primarily of still photographs, notably *The Movies*, by Richard Griffith and Arthur Mayer (1957).

From a rough draft,
not dated, but pre-
sumably written in
June 1935

Dear Nick [Schenck]:

The ants have conquered me again!

Under any circumstances you are a notoriously hard man to whom
to refuse anything; it is, then, doubly difficult to refuse you, in the face
of your very generous attitude and proposition. Hence, and also because it is easier for me to write you accurately my feelings than it is
to voice them, I send you this note instead of telling you personally
that I have decided that today is my last opportunity to try the things
I have wanted to do all my life—and that whatever the cost to me, I
must have my fling or regret it all my life.

I have weighed everything very carefully—both in the months
before your present trip and in the days that I promised myself I would
take, after you submitted your proposition, to coolly and calmly make
the decision. I am certain that there is no argument you can give me
which has not occurred to me. The amount of money I would definitely and certainly receive from MGM probably has few parallels in
all American industry; the association you offer me is one that would
be seized, I know, by any other individual in the picture business; the
freedom that I have had here, and presumably would continue to
have, is unknown elsewhere in the business; the additional care and
work that I must take on myself when I leave I know full well; the
independence from financial worry in making pictures is something
I may never have again; even the liberty of expression, in the making
of pictures, and the craving to do fine things in a fine way, which I have
here and undoubtedly will not have to the same extent elsewhere, I
have weighed and weighed—but I am at a crossroads where a sign
hangs high: "To thine own self be true, and it must follow, as the night
the day, thou canst not then be false to any man.". . .

I have no desire to go to work for anyone else. I have known employers now for several years and there just aren't any to be found anywhere like you and your associates. You are the employees' dream
men—but what I must do is get started on my own and try my wings,
and once and for all find out whether all by myself I cannot find what
I am looking for. I think I can make more money; but certainly the
additional money that I will make, if successful, cannot, from a busi-

ness standpoint, balance the fabulous insurance of your offer. So it is not the money that is involved. I am not trying to appear like a romantic artist, and certainly money is extremely important to me, because what I have accustomed myself to exceeds even reason. But I am prepared to do with less money if need be, if I fail in a commercial sense, in order to be absolute master from day to day and week to week and year to year of my instincts, my whims, my occasional desire to loaf, my time, and my destiny.

I should have tried this two years ago, but I allowed myself to be persuaded otherwise. If I hadn't been persuaded by MGM, I would have been persuaded by RKO; this I know, because I didn't have sufficient character to say "no" to both of you and go out and find whether I was right or wrong. During the past two years I have looked forward to the end of my contract as to the promised day. As the months went by, I was astonished to find myself slipping, slipping, slipping away from my long-established dream; recently I had even become reconciled and had decided that the ideas of my future that I had cherished were childish ones that I should have gotten over in my teens, or certainly in my twenties, and that certainly I was almost stupid not to realize that what I had was something that probably not a dozen men of my age in America could boast. But the hours came around again when I couldn't quite look myself in the eye without admitting that I was about to sell out for an easy life and a very high and steaming mess of pottage.

I have matured considerably, and with this maturing has come an acceptance that has almost made me into a different person—a person that I do not like very much. I want very much now to retrace my steps and to get back to the ambitious and vital and, if you like, even erratic, but at least free, person that I was.

I imagine you have received few business letters of this type, and to you it may seem that I have been reading too many plays and working on too many scripts, and that I am romanticizing and dramatizing to a nauseous degree. It may be that you will not even understand me, which I would regret very much because I want you to understand me. I want you to know of my appreciation and I want you to know I am not entirely insane in giving up what you offer me; and I want you to know that I recognize that I may be coming back in a year or two with my tail between my legs—but if that time should come, at least I will have had my fling, at least the ants will be forever banished, and at least the road I will travel for the rest of my life will be perfectly clear and the beautiful dancing ghosts that beckon now will have forever disappeared.

You and L.B. and Irving and Bob [Rubin] and David Bernstein[49] have my deepest and most sincere gratitude. Such recognition comes very seldom in any man's life and may never be mine again. When I finish my work here, my leave-taking will be both affectionate and tender, by contrast with the bitterness that would have characterized it had I left here when I wanted to—during the first months of my contract.

I should like to finish *Anna Karenina* and *A Tale of Two Cities*. . . . (It is possible that I can also finish *A Christmas Carol* at very little cost, before I leave.)[50]

I hope that your regard for my intelligence will not suffer as the result of my decision; and I trust that you will not think me unappreciative, and if you do, that you will forgive me.[51]

I should appreciate it if you would show this letter, or send copies of it, to each of the four other associates who have demonstrated such confidence in me.

Very sincerely and affectionately yours,

A Tale of Two Cities

To: Mrs. Kate Corbaley   June 3, 1935

Dear Kate:

. . . I know what you feel *A Tale of Two Cities* should be, but really, Kate, I am astonished myself at the fact that the more I work on it, the more I feel the difficulties of getting onto the screen what you and I both like to think is in the book. It is amazing that Dickens had so many brilliant characters in *David Copperfield* and so few in *A Tale of Two Cities*. There are twenty or perhaps forty living, breathing, fascinating people in *Copperfield* and practically none in *A Tale of Two Cities*, and herein lies the difficulty. The book is sheer melodrama and when the scenes are put on the screen, minus Dickens's brilliant narrative passages, the mechanics of melodramatic construction are inclined to be more

[49]Vice-President and Treasurer of Loew's, Inc. and MGM.
[50]This production was postponed for three years, and made by another producer.
[51]Selznick officially resigned on June 27, 1935. For a flat fee he stayed on at MGM for a few months to complete *Anna Karenina* and *A Tale of Two Cities*.

than apparent, and, in fact, to creak. Don't think that I am for a minute trying to run down one of the greatest books in the English language. I am simply trying to point out to you the difficulties of getting the Dickens feeling, within our limitations of being able to put on the screen only action and dialogue scenes, without Dickens's comments as narrator. I am still trying my hardest and think that when I get all through, the picture will be a job of which I will be proud—but it is and will be entirely different from *David Copperfield*.

My study of the book led me to what may seem strange choices for the writing and direction, but these strange choices were deliberate. Since the picture is melodrama, it must have pace and it must "pack a wallop." These, I think, Conway can give us as well as almost anyone I know—as witnessed by his work on [*Viva*] *Villa!*. Furthermore, I think he has a knack of bringing people to life on the screen, while the dialogue is on the stilted side. (I fought for many months to get the actual phrases out of *David Copperfield* into the picture, and I have been fighting similarly on *Two Cities*, but the difference is that the dialogue of the latter, if you will read it aloud, is not filled with nearly the humanity, or nearly the naturalness. . . .)

As to Sam Behrman, I think he is one of the best of American dialogue writers. Furthermore, he is an extremely literate and cultured man, with an appreciation of fine things and a respect for the integrity of a classic—more than ninety per cent more than all the writers I know. He can be counted upon to give me literacy that will match. On top of this, he is especially equipped, in my opinion, to give us the rather sardonic note in Carton.[52] If the dialogue is at times too modern, it is because I don't think many audiences, today, could quite believe the long, drawn-out, and maudlin speeches of Carton. . . .

There is a new danger which you might help us watch—which is that we do not have a miscarriage, within single scenes, of the Sam Behrman Carton and the Dickens Carton. Bear in mind that we have [Ronald] Colman playing the role and that there is the difficulty of getting him as anything but a rather gay, casual Colman—as he has always been. . . .

DOS

[52]Sidney Carton, the protagonist of *A Tale of Two Cities*.

Mr. Nicholas M. Schenck   October 3, 1935
Metro-Goldwyn-Mayer, Inc.
1540 Broadway
New York, N.Y.

Dear Nick:

We sneak-previewed *A Tale of Two Cities,* vastly overlength, before an audience of sailors and had a sensational success.

It has been reported to me that Mr. [Joseph] Vogel, of the Foreign Department, is tremendously enthusiastic about the picture and thinks it one of the biggest the company has ever turned out. Another member of the Foreign Department came to a member of my staff the other day to say that he just could not understand the apparent indifference of the studio to this obviously tremendous picture.

It is not quite so hard for me to understand this indifference. I have had to meet it on every picture, without exception, that I have made for the company and notably on *David Copperfield.* Had it not been for my trip to England on *Copperfield;* for the ballyhoo that attended this trip; for the bringing to this country of [author] Hugh Walpole; for my repeated daily insistences on the handling of every single item in connection with the production in an important way with the public and the trade; and for my willingness to stake my entire future on the picture by making clear the pains I was going to and the amount of the company's money I was spending, I am, in my own mind, convinced that *Copperfield* would have gone out as just another picture —with a probable loss to the company of somewhere between a million and two millions of dollars in revenue.

I write you this letter because I will not be here to fight the battles of *A Tale of Two Cities,* and I appeal to you for the company's sake to do something toward bringing it to the realization that it has in its possession a completed negative worth millions of dollars if properly handled—and only if properly handled.

If you ask me who it is among the executives who is indifferent to the picture, I answer you as follows: "Name me a single executive on the East or West Coasts who *is* excited about the picture."

Were this picture made by any other studio in the industry, the town would be agog about it, the Sales, Theater, and Advertising Departments would be frantic with excitement about it. Can you imagine if it were made by Zanuck? Just think back to the ballyhoo attendant upon *Clive of India* [1935] and how the whole trade was led to believe that this dreadful picture was a masterpiece. If *Clive of India* had been even a passable picture, its gross after its buildup would have been fabulous. As it is, I think whatever gross it did attain can be attributed largely to the loyalty of the Zanuck organization to its product, the excitement of Twentieth Century and United Artists executives about it, and the publicity campaign that accompanied every step of its production and release.

I think it a crying outrage that there has been not a word in either the trade or lay press about *A Tale of Two Cities* for months and months and I regard this as typical of the entire company's attitude. I hate to make my valedictory to the company a bitter complaint, and I assume that many of the executives, including the very able men who run the Publicity Departments, will be very annoyed with me. But I feel I owe it to the company to see that it gets its rewards for what looks like a very successful investment; and my pride in the completed production—the result of many many months of ceaseless effort—is such that I cannot just sit by and see what I regard as a picture second only to *Copperfield* among recent films, if indeed its popular appeal is even second to that, treated as just another output of a machine.

I should like also to call to your attention the danger of treating this picture as just another Colman starring vehicle. Granted that Colman is a big star; that any picture with him achieves a good gross; *A Tale of Two Cities*, even badly produced, would completely dwarf the importance of any star, and certainly it does any picture that Colman has appeared in since *Beau Geste*. The picture is beautifully produced. If I do not say this, no one else in the organization will. It has been splendidly directed by Jack Conway; and Colman is at his very top. Further, bear in mind that the book *A Tale of Two Cities* would without Colman have a potential drawing power equaled only by *David Copperfield, Little Women,* and *The Count of Monte Cristo* among the films of recent years because only these books have an even comparable place in the affections of the reading public. This is no modern best seller of which one hundred thousand copies have been published, but a book that is revered by millions—yes, and tens of millions of people here and abroad.

For the sake of a million dollars (if such a sum be important to

MGM), I beg you to call to the attention of the organization what it is it owns in *A Tale of Two Cities.*[53]

Cordially yours,
David O. Selznick

ROUGH DRAFT;
NOT DATED AND NOT SENT

Dear Nick [Schenck]:

I was considerably surprised to have you reply to a [the preceding] business letter with a personal attack. (From Howard Dietz[54] such a reply was quite another matter: Howard and I have been alternately abusing each other and getting drunk together for years.) But whether this be *lèse majesté* or not, I most respectfully question your right to indulge in invective when only reply is indicated.

I never for a moment suspected that you were so thin-skinned as to be upset by a criticism of any department. . . . The boys of the Publicity Department have been among the least reluctant to criticize our work; but turnabout doesn't appear to be fair play.

Your principal objection seems to be that I addressed copies to the people whose work I criticized, instead of complaining to you alone. I am very sorry, but I never have and never will do business that way. If I have any criticism to make, the people I am criticizing are immediately notified by me of it. I am aware that hypocritical and surreptitious attacks are customary in Hollywood, but I have never mastered the delicate art of knifing-in-the-back.

Howard and I had talked the whole matter over and wound up with some laughs and a mutual understanding, but as you have gone into matters totally unrelated and concerning my entire career before and since I came to MGM, I must claim the privilege of an answer.

First, as to my pictures:

You call attention to my failures for MGM without any comment on the successes. Let us deal with the failures first:

I took on *Vanessa* [*Vanessa: Her Love Story* (1935)] at the request of Eddie Mannix, after [producer] Walter Wanger's resignation; and

[53]Selznick had carbon copies of this letter sent to virtually all of the major executives of MGM and Loew's, Inc.
[54]MGM Director of Advertising and Publicity.

after working on the script, I advised L.B. that I thought its production a complete mistake—that I considered Helen Hayes no box-office asset —that the picture's cost could not, in my estimate, ever be returned —and that whatever punch there was in the story had been deleted by the Hays office. I asked L.B. to communicate my advice on the subject to you. The reply I received was that you were familiar with the book, that some close to you loved it, that I should proceed with it, that I should not worry at all about it.

Concerning *Meet the Baron,* I did not sign up Jack Pearl. The company signed Ed Wynn and Jack Pearl in a burst of enthusiasm for radio stars and I was asked to make the Pearl picture because I had had such a "break" with the *Dinner at Eight* cast, and it would "help studio morale" if I took it on. . . . However, I do not think I did a good job with it and I freely admit it. You can chalk this one against me.

For *Night Flight* I have no apologies: . . . the major mistake which I must share blame for is the casting of Clark Gable—but his casting was put up to you, personally, in L.B.'s office, and you approved it. In spite of everything, the picture (unless I am mistaken: foreign grosses, mysteriously, are denied MGM executives) did not lose money. As to its quality, I thought it was a fine picture when I made it, and I still think so.

As to *Reckless,* this was a musical designed for Joan Crawford. A week before we were to start, Miss Crawford was taken out of it by the executive office and Miss Harlow substituted. I thought she could do well by it and was for the substitution, even though I certainly never would have planned a musical for Jean Harlow. Even so, unless figures lie, it is one of the biggest, if not the very biggest, grossing pictures up to *China Seas* that Jean Harlow has appeared in.

So much for the failures.

I shall try to say as little as possible about the successes:

Dinner at Eight. Cost, including $110,000 for story, a total of under $400,000. Each star used from two to twelve days. No loss of star pictures whatsoever. "Properly Profitable," I believe.

Dancing Lady. Crawford, by common agreement, on the verge of ruin, thanks to *Rain* and *Today We Live.* Property had been shunted around for many weary months. Cost high because at your suggestion we waited weeks and weeks for Gable. Your reported words—very wise ones, so proven: "too important to Crawford's future that we have a fine picture, and have Gable with her." I was led to believe you were happy with the result.

Viva Villa! Cost high, due to the gods and Mexico. Result fine, I think. Can you point to a [Wallace] Beery success before or since, without a costar?

Manhattan Melodrama. Cost very low, indeed. Enormous money-maker. Brought Bill Powell to the company against everyone's protest, including your own.

David Copperfield. Cost high. I wish it were to be my next, my own, picture, at the same price.

Anna Karenina. Cost much less than *Queen Christina,* same as *Painted Veil.* I begged for Gable, but I got March. Yet the result, I am led to believe, is satisfactory.

A Tale of Two Cities. . . ?

I should, frankly, have thought that you would have been satisfied with such an average, at such a cost, from any producer, or for the entire program. I feel as though I were treading on eggs in making any comment or query, but—with a long breath, and even a confession of egotism, if you want—are there any better averages? Is the company's, or any individual's, return on investment more "properly profitable"? If you are not satisfied, I am mystified by the magnificent offer you made me to continue and which you repeatedly urged me to accept.

The cost of the pictures is, as everyone at MGM knows, very largely beyond the producers' control. I have my entire career been forced to work on budget, been trained to respect budget, been successful in keeping within budget. I asked for budgets at MGM; I was shocked at their absence; I urged (in vain) budgets for everyone there, including myself. Apart from this, I suggest you compare the costs of these pictures with others from MGM of a similar quality. Also, it might be interesting to compare the costs with my costs at Paramount and at RKO.

Furthermore, MGM's entire success and position, if I may as an outsider observe, is and has been built on pictures of costs as high and higher than these. (But then the man and men who made these successes have also had their successes minimized and explained.) Lose your leading producers, and your costs will still average $200,000 per picture higher than your competitors'. And you will then find the difference between cost with quality and cost without it.

Now to come to your comments concerning how MGM has put me over: when I accepted the offer which MGM urged upon me, the many arguments which were used included the facilities which would be put at my disposal, which you now seem to regret, disregarding the fact that the company has made a very substantial amount of money through putting these facilities at my disposal and that the same facilities are put at the disposal of other producers.

As to my reputation and standing at the time I accepted your offer, I can only remind you of the offer I turned down from RKO, an offer which has never been made before or since to any producer in the picture business, and the rejection of which conservatively cost me, in the two years I was with MGM, well over a million dollars. If you want some figures on this, I shall get them together for you.

My standing and reputation suffered a severe setback as soon as I joined MGM, thanks to the attitude of some of its staff, who went around town saying (without sending copies to me) that I had been given a fabulous salary by my father-in-law after being discharged by RKO. After I made *Dinner at Eight,* I did everything in my power to get a release from my contract. . . . Subsequently, and repeatedly, I again asked for a release from my contract, but was always refused. I saw no alternative to trying to make some fine pictures that would, in part, at least regain for me my reputation by the time my contract with MGM expired. If I have succeeded in doing this, it is because of a combination of the facilities which were put at my disposal and which were my promised due, and of my own abilities. Apparently, however, it is your impression that it was the pictures that made me and not me that made the pictures; although once again I must wonder at your offer if this be your real impression.

I said, in my letter, in so many words, "the very able men of the Publicity Department." They *are* able, very able. They do fine work, though their costs, mind you, are high. I stand on my comments about the prodding I have had to give them. I have heard Irving, who, in my opinion, knows more about exploitation—as well as production—than anyone else I know, make the identical comments. (If you think your organization automatically exploits and gets the most out of every great picture that it makes, how do you account for the returns on *The Thin Man?*)

It is true that the Advertising Department spends money with almost as prodigal an attitude as the Production Department. May I observe that perhaps there is waste there too? It's as generous as it is easy to dish out hundreds of thousands in magazines. It's a lot harder to spend it in a hundred local campaigns to really pull people into specific theaters on specific days. I don't think there's any trick, or much credit attached to the calling in of an advertising agent and making up a list of magazines to take space in. . . .

My letter about *A Tale of Two Cities* could gain me not one single penny, but could gain the company a fortune. It was prompted by purely unselfish motives and not so much with a view to being critical of the organization as with a desire to stimulate a justifiable interest in the picture. That it accomplished its objective is apparent in the completely changed attitude of everyone toward the picture since the letter. That it made me enemies is, of course, unfortunate.

To the publicity men who *were* my friends—this the claim, this I even believe—a short farewell. I like and admire them. When winter comes, they are welcome to join me.

I tried, to the literally bitter end, to make you money. I should have suffered smugness in silence. You have known me for a great many years and if your familiarity with my character could not stop you from writing such a letter, I am very, very sorry indeed.

Sincerely yours,

PART

SELZNICK INTERNATIONAL
(1935-1939)

GARBO'S LAST CONTRACT, before I left Metro, provided that her pictures had to be produced by either Thalberg or myself. She had a two-picture deal at that time: Thalberg did Camille (1936) and I did Anna Karenina. Then when it became known that I was leaving, she came to see me and pleaded with me to stay, and said that I could produce all her pictures. I said it would be a great honor, but I had my own ambitions.

Nicholas M. Schenck and Louis B. Mayer urged me to stay—and so did Thalberg, but I explained to them all that I simply had to fulfill my ambitions of starting my own company. It has always been an obsession of mine, unquestionably inherited from my father—and an obsession which Myron shared—that there be no interference with our work; that we must have authority.

Thalberg was my first investor in the new company. He said to me, "Have you raised your money?" I said, "Not a dollar." He said "Norma (Norma Shearer, his wife) and I would feel very pleased if you would let us be your first stockholders," and they put in $200,000. So I came East in the summer of 1935 to finance my own company with $200,000 from Thalberg and $200,000 from my brother, Myron.

Meanwhile, my friend and ex-associate Merian C. Cooper had sold John Hay Whitney the idea of backing him in Technicolor stock and in forming Pioneer Pictures. When I went to New York on behalf of my own company, to be called Selznick International, I got Robert and Arthur Lehman interested, John Hertz, and a few others. The big bulk of the money came from John Hay Whitney,[1] C. V. Whitney, and Mrs. Charles S. Payson (Jock Whitney's sister). Cooper was helpful, and for a time the Whitneys had money in with both Cooper and myself. (Incidentally, my first contact with the Whitneys had been when I tried to raise money from them during the period before I went to RKO.[2])

Cooper kept insisting that Pioneer would do better if he worked under me, and finally, at the insistence of C. V. Whitney, I took over the operation of Pioneer, along with Selznick International. To all

[1] Whitney became Chairman of the Board of Selznick International and continued to be President of Pioneer Pictures.
[2] Cooper had introduced Selznick to the Whitneys.

practical purposes, they were one operation, except as to ownership. I made A Star Is Born *and* Nothing Sacred, *which were known as Selznick International pictures, but which were owned by Pioneer and not by the Selznick International Company.*

A Star Is Born *was really a concept of my own to tell the story of a rising star and a falling star and to try to disprove what I had long believed had been a tradition until this time, that pictures about Hollywood could not succeed, although I had made a fairly successful one at RKO called* What Price Hollywood? *I believed that the whole world was interested in Hollywood and that the trouble with most films about Hollywood was that they gave a false picture, that they burlesqued it, or they oversentimentalized it, but that they were not true reflections of what happened in Hollywood. And my notion was to tell this in terms of a rising star in order to have the Cinderella element, with her path crossing that of a falling star, to get the tragedy of the ex-star, and we created this more or less as we went along. We started without anything more than a vague idea of where we were going, and it was really a relatively easy script to write. We had two sets of writers on it, curiously, and Dorothy Parker and her husband, Alan Campbell, did the final dialogue and some amendments in the scenes.[3] But I can say this, that ninety-five per cent of the dialogue in that picture was actually straight out of life and was straight "reportage," so to speak.*

During this period, I had asked my New York office to keep on the lookout for foreign pictures which we might purchase for either remake by ourselves, or as an investment for resale for remake purposes. Elsa Neuberger, Assistant Story Editor for me in New York, saw the Swedish Intermezzo *featuring Ingrid Bergman and shipped it out. I ran the picture at home with a group of friends, most of whom walked out in the middle of it. I wired Katharine Brown, my Story Editor in the New York office, to close immediately for the remake rights, and to take the next boat to Sweden and not come home without a contract with Miss Bergman.*

The pictures I produced during the Selznick International years were Little Lord Fauntleroy, The Garden of Allah, A Star Is Born, The Prisoner of Zenda, Nothing Sacred, The Adventures of Tom Sawyer, The Young in Heart, Made for Each Other, Intermezzo, Gone With the Wind, *and* Rebecca. *All of these films, with the exception of* Gone

---

[3]Robert Carson and William Wellman were the other credited writers. Budd Schulberg (son of B. P. Schulberg) and Ring Lardner, Jr., also worked on the script for a time.

With the Wind, *were released through a distribution arrangement with United Artists.*

:: :: :: :: :: :: :: :: :: :: :: ::

To: Mr. John Wharton[4]   December 16, 1935
cc: Mr. John Hay Whitney

. . . In connection with the cost of *Little Lord Fauntleroy* [1936],[5] which I should think should run around $525,000, I'd like to point out to you that we are selling our pictures for the top percentages in the business against the competition of the most costly pictures in the business. I think you and Jock [John Hay Whitney] should know just what our competition is:

I understand that MGM's average cost is now running around $590,-000 per picture. It was approaching this point some months ago. This average includes at least fifteen or twenty pictures produced for between $110,000 and $200,000—so you can have a rough idea of what their costs are on pictures for which they are demanding and securing terms from exhibitors comparable to what we are securing for our pictures. *Mutiny on the Bounty* cost $1,900,000, *A Tale of Two Cities* cost $1,000,000. Every Garbo picture, without exception, in the last several years has cost over a million dollars. The Norma Shearer pictures run on an average just as high. Pictures of the type of *The Broadway Melody of 1936* run well over a million dollars each. The Joan Crawford pictures, the Jean Harlow pictures—each run all the way from $500,000 to $800,000. They hope to finish *Ziegfeld* for $1,-500,000. The cost of *The Good Earth*, on which a camera has not yet been ground, is over $600,000 to date.

Paramount, I understand, had a great many pictures recently, each of which cost a million dollars or more . . . and several others that have run into $900,000 each. I am not talking about pictures that are in the *Mutiny* or *Two Cities* class as far as potential returns are concerned either—but rather about such pictures as *Peter Ibbetson, So Red the Rose, Rose of the Rancho, Anything Goes,* all the Dietrich pictures, etc.

Sam Goldwyn's average in his current five pictures is, I should esti-

[4]Treasurer of Selznick International and Comptroller of Pioneer Pictures.
[5]The first Selznick International film.

mate, well over $700,000 and probably closer to $800,000 or $850,000.

It is my opinion, generally speaking, and from long observation, that there are only two kinds of merchandise that can be made profitably in this business—either the very cheap pictures or the expensive pictures. I think you will find that eighty per cent of the pictures that have lost money for all the companies were the pictures that cost between $250,000 and $500,000.

We hope to get grosses over a million dollars on each picture, which I think is not at all an inordinate hope. We are going to have to be prepared to spend the money to get these—particularly when our hope is for at least an occasional picture that will gross a million and a half dollars or more, which is again not an inordinate hope.

One of the reasons why I am anxious to have you out here for a Board meeting, with Jock here, is to go thoroughly into this whole question of cost so that everyone will see eye to eye on what type pictures we are expected to make; what their costs will be; and so that no one will get any disappointments either in their grosses, the quality of the pictures, or their cost.

. . . If we don't deliver really topnotch product, we are not going to get terms and we are going to take a terrible beating after the first few pictures. There is no alternative open to us but to attempt to compete with the very best. This, in fact, I thought to be our intention all along. From my standpoint, I wish we could have five pictures a year, for which chances of success were as high as for *Fauntleroy*, at the same cost. . . .

DOS

The Garden of Allah

Mr. Gregory Ratoff[6]   August 27, 1935
Hollywood Knickerbocker
Hollywood, Calif.

Dear Gregory:

Thank you for your very long and interesting letter. . . .

As far as Marlene [Dietrich] goes, I am very pleased that she is interested in joining me, but if you want to do the job complete—and

[6]Actor, director, writer, and friend of Marlene Dietrich.

I know that you do, if only for my sake—you will have to get over to Marlene some facts which I doubt she at present appreciates. Any sales manager or important theater man will tell you—or indeed will tell her, if he is honest—that she has been hurt to such a terrible extent that she is no longer even a fairly important box-office star. There is no personality so important that he or she can survive the perfectly dreadful line-up of pictures that Marlene has had. Accordingly, she must realize the following:

1. To sign her up for one picture would be folly for me, in that, if I succeeded in making a fine picture for her, I would be taking the rap for those she has made in the last two years, and the benefits of the good picture would go to the producers of her subsequent picture instead of to me. Accordingly, I would not be interested in having her for one picture only.

2. She is in no position to command any fabulous salary—at least she is in no position to command it from me, although it is entirely possible that some other producer will give it to her. I am perfectly willing to give her a percentage deal whereby, if she thinks she is bigger than I think she is at the moment, she will get what perhaps she thinks she is entitled to: and, whereby, further, she will get all the money she can possibly want if, and when, she again becomes the star that she was after *Morocco,* and before the long line-up of *Dishonored, Song of Songs, The Blonde Venus, The Scarlet Empress,* etc. . . .

I don't mean to appear independent about the matter. I frankly want her on the right terms. I think she is one of the most magnificent personalities that the screen has had in many years and I think it a crying shame that she has been dragged down as she has been. . . .

Cordially yours,
DOS

To: Mr. Richard Boleslawski   April 14, 1936
[Director of *The Garden of Allah*]

Dear Boley:
. . . You do not have to be concerned about Marlene's lines. We carefully considered each of the points she brought up. Some of them we met and some we did not. She knows that we gave every consideration to each objection and, I think, appreciates it. In any event, she knows we expect to shoot the script as written, and unless I miss my guess, I don't think you will have trouble.

Incidentally and confidentially, Boyer told me this morning, before leaving, that she had kidded a couple of the lines to him and he had said—and very properly—that any line could be misread to make it sound comical; so apparently you can count on him in this, as well as every other, respect. . . .

When I had finished with Boyer . . . I asked Marlene to come over, and gave her a last-minute pep talk. I pointed out to her that our budget was fantastically high and put it more or less on a personal basis that it was up to her to keep it from going higher. I told her once more, frankly, about the tales around town about what she goes through between takes with her make-up, costumes, etc.—and as before, and curiously I believe in her sincerity—she told me this was all nonsense and that she *never* indulged in such carryings on and certainly would not on this picture.

I told Marlene that everyone was fearful that she would be the one stumbling block to speed; and that she would set the key for the time that the company would make. She promised the utmost cooperation and promised me too that she would do as I requested, even calling to the attention of anybody else who seemed to be slowing up the company, that she had to get through in order to get to England. She said further that quite apart from the fact that it is true she has to get through to go to England, she goes crazy with delays and with unnecessary shooting. So I honestly and sincerely believe her spirit is most helpful and what we all want it to be, and until we are proven wrong, I don't think we should look for any trouble in her direction.

I told her that my one other worry was about her performance— that she had demonstrated to the world that she was a beautiful woman, but that she had failed to demonstrate to the world, undoubtedly through lack of opportunity, that she was an emotional actress; that she had demonstrated very nicely in *Desire* that she was capable of an excellent comedy performance, but she had yet to make audiences cry. She said she had been wanting to prove this for years and certainly was anxious to make the attempt to show her stuff in this respect. I told her also, frankly, that I thought she worried most unnecessarily about her camera angles—that she was not Helen Hayes or Norma Shearer who had to worry about their faces, and that from any angle, it was impossible for her to be photographed as anything but beautiful and for God's sake and her own, she should forget about camera angles when it came to the playing of an emotional scene. She agreed with this also. Maybe I am just naïve!

However, here again, I think you should go right ahead as though you were directing some newcomer, and not worry about any legend of Dietrich difficulties. I think if this is in your mind and if you behave as if you expected difficulties, you will only encourage them; whereas if you assume that there is no reason for directing her differently than you would direct any other woman star, you will have no difficulty . . .

Marlene spent hours running the tests with [Director of Photography Harold] Rosson, and I think he got completely the manner in which we all decided the entire picture, including Marlene, should be photographed. . . .[7]

Marlene has been working extremely hard, never leaving the studio until twelve or one in the morning—having been here all day on costumes, etc. I think she has done a magnificent job on the costumes—better than could have been done, in my opinion, as well or as quickly without her supervision. . . .

Now as to your big worry—as demonstrated clearly by both your telegram and your letter—Joshua Logan.[8] I can say to you quite honestly that if you will only take advantage of Logan's services, I am absolutely positive you will have no trouble. I told him frankly that you were worried about the possibility of having "two captains" and the poor guy is worried sick for fear he is going to be in the way. I told him that he is only to try to help you and learn from you, and if anything, I think the danger now is that we have given him such an inferiority complex, and have frightened him so, that he will be afraid to contribute. I know this is not what you want either.

I went over with him in the greatest detail, and repeated two or three times, exactly how I want him to work—which is as follows:

He is never to discuss a scene with the actor without first having talked with you and respected your decisions on interpretations and readings. I told him he was to feel perfectly free to argue with you to the fullest extent as to the readings, especially on those scenes on which he sat in on conference with us, and that I knew you would be receptive to these arguments. (I hope you will consider all of his arguments most carefully, because I have found him most intelligent and most able, and I think his viewpoint on the readings will be most helpful to you.) However, I made it perfectly clear to him that *never* is he to argue with you in front of the actors; that he is never to side with an actor against you; that if perchance he is cornered and finds himself in a position where to disagree with an actor would be putting himself in a false position, he is to simply

[7] *The Garden of Allah* was one of the earliest features photographed in the new three-color Technicolor process, and Selznick's first color film.
[8] Engaged for the film as Dialogue Director.

withdraw and make it clear that you are the director of the picture and your word is final.

I even went so far as to consider whether or not Logan should even *be on* the set, but finally decided that if you were willing, it would be preferable for him to be there; first, to learn, and secondly, to listen—because of the accents etc. Also, it is clear to him that if he has any suggestions to make on the set, he is to make them only to you and never to the actor. . . .

Just one more word: I would like to recommend that you give the actors an opportunity to read their lines their way, either in the rehearsals that Logan conducts for you, or on the stage—if they don't agree with Logan—so that you can get the benefit of how some intelligent actors would play it. Also, occasionally, if you are in doubt, or if you think there may be something in what they say, or if it is the only way of ending the argument, I would suggest that you make two takes,[9] one each way. I certainly don't want to encourage this as a general practice, or you would not make any time at all; but I think it may at times be the only way to settle a difference of opinion. In any event, I feel that one of the great faults in this industry is the making of take after take with no difference in interpretation, and to me there are only two reasons for a number of takes—either because the director has not gotten it the way he wants it; or in order to give the producer and the director a choice of interpretations. . . .

Affectionately yours,

DOS

APRIL 28, 1936

DEAR BOLEY [Boleslawski]:

I AM GETTING TO THE END OF THE ROPE OF PATIENCE WITH CRITICISM BASED ON ASSUMPTION THAT ACTORS KNOW MORE ABOUT SCRIPTS THAN I DO, AND AM DISTURBED, WORRIED, AND UPSET BY TELEPHONE CALLS THAT ARE NOW POURING IN ON THE SCENE THAT PRECEDES THE CONFESSION, WHICH DEFINITELY INDICATE THAT ANOTHER SITUATION IS BREWING OF THE SAME KIND THAT HAPPENED BEFORE, WHERE THE ACTORS ARE GETTING TOGETHER AND GANGING UP ABOUT SCENES. WOULD APPRECIATE YOUR HAVING A FRANK HEART-TO-HEART TALK WITH MARLENE AND WITH BOYER, EITHER SEPARATELY OR JOINTLY, TELLING

---

[9]Photograph the scene twice from the same camera position.

THEM THE PROBLEMS THAT BOTH YOU AND I ARE UP AGAINST. . . .
MARLENE'S PICTURES HAVE BEEN NOTORIOUS FOR THEIR GHASTLY
WRITING, CHARLES IS YET TO HAVE AN OUTSTANDING AMERICAN
PICTURE, AND NEITHER OF THEM HAS EVER HAD A SINGLE
PICTURE COMPARABLE WITH ANY ONE OF FIFTEEN THAT I HAVE
MADE IN THE LAST YEARS. TELL THEM VERY BRUTALLY THAT THIS
COMES FROM ME. IT IS HIGH TIME FOR A SHOWDOWN, AND I AM
PERFECTLY PREPARED FOR IT BECAUSE I AM NOT GOING TO FACE,
OR HAVE YOU FACE, SIX OR SEVEN WEEKS OF THIS NONSENSE. I
WISH YOU WOULD LOSE YOUR TEMPER WITH THEM, AND I WILL
HAVE A LOT MORE RESPECT FOR YOU IF YOU TURN INTO A VON
STERNBERG WHO TOLERATES NO INTERFERENCE. I WISH YOU
WOULD MAKE IT CLEAR TO THEM JUST AS FIRMLY AND EVEN
VIOLENTLY AS YOU CAN THAT YOU HAVE PUT UP WITH ENOUGH
DIFFICULTIES AND WITH ENOUGH GANGING UP OF ACTORS, AND
THAT YOU HAVE RESPECT FOR ME AS AN EDITOR AND PRODUCER
IF THEY HAVE NOT: THAT THE SCENES WILL BE SHOT AS I
PREPARE THEM, THAT YOU HAVE A BIG JOB ON YOUR HANDS AND
DO NOT INTEND TO BE HURT PROFESSIONALLY BY THEM. AND
THAT SAME GOES FOR ME. I AM GOING TO MAKE PICTURES
ACCORDING TO MY OWN JUDGMENT AND NOT THEIRS. I WANT YOU
TO GET THIS OVER FLATLY TOO. I AM SORRY TO BOTHER YOU
WITH THIS AT THE BEGINNING OF A SHOOTING DAY, BUT I THINK
IT HIGH TIME FOR DISCIPLINE TO BE ESTABLISHED, AND THIS IS
ACTUALLY THE VERY FIRST TIME IN MY CAREER AS A PRODUCER
THAT I HAVE HAD TO PUT UP WITH THIS FANTASTIC STUFF THAT I
HAVE HEARD ABOUT FOR YEARS BUT NEVER HAD TO PERSONALLY
EXPERIENCE, AND I SHALL NEED YOUR COOPERATION AND
TOUGHNESS TO DO IT. IN THE STUDIO I WOULD FACE A
SHOWDOWN ON IT RIGHT NOW, BUT SINCE IT IS ON LOCATION[10] I
MUST ASK AND EXPECT YOU TO DO IT NOT MERELY FOR ME BUT
ALSO FOR YOURSELF. MAKE CLEAR TO THE ACTORS THAT IF THEY
CHOOSE TO SULK THROUGH SCENES AND GIVE BAD PERFORMANCES
I AM PERFECTLY PREPARED FOR THIS TOO AND AM NOT GOING TO
ADD HUNDREDS OF THOUSANDS MORE TO A FABULOUS COST TO
SATISFY THEIR TEMPERAMENT, BUT WILL RELEASE THE PICTURE
WITH THOSE PERFORMANCES. . . . I FEEL REINFORCED IN HAVING
YOU WITH ME ON THIS AND CAN THEREFORE TALK WITH
CONVICTION AGAINST RIDICULOUS ASSUMPTION THAT THEY KNOW
ANYTHING ABOUT SCRIPT. IF THEY WILL ONLY DO THEIR JOB AND

[10]The desert location near Yuma, Arizona.

GIVE A PERFORMANCE, THAT WILL BE ENOUGH. THAT IS ALL THAT
THEY ARE BEING OVERPAID FOR.

DAVID

To: Mr. Richard Boleslawski   June 17, 1936

Dear Boley:

Would you *please* speak to Marlene about the fact that her hair is
getting so much attention, and is being coiffed to such a degree that
all reality is lost. Her hair is so well placed that at all times—when the
wind is blowing, for instance—or when Marlene is on a balcony or
walking through the streets—it remains perfectly smooth and un-
ruffled; in fact, is so well placed that it could be nothing but a wig.

The extreme in ridiculousness is the scene in bed. No woman in the
world has ever had her hair appear as Marlene's does in this scene, and
the entire scene becomes practically unusable because everything is
so exactly in place that the whole effect of a harassed and troubled
woman is lost.

Even today, on the set, having the hairdresser rush in between takes
to put each last strand of hair in place looked so nonsensical, when you
could see the palms blowing in the background.

Surely a *little* reality can't do a great beauty any harm.

I wish you would go over the contents of this note with Marlene,
who, I am sure, will realize that what I say makes sense; and if you will
remind me, I will go into it with you and Marlene again when I am
next on the set.

DOS

A Star Is Born

To: Mr. Lowell V. Calvert[11]   December 19, 1936
cc: Mr. Ginsberg[12]

I have your letter of December 14, concerning Spyros Skouras's[13]
reactions to the future product [*A Star Is Born*].

[11]General Manager in Charge of Sales and Distribution for Selznick International and
Pioneer Pictures.
[12]Henry Ginsberg, Vice-President and General Manager of Selznick International.
[13]Fox West Coast Theatres executive.

Concerning the tragic ending, this is the sort of comment about pictures that dates back twenty years, and that I didn't think anybody seriously advanced today.

I will be satisfied with a long line of pictures that do as well as *Anna Karenina,* in which Garbo threw herself under a railroad train; or *A Tale of Two Cities,* in which Mr. Colman had his head chopped off; and if anybody wants further examples, I will sit down and list about fifty sensational successes with tragic endings.

I make the flat statement that pictures have reached the stage where audiences demand the proper ending to a story, whether it be happy or unhappy. If there is anybody in the business that hasn't learned this, it is high time they did. I can't think of a single success in Greta Garbo's long career that has had anything but an unhappy ending; and the same is true of practically all of Norma Shearer's recent successes, including *Smilin' Through.* I don't like to take the time to give you a complete list, but offhand, what about a few unimportant little trifles such as *Beau Geste, All Quiet on the Western Front, The Public Enemy,* etc., etc.? . . .

I think Mr. Skouras is probably the country's outstanding exhibitor, but over a long period of years I have seen producers go broke who failed to follow their own convictions, and followed instead the advance opinions of exhibitors, who cannot know what the producers have in mind in any given setup.

TO: KATHARINE BROWN   SEPTEMBER 28, 1936

HELLO KATHARINE. ABOUT TO BREAK SOME IMPORTANT PUBLICITY STORIES ON THE HOLLYWOOD PICTURE AND DON'T WANT TO WASTE THEM ON A TEMPORARY TITLE. . . . THEREFORE MEETING TO ATTEMPT TO GET SOMETHING THAT HAS FAIR CHANCE OF BEING PERMANENT. OUR FEELING IS THAT HOLLYWOOD HAS BECOME IDENTIFIED WITH CHEAP TITLES OF CHEAP PICTURES, AND THIS MORE TRUE TODAY THAN EVER BECAUSE OF "HOLLYWOOD BOULEVARD," WHICH HAS BEEN OUTSTANDING FAILURE AS PARAMOUNT QUICKIE, AND ALSO BECAUSE OF "HOLLYWOOD HOTEL," WHICH WARNERS ARE MAKING AS MUSICAL, AND WHICH WILL PROBABLY BE RELEASED BEFORE OUR PICTURE. BEARING IN MIND THAT ROMANTIC TITLE WOULD BE VALUABLE, ESPECIALLY LINKED WITH THE TWO STARS WE EXPECT TO SIGN, ANXIOUS TO GET REACTION FROM YOU PERSONALLY, MR. [John Hay] WHITNEY, MR. WHARTON, ALSO SIP [Selznick International

Pictures] AND UA [United Artists, distributors], TO TITLE "THE STARS BELOW," WHICH FITS PICTURE. WILL YOU LET ME HAVE THIS TODAY?

To: Mr. O'Shea[14]   January 7, 1937

I wish you would give immediate study to whether or not Wellman is entitled to a bonus on the story of *Star Is Born*. . . .

Star Is Born is much more my story than Wellman's or Carson's. I refused to take credit on it simply as a matter of policy, and if the picture is as good as we hope, they are the beneficiaries. Certainly Wellman contributed a great deal, but then any director does that on any story. The actual original idea, the story line, and the vast majority of the story ideas of the scenes themselves are my own.

Bill does everything possible to save us money, and will do so again on his next picture. I therefore don't want to seem ungrateful, and the matter should be handled with care. If, however, I am wrong in my recollection of our contract, and it states that Wellman is entitled to a bonus on *Star Is Born*, as it is his story, I would not for a moment quibble on whose story it is, and we should by all means pay him.

To: Mr. Wellman   January 25, 1937
cc: Miss Keon[15]

Dear Bill:

I wish you would give this some thought, until you see me tomorrow: . . .

I find that there is a reaction of uncertainty that [Fredric] March has committed suicide; and we particularly lose a very strong point if it is not clear to the audience that he has committed suicide, and that [Janet] Gaynor does not know that he has done so. As it is, even when the audience learns that it is so, it is too much for them to grasp at this minute the fact that Gaynor thinks it is an accidental death. . . .

I have been thinking about my new idea for the end, and I believe that we can retain Gaynor's entire approach up the aisle in front of the

[14]Daniel T. O'Shea was now assistant to Selznick and Secretary of Selznick International Corporation.
[15]Barbara Keon, Scenario Assistant and Production Secretary.

Chinese,[16] simply retaking the reaction to the footprints, more or less as is; with her then pulling herself together; the announcer asking her if she will say a few words; [Adolphe] Menjou saying something to the effect of "No, no—Miss Lester will not speak!"; Gaynor saying she will, advancing with all the pride in the world, throwing her head back, with tears in her eyes, and saying "This is Mrs. Norman Maine speaking"—with an alternate take on "This is Vicki Lester speaking." . . .[17]

To: Mr. Merian Cooper[18]   January 28, 1937

In connection with the suicide effects,[19] on which you are so kindly helping me, I have been thinking about the idea of a finish à la *Tabu*.[20] I wish you would give some thought to my fear that this is not the right note on which to finish. I am fearful the exhaustion and final drowning is too quiet a conclusion to the sequence.

My own feeling is that we should get a conclusion on a higher note. I feel we should get in scenes of his past, accompanied by an increasing tempo in the film, the music and sound effects; that these scenes of his past triumphs will have to be exceedingly brief and perhaps shot for the purpose; that they should be followed by such high spots of the story as we have seen—such as a piece of the trailer scene, the punch in the jaw at Santa Anita, the Academy scene, the night court (or perhaps only those high spots that have to do with Esther[21] so that we clarify what is troubling him—which is the misery he has brought and is bringing to Esther—thus confining ourselves perhaps to such things as the marriage scene, the trailer, the slap on the face at the Academy and the overhearing scene).

I feel we may be able to get a great effect out of the roar of the ocean, plus perhaps some trick effects such as the buzzing we had in *What Price Hollywood?* when Lowell Sherman shot himself—with perhaps even a note of triumph as his sacrifice reaches a conclusion.

All of this is very scattered and chaotic but I am groping as I suppose

[16]Grauman's Chinese Theatre in Hollywood.
[17]The former line was used in the final version.
[18]Now Vice-President of Selznick International and Executive Producer for Pioneer Pictures.
[19]For *A Star Is Born*, in which the leading man, played by Fredric March, drowns in the ocean.
[20]An F. W. Murnau film of 1931 in which the leading man drowns in the South Pacific.
[21]Earlier name of the character Vicki Lester, played by Janet Gaynor.

you are. However, the one thing I do feel is that this sequence should end on a high note instead of a low one.[22]

TO: JOHN WHARTON   FEBRUARY 12, 1937

HAVE RECEIVED FURTHER WORD FROM BREEN[23] ON THE SUICIDE QUESTION. HE CALLS ATTENTION TO THREE PICTURES WHICH HAD SUICIDE SEQUENCES, WHICH ENCOUNTERED NO TROUBLE IN ENGLAND, NAMELY, "ANNA KARENINA," "WHAT PRICE HOLLYWOOD," AND "DINNER AT EIGHT." ONLY SLIGHT DIFFICULTY WAS IN "DINNER AT EIGHT," IN WHICH DETAILS OF TURNING ON THE GAS WERE CUT. I DIDN'T REALIZE I HAD A SUICIDE COMPLEX UNTIL I SAW THIS LIST, ALL OF THE PICTURES WHICH I PRODUCED. IN ANY EVENT IT WOULD APPEAR THAT THERE IS NO REASON TO WORRY.

Mr. Fredric March   April 28, 1937
1026 Ridgedale Drive
Beverly Hills, California

Dear Freddie:

You must have heard from any number of people the most laudatory sort of opinions on your performance in *A Star Is Born*. Yet I fear that many of these statements may have seemed to you automatic flattery of a type you must be used to, and that perhaps you wonder which congratulations are on the level. It is for this reason that I thought I should send you this note to tell you that on all sides I have seldom heard such praise of any actor in any picture. In New York, as here, people are saying that your job is one of the most able and honest that has ever been done for the screen. That it will do a great deal for you, as it has for the picture and therefore for us, is a certainty.

May I add my congratulations (as well as my thanks) to the others? As to whether this is on the level, I remind you of what I told you about certain other performances.

---

[22]In the completed film, none of the effects mentioned above were used. The suicide was handled very simply. March walks out to the edge of the ocean at sunset. The camera follows his bathrobe as it drops by his feet, then the surf starts pulling the bathrobe out to sea. There follows a shot of March waist deep in the water, which became the end of the sequence.

[23]Joseph I. Breen, West Coast assistant to Will Hays.

At long last I salute you as I have wanted to through these years, with complete enthusiasm and unstinted admiration. . . .

Yours, etc.,

:   :   :   :   :   :

MR. JOHN WHARTON   APRIL 16, 1937
230 PARK AVENUE
NEW YORK CITY

I MUST CONCEDE MANY POINTS OF YOUR WIRE ARE SOUND. . . .
THE FACT IS, SIMPLY CANNOT KEEP UP AT THIS PACE FOR
INDEFINITE LENGTH OF TIME. HERE IT IS MIDNIGHT AND I DONT
KNOW WHEN I'M GOING TO GET THROUGH AND HAVEN'T HAD
DINNER. HOWEVER, A SOLUTION ISN'T CLEAR TO ME AS YET, AND
IF YOU WILL FORGIVE ME YOU YOURSELF MAKE CONTRADICTORY
STATEMENTS. YOU SAY IN WIRE THAT I'VE GOT TO TURN INTO
MORE OF AN EXECUTIVE PRODUCER AND IN ANOTHER PART OF
WIRE THAT YOU DO NOT THINK I CAN FIND PRODUCERS WHO DO
NOT REQUIRE CONSTANT DAILY SUPERVISION. MY OWN FEELING IS
THAT WE'VE SIMPLY GOT TO TRY TO FIND OURSELVES MEN WHO
WILL GROW INTO PRODUCERS EVEN IF THEIR DEVELOPMENT
COMES OVER LONG PERIOD. . . . I'D LIKE TO ATTEMPT TO LIGHTEN
THE BURDEN BY TRYING A COMBINATION ASSOCIATE PRODUCER
AND DIRECTOR POSITION FOR SUCH FEW MEN AS MIGHT BE
CAPABLE OF HANDLING SUCH DUAL RESPONSIBILITIES. OFFHAND I
SHOULD THINK LA CAVA MIGHT BE ONE. WHAT WOULD YOU THINK
OF MY TRYING TO MAKE A DEAL WITH LA CAVA? NINETY-NINE
DIRECTORS OUT OF A HUNDRED ARE WORTHLESS AS PRODUCERS,
PARTICULARLY FOR THEMSELVES. THE DIRECTOR-PRODUCER
SYSTEM HAS BEEN PROVEN TERRIBLY COSTLY AND FRUITLESS OF
GOOD RESULTS MANY, MANY TIMES AND IS BEING PROVEN WRONG
AGAIN RIGHT NOW AT PARAMOUNT, WHERE PRESUMABLY THEY
HAD NO ALTERNATIVE BUT TO TRY IT. HOWEVER, THERE ARE
EXCEPTIONS SUCH AS [Frank] CAPRA AND [Cecil B.] DE MILLE, AND
I BELIEVE THAT LA CAVA MIGHT ALSO BE AN EXCEPTION. HE GETS
ENORMOUS SALARY, BUT AFTER ALL IT WOULD BE FOR TWO JOBS,
AND I THINK I MIGHT BE ABLE TO WORK OUT DEAL WITH HIM
WHEREBY HE GOT SUBSTANTIALLY LESS THAN HE IS GETTING AND
IS OFFERED, AND TAKES A CUT IN PROFITS, WHICH WOULD BE
FURTHER PROTECTION ON COST ANGLE. LA CAVA WOULD DRIVE

ME CRAZY AS DIRECTOR WITH THE REWRITING HE DOES ON SET,
FOR AS YOU KNOW I DON'T LIKE ANY PROJECTION-ROOM SURPRISES
OR SHOCKS, BUT IF HE WERE HIS OWN PRODUCER WE COULD TAKE
CHANCE THAT HE WOULD SHOCK HIMSELF, AND I'D BE SEEING
FINISHED SCENES ON THE SCREEN AND WEIGHING THEIR VALUE AS
SUCH, INSTEAD OF BY COMPARISON WITH SCRIPT, ONCE I KNEW
THOROUGHLY AND HAD APPROVED WHAT HE WAS AFTER. . . .[24]

DOS

The Prisoner of Zenda

Excerpts from a speech given by Selznick on November 1, 1937, to a
Columbia University Extension Film Study Class, in conjunction with
the Museum of Modern Art.

In tackling *The Prisoner of Zenda*, the great criticism of most of
the people in Hollywood who heard we were going to make it, and
of most of the people in our own company, was that we were making a very dated piece of material; that we were making a story
that had no conceivable appeal to present-day audiences. It was an
old-fashioned fairy tale and melodrama. I felt that the affectionate
memories that most people had of *The Prisoner of Zenda* persisted, that audiences were ready for a great and clean love story
which contrasted with the sordid realistic pictures of which they
had had so many. And I have had, in any case, some success with
resurrecting some of the old books and in bringing them to the
screen. I also felt very candidly that the Windsor case had given
new life to an old problem—that of king and commoner, queen
and commoner; that it had become a topical problem, as a result of
the Windsor case.[25]

. . . I frankly would not have purchased the material if I hadn't had
Ronald Colman under contract, and if I hadn't determined in advance
that Colman would play the role. One of the thousand-and-one functions of the producer is to make sure that the star is happy with his

[24]Selznick did not make a deal with La Cava.
[25]Edward VIII abdicated the throne of England in December 1936 in order to marry
Mrs. Wallis Warfield Simpson, an American divorcée.

assignment, or face the prospect of losing him when the contract expires. Colman and I talked at great length about the picture, about its drawbacks, about what I saw in it and his fears concerning it. . . .

The big discussion with Colman was whether he should play the dual role. He has a dread of dual roles, based upon a picture he made some years ago, called *The Masquerader* [1933], which was not very successful. About two years ago I did *A Tale of Two Cities* with him, and at that time he agreed to do it provided he played Sydney Carton and did not play Charles Darnay. An examination of the book proved that it was really not necessary for both characters to look exactly alike, and that in the two places where the resemblance was necessary we could so avoid the issue to enable Colman to play only the one role. I am glad now that he held out for that, because I think a great deal of the illusion of the picture might have been lost had Colman rescued Colman and had Colman gone to the guillotine so that Colman could go away with Lucy. . . .

In the case of *Zenda* anything but the dual-role performance seemed obviously impossible. It was necessary that the entire kingdom should be fooled, including his brother, fiancée, and everyone else. We were fortunate in that Colman had the same voice for both roles so that he was able to fool them easier. . . .

Once Madeleine Carroll was cast for the role of Flavia, I had a problem, which was a complete change of make-up for her. She had been using her make-up since she had been in pictures with some degree of success. . . . She is building a popularity, and it is pretty hard to correct any woman's make-up on or off the screen, as you know, particularly when they have achieved international acclaim as a great beauty. I felt that it was vitally important that there should be no trace of artifice, no make-up visible, and I had a number of discussions with her, even arguments, about reducing the make-up on her mouth, eyebrows, and even taking the polish off her nails, so that she would seem like the virginal queen or princess of the 1880s—and not like a movie star of today. I think we achieved that through the largest part of the picture, although every now and then she would sneak something in when no one was looking. . . .

There was a great debate as to the style of the dialogue. . . . I felt that the picture would fall apart if just once, in the course of it, somebody spoke in slang or idiom or, let's say, in recognizable speech; that the whole story was based on such nobility of character and on such blacks and whites, of heavies and heroines and villains, that if we gave it, for even a few feet, the feeling of a story of today, the situations would not stand up. That is why the picture has the style that it has. . . .

In doing a picture like *The Prisoner of Zenda*, which is aimed at least fifty per cent toward a foreign market, it becomes important to get a director who at least has the judgment and taste to respect the sensibilities of audiences which are sensitive, particularly in England, about the behavior of royalty. In selecting John Cromwell, I was aware that he, being a stage-trained director, was not the best choice in the world for the action material in the picture. I tried it, however, supplying him with the help of other people who are expert at shooting action film.

Nevertheless, the fencing sequence originally came out very poorly. It lacked tempo, excitement, and all the things which are the only excuse for a sequence of that kind. So that when the picture was finished, and the fencing sequence was recut, I was still dissatisfied, and engaged Woody Van Dyke to come in and shoot just the fencing sequences. . . .

There originally were a prologue and epilogue to the picture, which were shot but never used. We began the picture in England with the old Rudolph[26] sitting lonely in his club, and we told the story backward, finishing with an epilogue in which he received a rose from Flavia, with a note from Fritz that told him she had died. It was a little bit better than that sounds, but we tried it and it didn't work. . . .

To: Mr. R. A. Klune[27] March 22, 1937
cc: Mr. Ginsberg, Mr. O'Shea

I am worried about various matters in connection with the fencing instruction for the actors in *Zenda*, as well as the actual scenes of fencing in the picture.

I feel that we must make certain that we have every possible guard against any injury to these actors, simply from the standpoint of the decent protection that we owe them; and that from the financial standpoint we should make certain that we are protected on insurance.

[26]Played by Ronald Colman.
[27]Selznick International Production Manager Raymond A. Klune.

I understand that [fencing instructor Ralph] Faulkner is having the actors take their lessons without masks, on the grounds that he can guard himself against injury. This seems to me utterly ridiculous. There is no reason to take this chance, and I feel we should insist upon every actor wearing a mask, every time that he is not fencing actually before the camera.

Have we insurance protection on this matter on the actors themselves, and shouldn't we have it on Faulkner as well?

During the making of the actual scenes, I think we must be careful that the sabers that are used are so constructed as to make the possibility of any injury remote.

Incidentally, Colman and David Niven should be brushing up on their fencing, along with the other actors. . . .

To: Mr. Wright[28]   April 12, 1937
cc: [Writer John] Balderston & [Director John] Cromwell

Dear Bill:

In connection with the shot of the horses in *Zenda* that we discussed last night, I assume the horses will come charging, and not merely over the drawbridge but into the hall. I think we might try three or four different angles on this, including one in which they charge directly into the camera; a buried camera shot; and reverse angles as well. I think, too, that we should get the effect of them riding right over Michael's[29] men, and that we should go in for saber thrusts. Perhaps one of our two "assistant heavies" is run down by a horseman, or perhaps one is killed by a saber, or perhaps both are killed by sabers. Perhaps, too, we should cue Zapt's[30] men into being so brutal by showing that the heavies start shooting first. Perhaps, too, one or more horsemen should go down, and I think it would be a grand effect if we could get one or two of the horses—horsemen and all—going headlong over the side of the bridge. Perhaps we should get shots on location shooting down into the water with the horses going down, just as we are going to do for Rupert's[31] dive—that is, either on location or into a tank. I'm not sure whether this can be done without being cruel to the animals, and if this is true, maybe there is some way of tricking it,

[28]William H. Wright, Production Associate on the film.
[29]Michael was played by Raymond Massey.
[30]Zapt was played by C. Aubrey Smith.
[31]Rupert was played by Douglas Fairbanks, Jr.

getting the horses going over on the stage: a fake horse going over (shooting straight down from the camera), with an actual man on his back, falling off as it nears the water. (It seems to me this could be done without cruelty, but this, too, should be checked.)

In any event, I think there are simply stunning effects to be obtained if we give the idea some thought. In fact, I've been thinking that while we're at it, we might as well do the thing up brown. (Incidentally, don't forget that we have to personalize it with excellent shots of Zapt and Fritz in the lead.)[32] . . . It is entirely possible that this charge could turn into one of the most outstanding things in the entire picture, and I don't think we should waste the opportunity to at least try to get something that's outstanding. . . .

The expense of doing it properly as against doing it slightingly would not, I think you will find, be much, because you could do an awful lot of these shots in a single day, and we have to get the horses and men anyway. We also have the sets. Accordingly, I can't see how extra expenses would run into much more than the film and lighting bill, and I think we might get an exciting climax to the attack sequence (pardon me—escape sequence), if we use our heads . . .

To: [Director of Photography James Wong] Howe   May 5, 1937
cc: Messrs. Wright and Ginsberg

Dear Jimmy:

On my departure for New York, I want to send you a few words about the remaining scenes to be shot on *Zenda*. While they constitute only a few days' work, the photography of these scenes is absolutely vital to the romantic side of the picture, and I am counting on you to do a grand job. . . .

On the Terrace Sequence, I am really hopeful that the set we discussed will permit you to get some really beautiful photography that will give us an idyllic quality in the love scene down the path and near the pool. I am counting on you to avoid the stagy appearance of most exterior sets that are built on the stage; to give us real night photography that will not hesitate to lose figures in deep shadows at the same time that it gives enough light for expressions on faces.

On the Renunciation Scene, you know the importance of really getting a mood that is indicated by the twilight hour that the scene is played in. Here, too, I am counting on something striking—with

[32]Fritz was played by David Niven.

gradually diminishing twilight, with decreasing light on the figures, and with only the face of Flavia showing in the final excellent tableau that Mr. Cromwell has devised for the end of the scene. . . .

DOS

Mr. Ronald Colman July 21, 1937
1003 Summit Drive
Beverly Hills, Calif.

Dear Ronnie:

I send you herewith copy of the Renunciation Scene on which Sidney Howard, George Cukor, and myself worked most of this afternoon. . . .

I am hopeful that you will consider my wish to have Cukor direct it in the light of his brilliant directorial talents, rather than through any mistaken notion that there is any other motive that has prompted me to assign him to it. As I said to you on the phone, I feel that this scene is necessarily and basically a Flavia scene—really her one scene, and while I think we have done well in preserving the position of Rassendyll [Colman] in the scene, it of course had to be written, and should be played, to Flavia's best advantage. I ask you to believe that with this thought in mind, and without any prompting from anyone whatsoever, I thought it would be folly not to take advantage of the fact that I have under contract, and available, a man who is generally conceded to be one of the finest directors in the world, and certainly unquestionably the best director of women in the world. He is also a man with a great sense of the style of a book and of a picture, as has been best evidenced by his work, including *Little Women* and *David Copperfield*.

There is the further advantage to be gained in Cukor directing the scene of your becoming acquainted with his style of direction, because on various occasions in the past when I have discussed him with you as a possible director for yourself, you could not express an opinion because you were not familiar enough with his work to judge how you would get along with him and how you would like his style of work. This gives us the ideal opportunity for you to find out, so that in any future discussions you will know him. This I advise you in advance— that you will find him the exact reverse of Van [Van Dyke], in his painstaking attention to subtleties and in his making clear to the performers exactly how he thinks the scene should be played. . . .

If by any chance you are unhappy at having George direct the scene, we can discuss it after the rehearsal; although I should rather that you said nothing about this, because I should not like so important and outstanding a director as George, who is after all doing us a great courtesy, to feel that there is any question of his being on trial. I think he would be justified in refusing, under such circumstances, to go ahead, and I should frankly hate to lose him on this scene; and I mention this only because in the final analysis I want you to be as happy about everything we do jointly as I like to feel you have been to date. Bear in mind that I am going to extra expense on a picture that is already terribly costly, and I certainly would not do this if I did not feel that there was a great deal to be gained from what I feel George can give the scene. In fact, I feel that the improvement is going to show itself much more through the direction than through our rewrite and rearrangement. . . .

I am depressed at feeling any slight unhappiness on your part over the program for this retake. I am only making it in the desire that *Zenda* shall be just as fine as it possibly can be, and I have no alternative but to hope that you will trust my judgment. I know that you are sick of it—but your own feeling should give you some idea of how sick of it I am. But I forget this in the realization of how important it is to you and to me that the picture be right. And at least we all have the consolation of knowing that Madeleine will leave for Europe as soon as this scene is finished, and that there is not another thing we can possibly cook up.

: : : : : :

TO: JOHN HAY WHITNEY   JUNE 12, 1937

"NOTHING SACRED" STARTED SHOOTING THIS MORNING. YOU WANTED COMEDY—BOY YOU'RE GOING TO GET IT, AND BE IT ON YOUR OWN HEAD. AFTER THIS ONE I AM EITHER THE NEW MACK SENNETT OR I RETURN TO DR. ELIOT.[33]

TO: MESSRS. WHITNEY AND WHARTON   JUNE 29, 1937

I SPENT A LONG TIME WITH COOP [Merian C. Cooper] TODAY AND . . . FEEL VERY STRONGLY, AS I EXPRESSED TO COOP, THAT WE MUST SELECT THE STORY AND SELL IT TO JOHN FORD, INSTEAD OF HAVING FORD SELECT SOME UNCOMMERCIAL PET OF HIS THAT WE

[33]Charles William Eliot, editor of the Harvard Classics. Selznick meant that he would go back to filming classics.

WOULD BE MAKING ONLY BECAUSE OF FORD'S ENTHUSIASM. I DO
NOT THINK WE CAN MAKE ANY PICTURE BECAUSE OF ANY
DIRECTOR'S ENTHUSIASM, AND IF THIS MEANS WE ARE TO LOSE
FORD, I WILL SUPPLY COOP WITH AS FINE A DIRECTOR AS
POSSIBLE. I SEE NO JUSTIFICATION FOR MAKING ANY STORY JUST
BECAUSE IT IS LIKED BY A MAN WHO, I AM WILLING TO CONCEDE,
IS ONE OF THE GREATEST DIRECTORS IN THE WORLD, BUT WHOSE
RECORD COMMERCIALLY IS FAR FROM GOOD. I SAW "WEE WILLIE
WINKIE" THE OTHER NIGHT AND IT IS ANYTHING BUT A GREAT
PICTURE, AND IF YOU WILL ANALYZE FORD'S RECORD YOU WILL
FIND THAT BALANCED AGAINST ONE REALLY GREAT PICTURE,
"THE INFORMER," WHICH CERTAINLY COULD NOT BE TERMED A
COMMERCIAL SMASH, AND A COUPLE OF GOOD PICTURES THAT DID
FAIRLY WELL, SUCH AS "THE LOST PATROL" AND "THE WHOLE
TOWN'S TALKING," ARE SUCH OUTSTANDING FAILURES AS "MARY
OF SCOTLAND" AND "THE PLOUGH AND THE STARS." I THEREFORE
FEEL THAT WE MUST DISMISS FORD AS A MAN WHO IS NO MORE
SURE-FIRE THAN IS CUKOR. BOTH ARE GREAT DIRECTORS AND
BOTH HAVE TO HAVE THEIR STORIES SELECTED FOR THEM AND
GUIDED FOR THEM, AND PRESUMABLY FORD NEEDS THE SAME
GUIDANCE IN SCRIPT THAT CUKOR DOES. . . . THE ONLY OTHER
STORY THAT I WOULD BE WILLING TO HAVE COOP AND FORD
MAKE IS "LAFAYETTE ESCADRILLE,"[34] WHICH I THINK COULD BE
OUTSTANDING IN COLOR WITHOUT STARS. COOP IS HAVING A
MEETING WITH FORD JUST AS SOON AS POSSIBLE.

To: Mr. O'Shea   July 16, 1937
cc: Mr. Ginsberg

As soon as you get back I want to go into the John Ford situation with
you. Coop tells me that Ford feels he is free of any commitment to us
as a company because of some clause in his contract with which I am
not familiar. . . .

Ford apparently has no desire to go through with his commitment
with us, evidently being annoyed because he could not do *The Stage
to Lordsburg*.[35] I don't think we should be chumps about this, and if
Ford actually has a commitment with us I see no reason for releasing

[34]A picture with the title *Lafayette Escadrille* was finally made by William Wellman
in 1957.
[35]*The Stage to Lordsburg* was eventually filmed by Ford in late 1938 as *Stagecoach*,
produced by Walter Wanger.

him. On the other hand, I have no particular desire to have him if he doesn't want to come here, and would be willing to trade him to some other studio for a director that we need. He is an excellent man, but there is no point in treating him as a god, and if he doesn't want to be here I'd just as soon have some other good director.

Please check his contract and advise me.

DOS

To: Mr. J. H. Whitney   August 11, 1937
cc: Mr. O'Shea

None of us can figure out what is in John Ford's mind. . . . I am somewhat wounded, since this is the first time in my career that anyone has said that he did not want to work for me, but I don't suppose there is anything I can do except bandage up the wound. Coop insists that Ford has nothing against me, and the man is hard to figure out, since immediately after announcements to the whole trade that under no circumstances would he ever work for either Zanuck[36] or Goldwyn, he proceeded to sign contracts with no one but Zanuck and Goldwyn. . . .

DOS

To: Miss Katharine Brown   August 30, 1937

. . . Answering your questions, and so that you will know about these matters for the future, the usual method of scoring pictures is for the arranger and scorer not to come near the picture until the editing is completed. The producer then turns the picture over to the music people, usually with the injunction to do a great job cheaply in a couple of weeks. This, on the fact of it, is silly, and I have tried to avoid working this way as well as to minimize the delays which are involved to get a picture released because of the time it takes to write, arrange, and record a score. Usually I have had the score in well ahead and I have tried to get these men to do the score from the script, having the weeks and months of production for the job—so that they are in a position to keep up with the changes as we edit the picture and to go with the least possible delay into the scoring, at the same time having

[36]Darryl F. Zanuck was now Vice-President in Charge of Production, Twentieth Century-Fox.

had sufficient time during the shooting of the picture to do a good job, instead of being rushed into doing it in a week or so when the picture is finished.

Incredibly, I have met resistance on this, particularly from [composer and conductor] Max Steiner, who found it difficult to do the work in this fashion, claiming that he had to have a finished picture. This was one of my long-standing arguments with Max, and his point in turn was based upon something else which was the root of our decision to get a divorce, which was my objection to what I term "Mickey Mouse" scoring: an interpretation of each line of dialogue and each movement musically, so that the score tells with music exactly what is being done by the actors on the screen. It has long been my contention that this is ridiculous and that the purpose of a score is to unobtrusively help the mood of each scene without the audience being even aware that they are listening to music—and if I am right in this contention, why can't the score be prepared from the script even though cuts and rearrangements may be necessary after the picture is edited—for the basic selection of music and general arrangement would not be affected by these cuts. I could go into this with you at further length but it would develop into an essay on musical scoring, about which I feel very keenly. I don't think there is another producer in Hollywood that devotes ten per cent as much time to the score as I do—and it may interest you to know that I was the first producer to use dramatic scores.[37] Max Steiner argued with me at the time, as he has since readily admitted, that musical scoring could not be used without the source of the music being explained to an audience.

I feel now that musical scoring is due for great improvement. Among other things, I feel that we have not had topnotch composers and conductors. I feel too that our pictures have been used as an exploitation ground for the second-rate talents of the composers who have been out here, and who have seen fit to substitute their own compositions for the practically untouched library of the world's music—which in my opinion is a gold mine for emotional effect that requires intelligent and educated selection and arrangement for our purposes by a man who has learned which music plays with most effect upon the emotions of the public. I am not

[37]Under dialogue in sound films.

certain that I would argue so much about the use of the world's classical and even nonclassical music if I had as an alternate really fine original composition. But too much of what has been composed for my pictures, and everybody else's pictures, has been second-rate—and I say this even though I am grateful for what I regard as the excellent composition in some of my pictures, notably Stothart's[38] work in *Viva Villa!* and Steiner's work in *The Garden of Allah.*

Newman[39] has been much more reasonable about working from script than Max was, but he too resisted the use of standard music that I thought could be used effectively and even help in achieving subconsciously a nostalgic mood. On occasion, notably in the score of *Anna Karenina,* I was able to force standard music. In the case of *Karenina,* Tchaikovsky selections—and with good effect.

Mr. Henry Luce[40]   December 7, 1937
135 East 42d Street   NOT SENT
New York, New York

Dear Harry:

I was shocked by the very tepid, if not actually damning review of *Nothing Sacred* in this week's *Time.* I was particularly surprised because the reviewer seemed to miss the whole point of the picture, a point which has been commented upon by magazine and newspaper critics across the country, which is that the picture strikes some entirely new notes in adult entertainment. It is the first comedy in Technicolor; it has been termed a very daring satire that has come off successfully; and it has been hailed from coast to coast as one of the best pictures of the year. I am asking Russell Birdwell[41] to send you reviews from leading cities all the way from New York to California, and from publications of varying kinds from *Newsweek* to Rob Wagner's *Script,* in support of these statements. I was pleased that the press responded to what I hoped and tried to make: something new and different; and, although it may be beside the point, it is gratifying to know that the public has supported the press opinion, as witness the picture's being held over a

---

[38]Herbert Stothart, composer and conductor, and MGM Musical Director.
[39]Alfred Newman, Musical Director. He composed and conducted the score for Selznick's *The Prisoner of Zenda.*
[40]Founder and Editor of *Time, Life,* and *Fortune.*
[41]Advertising and Publicity Director for Selznick International.

third week at [Radio City] Music Hall. . . .

I assure you that I would not be so upset about *Time's* review were it not for the fact that I still read the damned thing every week, and that you happen to be the only publisher whom I list among alleged personal friends. Perhaps it's the penalty of friendship—or perhaps it's the penalty of something else, because when I made inquiries concerning the review I found that the picture had been covered on the coast by an old friend, who, as I have previously advised you, has the ax to grind of my having refused repeatedly over a period of years to give him a job. I understand that you were good enough to have someone else cover the picture, which I appreciate enormously and very sincerely, but I cannot help but feel that the review must have been influenced by the original coverage.

Your men have been very friendly and helpful in the way of space on our pictures in the other papers,[42] and have certainly gone out of their way to repay friendship with friendship. And the only reason for this squawk is to ask whether, for the sake of my stockholders and your readers, you won't ask someone to cover my pictures who will sense the news values in them, and have some fair conception of their entertainment values as well, and who has no scenario-writing ambitions.

I hope to see you on the coast this winter.

Cordially yours,

The Adventures of Tom Sawyer

TO: KATHARINE BROWN   AUGUST 25, 1937

I REALIZE EVERYTHING YOU SAY ABOUT DIFFICULTIES
CONCERNING UNTRAINED CHILDREN, BUT I FEEL THAT THE
GREATEST PUBLICITY STORY AND HORATIO ALGER STORY IN THE
HISTORY OF THE PICTURE BUSINESS WOULD BE OUR FINDING TOM
SAWYER AND OR HUCK FINN IN AN ORPHAN ASYLUM, AND THAT
THIS WOULD RECEIVE SUCH TREMENDOUS ATTENTION AND AROUSE
SUCH A WARM PUBLIC FEELING THAT IT WOULD ADD ENORMOUSLY
TO THE GROSS OF THE PICTURE [*The Adventures of Tom Sawyer*

[42]Presumably meaning coverage of Selznick's films in Luce's two other publications, *Life* and *Fortune*.

(1938)]. I DON'T WANT TO TIP OUR HAND ON THIS BECAUSE WE ALL
FEEL THAT THE IDEA IS SO IMPORTANT THAT WE ARE AFRAID
THAT SOME QUICKY PRODUCER MAY GET BUSY ON THE SAME
ANGLE IF IT LEAKS OUT, SO THEREFORE KEEP OUR INTENTIONS TO
YOURSELF AS MUCH AS POSSIBLE, AT LEAST WITHIN TRADE AND
PRESS CIRCLES, UNTIL WE FIND OUT IF WE ACTUALLY CAN FIND
ONE OR MORE ORPHANS THAT FIT THE BILL.[43]

To: Norman Taurog[44]   January 8, 1938

. . . The only criticism that we had in the preview cards—and this
appeared in a number of them—was that the cave sequence[45] was
somehow too horrible for children. This worried me, because we certainly want the picture to be for a family audience, and I made it my
business both to study this criticism and to ask innumerable questions
of many people. My conclusion was that this horror was not based
upon the melodrama of this sequence, but upon two things: the bat
sequence, because of the feeling of horror born of weird and flying
animals; and upon what I had thought was your brilliant execution of
my hysteria idea for Becky.[46] I didn't like to lose the bat sequence
entirely, so for tonight's preview I have left it in, simply trimming it
—and if we get the same reaction we may have to cut it further.

Since I feel that the hysterical scene is one of the high spots of the
picture, I studied this even more carefully and came to the conclusion
that the offensive part was, hopefully, only the unusually horrible
close-up of Becky in which she is laughing hysterically and in which
her mind is obviously completely gone, and in which she looks like a
little witch rather than like a little girl—her hysteria perhaps a shade
too much that of a very ill woman, than that of a little girl. I found that
all the women I spoke to about this close-up were of one mind on it,
and hence I have dropped it with regrets.

I gave considerable study to the screams—their timing, volume,
placing, cueing, etc., and I am hopeful that you will find these improved in their effectiveness through not being used simply gratuitously. . . .

[43]The child eventually selected for the role of Tom was Tommy Kelly, a nonprofes-
sional (but not an orphan) from the Bronx. Huckleberry Finn was played by Jackie
Moran, a professional.
[44]Director of *The Adventures of Tom Sawyer.*
[45]The climax of the film.
[46]Becky was played by Ann Gillis.

Intermezzo

TO: KATHARINE BROWN   AUGUST 16, 1938

IN CONNECTION WITH BERGMAN,[47] WOULD STILL BE INTERESTED
EVEN IF SHE DOES NOT START UNTIL NEXT YEAR. AS MATTER OF
FACT THIS MIGHT BE AN ADVANTAGE BECAUSE SHE COULD BE
TAKING INTENSIVE ENGLISH LESSONS IN THE INTERIM. HOWEVER,
WOULD LIKE TO KNOW ALL ABOUT HER COMMITMENTS AS WE
MIGHT WANT TO GET HER OUT OF SOME OF THEM. IN CONNECTION
WITH TERMS FOR HER, I MIGHT POINT OUT THAT SHE WAS NOT
EVEN STARRED IN SWEDEN, SINCE THE MAIN TITLE OF
"INTERMEZZO" STARS GOSTA STEVENS AND GUSTAF MOLANDER.[48] A
COLD SHUDDER HAS JUST RUN THROUGH ME ON THE REALIZATION
THAT MAYBE WE ARE DEALING FOR THE WRONG GIRL. MAYBE THE
GIRL WE ARE AFTER IS GOSTA STEVENS. YOU HAD BETTER CHECK
ON THIS. . . .

To: Mr. Hulburd[49]   October 23, 1938
cc: Messrs. Ginsberg, O'Shea

Dear Merritt:

Before starting on notes on the [*Intermezzo*] script itself, I'd like to
make a few observations about the picture as a whole.

To begin with, we obviously cannot cast it in such a way as to insure
a big gross. This hope finished when Colman and Powell both refused
the lead. Maybe you can get some other important idea, in which case
I'd gladly add to the cost to give us the additional insurance value
of really big names. But so far, the best I have been able to think
of is the combination of Boyer and Loretta Young. This combination will cost us somewhere in the neighborhood of $150,000, which
is a good deal more than it's worth—but that's the way of the business; and I suppose we should be glad we're able to get this good a
combination. Boyer has already approved the role. Loretta has not
yet approved her role because I have not yet spoken to her about
it. But I don't anticipate any great difficulty with her, especially

[47]Swedish actress Ingrid Bergman, who had not as yet made an American film.
[48]The original Swedish version of *Intermezzo* (1936) featured, in addition to Ingrid
Bergman, Gosta Ekman and Inga Tidblad. The script was by Gosta Stevens and Gustaf
Molander; Molander also directed. Selznick had decided to remake it in English.
[49]Merritt Hulburd, Production Executive.

since she is most anxious to be with us. . . .

Now I ask you to bear in mind at all times that one of the principal reasons for buying foreign pictures to remake is that when they are good they save a very large part of the agonies of creative preparation and a large part of the cost as well. . . . The purchase price, incidentally, includes montage sequences which should save us a good deal of money, as well as any other negative which might be usable—although offhand I cannot think of anything but the montage.

Six months ago we would have been able to save a fortune by using the music tracks, but today with the union rule prohibiting the second use of music tracks, this is no longer possible. However, there is still a saving to be accomplished by using musical arrangements, etc., even though they have to be played again—because I think the score is, on the whole, quite good.

In passing, let me say that I think the "Intermezzo" strain is magnificent, and that we should not try to better it since it haunts everyone who sees the picture.[50] However, I do think that we should get in some other famous concert pieces such as "Humoresque," "Souvenir," etc., to get the full showmanship value of a violin solo of pieces that we know concert audiences are always screaming for; and to avoid the curious impression that one gets from the Swedish picture that the violinist plays nothing but "Intermezzo"! We should be glad to buy a really fine violinist without a big name for these renditions.

Incidentally, there is an unlooked-for advantage in the casting of Boyer in that I learn he plays the violin, and while he, of course, does not play it well enough to use the tracks he would make, his finger work would be all that would be necessary and we could really give the impression of his playing everything instead of having to fake it so much as we would have to with other actors.

To get back to where I was a few paragraphs ago, I want to impress on you strongly that the most important saving to be effected in remaking foreign pictures, a saving that more than offsets the doubtful foreign markets that have been used up by the original version, and that makes these remakes uniquely desirable—is in the shooting—by actually duplicating, as far as is practicable, the cut film. This should save weeks in shooting and a fortune in not shooting unnecessary scenes, and even more to the point, save on unnecessary camera angles. I think that the camera work in this picture and

[50]"Intermezzo" was composed by Heinz Provost for the Swedish production and retained for Selznick's version.

the use of angles, etc., was unusually good, and there is no reason at all for varying it if such varying is to mean extra cost. I do not mean to put the director in a strait jacket, but unless the director is willing to do a duplicating job to the extent, let us say, that John Cromwell did in *Algiers* of *Pepe le Moko*,[51] then we are better off to get a director who is willing to do such a duplicating job. If we are to bring the picture in at a price that accomplishes the original objective in having bought it, we must have a director who is willing to cooperate for this purpose, and to this end.

If you have not seen *Algiers* and *Pepe le Moko* you might arrange through Kay Brown to see them both. *Algiers*, contrary to general belief, was not a success at the box office. It did below-average business almost every place, and yet Wanger will come in with a nice profit, whereas if he had not done a frankly duplicating job and had gone to the expense of a more creative job on the script and on the shooting, he undoubtedly would have come out behind the eight ball.

We bought this picture because of my belief that a duplicating job on it could be done—that granted a good cast, direction that was at least as good as Molander's on the original, a somewhat faster tempo than his, for I think the pace is much too slow for an Anglo-Saxon audience, and some cuts—notably in the section of the affair between the first seeds of discontent and the girl's actual departure from Switzerland—we can practically duplicate the picture. . . .

Incidentally, the only reason we were able to get Lionel Barrymore is that he is now unfortunately crippled to such an extent (and I am sorry to say that I understand it is probably permanent) that he is unable to walk, and such appearances as the poor fellow is able to make in the future are going to have to be in a wheel chair (as in *You Can't Take It With You*), which naturally limits the number of things he can do, thereby making him more available than he was a few months ago when MGM was keeping him busy fifty-two weeks a year.

There is another good part which might be cast in some sort of showmanship manner to further the idea of an all-star cast, which is the manager (unless this is played by Lionel). As I recall the role, he has a great deal of acting to do and not very many lines of dialogue —which leads me to suggest that, if we can reduce the dialogue still further, it might be smart showmanship to cast John Barrymore in this role. . . .

[51] *Algiers* (1938) was the American remake of the French *Pepe le Moko* (1937).

You can clearly see what I have in mind if you list the following as possible casting:

> Charles Boyer
> Loretta Young
> Lionel Barrymore
> John Barrymore
> Gloria Swanson
> Freddie Bartholomew[52]

. . . Incidentally, in connection with the direction, we might do a lot worse than to have the picture codirected by Bill Menzies[53] and a good dialogue man. I think it possible that Menzies will be well enough advanced with his work on *Gone With the Wind,* particularly if the direction of the actors is in the hands of a good man. Maybe Danny [O'Shea] could arrange for [Garson] Kanin for this. If not, there are other good men around. I know of very few people in Hollywood who could direct the camera angles on this job as well as Menzies could, or who could give us as good a job pictorially. And we would have the advantage of being able to control and limit him without any difficulty whatsoever, as well as have the advantage of saving considerable money through both the control of shooting and through salary.

Still another idea on a codirection setup might be Lee Garmes,[54] who did a superb and most economic job in codirection with Hecht on *The Scoundrel.*[55]

DOS

To: Miss Katharine Brown   February 27, 1939
cc: Mr. Whitney, Mr. Ginsberg

Dear Kay:

I had a talk with Mr. Whitney today on the subject of changing Miss Bergman's name and asked him to discuss it further with you.

Since talking with him a few other thoughts occurred to me in connection with the subject:

I think you ought to check with a couple of the foreign departments as to the value of her present name abroad. Of course, there is nothing whatsoever to prevent our using her own name abroad and the new

[52]None eventually was cast.

[53]Production designer, art director, and occasional director William Cameron Menzies.

[54]Director of Photography, who received credit on *The Scoundrel* (1935) as Director of Photography and Associate Director.

[55]None of the above suggestions was realized.

name every place else—or at least it doesn't seem to me that there is anything against this, but this point might be checked too. . . .

If we change her name for only part of the world, then I think we can forget the idea of simply changing the spelling of it because I don't think Ingrid Berjman is a particularly good name either. Ingrid Berriman is a lot better but certainly this is no name that you would go out of the way to tack on to a personality either.

Ingrid Lindstrom[56] is also, I think, hard to remember. Perhaps the best thing to do would be to wait until she gets here, in accordance with the suggestion in the first paragraph of your letter. I don't think we ought to go into any big publicity campaign in advance of her appearance for us for several reasons, including the possibility of resentment against us as a company for importing another foreigner after the agitation concerning Vivien Leigh;[57] and also because build-ups on foreign importations have reached a point where the American public resents the players when they do appear. I think it a lot better to let them sneak in, more or less in the manner of Hedy Lamarr, who was discovered by the public through her appearance in *Algiers* rather than through any advance publicity build-up. I think that the best thing to do would be to import her quietly into the studio, go about our business of making the picture with only such publicity attendant upon her casting as would be the case with any unimportant leading woman, and then feed an important and favorable public reception of her when the picture is finished.

With this policy in mind, I think we should avoid interviews with her at the boat and should let her arrive in Los Angeles very quietly, which will give us the opportunity to discuss a change of name with her after she arrives at the studio. . . .

DOS

MISS KATHARINE BROWN   MARCH 18, 1939
SELZNICK INTERNATIONAL
230 PARK AVENUE
NEW YORK CITY

I NOTE BERGMAN IS 69½ INCHES TALL. IS IT POSSIBLE SHE IS ACTUALLY THIS HIGH, AND DO YOU THINK WE WILL HAVE TO USE STEPLADDERS WITH LESLIE HOWARD?

DAVID

[56]Miss Bergman's married name.
[57]By this time Selznick had already begun production on *Gone With the Wind* with Vivien Leigh.

To: Mr. Wyler[58]   May 8, 1939
cc: Messrs. [Leslie] Howard, Klune, O'Shea

Miss Bergman told me a very interesting thing about the way the more effective shots were made in the Swedish version of the violinist —those which gave a real illusion that the leading man was playing the violin.

The closer angles were made by having two violinists stand on either side of the leading man, whose arms were held closely at his side; one violinist had his arm outstretched and did the fingering and the violinist on the other side did the bow work.

I think we ought to do the same thing.

DOS

To: Mr. L. V. Calvert   May 19, 1939

Replying to your memo of the 16th, we are keeping the name Ingrid Bergman. I think Miss Bergman is justified in her attitude that after having spent so long to build it up in Europe, she feels reluctant to change it when there is no positive assurance that she will make any more than one picture here.

DOS

To: Miss Ingrid Bergman   June 8, 1939
cc: Mr. Ratoff

Dear Ingrid:

I understand you are disturbed about bad readings by yourself on lines that come through insufficiently in advance for you to be able to study them. Please don't worry about this unduly, since it is very easy for us to dub[59] any lines on which there are bad readings. In *Gone With the Wind* we are dubbing perhaps two hundred lines. In *Viva Villa!* I dubbed one of the principals all the way through. So you can see that it is a simple matter to dub any few lines that are badly read or in which the accent is, for any reason, bad.

DOS

[58]William Wyler originally was set to direct *Intermezzo*, but because the shooting script was delayed, he had to relinquish the assignment for a commitment with Samuel Goldwyn. Gregory Ratoff was then signed as Director.
[59]Rerecording dialogue at a later date.

To: Mr. Stradling[60]   June 9, 1939
cc: Mr. Ratoff, Mr. Klune, Mr. Westmore[61]

. . . There is no single thing about the physical production of the picture, including the photography, that even compares in importance with the photography of Miss Bergman. Unlike Mr. Howard, and unlike almost any player of importance that I know of, the difference in her photography is the difference between great beauty and a complete lack of beauty. And unless we can bring off our photography so that she really looks divine, the whole picture can fall apart from a standpoint of audience effectiveness.

I thought that we had the problem solved in one or two of the close-up tests that we made, but in the rushes we are right back to where we were on the first frightening tests. . . .

It is entirely possible that we haven't yet learned enough about her angles or about exactly how to light her and if this be the case, I urge that you make plans immediately (every day that we delay in solving this problem matters tremendously) to make another series of tests with her one evening, preferably on the evening of a day in which she had not worked. Or perhaps it would be better to do them tomorrow, Saturday night, or Sunday. These tests ought to be quite exhaustive as to lighting effects, make-up, angles, etc. As a matter of fact, on second thought, I urge that we make those tests at once regardless of whether you have confidence that the problem can be corrected without them or not.

I cannot tell you how strongly I feel about this matter or how important I feel it to be. I think it is the difference between a successful picture and an unsuccessful picture; the difference between a new star and a girl who will never make another picture here.

Actually, Hedy Lamarr was established purely by photography. And while I recognize that Miss Lamarr is comparatively easy to photograph and is a much more obvious type of beauty, whether or not we are going to have a star in Miss Bergman is equally dependent upon photography, especially because we know her capabilities as an actress.

The curious charm that she had in the Swedish version of *Intermezzo*—the combination of exciting beauty and fresh purity—certainly ought to be within our abilities to capture. It would be shocking

[60]Harry Stradling, the original Director of Photography on *Intermezzo*, who was replaced after filming started by Gregg Toland.
[61]Make-up artist Monty Westmore.

indeed if some cameraman in a small Stockholm studio was proven to be able to do so much more superior work with her than we are. . . .

DOS

To: Mr. Hebert[62]   June 12, 1939

I think Miss Bergman's interview in the [*Los Angeles*] *Examiner* was awfully bad publicity, as I am sure you will agree. In the first place, our being quoted as thinking she is sexy puts us in a rather silly position and furthermore is not the way we should publicize her. The dentist husband doesn't help any, nor does the publicity that she is too tall, especially in relation to Leslie Howard, which is incidentally not the case.

Please don't have her interviewed in the future unless somebody you can rely on, or you yourself, can be present.

DOS

To: Mr. Gregory Ratoff   June 22, 1939
cc: Mr. Gregg Toland

Dear Greg:

The Toland tests of Miss Bergman prove indubitably what we have been saying since before the picture started—that more than with any other girl that I know of in pictures, the difference between a great photographic beauty and an ordinary girl with Miss Bergman lies in proper photography of her—and that this in turn depends not simply on avoiding the bad side of her face; keeping her head down as much as possible; giving her the proper hairdress, giving her the proper mouth make-up, avoiding long shots, so as not to make her look too big, and, even more importantly, but for the same reason, avoiding low cameras on her, as well as being careful to build people who work with her, such as Leslie Howard and Edna Best (as well, of course, as the children, beside whom she looks titanic if the camera work isn't carefully studied); but most important of all, on shading her face and in invariably going for effect lightings on her. This means that there should not be a single sequence of the picture that is not staged for real effect lighting—whether it be morning, afternoon, or night. One might say with justice that almost any dramatic picture benefits from

---

[62]William Hebert, Advertising and Publicity Director for Selznick International.

this sort of careful attention to lighting effects, but in the case of
Intermezzo the mood of the picture is dependent upon it to an extent
far greater than what is true of most pictures. Thus, in photographing
Miss Bergman properly we will be benefiting the picture as a whole.
And I consequently urge you to give Mr. Toland every assistance in
going for the type of job which some large studios might consider arty,
but which in the case of this particular picture I regard as equally
important as the dialogue and the performances if we are to get the
artistic gem that we hope out of our simple little story.

DOS

To: Mr. Hebert   June 22, 1939

I think there is a publicity angle on Ingrid Bergman which could be
widely built up and which could be used with her for years.

Miss Bergman is the most completely conscientious actress with
whom I have ever worked, in that she thinks of absolutely nothing but
her work before and during the time she is doing a picture, and makes
no engagements of any kind and no plans that for one minute would
distract her from her picture work. She practically never leaves the
studio, and even suggested that her dressing room be equipped so that
she could live here during the picture. She never for a minute suggests
quitting at six o'clock or anything of the kind, and, on the contrary, is
very unhappy if the company doesn't work until midnight, claiming
that she does her best work in the evenings after a long day's work.

More to the point of my first paragraph, she is simply frantic about
spending any of the company's money. She was terribly upset about
a dress being thrown out because the test proved it was not becoming
to her, and suggested that perhaps a new collar could be built for it
to make it more attractive, or that it could be dyed, or that something
else could be done with it so that the money wouldn't be wasted.

She was amazed about having a stand-in and said that despite the
fact that she was starred in ten pictures in Sweden she has never had
a stand-in and did all of the standing-in for lights, etc., herself.

Because of having four stars in *Gone With the Wind*, our star dress-
ing-room suites were all occupied and we had to assign her a smaller
suite. She went into ecstasies over it and said she had never had such
a suite in her life.

When I found it necessary to switch cameramen, taking a staff man
[Harry Stradling] off *Intermezzo* and putting him on *Rebecca*, tears
came to her eyes and she wanted to know whether it would hurt his

standing, because after all he was a very good cameraman and it didn't matter if she was photographed a little worse—she would rather have this than hurt him.

All of this is completely unaffected and completely unique and I should think would make a grand angle of approach to her publicity, spreading these stories all around, and adding to them as they occur, so that her natural sweetness and consideration and conscientiousness become something of a legend. Certainly there could be nothing more popular, and nothing could win for her the affection of fans more than this, particularly in view of the growing nonsense that stars are forcing us to put up with, and more pertinently, because of the general public conception, which is largely true, that foreign stars are a goddam nuisance with their demands and their temperament.

This is the first approach to publicity on her that I would be willing to spring now without waiting for the picture's release. It is completely in keeping with the character she plays in the picture and completely in keeping with the fresh and pure personality and appearance which caused me to sign her, so that the publicity would be completely consistent, and would be the opposite of the comparisons which would be untrue, which would be extremely bad for her, and which I abhor —comparisons with Garbo, Dietrich, and other exotic numbers with whom she cannot compete, any more than, in my opinion, they can compete with her. . . .

TO: JOHN HAY WHITNEY   JULY 25, 1939
    AND LOWELL V. CALVERT

ANXIOUS TO HAVE SOME HELP AND ADVICE ON "INTERMEZZO"
TITLE SITUATION. . . . MANAGER OF PREVIEW THEATER, WHO
LIKED PICTURE ENORMOUSLY, FELT TITLE "INTERMEZZO" WOULD
HURT IT,[63] BUT THIS MAY BE TYPICAL OLD-FASHIONED
THEATRICAL OR DISTRIBUTION VIEWPOINT, AND I AM STILL
WORRIED AS TO WHETHER OR NOT WE ARE GIVING UP THE BEST
TITLE IN CHANGING "INTERMEZZO." I'M SORRY TO APPEAR
VACILLATING ON THIS POINT, BUT MY FEELING THAT PERHAPS WE
SHOULD AGAIN CONSIDER RETAINING IT IS BORN OF MISS
BERGMAN'S STATEMENT TO ME THAT IN SWEDEN THEY WENT
THROUGH SAME THING WE ARE GOING THROUGH. THERE WERE
VIOLENT OBJECTIONS TO THE TITLE DURING PRODUCTION, AND
MUCH FEELING EVEN WHEN IT WAS FINISHED THAT IT SHOULD BE

---

[63]Because of the relative obscurity of the word.

CHANGED. BUT THE TITLE WAS RETAINED AND BECAME MUCH
DISCUSSED AND WAS VERY SUCCESSFUL. INCIDENTALLY, WHAT
WOULD YOU THINK OF CABLING UNITED ARTISTS IN SWEDEN
IMMEDIATELY TO ASK THEM FURTHER ABOUT POPULAR REACTIONS
TO THE TITLE OF ORIGINAL VERSION, SINCE I CANNOT IMAGINE IT
WOULD BE ANY MORE DIFFICULT FOR SWEDISH AUDIENCES TO
ABSORB AS A TITLE THAN FOR AMERICAN OR ENGLISH AUDIENCES.
. . . THE STUDIO STAFF IS ABOUT EVENLY SPLIT BETWEEN
RETAINING IT AND CHANGING IT. A GREAT MANY HERE LIKE THE
TITLE "LOVE STORY." OF THOSE WE HAVE CONSIDERED I LIKE
VERY MUCH THE IDEA OF CALLING IT "SACRED AND PROFANE
LOVE." THIS IS THE TITLE OF AN ARNOLD BENNETT PLAY OWNED
AND ONCE PRODUCED BY PARAMOUNT MANY YEARS AGO. . . . MR.
WHITNEY AND I BOTH COMMENTED ON WHAT A LOVELY TITLE RKO
HAD IN "MEMORY OF LOVE." I NOTICED THIS MORNING THAT THEY
HAVE CHANGED THE TITLE OF THIS PICTURE AND IT IS THEREFORE
PRESUMABLY AVAILABLE. . . . ANOTHER SUGGESTION I THINK IS
SPLENDID IS SIMPLY THE ONE WORD "LOVERS," OR PERHAPS "THE
LOVERS." WE HAVE NOT LOST SIGHT OF THE IDEA OF CALLING IT
"INTERMEZZO" WITH "A LOVE STORY" IN PARENTHESES, BUT THIS
IS PERHAPS BEGGING THE ISSUE. EVEN THOUGH THIS WOULD
RETAIN PUBLICITY VALUE WE HAVE HAD, IT STILL DOES NOT
ANSWER THE QUESTION AS TO WHETHER OR NOT WE SHOULD
RETAIN "INTERMEZZO," AND I DO NOT THINK OUR DECISION AS TO
WHETHER OR NOT TO RETAIN IT CAN REST UPON THIS SUBTITLE
SUGGESTION . . . SINCE OBVIOUSLY THE PICTURE WILL BE
ADVERTISED ON THEATER MARQUEES, ETC., WITH JUST THE ONE
WORD. IF, HOWEVER, WE DID DECIDE TO RETAIN IT, I DO NOT
THINK WE COULD LOSE ANYTHING BY USING THE SUBTITLE AND
WE MIGHT GAIN.[64]

To: Mr. Birdwell   November 8, 1939

. . . The item about Leslie Howard's having possibly discovered
Bergman is, of course, amusing in view of the fact that Howard was
engaged for *Intermezzo* months after Bergman was signed for it.

Ann Rutherford,[65] whom I saw on the train, told me something
which might be the basis of some excellent publicity, which is that all
the girls she knows are letting their eyebrows grow in as a result of

[64]The film was released with the title *Intermezzo: A Love Story.*
[65]Ann Rutherford played one of Scarlett O'Hara's sisters in *Gone With the Wind.*

Bergman's unplucked eyebrows, and that she herself now feels very strongly about unplucked eyebrows, not merely because of Miss Bergman but because of Miss Leigh, whom we also should have eyebrows *au naturel.* So apparently our decision about Miss Bergman's eyebrows, based upon this studio's feeling that the public was sick and tired of the monstrosities that had been inflicted on the public by most of Hollywood's glamour girls, is going to have a national reaction!

I would just as soon not be identified with this startling national movement personally, but I think it might make for good publicity about Bergman and Leigh.

Selznick International Studio in Culver City in the late thirties.

Ronald Colman and Madeleine Carroll in *The Prisoner of Zenda* (1937).

Director W. S. Van Dyke II and Selznick
on the set of *The Prisoner of Zenda.*

Ronald Colman and fencer Ralph Faulkner in *The Prisoner of Zenda.*

Carole Lombard and Fredric March in *Nothing Sacred* (1937). *(To be continued—)*

(—continued)

Tommy Kelly as Tom and Ann Gillis as Becky
in *The Adventures of Tom Sawyer* (1938).

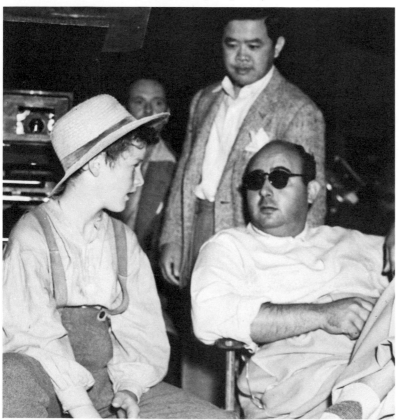

Tommy Kelly and Director Norman Taurog (seated) on the set of
The Adventures of Tom Sawyer, with Director of Photography
James Wong Howe.

Val Lewton, Selznick International
West Coast Story Editor (1938).

Stage star Maude Adams and Selznick in front
of Selznick International Studio (1938).

Roland Young, Billie Burke, Douglas Fairbanks, Jr., and Janet Gaynor in *The Young in Heart* (1938).

On the set of *The Young in Heart* (1938). Top center: Billie Burke. Clockwise: Douglas Fairbanks, Jr., Janet Gaynor, Roland Young, script clerk Geraldine Wright, actress Minnie Dupree, Director Richard Wallace, writer Paul Osborn.

James Stewart and Carole Lombard in *Made for Each Other* (1939).

Ingrid Bergman and Erik Berglund in the original Swedish production of *Intermezzo* (1936).

Ingrid Bergman and Leslie Howard in *Intermezzo* (1939).

Director of Photography Gregg Toland
on the set of *Intermezzo* (1939).

Ingrid Bergman and Director Gregory Ratoff rehearsing a scene for *Intermezzo* (1939).

Selznick dictating a memo to secretaries Frances Inglis (on Selznick's right) and Virginia Olds (1941).

Director George Cukor (left) and dramatist Sidney Howard on a sound stage at Selznick International in 1937, during the preparation of *Gone With the Wind*.

Louis B. Mayer signs contracts for the loan of Clark Gable to Selznick International to play Rhett Butler in *Gone With the Wind,* and for MGM to release the film. Gable is seated. Standing: Selznick and MGM executive Al Lichtman (1938).

Production Designer William Cameron Menzies working on sketches for *Gone With the Wind*.

Art Director Lyle Wheeler with the model of the portions of Atlanta to be re-created on the back lot of Selznick International.

Bette Davis as *Jezebel* (1938).

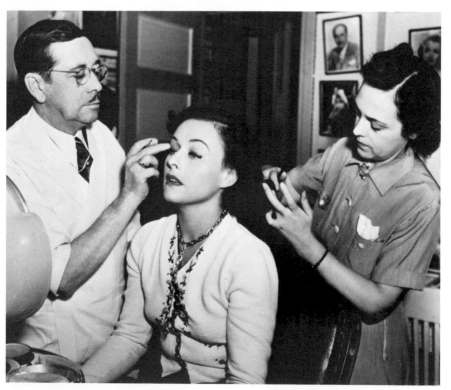

Paulette Goddard preparing to test for the role of Scarlett in *Gone With the Wind*. Paul Stanhope and Hazel Rogers are applying make-up and dressing her hair.

The burning of Atlanta on the back lot of Selznick International, marking the start of production on *Gone With the Wind* (December 1938).

Party at Myron Selznick's home, December 1938. Left to right: Vivien Leigh, Laurence Olivier, David O. Selznick, George Cukor, Irene Selznick, John Hay Whitney, Merle Oberon.

Selznick, Leslie Howard, and Olivia de Havilland watching Vivien Leigh sign the contract to play Scarlett in *Gone With the Wind*.

Scarlett at Tara in the opening sequence of *Gone With the Wind*.

The O'Hara family and servants at prayer in *Gone With the Wind*.

Scarlett (Vivien Leigh) and Ashley (Leslie Howard).

George Cukor registering delight while directing Clark Gable and Vivien Leigh in the benefit bazaar sequence for *Gone With the Wind*.

Vivien Leigh, Clark Gable, and Director Victor Fleming between scenes on *Gone With the Wind*.

Sam Wood, who directed portions of *Gone With the Wind*.

Filming the evacuation of Atlanta in *Gone With the Wind*.

Rehearsing the spectacular crane shot of Scarlett amidst the wounded at the Atlanta depot in *Gone With the Wind*.

Scarlett and Rhett.

Photographing Mr. and Mrs. Rhett Butler with daughter on a Sunday stroll in Atlanta (the back lot of Selznick International).

Composer Max Steiner conducting his score for *Gone With the Wind*.

Selznick and Will H. Hays, President of the Motion Picture Producers and
Distributors of America, Inc. (1939).

Tara in the background; Selznick in the foreground.

Arriving in Atlanta for the world première of *Gone With the Wind* on December 15, 1939. Left to right: Olivia de Havilland, Selznick, Laurence Olivier, Vivien Leigh, and Mayor William B. Hartsfield.

Margaret Mitchell, author of *Gone With the Wind*, and Clark Gable.

The Hollywood première of *Gone With the Wind*. Left to right: John Hay Whitney, Irene Selznick, Olivia de Havilland, Selznick, Vivien Leigh, and Laurence Olivier.

Selznick, Vivien Leigh, and one of ten Academy Award
Oscars received for *Gone With the Wind* (1940).

Selznick at home. Above him is a caricature
of the producer as Rhett Butler (1940).

Joan Fontaine, Laurence Olivier, and Judith Anderson in *Rebecca* (1940).

On the set of *Rebecca*. Left to right: Director Alfred Hitchcock, Assistant Cameraman Jack Warren, Laurence Olivier, C. Aubrey Smith, and Joan Fontaine.

Alfred Hitchcock and Selznick on the set of *Rebecca*.

Laurence Olivier, Joan Fontaine, and Alfred Hitchcock rehearsing *Rebecca*.

The miniature exterior of Manderley built for *Rebecca*.

The only portion of Manderley's exterior built full-scale for *Rebecca*.

Rebecca: Joan Fontaine, Laurence Olivier, and Reginald Denny.

Irene and David Selznick
at home (1940).

Irene Selznick, Jeffrey, Daniel, and David Selznick (1941).

Selznick and Daniel T. O'Shea, his close associate for many years.

Selznick becoming a partner in United Artists and joining Charlie Chaplin, Mary Pickford, and Alexander Korda (1941).

Phylis Isley (Jennifer Jones) and Sammy McKim in *New Frontier* (1939).

Story conference on *Jane Eyre* in 1942. Behind Selznick is Director Robert Stevenson. Left to right: Production Designer William Pereira, Scenario Assistant Barbara Keon, author Aldous Huxley.

PART

GONE WITH THE WIND
(1936–1941)

WHEN I HESITATED about paying $50,000 for a novel about the Civil War—the largest price ever paid for a book that was not even established as a success—Jock Whitney wired me that if I didn't buy it for Selznick International, he would buy it, and hold it for the company if I wanted it. This was all the encouragement I needed, and rather than have Jock have the last laugh on me, we went ahead and bought Gone With the Wind. I then went to Hawaii on vacation and read the novel on board ship.

Much later, Metro demanded half the film, and secured it, for a loan of Clark Gable. They put up $1,250,000—and we took all the gamble. (The picture cost $4,250,000.) The risk money was entirely ours, secured from the banks, due to the great support I had from Jock Whitney, who approved enthusiastically everything I did in this particular.

Whitney had the last laugh on all the self-appointed critics who picked on him and on the company for what looked like a foolish endeavor in attempting to have our little company try to make the biggest picture of all time, a film that would have strained the resources of the largest of studios.

MGM had no controls whatsoever over the making of Gone With the Wind, and indeed we produced it at our own studio, Selznick International, without even any of their staff. MGM had urged me to make the picture with Joan Crawford as Scarlett, Maureen O'Sullivan as Melanie, and Melvyn Douglas as Ashley. I said they were all very good people, but they would all be miscast. Fortunately, I had the authority to cast it as I saw fit, as I did with all my other pictures.

A producer can only find and put over new personalities when he has patience, and the money for overhead, and the authority to refuse to be rushed into making his judgments. If you have to get somebody by Wednesday when shooting starts, you take the best available and cross your fingers and pray. The pressure for haste on Gone With the Wind was severe, but I knew that seventy-five million people would want my scalp if I chose the wrong Scarlett, and that there was no agreement on who, among all the girls in pictures, was the right Scarlett. For instance, there were just as many people against Bette Davis as there were for her; maybe more. So I had no alternative to sticking to it and looking everywhere.

In addition to her vitality and beauty, her striking personality and enormous natural ability, Vivien Leigh had a background of training and acting experience that made her a fine actress. Vivien made no secret of her opinion of certain scenes as she went along: during the 122 days she was on the set during Gone With the Wind, *she groused plenty: before a scene, she would be muttering deprecations under her breath and making small moans. According to Vivien, the situation was stupid, the dialogue was silly, nobody could possibly believe the whole scene. And then, at a word from Victor Fleming, who was not merely a very fine director but a man who had the ability to conceal the iron hand in the velvet glove, she would walk into the scene and do such a magnificent job that everybody on the set would be cheering.*

:: :: :: :: :: :: :: :: :: :: :: ::

TO: KATHARINE BROWN   MAY 25, 1936

HAVE GONE OVER AND CAREFULLY THOUGHT ABOUT "GONE WITH THE WIND." THINK IT IS FINE STORY AND I UNDERSTAND YOUR FEELING ABOUT IT.[1] IF WE HAD UNDER CONTRACT A WOMAN IDEALLY SUITED TO THE LEAD, I WOULD PROBABLY BE MORE INCLINED TO BUY IT THAN I AM TODAY, BUT I DO FEEL THAT ITS ONLY IMPORTANT SHOWMANSHIP VALUES WOULD BE IN EITHER SUCH STAR CASTING OR IN A TREMENDOUS SALE OF THE BOOK. TO PAY A LARGE PRICE FOR IT NOW IN THE HOPE WE COULD GET SUCH A STAR AND-OR IN THE FURTHER HOPE BOOK WILL HAVE TREMENDOUS SALE IS, I FEEL, UNWARRANTED. PERHAPS ONE OF THE LARGER COMPANIES CAN AFFORD BUY IT NOW IN THE HOPE OR EXPECTATION OF SUCH CASTING OPPORTUNITIES AND SUCH A SALE, BUT I DO NOT FEEL WE CAN TAKE SUCH A GAMBLE. IF IT IS NOT PURCHASED IMMEDIATELY THEN I KNOW YOU WILL WATCH ITS SALES CAREFULLY, AND IF IT THREATENS TO BECOME AN "ANTHONY ADVERSE" . . . THEN WE PRESUMABLY WILL BE IN AS CLOSE TOUCH AS ANY OTHER COMPANY, BUT IF IT IS BOUGHT IN INTERIM, WE MUST HAVE NO REGRETS.[2] I FEEL, INCIDENTALLY,

---

[1]Selznick was referring to a synopsis he had been sent. The book was first published one month later.

[2]*Anthony Adverse*, a huge success when it was published in 1933, has sold approximately one million hardcover and paperback copies in the United States to date.

THAT ITS BACKGROUND IS VERY STRONGLY AGAINST IT, AS
WITNESS "SO RED THE ROSE" [1935, Paramount], WHICH ALSO
THREATENED TO HAVE TREMENDOUS SALE AND WHICH IN SOME
PARTICULARS WAS IN SAME CATEGORY AND WHICH FAILED
MISERABLY AS A PICTURE. MOST GRATEFUL FOR YOUR INTEREST
AND EARLY ACTION ON THIS AND DO NOT WANT DISCOURAGE YOU
FROM BRINGING TO OUR ATTENTION THIS FORCIBLY ANY NEW OR
OLD STORY WHICH YOU RUN ACROSS, AND THEREFORE MOST
SORRY TO HAVE TO SAY NO IN FACE OF YOUR ENTHUSIASM FOR
THIS STORY.

TO: KATHARINE BROWN   MAY 26, 1936

WANT YOU TO NOTE THAT I HAVE THOUGHT FURTHER ABOUT
"GONE WITH THE WIND" AND THE MORE I THINK ABOUT IT, THE
MORE I FEEL THERE IS EXCELLENT PICTURE IN IT. SUGGEST YOU
CALL THIS TO MR. [Merian C.] COOPER'S AND MR. WHITNEY'S
ATTENTION FOR PIONEER AS POSSIBLE COLOR PICTURE,
ESPECIALLY IF THEY CAN SELL THE VERY COLORFUL MAN'S ROLE
TO GARY COOPER. WERE I WITH MCM, I BELIEVE I WOULD BUY IT
NOW FOR SOME SUCH COMBINATION AS GABLE AND JOAN
CRAWFORD.

TO: KATHARINE BROWN   MAY 28, 1936

I AM IN TOUGH SPOT ON "GONE WITH THE WIND." PROBLEM IS AS
FOLLOWS: WHAT DO YOU THINK ABOUT RONALD COLMAN FOR THE
LEAD? SPENT LATE LAST NIGHT TALKING STORIES WITH HIM AND
FOUND MYSELF SELLING HIM THIS STORY. HE SEEMED VERY
INTERESTED INDEED, AND WE DISCUSSED MATTER OF SOUTHERN
ACCENT. HE THINKS HE WOULD LOVE TACKLE IT AND SAYS HE
WOULD SPEND NEXT SEVERAL MONTHS MAKING STUDY OF IT AND
IS SURE HE COULD MASTER IT, AND I DON'T DOUBT THAT HE
COULD. . . . FOR THE LEAD MIGHT TRY SOMEONE LIKE [Miriam]
HOPKINS OR [Tallulah] BANKHEAD. I ONLY KNOW THE STORY FROM
SYNOPSIS. YOU KNOW THE BOOK. DO YOU THINK COLMAN IS
INSANE FOR IT? EVEN IF COLMAN IS RIGHT, THE PROBLEM IS THAT
IT TAKES HIM FOREVER TO MAKE UP HIS MIND. IF METRO DEAL
FALLS THRU—AND INCIDENTALLY I UNDERSTAND THERE IS NO
EXECUTIVE THERE WHO HAS ANY PARTICULAR INTEREST IN IT,
(BUT THALBERG IS LIABLE TO TAKE GAMBLE WITHOUT EVEN

READING IT)—COULD YOU POSSIBLY GET A ONE WEEK OPTION
PAYING 1000 BUCKS OR SOMETHING OF SORT FOR IT, IF
NECESSARY? IT IS ALSO POSSIBLE IF WE HAVE TO BUY IT, TO GET
IT AT ALL, WE WOULD HAVE TO TAKE CHANCE THAT IF WE DIDN'T
USE COLMAN, WE COULD GET GARY COOPER OR SOMEONE ELSE
LATER ON, UNLESS BOOK DEVELOPS IMPORTANTLY ENOUGH TO BE
BIG ATTRACTION ON THE BOOK ALONE, AS IN CASE OF
"MAGNIFICENT OBSESSION." THINK YOU OUGHT TO TALK THIS ALL
OVER WITH MR. WHITNEY IMMEDIATELY, ALTHOUGH I STILL THINK
. . . 65,000 IS TERRIFIC PRICE AND IF METRO DEAL FALLS THRU, I
CAN, IF YOU WISH AND IF IT WILL BE OF ANY VALUE, GET A LINE
ON JUST WHAT THEY MIGHT HAVE PAID.

DOS

TO: KATHARINE BROWN   JULY 7, 1936

IF YOU CAN CLOSE "GONE WITH THE WIND" FOR 50,000, DO SO.
ALTERNATE PROPOSITION 5500 AGAINST 55,000 FOR 90- OR 60-DAY
OPTION. . . . I CANNOT SEE MY WAY CLEAR TO PAYING ANY MORE
THAN 50,000. KNOW HOW HARD YOU HAVE WORKED ON THIS, AND
HOPE THIS WILL NOT MEAN OUR LOSS OF PROPERTY, BUT IF IT
DOES IT JUST CAN'T BE HELPED. YOU MAY ASK WHAT DIFFERENCE
AN EXTRA FIVE OR TEN THOUSAND DOLLARS WOULD MAKE ON A
PROPERTY LIKE THIS, BUT THE POINT IS THAT I FEEL WE ARE
EXTENDING OURSELVES CONSIDERABLY EVEN TO PAY SUCH A
PRICE FOR IT IN VIEW OF FACT THAT THERE IS NO CERTAINTY WE
CAN CAST IT PROPERLY.[3]

DOS

TO: KATHARINE BROWN   SEPTEMBER 25, 1936

ON SIDNEY HOWARD MY SUGGESTION IS THAT YOU ADVISE HIM
THAT I WOULD LIKE VERY MUCH TO HAVE HIM COME OUT AND DO
A SCRIPT WHENEVER HE IS AVAILABLE, AND IF HE DOES NOT LIKE
THE ONE I HAVE FOR HIM RIGHT NOW, PERHAPS I WILL HAVE
SOMETHING ELSE TO OFFER HIM. . . . ALTHOUGH HE NEED NOT
KNOW THIS, I FEEL THAT HE AND BEN HECHT ARE PROBABLY THE
TWO BEST WRITERS FOR PICTURES WHO ARE NOT TIED UP WITH
STUDIOS, AND THEY ARE BOTH RARE IN THAT YOU DON'T HAVE TO

[3]Selznick did obtain the rights for $50,000.

COOK UP EVERY SITUATION FOR THEM AND WRITE HALF THEIR
DIALOGUE FOR THEM. . . .

TO: KATHARINE BROWN   SEPTEMBER 28, 1936

ON MR. [MERIAN C.] COOPER'S ARRIVAL PLEASE IMMEDIATELY
DISCUSS WITH HIM THE SIDNEY HOWARD SITUATION. COOP IS VERY
INTIMATE FRIEND OF HOWARD'S, WITH WHOM I BELIEVE HE FLEW
DURING THE WAR. I HAVE JUST RECEIVED NOTE FROM COOP IN
WHICH HE ASKED IF HE SHOULD HELP IN HOWARD ARRANGEMENT,
AND I WISH YOU WOULD TELL HIM THAT BY ALL MEANS I WISH HE
WOULD DO THIS. . . .

TO: KATHARINE BROWN   SEPTEMBER 29, 1936

HAVE JUST SPOKEN TO CUKOR[4] AND HE SHARES MY ENTHUSIASM
FOR SIDNEY HOWARD ON "GONE WITH THE WIND."

TO: KATHARINE BROWN   OCTOBER 8, 1936
     AND MR. [MERIAN C.] COOPER

I AM VERY HAPPY ABOUT THE SIDNEY HOWARD DEAL. CARRY IT
THROUGH AS BEST YOU CAN. HOWEVER, I DO WISH YOU WOULD
TRY TO MAKE SUCH CHANGES IN THE TIME AND AVAILABILITY
ELEMENTS AS ARE POSSIBLE, IN LINE WITH WHAT I AM ABOUT TO
SAY. I HAVE NEVER HAD MUCH SUCCESS WITH LEAVING A WRITER
ALONE TO DO A SCRIPT WITHOUT ALMOST DAILY COLLABORATION
WITH MYSELF AND USUALLY ALSO THE DIRECTOR. ACTUALLY, THE
ONLY EXCEPTION IN MY ENTIRE PRODUCING CAREER IN WHICH I
HAVE HAD ANY SUCCESS IN LEAVING A WRITER MORE OR LESS
ALONE HAS BEEN IN THE CASE OF HECHT, AND THEN STRUCTURAL
CHANGES IN THE SCRIPT HAVE BEEN NECESSARY AS HE WENT
ALONG, EVEN AFTER ORIGINAL DISCUSSIONS AND AGREEMENT ON
TREATMENT. I AM HOPEFUL AND EXPECTANT THAT THIS WILL BE
EQUALLY AND POSSIBLY EVEN MORE TRUE WITH HOWARD.
NOTHING WOULD DELIGHT ME MORE THAN TO HAVE THIS HOPE
MATERIALIZE, FOR IT WOULD CERTAINLY BE A DELIGHT TO BE
ABLE TO AVOID THIS EFFORT, AND FURTHER TO BE ABLE TO
RETAIN AN EDITORIAL PERSPECTIVE THROUGH NOT HAVING TO

[4]Selznick had interested George Cukor in directing the property.

MAINTAIN THIS CONSTANT COLLABORATION. NEVERTHELESS, I AM FEARFUL ABOUT NO CONTACTS BETWEEN HOWARD, CUKOR, AND MYSELF BETWEEN THE TIME HE HAS HIS CONFERENCES WITH US ON THE TREATMENT AND THE TIME HE COMPLETES THE SCRIPT. THEREFORE, ANYTHING YOU CAN DO TO MAKE HOWARD AVAILABLE FOR CONFERENCE WITH US DURING THE ACTUAL WRITING OF THE SCRIPT WILL, I THINK, BE SAFEGUARDED. . . . ALSO, ASSUME THAT HE WILL BE AGREEABLE TO VISITING MARGARET MITCHELL[5] WITH CUKOR, BUT PLEASE CHECK THIS. ALSO, WISH THAT YOU WOULD HAVE A TALK WITH HIM ABOUT NOT GOING OVERBOARD ON SIZE AND EXPENSIVE PRODUCTION SCENES OF THE CIVIL WAR, WHICH I THINK SHOULD BE SHOWN MAINLY IN TERMS OF ITS EFFECT ON OUR PRINCIPALS. . . .

To: Miss Katharine Brown   November 7, 1936

Dear Katharine:

It looks as though George Cukor will be coming East about November 17. Present plans are for him to have conferences with Sidney Howard and then go South on research, location hunting, and—much more important—on the quest for some actors, particularly a Scarlett.

I wish you would advise Sidney Howard of this plan, and if it is at all possible, I would like Sidney to accompany George. This would give them plenty of time to talk about the adaptation, and at the same time would give us the benefit of Sidney's help in the search. . . .

In view of this, I think that George's search for actors in New York and his search in the South should be so laid out as to have him see as many prospects as possible, and to make such tests as he wishes within his limited time. I presume that insofar as New York is concerned, you will have such prospects as there may be lined up and ready for George to interview, either for Scarlett or for the other roles; and that you will arrange all tests that may be necessary. . . .

You should also be starting now to make the necessary arrangements for tests during the trip, either taking along a cameraman and sound man; or, if it appears more practical and cheaper (as it most likely will), using such commercial studios as there may be in the

[5]Author of *Gone With the Wind.*

South. Lists of such studios you can probably secure from the Hays Association and/or the film trade papers.

Incidentally, the itinerary should of course include the visit to Miss Mitchell. . . .

DOS

TO: MR. J. H. WHITNEY   DECEMBER 24, 1936

DEAR JOCK, HAVE WIRED TALLULAH [Bankhead] AS FOLLOWS—
"DEAR TALLULAH, THE TESTS ARE VERY PROMISING INDEED. AM
STILL WORRIED ABOUT THE FIRST PART OF THE STORY, AND
FRANKLY IF I HAD TO GIVE YOU AN ANSWER NOW IT WOULD BE
NO, BUT IF WE CAN LEAVE IT OPEN I CAN SAY TO YOU VERY
HONESTLY THAT I THINK THERE IS A STRONG POSSIBILITY. I
SHOULD LIKE TO CONTINUE LOOKING AROUND AND A LITTLE
LATER ON CONSIDER THE ADVISABILITY OF MAKING FURTHER
TESTS WITH YOU EITHER IN NEW YORK OR HERE USING DIALOGUE
SCENES FROM SCRIPT DIRECTED BY GEORGE. THESE TESTS SHOULD
BE BENEFICIAL TO YOUR CHANCES, BECAUSE CERTAINLY ONCE
YOU GET A CHANCE TO ACT, YOU SHOULD BURN UP THE SCREEN,
AND FROM OUR STANDPOINT THEY WOULD REALLY GIVE US CLEAR
IDEA AS TO HOW YOU WOULD BE AS SCARLETT AND HOW MUCH
YOUR PERFORMANCE WOULD OFFSET OTHER POSSIBLE
DRAWBACKS. IN SHORT, I SHOULD LIKE TO SAY TO YOU VERY
SINCERELY THAT I THINK YOU ARE A DEFINITE POSSIBILITY, BUT I
CANNOT GIVE YOU AN ANSWER FOR SOME TIME. CORDIALLY—
DAVID SELZNICK". . .

To: Mr. O'Shea   January 4, 1937

One of our strongest possibilities for the lead in *Gone With the Wind* is Errol Flynn.

Myron[6] is going to determine from Warner Brothers whether they would give us a picture a year with Flynn, if we gave him this lead. Please follow him up on this.

For your confidential information, Cukor and I jointly feel that the choice is in the following order: 1. Gable. 2. Gary Cooper. 3. Errol Flynn. This is so you may guide yourself accordingly.

[6]Myron Selznick had developed his own large—and successful—talent agency.

To: Mr. Wm. Wright   January 5, 1937
cc: Mr. M. C. Cooper

. . . Even more extensive than the second-unit work on *Zenda* is the
work on *Gone With the Wind*, which requires a man really capable,
literate, and with a respect for research to re-create, in combination
with Cukor, the evacuation of Atlanta and other episodes of the war
and Reconstruction Period. I have even thought about [silent-film
director] D. W. Griffith for this job.

Mr. Sidney Howard   January 6, 1937
157 East 82nd Street
New York City, N.Y.

Dear Sidney:

As I wired you, I had the opportunity to spend some time with
George [Cukor] going over my general feelings about the adaptation,
but I'll send them along to you anyway, in case George has forgotten
them.

To begin with, I'd like to say that I am very happy indeed over your
approach to the story, rough as it is. Since it is so rough, I won't go in
for many detailed comments.

I recognize, perhaps even more than you, the problem of length. I
am prepared for a picture that will be extremely long in any case,
perhaps as much as 14,000 feet,[7] which I believe the subject might
stand. But even getting down to this length is going to be tough. We
must prepare to make drastic cuts and these drastic cuts, I think, must
include some of the characters because my feeling, based on experience in adapting well-known and well-loved books, is that it is much
better to chop out whole sequences than it is to make small deletions
in individual scenes or sequences. We had this problem in *David
Copperfield* and we got away with it very successfully indeed. It was
astonishing even to me how successful we were in cutting out such
chunks as the whole school sequence in which we met Steerforth as
a boy, and the whole Steerforth love story, as well as his mother. Dr.
Strong and his wife also went by the boards. Yet we had no criticism
of any kind and were universally congratulated upon giving them the
book they knew so well and loved so well, and I feel that this is
not merely because of the care that we exercised in creating the

[7]Two hours and thirty-five minutes.

atmosphere, or because of the splendid performances, or because of George's masterful job of direction; but also because such cuts as we made in individual scenes defied discernment.

We have an even greater problem in *Gone With the Wind*, because it is so fresh in people's minds. In the case of ninety-nine people out of a hundred who read and saw *Copperfield*, there were many years between the reading and the seeing. In the case of *Gone With the Wind* there will be only a matter of months, and people seem to be simply passionate about the details of the book.

All of this is a prologue to saying that I urge you very strongly indeed against making minor changes, a few of which you have indicated in your adaptation, and which I will note fully.

These minor changes may give us slight improvements, but there will be five or ten million readers on our heads for them; where, for the most part, they will recognize the obvious necessity of our making drastic cuts.

I feel, too, that we should not attempt to correct seeming faults of construction. I have learned to avoid trying to improve on success. One never knows what chemicals have gone to make up something that has appealed to millions of people, and how many seeming faults of construction have been part of the whole, and how much the balance would be offset by making changes that we in our innocence, or even in our ability, consider wrong.

I am embarrassed to say this to you who have been so outstandingly successful in your adaptations, but I find myself a producer charged with re-creating the best-beloved book of our time, and I don't think any of us have ever tackled anything that is really comparable in the love that people have for it.[8]

I agree with your very sound conclusion, which, frankly, had not occurred to me before, that Miss Mitchell does everything "at least twice." An outstanding case of this is the repetition of what you might describe as "nights of love." Certainly, I think one scene of husbandly rape is enough. How the hell we can even use one is going to be a problem. . . .

I don't think that George agrees with me, but I should share your regret if we omitted (p. 6 of your treatment) the passage dealing with Mammy's devices about Scarlett's clothes, appetite, etc. I think it is

---

[8] *Gone With the Wind*, shortly after publication, became an unprecedented best seller. It has sold over seven million hardcover and paperback copies in the United States to date (over eleven million throughout the world).

superb indication of Scarlett's life in the first part of the story and is original and charming.[9] I recognize that it holds up the story at this point and suggest that perhaps you might be able to work it in right at the start of the picture. (I don't think there is much harm in rearranging sequences so long as the sequences are as the readers remember them and so long as cuts in these sequences are made so carefully that the losses are not discernible.)

. . . I shall comment about your suggestion concerning the series-of-dissolves technique. There are times when I think these can be used to great advantage, but there are other times when I think that everything possible should be done to avoid them. I feel that where they tell one thing, such as the walk of David Copperfield from London to Dover, they are not only acceptable but are absolutely necessary. But I do not feel they should ever be used to tell a great many things; when the technique is utilized purely to solve a problem of footage, using ten or fifteen feet to tell each of many scenes, I think it becomes obvious and is a distraction to audiences, who immediately become aware of movie tricks instead of being immersed in the story and forgetting that they are watching a picture.

I certainly urge most strongly against including any sequence in which Rhett is shown "doing his stuff" as a blockade runner.[10] We will be forgiven for cuts if we do not invent sequences. Quite possibly we will have to invent a few sequences as we did in *Copperfield*, including in these new sequences material from those we had cut, so that the illusion was complete as to including only material from the book. ([Hugh] Walpole did a fine job in re-creating even the actual Dickensian type of phrasing.)

It is true that there is a "lack both of variety and of invention in what Rhett does," but here again I urge that we abide by Miss Mitchell's failures as well as her successes, because I am frankly nervous about anybody's ability—even Miss Mitchell's—to figure out which is which. I think that she herself might very well rewrite the book into a failure.

P. 15: I urge against any change in Rhett's character that might be indicated by the suggested apology. I think his boorishness and bad manners, if that's what they are, are as much a part of Rhett as his charm, and I don't think we should attempt to white-wash him in the least. The balance of Rhett's behavior and Scarlett's behavior has come off brilliantly and I am afraid to tamper with it. . . .

[9]This material ultimately was retained.
[10]This was not included.

P. 28: I have had a little discussion with George, who shares your lack of belief in Rhett's sudden decision to enlist in the army, on whether to make any change here. I personally think that this can be made completely believable if what we see of the plight of his fellow Southerners immediately before this is sufficiently heart-wringing to make everyone in your audience want to get out and fight with them. If we can do this, and I don't see why we should have any inordinate trouble about it, I think Rhett will be behaving exactly as your audience will be wanting him to behave, regardless of his previous attitude.[11]

P. 30: I think we must definitely keep the killing of the Yankee cavalryman. I feel that this is one of the most exciting and dramatic scenes in the book and that we simply cannot do without it. . . .[12] I feel quite the opposite, however, about the Yankee's attempt to burn Tara. As far as I am concerned, this can be lost. . . .[13]

P. 37: Here we come to a very touching point and I am hopeful that you share my feelings on it. I have already discussed it with George and he agrees—but then, our feelings are prejudiced. I refer to the Ku Klux Klan. I personally feel quite strongly that we should cut out the Klan entirely. It would be difficult, if not impossible, to clarify for audiences the difference between the old Klan and the Klan of our times. (A year or so ago I refused to consider remaking *The Birth of a Nation,* largely for this reason. Of course we might have shown a couple of Catholic Klansmen, but it would be rather comic to have a Jewish Kleagle; I, for one, have no desire to produce any anti-Negro film either. In our picture I think we have to be awfully careful that the Negroes come out decidedly on the right side of the ledger, which I do not think should be difficult.) Furthermore, there is nothing in the story that necessarily needs the Klan. The revenge for the attempted attack can very easily be identical with what it is without their being members of the Klan. A group of men can go out to "get" the perpetrators of an attempted rape without having long white sheets over them and without having their membership in a society as a motive.

I do hope that you will agree with me on this omission of what might come out as an unintentional advertisement for intolerant societies in these fascist ridden times. . . .[14]

P. 40: I don't see quite eye to eye with George on the matter of

[11]This point was observed.
[12]The scene was retained.
[13]The incident did not appear.
[14]No reference to the Klan was kept.

Scarlett's first child. George feels we should eliminate it, as you do. I am nervous about this. I feel that everybody remembers that Scarlett had the two children, and that to rob her of one in such cavalier fashion would not be easily forgiven. I admit this first child is a nuisance, but I don't know as yet what to do about it. I also feel that we might be forgiven more easily if we cut out her marriage to Frank and therefore not have the first child. You might give some thought to the possibility of dropping out entirely this second marriage, because Frank is certainly not one of our best characters; if we cut out the child and keep the marriage, it becomes even more dull. Offhand, however, my advice is to attempt to retain both the marriage and the child.[15]

I know just what you are up against in portraying the Reconstruction tragedy accurately and vividly, but here again this will have to be forced into each scene in this section of the story instead of creating scenes or retaining scenes that give us nothing but his attitude. Throughout the picture our great problem is going to be to get the background in unobtrusively while we concentrate on the personal story. . . .

P. 46: I think we can, and must, definitely lose the miscarriage. These infallible pregnancies at single contacts are a bit thick, and in any event I don't think the miscarriage gets us anywhere.[16]

P. 47: I know your problem about Rhett's character and I agree thoroughly that we must retain every bit we can of Rhett in the last part of the book. The fact that the book and the picture may be somewhat out of balance in stressing Scarlett for two-thirds and Rhett through the last third doesn't worry me.

P. 50: I beg you not to consider further the omission of Bonnie.[17] I feel that she is absolutely vital to the heartrending quality of the portrayal of Rhett in this section of the book and I know that you, too, would finally come to this conclusion, as indicated by the last paragraph of your treatment in which you quote the magnificent speech about Rhett's seeing in Bonnie the resemblance to Scarlett before things happen to change her.[18]

Please do not feel that anything I have said must of necessity be followed. But until we get a chance to have discussions this is the only way in which I can transmit to you my general feelings about the script. I am hopeful that the conferences in which we really

[15]The marriage was retained; the child was not.
[16]The miscarriage remained.
[17]Scarlett's child by Rhett.
[18]Bonnie was retained.

get down to a more detailed attack won't be long postponed.

With most cordial regards,

Sincerely,

David O. Selznick

To: Mr. John Wharton   January 13, 1937

Dear John:

I understand you perfectly about *Gone With the Wind*. I am aware that we can spend a lot of money unnecessarily on the picture. On the other hand, it is one picture which, if done perfectly, can almost with certainty return an enormous profit, in my opinion; and which, if cheated on, can cut down these potential profits substantially.

I think, however, I know what you have in mind, and you may be sure that we are not approaching the picture with any foregone conclusion that it has to be enormous in size and has to have an exceptionally high cost, even for big pictures.[19] I myself have no idea what the picture will cost, but as soon as we get closer to a first script, I will see if we can arrive at a preliminary budget.

TO: KATHARINE BROWN   FEBRUARY 3, 1937
      AND OSCAR SERLIN[20]

CORRECTING ON MATTER IN TELETYPE, I HAVE NO ENTHUSIASM FOR VIVIEN LEIGH. MAYBE I WILL HAVE, BUT AS YET HAVE NEVER EVEN SEEN PHOTOGRAPH OF HER. WILL BE SEEING "FIRE OVER ENGLAND"[21] SHORTLY, AT WHICH TIME WILL OF COURSE SEE LEIGH. . .

Mr. W. R. Wilkerson[22]   March 23, 1937
The Hollywood Reporter
Hollywood, California

Dear Bill:

There have been so many errors appearing in print, in connection with our plans for *Gone With the Wind*, and so much comment on

---

[19]The top figure in discussions within the corporation at the time of this memo was $1,500,000.

[20]Employed as a talent scout by Selznick International.

[21]*Fire over England* (1937) was produced in England by Alexander Korda and featured Miss Leigh and Laurence Olivier.

[22]Editor and Publisher of *The Hollywood Reporter*, a daily film-industry publication.

what we are supposed to be intending, climaxed by your Tradeview of today, that I have decided to clarify our objections on the casting of this picture, especially since this casting has turned into something of a national game. If this letter does nothing else, it should relieve me of the necessity of long-winded discussions on this subject with everyone I meet socially and professionally.

To begin with, I should like to take up your comments which, apparently, are based upon the printed report that Miss Norma Shearer might be playing "Scarlett."

My conversations with Miss Shearer have been most informal. This great artist and very beloved star has flattered me by publicly expressing pleasure over the prospect of doing *Gone With the Wind* or another picture for me. She has, at the same time, publicly expressed what she and I have privately agreed: that a new star could and should be made by "Scarlett"—as, indeed, could others of Miss Mitchell's brilliantly drawn and already celebrated characters. . . .

You forget, among other things, the foreign market. . . .

At the very moment of your paternal suggestion, George Cukor was preparing an extensive Southern trip to look for new personalities; Oscar Serlin was doing the same in the sticks up North; and Charley Morrison the same out here—all searching for Scarletts and Rhetts and Ashleys and Melanies and Bonnies and Pittypats. If they find them, grand! So far, no luck. . . .

Yours for new faces,

TO: KATHARINE BROWN   MARCH 25, 1937

MUST REGRETFULLY INFORM YOU . . . THAT CHANCES OF GETTING GABLE ARE PRACTICALLY NIL, IF NOT IN FACT ACTUALLY NONEXISTENT.[23] THEREFORE, IT LOOKS AS THOUGH WOULD HAVE TO GET ENTIRE CAST OF NEWCOMERS, WHICH MEANS THAT "TOM SAWYER" HAS BEEN CHILD'S PLAY BY COMPARISON; SO YOU HAD BETTER GET YOURSELF EQUIPPED ACCORDINGLY.

TO: MR. LOWELL V. CALVERT   AUGUST 9, 1937

IT IS CORRECT THAT I ASKED GEORGE SCHAEFER[24] TO SECURE FOR ME A PRETTY COMPLETE OPINION AS TO THE ADVISABILITY OF MAKING "GONE WITH THE WIND" AS TWO PICTURES. I SHOULD

[23]Clark Gable was under contract to MGM. Selznick International had a releasing arrangement with United Artists.
[24]Vice-President and General Manager in Charge of Sales for United Artists.

LIKE TO HAVE THIS INFORMATION AND OPINION AGAINST THE DAY WHEN IT APPEARS IMPOSSIBLE TO DO A SATISFACTORY ADAPTION AS ONE PICTURE. SCHAEFER PERSONALLY WAS EXTREMELY ENTHUSIASTIC ABOUT THE IDEA AND SAID THAT HE WAS CERTAIN IT WOULD ADD ENORMOUSLY TO THE GROSS TO HAVE IT AS TWO PICTURES. I, MYSELF, AM DUBIOUS AND AM BENDING MY PRESENT EFFORTS TOWARD GETTING IT WITHIN THE LIMITATION OF ONE PICTURE, EVEN IF IT IS A LONG ONE. . . . I FEEL THAT THERE IS ONLY ONE WAY THAT THE PICTURE CAN BE BROKEN INTO TWO, AND THAT IS IF EACH IS COMPLETE SO THAT IT WILL BE UNNECESSARY WITH THOSE AUDIENCES THAT HAPPEN TO SEE ONLY ONE HALF TO SEE THE OTHER, AND WITH THIS IN MIND, THE ONLY POSSIBLE BREAK THAT I CAN SEE IS THE MARRIAGE OF RHETT AND SCARLETT, WITH THE SECOND PICTURE PICKING UP THE HONEYMOONING COUPLE IN NEW ORLEANS. SINCE THE FIRST PART WOULD COVER ALMOST THREE-FOURTHS OF THE BOOK, YOU CAN SEE THAT IT WOULD BE A GOOD DEAL LONGER THAN THE SECOND PART. HOWEVER, THIS WOULD PERMIT US TO TELL FULLY AND FOR ALL ITS VALUE THE STORY OF RHETT, SCARLETT, AND BONNIE, WHICH OTHERWISE WE WILL HAVE TO TELESCOPE TERRIFICALLY. . . .[25]

To: Messrs. Whitney and Wharton　　　　　September 1, 1937

. . . I had not intended to tell you of my plan concerning Menzies until it was more clear in my own mind, which it will be when I see the results of the Cave sequence in *Tom Sawyer*, which is now being photographed and which will be on the shooting stages for the next ten days or so. However, since you have inquired I shall advise you what I have in mind. . . .

I feel that we need a man of Menzies's talent and enormous experience on the sets of this picture, and on its physical production. I hope to have *Gone With the Wind* prepared almost down to the last camera angle before we start shooting, because on this picture really thorough preparation will save hundreds of thousands of dollars. Accordingly, if we do go ahead with Menzies, he will start on the *Wind* sets directly he finishes his work on the Cave sequence of *Tom Sawyer*. . . .

While our script is not completed, and we are not yet certain of what we will have to cut, we know that there are half a dozen things . . . such as Tara, the Wilkes home, Miss Pittypat's home, the ball in At-

---

[25]All the material ultimately was included in the one film.

lanta . . . that must of necessity stay in, as well as the streets of Atlanta for the news of Gettysburg and the big evacuation scene which involve great physical problems and which will more than utilize all of Menzies's time until we can give him a complete script. When he gets the complete script, he can then do all the sets, set sketches, and plans during my absence, for presentation to me upon my return, and can start on what I want on this picture and what has only been done a few times in picture history (and these times mostly by Menzies)—a complete script in sketch form, showing actual camera setups, lighting, etc. This is a mammoth job that Menzies will have to work on very closely with Cukor. There is also the job of the montage sequences, which I plan on having Menzies not merely design and lay out but also, in large degree, actually direct. In short, it is my plan to have the whole physical side of this picture, with many phases that I have not dealt with in this paragraph (such as the handling of the process shots) . . . personally handled by one man who has little or nothing else to do—and that man, Menzies. Menzies may turn out to be one of the most valuable factors in properly producing this picture. One of the minor problems in connection with this arrangement is the matter of Menzies's credit. Menzies is terribly anxious not to get back to art direction as such, and of course his work on this picture, as I see it, will be a lot greater in scope than is normally associated with the term "art direction." Accordingly, I would probably give him some such credit as "Production Designed by William Cameron Menzies" or "Assistant to the Producer." . . .[26]

DOS

TO: O'SHEA   OCTOBER 14, 1937

PLEASE OPEN NEGOTIATIONS WITH MIKE LEVEE[27] FOR LESLIE HOWARD TO PLAY ASHLEY IN "GONE WITH THE WIND." I SUPPOSE YOU DO NOT NEED ANY COACHING ON SALES TALKS OR ON ATTITUDE. . . . CAN YOU POINT OUT TO LEVEE WITH COMPLETE ACCURACY THAT HOWARD HAS BEEN A BOX-OFFICE FAILURE IN ALL OF HIS PICTURES IN RECENT YEARS WITHOUT EXCEPTION, AND YOU MIGHT START OUT BY DEMANDING OPTION FOR COUPLE OF PICTURES AT LEAST, EVENTUALLY RELINQUISHING THIS POINT IF TERMS ARE RIGHT. IF PERCHANCE HE SHOULD BRING UP ANYTHING ABOUT APPROVAL OF SCRIPT OR ROLE, YOU MAY BE AS

[26]Selznick eventually settled on the former.
[27]Leslie Howard's manager.

DIFFICULT AS YOU PLEASE ABOUT THIS, AS CERTAINLY WE DO NOT
HAVE TO CATER TO ANYBODY THAT WE WANT FOR ONE OF THE
LEADS IN THIS PICTURE. CONCERNING BILLING, WE CAN AGREE
THAT NO ONE WOULD RECEIVE LARGER OR MORE PROMINENT
BILLING, BUT IN THE EVENT HE BROUGHT UP ANYTHING ABOUT
SIZE OF TYPE OR THE WORD "STARRING" OR ANYTHING OF THIS
KIND, YOU MUST REFUSE THIS BECAUSE WE WILL CERTAINLY STAR
THE PICTURE AND ANY ACTORS' NAMES WILL UNDOUBTEDLY
FOLLOW THE TITLE, AND IF THEY SHOULD PRECEDE THE TITLE,
THEY WILL BE IN MUCH SMALLER SIZE THAN THE TITLE. I WOULD
NOT BE AVERSE TO DISCUSSING POSITION HOWARD SHOULD HAVE
IN THE LIST, ALTHOUGH I THINK IT SHOULD BE THIRD WITH
RHETT AND SCARLETT PRECEDING HIM IN THE SAME-SIZED TYPE,
BUT I WOULD BE AGREEABLE TO MAKING THIS HIGHER IF IT
SHOULD SUBSEQUENTLY DEVELOP THAT WHOEVER PLAYS RHETT IS
NOT A BIGGER STAR THAN HOWARD. . . .

To: Mr. O'Shea   November 26, 1937
cc: Mr. Cukor

. . . Will you please try to set the following casting in connection with
Gone With the Wind.

Definitely set Lionel Barrymore as Dr. Meade. . . . I want to test
Billie Burke for Aunt Pittypat. Ditto Gladys George as Belle Watling.
Ditto Janet Beecher for Mrs. Merriwether or Mrs. Meade. Ditto Judy
Garland for Carreen. Ditto Shepherd Strudwick for Ashley. . . .[28]

                                                            DOS

Mr. Harry M. Warner, President   December 1, 1937
Warner Brothers Pictures, Inc.
Burbank, California

cc: Mr. Will H. Hays

Dear Mr. Warner:

I do not mean to prolong unnecessarily any discussions on the *Jezebel* [Warner Bros., 1938] matter, especially since in your relations with
me you have always been so friendly and so fair. . . .

The article which you enclosed with your letter gives complete

[28]Harry Davenport later was cast as Dr. Meade, Laura Hope Crews as Aunt Pittypat,
Ona Munson as Belle Watling, Jane Darwell as Mrs. Merriwether, Leona Roberts as Mrs.
Meade, Ann Rutherford as Carreen, and Leslie Howard as Ashley.

confirmation to the warning I expressed to you some time back that your studio, if not cautioned by you, would stoop to publicizing its picture on the strength of *Gone With the Wind:* Certainly, there can no longer be any question on this fact since Jack[29] is actually quoted, and since the publicity material from your studio goes so far as to say that around the studio Bette Davis is now known as "Scarlett."

May I remind you that the rights to *Jezebel* were repeatedly turned down by your studio, as by all other studios, until after the public's attention was directed to *Gone With the Wind?*

As to your inferences concerning the rumors on Bette Davis, and the source of these, if you are interested I will dig up and send to you the articles which started these rumors, including statements sent out by your Publicity Department quoting Bette Davis on a comparison of the two roles.

I do not know how far your organization intends to capitalize upon the work and investment of others, and since I think you will agree that the picture business has been happily free of such tactics for many years, I can only hope that your studio will not find itself in a position where it is "forced" to issue statements comparing your picture with that of another studio.

Cordially and sincerely yours,
David O. Selznick

To: [Director Richard] Wallace, Mr. Wright   February 17, 1938

I saw *Yank at Oxford* last night, which, by the way, is a swell picture. While I think Vivien Leigh gave an excellent performance and was very well cast, I don't like her for the part in our picture[30] as well as Margaret Lindsay, Pat Patterson, or Dorothy Hyson.[31]

DOS

To: Mr. George Cukor   February 25, 1938

Dear George:

Sidney and I have a terrific job on our hands, as is apparent from our work today when we spent the whole morning up to one-thirty on

---

[29]Jack L. Warner, Vice-President in Charge of Production, Warner Bros.-First National, and brother of Harry.

[30]*The Young in Heart* (1938), which was being prepared by Selznick in conjunction with *Gone With the Wind.*

[31]Paulette Goddard eventually played the role.

nine pages of the script. I am weighing every word and every line most carefully; and Sidney's ideas are, as usual, excellent. I am also double checking against the book once more and substituting valuable lines wherever I can for ordinary lines in the script. We are also double checking against our Story Department's notes on things that they missed from the book; on Kurtz's[32] notes; on production notes; on Hal Kern's[33] cutting suggestions; on research notes from a society that complains about inaccuracies; and on Hays office notes.

Obviously we have weeks ahead of us, but I think that by the time you finish with *Holiday* [Columbia, 1938] we will have a perfectly swell script and, hopefully, one that is near the proper length.

Now, Sidney and I are both extremely worried that all this painstaking work is going to be largely in vain unless we have a pledge from you now that you won't use the book during the course of production to add three lines here and four lines there, as has been done in the test scenes. Even the addition of five or six words per scene is going to count up to a thousand feet or more that we have taken out with terrific agony, intense work, and tremendous loss to the company through my devoting my time to this instead of to other pictures that we sorely need.

Certainly I am not going to have any objection to your raising any points about lines or cuts or anything else in advance of our starting in production; but when we get all through the script I think you will be delighted with it—and I am hopeful that you will, on completion of *Holiday,* take a couple of days off by yourself with only Bobby [Barbara Keon] to take your notes on what if anything you miss, or what if anything you object to—which we can then thrash out in a few final conferences with Sidney—if, as I hope, he will still be here. But I do want to know now that the torture that Sidney and I will be going through for the next several weeks will not be in vain. . . .

Sidney's worries on this are greater than mine, and it will help build the enthusiasm that he puts into our present labors for him to have a reassurance from you on this.

I am more enthusiastic than ever about the script, and will be calling Menzies in to conferences practically each day so that by the time we finish the script, we will have almost all of the physical production mapped out, as well.

[32]Wilbur G. Kurtz, historian for *GWTW.*
[33]Supervising Film Editor for *GWTW.*

And I hope that the next picture that we do together will be something more nearly like *Holiday* than this one.

DOS

MR. JACK WARNER   MARCH 8, 1938
WARNER BROTHERS STUDIOS
4000 S. OLIVE AVENUE
BURBANK, CALIFORNIA

DEAR JACK: REITERATING WHAT I TOLD YOU LAST NIGHT, I THINK IT WOULD BE A VERY GREAT PITY INDEED FROM YOUR OWN STANDPOINT IF SO DISTINGUISHED AND COSTLY A PICTURE AS "JEZEBEL" SHOULD BE DAMNED AS AN IMITATION BY THE MILLIONS OF READERS AND LOVERS OF "GONE WITH THE WIND." AND I AM FEARFUL THAT THIS IS WHAT MAY HAPPEN, DUE TO A FEW COMPLETELY UNNECESSARY BITS. THE PICTURE THROUGHOUT IS PERMEATED WITH CHARACTERIZATIONS, ATTITUDES, AND SCENES WHICH UNFORTUNATELY RESEMBLE "GONE WITH THE WIND," REGARDLESS OF WHETHER OR NOT THEY WERE IN THE ORIGINAL MATERIAL. BUT I AM REFERRING TO A FEW SPECIFIC THINGS, SUCH AS THE VERY WELL-REMEMBERED PIECE OF BUSINESS IN WHICH SCARLETT PINCHED HER CHEEKS TO GIVE THEM COLOR. MORE IMPORTANTLY, THERE IS THE SCENE OF THE MEN AROUND THE DINNER TABLE, WHICH ACTUALLY IS A SLOW SPOT IN YOUR PICTURE, IF YOU WILL FORGIVE MY SAYING SO. I REFER TO THE DIALOGUE SCENE DEALING WITH THE DIFFERENCE BETWEEN THE NORTH AND SOUTH, THE DISCUSSION OF AN IMMINENT WAR, AND THE PREDICTION BY THE SOUTHERNER THAT THE NORTH WILL WIN BECAUSE OF ITS SUPERIOR MACHINERY, ET CETERA.[34] THIS SCENE IS LIFTED PRACTICALLY BODILY OUT OF "GONE WITH THE WIND," IN WHICH IT IS AN IMPORTANT STORY POINT LEADING TO RHETT BUTLER'S ENTIRE BEHAVIOR DURING THE WAR. . . . IF YOU LIKE, I WOULD BE VERY HAPPY INDEED TO STUDY YOUR PICTURE FURTHER AND TO GIVE YOU PAGE REFERENCES FROM "GONE WITH THE WIND" ON OTHER POINTS, BECAUSE I SINCERELY THINK IT IMPORTANT FROM YOUR OWN STANDPOINT AS WELL AS OURS THAT THE SUCCESS WHICH YOUR PICTURE DESERVES SHOULD NOT BE MARRED BY ANY APPEARANCE

---

[34]This scene later was deleted from *Jezebel*.

OF AN ATTEMPT TO CAPITALIZE ON A WORK FOR WHICH THE
AMERICAN PUBLIC HAS DEMONSTRATED SUCH A GREAT LOVE. I AM
ASSUMING THAT THESE SUGGESTIONS, WHICH ARE ADVANCED IN
GOOD FAITH, WILL BE GIVEN NO PUBLICITY BY YOUR PEOPLE.
ONCE AGAIN MY CONGRATULATIONS TO YOUR ORGANIZATION ON A
FINE JOB. CORDIALLY YOURS

DAVID O. SELZNICK

To: Mr. J. H. Whitney   March 14, 1938

. . . I feel that we must get the production and release plans of this
picture settled before you leave California, and also that any plans
involving Gary Cooper should be settled, if possible, before Goldwyn
goes to Europe on Friday.

I therefore urge that you make clear to Mr. Goldwyn that there is
no chance whatsoever of our distributing the picture through United
Artists unless it is clear before he leaves for Europe that in any negotiations that may take place during his absence for the release of the
picture through United Artists, we are to have Gary Cooper for the
lead. If he is in no position to say that we can count upon this in such
a release deal, then I think it should be further made clear to him that
by the time he gets back from Europe we may have made a deal which
involves other casting. . . .

DOS

MR. JOHN HAY WHITNEY   MAY 27, 1938
230 PARK AVE.
SELZNICK INTERNATIONAL PICTURES
NYC

L. B. [Mayer] CALLED ME TODAY TO SUGGEST THAT THEY [MGM]
WOULD BE INTERESTED IN BUYING "GONE WITH THE WIND"
TOGETHER WITH MY SERVICES AS PRODUCER ON AN OUTRIGHT
PURCHASE INCLUDING, OF COURSE, REPAYMENT OF OUR COMPLETE
INVESTMENT PLUS A SUBSTANTIAL PROFIT. HE ASKED ME TO GIVE
SOME THOUGHT TO THIS AND ADVISE HIM WHETHER WE WOULD
BE WILLING TO MAKE SUCH A DEAL ON BASIS OF A PROFIT TO US
THAT THEY COULD STAND. I WILL GIVE THIS SOME THOUGHT
OVER WEEKEND AND WISH YOU WOULD DO THE SAME. I
MENTIONED IMPOSSIBILITY OF OUR CLOSING OUR STUDIO WHILE I

PRODUCED "WIND" FOR THEM, AND HE COUNTERED WITH
SUGGESTION THAT I BELIEVE YOU AND I HAVE PREVIOUSLY
DISCUSSED, WHICH IS THAT BECAUSE OF CLOSENESS OF TWO
STUDIOS IT MIGHT BE POSSIBLE FOR US TO CONTINUE HERE WITH
MY SIMPLY SPENDING AN HOUR OR TWO A DAY UP THERE WHILE
PICTURE WAS SHOOTING, PROBABLY EVEN LESS SINCE I SPEND
MUCH LESS TIME ON THE SET WITH GEORGE THAN WITH ANY
OTHER DIRECTOR, AND I COULD SEE RUSHES HERE AS WELL AS
HAVING CONFERENCE ON SETS, COSTUMES, CASTING, ET CETERA
HERE. NOW THAT THE FINANCING PROBLEM ON THE PICTURE IS
SEEMINGLY ON THE WAY TO BEING SOLVED, I DISLIKE SEEING OUR
COMPANY NOT MAKE THE PICTURE, BUT THERE IS OF COURSE TO
BE CONSIDERED THAT IF THE PROFIT WERE SUBSTANTIAL ENOUGH
IT WOULD GREATLY EASE OUR FINANCIAL PICTURE AND WOULD
GIVE US A CERTAIN PROFIT INSTEAD OF A RISK, IF YOU FEEL
THERE IS ANY RISK. I MYSELF FEEL THE RISK IS SLIGHT, AND THAT
IF ANY COMPANY CAN'T MAKE "GONE WITH THE WIND" POSSIBLY
IT SHOULDN'T MAKE ANYTHING. ANOTHER FACTOR IS CASTING
PROBLEM, WHICH WOULD OF COURSE BE MUCH SIMPLER THERE,
AND WHICH WOULD MAKE PICTURE LESS OF A RISK FOR THEM
THAN IT WOULD FOR US, SINCE GABLE WOULD GIVE THEM AN
INSURANCE WE WOULD NOT HAVE. FROM MY PERSONAL
STANDPOINT, I COULD PROBABLY MAKE PICTURE WITH LESS
TROUBLE THERE AND, INDEED, PROBABLY MAKE A BETTER
PICTURE WITH THEIR RESOURCES THAN WITH OUR OWN. I MAY
SEEM TO BE ARGUING BOTH SIDES OF QUESTION. FROM
STANDPOINT OF OUR PRESTIGE, I THINK THE HARM WOULD BE
MINIMIZED BY FACT THAT I PERSONALLY WAS PRODUCING
PICTURE, AND I BELIEVE AN ANNOUNCEMENT WOULD BE
ACCEPTED THAT WE HAD MADE DEAL BECAUSE OF MY FEELING
THAT THE PUBLIC DEMANDED GABLE AND WE COULD HAVE HIM IN
PICTURE NO OTHER WAY. I MIGHT ALSO BE ABLE TO HANDLE IT SO
THAT PICTURE WAS PRESENTED BY MGM IN ASSOCIATION WITH
SELZNICK INTERNATIONAL.[35]

DAVID

[35] For a time Selznick and Whitney seriously considered letting MGM back the entire
picture, due to the financial plight of Selznick International. However, Whitney arranged to put up additional money, and an arrangement for MGM's partial backing of
$1,250,000 and Gable's services were made in exchange for distribution rights and fifty
per cent of the profits.

MR. GEORGE SCHAEFER   AUGUST 25, 1938
UNITED ARTISTS CORP.
729 SEVENTH AVE.
NYC

DEAR GEORGE: WE HAVE SIGNED CONTRACTS WITH METRO
CALLING FOR THE RELEASE OF "GONE WITH THE WIND" AND FOR
GABLE AS RHETT BUTLER. THE ONLY REGRET I HAVE ABOUT THE
DEAL IS THAT YOU AND I WILL NOT BE ASSOCIATED IN THE
HANDLING OF THIS PICTURE. I CANNOT HELP BUT FEEL THAT THE
PICTURE WOULD HAVE BEEN MADE BY NOW AND WOULD HAVE
BEEN RELEASED THROUGH UNITED ARTISTS HAD WE BEEN ABLE TO
SECURE THE LONG-SOUGHT COOPERATION ON GARY COOPER, BUT
THAT IS WATER OVER THE DAM, AND WHILE I CANNOT HONESTLY
SAY I AM ANYTHING BUT VERY HAPPY WITH GABLE AND THE
ENTIRE ARRANGEMENTS INCLUDING METRO DISTRIBUTION, I STILL
WANT YOU TO KNOW MY PERSONAL FEELINGS ABOUT YOU. . . .
                                     DAVID SELZNICK

To: All Department Heads   August 26, 1938

The contracts that have been signed with Loew's, Inc. for the release of *Gone With the Wind* in no way affect its identity as a Selznick
International picture or its production on this lot. You will, accordingly, please continue uninterruptedly on your work on this picture,
which will definitely start in production between November 15 and
January 15, the exact date to be determined at the latest during the
month of October.

Mr. Ed Sullivan[36]   September 20, 1938
621 Alta Drive
Beverly Hills, Calif.

Dear Ed:
I haven't commented upon the thousands of mistaken items that
have appeared throughout the country in connection with *Gone With
the Wind*. In the first place, people don't print denials; in the second
place, I wanted to hold to my policy of saying absolutely nothing about
Gone With the Wind except things that were official and final; and

[36]Hollywood columnist for the *New York Daily News*.

finally, I wouldn't have had the time to do anything else.

However, in view of what I had thought was a friendship existing between us, I don't like to let your attacks upon me personally go by without putting certain things squarely up to you, so that you can determine for yourself whether you are being fair.

It may be folly on my part to send you this letter, since the man behind the linotype machine has the last word—but I'm willing to take the chance that after you've read it you will feel that you have quite gratuitously offended me, instead of my offending you by writing you as I am.

You say, among other things, that I have messed up *Gone With the Wind*. Now since *Gone With the Wind* hasn't yet been made, as I think you know, it is not clear to me how I could have messed it up. You might with as much justice attack the French generals for their conduct of the next war, or the war after that.

Perhaps what you mean is that I've messed up the preparation. But how can you know anything about this? Have you any familiarity with just what I've done? Have you seen the script or any of the production plans?

Let's review the history of exactly what I have done:

We bought the book from the galleys, paying a big price for it. . . .

I assigned George Cukor to direct the picture. I have stubbornly held to this decision through difficulties which you cannot imagine, because I felt that Cukor was the ideal man to do it, this judgment being based upon his work on *Little Women, David Copperfield, Camille,* and *Romeo and Juliet.* Is Cukor a satisfactory choice, in your opinion?

I engaged Sidney Howard for the script. He is one of America's most distinguished playwrights, a Pulitzer Prize winner among other things, and, in my opinion—which I don't think anyone will challenge—one of the best scenarists in the world. (His last job was *Dodsworth.*) I have personally spent four or five hours a day for a period of about twenty-five weeks on the script, in close collaboration with Sidney Howard and with George Cukor. We have been as rigidly faithful to the book as possible—although you will understand that putting the book, as written, on the screen would make about a hundred-reel picture. However, I have stubbornly insisted in all my dealings on the picture for release, etc., on the privilege of making the picture as long as perhaps sixteen or seventeen reels—the longest picture ever made, because I want to give the public just as much of the book as is endurable at one sitting. (We played around with the idea of making it as two or three pictures, but were fearful that the public might misunderstand our motives and think we were trying to capitalize inordinately, so we dropped this idea.)

. . .Regardless of the extra cost, I have insisted upon the picture's being made in Technicolor.

Now, to the casting. You have been in Hollywood enough to realize that players under contract to a studio cannot be secured by another studio just for the asking, even for a project such as *Gone With the Wind.* The public's choice was clearly Gable for Rhett Butler. For two years I tried everything on earth to get Clark Gable. But you ought to have a rough idea as to how willing MGM would be to give up Clark Gable for a picture to be released by another company—and bear in mind that my company was under an exclusive contract for distribution with United Artists.

Accordingly, the only way I could get Gable was to distribute the picture through MGM, and this meant that I had to wait to start the picture until my contract with United Artists had expired, which it does with *Made for Each Other,* which we are now shooting. Therefore, *Gone With the Wind,* with Clark Gable as Rhett Butler, couldn't under any circumstances have been made one day sooner.

Now as to Scarlett: please believe me when I say that I have at my disposal more information as to whom the public wants in this picture than has anyone else. And the public's choice is clearly and very strongly for a new girl as Scarlett. I have spent a fortune trying to find this new girl—not $500,000 as was reported, but actually very close to $50,000, and $50,000 buys a lot of talent searching. I had the best talent scouts in the country; I sent George Cukor and a whole crew all through the South; between Cukor and myself we have seen personally every bit player and young actress that was even remotely a possibility, as well as hundreds and even thousands that weren't. We have had readings, we have made tests, we have trained girls who looked right but whose talent was uncertain, we've done everything conceivable. Not alone that, but we have had the cooperation of every other studio in town in trying to find a new girl, since I promised other studios that if they succeeded in finding me a girl they could have an occasional picture with her—which, of course, is a great incentive, since a new girl playing Scarlett ought to be an overnight star if she's any good. This search is on again with renewed vigor—since I am under contract to start with Gable immediately after he finishes in *Idiot's Delight*—the very earliest date that I could get him. And the best Scarlett that shows up by that time will play the role willy-nilly.

You may inquire why I didn't give up the idea of a new girl and get Bette Davis, for instance. But certainly you ought to know that Warner Brothers wouldn't give up Bette Davis for a picture to be released through MGM, even had we wanted Miss Davis in preference to a new personality. Warner Brothers offered me Errol Flynn for Butler and Bette Davis for Scarlett if I would release the picture through Warners —and this would have been an easy way out of my dilemma. But the public wanted Gable, and I was determined that the public should have Gable. And Gable it is going to have, at the very earliest date it could have had him.

There is no point in going through the strings tied to other stars who might have played Scarlett, because either they were choices whom the public would have hopped all over, or it was utterly impossible to get them. MGM and my company played around with the idea of having Norma Shearer do the role. It was never finally settled, but it leaked out that we were thinking about it and you know yourself what an outcry was raised. Mind you, I think the outcry was unfair, and I think people might have withheld their judgment until they saw her play the part. Norma is a grand woman and a grand actress, and out of deference to her oft-demonstrated versatility, and to the many years of loving care, and faithfulness to an ideal that have been given to her career by herself and by the late great Irving Thalberg, I think that she might have been treated with a little more considera-tion. . . .

But let us say that all of the absolutely unavoidable delays could have been avoided, which is, of course, not so. What of it? Why shouldn't the book be picturized a couple of years after it first appeared? There are still millions of people who haven't even read the book; its newspa-per serialization hasn't even yet appeared; its cheaper edition hasn't even yet appeared. . . .

Please bear in mind, Ed, that I am not seeking any publicity on this picture. Almost two years ago I instructed my Publicity Department that they were to send out not one single word about the picture that was not an official and final announcement, and, on the contrary, I have done everything possible to stop publicity, because I anticipated two years in advance that the public might get tired of reading about it. (Maybe even now they're not tired of reading about it, but that has been my attitude and I mention it now so that you will know that I have in no sense been responsible for the campaign that has gone on about it in relation to its cast, etc.) . . . Therefore, when I am attacked by someone such as you, especially when that person is, to the best of my knowledge, a friend of mine, I am grieved and mystified.

Now really, Ed, don't you think you've done me an injustice? And don't you think you owe it to me to straighten this out?

Cordially and sincerely yours,

To: Mr. Dan O'Shea   September 21, 1938
CONFIDENTIAL

I have reluctantly, and at long last, come to the conclusion that we have simply got to do something, and promptly, about the Cukor situation. I have thought that George was a great asset to the company, but I am fearful that he is, on the contrary, a very expensive luxury . . . regardless of his great abilities. . . .

George has been with us now for a long time and we have yet to get a picture out of him. We are in danger actually of winding up paying him about $300,000 for his services on *Gone With the Wind.*

There is a large measure of justice in George's statement that this is not his fault—and that he could have done pictures; and this is because we have not forced him to do pictures. But it is also because we have deferred to his own wishes—and we have got to make our position clear so that the same thing does not occur in the future. . . .

When I first tackled *A Star Is Born* I spoke to George about doing it and he didn't feel that he wanted to do a Hollywood picture. When we took [director H. C.] Potter off *Tom Sawyer* I spoke to George about doing it, and he didn't want to. When we needed him for another picture, he preferred to direct Garbo. Probably when we need him for another picture later, he will prefer to do another Garbo. . . .

Let's take the immediate situation: We have quite a period of time before George will be required on *Gone With the Wind*—time enough for any director in the business to make a picture. We have only one picture for him to direct, and that is *Intermezzo.* George doesn't like it. . . .

But let's say that we are nice enough not to force him to direct it. Then we offer him an outside picture with [Claudette] Colbert: he doesn't like it. We offer to try to get him a picture at Columbia: he doesn't want to work for Columbia. . . .

As to *Gone With the Wind,* I would be willing to negotiate a new deal with him for this particular picture, without, however, the obligation to make such a deal if his terms are exorbitant. We must bear in mind that we could get great benefits for the future in the way of a contract director of importance if we were able to offer *Gone With the Wind*—by contrast with George, who is willing to do *Gone With the Wind* for us but isn't willing to take our other pictures. For instance, I am confident that we could sign Victor Fleming if we would give him *Gone With the Wind* as his first picture—and if we wanted him instead of borrowing [Jack] Conway from MGM. I am sure that we could even sign Frank Capra, who is dying to do *Gone With the Wind*— although offhand I don't think I would want him to do it as I don't think we need him on it, and I mention this only to show the buying power of a directorial assignment on *Gone With the Wind*.

In any event, I think the biggest black mark against our management to date is the Cukor situation and we can no longer be sentimental about it. . . . We are a business concern and not patrons of the arts. . . .

DOS

To: Mr. Butcher[37] September 23, 1938

Thanks for your report on the comparative estimates on *Gone With the Wind*. I am hopeful we can bring the picture in for $2,250,000 at the outside, and in cutting the script I will aim at a $2,000,000 cost— hence my desire for a breakdown of the estimated cost of the script by sequences, so that I may have this in front of me in making cuts.[38]

DOS

TO: JOHN HAY WHITNEY OCTOBER 12, 1938
AND KATHARINE BROWN

. . . WE MUST NOT LOSE SIGHT OF THE FACT THAT I AM GOING AWAY FOR TWO PURPOSES AND TWO PURPOSES ONLY, THE PRINCIPAL ONE OF WHICH IS TO CONCENTRATE ON FINISHING THE SCRIPT OF "GWTW," AND THE SECOND AND INCIDENTAL REASON OF WHICH IS, HOPEFULLY, TO GET A LITTLE REST. IT WOULD PROBABLY BE DIFFICULT OR EVEN IMPOSSIBLE TO ACCOMPLISH THESE OBJECTIVES ON A EUROPEAN TRIP WITH ALL ITS DISTRACTIONS, AND IT THEREFORE SEEMS THAT THE SMARTEST THING TO DO WOULD BE TO HOLD TO OUR ORIGINAL SELECTION

---

[37]Edward W. Butcher, Production Manager of Selznick International.
[38]The production cost, exclusive of prints and advertising, eventually came to $4,250,000.

OF BERMUDA, UNLESS THE REPORT KAY GETS ON THE WEATHER IS
TOO FRIGHTENING. CONCERNING THE WRITER, IT WOULD, OF
COURSE, BE SIMPLY WONDERFUL IF YOU COULD TALK MARGARET
MITCHELL INTO A BRIEF BERMUDA JAUNT AT OUR EXPENSE.
PERHAPS IF HER HUSBAND COULD GET A WEEK OR TWO OFF AND
COULD GO ALONG IT WOULD BE HELPFUL. IF I COULD HAVE
MITCHELL FOR SO MUCH AS EVEN A WEEK TOWARD LATTER PART
OF MY TRIP I FEEL CONFIDENT I COULD DO WHAT REMAINS TO BE
DONE ON THE SCRIPT BY MYSELF, PERHAPS WITH THE AID OF BILL
MENZIES, AND I THINK THE MOST WONDERFUL THING WE COULD
POSSIBLY ACCOMPLISH FOR "GWTW" WOULD BE AN
ANNOUNCEMENT THAT THERE WILL NOT BE A SINGLE ORIGINAL
WORD IN THE SCRIPT THAT IS NOT WRITTEN BY MARGARET
MITCHELL. HOWEVER, EVEN IF SHE WOULD NOT PERMIT US TO
MAKE SUCH AN ANNOUNCEMENT, SHE WOULD STILL, OF COURSE,
BE INFINITELY PREFERABLE TO ANYBODY ELSE, AND SUCH A TRIP
MIGHT NOT FRIGHTEN HER SO MUCH AS ONE TO HOLLYWOOD.[39]

TO: KATHARINE BROWN   OCTOBER 14, 1938

SUGGEST YOU TELEPHONE SIDNEY HOWARD IMMEDIATELY AND
INFORM HIM THAT I AM LEAVING FOR BERMUDA AND THAT I
CANNOT CONSIDER THE IDEA OF WORKING IN NEW YORK.
FURTHER, THAT I MUST KNOW DEFINITELY WHETHER HE INTENDS
TO BACK DOWN ON ALL THE PLANS HE MADE WITH ME AND THAT
I CHECKED AND RECHECKED REPEATEDLY WITH HIM, AND IF THIS
IS THE CASE, I MUST GET ANOTHER WRITER IMMEDIATELY. PLEASE
GIVE HIM NO ARGUMENTS OTHER THAN TO MAKE THE ABOVE
STATEMENT ONCE, AND SIMPLY.[40]

To: Mr. Henry Ginsberg and Mr. Butcher   October 18, 1938
cc: Mr. O'Shea

To get the right cameraman on *Gone With the Wind* we will have
to work far ahead. As a matter of fact, with our starting date now

---

[39]Miss Mitchell declined.

[40]Howard did no further work on the script. He was a precise, orderly man who
delivered material on time and was used to little interference. Selznick insisted upon
revisions in Howard's script, but Howard felt the assignment complete and proper, did
not want to involve himself in further revisions, and left for New York and his next
scheduled Broadway play commitment.

Screenwriter Jo Swerling worked in Bermuda on revisions with Selznick.

known to us, there is no reason why we should not settle on the cameraman immediately.

I certainly want to avoid having the dual setup of a black-and-white cameraman and a color cameraman because of the black-and-white cameraman's lack of knowledge of Technicolor—although perhaps this is unnecessary because I hear that MGM has been putting its black-and-white cameramen on color right from scratch, although, on the other hand, I understand the results have in some cases been none too happy. . . .

I should like the two of you to follow up on this at once, consulting with Mr. Cukor on the question. We obviously should have the best man in the business, and it may be that if the man we select has no familiarity with color work we could train him in the interim.

I think that MGM would be glad to cooperate in lending us any of their men, even if they were scheduled for important pictures. Among their men who I think are possibilities are Hal Rosson, Oliver Marsh, Ray June.

Incidentally we should, of course, avoid any man who has any reputation for being slow.

Charlie Lang at Paramount, about whom Mr. Cukor is so enthusiastic, is, in my opinion, one of the two or three top men of the business and should also be on the list.

Tony Gaudio's work on *Robin Hood*[41] was, in my opinion, the best photographic job in color that has yet been done.

Other possibilities are [Karl] Struss, [Karl] Freund, Toland and [Rudolph] Maté.

I am extremely worried about this situation, for fear that at the last minute we will have to take a second-rate man, and I therefore should be grateful if you would keep me informed both before and after my departure.

A minor point in connection with the camera work is that I should like whichever cameraman is finally decided upon to make some tests at an early date to see if we cannot do better about accomplishing a lighting effect of candlelight and other methods of illumination during the period of *Gone With the Wind*. All the period pictures that have been done in Technicolor to date look as though the scenes were lighted by electric light, and a great deal of mood is lost in conse-

[41]The 1938 version. Sol Polito and W. Howard Greene shared photographic credit along with Gaudio.

quence. I wish Mr. Butcher would follow this up and report to me on it.

DOS

P.S. Since dictating the above, I have spoken to Eddie Mannix,[42] who states that he will definitely hold Hal Rosson for us if we wish, and that he will be very happy to give us any of his top men if they are not busy with their three or four top women stars who always demand the same cameraman. Certainly one or two of these is likely to be available, among them possibly Bill Daniels, whom I inadvertently omitted above but who is certainly among the best; and Oliver Marsh, who, from a standpoint of speed, would probably be better than any of the others.

DOS

To: Mr. O'Shea   October 20, 1938

Confidentially, I think it extremely unlikely that we will find any Ashley that will be as satisfactory to me, or that any of the Ashleys that we are testing will prove on film to be as right as Leslie Howard seems to be in my imagination. My worry about Howard is purely and simply concerning his age, and I wonder if you would not persuade Howard to make a silent test in costume in color in England, which I am sure [producer Alexander] Korda would be able to make for us in color.

Howard is an unusually intelligent actor, and I think that if it were explained to him that he would be leading with his chin as much as we would if he were not right pictorially for the part, and that I have not the slightest desire to give him an acting test, nor the slightest doubt as to his ability to give a great performance, but have simply the necessity, from his standpoint and my own, of making sure that he is right pictorially, Howard would make this test. I think, further, that if he were told to make himself look as young and handsome as possible, with particular attention to his hair, he is an experienced enough producer and director himself to handle his own test for the purpose we have in mind. . . .

I know you will agree that there is nothing in connection with *Gone With the Wind* that is as much of a worry at the moment as the casting of Ashley—not even the casting of Scarlett, because we have, after all, a few good Scarletts in reserve if necessary, but we haven't one Ashley that I can really throw my hat in the air about.

DOS

[42]Vice-President and General Manager of MGM Studios.

To: Mr. Cukor and Mr. O'Shea   October 21, 1938
cc: Mr. Ginsberg   CONFIDENTIAL

. . . I am still hoping against hope for that new girl. . . . If we finally wind up with any of the stars that we are testing we must regard ourselves as absolute failures at digging up talent; as going against the most violently expressed wish for a new personality in an important role in the history of the American stage or screen; as wasting the opportunity to create a new star; as actually hurting the drawing power of the picture by having a star instead of a new girl, in whom there would be infinitely more interest in this particular picture; and as actually, in my opinion, hurting the quality of the picture itself by having a girl who has an audience's dislike to beat down, as in the case of Hepburn,[43] or identification with other roles to overcome, as in the case of Jean Arthur. (Paulette Goddard also has plenty against her in the way of the public's attitude, but I think that when it comes time for the final decision she at least has in her favor that she is not stale. For this reason, I think George ought to devote particular attention to the dramatic sections of the Goddard test.)

                                                            DOS

To: Mr. Henry Ginsberg   Bermuda
                                                November 7, 1938

Dear Henry:
. . . I think you ought to get hold of Dr. Kalmus,[44] wherever he is, and say to him that we feel very strongly indeed the important part we have played in putting Technicolor over at the crucial period in its history; and that, further, we feel very strongly that we require, as a company, the appreciation of Technicolor for our insistence upon producing *Gone With the Wind* in Technicolor. You might, if you care to, drop en route very casually that there is still time for us to change and to make *Gone With the Wind* in black and white, which we have no intention of doing, but that MGM, our partners in the enterprise, are still far from being sold on color as an economic proposition; and, on the contrary, I have spent hours with Eddie Mannix recently in the

[43]A group of exhibitors had labeled Hepburn "Box Office Poison" in 1938. Her more recent films—for the most part—had been flops; e.g., *Mary of Scotland* (1936), *A Woman Rebels* (1936), and *Quality Street* (1937). Even *Bringing Up Baby* (1938) was commercially disappointing.
[44]Dr. Herbert T. Kalmus, President of Technicolor. Selznick was seeking better cooperation from Technicolor executives.

presence of the entire MGM executive staff, debating the value of color by comparison with its extra cost. . . .

I have believed in the future of Technicolor and I have believed in the Technicolor company as our allies, who would do everything possible to assist us in our fight to prove to MGM and to the rest of the industry the practicability of color from a commercial standpoint, and the wisdom of adding such a fabulous expense to a picture like *Gone With the Wind,* which seemingly needs nothing from an attraction standpoint to give it extra importance. . . .

DOS

TO: O'SHEA   BERMUDA
SELZNICK INTERNATIONAL   NOVEMBER 11, 1938
CULVER CITY

WILL REQUIRE DIALOGUE WRITER "WIND," PREFERABLY STARTING ON MY ARRIVAL NEW YORK. WISH YOU AND NEW YORK OFFICE WOULD HAVE LIST AVAILABLE ON MY ARRIVAL WHICH WILL BE NEXT THURSDAY. PARTICULARLY INTERESTED ROBERT SHERWOOD, STARK YOUNG. NOT INTERESTED SIDNEY HOWARD. UNDERSTAND [Oliver H.P.] GARRETT'S PLAY TERRIBLE FLOP, SO SHOULD BE ABLE BUY HIM CHEAPLY. FIND OUT PRICE WEEK-TO-WEEK JOB ON "WIND." THIS APART FROM NEED OF DIALOGUE WRITER, AS WELL. WANT GARRETT DO CONTINUITY CERTAIN SEQUENCES, MAYBE ONLY FEW, MAYBE THROUGHOUT PICTURE. IF PRICE RIGHT, WOULD WANT HIM FAMILIARIZE HIMSELF BOOK AND SCRIPT AND PREPARE WORK ON MY ARRIVAL NEW YORK, PROBABLY ALSO EN ROUTE HOME AND AT STUDIO. IF WORK SATISFACTORY, CAN PROBABLY USE HIM ON ANOTHER JOB SUBSEQUENTLY, BUT MAKE NO SPECIFIC PROMISES.

DAVID

To: Marcella Rabwin[45]   November 12, 1938

. . . I have long felt that there is a very good chance that we have passed up Scarlett with our cavalier attitude about a number of the girls that have applied, through not taking sufficient pains to see personally more of these applicants. . . .

While it is almost too late, I think that for the remaining time Mr.

[45]Executive Assistant to Selznick.

Cukor should set aside an hour daily during which he will interview applicants personally. Actually, if the thing were organized properly as many as fifty girls could be in and out of his office in an hour. Mr. Cukor could, by exchanging two sentences with each of the girls, determine whether she was worth chatting with further, whether she had striking looks, or striking personality, or that "something" which makes for an outstanding theatrical personality, which an expert such as Mr. Cukor could detect instantly—but which our young and inexperienced punks cannot detect in four hours. I feel that our failure to find a new girl for Scarlett is the greatest failure of my entire career. I feel very keenly about it and I feel that everyone in the company is to blame, including myself.

And for the few weeks remaining, let's be sure that we do a better job than the messy, even stupid job we've done to date.

In the final analysis, the fault is directly traceable to my office, and I wish, therefore, that you would immediately have Mr. Cukor read this letter and go over with him what he personally might do in a final, last-minute attempt. . . .

Every other studio in town is making new stars in pictures of comparative unimportance, and it would be shocking if the starting date of *Gone With the Wind* rolls around and we have found neither a Scarlett nor an Ashley nor a Melanie and have to resort to girls that have been dug up from high schools and God knows where else by directors, producers, and casting directors.

DOS

To: Mr. Daniel T. O'Shea   November 18, 1938
cc: M. Rabwin

I am sending you only one copy of this so that too many people will not see it and so that there will not be any risks. Please send for George and go over the contents of this letter with him, as well as familiarizing Henry with its contents, of course.

As I wired you, I saw the Paulette Goddard–Jeffrey Lynn test and thought there was an enormous improvement in her work—so much so that I think she is still very strongly in the running as Scarlett, and I think we ought to take the chance that if she doesn't play Scarlett, we will be able to find other engagements for her besides the Universal job. . . .

I was completely unimpressed by Jeffrey Lynn and I think we should forget him as Ashley.

Incidentally, I should appreciate it if Hal and George would bear in mind in future tests in the cutting and shooting, respectively, that the huge close-ups, such as are used in the Goddard test, should be used with great discretion and very rarely, as it is difficult to form impressions of the artist involved without seeing how they handle their bodies, how they move, etc.

I am going to summarize below my present impressions and conclusions concerning the casting possibilities of *Gone With the Wind,* which should of course be kept strictly confidential . . . nor should the artists involved be told anything more than is necessary.

Concerning Scarlett, I think that at the moment our best possibilities are: Paulette Goddard, Doris Jordan,[46] Jean Arthur, Katharine Hepburn, and Loretta Young. . . .

It must be borne in mind that Jordan is a complete amateur who had not even had a single day's experience and didn't have good direction, to speak of, at the time she made this scene. . . .

Presumably, by the time you receive this, you will have determined whether or not it is possible to conclude an agreement with Hepburn. If an agreement has been concluded, Hepburn should be sent for immediately and her test should be carefully selected to include the scenes that require the most sex, because I think Hepburn has two strikes against her—first, the unquestionable and very widespread intense public dislike of her at the moment, and second, the fact that she is yet to demonstrate that she possesses the sex qualities which are probably the most important of all the many requisites of Scarlett. . . .

As to Melanie, as I previously advised you, I think Dorothy Jordan[47] is our best Melanie to date. . . .

It is still difficult for me to visualize Lew Ayres as Ashley, in spite of his recent rebirth, but I have no objections to testing him. . . .

Never having seen Geraldine Fitzgerald, I can't make any comment about her.

Ditto for Priscilla Lane. However, I note that George saw *Brother Rat,* which I think is wrong. I think he should see *Four Daughters,* which is the picture that overnight established her as a big favorite. . . .

Certainly I would give anything if we had Olivia de Havilland under

---

[46]She later played opposite Gary Cooper in *The Westerner* (1940), using the name of Doris Davenport.

[47]Mrs. Merian C. Cooper; not to be confused with Doris Jordan mentioned above.

contract to us so that we could cast her as Melanie. . . . It should also be borne in mind that it is a long time since George has seen [her sister Joan] Fontaine. . . . She certainly should have readings. . . .

The same is true of Jane Bryan. I think it is silly to rule these girls out on the strength of a picture which was probably shot in three or four weeks and in which they play straight for some young boy. We would be just as entitled to rule out Goddard on the strength of *The Young in Heart* or Jean Arthur on the picture *You Can't Take It With You*, if we were silly enough to judge these girls without considering the limitations of opportunities. . . .

I think we can forget about Susan Hayward because we don't even need her any more as a stand-in for Scarlett, or to work with people we are testing for the other roles, what with others around. . . .

I hear sensational things about Ann Sheridan and think we should check doubly to make sure we are not passing up a girl who many people think is slated for great stardom. It must be remembered that in a couple of years, these girls are going to take the place of the present-day stars, and it must also be remembered that Bette Davis, who today is probably the outstanding feminine star of the screen, was in no different position a couple of years ago than Ann Sheridan is today. Warners seem to have a sensational knack for the discovery of new people and also have the courage to give them opportunities. In the case of Bette Davis it is true that it was RKO who gave her a chance, but the fact remains that if we had seen Bette Davis just before *Of Human Bondage* and had judged her on the strength of some of the silly ingenue parts she had played, we probably would have passed her up as we are passing up girls who six months from now are likely to be more important stars than Katharine Hepburn. . . .

I think Ann Sheridan is definitely a clear possibility and should be followed up.

I understand Lana Turner and Melvyn Douglas are being tested today and will look forward to seeing this test.

I am as depressed about the Ashley situation as I am about Scarlett and Melanie, and I feel that here our snobbish attitude about newcomers may have cost us a great performance of a great star. We have simply got to stop living in the past.

If we don't find a new Ashley, I suppose our best possibilities, depressing as it seems, are Leslie Howard and Melvyn Douglas. All we have to do is line up a complete cast of such people as Hepburn and Leslie Howard, and we can have a lovely picture for release eight years ago. However, in the circumstances of our failure, we had better exert every effort in connection with Leslie Howard and Melvyn Douglas, as we have a starting date staring us in the face now and we have to go ahead even if we pay the same penalty for casting one of these men for Ashley that MGM paid on *Romeo and Juliet* for casting Leslie Howard as Romeo, when Bob Taylor was wandering around the lot waiting for an opportunity which it took [director] John Stahl to give him [in *Magnificent Obsession* (1935)].

I think Billie Burke should definitely be tested for Aunt Pittypat, but I'm afraid she's too young. . . .

I don't know anything about Evelyn Keyes and will be interested to see her on my return. . . .

I think Ann Dvorak is a very remote possibility indeed for Melanie. . . .

I don't know why it was decided to rule out Julie Haydon, Lewis Stone, and Robert Young. We certainly should consider Stone for one of the older roles, and he should be kept on the list. Julie Haydon is, I think, a Melanie possibility, and Robert Young, while he's no Barrymore, is about on a par with Lew Ayres. . . . I should like to say a word of caution against judging Young for what he was a couple of years ago. I was among those who thought he should be thrown out of Hollywood; since then, I have had to eat my words after seeing him give some really fine performances.

I haven't had any word from you as to whether Janet Gaynor will cut her salary to play Melanie.

Warners have so far definitely refused to consider letting us have [Olivia] de Havilland for Melanie, but I think they might be persuaded, especially if we offer Goddard in trade,[48] since I understand Jack Warner thinks well of Goddard. This would mean giving a star-making role to a Warner player, but it looks as though we may be stuck, in which case we may want to break our necks to get de Havilland. . . .

Almost the same thing is true of Andrea Leeds, although I don't think she's as good as de Havilland for the role. . . .

I feel strongly that Ray Milland should definitely not be forgotten. On the contrary, I think he's probably as good an Ashley possibility as has yet been suggested, even though the suggestion did come from my

---

[48]Paulette Goddard was under contract to Selznick for a short while. She had appeared in *The Young in Heart*.

wife, whose casting ideas I rarely agree with. I am aware of the deficiencies of Milland's accent, which are almost as great as those of Clark Gable! I think Milland very definitely is a sensitive actor, possessing the enormous attractiveness and at the same time the weakness that are the requirements of Ashley. . . .

I agree that Sara Haden and Humphrey Bogart can be forgotten.

Concerning Joan Bennett, I will be agreeable to her demands for a test instead of a reading if you can work out sensible terms. . . .

The Richard Carlson and Shepherd Strudwick tests will be made in New York, probably while I am here.

I think that George is right to test Eddie Anderson for Pork. . . .[49]

To: Mr. Daniel T. O'Shea   November 20, 1938

What is the news on Garrett? I had hoped the deal would be made by now, so that Garrett would be thoroughly familiar with both the book and the script before we leave, so that we could work on the train. . . .

With Kay [Brown] away, you had better handle the dialogue-writer situation. I am interested in Robert Sherwood, Stark Young, James Boyd, Rachel Field, Evelyn Scott, MacKinlay Kantor. I suggest that you reach Stark Young through publishers.

The job is not really an extensive one, but it is obviously important that in those places where we need new dialogue, we have someone who can match the quality and flavor of Miss Mitchell's work. I am going to take a stab at getting Miss Mitchell to do it, but I am not too sanguine. I'd be interested in having by wire or telephone the availability and salaries of those in whom I have indicated interest, together with George's opinion and preferences. . . .

It may be that Garrett will give us good enough scratch dialogue that, together with our efforts to use Mitchell dialogue wherever possible (even transposing it from scenes in the book that we are not using to our originally created scenes), will mean that the whole thing will not involve more than a hundred lines of dialogue. . . . We need to match Mitchell's dialogue, at least as well as [Hugh] Walpole matched Dickens, or at least caught the Dickensian flavor in such new dialogue as we had in *David Copperfield*. Obviously we have no time to waste and I am even in hopes that we can line this thing up in time for the

[49]Eddie Anderson was cast as Uncle Peter.

dialogue writer to be on the train with Garrett and myself, so that as I finish a scene with Garrett, I can turn it over to the dialogue writer, and so that the dialogue writer's draft will be ready for George and me to go over for whatever revisions will be necessary on at least the first few scenes by the time I get back.

Because we will know very specifically almost the exact content of the new lines we are going to require, it is necessary that we have someone that will be easy to work with and that will be pliable. . . .[50]

DOS

To: Mr. O'Shea

New York
November 21, 1938
CONFIDENTIAL

Dear Danny:

In connection with Scarlett: we're getting so close to the starting date of the picture that I'm commencing to grow fearful of losing any of our really good possibilities and I think we should make clear to Katharine Hepburn, Jean Arthur, Joan Bennett, and Loretta Young that they are in the small company of final candidates; and on my return I hope you will be able to tell me immediately the situation in relation to each of these.

I think the final choice must be out of this list plus Goddard and our new girl [Doris Jordan], plus any last-minute new-girl possibility that may come along.

DOS

To: Mr. O'Shea

November 21, 1938

. . . I saw Lana Turner and Melvyn Douglas test. I think that Turner is completely inadequate, too young to have a grasp of the part apparently. . . . I'm afraid we'll have to forget her.

I think that Douglas gives the first intelligent reading of Ashley we've had, but I think he's entirely wrong in type, being much too beefy physically—suggesting a lieutenant of Rhett Butler's rather than an aesthetic, poetic, and defeated Ashley. I'm afraid that we'll have to forget him, too, which is particularly frightening since this narrows down our Ashley list still further. It makes the Leslie Howard matter

---

[50]No dialogue writer was signed at this point.

even more vital and pressing. . . . If possible, I'd still like this to be subject only to a photographic test. . . .

I am anxious about Doris Jordan because I think, apart from the photography and hairdress, her new test is even more promising than the first one and shows decided promise. I think that George has done wonders with her since her New York test, and I hope he is continuing to work with her daily. . . .

No pains should be spared in connection with the girl, since she is certainly one of our four or five final possibilities.

I have looked at the new Goddard test—the one she made with Jeffrey Lynn—practically daily since it arrived, to see whether my first impression of the great improvement in her remained; and I must say that each time I see it I am more and more impressed. As much work as possible should be done with her. Incidentally, the point in her contract about which I have written you, concerning Chaplin's rights,[51] should be straightened out immediately if it needs straightening out. It might be wise for you to make clear to Goddard that unless this point is straightened out (provided you feel it needs straightening) and unless we get a further extension of the contract to a full seven years, she is not going to play Scarlett.

DOS

To: Miss Katharine Brown   December 5, 1938
cc: Mr. O'Shea

The wire from Miss Reissar[52] concerning Lee Garmes on *Gone With the Wind* was a curious coincidence, since just yesterday I was discussing the possibility of bringing him over for this. I suggest you cable Reissar immediately, saying that we would be interested in Garmes if his salary were low enough, and asking her to determine further whether he has had any experience in Technicolor, and also whether he would give us options. His salary on *Wind* ought to be in the neighborhood of five to six hundred dollars weekly, and the options could be for fifty to a hundred dollars weekly more than this, but should never get above $750, which is the top cameraman's salary in the entire business. . . .

DOS

51Paulette Goddard was Chaplin's wife.
52Jenia Reissar, Selznick International's London Representative.

To: Miss Macconnell[53]   December 5, 1938
cc: Miss Keon

. . . I would like you to make suggestions as to where we might be able to drop in any minor characters that we have eliminated for brief appearances, in the manner in which we used "Barkis" in *David Copperfield,* or for additional appearances of minor characters that we have retained but briefly, or for transferring to minor characters that we have either retained or dropped from the picture any action or dialogue that we have given to other minor characters.

Also, please secure from Bobby [Barbara Keon] a copy of the book with markings that duplicate my own, and I am particularly anxious for you to call to my attention, as the next draft of the script progresses, dialogue, business, and complete scenes that I marked but that we have not included in the script. Even sections of the dialogue that we have dropped I want to recheck, and for this purpose I will prefer that you cut out pages of the book and paste them on sheets, marking what I have retained and what I have dropped—as it will be easier for me to read it in this form. You had better have available an extra copy of the book so that in the event there is dialogue or business on both sides of a single page, you will be able to paste onto the sheet sections from both sides of the page.

Also, and more on the creative side, I should like you to call to my attention—and this is perhaps the most important phase of your work —dialogue or action that I have marked, or that I have not marked, that is not included in the script but that might be transferred and used in scenes where we have created original dialogue. The ideal script, as far as I am concerned, would be one that did not contain a single word of original dialogue, and that was one hundred per cent Margaret Mitchell, however much we juxtaposed it. With this objective, or something at least approaching it, in mind, call to my attention even individual lines that might be substituted for original lines that we have created.

The same is true of sets. Where we have indicated a set that does not appear in the book, and we can transfer the action to a setting that does appear in the book, I am anxious to attempt to do this.

Miss Gerry Wright has been engaged in making a most careful index of the entire book, which should be enormously helpful to you. As an

[53]Franclien Macconnell, Assistant Story Editor.

example, Rhett's attitude toward the war is dealt with in many dialogue passages in the book. Obviously it will be dealt with in fewer passages in the script. I would be anxious to examine all such passages in the book to make sure that we have used the best of this dialogue in those places where we deal with it in the script. The same is, of course, true of all subjects with which we deal, and of all scenes between important characters. As a further, and even more important example, practically all the scenes between Rhett and Scarlett in the book are wonderful for picture purposes, and it is unfortunate that we are going to lose a number of them. I want to examine all the dialogue between Rhett and Scarlett in the book and make sure that we have done the best possible editing job, and have retained the best of it, within our footage limitations.

DOS

To: Miss Katharine Brown   December 6, 1938

Would you care to brave the lioness's den and inquire from Miss Tallulah Bankhead whether she would like to play Belle Watling? As a disappointed Scarlett she's likely to bite your head off—and for God's sake, don't mention my name in connection with it, simply saying that it is an idea of your own that you haven't yet taken up with me.

My own feeling is that she would do wonders with this bit, making it stand out, and that she would be a perfect illicit mate for Rhett Butler. However, if she betrays any interest you had better explain that it is an extremely small part, having only about three or four appearances.

The reason I think she might go for it is simply as a stunt, just as it has been suggested that Mae West (who is out of the question, of course) might be glad to do it as a stunt.

Do I hear you muttering obscenities?

DOS

TO: KATHARINE BROWN   DECEMBER 6, 1938

AM NOT AT THIS STAGE INTERESTED IN SIDNEY HOWARD FOR "REBECCA." HOWEVER, WITH A BIG EFFORT I HAVE BECOME BROAD-MINDED AND FORGIVING AND AM WILLING TO HAVE SIDNEY DO DIALOGUE WORK ON REVISED SCRIPT OF "WIND" IF HE WISHES TO. I SHOULD ESTIMATE THIS JOB WILL RUN SOMEWHERE

BETWEEN ONE AND TWO WEEKS, STARTING SOMETIME WITHIN NEXT
TWO WEEKS. YOU MIGHT TELL LELAND[54] THAT I SHOULD THINK
SIDNEY WOULD HAVE THE GRACE TO HUMBLY ASK TO DO THIS JOB
ON ANY TERMS IN VIEW OF THE WAY HE LET ME DOWN. I WOULD
NOT PAY HIM ANY MORE SALARY THAN HE RECEIVED FROM US
BEFORE, WHICH IS WHAT HE WOULD HAVE GOTTEN HAD HE LIVED
UP TO HIS OBLIGATIONS. THIS WAS $3000 WEEKLY, AND I WOULD
NOT GUARANTEE MORE THAN ONE WEEK. ALSO MAKE CLEAR THAT
OUR PRESENT SCRIPT IS SO MATERIALLY REVISED FROM HOWARD
SCRIPT THAT WHEN COMPLETED IT MAY BE NOT MERELY THE
DECENT THING TO DO BUT THE NECESSARY THING TO GIVE
GARRETT COCREDIT WITH SIDNEY. . . .

To: Mr. Cukor   December 8, 1938

For your information, I am informed by MGM that Clark Gable
refuses under any circumstances to have any kind of a Southern accent.

I am very anxious to talk to you generally about this entire accent
problem, and would appreciate it if you would make a note to take it
up with me when you see me tomorrow.

DOS

MR. JOHN HAY WHITNEY   DECEMBER 10, 1938
230 PARK AVENUE
NEW YORK CITY

YOU HAVE MISSED A GREAT THRILL. "GONE WITH THE WIND" HAS
BEEN STARTED. SHOT KEY FIRE SCENES AT EIGHT-TWENTY
TONIGHT, AND JUDGING BY HOW THEY LOOKED TO THE EYE THEY
ARE GOING TO BE SENSATIONAL.[55]

DAVID

---

[54]Leland Hayward, talent agent, whose New York company was associated with
Myron Selznick's West Coast talent agency. Howard did not work for Selznick again.

[55]The burning of Atlanta was re-created on the back lot of the Selznick (Pathé) Studio.
Old sets were given false fronts and new profiles in order to simulate buildings of the
period. Seven Technicolor cameras photographed doubles for the characters of Rhett
and Scarlett in medium and long shots against the fire background. It was necessary to
shoot this sequence ahead of the start of actual production in order to clear the area and
allow for construction of the exterior Tara set, sections of Atlanta, and various other
exteriors to be used during the course of filming.

Mrs. David O. Selznick   December 12, 1938
Sherry-Netherland Hotel
New York City

Darling:

. . . Saturday night I was greatly exhilarated by the Fire Sequence. It was one of the biggest thrills I have had out of making pictures— first, because of the scene itself, and second, because of the frightening but exciting knowledge that *Gone With the Wind* was finally in work. Myron rolled in just exactly too late, arriving about a minute and a half after the last building had fallen and burned and after the shots were completed. With him were Larry Olivier and Vivien Leigh. Shhhhh: she's the Scarlett dark horse, and looks damned good. (Not for anybody's ears but your own: it's narrowed down to Paulette, Jean Arthur, Joan Bennett, and Vivien Leigh.

We're making final tests this week, and I do frantically hope that you'll be home in time to sit in on the final decision. . . . At least when I am lynched I want you to be able to shout sincerely that I did the best I could.) . . .

INTERPOLATION[56]

Before my brother, Myron, Hollywood's leading agent, brought Laurence Olivier and Miss Leigh over to the set to see the shooting of the Burning of Atlanta, I had never seen her.[57] When he introduced me to her, the flames were lighting up her face and Myron said: "I want you to meet Scarlett O'Hara." I took one look and knew that she was right—at least right as far as her appearance went—at least right as far as my conception of how Scarlett O'Hara looked. Later on, her tests, made under George Cukor's brilliant direction, showed that she could act the part right down to the ground, but I'll never recover from that first look.

[56]Correspondence regarding Selznick's initial meeting with Vivien Leigh, her testing for the role of Scarlett, the reactions to the tests, the unofficial selection of her for the role, and the subsequent negotiations with Alexander Korda, the noted European producer and director who held her contract, is all conspicuous by its absence in the Selznick files. Whatever material in this regard was put in writing at the time was probably marked the equivalent of "highly confidential" for fear of a premature leak to the press and members of the industry. It is possible that file copies were not made. The interpolated excerpt above was taken from a magazine piece written in 1941 called "Discovering the New Ones" by Selznick.

[57]In person; but based on previous correspondence he had seen her work in *Fire over England* and *A Yank at Oxford*.

To: Mr. Ginsberg   December 12, 1938

I wish you would . . . lay out the schedule of the remaining tests of our principals for *Wind*, which are much the most important that we have made. Scarlett will definitely be decided upon as the result of this next group of tests, which I hope we will be able to see by Monday or Tuesday of next week. The boys should be cautioned to keep things as confidential as possible.

The girls to be tested in these scenes are Miss Goddard, Joan Bennett, Jean Arthur, and Vivien Leigh. . . .

The Mammy scenes should be made with our two principal candidates for this role, Hattie McDaniel and Hattie Noel. However, since the scene will be shot four times, it would be highly desirable to bear down at once on other possible Mammy candidates and take advantage of this opportunity to see two others, one of whom I should like to be Louise Beavers.[58] . . .

Mrs. David O. Selznick   December 17, 1938
Sherry-Netherland Hotel
New York City

Darling:

. . . I can't seem to get going full steam on *Gone With the Wind*—maybe because I had such tough evenings on *Made for Each Other*. However, that's now practically out of the way, and next week I will be more *Wind* conscious. You'll see the next—and what I hope will be the semifinal—preview of *Made for Each Other*, which we're trying to make Friday night. Retakes have been comparatively simple—just two days of bits and pieces.

George is busily engaged on the Scarlett tests. All day today with Jean Arthur, who has been no end of trouble (I look at her as though I had never known her before!), but who looks on the set as though she may be wonderful—although I have seen only a small part of one scene rehearsed. The tests of each of the four girls will consist of three scenes—and we'll then intercut them so that we'll see each of the four girls consecutively playing each of the three scenes. And what happens if they're all no good? You can give me back to the Russians, I suppose. . . . George will have all day Monday with Joan, all day Tuesday with Paulette, all day Wednesday with Vivien Leigh—which means that you'll be back in time for the final knockout blow. George

[58]Hattie McDaniel played the role.

and everybody are being so well behaved that Danny O'Shea has suggested we give a *Gone With the Wind* party when the picture starts—to celebrate the last time when we're all talking to each other.

By the way, I think I forgot to tell you that Irving Berlin, in all seriousness, made a remark that's worthy of Goldwyn or Wurtzel.[59] At the Goetzes[60] last Sunday night he asked what picture they were running, and the reply was *Christmas Carol.* Irving said, "Christmas Carol? What a swell title!"

To: Mr. Ginsberg—Mr. O'Shea   December 19, 1938

The more I think about Lee Garmes, the more I feel that he might be much the best man for us, especially in view of his skill with angles and his ability to get the sort of effects which are so essential to our picture.

What is the status of the negotiations with him?

DOS

To: Mr. Ginsberg—Mr. Klune   December 20, 1938

Contrary to my attitude with most directors on the question of set-dressing,[61] about which I think I know more than most directors, I think that George Cukor knows a great deal more about set-dressing than I do and has better taste and judgment in his department. Therefore, I would not want any set-dresser that George did not want on *Gone With the Wind.* . . .

DOS

TO: KATHARINE BROWN   DECEMBER 23, 1938

CASTING FULL BLAST. DID ANYTHING COME OF YOUR TALK WITH LILIAN GISH? SHE AND BARBARA O'NEIL ARE AMONG OUR VERY FEW CONTENDERS FOR THE ROLE OF ELLEN.[62] ANOTHER IS CORNELIA OTIS SKINNER, WHO WE UNDERSTAND IS VERY INTERESTING, AND WOULD LIKE TO HAVE AN IDEA AS TO HER AVAILABILITY AND MONEY.

[59]Sol Wurtzel, Twentieth Century-Fox Executive Producer.
[60]William Goetz was Vice-President and assistant to Darryl F. Zanuck at Twentieth Century-Fox. His wife, Edith, was Irene Selznick's sister.
[61]The furniture, rugs, pictures, draperies, and other interior decorations used in a setting.
[62]Scarlett's mother. Barbara O'Neil played the part.

To: Mr. John Hay Whitney   January 4, 1939
                                                          CONFIDENTIAL

Dear Jock:

I send you herewith draft of the announcement.[63] Please guard this with your life. . . .

Korda specially and repeatedly has requested that we get him as much as possible in the announcement. Hence those sentences dealing with him.

There are still last-minute changes and demands to be coped with in the negotiations. It looks now as though . . . Korda is going to wind up with the choice of having the second picture [with Viven Leigh] beyond *Gone With the Wind*—in other words, we would have *Gone With the Wind* and one picture, then one to Korda, then one to us. The lucky Hungarian has fallen into something, and we're going to make a fortune for him. However, if she's really as good as we hope, I suppose we're lucky too, and shouldn't be greedy that someone else gets something out of it.

Hastily,
DOS

To: Mr. Ginsberg   January 6, 1939
                                                          CONFIDENTIAL

Directly the Scarlett contract is signed, if indeed it ever is signed, the girl [Vivien Leigh] should report regularly at nine or nine-thirty, or at the latest, ten o'clock each morning; work at least two hours on her accent, then report for fittings, then report for rehearsals with Mr. Cukor and for any photographic tests that may be necessary; then work two hours more on her accent.

I am terribly worried about the accent problem receiving enough attention and regularly, and without fail, she should have at least four hours instruction daily on it. . . .

Directly Garmes arrives and the contract is signed with the girl, photographic tests should be made that will include experiments with her eyebrows and hair. Strict orders should be given, however, that nothing should be done that cannot be remedied: in other words, her hair should not be cut or the color changed, nor should her eyebrows be plucked in any way.

[63]Regarding the signing of Vivien Leigh for the role of Scarlett O'Hara.

I should like the photographic tests to include various experiments with ways of making up her eyebrows to make them look more natural and more in the period; different make-ups; experiments with her figure, including particularly her bosom. . . .

To get back to the accent problem, we will certainly have to get busy with accent work with Rhett, and we may have the same accent problem with Ashley, Melanie, and others—almost certainly with Ashley and Melanie. Accordingly, regular instruction should be arranged for all of them—perhaps classes including all of them jointly, as well as individual work. . . .

DOS

To: Mr. O'Shea   January 6, 1939

Fitzgerald[64] starts with us today, 1/6/39, at $1250 week, on loan from MGM. He will work on *GWTW* dialogue.

He will undoubtedly be here all day Saturday and Monday, but it is possible that after that we may use him only an hour or two each day—however, I will let you know about this later.

DOS

To: Messrs. Cukor, Garrett, Fitzgerald   January 7, 1939

In relation to our length problem, the only way that we can really cut down may be through the elimination of some of the very best scenes in the whole picture—also some of the best-remembered scenes in the book.

I will note in this memo as I go along those scenes which from a standpoint of storytelling we can lose; and we should have a discussion on this before we start shooting, possibly postponing the shooting of these dubious scenes until the completion of the picture and until we see how long we actually are. It breaks my heart to consider losing any of them but I don't see any other alternative, and certainly the very least we should do is discuss them.

We are a couple of reels before we get to the story of Scarlett and Rhett, which is, after all, the stuff on which the book is built and upon which the success of the picture will depend. These couple of reels are made up of the following:

[64]Author F. Scott Fitzgerald worked on a few scenes, contributing criticisms, suggestions, and some revised dialogue until on or about January 24, 1939. Virtually none of his material appeared in the final version of the script.

1. Scene with the Tarleton twins, which is defensible on only two grounds; first, that it is remembered that the book opens this way, and second, that it introduces talk of the war.
2. The scene with the father, which is undoubtedly necessary.
3. The scene of the mother's return from the Slatterys, which has the following necessary points which perhaps could be handled elsewhere:

   Introduction of the sisters;
   Introduction of Jonas Wilkerson;
   Introduction of the house servants.
4. Prayer Scene—which certainly is in no sense essential, and which I have included only because it is so well remembered and should be effective pictorially, and also because we see Ellen as the mistress of the house and the great lady in charge of her family and domestic servants—and performing her functions as the mistress of a Southern establishment. This scene has the additional point which is desirable but not essential—of planting Scarlett's intentions about the next day—because the scene with Ashley actually does not need this plant.
5. There is a considerable chunk of film that might be saved by going straight from the prayer scene to Twelve Oaks—because, actually, the intervening scene between Scarlett and Mammy, and the bits that surround it, do not progress our story one iota and, in fact, hold it up. It is an absolutely wonderful scene, one of the best we have, but there is no justification for it from a standpoint of storytelling or footage.
6. The arrival at Twelve Oaks and the scenes that precede the barbecue are not very exciting, and are justified only by the introduction of Ashley and Melanie, plus some minor relationships such as that between India and Charles Hamilton (the importance of which is not very great and which, actually, the picture can live without), as well as the relationship between Frank Kennedy and Suellen, which is also not terribly important if our footage problem continues to be as great as it presently appears.

   Rhett's introduction could very easily be handled in the barbecue or in the library. As a matter of fact, a very good introduction is his popping up out of the couch.[65]
7. Similarly, the barbecue scene is completely unnecessary. Actually

---

[65]Rhett's introduction took place immediately following the arrival at Twelve Oaks, as it occurred in the novel.

it has not any real value of any kind, except in relation to Scarlett's return to the scene of the barbecue on her way from Atlanta to Tara—and even this effect could be duplicated by having her in the house instead of at the barbecue pits. The only conceivable reason for the barbecue is that it is well remembered. (Note: if we drop the barbecue, perhaps we should change the dialogue in the sequence at Tara, with reference to the barbecue.)

8. The scene of Scarlett tiptoeing out of the girls' room is also not necessary, but presumably the dialogue about the war and Rhett's attitude toward it is essential. We may be able to reduce it considerably, but our present method of handling it seems rather adroit, in that it keeps the Ashley-Scarlett story going while the war talk and Rhett's attitude is being slipped to the audience.

From all of the above something can be dropped[66]—just what, I haven't finally concluded, but I think we should have a meeting immediately to decide which, if any of these scenes, we should lose.

I think we must realize that if the book were 2000 pages long instead of 1000 pages, we would obviously have to throw away many, many great scenes; and I think there is only one policy to follow in concluding what we can and cannot retain—and that is, that we must retain scenes that are essential to the story, and lose scenes, however valuable, that are not essential. . . .

DOS

Mr. Ed Sullivan   January 7, 1939
621 North Alta Drive
Beverly Hills, California

Dear Ed:
    . . . I think the following answers your question:

1. Scarlett O'Hara's parents were French and Irish. Identically, Miss Leigh's parents are French and Irish.
2. A large part of the South prides itself on its English ancestry, and an English girl might presumably, therefore, be as acceptable in the role as a Northern girl.
3. Experts insist that the real Southern accent, as opposed to the Hollywood conception of a Southern accent, is basically English.

[66]None of the possibilities mentioned was dropped.

There is a much closer relationship between the English accent and the Southern accent than there is between the Southern accent and the Northern accent, as students will tell you, and as we have found through experience. . . .

Miss Leigh seems to us to be the best qualified from the standpoints of physical resemblance to Miss Mitchell's Scarlett, and—more importantly—ability to give the right performance in one of the most trying roles ever written. And this is after a two-year search.

. . . I like to think that you'll be in there rooting for her.

Cordially and sincerely yours,

MRS. JOHN R. MARSH [Margaret Mitchell]   JANUARY 13, 1939
4 EAST 17TH STREET N.E.
ATLANTA, GEORGIA

DEAR MRS. MARSH: WE ARE ABOUT TO GIVE STORY ON SCARLETT, ASHLEY, AND MELANIE TO THE PRESS AND ARE HOLDING IT UP FOR ONE HOUR IN ORDER TO GIVE YOU TIME TO RELEASE IT TO ATLANTA PAPERS AND CORRESPONDENTS. WOULD ACCORDINGLY APPRECIATE IT ENORMOUSLY IF YOU WOULD IMMEDIATELY UPON RECEIPT OF THIS TELEGRAM SEND FOR THE PRESS. SENDING YOU FULL STORIES IN SEPARATE WIRES. I DO HOPE YOU ARE AS HAPPY ABOUT THE FINAL OUTCOME AS WE ARE. ONE OF MY GREATEST HOPES AND DREAMS IS THAT YOU WILL BE COMPLETELY SATISFIED WITH THE FILM VERSION OF YOUR MAGNIFICENT WORK. CORDIALLY AND APPRECIATIVELY

DAVID O. SELZNICK

MRS. JOHN R. MARSH
4 EAST 17TH STREET, N.E.
ATLANTA, GEORGIA

DEAR MISS MITCHELL: FOLLOWING IS THE SCARLETT ANNOUNCEMENT: QUOTE VIVIEN LEIGH, WHOSE FATHER IS FRENCH AND MOTHER IRISH, WILL PLAY THE ROLE OF SCARLETT O'HARA, WHOSE FATHER WAS IRISH AND MOTHER FRENCH. . . . CLARK GABLE ALREADY HAS BEEN ANNOUNCED FOR THE ROLE OF RHETT BUTLER. . . . THE PICTURE, TO BE FILMED ENTIRELY IN TECHNICOLOR, GOES BEFORE THE CAMERAS WITHIN THE NEXT

TWO WEEKS. IN HER PHYSICAL CHARACTERISTICS, AS WELL AS HER
ANCESTRY, MISS LEIGH RESEMBLES THE HEROINE OF MISS
MITCHELL'S BOOK. . . .

PRIOR TO HER RECENT SCREEN WORK IN ENGLAND, MISS LEIGH
HAD A GREAT DEAL OF EXPERIENCE ON THE STAGE. . . . IN
PRIVATE LIFE, MISS LEIGH IS MRS. LEIGH HOLMAN, WIFE OF A
LONDON BARRISTER AND MOTHER OF A FIVE-YEAR-OLD DAUGHTER,
SUZANNE. MISS LEIGH WAS BORN IN DARJEELING, INDIA, AT THE
FOOT OF MT. EVEREST, ON NOVEMBER 5, 1913. . . . SHE WAS
SCHOOLED IN PARIS, LONDON, SWITZERLAND, ITALY, AND
GERMANY. . . . MISS LEIGH'S NAME IS PRONOUNCED AS THOUGH
SPELLED "LEE." UNQUOTE

DAVID O. SELZNICK

To: Mr. John Hay Whitney   January 25, 1939

Dear Jock:

Herewith the Sidney Howard script, the so-called Howard-Garrett
script, and the script that we are shooting, as far as we have revised
it.

Don't get panicky at the seemingly small amount of final revised
script. There are great big gobs that will be transferred from either the
Howard script or the Howard-Garrett script, and it is so clearly in my
mind that I can tell you the picture from beginning to end, almost shot
for shot. I was about to say "line for line," but this I won't say because
I want to match up the best things from the book and from Garrett
and Howard, as well as try to make cuts.

The important thing to remember is that the creative work that
remains to be done is not of the type that leads to trouble. We have
everything that we need in the book and in the Howard and Howard-
Garrett scripts. The job that remains to be done is to telescope the
three into the shortest possible form. . . .

The only thing that I can see that might get us into trouble would
be for me suddenly to be run down by a bus, so you'd better get me
heavily insured. As long as I survive the whole situation is well in hand:
the whole picture is in my mind from beginning to end; all the sets
for the first six weeks of shooting approved in detail; all the costumes
approved; the entire picture cast with the exceptions only of Belle
Watling and Frank Kennedy, who don't work for some time; and
generally the picture is, I assure you, much better organized than any

picture of its size has ever been before in advance of production.

You must bear in mind that I am aware that I am in a terrific spot and that the company is in a terrific spot. Also, that a picture of this size and importance cannot be created to the last inflection in advance of production; there must be a certain leeway in production as we go along. Otherwise, I could simply leave town and drop the picture into the lap of anybody to execute.

A couple of days ago I was sick with trepidation, but as of tonight —the night before we start shooting[67]—I am filled with confidence and certain that we will have a picture that will fulfill all the publicity and will completely satisfy all the readers of the book as well. But you are going to have to bear with me for the next couple of months, which will be the toughest I have ever known—possibly the toughest any producer has ever known, which is the general opinion of the whole industry.

I think you will find the Garrett script infinitely better as to continuity and as to storytelling generally, but inferior to the Howard script as to each individual scene. Therein lies my job.

By the time you get here next Tuesday we will be able to show you three or four sequences, and I think you will be completely happy. Certainly we ought to feel pleased that as small an outfit as ours is making the most important picture since sound came in—and, more astonishingly, that we have wound up with a cast that could not be improved if we had all the resources of all the big studios combined.

You have had faith in me to date, and I beg you to continue to have this faith until the picture is finished. I must refuse to be judged until the final result is in—at which time if the picture isn't everything that everyone wants, I not alone am willing, but am anxious to leave the whole goddam business.

DOS

LOWELL V. CALVERT   JANUARY 26, 1939
SELZNICK INTERNATIONAL PICTURES
NYC

STARTED SHOOTING "GONE WITH THE WIND" TODAY.

DOS

---

[67] Referring to the shooting of the film proper. The burning-of-Atlanta long shots, done with doubles for the leading players, took only one evening's filming on December 10, 1938.

To: Mr. Menzies   January 28, 1939
cc: Messrs. Ginsberg, Cukor, Garmes, Klune

It is obvious that something must be done immediately to correct the situation of the conflicting opinions about color among members of the art departments, officials of the Technicolor company, etc., if we are to avoid confusion, loss of time, and waste of money through such ridiculously unnecessary things as repainting sets, etc.

I should like to reiterate that Mr. Menzies is the final word on these matters and should be the arbiter on any differences of opinion. I hold Mr. Menzies responsible for the physical aspects of the production and for the color values of the production, and any difference of opinion should be settled by him, hopefully without delay or equivocation.

It is up to Mr. Menzies to decide whether a pattern or color is going to be too obtrusive or is dangerous from any standpoint, after listening to the opinions of everyone, including the Technicolor representatives, Mr. Garmes and Mr. Cline.[68] He has the privilege of making a test of any material or color any time he sees fit and any time that he is in doubt—although I am hopeful that with the wide experience the studio has already had in color, we can cut down and largely eliminate the extravagance which has been indulged in regarding tests. Where he feels reasonably safe, his decision should be made without tests—but in any event, his decisions should be final and should be made sufficiently in advance to obviate all possibility of confusion or waste.

As to the obtrusiveness of sets, it is my opinion, based upon very solid experience in Technicolor, that this is largely, if not entirely, a matter of the photography and lighting. Mr. Garmes is familiar with our desires in this respect, and is completely in accord with Mr. Cukor and myself on the obvious folly of the old-fashioned Technicolor photography that indulged in lighting of every detail of a set with resultant great distraction from the scene and from the players.

DOS

To: Mr. George Cukor   February 8, 1939

Dear George:

You will recall that before we started the picture we had a long discussion concerning my anxiety to discuss with you in advance the

---

[68]Wilfrid M. Cline, Technicolor Cinematographer. In the early years of three-color Technicolor, it was customary to have a Technicolor cinematographer work in association with the director of photography assigned to a film.

points that I personally saw in each scene. We had both hoped that we would have a period of rehearsals and that we would have a chance to see the whole script rehearsed. This, for many reasons, was impossible. Then we discussed seeing each scene rehearsed, and this idea was in turn lost sight of in the pressure of many things.

Now the idea becomes more important than ever, because we have little or no opportunity in most cases even to discuss each re-written scene before you go into it. I therefore would like to go back to what we discussed, and to try to work out a system whereby I see each block scene rehearsed in full before you start shooting on it. I am worried as to the practicability of this and as to whether it would lose too much time, but I should appreciate it if you would give some thought to it, as it might even save time in the long run. Also, it would avoid the necessity of my coming down on the set at any other time; any feeling on my part that I ought to go down to make sure a point we had intended has been made clear to you; would avoid projection-room surprises for me; and, conceivably, would be of considerable service to you. Therefore, unless you see something in the way of the plan, I'd like, commencing immediately, to be notified when you are rehearsing each block scene. If this means I have to get in at the same time as the rest of you, so much the better—I'll get home earlier and Irene will appreciate it!

DOS

To: Mr. John Hay Whitney   February 13, 1939

The following is being released immediately:

George Cukor and David O. Selznick last night jointly issued the following statement:

"As a result of a series of disagreements between us over many of the individual scenes of *Gone With the Wind*, we have mutually decided that the only solution is for a new director to be selected at as early a date as is practicable."

Selznick added: ". . . Mr. Cukor's withdrawal . . . is the most regrettable incident of my rather long producing career, the more so because I consider Mr. Cukor one of the very finest directors it has ever been the good fortune of this business to claim.[69]

[69]See page 433. The exact circumstances behind the removal of Cukor from the film are, unfortunately, not in any of the Selznick files. Perhaps they were not referred to in writing at the time; or it is conceivable that any correspondence relating to the

"I can only hope that we will be so fortunate as to be able to re-place him with a man of comparable talents."[70]. . .

DOS

To: Mr. R. A. Klune   February 20, 1939

We will start shooting again on Monday. Please get together with Mr. Fleming immediately in connection with the opening scene. We should start with the twins and then go to Gerald and Scarlett to permit you to change the condition of Tara. It would be my prefer-ence, if there is no reason against it, and if Fleming is agreeable, to then jump into retakes in the Bazaar, followed by Rhett and Scarlett on the McDonough road.

DOS

---

incident was deemed to be of such a highly confidential nature, for various reasons, that all copies were destroyed.

Selznick was quoted in 1947 by Lloyd Shearer in *The New York Times Magazine* as follows: "We [Cukor and himself] couldn't see eye to eye on anything. I felt that while Cukor was simply unbeatable in directing intimate scenes of the Scarlett O'Hara story, he lacked the big feel, the scope, the breadth of the production."

Speculation in the industry at the time centered about MGM being dissatisfied with the speed at which the scenes were being photographed, Cukor objecting to Garrett's revision of Sidney Howard's script, changes in the dialogue by Selznick being delivered on the set continuously, and Clark Gable's unhappiness over Cukor's supposed preoccu-pation and fastidiousness with the characters portrayed by Vivien Leigh and Olivia de Havilland.

Cukor was quoted by Gwen Robyns as saying that "it is nonsense to say that I was giving too much attention to Vivien and Olivia. It is the text that dictates where the emphasis should go, and the director does not do it. Clark Gable did not have a great deal of confidence in himself as an actor, although he was a great screen personality; and maybe he thought that I did not understand that. My own theory after all these years is that for David Selznick *Gone With the Wind* was the supreme effort of his career; he was enormously nervous about the whole thing . . . it was a great trial, but also his undoing, and he did things he had never done before. For the first time he wanted to come down on the set and watch me direct something that we had worked out together. It was very nerve-racking."*

Vivien Leigh, in correspondence at the time with her husband, Leigh Holman, men-tioned that Cukor was "a very intelligent and imaginative man, and seems to under-stand the subject perfectly." After Cukor left the film she wrote, "He was my last hope of ever enjoying the picture."†

†Quoted from Alan Dent, *Vivien Leigh: A Bouquet* (London: Hamish Hamilton, 1969).

[70]The directors mentioned at the time as possibilities were Robert Z. Leonard, Jack Conway, King Vidor, and Victor Fleming (all MGM contract directors). The day follow-ing Cukor's exit, Victor Fleming, a good friend of Gable's, was taken off the completion of *The Wizard of Oz* and signed to direct *Gone With the Wind*. The *Wind* company resumed shooting two weeks later (March 1, 1939).

*From Gwen Robyns, *Light of a Star* (London: Leslie Frewin Publishers, Limited, 1968).

To: Mr. Victor M. Shapiro[71]   February 20, 1939

In respect to any inquiries concerning Hecht and [playwright John] Van Druten and the script of *Gone With the Wind*:

Van Druten is working on the script of *Intermezzo,* and he together with Hecht are simply spending a couple of days with us in an attempt to get a little footage out.

Do not, however, give even this information unless you are asked.

DOS

To: Mrs. Rabwin   February 21, 1939

Please talk to Mr. Fleming, who, I discovered to my pleasure, feels even more keenly about the breastwork situation than I do, and ask him if he would kindly make this his personal department, in which case turn over to him the woman that Mrs. Selznick told us about and arrange a meeting between her, Miss Leigh, and Mr. Fleming—but I have pestered poor Vivien so much about this, please explain to Victor that I would rather he became the sole heavy from now on (he is worried about it personally, which is a fact); tell him that if she doesn't look at least as good as Alice Faye in this particular department, I'll consider that his whole life has been wasted. Please keep me advised on this.

DOS

To: Mr. Henry Ginsberg   March 8, 1939

I think that whoever is going to do the score on *Gone With the Wind* ought to know about it now so that he can be spending whatever time he has free in study of the music of the period and generally doing preparatory work that would save us time and money before he came on our payroll—and that should do much to expedite the final score when we are ready for it.

My first choice for the job is Max Steiner, and I am sure that Max would give anything in the world to do it. I should think the approach should be through Forbstein[72] and Forbes,[73] but use your own judgment on this.

DOS

[71]Selznick International Advertising and Publicity Director for a three-month period.
[72]Leo F. Forbstein, head of Warner Bros. Music Department. Steiner was under contract to Warner Bros.
[73]Lou Forbes, Music Director of Selznick International.

To: Mr. Henry Ginsberg   March 3, 1939

The general feeling of laymen, such as Mr. and Mrs. Payson,[74] and experts, such as Ted Curtis,[75] who see our cut stuff, is that two or three of the sequences, such as (but not confined to) the arrival of Ellen at Tara and the prayer scene, are much too dark. . . .

It may be my fault for insisting on effect photography but I cannot seem ever to be able to drive into people's heads that when I ask for effect photography, I do not mean that the whole screen should be so dark that we cannot tell what is going on. Before the picture started, I made very clear to Lee Garmes and everybody connected with it that wherever there is effect photography, that sections of the screen which we want well lighted should be as strongly and brilliantly lighted as the whole screen would be if we did not want effect photography. I would appreciate it if you would get together with Garmes and [Ray] Rennahan [Technicolor Cinematographer] and make clear that we simply cannot tolerate any more photography that is so dark as to bewilder an audience—and that if they cannot get effect lighting without avoiding this risk, they should forget the effect lighting and light everything as though it were a newsreel. If we can't get artistry and clarity, let's forget the artistry.

                                                        DOS

To: Mr. Ginsberg   March 9, 1939
cc: Mr. Klune

For your information, I had a very nice talk with Lee Garmes, who behaved beautifully about the whole thing and took the change with considerable grace. He had no alibi to offer other than to say that he felt he was being blamed in a large part for work of the Technicolor company. . . .

                                                        DOS

To: Mr. Ginsberg   March 9, 1939
                                                       IMMEDIATE

In case by any unfortunate chance we should have to make still another change in the cameraman setup, if we can avoid a contract

[74]Mrs. Charles S. Payson (sister of John Hay Whitney), was one of the original backers of Selznick International.
[75]Edward P. Curtis, Eastman Kodak executive.

on Haller[76] we should do so. Did you make a commitment for any particular number of weeks? I have every confidence that Haller will come through, but we have been disappointed before and might be again. . . .

DOS

To: Mr. Klune   March 9, 1939
    Mr. Menzies

The more I see of our film, and compare it with film in color pictures such as *Robin Hood* and black-and-white pictures such as *The Great Waltz*, the more I realize how much we have been kidding ourselves in feeling that we could get really effective stuff on the back lot that should have been made on location. The walk of Gerald and Scarlett, which was specially written by Margaret Mitchell, and copied by us, to sell Tara looks on the screen as though it were the back yard of a suburban home. It is my feeling that before we get through, we are going to have to go out on location and retake this sequence. I wish you would immediately get together with Mr. Menzies and see what we can do about the remaining exterior sequences to get better results.[77] Frankly, I am now terribly sorry we didn't build Tara on location. . . .

I'd like you and Mr. Menzies to get together immediately to make sure that our remaining exteriors, such as the exterior of Twelve Oaks,[78] and the shot in which Gerald talks about the land being the only thing that matters (even if this is shot on the stage), have real beauty instead of looking like "B" picture film. This is quite apart from the photography—I don't see how the greatest cameraman in the world could get much beauty out of what we have given him for the exterior of Tara. (I am not speaking now of the set itself but of the landscaping, the line of trees, etc.) Please go over this memo with Mr. Menzies when you meet with him, and give me a report on the results. After all the expense and trouble we have gone to, I feel that other studios are making monkeys out of us on our pretentious effort. . . .

Incidentally, I would also like you to consider whether your second unit should go immediately to Georgia, or any place else, to pick up

[76]Ernest Haller, Director of Photography, who replaced Lee Garmes.
[77]Some material eventually was shot by a second unit, directed by Chester Franklin, in Chico, California.
[78]Some of which was later shot in the old Busch Gardens, Pasadena.

some shots for the opening sequences. This would include the shots of the Negroes returning from their work at quitting time. I wish you would make a note for the director and cameraman for the second unit, in connection with these particular shots, to see the opening of *Viva Villa!* with the peasants leaving their work as the bell rings. . . .[79]

DOS

To: [Supervising Film Editor] Hal Kern   March 9, 1939
cc: Messrs. Fleming and Klune

. . . I am extremely anxious, without delay, for our entire technical group to see *The Great Waltz*, which is in my opinion Hollywood's best technical achievement in many ways in several years. The photography, in particular, is the most outstanding job I have seen in a long, long time, as well as the way the camera is handled and the values that are got out of both sets and location shots. I would like this to be seen by the entire unit. . . .

DOS

To: Mr. Klune   March 9, 1939
cc: Mr. Fleming

For your information, I had a talk with Mr. Fleming today about going after various effects photographically, and going in for various camera angles, on *Gone With the Wind* that will at least compare with those that Mr. Fleming got for *The Great Waltz*.[80] Mr. Fleming explained that the difficulties of having as much flexibility are because of the Technicolor equipment; and during this talk we discussed the greater freedom that he would have if he went in for more shots in which we dubbed the dialogue so that they could be made silent. I have encouraged him to feel no inhibitions about making as many of these shots as he sees fit, wherever he can get an improved photographic effect.

DOS

[79]Producer James A. FitzPatrick (of *Traveltalks* short subjects) went with a unit to Georgia to shoot some atmospheric footage, a little of which was included in the final version of the film.

[80]Fleming received no official credit on *The Great Waltz*, but he did direct portions of the film. Julien Duvivier received sole directorial credit.

To: Messrs. Fleming, Haller, Klune, Menzies, [Art Director Lyle] Wheeler, [Costume Designer Walter] Plunkett, [Wardrobe Supervisor Edward P.] Lambert and [Set Decorator Edward G.] Boyle

March 11, 1939

There has been a great deal of comment recently about the difference between the outstanding foreign pictures, particularly the French pictures, and the American pictures, in that the better foreign pictures seem to capture a quality of reality in the photography, sets, and costumes that is lacking even in the best of American pictures. I personally feel that this criticism is a justifiable one.

I feel that our sets always look exactly what they are—sets that have been put up a few hours before, instead of seeming in their aging and in their dressing to be rooms that have existed for some time and that have been lived in. The same is true of the costumes. They always look exactly what they are—fresh out of the Costume Department, instead of looking like clothes that have been worn.

I do hope that we can correct this common fault of all American pictures to some extent in *GWTW*, and I should appreciate it if the Art, Set-Dressing, and Costume Departments would give this their attention.

To: Mr. R. A. Klune
cc: Mr. Fleming

March 13, 1939

. . . The costumes of the picture, and the sets also, should have dramatized much more than we have done to date, and much less than I hope they will do in future, the changing fortunes of the people with whom we are dealing. The first part of the picture—especially the sequences at Twelve Oaks—have been so neutralized that there will be no dramatic point made by the drabness of the costumes through the whole second half of the picture. We should have seen beautiful reds and blues and yellows and greens in costumes so designed that the audience would have gasped at their beauty and would have felt a really tragic loss when it saw the same people in the made-over and tacky clothes of the war period. The third part of the picture should, by its colors alone, dramatize the difference between Scarlett and the rest of the people—Scarlett extravagantly and colorfully costumed against the drabness of the other principals and of the extras.

I am hopeful that this will be corrected in such things as the bazaar retake. I am aware that the former scene at the bazaar looked like a cheap picture postcard in its color values—but this was because we were foolish enough to overdress the set so that it looked cheap and garish, instead of neutralizing it as to its color values, so that it was obviously an armory, and playing against this the beauty of the costumes, which gave us a marvelous opportunity for beautiful colors against the set, which obviously gave us no opportunities. The shots that Mr. Fleming has in mind on the waltz will fulfill their complete promise of beauty only if the costumes are lovely and colorful—so that Scarlett's black is a complete contrast and so that the colors of the costumes of the others are a complete contrast with the neutral colors that we should see as the war goes on, and in fact throughout the entire picture. Twelve Oaks and the bazaar were, and to a degree still are, our only opportunities for beautiful color for the entire race of people we are portraying in the entire film. . . .

I cannot conceive how we could have been talked into throwing away opportunities for magnificent color values in the face of our own rather full experience in Technicolor, and in the face particularly of such experiences as the beautiful color values we got out of Dietrich's costumes in *The Garden of Allah*, thanks to the insistence of Dietrich and [wardrobe designer Ernest] Dryden, and despite the squawks and prophecies of doom from the Technicolor experts. . . .

Examine the history of color pictures: the one thing that is still talked about in *Becky Sharp* is the red capes of the soldiers as they went off to Waterloo. What made *La Cucaracha* a success, and did so much for the Technicolor company, were the colors as used by [stage and screen designer Robert Edmond] Jones for his costumes. The redeeming feature of *Vogues of 1938* was the marvelous use of color in the women's styles. The best thing about the [*Goldwyn*] *Follies* [1938] was the beautiful way in which colors of sets and costumes were blended, as in the ballet. . . .

Presumably Bill Menzies is sufficient of an artist to so blend the colors that the scenes won't look like Italian weddings and so that where we use striking color, it will be used as effectively as Dietrich's costumes against the drab sand, or as the [Vera] Zorina ballet [in *Goldwyn Follies*]. . . .

Neutral colors certainly have their value, and pastel colors when used properly make for lovely scenes, but this does not mean that an entire picture—and the longest picture on record—has to deal one hundred per cent in neutral colors or pastel shades. This picture in particular gives us the opportunity occasionally—as in our opening scenes and as in Scarlett's costumes—to throw a violent dab of color at the audience to sharply make a dramatic point.

I know from talking to Walter Plunkett that no one feels as badly about the limitations that have been imposed upon him as he does. But if we are going to listen entirely to the Technicolor experts, we might as well do away entirely with the artists that are in our own Set and Costume Departments and let the Technicolor company design the picture for us. The result will be the unimpressive pictures that have been made in color by contrast with new and startling color combinations such as we achieved in *The Garden of Allah* and such as I had hoped we were going to vastly improve upon in *Gone With the Wind*.

... I have tried for three years now to hammer into this organization that the Technicolor experts are for the purpose of guiding us technically on the stock and not for the purpose of dominating the creative side of our pictures as to sets, costumes, or anything else.

DOS

To: Will Price[81]　　　　　　　　　　　　　　　　　March 25, 1939

... I had a talk with Mr. Gable the other day about his accent and told him that I didn't think as yet we were getting the occasional accented word and I urged him to go a step further on this without getting into a really noticeable accent, such as we had in the early scenes with Mr. Cukor and which seemed all wrong coming from Mr. Gable. I also mentioned to him and to Mr. Howard that I thought Mr. Howard's accent in the dining-room scene was exactly what it should be, in my opinion. However, he has fallen away from this in subsequent scenes.

I don't think we are doing enough with our bit actors[82] in the accent. For instance, Harry Davenport, Jr., who played the one-armed soldier in the bazaar scene, had no trace of accent whatsoever. I wish you would watch these bit actors more carefully.

DOS

[81]Southern Dialect Coach and Technical Adviser on *GWTW*.
[82]Actors playing very small parts.

To: Mr. R. A. Klune   March 29, 1939

While we are all sympathetic with Mr. Fleming's desire to shoot in continuity, I would like to see you with him to discuss the holding of several sequences until we have disposed of Gable, Howard, and Miss de Havilland. It seems silly to be shooting such things as the hospital sequences while Gable and Howard are on the payroll doing nothing. We have the further factors that we must get through with Leslie Howard in order to start *Intermezzo* and that we may run into difficulties in keeping Miss de Havilland. . . .

DOS

To: Mr. Lambert   April 3, 1939

I spoke today to Walter Plunkett about Gable's costumes. I think there is no excuse for their fitting him so badly, especially around the collar. . . . I think it is very disappointing indeed to have the elegant Rhett Butler wandering around with clothes that look as though he had bought them at the Hart, Schaffner, and Marx of that period and walked right out of the store with them.

I have also asked repeatedly for all our clothes to be aged sufficiently and worn sufficiently to look as though they had been worn and not to look what they are—fresh out of the tailoring shop. But nothing seems to be done about this either.

To get back to the fitting on Gable, if he is being fitted according to the way he stands in the shop, I'd like to call to your attention that his carriage is quite different when he is relaxed, and that necessarily he has to do a great deal of bending because of the difference between his height and Miss Leigh's, etc., and that a little more imagination should be used as to how he is going to wear them, without taking it for granted that he is going to stand stiff as a ramrod in all the scenes.

Also, his collars shouldn't be fitted so tightly that he looks as though he is overweight. The trick about collars on any man with a large neck, a trick which should be known to any costumer, is to make the collars slightly large so that they don't press against the neck and make it look as though it is bulging. Look at Gable's own collars in private life and see how well he looks in them, and then compare them with our collars. As a matter of fact, look at how well he looks in his own clothes generally, and compare the fit and the tailoring and the general attractiveness with what I regard as the awful costuming job we are doing with him.

DOS

To: Mr. Klune   April 7, 1939
cc: Mr. Ginsberg

Dear Ray:

. . . I have always felt that it is the falsest kind of economy to save on bit actors. The time that cheap and inexperienced actors cost, through the director's inability to get performances out of them, alone more than makes up the difference between their salaries and the salaries of good actors; film shot with cheap actors for a picture requiring the perfection of *Gone With the Wind* obviously cannot be used, where the cheap actors fail to deliver what is demanded of them; and even if the cheap actors should work quickly and should give adequate performances, it is still false economy because nothing is as important on the screen as the actor. To save money on actors and spend it on sets is silly—the audiences are looking at the actors, not at the sets, if our action means anything. And while a bit actor is on the screen, if it is for only two seconds, he is as important as the star. . . .

DOS

To: Mr. Ginsberg—Mr. O'Shea   April 14, 1939

We may soon have a serious worry to face that I think we should be prepared for if we are not going to be met with the possibility of again halting production. We should keep our worry confidential, but should be active on it none the less.

I have for some time been worried that Fleming would not be able to finish the picture because of his physical condition. He told me frankly yesterday that he thought he was going to have to ask to be relieved immediately, but after talking with his doctor was told that it would be all right for him to continue. However, he is so near the breaking point both physically and mentally from sheer exhaustion that it would be a miracle, in my opinion, if he is able to shoot for another seven or eight weeks. Since it would be difficult, if not actually impossible, for any substitute director to step in without taking the time to thoroughly familiarize himself with the book, the scripts and the cut stuff, I think we ought to start now selecting an understudy and familiarizing him with the material, so that he could step in on brief notice.

I have also discussed with Fleming the possibility of throwing in a substitute almost immediately for perhaps a week's shooting, to give him a chance to get a little rest and also to secure the benefit of his help on the script of the final part of the picture. As a matter of fact, this suggestion came from Fleming, and if we went through with it it would have the double advantage of having another man familiar with the material and actually having shot on the picture, and consequently prepared to step in should Victor have to quit.

I'd like you to talk this over between yourselves, and then one of us, I think, should discuss it with MGM to see if we can get some help from them.

One of the best possibilities would be Bob Leonard, since Bob knows the books thoroughly and told me at the time Vic went on the picture that if we ever needed him to shoot any particular sequences on the picture, he would be happy to stop in and help out. Leonard is also unusually adept, and completely without any nonsense about stepping in in a hurry. I once dragged him in on *A Tale of Two Cities* when Conway fell ill and he started shooting for me on twenty minutes notice. I think it might be wise for Henry [Ginsberg] to run up the street and have a discussion with Mannix and Thau[83] about the possibility of Leonard coming down and shooting for a while.

Another very good possibility would be Bill Wellman, if we could arrange to get Bill for a brief period in between his two pictures. I am sure Bill would do this as a favor for me, and I think Paramount owes it to us.[84] . . .

April 14, 1939

Darling [Irene Selznick],

. . . I wish I could just be with you somewhere, away from need of money, habit of work, drive of years' silly hopes. Maybe—oh, I hope so—we can map a program: months, eight or ten, of hard work and drive for financial freedom, then some place where there is neither . . . Clover Club[85] nor synopses.

. . . I don't think any more my Fate is millions, and Leadership. I hope it isn't (as though the hope were not gratuitous!). I'm damned if I know quite what's the alternate hope. . . .

---

[83]Benjamin Thau was now MGM Executive Producer.

[84]On April 26, Fleming collapsed and was out for two weeks. Sam Wood took over and continued to shoot material after Fleming's return in order to expedite the picture's completion.

[85]Popular Hollywood gambling club of the period.

To: Mr. Klune   April 17, 1939
    Mr. Lambert

I made it a point to go to the bottom of the terrible mess we have made of Gable's clothes, and was surprised to find that the reason why Gable looks so much worse in the clothes he has had so far in the picture than in all the pictures he has made (including such costume pictures as *Parnell*) is that Gable was told when he first came here that he could have any tailor he wanted except *Schmidt*. Since Schmidt has been Gable's tailor all through his career, from the time he started as an obscure actor to the time he became the biggest star in the world, this was an insane order to begin with. And it had the further effect of making Gable take a what-the-hell attitude and not bother with his own clothes, whereas normally he takes complete charge of his own clothes, has sketches made, works on them, etc.

I would like to know why, in the first place, the one tailor that should have outfitted Gable was ruled out. As for the future, and in the hope that we will do a decent job with him and not have a repetition of what we have had in the past, I am in hopes that you will sit down with Gable, determine exactly how he has worked in the past, and make sure this is the way he works in the future on his clothes.

The clothes that I have been complaining about in the past are masterpieces of tailoring compared to the horrible outfits that I saw tried on him Saturday. A more ill-fitting and unbecoming group of suits I have never seen on a laboring man, much less on a star. . . .

                                                                DOS

Mr. Howard Dietz   May 2, 1939
Metro-Goldwyn-Mayer
1540 Broadway
New York, New York

cc: Mr. Al Lichtman[86]

Dear Howard:

I was surprised to note in the excellent ads which your boys got up announcing the new year's product, the inclusion of *Gone With the Wind*.

You do whatever you see fit on this, but I should like most respectfully to suggest that it might be preferable if *Gone With the*

---

[86]MGM executive and Loews, Inc. Vice-President.

Wind were omitted from these announcements for a couple of reasons: to begin with, Al Lichtman shares my hopes that the picture is turning out so brilliantly that its handling will have to be on a scale and of a type never before tried in the picture business. The only close approach to it would be *The Birth of a Nation*. Al has a lot of wonderful ideas as to different experiments in road showing[87] and shares my hopes that the picture will be road shown in every town and hamlet in America, undoubtedly not reaching the regular theaters for a year, most probably not reaching them for two years, and quite possibly not reaching them for three years or longer. Al has stated on several occasions that there is no telling what the gross of the picture may be—perhaps ten million dollars, perhaps twelve or thirteen million, perhaps fifteen million.[88] I know all this sounds like Hollywood insanity to you, but if these expectations and hopes are insane, then I have been insane in the manner in which I have approached the picture (which I grant you is possible), because I have staked everything on it, including my personal future and the future of my company. For your confidential information, the cost is presently only a little under three and a half million dollars—how much more than this it will go we don't know. This means that its cost is almost twice that of any other picture ever made, with the possible exception of *Ben-Hur* [1925, silent], the cost of which I don't know (and I doubt that anybody else does: the boys were still charging luncheon checks to it a couple of years ago!). You can see that we're going to have to have the largest gross any picture has had in the last ten years simply to break even.

Incidentally, it will be the longest picture ever made—running somewhere between three and four hours. Obviously, the very least we will have to have will be two intermissions. Plans I have discussed with Al include showings with two intermissions; and perhaps even experiments with the picture running in two theaters simultaneously—the first half in one theater and the second half in another theater, with one admission ticket sold for both theaters. . . .

I am more grateful than I can say that the picture is in the hands of Loew's, because I think it needs the vision of men such as Al and

[87]Increased admission prices, reserved seats, and usually only one or two performances a day in selected theaters in large cities prior to the general release of a special feature.

[88]As of December 1971, *GWTW* has paid $74,200,000 in rentals in the United States and Canada alone. The total world-wide rentals are approximately $116,000,000.

yourself to feel the picture's way as it is completed and as it goes along. You know from experience that I am not in the habit of bulling you, or of salving anybody, so please believe what I say about the large measure of relief it gives me through these sleepless weeks and months to know that the finished product will have loving and expert care in its handling.

It is for all of these reasons that I think it is a mistake to include the picture with the rest of your product in any announcements. I think that psychologically it is a mistake to have it grouped with any pictures, however important. Certainly films like *Wizard of Oz* and *Northwest Passage* and *The Women* should be enormous grossers— probably the biggest of the year; but forgive me if I feel that these are mere pygmies alongside of *Gone With the Wind. San Francisco* and [*The Great*] *Ziegfeld* (1936), for instance, were enormous pictures, but you would scarcely group them with *Ben-Hur* and *The Big Parade.* And I am hoping that *Gone With the Wind* will make even *The Big Parade* and *Ben-Hur* seem like small grossers. I think that in the handling of the picture by Al, as against another distributor, there is literally a difference of millions of dollars, and I think that Al is out to get a record on the gross of the picture that is not likely to be approached by any other film for many years. I feel, too, that in the psychological approach to the picture of the trade and of exhibitors, particularly, there is also a difference that may amount to hundreds of thousands or even millions. It is for this reason that even a single inclusion of the film on the same basis as other films in any ad seems to me to be wrong.

Of course it is entirely possible—God forbid!—that I am wrong; that the picture will not be what Al and I hope. . . .

As you have no doubt heard and read, our troubles are by no means over. Vic Fleming collapsed on us, and we had to make another directorial switch. But Sam Wood seems to have taken over beautifully and I don't think there is going to be any letdown in quality. I have two other units shooting presently, and there is one stage of the picture at which five units will actually be shooting simultaneously! It looks to me as though we will be finished with the picture, exclusive of montages and an enormous amount of trick [special-effects] work, about the middle of June.

Are you likely to be out here soon? I'm dying for you to see some of the stuff.

Cordially,
David O. Selznick

To: Mr. Klune   May 5, 1939

When are we planning on doing the big pullback shot?[89] It is uncertain yet whether or not Mr. Fleming is coming back on the picture, and until we know, I think it might be preferable to hold this for him. We should know by Monday.

I am not at all satisfied that the fire sequence is as good as it ought to be, and I think that at comparatively little expense we could improve it enormously. Until we get a chance to study this, therefore, I think it would be wise to hold the shooting of the plates[90] for it. Do you see any reason why this couldn't be scheduled as the last thing that Gable and Leigh do, or as one of the last?

                                                                      DOS

To: Mr. Ginsberg   May 19, 1939

I have had a very long talk with Vic about speeding up on the rest of the picture and he, as always, expressed himself as ready to do anything and everything.

He was more than agreeable to having Sam Wood set up a unit for shooting nights or Sundays or any other time, and expressed himself as being willing that we should have five units going if we could expedite the completion of the picture.

He asked me to suggest anything and everything that could be done for him to speed things up. I think it might be a good idea if you had a talk with Vic immediately. Read him this note if you wish, and in any event, express my appreciation for his attitude and for his desire to cooperate.

Among other things that I think could be done are the following:

I think that Hal Kern should spend practically his entire time on the set, figuring out ways and means of cooking up suggestions and of gathering them from Menzies and myself, etc., to substitute simple angles that do not take time for elaborate angles, where these elaborate angles are not materially helpful to the scene. As I told Vic, when we get into the hall, I think we are going to have to use a boom to get the proper effects, and actually the boom will probably save time. But in the simple, intimate scenes, I think we can use pans and dollies in

---

[89]The famous scene at the Atlanta railroad depot, showing Scarlett amid scores of wounded Confederate soldiers as the camera pulls up and back on a construction crane (no camera crane extant would go high enough, and helicopter rigs were decades away).
[90]Scenes to be used for background projection in process photography.

substitution for difficult boom shots with no perceptible loss of value on the screen but with an enormous saving in cost.[91]

I also think that if Hal were on the set, he could discuss with Vic between setups ways and means of reducing the shooting, such as, for instance, by not worrying about a complete approved take of an angle which we are only going to use partially; eliminating close-ups which are likely never to be used; conceiving two-shots instead of individuals, etc., etc.

I think also that it is important that Vic be more precise about setting the exact first setup[92] for the next morning the night before, instead of so often changing this setup in the morning. On this, too, I think he might feel better if Hal were with him and if Hal could send for Menzies—but only when and where he thought this would be an advantage. To me there is no reason for changing setups in the morning except on the rarest occasions.

I think that the day's work could be laid out so that shots involving players other than Gable are left until after six o'clock, so as to get a longer day.

I do not think that anybody in the unit realizes the cost of the delays. Each of the items above may seem like very little, but I think it would be staggering to the unit if they realized that a saving of four days, let us say, would save between $60,000 and $75,000. I know that Hal Kern was shocked today when I explained to him that one half a day lost on an elaborate boom shot means a loss of $7500, and certainly the perceptible difference on the screen is worth not a tiny fraction of this amount, especially in view of the unprecedented production values we have in the picture now, as well as those we will have in future sequences, where we will not have these restrictions. . . .

I seriously think that unless you and I personally both drive on through the remaining weeks with daily pressure, we are going to run into serious trouble. I think it is going to take the combined efforts of yourself and myself to accomplish a difference in cost that could well amount to $100,000. . . . Quite apart from the cost factor, everybody's nerves are getting on the ragged edge, and God only knows what will happen if we don't get this damn thing finished. . . . If it weren't for

---

[91]"Panning" the camera is sweeping it horizontally; "dollying" involves wheels on the camera unit allowing it to move about on the floor while photographing. "Boom shots" are made with a crane, which enables the camera to sweep up, down, or laterally during filming. A boom shot requires more time to set up, light, rehearse, and shoot.

[92]The positioning of camera, lighting, sound equipment, actors, etc., for any given shot.

the pressure of the remainder of the script and on *Intermezzo*, I personally would devote myself almost exclusively to the precutting of each scene and to figuring out ways and means of shortening the shooting time on each sequence. . . .

DOS

To: Mr. Klune   May 25, 1939

Despite my various precautions in the matter, in looking at the cut stuff, it seems to me that the doubling of Gable by [stunt man and later second-unit director] Yakima Canutt, and even more so by the other double, is in some cases quite apparent, and I think it is going to cause us eventually to cut out some effective shots or to have to trim them greatly.

Judging by the film, there was little or no effort exerted to study an exact duplicate of Gable's costume, how it was creased, etc. . . . I wish that on the remaining shots to be made with the doubles, particularly those which Menzies does, you will see to it that more care is taken about this matter. . . .

Also please charge some one individual with the responsibility of approximating the way Gable carries himself, the way he wears his hat and costume, the way he walks, etc., and also, changing with clothes the figures of the doubles to get a more exact match of Gable's figure.

DOS

To: Mr. Leslie Howard   May 27, 1939

Dear Leslie:

I send you herewith a copy of that book you ought to get around to reading some time, called *Gone With the Wind.* I think the book has a great future and might make a very good picture.

Seriously, you will remember that you promised me faithfully not merely to know the paddock scene backward, but also to read those pages of the book from which it was taken, in order to get the true import of the scene, and in order to understand the full-length portrait of Ashley that these pages give. You won't have to read a great deal —only pages 525 to 535 inclusive.

Promise?

I'll check up on you!

Cordially,
DOS

MR. JOHN HAY WHITNEY   JUNE 27, 1939
630 FIFTH AVENUE
NEW YORK, N.Y.

SOUND THE SIREN. SCARLETT O'HARA COMPLETED HER
PERFORMANCE AT NOON TODAY. GABLE FINISHES TONIGHT OR IN
THE MORNING, AND WE WILL BE SHOOTING UNTIL FRIDAY WITH
BIT PEOPLE. I AM GOING ON THE BOAT FRIDAY NIGHT AND YOU
CAN ALL GO TO THE DEVIL. WE ARE TRYING TO KEEP VIVIEN'S
ARRIVAL IN NEW YORK THURSDAY A SECRET. . . . VIVIEN IS
EXPECTING A CALL FROM YOU, SO IF YOU CAN ARRANGE ONE
EVENING OR SUNDAY FOR HER AND LARRY [Olivier], I THINK IT
WOULD BE A NICE THING TO DO. . . .

                                                                  DAVID

The Hon. William B. Hartsfield, Mayor   July 17, 1939
Atlanta, Georgia

Dear Mayor Hartsfield:

I am in receipt of your telegram concerning the première of *Gone With the Wind*.

The rumors which you have heard have no foundation. Neither we, nor Loew's, Incorporated (the distributors of the picture), have ever given any thought to opening in any place but Atlanta, as I have repeatedly assured Governor Rivers, yourself, Miss Mitchell, and other important Georgians. . . .

For your information, I am afraid that I am going to have to ask the public, which has been so kind in its attention to the production, to be patient. The picture proper is completed, but some of the important effects including montage and battle scenes remain to be photographed. Furthermore, the picture is presently four and a half hours long in its rough assembly, and it is going to take me a considerable length of time to edit at least one hour out of the picture. When all this is finished, there remain the scoring and sound effects, which take a great deal of time; the matching of the Technicolor, which is an elaborate, painstaking, and time-devouring procedure; and the making of the prints themselves. It is my hope that all of these processes will be completed by the end of November, but even this is going to take backbreaking effort on the part of my entire organization. It has been my hope that we might make the première in Atlanta November 15, which, as I understand it, is the 75th anniversary of the burning of

Atlanta. While this is, at the moment, much more of a hope than an expectation, I mention it here, if only to show you the thought which we have given to the Atlanta première. . . .

Cordially and sincerely yours,

To: Mr. Whitney   August 25, 1939

I feel that one of the shrewd things that we have done from a showmanship standpoint has been the manner of our handling the publicity on the picture, so that the public does not know today what the characters look like. I am certain that if we had opened the flood-gates of publicity on the picture at the time we started it, as we were sorely tempted to do, and as is usually not merely done but eagerly sought-after with pictures, the public would by now be thoroughly familiar with the characters and the scenes, and by the time we release the picture some months hence, it would seem like a reissue. This is still my attitude about the picture edition,[93] and about many other publicity ideas which we have turned down.

I have wakened in the middle of the night with the temptation to come over and set a match to all the stills on the picture so that they would never be published or seen anyplace, anywhere. I am more convinced that I can properly express that the more we can keep under cover exactly what the characters and scenes look like, the more avid the public will be to see the picture itself—and, equally impor-tant, the more excited it will be when it does see the picture.

It has been no small task of negative handling of publicity to keep the picture fresh and alive. We have succeeded in doing this, I think you will agree. Suddenly to do a rightabout-face after the struggle we have been through on this score, and to let down the bars, would in my opinion be madness and would be hurting the picture to an extent that we cannot guess. However strong the at-traction of the picture, we must bear in mind that its continuing attraction value, over what we hope will be a couple of years, is dependent upon word-of-mouth advertising, and this word-of-mouth advertising is going to be dependent, of course, upon how much the public enjoys the picture, and its enjoyment in turn is going to be dependent to some indeterminable degree upon how

[93]The motion-picture edition of the novel, which would include still photographs from the film.

fresh the picture will be when it sees it, and the extent of its excitement over finally having the thrill of seeing the characters and scenes come to life. . . .

As to your inquiry about my statement that we are "not after publicity on *Wind*": My attitude is simply that we should never be in the position of *seeking* publicity on the picture. Unless something suddenly happens that we cannot foresee, we are going to get all the publicity that we want, even on this picture, by simply properly supplying the demand—without ever having to go out to plant anything. . . .

DOS

To: Mr. Howard Strickling[94]   August 30, 1939
cc: Mr. Hebert

Dear Howard:

. . . It may interest you to know that I have Mr. [Nicholas] Schenck's support in my attitude about the length. He saw it in 24,300 feet[95] and told me that it was his judgment that I should not attempt to get it down to any length just for length's sake—that I should cut it purely for quality. Since that running, I have reduced it to slightly under 20,000 feet[96] but this without montages, which will probably swell it another 500 feet. I frankly think we are going to have a hell of a job getting more than 1000 feet out of it from this point on without materially damaging it, and this I wouldn't do for anything or anybody on earth. And I feel that if anything, the length of the picture is added showmanship, just as the length of the book was, according to the publishers, a factor in its fabulous success.

I didn't go after length any more than Margaret Mitchell did, but the story naturally required extreme length, and I regard it as old-fashioned to feel that there is anything wrong with having a picture of this importance and quality in such a length for the public that it gets its entertainment in one fine picture instead of two weak or average pictures. . . .

Cordially and sincerely yours,
DOS

[94]Director of Publicity for MGM on the West Coast.
[95]Four hours and twenty-seven minutes.
[96]Three hours and forty minutes. This was to be the length of the final version.

To: Mr. Howard Dietz   September 12, 1939
cc: Miss Katharine Brown

We sneak-previewed the picture at Riverside Saturday night with sensational success. Jock can tell you all about it, since he was there. The reaction was everything that we hoped for and expected.

DOS

To: Miss Katharine Brown   September 20, 1939
                                        NOT SENT

Dear Kay:

Please tell Miss Mitchell that I was terribly worried about the ending of the picture, as we found it impossible to get into script form even the hint that Scarlett might get Rhett back that is inferred in the book. We tried two or three ways, and even shot one indicating something of the kind after she went back to Tara, but it didn't work; and I finally cooked up an ending of my own which was pretty loudly jeered at on paper, and which I imagine will sound pretty awful to you and Miss Mitchell on paper, but which, believe me, worked like a charm. My own feeling always was that the whole picture led up to Rhett's saying, "Frankly, my dear I don't give a damn." (Incidentally, one of my greatest disappointments about the picture is that Breen[97] has forbidden the use of this line, and to my disgust, and I imagine Miss Mitchell's, Rhett says, "Frankly, my dear I just don't care.") He has taken such a beating from Scarlett that I think it would be the most puerile sort of ending to negate everything that has preceded it by bringing them together, and I did not succumb to this temptation, despite the coaxing of many Hollywoodites. In reaching for a satisfactory ending for motion-picture purposes, I felt that the one thing that was really open to us was to stress the Tara thought, more even than Miss Mitchell did. Accordingly, the ending is as follows (and I beg you and Miss Mitchell not to judge this until you see it in the film itself, because on paper I imagine it will sound as bad to you as it did to everyone else I tried it on):

After Rhett leaves Scarlett she turns from the door reading the lines, sobbingly, "I can't let him go. I can't. There must be some way to bring him back. Oh, I can't think about this now. I'll go crazy if I do. . . . I'll . . . I'll think about it tomorrow." Still crying, she sinks on the steps,

[97]Joseph I. Breen, West Coast assistant to Will H. Hays.

moaning, "But I must think about it, I must think about it. What is there to do? What is there that matters?" with her head in her arms; suddenly we hear the ghostlike voice of Gerald saying, "Do you mean to tell me, Katie Scarlett O'Hara, that Tara doesn't mean anything to you? Why, land's the only thing that matters. It's the only thing that lasts."; then the ghostlike voice of Ashley: "Something you love better than me, though you may not know it. Tara."; then the ghostlike voice of Rhett: "It's this from which you get your strength; the red earth of Tara." Then part of each speech is repeated in turn with increasing tempo and volume; then the last phrase of each speech is repeated with still more tempo and volume; and finally, the voice of each of the three men saying in turn, "Tara." During this Scarlett has been emerging from her despair, raising her head slowly and reacting to the realization that she still has Tara. She lifts her head and, as the camera moves in to a big close-up of her, says, "Home, to Tara! After all, tomorrow is another day." We immediately dissolve to Scarlett standing at Tara in silhouette in the very spot where we saw her standing with Gerald earlier in the picture as he spoke to her about the land. The camera pulls back just as it did on Gerald and Scarlett to an extreme long shot as we come to our end.

I had a couple of other endings in mind, and I tried this one out with considerable trepidation, but to my delighted surprise, not one single preview card made any comment against it, and it seemed to give the picture a tremendous lift at the end where it was necessary, and where, without something of the kind, we might have ended on a terrifically depressing note.

Apparently there is no thought in the minds of anyone that this is not exactly faithful to the book, in spirit at least, even though it isn't one hundred per cent book material, as is true with so much of the picture.

I think Miss Mitchell will also be interested to hear that our preview cards, which were probably the most amazing any picture has ever had in their praise (a good two thirds of which used such phrases as "Greatest picture ever made," "Greatest picture since *The Birth of a Nation*," "Screen's greatest achievement of all times," etc.) were largely filled with praise for the faithfulness of the picture to the book, any number saying that they had no conception and no hope that they could get as much of the book as this, or as faithful a job as this. . . .

To go back to the matter of the ending, and to answer a little more specifically Miss Mitchell's question, to my great pleasure not one preview card mentioned that they wanted to see Rhett and Scarlett together again. I think they still hope that they will get together, but it leaves them something to discuss, just as the end of the book did.

DOS

MR. BEN HECHT   SEPTEMBER 25, 1939
PERRY LANE
NEW YORK

DEAR BEN: THERE ARE ONLY SEVEN TITLES[98] NEEDED FOR "GONE
WITH THE WIND" AND I AM CERTAIN YOU COULD BAT THEM OUT
IN A FEW MINUTES, ESPECIALLY SINCE A FEW OF THEM CAN BE
BASED ON TITLES YOU WROTE WHILE HERE. WILL YOU DO THESE
FOR ME IN ACCORDANCE WITH YOUR PROMISE? COULD SEND THEM
TO YOU IN SUCH FORM THAT YOU WOULD KNOW EXACTLY WHAT
WE NEEDED. VERY ANXIOUS TO GET PICTURE INTO LABORATORY
AT ONCE AND WOULD APPRECIATE IT IF YOU COULD TACKLE THEM
IMMEDIATELY UPON THEIR RECEIPT. PLEASE WIRE REPLY.
CORDIALLY

DAVID

To: Miss Katharine Brown   October 7, 1939

I am in receipt of Howard Dietz's letter to you concerning the billing on *Gone With the Wind*. . . .

Frankly, I don't understand Dietz's attitude about segregating Gable. I suggest you call to his attention that they costarred Gable with Constance Bennett, of all people; that he was costarred with Marion Davies, with his name coming second; also that they have costarred Norma Shearer and other important stars with everybody but Baby Sandy.

Personally, I think that it is all a lot of nonsense, and I think the smartest actor in the business is Bing Crosby, who, through his entire starring career, has insisted that they costar somebody, even if it was a bit player, so that he couldn't be blamed alone if the picture failed. But regardless of how I feel about it, we are bound by contracts, so let's start out by saying that whatever is done for Gable must also be done

[98]The written introductory sequence and other titles which set the scene and condense the narrative throughout.

for Leigh, [Leslie] Howard, and de Havilland. It is not a matter of discussion, or of MGM's wishes, or of my own wishes—we have contracts, and if they think they are going to get Leslie Howard to agree to a change, or Warners to agree on a change with reference to de Havilland, I suggest they try it. . . .

It accordingly comes down to whether we use the four stars' names before the title or after the title, on the main title, and in advertising; and the relative size of the names of the four stars to the name of the picture.

As to the main title, I will take this up with Al Lichtman, as Dietz suggests. We have our main title all laid out on the basis of having *Gone With the Wind* come first, and in a unique manner; but if MGM for some strange reason thinks that Clark Gable is more important than *Gone With the Wind*, and should come first, and wants to bitch up our main title layout, I suppose there's nothing I can do but get up a new main title, since under our contract with MGM Gable's name must precede *Gone With the Wind*.

As to the advertising, I still think that to use the names of four stars in anything more than fifty per cent of the height, width, and heaviness of type that is used for *Gone With the Wind* would be the equivalent of having done the same thing with Henry Walthall and Lillian Gish and Bobby Harron on *The Birth of a Nation*. What was sold was *The Birth of a Nation*, and what should be sold is *Gone With the Wind*. I would prefer that their names come under the title with the word "starring," but if they insist upon putting them above the title, here again I don't suppose there is anything we can do about it, and the important thing is to make sure that *Gone With the Wind* is not minimized. If Gable alone were starred in the picture, I would still feel this way, but since we must use the names of four stars, if we try to use each of them [in a size] seventy-five per cent of the title we are going to have very messy advertising, and the names of the four stars will occupy much more room on the billing than *Gone With the Wind*. . . .[99]

Also, in case Mr. Dietz does not know it, it is important that he should know that MGM receives no credit on advertising, other than its distribution. . . .

You can tell Howard for me that after what I, personally, and our company have gone through, and after the investment we have made,

---

[99]The names of the four stars, in a size fifty per cent of the film's title, followed the film's title on the screen and in all advertising.

we expect our company to benefit and the picture to be known as a Selznick International picture, and not as an MGM picture. . . .

DOS

To: Mr. O'Shea   October 9, 1939

Some time ago, it was my intention to have, in addition to the Sidney Howard credit on *Gone With the Wind*, a list of contributing writers. I would rather now abandon this idea, first because while it is true that Sidney Howard did only a portion of the script, there is no other writer who worked on it whose contribution is worth serious mention; second, because our titles are cluttered enough as it is; and third because I don't want to deprive Sidney Howard, and more particularly his widow,[100] of any of the glory that may be attendant upon his last job.

When I mentioned to Oliver Garrett that I had some intention of giving him a contributory credit, he seemed rather upset and felt to my amazement that the credit ought to read: Adaptation by Sidney Howard and Screenplay by himself, which would of course be ridiculous. But rather than get into any argument at that time, I told him that when the script was finished, I would take it up further. Since that time, I myself did the last half or two thirds of the script without anybody's help, and Garrett's claim has become even more ridiculous. However, I want to avoid the possibility of any trouble with him about this, and I wonder what we should do about it. It would be most unpleasant if Garrett started filing claims after the picture was released; and most difficult and expensive if we had to revise our credits subsequent to the making of the prints and the advertising. Since the advertising must go into work at once, and the main title cards are now being lettered, I regret that I have let this go so long, but it frankly hasn't occurred to me recently until today.

What is your advice in the matter? Do you think you ought to call Garrett? Or should we simply ignore him? Or should we take it up with the Writers Guild, or what?

I don't think there is a chance of anybody else advancing any claim in connection with it even though, if you should discuss it with Garrett, you can say frankly that of the comparatively small amount of material in the picture which is not from the book, most is my own personally, and the only original lines of dialogue which are not my own are a few from Sidney Howard and a few from Ben Hecht and a couple more

---

[100]Howard died in August 1939, after an accident on his farm in Massachusetts.

from John Van Druten. Offhand I doubt that there are ten original words of Garrett's in the whole script. As to construction, this is about eighty per cent my own, and the rest divided between Jo Swerling and Sidney Howard, with Hecht having contributed materially to the construction of one sequence.

If necessary, Bobby [Barbara Keon] could send the script of the picture as it stands, but this might take some time that we could not afford; and even this wouldn't prove anything to Garrett unless he saw that the only things from his script which are in the finished picture are construction points which were laid out by myself with Jo Swerling. He might try to prove his point by showing that the picture is a lot closer to his script from a construction standpoint than any script of Howard's, which is a fact; but the construction of his script is based on the notes taken by Bobby of the conference between Swerling and myself in Bermuda, which notes are available. And in any discussion with Garrett, if he gets tough, you might say that we have examined the notes taken by Bobby of the conferences between Swerling and myself, that these are available, and that his contribution could be proved before any arbitrators as being practically nonexistent.[101]

DOS

To: Mr. Max Steiner, Mr. Lou Forbes   October 9, 1939

The score on *Intermezzo* is receiving a great deal of comment and extraordinarily favorable attention, for which I thank and congratulate you both.

The outstanding point that has been commented on by so many, and that certainly has served to make the score so beautiful, is its use of classical music to such a great extent instead of original music hastily written. This is a point on which I have been fighting for years, with little success. . . .

I have had a dozen people ask me hopefully whether *Gone With the Wind* will give the feeling of the Old South in its whole score— whether the score will be based entirely, or to a large extent, upon the strains and songs and compositions of that particular period and civilization. And I am increasingly depressed by the prospect that we are not going to use the great classical music of the world for our score, nor are we even going to use the great Southern pieces for a large section of our score. But if we don't, we will have failed to learn the

[101]Sidney Howard received sole writing credit.

lesson of concert managers, radio broadcasts, and of our own *Intermezzo*.

I should like you both to give this your immediate thought and I should appreciate it if Mr. Steiner would adapt whatever his plans are for the score to use, instead of two or three hours of original music, little original music and a score based on the great music of the world, and of the South in particular.[102]

After you have discussed this between yourselves, I should like to see both of you.

DOS

To: Mr. Kern, Mr. Forbes   October 10, 1939
cc: Mr. Ginsberg

I am very serious about wanting the whole score of *Gone With the Wind* played for me before it is recorded, by as small an orchestra as is practicable for the purpose. This should be as far ahead of the recording as is possible, to permit me to express opinions on anything I don't like. I don't mind hearing it in sections if this will expedite matters. And further, if it will help avoid any arguments or waste of time later, perhaps two or three musicians could be gotten in to play the themes for me before we go into the expense of arrangements.

DOS

To: Mr. John Hay Whitney   October 12, 1939

Dear Jock:

I am about to go to work on the struggle on "Frankly, my dear, I don't give a damn." Can I count on your help if I need it? If I can't persuade the Breen office here to see reason on it—particularly since the *Oxford Dictionary* clearly indicates that this use of it is not considered even mild profanity, but simply a colloquialism—then I think the best way of getting it through would be for you to advise Hays that you insist upon a special Board of Directors meeting being called immediately for the purpose of ruling on it. I question that the company heads would waste time at a meeting on a silly point like this, and if you call two or three of them personally, I imagine they would tell Hays to forget it. Nick [Schenck] won't be much help to us because he doesn't

---

[102]The final score consisted of mostly original music with "Southern pieces," and military and patriotic tunes interspersed for poignancy and historical propriety.

think there is any value to it—but he hasn't had the advantage that I have had of seeing it both ways and of appreciating the vast difference to the finish of the picture. (You know, confidentially, we shot it both ways—if they knew about this, they might get sore.) . . .

We are, of course, fighting time—but I am cutting the negative in such a way that up to the last few weeks before the picture goes East, we can still cut it in. At this moment all I want to know is whether you are with me, suh!

DOS

Mr. E. J. Mannix   October 17, 1939
Metro-Goldwyn-Mayer Studios   NOT SENT
Culver City, California

Dear Eddie:

I have been informed, hopefully mistakenly, that you have done some barking about an alleged intent on my part to do in Vic Fleming on the matter of credits. I would be happy to hear that there has been a misunderstanding.

I like to believe there would be very little trouble about credits in this business if all producers had the generosity about credits that I always insist upon from the people who publicize, advertise, and distribute my pictures. I have always gone out of my way to build up the work of the director. . . . And it may perhaps be pertinent to call to your attention that it was I who originated the system at MGM of giving a separate card to the directors, insisting upon this for my productions despite the long-standing MGM custom of slipping them in on one line on the main title.

The truth of the matter about credit for the other directors is this: I asked Vic Fleming whether he would like to see us include a card crediting people who had contributed greatly to the picture, but who had no place in the program credits—among them, George Cukor, who spent over two years in the preparation of the picture, worked with me on most of the sets and most of the costumes, and through the long, agonizing months of casting, and who, further, has practically all of his scenes still in the picture; Sam Wood, who stepped in so graciously when Vic was taken ill, and who has a great many sequences in the picture; Ben Hecht and Oliver Garrett, if upon investigation their contributions to the script would have seemed to warrant their inclusion even on such a card; cameramen of second units who contributed some of the most magnificent individual shots ever seen on the screen; Katharine Brown, to whose insistence and foresight I owe the purchase of the story. . . . I was motivated in this idea by the gracious gesture of crediting Sidney Franklin on [*Goodbye,*] *Mr. Chips* [1939]. . . . My conversation with Vic on the subject literally didn't last thirty seconds. I asked Vic how he felt about it, but I got no further than the names of Cukor and Wood; Vic obviously, and no doubt understandably, wasn't happy about the idea, saying in so many words that he didn't think it was necessary to credit them on the screen. I immediately, and without further discussion, told him to forget about it; and as far as I was concerned, it was a closed issue.[103]

Actually, I am not even sure that all of these people would have liked credit. I know that George has particularly requested me never to use his name in connection with the picture, as the incident concerning him is a closed one—and happily, and as I predicted when I urged that he be given *The Women,* he has emerged at least as important in the trade as ever before. . . . Sam Wood has stepped in on other jobs before, and has had other people step in to help on his jobs, so I am certain that he expects nothing. . . . But in my happiness over the picture—and, far from my desire to do anyone out of credit, in my eagerness to give credit to everyone who contributed—apparently I was misunderstood. I am sorry, not so much at being misunderstood, because this seems to be a particular characteristic of Hollywood, but over the apparent disappointing unfamiliarity with my character.

Vic Fleming will receive enormous credit for *Gone With the Wind.* I told him at the time that we persuaded him into doing it, and all through the months when he was uncertain—to say the least—about the result of both my labors and his own efforts, that it would make him far more outstanding in the industry than ever before in his career. . . .

Candidly, Eddie, I don't like interference in what is this studio's business; and my feelings are considerably stronger than this when it comes to any inference that Vic Fleming needs protection from me by anybody. There is no occasion for this, and the only conclusion I can draw, if the facts are as reported to me, is that somebody is trying to build themselves up as Vic's friend against an enemy from the Land of Oz. My relations with Vic were completely pleasant and cordial. I don't recall a single unpleasant moment between us through what was probably the most nerve-racking experience any producer and director have had to share in the history of Hollywood. And it would be a

[103]Victor Fleming received sole directorial credit.

great pity indeed if, having gone through the war together, his peace-time pals gave rise to even a rumor of difficulty, or differences, or of doing each other in. . . .

Sincerely yours,

To: Mr. Klune   October 17, 1939

I have been thinking about how difficult I must be to live with these days, and the amount of barking that I have done, both verbally and by memo, at you, Lyle Wheeler, and some of the other boys around the lot. I should appreciate it if you would explain to them that I am uncomfortably aware that I must have been pretty awful; that it doesn't mean that I am not appreciative of all their efforts; and that the only excuse I can offer is that I am simply worn out, and I suppose my nerves are pretty well shot. You can do me a service if you will explain this to any of the boys that I may have made unhappy.

DOS

Mr. Will H. Hays   October 20, 1939
Motion Picture Producers and Distributors of America, Inc.
28 West 44th Street
New York, N.Y.

bcc: Mr. Whitney, Mr. Calvert

Dear Mr. Hays:

As you probably know, the punch line of *Gone With the Wind*, the one bit of dialogue which forever establishes the future relationship between Scarlett and Rhett, is, "Frankly, my dear, I don't give a damn."

Naturally I am most desirous of keeping this line and, to judge from the reactions of two preview audiences, this line is remembered, loved, and looked forward to by the millions who have read this new American classic.

Under the code, Joe Breen is unable to give me permission to use this sentence because it contains the word "damn," a word specifically forbidden by the code.

As you know from my previous work with such pictures as *David Copperfield, Little Lord Fauntleroy, A Tale of Two Cities*, etc., I have always attempted to live up to the spirit as well as the exact letter of the producers' code. Therefore, my asking you to review the case, to look at the strip of film in which this forbidden word is contained, is not motivated by a whim. A great deal of the force and drama of *Gone With the Wind,* a project to which we have given three years of hard work and hard thought, is dependent upon that word.

It is my contention that this word as used in the picture is not an oath or a curse. The worst that could be said against it is that it is a vulgarism, and it is so described in the *Oxford English Dictionary.* Nor do I feel that in asking you to make an exception in this case, I am asking for the use of a word which is considered reprehensible by the great majority of American people and institutions. A canvass of the popular magazines shows that even such moral publications as *Woman's Home Companion, Saturday Evening Post, Collier's* and the *Atlantic Monthly,* use this word freely. I understand the difference, as outlined in the code, between the written word and the word spoken from the screen, but at the same time I think the attitude of these magazines toward "damn" gives an indication that the word itself is not considered abhorrent or shocking to audiences.

I do not feel that your giving me permission to use "damn" in this one sentence will open up the floodgates and allow every gangster picture to be peppered with "damns" from end to end. I do believe, however, that if you were to permit our using this dramatic word in its rightfully dramatic place, in a line that is known and remembered by millions of readers, it would establish a helpful precedent, a precedent which would give to Joe Breen discretionary powers to allow the use of certain harmless oaths and ejaculations whenever, in his opinion, they are not prejudicial to public morals.

Since we are trying to put *Gone With the Wind* into the laboratory this week, I should appreciate your taking this matter under immediate consideration. Mr. Lowell Calvert, our New York representative, has a print of the scene referred to, which will take you literally only a few seconds to view. . . . However, you may feel it possible to give the consent without viewing the film.

The original of the line referred to is on page 1035 of the novel, *Gone With the Wind,* and you might have your secretary secure it for you.

We have been commended by preview audiences for our extremely faithful job on *Gone With the Wind,* and practically the only point that has been commented on as being missing is the curious (to audiences) omission of this line. It spoils the punch at the end of the picture, and on our very fade-out gives an impression of unfaithfulness after three hours and forty-five minutes of extreme fidelity to Miss Mitchell's work, which, as you know, has become an American Bible.

Thanking you for your cooperation in this,[104]

Cordially and sincerely yours,

Mr. Al Lichtman, Vice-President   October 20, 1939
Metro-Goldwyn-Mayer   NOT SENT
Culver City, California

Dear Mr. Lichtman:

I have listened to all the arguments, and I am more strongly than ever opposed to the policy that is presently planned on the selling of *Gone With the Wind*. I intend to do everything that is within my power to stop it. I am hopeful that you will not regard this as a personal issue between us, but will understand that it is entirely a matter of business. . . .

I think it is as wrong not to road show *Gone With the Wind* as it would have been wrong not to road show *The Big Parade* or *Ben-Hur*. In fact, I do not think there is anyone who will disagree with the argument that there is a vastly greater audience waiting in advance for *Gone With the Wind* than there was for either of these two pictures. And I do not believe that there is anything in present-day times or conditions to warrant the belief that the public will not go to see *Gone With the Wind* at road-show prices.

I think it is as wrong not to road show *Gone With the Wind* as it would have been not to road show *The Birth of a Nation*. In fact, I think it is infinitely more wrong. It is not for me to say that *Gone With the Wind* is as outstanding a picture for its day as *The Birth of a Nation* was when it was made; however, your own people have said this, and much more. But what I do claim is that *Gone With the Wind* actually has an infinitely greater audience waiting for it than *The Birth of a Nation* had in advance of its release. And I call to your attention that the public paid road-show prices to see *The Birth of a Nation* to an amount, I understand, of between $10,000,000 to $15,000,000, at a time when motion-picture theaters were charging five to fifteen cents per ticket. It is inconceivable that the American public, which was willing to pay road-show prices at that time, is not willing to pay them now. The failure, or the mild success, of dozens of other road shows is no criterion. There were dozens of road-show failures at the time of

[104]Permission was granted to use "damn."

Ben-Hur and *The Big Parade*. Clearly the pictures did not warrant road showing. . . .

I regard your ownership of fifty per cent of the profits of *Gone With the Wind* as the most generous deal ever made by a producer in the history of the picture business, and I don't think you need *more* than the original terms to make the deal a good one for you! . . .

It is possible that it is better for your company to get the money in quickly, but it is not a determining factor with us. And in any event, it is not clear to me that there would be any material difference in the speed of revenue if the picture were played two-a-day, at road-show prices, instead of three-a-day at lesser prices: there might be a few months' difference at the most. . . .

On a short picture one argument against road show is in the number of performances: there can be five or six turnovers daily on a picture of average length. It is utterly impossible to have more than three shows on *Gone With the Wind* daily unless the first performance is held for night watchmen. It is conceivable that an early-morning show might do some business—although the argument that has been advanced in relation to *The Wizard of Oz* in New York has no bearing whatsoever in this case. In the first place, Mickey Rooney was appearing in person for a limited length of time, and people knew that if they did not catch him during this particular engagement, they might never be able to see him again. In the second place, it was vacation time, and the morning crowds were traceable to the inclusion of great numbers of children—as witness the falling-off of business on *The Wizard of Oz* as the day went on. And in the third place, *Gone With the Wind* is *not* a picture for children, by the widest stretch of the imagination.

I understand that Mr. Rodgers[105] has agreed to have an intermission in the picture. It would be a defiance of the laws of nature to assume that there would not be a substantial percentage of the audience who would find it necessary to go to the lavatory in the course of almost four hours of film. Since the time of ancient Greece, theatrical managers have known the wisdom and even the necessity of intermissions where the performance deals with one story. To make a guinea pig of *Gone With the Wind*, which you state is the greatest picture ever made, and make it the great experiment of the no-intermission entertainment, would, in my opinion, be unthinkable. . . .

But Mr. Rodgers has warned us that in his opinion, the intermission plan will not prevail after it is tried out. It is not hard to understand

[105]William F. Rodgers, Loew's, Inc. General Sales Manager.

why he makes this prediction. If tickets are going to be sold for un-reserved seats, and standing room is going to be sold to an unsuspecting public, there would at intermission time be a mad scramble for the seats of those people who had gone to the lavatories. The members of the audience would be faced with the alternatives of sitting miserably through the second half of the picture, and taking a chance on bladder trouble, or of losing their seats, and for this alternative they have paid .75¢ to $1.10. Obviously, if an intermission is necessary, and I can tell you point-blank, without the slightest equivocation, that an intermission is not merely desirable but essential, the only answer is reserved seats.

Since no amount of argument could convince me that an intermission was not an absolute essential to the enjoyment of the picture, and to the health and comfort of the audience; and since reserved seats are a necessity if there is to be an intermission, a scale of road-show prices becomes the obvious choice as to policy, if only in order to give the theater a large enough revenue.

This picture represents the greatest work of my life, in the past and very likely in the future. I am associated with it in the public mind, and will be further associated with it. I do not intend, without every struggle that it is possible for me to put up, to be blamed for making a miserable botch of its exhibition to the point where a large part of the audience sees it backward, or a large part of the audience sees it incomplete, or a large part of the audience stands in line, and then in back of the theater, for part or all of its four hours running time. I certainly shall fight to the end that the public may see the picture as we have produced it, and may enjoy the picture in accordance with its merit. . . .

You will recall that you laughed at the incident I reported to you of the woman who said she had been saving her money to pay $1.65 per seat to see *Gone With the Wind*, and to pay $1.10 per seat for the members of her family for "second-best tickets"; but who, upon hearing that she would be able to buy the best seats, unreserved, for $1.10, said that she certainly would not do this, and that if this was to be the price of the best tickets, obviously the picture wasn't what it was cracked up to be, and would soon be playing at lesser prices, and she would wait until it got to the neighborhood houses at the regular price. Since then, I have had occasion to cross-examine a number of other people in the middle-class and lower-middle-class brackets. The reaction has in each case been identical, and has, in addition, been one of great disappointment that an event which they had looked forward to for so long was evaporating. I firmly believe that there are countless thousands of people who will be eager to pay $1.10 for "second-best tickets" and $1.65 for the best seats, provided they can get reserved seats and it can be a gala event; but who will refuse to pay .75¢ to $1.10 for unreserved seats at something that is not an event. I believe that there are countless thousands of people who will be enraged at being gouged for advanced prices to stand in line, to take their chances at seeing the picture partially, to see the picture in discomfort—but who would storm the box offices to pay $1.65 to be sure of a seat, and to see it under the proper circumstances. . . .[106]

Actually, my principal present objection is to the folly of leaping into a distribution plan, and an exhibition plan, on *Gone With the Wind* without experimentation, and from which there can be no retreat. Nobody on earth knows how *Gone With the Wind* should be handled; and nobody on earth can find out without experimentation. Even the hours at which the picture should be exhibited should, if the merchandising is to be sound and thorough, be determined by a nation-wide Gallup poll, so that in each city it could be learned what hours were most convenient for the public to see this extraordinarily long film. In one city there might be as much as an hour's difference from another city, according to the working hours of the greatest number of the population. . . . It might even be found necessary—in fact I believe that it *would* be found necessary—to exhibit the picture simultaneously in two or more theaters in each city, with different starting times, so that the individual members of the public could choose the hours that fitted into their working hours, their retiring hours, and their family plans for lunch, for dinner, for taking care of the children, and for any number of other things. To assume that we can sit in Hollywood, or in New York, and decide at what hours the American public should see *Gone With the Wind* is in itself a fantastic presumption. . . .

I am aware that the picture will do tremendous business under your plan, or under *any* plan, but we would never know what we had passed up; and if your plan should be proven wrong, we are doomed and must immediately fall back upon runs in regular theaters at regular prices. . . .

Very truly yours,

[106]The modified road-show policy eventually agreed to specified an absolute minimum admission charge of .75 cents for the morning and afternoon performances, $1.00 for evenings, and $1.50 for preferred seats. Reserved seating was optional, but MGM demanded that a thirty-minute lapse of time be provided between each showing. The intermission time during the film was decided by the exhibitor and distributor representative.

To: Mr. John Hay Whitney, Mr. John Wharton   October 30, 1939

Most of the complaints that have come to us from various patriotic organizations are based on an alleged distortion of history by us to the detriment of the Northern troops. We have not only followed Miss Mitchell, but we have also been careful to have each of our historical facts checked thoroughly by a historian, Mr. Kurtz. Further, we have actually toned down considerably Miss Mitchell's portrait of the depredations of the invaders. I have had compiled by Mr. Kurtz an answer to the detailed charges of inaccuracy and I should appreciate having the opinion of each of you as to whether you think we should get up a form letter, to be individually typed of course, replying to these charges; or whether you think we should simply ignore them.

Mr. W. F. Rodgers   November 2, 1939
Loew's, Incorporated
1540 Broadway
New York City

cc: Mr. Whitney, Mr. Dietz, Mr. Rubin, Mr. Calvert

Dear Bill:
. . . I am anxious to do everything possible that the picture should be presented everywhere with taste and with showmanship. The old Belasco tradition of the theater, the Griffith and [theater managing director Samuel L. ("Roxy")] Rothafel method of presenting a picture as though it were a jewel, have been too long lost; and as in everything else that is offered the public, the way in which a production is presented is highly important. I regard it as doubly important in this case because I don't think the individual members of the audience feel that they're getting something that is worth extra money unless the method of presenting it indicates that we feel we have something extraordinary. I am hopeful that I personally will be able to supervise the details in New York, Los Angeles, and Atlanta; I'd like to feel also that when you see the picture under such circumstances, you will agree that these details should be watched closely everywhere. . . .

Cordially and sincerely,
David O. Selznick

To: Mr. Lou Forbes   November 7, 1939
cc: Mr. Ginsberg, Mr. Kern

Commencing today, and daily until the score of *GWTW* and the score of *Rebecca* are completely finished, I should like a *daily* report from you, without fail, telling me the exact progress of each score. In the case of *Gone With the Wind*, this should include exactly what Mr. Steiner and his associates have accomplished, and exactly, also, what has been accomplished by [composer and conductor Franz] Waxman on the so-called insurance score that we are having him write against the possibility that Max will not be ready by our deadline date. Please be sure that this report does not include hearsay information, but only facts that you yourself have checked.

DOS

To: Mr. Birdwell[107]   November 8, 1939

. . . The nation is now burdened with snoods for women's hair as a result of the Scarlett and Melanie snoods. I assume you know that the costumes of *Gone With the Wind* are the basis of at least fifty per cent of fashions at this present moment, and I am sure the whole business of the return to corsets is due to *Wind*. All of this is trivial and laughable in a world that is shaken by war, but women being what they are, I think it could make for excellent publicity. Because of my feeling about its trivial nature, though, I would suggest that the publicity be confined to the women's magazines, fan magazines, etc.

DOS

MR. JOHN HAY WHITNEY   NOVEMBER 9, 1939
SELZNICK INTERNATIONAL
630 FIFTH AVENUE
NEW YORK CITY

STEINER HAS AGAIN TOLD US HE CANNOT MEET THE DATE. WE DISCOUNT THIS VERY LARGELY BECAUSE STEINER IS NOTORIOUS FOR SUCH STATEMENTS AND WORKS WELL UNDER PRESSURE, AND I AM INCLINED TO TAKE THE CHANCE THAT WE CAN DRIVE HIM THROUGH, PARTICULARLY WITH THE PRECAUTIONARY MEASURES WE ARE TAKING WITH WAXMAN AND OTHERS. HOWEVER, THE

---

[107]Russell Birdwell and Associates, publicity and public-relations organization.

REASON WE ARE CONTINUING WITH HIM IS BECAUSE OF MY
BELIEF, TO WHICH I STILL CLING IN SPITE OF EVERYTHING, THAT
HIS WORK WILL BE A GREAT DEAL BETTER THAN IT SOUNDED ON A
FEW PIECES. TOMORROW, FRIDAY, HE IS RECORDING THE FIRST
SEVERAL REELS. IF QUALITY IS DISAPPOINTING, THIS, TOGETHER
WITH HIS PESSIMISTIC STATEMENTS, WOULD WARRANT PULLING
HIM OFF, PARTICULARLY IN VIEW OF FACT HERBERT STOTHART IS
DYING TO DO THE JOB AND GUARANTEES HE WOULD GET IT
THROUGH ON TIME, AND FROM INTIMATE KNOWLEDGE OF
STOTHART I KNOW HIS STATEMENTS CAN BE RELIED UPON.
STOTHART WAS MY SECOND CHOICE FOR THE JOB AND IT IS MY
REGRET NOW OF COURSE THAT HE WAS NOT FIRST CHOICE,
ALTHOUGH A COUPLE OF MONTHS AGO WHEN WE WERE READY TO
SWITCH, DUE TO FIRST INDICATIONS OF WARNER MANEUVERS
WITH STEINER, WE WERE TOLD BY MGM STOTHART WAS NOT
AVAILABLE AND THEREFORE CLUNG TO STEINER, BECAUSE I DO
NOT FEEL THERE IS ANYONE SCORING PICTURES WHO IS IN SAME
CLASS WITH STOTHART AND STEINER. IN CASE YOU ARE NOT
FAMILIAR WITH STOTHART'S WORK, YOU MAY PERHAPS RECALL HIS
SCORES FOR ME ON "NIGHT FLIGHT," "VIVA VILLA!," "DAVID
COPPERFIELD," AND "TALE OF TWO CITIES." I HAVE JUST HEARD
FOR THE FIRST TIME THAT STOTHART IS A NATIVE GEORGIAN.
VERY SECRETLY WE RAN THE PICTURE FOR HIM TODAY AND HE IS
SIMPLY FRANTIC WITH EAGERNESS AND ENTHUSIASM TO DO IT. HE
IS UNDER CONTRACT TO MGM BUT IS PRESENTLY DOING NOTHING,
WAITING FOR THEM TO DECIDE WHAT THEY ARE GOING TO DO
ABOUT "NORTHWEST PASSAGE," WHICH APPARENTLY IS A
HEADACHE. SINCE WE DO NOT WANT TO DECIDE ON THE SWITCH
UNTIL WE HEAR STEINER'S WORK OVER WEEKEND, WE ARE LOSING
PRECIOUS TIME WITH STOTHART IF HE IS TO DO JOB. WHAT I
WOULD LIKE TO DO IS TO START STOTHART SELECTING AND
WRITING IN THE MORNING WITH HIS FULL KNOWLEDGE THAT HE
MAY NOT GO AHEAD IF WE DECIDE TO PROCEED WITH STEINER
SUNDAY OR MONDAY. OR IT MIGHT BE DESIRABLE TO HAVE HIM GO
AHEAD AND WRITE THOSE REELS WHICH STEINER IS NOT WORKING
ON, IN CASE OF FURTHER TROUBLE WITH MAX AND AS OUR BEST
POSSIBLE INSURANCE OF COMPLETION. AS A THIRD ALTERNATIVE,
WE MIGHT HAVE HIM COLLABORATE WITH STEINER ON SCORE,
ALTHOUGH NOT AT ALL CERTAIN THIS WOULD WORK OUT. IN ANY
EVENT, I WOULD BE SOMEWHAT RELIEVED OF MY DEPRESSION
ABOUT THE QUALITY OF SCORE AND CONSIDERABLY RELIEVED OF

ALL OUR WORRIES ABOUT COMPLETION OF SCORE IF STOTHART
COULD START TO WORK WITH US IN THE MORNING. . . .

DAVID

To: Mr. Howard Dietz   November 9, 1939

Replying to your memo, it is not our intention to have a technician
accompany the print. The sound will be set, and I should like personally to supervise a rehearsal at the Atlanta theater. It won't be necessary for me to run the whole picture, but the night before the
première, or even the day of the première, I could see and hear
sections of it.

Would it, however, be possible to have any sort of hook-up from
wherever I am sitting to the booth the opening night? Or perhaps it
would be preferable to have some member of the theater staff seated
directly in front of me on the aisle so that I could chase him out during
the picture for anything that bothered me in connection with projection, sound, house lights, etc. Perhaps you could arrange this for me,
both as to the member of the house staff and reserving the seat for him.
I should like to be on the aisle and have him on the aisle directly in
front of me. The very least there should be, however, is a phone from
the back of the orchestra or the loges or wherever we will be sitting,
from which either I or this member of the house staff could telephone
to the projectionist, the house manager, etc. during the opening performance.

DOS

To: Mr. John Hay Whitney   November 13, 1939

The Stothart situation was all worked out beautifully, and then over
the weekend two things occurred: first, Stothart had a few drinks on
Saturday night, apparently, and did a lot of loose talking about how he
was going to have to fix up Max's work. In case you don't know it, the
musicians out here are even more jealous of each other, and there are
even more cliques among them than is true about producers, directors, actors, etc. The result was that within ten minutes it was back to
Max, and he was in a rage.

Second, Sam Katz,[108] with whom Stothart has been working, started
raising holy hell about Stothart's being taken off his present alleged
assignments. Apparently, no two MGM executives could agree

---

[108]MGM and Loew's, Inc. Vice-President.

on whether or not Stothart was working at the moment, and on what.

However, Max, spurred on by the Stothart episode, really went to town, and the result is that by tomorrow we will have considerably more than half the picture scored. And it looks as though we are going to be okay without Stothart. I am sure that in any case we can credit all our attempts to get Stothart with leading Max to faster and greater efforts.[109]

DOS

To: Mr. Forbes, Mr. Steiner, Mr. Kern   November 17, 1939
cc: Miss Keon

. . . I think the score is coming along fine and if you will just go mad with schmaltz in the last three reels I will undoubtedly be as happy through the years with the memory of a great Steiner score as has always been the case in the past.

DOS

To: Mr. Hal Kern, Mr. Lou Forbes   November 18, 1939

. . . I should like about one minute of overture before the second half starts, which might commence with something such as the Tara theme and toward the end go into something very threatening, leading into what should be a very big and gradually mounting wind effect (Hal might be able to use some of *The Hurricane* sound effects, and thereby save a little time since an effect as good as we want might take too long to build from scratch); the music should also sell a frightening wind and dust storm and an approaching hurricane to synchronize with the approaching cloud of red dust. Music and effects on the fire are obvious and the word "Sherman" (the second title) should be punctuated in music and effects terrifyingly. Out of this should grow all the effects we can merge of an approaching horde of invaders—the clatter of artillery caissons; the horses hooves; bugles; an enormous number of marching feet—all scored with violent military music. (Under no circumstances use any patriotic American music, with the possible exception of "Marching Through Georgia," the strain of which—you might consider having it off key—could recur through the other effects and music. This ought to blend off into the Tara theme as we dissolve to the cotton fields at Tara.)

---

[109]Stothart did not contribute to the final score.

Both for music and sound effects, I think this is practically the best opportunity we have in the whole picture. I wish that Lou would get together with Max Steiner immediately, show him this note, and discuss the matter with him.

DOS

To: Mr. Russell Birdwell   November 24, 1939

Dear Russ:

I have succeeded in persuading Mr. Whitney that he should associate himself publicly with *Gone With the Wind*, and overcome his long-standing resistance to personal publicity. . . .

I am anxious, if possible, to associate Mr. Whitney with articles such as those appearing in *Life, Time, Look,* etc. Among the other things that I think should be brought out are . . . that he insisted *Gone With the Wind* should be made in its full length; that as chairman of the company, he refused to consider any offers to purchase it, even when these offers got up to the million dollar mark; that throughout the picture his faith in it never wavered; that he kept in touch with me by telephone almost every day as to its progress, and that never for a moment did he have any doubt about the outcome, or any worry about its cost, assuring the members of our Board at all times that he was confident of the final result, and that he would share responsibility for it; that every major decision was made jointly with him, including the one whereby we made the deal with MGM for release through them, and securing Gable. . . .

DOS

To: Mr. Russell Birdwell   November 25, 1939

Dear Russ:

. . . In all candor, is this what you would call a publicity report on the greatest theatrical attraction of all time, a couple of weeks in advance of its release? For the love of Pete, let's get someone in to do some work here. . . .

If you would like to make me a little bet, or a large one, I will undertake, busy as I am, to devote fifteen minutes a day to publicity on *Gone With the Wind* for the next week, and at the end of that week, to have accomplished personally five times as much as is covered on this report. Do you want the bet?

DOS

To: Miss Katharine Brown   November 27, 1939

As I have wired you, I hope you are discouraging any idea of an earlier arrival in Atlanta. . . .[110]

You must bear in mind that Gable has been opposed to this whole trip from the outset. He is still squawking about the ball, claiming that going to the opening is bad enough, but that selling thousands of tickets because of a personal appearance by him at a ball is a little thick. I understand his viewpoint, especially since he is very self-conscious and shy with crowds and obviously is going to have an uncomfortable time. Strickling[111] assures me that the ball will be all right, since he is sure Clark will go through with it once it is clear to him that it is for charity, etc., and once we have him in Atlanta. But now to go back to him, in view of his feelings about the entire trip, and try to tell him that a few hours before the ball, the ball itself, *the entire next day*, and the opening are not enough is something that *I* won't do.

Clark is a very nice fellow, but a very suspicious one, and very quickly and not infrequently gets the notion in his head that people are taking advantage of him. All we have to do is to have this happen through trying to get too much, and anything can happen, from not having him show up at all to having him very difficult when he does get there. Carole Lombard's[112] nonappearance is solely the result of the Gables getting the idea that MGM is not behaving properly about the trip. It's not a question of whether his attitude on these matters is right or wrong: It's simply that we are going to put him through enough torture for the time he will be in Atlanta without aggravating it simply because the mayor and half-a-dozen other Atlantans decide it would be nice to have him there for the better part of still another day. I am surprised they didn't decide they would like to have him there for the whole week. This would have made just as much sense. . . .

I would like you to consider whether it wouldn't be a smart thing to have the arrival in town a complete secret from the public, with a dramatic entrance of Gable and Leigh at the ball, where they would be seen for the first time in Atlanta with all the glamour that we can surround them with. It seems to me this would be much better show-manship, especially since there will be plenty of festivities the next

[110]For the gala première of *GWTW*.
[111]Howard Strickling, Director of Publicity for MGM on the West Coast.
[112]The actress was Mrs. Clark Gable in private life.

day, and probably a mob at the airport when he leaves. I would like to be in a position to be able to tell Clark the exact reverse of his going through additional things—and rather that, at our insistence, we have spared him festivities that were planned for the afternoon of his arrival.

In all of this I haven't mentioned Miss Leigh. No mention is necessary. You know her as well as I do, and she's not going to be exactly Pollyanna about what we put her through. But in her case I feel that she owes it to herself, and to the picture. In Clark's case I feel that whatever he does for us is in the nature of a great favor, and that we should regard it as such. He doesn't need Atlanta and he doesn't need us and he doesn't need these idiotic festivities. He is the biggest star in the world, and any time he wants to show his face for three minutes, he can get a fortune for it. . . .

I checked with Larry Olivier this morning, and it is satisfactory with him if we announce that he is coming to Atlanta as a trailer[113] for *Rebecca*. We will arrange today to send photographs of Olivier and stories concerning him in *Rebecca*, as you suggest. . . .

My sister-in-law, Edith Goetz, informed me last night that Claudette Colbert is coming with her and Mr. Goetz. . . . Poor deluded Claudette is coming under the notion that she is going to have a good time. It is okay with me, as she is really a terribly sweet girl and we will have no trouble with her of any kind. . . .

DOS

To: Miss Katharine Brown   November 28, 1939

. . . Before I could say anything whatsoever about the Atlanta hope of getting Gable there earlier, Strickling mentioned that if just one more request were made of Gable, we wouldn't have him at all.

Strickling went on to say, interrupted every few seconds by Birdwell speaking in agreement, that in his opinion the plans that he has heard about concerning the festivities on arrival should not be gone through with. He and Birdwell both feel, and I must say I agree with them one hundred per cent, that the parade, or anything else in connection with the opening festivities that smacks of the reception of a conquering hero, is going to be so ridiculous as to make Gable, the picture, the entire trip, MGM, and ourselves laughingstocks of the whole country. After all, we have only made a motion picture, and we

---

[113]Industry term for previews of coming attractions.

are only motion-picture people, and the idea of a town receiving us as though we had just licked the Germans is something that I for one will not go through with. You couldn't get me into one of those cars for a million bucks, and I daresay you won't get Gable into any of them either, so the parade will probably wind up with Nick Schenck and [Loew's, Inc. Vice-President] Charlie Moskowitz being received with rotten eggs by an outraged Southern citizenry. . . .

As far as I am concerned, and anybody else other than the stars, for God's sake, don't let us in for any nonsense that makes us ridiculous. The public isn't interested in us as personalities, and if the press wants us, they can get us at the hotel.

Furthermore, I am thinking of coming by train with Irene and some of the others, for various reasons—first, because I see no reason for going by plane when I can go by train, getting a little rest, and some sleep; second, to avoid a great deal of the nonsense (and I hope that my arrival by train won't be publicized either); and third, to avoid the one-in-a-hundred chance that something would delay the plane so that I wouldn't be there for the opening. My anxiety to be at the opening is not to be seen, but to see. I want to be present to enjoy (hopefully) the first opening of the picture, but not to make a horse's ass of myself.[114]

I hope all of this doesn't upset His Honor and various others who want to make a Roman holiday out of this. Let's satisfy Atlanta in a dignified way.

DOS

Mr. William S. Paley[115]   December 6, 1939
485 Madison Avenue
New York, N.Y.

Dear Bill:

The thought occurs to me that you might like to have one of your record companies get out one or more records of the musical score of *Gone With the Wind*. I know that under ordinary circumstances the musical score of a picture couldn't be expected to sell records, but everything in connection with *Gone With the Wind* is apparently attracting such unprecedented attention that this may be the exception. And incidentally, the score is quite beautiful.

[114]Selznick flew to Atlanta.
[115]Chairman of the Board of Columbia Broadcasting System.

Is there anything in union rules that prevents your making a record and selling it from motion-picture sound track? If there is no such rule, then the record might be made very cheaply.[116]

Cordially,

MISS KATHARINE BROWN ˙   DECEMBER 11, 1939
GEORGIAN TERRACE HOTEL
ATLANTA GEORGIA

HAVE JUST FINISHED "GONE WITH THE WIND." GOD BLESS US ONE AND ALL.

DAVID

Mr. Frank Capra[117]   January 22, 1940
9336 Washington Boulevard
Culver City, California

Dear Frank:

I have been brooding about our talk of last week, and burning over the cause of it. There are several conclusions I have reached, and several points that I should like to make. I want first of all to express my very sincere appreciation of the frankness with which you replied to my questions, and of the characteristic honesty of your discussion. It is only because of my knowledge of your character that I write you as I do, and only because of my knowledge of the unselfishness with which you have devoted yourself to industry problems, large and small, that I ask your patience in wading through this letter. I write as I do in acceptance of your statement that matters of this kind are held in the strictest privacy by your Board [Screen Directors Guild Board]. As you know, there have been leaks about previous discussions, but I am confident that you will be able to avoid a repetition of this.

I leave it entirely with you as to what you do with this letter. You may use it in whole or in part with your group; you may destroy it; or you may use it for the excrescence of the Guild, which is a suggestion that may be made to you if any of your confreres hear that I have

[116]Background scores from dramatic films produced in America were not made available on commercial recordings until the 1940s, primarily because it was thought there was not a sufficient market. The score from *GWTW* (a re-creation, not the sound track), was not issued until 1954, although various short renditions of the Tara theme had been available for several years.
[117]At this time Capra was President of the Screen Directors Guild.

written a letter. There is only one thing that I wish you would do, and that is to check its accuracy with everyone who worked on *Gone With the Wind,* including particularly Victor Fleming. Until recently, I would have acted under the assumption that my word was good enough, and that my integrity was unquestioned in this business. As a few of my friends know, I have tossed away millions of dollars in the protection of this integrity, and of my reputation, which a few of your men seem inclined so casually to impair. But apparently there is a new grand jury in the business, composed of your associates, that either does not know me, or that wishes to disabuse me of any notions I may have about my reputation. And it is for this reason that I suggest that you check up, particularly with Vic.

It is a pretty sad commentary on Hollywood that a group of important leaders in an important industry can spend their time trying to figure out how to correct a situation they deem important, a situation in which a member of the industry is receiving credit for his own work, a credit which is apparently not to the liking of this group.

I say that I am receiving credit that is properly mine. Since I am not expectant that my statement would be accepted by a group of directors, I quote one of their group, Victor Fleming (in speaking to a group at his own studio, whose testimony is available): "David not alone produced the picture; he wrote it, and he half directed it."

But whatever credit is being given me is a credit that comes almost entirely voluntarily from the press, a credit that could no more have been stopped than could the blame that would have attached to me, and me solely, if the picture had been a disappointment. . . . Since the picture has been finished, I have tried very honestly and sincerely not to blow my own horn. I have turned down all kinds of interviews and other publicity that was offered, since my satisfaction with the finished job, and my knowledge that I was inseparably connected with the picture in the public mind, made it completely unnecessary for me to seek any publicity. However, I am forced into the details of my contribution by your men; and, frankly, if it is Victor Fleming they are trying to serve, I can only say that the more they talk about it, the more they are going to reveal just how much this was a producer-made picture. . . .

We went ahead with the script, with the casting, with the sets, with the color plans, with the staff, and with all the fabulous preparation involved in a picture of this size, long before Victor Fleming ever came near it. When Victor did come on the picture, and often subsequently, he said, "This is your picture, David. I am doing exactly what you tell me to do, and I hope it turns out all right."

I do not mean in any way to detract from the brilliant job that Victor did. I have gone on record with the press many times, starting with almost the first rushes that he directed, that in my opinion he was doing one of the greatest directorial jobs the industry has ever seen. I regard it as doubly brilliant because he did not know the complete story, and did not have time to finish reading the book until the picture was almost completed; because he did not have any preparation; because he was fighting actors who did not want him, and whose feelings I had to assuage morning, noon, and night, and who did not appreciate what he was doing; because he was a sick man who undertook the job unwillingly, and despite the fact that he was physically and mentally worn out; and because he executed with such brilliant perfection every single conception of Margaret Mitchell, of myself, and of a staff which knew the subject backward, had devoted two years to thought of it, and which would have been horribly critical if Victor's work had been anything short of perfection. I think that if Victor does not win the Academy Award for his job on this picture—probably the most difficult, particularly under the circumstances, in many, many years— it will be in large measure traceable to the detraction from his work that has been occasioned by his well-meaning friends, particularly if they persist in forcing the exact facts about the picture to become more widely known.[118] As you well know, this town is filled with envy and hypocrisy, and there are many people who would leap at the knowledge of the extensive work done on the film by other men to attempt to minimize Victor's outstanding job. . . .

The billing of the picture was entirely in my control, and if you will investigate the advertising, you will find that his name and my own are in exactly the same size. The same is true of the screen credit, and I showed Victor the two places where I wanted to use the direction and production credits and asked him which he would like to have, and I followed his choice. I even went to the extent of retaking the entire main title to give Victor's name additional prominence, which is also a matter of record. . . .

I pleaded with Victor to go to the Atlanta and New York openings, and one reason why he has not received more publicity is that he did not attend either, because of his pique over a piece of literature prepared and issued not by me, but by the studio to which he is under long-term contract. I straightened this all out with Victor; we had

[118]Fleming did receive the Academy Award for *GWTW*.

some very nice talks in which we expressed mutual regrets that anything had ever come up to separate us after the trial we had been
through together; and we literally threw our arms around each other
and decided not to let any outsiders spoil a long and warm friendship;
and I thought that this was the end of it, until some others took the
matter up and decided to make it their issue, even when it was obviously of no interest to Victor. . . .

Now permit me to comment on the treatment of the other directors
who worked on the film. There were some things said about George
Cukor which were untrue and possibly damaging. I did my very best
to contradict these errors, as I can prove. I was extremely careful at
the time George and I came to a disagreement that he should not be
harmed. . . . I was made the subject of a great many nasty remarks,
both in the press and privately, and I am glad to be able to look back
upon my behavior and know that I kept silent and took the rap along
with the knowledge that my silence increased the difficulty of the spot
I was in in relation to the whole endeavor. I must say that George's
behavior was exemplary, and I was glad to have it proven that my
long-standing friendship with him had not been misplaced. Neither
then, nor since, has George been anything but sympathetic and unselfish; and one of my most cherished mementos of *Gone With the
Wind* is an affectionate wire from George to me at the Atlanta opening expressing his most fervent hopes for the picture's success. I could
wish that all people in the business behaved as well.

I might inquire in passing as to just how much I held down George
Cukor's publicity and credit through all the long years we were associated.

Before George left *Gone With the Wind,* I made very sure that his
future was protected, and spent days securing for him his next assignment [*The Women* (1939)]. I urge that you call George Cukor and ask
him, first, whether he holds me in any way accountable for unfortunate things which were said in some of the papers; and second, how
he feels about the treatment that I accorded him generally, during the
long years of our association and right up to and including the time
that he resigned from *Gone With the Wind,* and also since then.

Sam Wood, I believe, came off without either credit or
blame. . . .

I wanted very much, and I freely admitted, to see George and Sam
get some credit out of their labors; but they didn't want it, and Vic
didn't want it. Vic did suggest, when I discussed the matter with him,
that they be credited in the program; but when this credit appeared,

it was so phrased—not by me, but by the MGM people in New York —as to offend Vic.

I say I wanted to give George and Sam credit because if anyone has been done an injustice in connection with the credits on *Gone With the Wind*, it is these two men and Bill Menzies. I think there is an ironic note in any complaints about Victor's credits, when the fact of the matter is that Victor is receiving enormous credit, not simply for his own brilliant work, but also for the work of these other men. Frankly, a complaint as to improper credits to Cukor, Wood, and Menzies would make much more sense; and against such a charge, I would have no defense except the precedent of the business, and the extent to which I went to protect Victor.

Cukor . . . has several sequences still in the picture—several very important ones.

Three solid reels[119] of *Gone With the Wind*, as it stands today, were directed by Sam Wood, including several of the most important sequences in the film.

Bill Menzies spent perhaps a year of his life in laying out camera angles, lighting effects, and other important directorial contributions to *Gone With the Wind*, a large number of which are in the picture just as he designed them a year before Vic Fleming came on the film. In addition, there are a large number of scenes which he personally directed, including a most important part of the spectacle. Day and night, Sundays and holidays, Menzies devoted himself to devising effects in this picture for which he will never be adequately credited.

Since your associates are so concerned about the directorial credit, does it not occur to them that they might also be concerned about Cukor, Wood, and Menzies? It seems to me that if the directors are honest with themselves, or were to be psychoanalyzed, it would develop that what they really resent is the increased credit that has recently been given to producers, rather than what has happened to Vic Fleming; and that what they really fear is that some producers may get credit for work that directors have done. I sympathize with their fears, and I even understand their resentment. I think that there are many producers in this business who are receiving credit for directors' work; but I also think there are some directors who are getting credit for producers' work; and I think that there are too few of the ideal collaborations, where both director and producer contribute, and both receive credit.

[119]Approximately thirty-three minutes.

And furthermore, I have never understood why it is impossible for two men to get credit for different jobs. I have known of no case where a director has suffered through a producer also getting credit for a fine picture, any more than the director has suffered through a writer getting credit. Attempts to eliminate such collaborations can only be harmful to the business as a whole. I say without fear of refutation that neither Victor nor myself could have done as well on *Gone With the Wind* without the other. The growing obsession of the one-man jobs is based on vanity, as some men who are attempting to write, direct, and produce will to their sorrow learn, and, in fact, have in some cases already learned. The reaction is already setting in, and two or three splendid directors have had the good sense to give up their vanity, rather than let it destroy them, and return to direction, working in collaboration with fine producers.

In any event, I do not think that a group of men who have set themselves up as a Guild in pursuit of equity, and presumably with the avowed purpose of protecting the individual against the group, should this early in its career turn around and so distort its objectives as to have the group attack the individual, in this case myself, without regard to equity. . . .

The last time a gang sat around and decided to cut me up was at a producer meeting some years back, after I had stated that the business should be broken up into units, and that I proposed to start this movement by forming a company with Lewis Milestone. The producers temporarily succeeded, and I had to await my chance for independence. One would think that the success of my independence was something to be rooted for by the directors who have so long fought factory methods, as I have fought this. (Perhaps your gang can harm me. But I suggest that they consider whether in harming me they are not harming a leading advocate of so much that they have stood for.)

If it be one of the purposes of the Directors Guild to attempt to tear down producers, despite repeated assurances to the contrary during discussions I had with your members, and regardless of whether or not they have benefited the business, regardless of their record with directors, and without even the most cursory investigation, then I am very sorry indeed that I have had any dealings with the Directors Guild. I was thrown out of producer meetings, and have never been invited back, since I fought violently and singlehandedly on behalf of the Guilds; I can only say that I am sorry at this late date to discover that the producers en masse were right, and that I was wrong. . . .

I suggest also that the Guild investigate my dealings with directors in the past. To go back to MGM, I should like to remind any of your group who were with that company that for many, many years the director received a very small credit, along with many other credits, on all MGM pictures. My contract with MGM gave me control of my pictures, and I insisted, despite considerable argument, that whatever was done on other MGM pictures, the director would receive a separate card[120] on my pictures. As a result of this, MGM was forced to give a separate card to the director on all its pictures. . . .

I suggest that you ask John Cromwell what treatment he received from me on *Little Lord Fauntleroy*, *Prisoner of Zenda*, and *Made for Each Other* [Selznick International (1939)]. . . .

I suggest that you ask William Wellman what treatment he received from me on *A Star Is Born* and *Nothing Sacred*. I also call to your attention that if credit-stealing were in my line, Billy Wellman would not have found it in order to say, upon receiving the Academy Award for the story of *A Star Is Born*, that the Award should have been given to me.

I suggest that you ask Norman Taurog what treatment he received from me on *Tom Sawyer*. . . .

I might comment that I have had any number of directors seek the opportunity to work with me, if only for one picture, and they mention, among other things, the tremendous credit that they receive as a result of having made a picture under the perfection ideal that I always seek.

I suggest that you give particular attention to the case of Alfred Hitchcock,[121] and decide for yourself whether any studio in your knowledge, in the entire history of the business, has ever given the publicity build-up to a director that I have given to Alfred Hitchcock, and the proof of this build-up is that whereas his agent could not get bids for him at the time I signed him, he is now in tremendous demand, despite the fact that his first picture since that time has not even been seen . . . and is not yet even edited! . . .

I daresay that in checking with the directors who have worked with me, you will find that I have increasingly become a supervisor of every detail of production and direction. This reached its climax on *Gone With the Wind*, because of the spot I was on, and because I alone had the reins of the picture in my hands. . . .

[120]A single name on the screen during the credit titles which precede a film.
[121]Director Alfred Hitchcock had not worked on an American film until Selznick hired him to direct *Rebecca* (1940).

I say that I have increasingly supervised every detail, and I am aware that there have been complaints from directors on this score. But this happens to be my production method, and if directors resent this method, they don't have to work with me. They are free men, and until advised to the contrary by the Directors Guild, I am also a free man. I have had a long and difficult struggle in this business, particularly since starting my own company, which I like to think has, in itself, been a very fine thing for the business as a forerunner of other independent units, and particularly in proving to financiers the feasibility of such units. I went ahead and made *Gone With the Wind* according to my own lights, against the advice of every single person who had any contact with me in or outside my company, and including *without exception* every single other person connected with the more important phases of the production. I was told by the most important people in this business that no independent company could hope to achieve the result I was after; and I replied that *only* an independent company could achieve such a result, that it was impossible in a factory. Everything in *Gone With the Wind*, without exception, is as I wanted it to be. I took the gamble on my own conceptions, and on my own methods. So let's not becloud the issue. Let them attack me on the grounds of too much interference, or let them attack me on their personal animosities to my face. . . .

Whatever I have been accused of, I am not aware that anyone has yet charged me with being yellow; and I could not sit by and let attacks upon me take place without fighting back. I have not been terrified by producer groups, and I don't intend at this stage of my career to be terrorized by director groups. I will meet them fairly and squarely on any issue any time. . . .

January 22, 1940
PERSONAL

Dear Carole [Lombard]:

I have received your messages through Myron [Selznick], and am anxious to get together on the [writer Norman] Krasna idea as soon as possible. . . .

Before we proceed, there is something I would like to discuss with you very frankly. Are you sure, Carole, that we should make another picture together?[122] I know from countless sources how highly you

---

[122]Carole Lombard had appeared in *Nothing Sacred* and *Made for Each Other* for Selznick.

think of me, both as a person and as a producer, and this is a source of great gratification to me. And I shall always look back on our past associations as among the most pleasant of my career. Certainly I have always held you up as the shining example of what a joy it can be to work with a star when that star appreciates a producer's problems and cooperates in their solution. But I must face the fact that you are married to Clark, and that Clark obviously feels quite differently about me.

I had hoped that my dealings with Clark on *Gone With the Wind* would once and for all disabuse him of any notions he had about me. I cannot think of any particular in which I could have gone further to make him happy in anything ranging from such details as his costumes to such important factors as the script and direction. I even cost myself a very substantial amount of money through keeping him idle, and paying his salary, in order to accommodate him on the schedule as he desired. All through the picture he was frank in expressing his suspicions that I intended to do him in, and I kept pleading with him to wait until the picture was finished and then tell me his opinion. I was under the impression that he was delighted with the final result, but he apparently disassociates me from this final result, if I am to judge from what has been reported back to me, and from items in the press. I regret all this more than I can say, because there has been nothing whatsoever on my side against Clark; and because, as I have repeatedly told him, he contributed in my opinion a really great performance to the effort that meant so much to me.

But if I couldn't and didn't satisfy Clark about myself, as person or producer, on *Gone With the Wind,* it is not likely that anything I could ever do with him or with his wife would change his opinion. On the contrary, it is much more likely that anything we did together would be regarded with suspicion by him; that you would forever have to be in the position of defending me and my moves to him; that if everything turned out all right, it would still not obviate any embarrassment you may be under through working with me, any more than *Gone With the Wind* did; and that, if, as can happen to everyone, things turned badly, he would have confirmation of his opinions and suspicions to point to. . . . Neither of us is used to such strained and peculiar situations as that on the night of the local opening of *Gone With the Wind,* when I like to believe we should have been in each other's arms. I certainly recognize the awkward position you are in, and cannot expect to come out on the right side when your loyalties are divided. And perhaps some day in the future, attitudes may change, as they do in this business, and it will again be possible for you to do a picture for me with the wholehearted pleasure that we once both knew in our endeavors.

The decision, however, is entirely yours. You would suffer much more from the repercussions in your personal life than would I; and I can stand it if you can. My principal thought in writing this letter is to tell you that freely, and with my blessings and steadfast affection, I will relieve you of your obligation to do a picture for me, provided only that I know in sufficient time to avoid making any commitments for it. . . . And believe me, whichever way you decide,[123] Carole Lombard can have no more earnest fan, personally or as an actress, than

Yours, affectionately and sincerely,

To: Miss Katharine Brown   February 1, 1940

Dear Kay:

. . . Whether or not we ourselves ever make the sequel [to *Gone With the Wind*], there is a fortune to be made on a deal under which Metro would make the picture, if we didn't want to make it ourselves. And there is literally nothing in our projected future comparably important from a financial standpoint with the securing of these sequel rights. . . .

I am anxious to get it lined up just as soon as possible. Actually, we might want it to be Miss Leigh's next contractual picture with us this coming winter, and this would necessitate getting an early start on it . . . All we need is consent.[124]

DOS

To: Mr. Daniel T. O'Shea   October 15, 1940
cc: Mr. Whitney, Mr. Altstock[125]

With reference to Vivien . . . for cooperation on the *Wind* second play-off:

Metro would like her to make personal appearances in several cities, but even I am not brazen enough to ask for this. . . . But it should be understood, and perhaps even be in writing, that she will grant all interviews asked for by the Metro Press Department, etc. You might

[123]Carole Lombard did not make another film for Selznick. She died two years later.
[124]Miss Mitchell declined to give consent.
[125]L. F. Altstock, Selznick International Comptroller.

as well also tell her that it is our intention to use her tests for the role of Scarlett very widely, in showings for the press and elsewhere, which we are confident will get us a lot of space that otherwise might not be available to us on the second play-off. I don't think Vivien will mind this in the least, since she was so good in them, and while I don't agree with her, she prefers the black-and-white photography to the color photography. You will recall that she was directed by Cukor, and to this day she believes she was better in the tests, under Cukor, than she was in the finished picture. In one scene in particular, the scene in which she tries to persuade Ashley to run away with her, there is no question that she was infinitely better in the test, and we were never able, despite a retake, quite to capture the magnificent performance she gave in this test scene. . . .

DOS

To: Miss Brown October 7, 1941
cc: Mr. O'Shea

Dear Kay:

. . . If we can't get a sequel I would still be delighted to have a story to be called *The Daughter of Scarlett O'Hara*, with Vivien playing the daughter. . . .

Don't you think we might persuade Mitchell to write such a story as a novel, or a novelette, or even as a short story?[126] She could no doubt get a good deal of money for it, and while I wouldn't be prepared to pay what I would for a sequel, I would still pay her plenty. As a short story, it wouldn't need to have the action which she speaks of for a novel—and she could probably write it in a few weeks at the most. . . .

I realize that we killed off Bonnie Blue, and it is not clear to me as to how Scarlett would get herself pregnant again, but then Scarlett, after all, was Scarlett, and there must have been other men in her life after Rhett walked out the door. Maybe we could talk about a marriage beyond Rhett, or perhaps even have an opening sequence in the story and in the picture dealing with her fourth husband.

As for remake rights of *GWTW*, I don't think this should be a consideration, because Jeffrey and Danny [127] will have to worry about this, and hopefully they will want to venture into new fields. I think it will

[126]Miss Mitchell declined.
[127]Selznick's sons, born in 1932 and 1936, respectively.

be many, many years, if ever, before anybody wants to think about remaking *GWTW*. Imagine, for instance, somebody remaking *The Birth of a Nation*. Although, on second thought, this isn't a bad idea! . . .

DOS

REBECCA
(1938–1941)

ALTHOUGH THE PUBLIC FUROR *about it was not so great as with* Gone With the Wind, *my experience with* Rebecca *was almost as exciting. For a year I had been talking with Joan Fontaine and trying her in tests. At one point in the proceedings, I tried to get Sam Goldwyn and producer Hal Roach to join me in a three-way deal on a contract with her, but they looked at her other pictures and would have none of her; RKO gave her a couple of important opportunities and then let her out. She was thought by some people in Hollywood to have so little talent that they called her "the wooden woman." Nobody at our place could see her for dust in this role, nor could they understand why I kept turning down the great and important stars that were dying to play the part. (Bear in mind that the part was considered the biggest plum in years, second only to Scarlett; and one prominent star pleaded with me to let her play it with no salary whatever.)*

At one point, I weakened and decided I couldn't be the only sensible person in the world, and allowed Miss Fontaine's option to drop. Then, a week before shooting was to start, I got my back up again. I paced the floor one night and brooded over the fact that if the lead in Rebecca *was miscast, the whole picture would be wrong; and that if I had enough nerve to cast an English girl as Scarlett O'Hara, why couldn't I have the courage of my own convictions about Fontaine? I reminded myself that she would have the benefit of the guidance of the great director I had assigned to the picture, Alfred Hitchcock. And I went to the studio bright and early the next morning, determined to use her.*

:: :: :: :: :: :: :: :: :: :: :: ::

TO: KATHARINE BROWN   AUGUST 23, 1937

I AM DEFINITELY INTERESTED IN HITCHCOCK AS A DIRECTOR AND THINK IT MIGHT BE WISE FOR YOU TO MEET AND CHAT WITH HIM. IN PARTICULAR I WOULD LIKE TO GET A CLEAR PICTURE AS TO WHO, IF ANYONE, IS REPRESENTING HIM AND WHAT HE HAS IN MIND IN THE WAY OF SALARY; ALSO, WHETHER HE IS DEALING WITH MGM. . . .

ALFRED HITCHCOCK   JANUARY 9, 1938
153 CROMWELL ROAD
SW 5
LONDON (ENGLAND)

DEAR HITCH: THANKS FOR YOUR KIND MENTION OF ME ON RADIO.
SAW "LADY VANISHES" LAST NIGHT AND I LOVE YOU. REGRET
HAVE TO INFORM YOU COLMAN SO FEARFUL ABOUT MURDER
ANGLE AND ALSO ABOUT POSSIBILITY OF PICTURE[1] EMERGING AS
WOMAN-STARRING VEHICLE THAT HE WILL NOT DO IT UNLESS HE
SEES TREATMENT, AND WE MIGHT FIND OURSELVES IN JAM BY
WAITING. IF MOVE WITHIN NEXT FEW HOURS CAN SIGN LESLIE
HOWARD FOR IT; OTHERWISE WILL LOSE HIM TOO. BILL POWELL
HAS BEEN ABSOLUTELY WILD ABOUT ROLE AND ANXIOUS TO DO IT,
BUT I TURNED HIM DOWN ON EXPECTATION OF GETTING COLMAN.
. . . WISH YOU WOULD DICTATE REPLY IMMEDIATELY UPON
RECEIPT OF THIS, GIVING ME YOUR REACTIONS.

                                                        DAVID

L. C. HAM[2]   MAY 4, 1938
SELJOY
LONDON, ENGLAND

IS HITCHCOCK IMMEDIATELY AVAILABLE? IF HE IS AND WHILE IT IS
BY NO MEANS DEFINITE, I SHOULD LIKE TO DECIDE WITHIN NEXT
FEW DAYS WHETHER TO BRING HIM OVER TO DIRECT A
PRODUCTION TO BE BASED UPON AND CALLED "TITANIC." I
SHOULD LIKE HITCHCOCK TO UNDERSTAND THAT FOR CERTAIN
REASONS WE WOULD HAVE TO START IN PRODUCTION BY
MID-AUGUST AND WE WOULD THEREFORE HAVE TO PRESS VERY
HARD IMMEDIATELY ON WHAT AMOUNTS TO AN ORIGINAL STORY.
IF IT WORKED OUT HITCHCOCK COULD BRING A WRITER WITH HIM
AND WORK EN ROUTE TO SAVE THIS TIME. . . .

                                                        DAVID

[1] *Rebecca.* Hitchcock had an opportunity to purchase the property while still in England, but eventually declined due to the asking price. Selznick was only partially involved at this point, and did not buy the film rights of the novel until several months later.
[2] London Representative for the (Myron) Selznick–(Frank) Joyce talent agency.

TO: JOHN HAY WHITNEY   JUNE 29, 1938
    AND KATHARINE BROWN

I THINK "REBECCA" PRESENTS PROBLEMS. . . . IT IS NOT CLEAR TO
ME HOW WE COULD GET A SATISFACTORY DEVELOPMENT IN
WHICH THE MAN IS NOT SURE WHETHER OR NOT HE HAS KILLED
HIS WIFE. AND IF THIS DEVELOPMENT WERE SUCH THAT HE HAD
INTENDED TO MURDER HER, OUR CENSORSHIP PROBLEM WOULD BE
ALMOST IDENTICAL. . . . SUGGEST YOU SECURE PRICE AND
FURTHER INFORMATION AS TO ITS LIKELY SALES. IF IT IS A REALLY
BIG SELLER, IT CERTAINLY WILL BE BOUGHT, AND IT WOULD BE
WORTH THE EFFORT TO LICK THE MAJOR PROBLEM. IF IT IS NOT A
REALLY BIG SELLER, IT IS STILL WORTH PLAYING WITH. . . .[3] I
WILL GIVE FURTHER THOUGHT TO THE CENSORSHIP PROBLEMS
HERE, AND WILL AWAIT WORD FROM YOU AS TO WHETHER YOU
CAN SECURE IT ON AN OPTIONAL BASIS AND AT WHAT PRICE.

NLT ALFRED HITCHCOCK   SEPTEMBER 7, 1938
CARE SELJOY
LONDON (ENGLAND)

DEAR HITCH: PLANNING ON HOLDING "REBECCA" FOR YOU IF THIS
IS ALL RIGHT WITH YOU. . . . IF ANYTHING SHOULD UNEXPECTEDLY
GO WRONG ON "TITANIC," WHICH I SINCERELY HOPE WILL NOT
OCCUR, THIS COULD SUBSTITUTE. OTHERWISE "REBECCA" COULD
BE YOUR SECOND PICTURE. . . .[4] WARMEST REGARDS
                                                       DAVID

MR. JOHN HAY WHITNEY   SEPTEMBER 26, 1938
230 PARK AVENUE
NEW YORK CITY

. . . WHAT DO YOU THINK ABOUT LORETTA YOUNG FOR THE
GIRL? . . . I FEEL WE HAVE TWO PICTURES FOR HER IN "REBECCA"
AND "INTERMEZZO." ALSO THINKING ABOUT MAKING A DEAL WITH
HECHT TO DO SCRIPT OF THIS WITH HITCHCOCK
                                                       DAVID

---

[3] *Rebecca* did become a very big seller in the United States and England. Approximately three million combined hardbound and paperback copies have been sold in the United States to date.
[4] Selznick decided not to produce *Titanic*.

Mr. Merritt Hulburd   September 30, 1938
Box 161
Ambler, Pennsylvania

cc: Miss Katharine Brown

Dear Merritt:

I have your letter about *Rebecca*.

I, too, worried about the title, and at the time I bought it I offered to give a little extra money if they would change the title of the book. However, they refused, and the title does not seem to have hurt the book in England or to be hurting it here—and, actually, my experience has been that if a book has succeeded with a title that seems a bad picture title, picture producers are foolish to worry about it. At the time we bought *Gone With the Wind* from the galleys, we were actually worried about paying so much for a book, the title of which we would obviously have to change! I know that it is pretty difficult to think of anybody walking into your office and suggesting that you call a picture *Rebecca*—unless it was made for the Palestine market —but it is equally difficult to think of asking for a new title for a picture and accepting a suggestion of *Gone With the Wind*. So let's forget our worries about the title and hope that the book clicks as importantly as it looks as though it's going to.

As to the other phases of the material, I think your worries are entirely groundless, because it is clear that, perhaps more than any other book of this type in our times, it has an enormous appeal to women, and, for my part, I am convinced that it is really great box office and that, after all, is my worry and not yours. . . .

I have exchanged a few cables with Hitchcock concerning possible writers.

My own suggestions have been Ben Hecht, Clemence Dane, and John Balderston, about whom I wired to Hitchcock; and Sidney Howard and Richard Blaker, about whom I have not yet wired Hitchcock.

Clemence Dane did *Anna Karenina* for me, and while it needed rewriting [by S. N. Behrman], I think the mood of her novels would indicate that she ought to be just about right for this, and I think she could draw the girl beautifully. Also, she will always rank high in my mind because of *A Bill of Divorcement*, which I think is one of the most perfectly constructed and best-written plays of the last twenty-five years. . . . However, Hitchcock, who has worked with her, has no particular enthusiasm for her and has wired me as follows:

"Writer you mention (Dane) not at all satisfactory as shown by my current experience. Will cable suggestions shortly."

and again as follows:

"Undoubtedly prefer Hecht of three suggested but is he right from emotional standpoint? What about Lillian Hellman? Another question which concerns me is the writing of small parts English characters to provide ingredient of humour. If you agree with me would suggest employing English writer Sidney Gilliat, who was responsible large amount of humourous characterizations 'Yank at Oxford'."

. . . I think Ben is a great master of the mood that we should have in this picture—but I question whether he's right because of the English atmosphere.

John Balderston did an excellent job for me on *The Prisoner of Zenda,* and the range of his work extends from the horror pictures, all of the best of which—including *Frankenstein* and *Dracula*—he wrote, to as tender and odd a play as *Berkeley Square.* And while not English, he knows the English scene thoroughly.

You know more about Lillian Hellman than I do. I have never met her and have never worked with her, and know her only from *The Children's Hour.*

I have been trying to get Jack Conway to check with him on Sidney Gilliat, since I know how closely Jack works on script; he directed *Yank at Oxford,* and unquestionably knows exactly what Gilliat contributed; and is a very close friend of mine, whose judgment and honesty I can trust in reply to a question of this kind.

Of course Sidney Howard is about as good as anyone I know in getting a book into script form. And as to the mood of this particular piece, *Bulldog Drummond* the first [a Samuel Goldwyn film of 1929] would seem to qualify him in this regard, also.

Leland [Hayward] has managed to get Sidney's salary up out of all proportion, but he has the virtue of being fast—in some ways as fast even as Hecht, where there is a good original piece of work to be adapted, and therefore the total price might not be prohibitive.

Against Sidney is Hitchcock's feeling about wanting an English writer, which feeling I think we should seriously consider.

Richard Blaker I know very little about, but he comes to me recommended by Hugh Walpole, who is really one of my closest friends, and who would not give me a bad steer. . . .

It has always been my feeling that many pictures go wrong because insufficient time and consideration are given to the casting of the scenario writer, and I always spend as much time deliberating on the selection of this particular piece of manpower as I do to the casting of the star. I am warning you that you will find me something of a nuisance in this particular.

I should appreciate it if you would let me know just how you feel about the writers suggested by both Hitchcock and myself, whether you have any other suggestions, and, if not, the order of your personal choice for it.

Cordially,

To: Miss Katharine Brown   October 6, 1938

Dear Kay:

I'd love to have an autographed copy of *Rebecca*. If you can make it one of the first copies of the first edition—securable from the English company—so much the better.

Incidentally, I'd like to get for framing in my room a page of manuscript or galleys or proof with author's corrections—preferably of a title page or something of the sort, signed by Miss du Maurier.[5] This was what I am also in hopes you will be able to get for me from Margaret Mitchell. I know these matters are a nuisance, but since you have been so kind as to volunteer on this one, perhaps you could get me the other thing.

DOS

Mr. Alfred Hitchcock   December 12, 1938
153 Cromwell Road
London, S.W. 5, England

Dear Hitch:

Separately I am sending you a transcription of last week's radio broadcast of *Rebecca*, which created a minor sensation in this country and about which everyone is talking. . . .

I think it was exceptionally well timed, and there are certain phases of it which I should like you to study. In particular, I have been thinking about the idea of the first-person method of telling the story in part, which you will note [Orson] Welles (who wrote and produced

[5]Daphne du Maurier, author of *Rebecca*.

the program, in addition to appearing in it) used, following the book in this method. It has never, to my knowledge, been used in a picture —except to a minor extent in [director] Bill Howard's Fox picture of some years back called *Power and the Glory.* . . .

I wish you would give some thought to this idea. We might accomplish it by having the girl start to tell the story, and using her as the narrator over silent film until we slip into the picture proper, reverting to the technique at the end of the picture. . . .[6]

Cordially and sincerely,

To: Miss Katharine Brown   March 25, 1939
cc: Mr. O'Shea

Dear Kay:

I am very interested in the idea of having Nazimova play Mrs. Danvers. She had previously communicated her desire to play this role to me through George Cukor.

I think that Nazimova is one of the greatest actresses in the world and, despite her accent, I think she would be magnificent. Other possibilities include Flora Robson and Judith Anderson. I wish you would get hold of Hitchcock and see how he feels about this because it might be wise to line up one of these women well ahead of time. . . .[7]

DOS

To: Mr. Alfred Hitchcock   June 12, 1939

Dear Hitch:

It is my unfortunate and distressing task to tell you that I am shocked and disappointed beyond words by the treatment of *Rebecca.*[8] I regard it as a distorted and vulgarized version of a provenly successful work, in which, for no reason that I can discern, old-fashioned movie scenes have been substituted for the captivatingly charming du Maurier scenes. This is particularly true in the Riviera sequence.

We bought *Rebecca,* and we intend to make *Rebecca.* The few million people who have read the book and who worship it would very properly attack us violently for the desecrations which are indicated by the treatment; but quite apart from the feelings of these few mil-

[6]This technique was used at the opening, but not at the closing in the final version.
[7]Judith Anderson eventually was cast.
[8]Written by Philip MacDonald and Joan Harrison under Hitchcock's supervision.

lion, I have never been able to understand why motion-picture people insist upon throwing away something of proven appeal to substitute things of their own creation. It is a form of ego which has very properly drawn upon Hollywood the wrath of the world for many years, and, candidly, I am surprised to discover that the disease has apparently also spread to England.

I don't hold at all with the theory that the difference in medium necessitates a difference in storytelling, or even a difference in scenes. In my opinion, the only thing that is justified by the difference in medium is a difference in the manner in which a scene is told; and the only omissions from a successful work that are justified are omissions necessitated by length, censorship, or other practical considerations. Readers of a dearly loved book will forgive omissions if there is an obvious reason for them; but very properly, they will not forgive substitutions.

Nor do I hold with the theory that stories should be changed for motion pictures because they fall into a so-called narrative classification. I have made too many classics successfully and faithfully not to know beyond any question of a doubt that whether a film is narrative or dramatic it will succeed in the same manner as the original succeeded if only the same elements are captured and if only as much as possible is retained of the original—including alleged faults of dramatic construction. No one, not even the author of an original work, can say with any degree of accuracy why a book has caught the fancy of the public; if it were this easy, the author of the original could duplicate these elements and duplicate the success, which we know very few authors of successful works are able to do. The only sure and safe way of aiming at a successful transcription of the original into the motion-picture form is to try as far as possible to retain the original, and the degree of success in transcribing an original has always been proportionate to the success of the transcribers in their editing process and the qualities that are gotten into the casting, performances, direction, settings, etc.—as well, of course, as in the proper assembly for motion-picture purposes of the original elements.

This is not theory. I have too long and too successfully resisted attempts to movie-ize successful works not to be sure that my process of adaptation is sound. While others monkeyed around distorting original works, I insisted upon faithfulness in a long list of transcriptions. . . .

This is the process that I had hoped was being engaged in on *Rebecca*. This is why I have kept warning you to be faithful. I have my own ego and I don't mind letting my own creative instincts run wild either on an original, as in the case of *A Star Is Born,* or in the adaptation of an unsuccessful work, as in *Made for Each Other.* But my ego is not so great that it cannot be held in check on the adaptation of a successful work. I don't think I can create in two months or in two years anything as good with the characters and situations of *Rebecca* as du Maurier created; and frankly, I don't think you can either. I want this company to produce *Rebecca,* and not an original scenario based upon *Rebecca.*

The medium of the radio is certainly no closer to the novel form than is the motion picture. And yet Orson Welles, throwing together a radio script on *Rebecca* in less than a week's time, had one of the greatest dramatic successes the radio has ever known by simply assembling ten or fifteen scenes from the book word for word—thereby proving that du Maurier's *Rebecca* in any form has the identical appeal that it had in book form. A clever showman, he didn't waste time and effort creating anything new but simply gave them the original. I hope we will be equally astute. If we do in motion pictures as faithful a job as Welles did on the radio, we are likely to have the same success the book had and the same success that Welles had. If we create an original script, we can only pray that we'll get something that is as good and as appealing as what we had and threw away.

Now the lecture having ended, let's get down to individual instances —some very minor, some very important—of what I am talking about. I will make these comments, trivial or important, in the order of the scenes to which they apply in the treatment:

I hope that it is not our intention to use the name Daphne or any other name for the girl. Next to the fact that the title character Rebecca never appeared, one of the most talked-about things in connection with the book was that the principal character had no name. Again, Welles shrewdly capitalized on this point, and the ten or fifteen million people who were fascinated by the story on the air also know that the leading character never appeared by name. We certainly would be silly to give her a name in our picture. This is not a point of storytelling but simply of showmanship.

I think the scenes of seasickness are cheap beyond words, and old-fashioned in the bargain. If there is any humor left on the screen in seasickness, let's for God's sake leave it to the two-reel comedies and not get our picture off on a low note by indulging in such scenes. And the first portrait of Max smoking a cigar that makes the other passengers ill is not my idea of an introduction for a romantic and mysterious figure. On the contrary, it would be a good introduction for a boor.

And quite apart from this, I don't know what we gain with our principals on their way to the Riviera, and I know a great deal that we lose: in the first place, we lose the idea of the brooding, introspective man who has for some time been away from England, trying to forget and wipe out the past. In the treatment he has apparently only just left England. In the second place, we lose the idea of the girl who has been living on the Riviera for some time with her vulgar employer, apparently having led a miserable existence for at least months. In the treatment, she has no background of existence at all with her vulgar employer because she meets de Winter the very night she leaves England.

The opening of the book is excellent, and why it requires any change for motion pictures or any other medium I am sure I don't know—with its picture of snobbish Mrs. Van Hopper and her unhappy companion, and the ever-so-slight and romantic first hint of de Winter in the distance. . . .

And Max in a speedboat, driving out to his friends on an anchored yacht—what in God's name does this do to the portrait of the man who is wandering alone, trying to get away from everything? (The repeat on the seasickness isn't even worthy of comment.) Whatever happened to the construction that we discussed and agreed upon—that we were going to follow his moods and his being difficult and distant exactly as in the book until the honeymoon, when for the first time we saw a gay man, snatched out of his depression and his bitterness and his sour humor at long last by his new young wife, and returning to his old mood as Manderley obtrudes into his life on their return? . . .

Even such wonderful little things as the girl tearing out the page of the book, trying this early and in this futile fashion to erase Rebecca; and the little scene in which Mrs. Van Hopper predicts doom to the girl—at the end of Chapter Six: these are wantonly thrown away too, for what reason I don't know.

So much for the Riviera sequences. As for Manderley, every little thing that the girl does in the book, her reactions of running away from the guests, and the tiny things that indicate her nervousness and her self-consciousness and her gaucherie are all so brilliant in the book that every woman who has read it has adored the girl and has understood her psychology, has cringed with embarrassment for her, yet has understood exactly what was going through her mind. We have removed all the subtleties and substituted big broad strokes which in outline form betray just how ordinary the actual plot is and just how bad a picture it would make without the little feminine things which are so recognizable and which make every woman say, "I know just how she feels . . . I know just what she's going through . . ." etc.

It would take too long to go into the details of my resentment toward the other changes. Obviously there are sections of the book which are repetitious, and which need to be telescoped. But this is no excuse for making Max's sister into another Mrs. Van Hopper; for throwing away the wonderfully etched and extremely entertaining portraits of his sister and her husband; for substituting some slapstick comedy about her hole-in-one on a golf course for the mood of the walk through the estate, with a very human little argument about the dog running over the rocks, and Max's curious subsequent behavior.

The steps by which the readers of the book are intrigued by the mysterious behavior of Mrs. Danvers, and by Max's curious reactions to little things—all these have been distorted in a lesser or a greater manner, and it would take days to comb through them and see just where point after point has been lost, just as they have in the Riviera sequence. I would rather say very flatly that I think the treatment is pretty bad, and that it is easier to do a new one than to repair this one. Apparently the original had very little charm for the people who worked on this treatment, because if they felt about it as I do, and as all the other readers of the book that I have ever spoken to do, all their efforts would have been toward seeing exactly how much of the original they could preserve as to incident, reactions, characterizations, and all the other things that have made the book the most successful love story next to *Gone With the Wind* that has appeared in the last five years. . . .

I can't think why you avoid showing the interior of the cottage on the beach.

Nor can I understand particularly why you want the grandmother in the tower of Manderley. If for no other reason, she and her own home have value as something to break the monotony of always being in the Manderley settings. However, this value may not be important, since we have plenty of sets within Manderley, its grounds, etc., and there may, on the contrary, be a value in staying entirely within Manderley. In this case, I am not sure that grandmother serves any purpose at all, and perhaps she ought to be eliminated from the story.[9]

Other little things that I miss are the many comparisons between

[9]She was.

the girl and Rebecca which the girl observes and which make her feel her own gaucherie. I refer to such things as the comparison of handwriting between her own and Rebecca's. . . .

Also, in the book more than in the treatment, I understand why Max puts up with Mrs. Danvers, and this is weak even in the book. . . .

I don't know why you have changed the converted boathouse into a small stone cottage. This, to me, is just a gratuitous change which is for no reason unless it is to annoy the readers of the book. . . .

I don't think the breaking of the china cupid in violence is as good as its being broken through awkwardness. In the one case it is fortuitous, and in the other case it is in character.

Max's scolding of the girl in front of Mrs. Danvers, while it may be a little ill-bred, is much more heartbreaking than after Mrs. Danvers leaves.

I don't know what Max is doing in Rebecca's room when the girl visits these rooms. I think this is cheating the audience. Du Maurier accomplishes the result of having her readers and the girl think that Max is still in love with Rebecca without such cheating.

Also, Mrs. Danvers's appearance in this room turns the readers' blood cold, and I don't think the substitution of Max is comparably good. In fact, I don't think Mrs. Danvers comes through in the treatment half as well as she does in the book. . . .

I personally don't think you could get Olivier or any other good actor to play this role as indicated in the treatment. The character has no charm, no mystery, and no romance.

It is my regretful conclusion that we should immediately start on a new treatment, probably with a new writing setup.[10]

DOS

TO: MR. LOWELL V. CALVERT   JUNE 15, 1939

WE ARE ABOUT TO CLOSE FOR LAURENCE OLIVIER FOR "REBECCA," BUT BEFORE DOING SO, ANXIOUS TO HAVE IMMEDIATE CHECK ON THE FOLLOWING. SINCE I CANNOT DELAY OLIVIER NEGOTIATIONS, WOULD LIKE TO HAVE SOME WORD EARLY IN THE MORNING. WILLIAM POWELL IS STILL EXTREMELY ANXIOUS TO PLAY THE PART; HE WOULD COST $100,000 MORE THAN OLIVIER, WHICH

[10]Virtually all of Selznick's criticisms were accepted, and his suggestions were incorporated in the final version of Rebecca. Philip MacDonald and Joan Harrison continued to work on the adaptation.

MEANS WE WOULD HAVE TO GROSS $150,000 ADDITIONAL TO
BREAK EVEN ON THE EXPENDITURE. EVEN IF WE WANT HIM THERE
IS STILL NO CERTAINTY WE CAN GET HIM, SINCE IT WOULD
REQUIRE MGM'S CONSENT. HOWEVER, POWELL IS HOPEFUL THIS
MIGHT BE OBTAINED. OBVIOUSLY I DO NOT WANT TO MAKE THE
ATTEMPT UNTIL AND UNLESS WE ARE SURE WE WANT HIM. THIS IS
NOT A QUESTION OF CASTING, AS WE CAN MAKE THIS DECISION
OURSELVES, AND ON THIS POINT THERE IS MUCH TO BE SAID ON
BOTH SIDES. FOR INSTANCE, POWELL IS MUCH MORE RIGHT AS TO
AGE, WHEREAS OLIVIER IS BETTER PERHAPS FOR THE MOODY
SCENES, ALSO HIS ENGLISH, AND PERHAPS HE HAS THE MORE
OBVIOUS EDGE ROMANTICALLY. THE DECISION SHOULD PROBABLY
REST NOT AT ALL UPON WHICH ONE IS BETTER FOR THE ROLE,
SINCE COLMAN IS THE ONLY PERFECT MAN AND WE CANNOT GET
HIM AND THEREFORE WE ARE POSSIBLY EQUALLY WELL OFF WITH
EITHER OF THESE SECOND CHOICES FROM STANDPOINT OF
ACCURATE CASTING. THE DECISION INSTEAD SHOULD BE BASED
SOLELY ON WHETHER WILLIAM POWELL IS LIKELY TO ADD
HUNDREDS OF THOUSANDS OF DOLLARS TO THE GROSS. HE WILL
HAVE HIS NEXT "THIN MAN" PICTURE IMMEDIATELY BEFORE. . . .

DAVID O. SELZNICK

To: Miss Katharine Brown   June 21, 1939

Please inform Miss du Maurier . . . that my feelings about showing
the dead wife coincide entirely with her own—and that apart from the
reasons she gives, I have always had the additional feeling that there
is no woman we could show who could possibly satisfy everybody's
conception of what the dead wife looked like.

We have given a good deal of thought to the possibility of some
treatment of the type she talks about, such as showing her back in a
dissolve which we may find it necessary to use when Max tells his story
to the second wife. However, I am hopeful that we won't even have
to do this and that we will accomplish what we want either only with
dialogue or with a flashback limited to Max.[11]

It will probably interest you, and it may interest Miss du Maurier,
to know that I have thrown out the complete treatment on *Rebecca*

[11]Rebecca, the dead wife, was not seen or heard at all in the final version. Max relates
the story with dialogue—not a flashback.

because of its insufficient faithfulness to the book; and that it is my intention to do the book and not some botched-up semioriginal such as was done with *Jamaica Inn*.[12]

DOS

To: Mr. John Hay Whitney   June 27, 1939
cc: Miss Katharine Brown

. . . Vivien is still anxious to play in *Rebecca* for obvious reasons. She really thinks she could knock us dead in another test and that the former test was unfair in that she had to hop right out of Scarlett O'Hara into the girl in *Rebecca* in ten minutes. It is my personal feeling that she could never be right for the girl, but God knows it would solve a lot of problems if she was right, and I have too much respect for her ability as an actress, too much consideration for my own peace of mind during the months of August and September when a certain young man [Laurence Olivier] is in these parts, and too much appreciation of how good it would be for her future with us if she were to play *Rebecca*, to close the door on the possibility of her being right for it. I have therefore said that we would not close with anybody to play the role for a period of ten days from today, during which time she could if she wished make a test with Larry Olivier in New York . . .

To: Mr. Hebert   July 10, 1939

Stradling has definitely been assigned to photograph *Rebecca*, and we have taken up our option on him, so if you could get him some sort of break in the trade papers on this I wish you would, to offset any harm or even hurt feelings that he may have through any misunderstanding of why he was taken off *Intermezzo*. (I would not, however, refer to *Intermezzo* in the story.)

DOS

To: Miss Katharine Brown   July 18, 1939

I can't tell you what we have been through for the past couple of months trying to line up a good dialogue writer for *Rebecca*. You know part of it because of our attempts to get Sam Behrman.

Most of our difficulties have been caused by the necessity of having

[12]Another du Maurier novel filmed by Hitchcock in 1939.

a man who had the required good taste for the job as well as the necessary playwriting ability. (We did not and do not now need a screenwriter, but simply someone to fill in that dialogue which we are not using from du Maurier.)

Preferably our requirement would have been filled by an English-man, and an Englishman familiar with this class of society, but most of those who would immediately come to mind, such as Hugh Walpole, Clemence Dane, and Rosamond Lehmann, were either unwilling to come over, as in the case of Walpole and Miss Lehmann, or we turned down because either Hitch or I didn't think either he or she was right for the job for reasons other than their background.

Now we are trying a man named Michael Hogan, but I know very little about him and I have only a hope that he will work out properly, so we will be in a terrible jam for good dialogue on the picture unless right now we start lining up somebody for it.

I am sick of going through agents' lists out here, and the thought occurred to me that you might be able to dig up someone in New York who has escaped our notice. . . . Also, you may have covered English plays in New York that we haven't seen which failed for reasons other than their possession of good dialogue of the type we require. Also, it might be worthwhile for you to wire Miss Reissar asking her to make a final stab at du Maurier to see whether she herself wouldn't like to come over,[13] and asking further whether either Miss Reissar or Miss du Maurier has any suggestions as to someone who could leave im-mediately. Anyone who is here later than about ten days from now would be useless to us, and even this is playing pretty close to the line. If we don't get someone awfully good and very soon, we will have to struggle through as best we can with the best we can get in Hollywood. You might, however, make another stab on the Behrman situation.

DOS

To: Mr. Ginsberg July 25, 1939

. . . Hitchcock agrees with me that the physical production cost on the picture is ridiculous, and while he doesn't know much about American costs, of course, he wants to cooperate fully to get the cost of the picture down considerably. He speaks about getting it down to $750,000, even though I have told him that this is impossible. How-

[13]Miss du Maurier declined.

ever, I do think that we can get the cost down $75,000 to $100,000 below the $947,000 estimate, and it is conceivable that we can get it down more. . . .

I think the staff that is maintained in Men's and Women's Wardrobe is untenable and should be chopped to the bone. All I can say is that when I personally was running these departments and supervising every item, as was the case with *Fauntleroy*, we didn't have such staffs, and this picture is about ten times as simple from a wardrobe standpoint as was *Fauntleroy*, which was in period. . . .

I can't help but feel that our departments are trained to do things in the most expensive possible way and that nobody even gives a thought to the cheaper way of doing things, even if a picture, such as *Rebecca*, has a comparatively short cast, practically no physical problems, and a simple wardrobe problem, etc. A picture like *Intermezzo* or *Rebecca* is handled as though it were a big costume endeavor.

I think that after some study you ought arbitrarily to set a budget of $850,000 top, and hopefully of less than this, and so lay it out that each department is budgeted and must keep within this budget and that it should be made clear once and for all that any department head that does not keep within the budget, and thereby proves his right to a future here, is going to be fired. I think something as drastic as this is needed at this time to once and for all prove to the organization that *Gone With the Wind* is finished, and that we are trying to make some pictures that will make some money. I am personally sick and tired of working my head off to support a lot of people who won't give a thought as to how to save money. And I think that the presentation of an estimate such as the one I have in front of me on *Rebecca* is a disgrace and proves pretty conclusively that we are desperately in need of some sort of production and cost management. There is not a first-class production manager in town in my opinion who would dare to present an estimate of $947,000 on this picture. The excuse of not having a script is no excuse at all. The treatment is available and so is the book, and such items as those that I have mentioned in this memo couldn't conceivably be seriously estimated at the figures they are, regardless of the script. . . .

Perhaps the point of the Production Department in presenting this kind of an estimate is to play so safe that under no circumstances will they ever be in the position of having estimated the picture at less money that it winds up at—which is, of course, an untenable attitude, since it inevitably results in extravagances through the delusion that we are keeping within our budget. What other excuse can there be for the inclusion of such an item as $10,000 for the casting of Beatrice?[14] This item is so ridiculous that I would like to know who is responsible for it. The reason that the inclusion of such items maddens me so is that department heads come back at me from time to time and tell me that they are within budget, when the budget in the first place is something for which they should have been fired then and there.

Who is responsible for this budget, and what was the sense in its presentation?

. . . I would like to know as promptly as possible whether there is any difficulty in reaching an $850,000 figure, because if there isn't, I intend personally to clean out the whole place and get in competent people who can produce pictures for a price. If there is going to be any extravagance in our picture-making, it is going to be indulged in by me personally to improve the quality of the pictures, and I am not going to have it thrown away through sloppy management. I can't tell you how very deeply upset I am to be faced with this at a time when I am overwhelmed with creative and editing work.[15]

DOS

To: Mr. O'Shea   August 1, 1939

Before we finally decide on who is to play the lead in *Rebecca*, which I think we must do within the next couple of days, I want to be sure we have exhausted very possible means of getting Olivia de Havilland.

I wish you would discuss with Henry [Ginsberg] whether it wouldn't be smart for him to run over and see Harry Warner about it at the Warner Studio.

The situation is complicated by four things:

1. Warners' unwillingness ever to cooperate on these things, which I think Henry might overcome in a personal interview. Incidentally, at the moment I think Jack Warner is very kindly disposed.

2. Her commitment for a Goldwyn picture, *Raffles*, which however, I think she and Leland [Hayward] would do a great deal to overcome. I think that if sufficient pressure were put on Goldwyn and he knew he was going to get her for a later and more important picture, he might be made to see reason in it.

3. Leland acting as her agent when he knows of our interest in Margaret Sullavan, his wife. I don't think he will do much about de

---

[14]Max de Winter's sister. Gladys Cooper eventually was cast.
[15]The final cost of *Rebecca*, exclusive of prints and advertising, was a little over $1,000,000.

Havilland while Sullavan is in the running, and if we spoke to him now about de Havilland he might think we were kidding about Sullavan. I think what you would have to say to Leland is that our second choice, if we can't get together with MGM, would be de Havilland, and see if we can't get him for once in his life doing something active for a client.

4. Miss de Havilland's unwillingness to be considered because of her sister, Joan Fontaine, being up for it. I think that we would frankly have to tell Leland that Miss de Havilland would be foolish to take this attitude, since it might very well wind up that she would make the sacrifice for her sister only to have someone else play it, perhaps Vivien Leigh. . . .

DOS

MISS KATHARINE BROWN   AUGUST 3, 1939
SELZNICK INTERNATIONAL
630 FIFTH AVENUE
NEW YORK CITY

. . . PLEASE TELL JOCK THERE ARE MANY PEOPLE HERE WHO FEEL STRONGLY THAT AN IDEAL SELECTION WOULD BE LORETTA YOUNG, WHOM IT WOULD BE EASY TO DEGLAMORIZE AND WHO WOULD HAVE THE ADVANTAGE OF YOUTH, AND WHO IS A MUCH BETTER ACTRESS, I AM SURE, THAN MOST PEOPLE THINK. WE ARE PLANNING A TEST OF LORETTA ON MONDAY, BUT WE MAY HAVE TO CALL THIS OFF IF IT BECOMES NECESSARY TO GIVE A DECISION TO THE OTHERS, ESPECIALLY SULLAVAN, BEFORE THEN.

DAVID

To: Mr. Hitchcock   August 4, 1939
cc: Mr. Klune

I think we must be very careful in *Rebecca* in both the script and in the reading of the lines by English actors . . . to avoid anything which might be difficult for an American audience to understand—as to actual phrasing and as to dialect. I am afraid that you wouldn't be a very good judge of this since things which you have heard many times during your life and which would seem perfectly easy to understand to you might be very difficult for Americans to understand. I will watch the script myself in this particular but I think we should commission the script girl, or some other American, to watch this point carefully throughout the making of the picture and to call to your attention anything which she thinks is dangerous from this standpoint.

DOS

August 9, 1939

Angel [Irene Selznick]:[16]

. . . I took Hitch to the preview;[17] saw Edie [Goetz] for a brief moment at the outside of the Troc[adero], where I went just long enough to congratulate Vic [Fleming] and Mervyn [Le Roy],[18] both of whom I missed at the theater; and then went on with Hitch, for a drink and some dinner to Lamaze. . . . We talked—stories!! *Rebecca* and *Titanic* and Benedict Arnold were my gaiety. He's not a bad guy, shorn of affectations, although not exactly a man to go camping with . . .

I've been thinking of you, and have decided to marry you if you'll have me. I'm a little middle-aged, to be sure; I have a hammer toe and I run into things; I'm ex-arrogant, and once I wanted to be a big shot; I snore loudly, drink exuberantly, cuddle (i.e., snuggle) expansively, work excessively, play enthusiastically; and my future is drawing to a close, but I'm tall and Jewish and I do love you. . . .

David-in-Quest-of-His-Mate

To: Mr. Ginsberg

August 11, 1939

I cannot tell you how strongly I feel that [Gregg] Toland is worth his weight in gold to *Rebecca*. I will be agreeable to paying a very fancy bonus for having him on the picture. I don't feel there is any other cameraman in town comparable with him for this job—and while there may be other men of equal ability, they would take twice as long to get the same result. . . .[19]

DOS

[16]Mrs. Selznick was in New York briefly.
[17]*The Wizard of Oz* preview.
[18]Director and producer, respectively, of *The Wizard of Oz*.
[19]George Barnes eventually replaced Harry Stradling as director of photography. Stradling had requested and was granted a release from his contract. In a teletype to Selznick, he stated that "with the mental strain of wondering whether I was satisfying you and with thoughts of being taken off the picture, I honestly don't feel I could do justice to you and your organization in making *Rebecca*."

VIVIEN HOLMAN[20]   AUGUST 18, 1939
ÎLE DE FRANCE
NEW YORK RADIO

DEAR VIVIEN: WE HAVE TRIED TO SELL OURSELVES RIGHT UP
UNTIL TODAY TO CAST YOU IN "REBECCA," BUT I REGRET
NECESSITY TELLING YOU WE ARE FINALLY CONVINCED YOU ARE AS
WRONG FOR ROLE AS ROLE WOULD BE FOR YOU. YOU MUST
REALIZE IT IS THIS SAME PATIENCE, CARE, AND STUBBORNNESS
ABOUT ACCURATE CASTING THAT RESULTED IN PUTTING YOU IN
MOST TALKED-OF ROLE OF ALL TIME IN WHAT EVERYONE WHO
HAS SEEN IT AGREES IS GREATEST PICTURE EVER MADE. IT WOULD
HAVE BEEN VERY SIMPLE TO CAST BETTE DAVIS AS SCARLETT,
THEREBY SATISFYING MILLIONS OF PEOPLE INCLUDING EVERYONE
IN THE PROFESSION. IT WOULD BE MUCH SIMPLER TO CAST YOU,
WHO ARE UNDER CONTRACT TO US, IN "REBECCA" LEAD, AND
THEREBY HAVE SAVED US ALL GREAT DEAL OF EXPENSE AND
AGONY SEARCHING FOR RIGHT GIRL. AND EVEN THOUGH YOU MUST
BE COMPLETELY WRONG CASTING, WE MIGHT STILL HAVE PUT YOU
IN IT HAD WE THOUGHT IT WAS GOOD FOR YOU, REGARDLESS OF
THE PICTURE. BUT I AM POSITIVE YOU WOULD BE BITTERLY
CRITICIZED AND YOUR CAREER, WHICH IS NOW OFF TO SUCH
TREMENDOUS START WITH SCARLETT, MATERIALLY DAMAGED.
ALTHOUGH HITCHCOCK FEELS EVEN MORE STRONGLY THAN I DO
ON THIS QUESTION, I WAS STILL NOT SATISFIED AND THEREFORE
RAN THE TESTS OF ALL CANDIDATES FOR [playwright and
screenwriter] ROBERT SHERWOOD, WHO IS WORKING ON SCRIPT,
WITHOUT GIVING HIM ANY HINT OF OUR FEELINGS. HIS FIRST AND
IMMEDIATE REACTION WAS HOW COMPLETELY WRONG YOU WERE
FOR IT. STILL NOT SATISFIED, I REPEATED THE PROCEDURE WITH
GEORGE CUKOR, KNOWING HIS HIGH REGARD FOR YOU, AND
GEORGE'S FIRST AND IMMEDIATE REACTION WAS IDENTICAL WITH
SHERWOOD'S. AM HOPEFUL OF HAVING SOMETHING SOON FOR YOU
THAT WE WILL BOTH BE HAPPY ABOUT, AND ALSO HOPEFUL YOU
WILL RECOGNIZE THAT SAME CARE THAT HAS GONE INTO "WIND"
AND "REBECCA" WILL GO INTO SELECTION AND PRODUCTION OF
YOUR FUTURE PICTURES, WHICH IS SOMETHING I HAVE NO
HESITANCY IN SAYING DOES NOT EXIST IN MANY STUDIOS.
AFFECTIONATELY,

                                                    DAVID

[20]Vivien Leigh's married name.

LAURENCE OLIVIER   AUGUST 18, 1939
ÎLE DE FRANCE
NEW YORK RADIO

DEAR LARRY: PLEASE SEE MY WIRE TO VIVIEN. I KNOW YOU MUST
BE DISAPPOINTED, BUT VIVIEN'S ANXIETY TO PLAY ROLE HAS, IN
MY OPINION, BEEN LARGELY, IF NOT ENTIRELY, DUE TO HER
DESIRE TO DO A PICTURE WITH YOU, WHICH WAS BEST
DEMONSTRATED BY HER COMPLETE DISINTEREST IN PART WHEN I
FIRST MENTIONED IT TO HER AS POSSIBILITY AND UNTIL SHE KNEW
YOU WERE PLAYING MAXIM. YOU WILL, AFTER ALL, BOTH BE
WORKING HERE, SO I THINK HER EAGERNESS HAS BECOME
EXAGGERATED AND NOT RATIONALIZED. BECAUSE OF MY
PERSONAL AFFECTION FOR VIVIEN AND MY HIGH REGARD FOR YOU
BOTH, AM HOPEFUL YOU WILL RECOGNIZE THAT MY JUDGMENT
HAS BEEN FAIRLY SOUND AND SUCCESSFUL IN THESE MATTERS FOR
MANY YEARS. HOPEFUL WE WILL BE ABLE TO FIND SOMETHING
FOR THE TWO OF YOU TO DO TOGETHER FOR US AT SOME FUTURE
DATE. SCRIPT IS COMING ALONG SPLENDIDLY, AND GLAD BE ABLE
TELL YOU ROBERT SHERWOOD IS DOING FINAL DIALOGUE
REWRITE. BELIEVE WE ARE ASSEMBLING EXCITING CAST
INCLUDING JUDITH ANDERSON AS MRS. DANVERS, GEORGE SANDERS
AS FAVELL, REGINALD DENNY AS FRANK, AND NIGEL BRUCE AS
GILES. POSSIBLE MAY BE ABLE LET YOU HAVE DAY OR TWO IN NEW
YORK IF YOU WANT IT AND IF YOU WILL CONTACT US BEFORE
LEAVING FOR COAST. CORDIALLY,

                                                       DAVID

To: Mr. John Hay Whitney   August 18, 1939

. . . The situation on the lead for *Rebecca* is as follows:

We have definitely ruled out Anita Louise as giving a very good
performance and one that we should bear in mind for the road company.[21]

. . . I feel Loretta Young is a very good bet, and that with a few good
pictures, she is the logical successor to Joan Crawford—but we don't
think she is right for *Rebecca*. . . .

Olivia de Havilland, despite our conviction that she might be superb
in the role, and her own anxiety to play it, we have had to rule out because it would mean dealing with Sam Goldwyn and the Warners. . . .

[21]Intended humorously.

Our feelings about Vivien are very clearly expressed in the attached radiograms which I have sent today in answer to a series of them from Larry and Vivien respectively. Sherwood and Cukor respectively, and without any prompting whatsoever, made the same comments that Hitchcock and I made—that she doesn't seem at all right as to sincerity or age or innocence or any of the other factors which are essential to the story coming off at all. Sometimes you can miscast a picture and get away with it; but there are certain stories, such as *Rebecca,* where miscasting of the girl will mean not simply that the role is badly played but that the whole story doesn't come off—with, in some cases, the maddening result that the player who has been miscast is credited with a great performance and the picture is considered very bad.

I am convinced that we would be better off making this picture with a girl who had no personality whatever and who was a bad actress but was right in type than we would be to cast it with Vivien. Bette Davis is also an enormously effective actress and she would, in our opinion, be just about as right for it as Vivien would—in fact, more right, since she doesn't have the wrong qualities that Vivien has, and apparently can't get away from.

This brings us down to three candidates, apart from any that may show up from Reissar or from New York or Hollywood at the last minute, which is, of course, an extremely long-shot chance—which never comes true except in the case of Vivien Leigh and *Gone With the Wind!*

The three candidates are Margaret Sullavan, Joan Fontaine, and Anne Baxter.

Most of the people in the studio who haven't studied the picture or its casting, as have Hitch and Sherwood and myself, were more enthusiastic about Margaret Sullavan than about anyone else (until they saw the Anne Baxter test, which changed the opinion of a large number of them). Apparently, her voice and her personality are so appealing that they don't stop to think that there is practically not one scene in the picture the qualities of which would not be affected by casting Sullavan. Imagine Margaret Sullavan being pushed around by Mrs. Danvers, right up to the point of suicide! Imagine Margaret Sullavan wishing she were a woman of thirty in a long black dress!! . . .

This then reduces it to two candidates. The first is Joan Fontaine. I had pretty well decided to forget her for the role since I couldn't get anybody on the studio staff, excepting only Hal Kern, or anybody in the New York office to agree with me that she was physically an ideal choice for the role and that from a performance standpoint she obviously (or, at least, so *I* thought) was the only one who seemed to know completely what the part was all about. However, several things happened in succession—Hitchcock started swinging around to her after listening to discussions of the part by Sherwood, myself, etc.; John Cromwell (who had made her first test) in the course of a conversation stated that he thought we were out of our minds not to put her in the part; and when I ran the tests for Bob Sherwood, he stated unequivocally and without the slightest prompting on our part of any kind that apart from his liking for Sullavan, there was no question but that Fontaine was far and away the best for the role. Encouraged by this, I decided to get George Cukor over here to run all the tests, bearing in mind that George is a great enthusiast of Vivien's and a great personal friend of hers, and also that he and Cromwell are the two men who, in my career of producing, have demonstrated the most accurate sense of casting. I was careful not to give George any prompting whatsoever, and he looked at them all very seriously and quietly and conscientiously and with no comment at all during the running, except for some loud guffaws at Vivien's attempts to play it. When they were all over, he said that in his opinion the most touching test was that of Anne Baxter, but that if it were up to him and he had to start the picture immediately, he would without any hesitation select Fontaine from this group of six. (Leigh, Fontaine, Sullavan, Louise, Young, and Anne Baxter.)

I neglected to mention above that Sherwood saw this same group, including the Baxter tests. But Sherwood voted third for Baxter.

Now, the situation on Fontaine is curiously complicated since her engagement to Brian Aherne, whom she is marrying tomorrow, Saturday. I have told her of my feelings that she could not sustain the part and that she might be monotonous through the entire picture; and that as a consequence we would be very hesitant about casting her in the role until and unless we saw other tests of her which she had, for a couple of days before I spoke with her, refused to make (saying that she would be delighted and honored to play the part but that she didn't want to make any more tests). I said to her yesterday that what we would like to see is three or four scenes from various parts of the picture to get the full range of her performance. Unfortunately, her face is swollen with an impacted wisdom tooth (and not so good for a honeymoon), and therefore she couldn't make the tests today or any time before her marriage tomorrow. She said that she would be delighted to cut her honeymoon short, coming back after a week if we decide to put her in the part; and further that she would cut her honeymoon short to make further tests. . . .

As to Anne Baxter versus Fontaine: I think she has more sincerity than Fontaine, and that she is much more touching, in the word of Cukor, in the scenes. I think she is a shade young, although it is entirely possible that this would turn into an advantage. She is ten times more difficult to photograph than Fontaine, and I think it is a little harder to understand Max de Winter marrying her than it would be Fontaine. Yet I have decided that the best thing to do would be to try to work out a deal today with Baxter, closing with her, and gambling the comparatively small amount of money that would be involved if we don't use her. . . .

So at the moment, it looks as though the setup is about two thirds in favor of Baxter, one third in favor of Fontaine. (Incidentally, Irene's vote is for Fontaine, with Baxter second.)

I do wish that you would be very careful not to let on anything about this final choice since it might affect our negotiations with one or both girls, since it would completely spoil our publicity breaking, and since it might get us in wrong with the press if it leaked and we should subsequently change our minds.

. . . I am in agreement with your comment that it would be a mistake to show the Baxter test to Vivien or Larry. And further, I think that if Vivien and Larry ask, as they almost certainly will, who is up for the role, it would be better if you both said that we have several girls from whom we haven't made our final selection.

If there are any last-minute choices that turn up, please wire or telephone.[22]

DOS

To: Mr. Ginsberg, Mr. O'Shea   August 23, 1939

I think you ought to investigate what would happen in the case of *Rebecca* in the event of war and in the event that Larry Olivier, George Sanders, etc., were ordered to report. I don't know whether they would be able to finish the picture, and we would be in a fine pickle if they walked out in the middle—not so much of a pickle as Poland, I grant you, but still a pickle.

You might talk this over with the British consul. Also, is there any

[22]Joan Fontaine was chosen a short while later.

form of insurance we ought to take out that would cover us in such an emergency?

DOS

To: Mr. John Hay Whitney   September 6, 1939

. . . In view of the United Artists fight with the Hays Association, about which you told me on the phone, and before this fight is settled, I think we have the ideal occasion to secure United Artists' support to telling the Hays Association that we want no part of them or their Code. As I see it, the only recourse they would have would be to instruct their theaters not to play our pictures—and it seems to me (but this is a legal question on which John [Wharton] should rule) that if we made decent pictures that passed all authorities, including censor boards, it would be a combination in restraint of trade to stop us from making anything we saw fit, or releasing anything we saw fit; and I doubt very much that the big companies with all the conspiracy and trust trouble that they are already in would dare to chance anything else along these lines. If it weren't for our contract with MGM we would have the ideal picture with which to fight them in *Gone With the Wind,* but I am not sure that we haven't something comparatively good to fight them with in *Rebecca.* Here is a story that has appealed to Americans by the hundreds of thousands and even millions—that was one of the three or four most popular books of the last five years, and that a family publication like the *Ladies' Home Journal* saw fit to reprint without fear that it was anything immoral. I think that if we made *Rebecca* as written, without adding anything censorable beyond what du Maurier wrote, and if the big companies tried to gang up to stop us from showing it in their theaters because it hadn't been passed by Breen, we would have a pretty good case to take to the courts and —more importantly—to the press and the public, because I don't think Mr. Hays and his cohorts would very much relish the thing being fought out in the public prints. I could almost certainly guarantee tremendous support from the Guild groups here, actors, directors, and writers, and in fact, I think we would become heroes with them for having led the fight against so insane and inane and outmoded a Code as that under which the industry is now struggling.

The whole damned Code becomes doubly onerous now that we are in danger of losing our foreign market. It was bad enough trying to make pictures that would break even when we had a world market to play to and with many of our best possibilities ruled out by the Code.

But now, when we need at least to have something like the freedom that newspapers and magazines and book publishers and the legitimate stage have, when we need this freedom desperately, to have the industry itself strangle us is something which would be tolerated only by this shortsighted industry. . . .

The whole story of *Rebecca* is the story of a man who has murdered his wife, and it now becomes the story of a man who buried a wife who was killed accidentally! . . .[23]

DOS

To: Mr. Hitchcock   September 14, 1939
cc: Mr. Kern, Mr. Newcom[24]

With reference to our talk today about tempo, which is obviously of vital importance, various directors who have worked for me in the past have found it a benefit to have the cutter spend more time on the set with them to constantly prod the director about tempo. I know, for instance, that George Cukor used to ask Hal Kern to drive him crazy by insisting that every scene was too slow while he was actually shooting on it. I personally don't think there is any danger of this picture being played too fast, and I think that if you speed the pace a little more, even, than you think is right we will be a lot better off, and in any event I would much rather err on the side of too fast a tempo than on the slow side.

As I told you today, I feel that the dialogue tempo throughout, and without exception, is too slow, but that in speeding it up I would suggest you speed the other characters more than Mrs. Danvers, even though even she could be a bit faster than she has been. . . .

DOS

To: Mr. Hitchcock   September 19, 1939
                                                    NOT SENT

Dear Hitch:

I am putting this in writing because there seems to be some difficulty on the part of Henry [Ginsberg] and the Production Department

[23]In the novel, Rebecca was shot by her husband, Max de Winter. He then put her in their small boat, sailed out on the bay, opened the seacocks, drilled holes with a pike, and left the boat to sink. In the film—at the suggestion of Joseph Breen of the Hays office —Rebecca trips during a confrontation scene with Max and kills herself in falling. Then Max proceeds to take her body to the boat as described above.

[24]James Newcom, Associate Film Editor on *Rebecca*.

in making our complaints clear, and I want there to be no misunderstanding of any steps if they eventually become necessary because of your failure, or (and I dislike to think this) your refusal, to understand what it is that we are complaining about. . . .

Cutting your film with the camera[25] and reducing the number of angles required is highly desirable, and no one appreciates its value more than I do; but certainly it is of no value if you are simply going to give us less cut film per day than a man who shoots twice as many angles. Eliminating additional angles without eliminating the time that is spent on these additional angles, and actually through increasing the time that would be spent by other men if they secured these additional angles, is no feat. As somebody said the other day, "Hitchcock shoots like Van Dyke—except that he gets one third as much film," which means that you cut your film with your camera the way Van Dyke does but that he gets three times as much cut film per day.

I am aware that it takes time to get the performance out of Joan Fontaine, but every picture I have ever worked on had some such difficulty, and you are fortunate in having a completely competent cast of highly expert actors. . . . Miss Fontaine . . . requires work—but so has every other girl who has been aimed at stardom and who requires an enormous amount of work in her first big opportunity. Your difficulties in shooting this picture are a great deal less than the difficulties on the usual picture. And in most studios you wouldn't have anything like the cast you have now: you would have a great deal cheaper actors, and would have great difficulties with a great many of your roles . . . and you would be expected to make about twice the time you are making.

Nor do I feel that the condition of the script is even a factor. I will not go into the fact that the condition of the script is in my opinion largely due to your reluctance to do a more faithful job on scenes from the book, despite my pleas that you should do so over a period of months. Perhaps you can charge me with the condition of the script. But whether you or I is responsible, or we are responsible jointly (which is probably closer to the truth), does not dismiss the fact that on every scene that you have made you have had the script many days ahead and there has been no question of it coming out at the last minute. Actually, the script of each scene on this picture has in every

---

[25]A method of working from a predesigned plan to shoot only the camera angles (setups) thought to be needed for eventual editing, and only certain portions of the scenes from these angles. This system affords little or no "protection" footage for flexibility or second thoughts during editing.

case been out very much earlier than on almost any picture we have ever made, including *Gone With the Wind, A Star Is Born, The Prisoner of Zenda*, etc. And there are some good directors in this town who, for some reason unknown to me, persist in having each scene rewritten after it is rehearsed on the stage, and who still manage to make infinitely better time than we are making on *Rebecca*.

This complaint would have been identical a month or six weeks ago. Today, when we are faced with the probability of a large loss on *Rebecca* because of war conditions, it is no longer a matter of better time being desirable, it is a necessity. In all other studios in town producers and directors are trying to figure out how they can cut down their normal shooting schedules and budgets by twenty-five to fifty per cent. And their normal schedules and budgets are a great deal higher than what we have been hoping for on *Rebecca*. Good average time on *Rebecca* would be acceptable in normal conditions, although regrettable today; bad time on *Rebecca*, regrettable and untenable as it might be in normal times, is impossible of acceptance today.

There are various things about your methods of shooting which I think you simply must correct, because even if we permitted you to follow them on *Rebecca*, you would have to cure them on your next picture and succeeding pictures because nobody in Hollywood would stand for them, so we might as well clamp down on you for this picture. I refer to such things as letting the actors remain idle while the camera crew lines up, and the camera crew remain idle while the actors are being rehearsed. It is just infantile not to realize that these two processes must go through simultaneously, and if the noise disturbs you, then rehearse them on the sidelines or somewhere.

God knows that this studio has never been famous for its speed of production. In fact, our pictures have always been made more slowly than comparable pictures in almost any other studio in town. We had hoped to correct this on *Rebecca*. Instead, we find that we are behind even normal-prosperity-time speed. . . .

I know that you are working late evenings, but working late means overtime and overtime means additional cost—and these additional hours in the evening are only justified to improve normal shooting time. They are certainly not justified to make up shooting time that has been wasted in the course of the day, particularly when these extra hours don't even make up for the lost time. We want these extra hours, although they perhaps might not be necessary if we had achieved real John Ford type of speed in the course of the day; but we want them, in addition, to do a good full day's work and not as an inadequate and expensive substitute for it.

... My fondness for you personally, and my respect for your abilities, cannot blind me to my responsibility to the people who are financing these pictures, and to the employees whose jobs depend upon efficient shooting on the stage. ...

I will be very happy to discuss this with you tonight at the studio, or at my home, or over a drink, or tomorrow, or any other time. Or, if you wish, we will say no more about it and just look to a difference in result.

DOS

To: Mr. Calvert   September 28, 1939

While pressing on with *Gone With the Wind,* we of course do not want to lose sight of the picture which, but for *Wind,* we would all consider the most important picture we have made—*Rebecca.*

You are familiar, I believe, with the fact that the studio will be shut down for a period upon the completion of *Rebecca.* To save money on overhead, I have notified everybody in the studio that we want to get *Rebecca* completed and prints out with unusual speed; but another reason for this, equally important, is that I feel we ought to go after Christmastime [release] everyplace on *Rebecca.* ...

DOS

October 3, 1939

[To Irene Selznick]

... You might start thinking about January. Jock is now as determined as I about the proposed [production] hiatus. Make some definite plans, and I'll work toward them. My mood is the Riviera— the Nile —houseboat—Greek Islands—yacht—Palestine—to hell with expenses. I want to go gloriously in debt for a Great Cause. I want to loaf and play and write and love. I don't want to even try to make any money during the period. I'd like people if they're strictly fun-people, otherwise none. Maybe different people in different places. I think it would be grand if we had Myron part of the time, Jock part. Maybe London for the *Wind* première (King and Queen there, I believe). I want to see you curtsy. I want to be gone three months, four months, six months—no plans for return—plans only for the first couple of months—stay as long as we like—come home when we miss it. And I'll never forgive either of us if we let *anything* interfere. . . .

Aviday

To: Mr. Hitchcock   October 9, 1939
cc: Mr. Wheeler

I am very disappointed in the second-unit stuff on the opening sequence. . . . I think it lacks mood, and I think this sequence is worthless unless we have a foreboding quality even in the photography. I think it requires filtered skies and silhouettes of the people, and I think we should go back for the opening shot to the idea of sweeping around the bay, perhaps opening on the waves dashing on the rocks, and moving back by camera to reveal in the far distance a lone figure of a silhouetted man against a very dark sky; and straight cutting to a low camera on Larry against a plate[26] of the same sky.

Also I think the action as shot by the second unit is all wrong, and I would like to go over this with you before you shoot it.

I believe we might be able to get something of what we want with a different cameraman, shooting at Palos Verdes.[27] I have asked Lyle Wheeler to prepare some sketches and I wish that one day at lunch, perhaps Wednesday, you would come up to discuss this sequence.

DOS

To: Mr. Monty Westmore   October 9, 1939

Thanks to clubbing everybody on the head about avoiding make-up on Miss Bergman, it looks as though we have a new star in her, with the public and the press all commenting widely on the fact that her eyebrows look natural, and that she isn't smeared with Hollywood make-up. However, we don't seem to have learned our lesson and we are still doing tricks with Miss Fontaine.

In one of the most important close-ups in the picture, the one in today's rushes where the character is almost driven to suicide, she has on eyelashes that compare with Marlene Dietrich's at her worst (even if they are her own eyelashes, they are made up in such a fashion as to look fake), and her eyebrows are all plucked out to a point at the

[26]Background projection shot.
[27]Near Los Angeles.

end, so that the whole idea of this sweet young girl being at Manderley fighting a memory of the sophisticated Rebecca is materially hurt. Please correct this for the future, and immediately. And what can I do to get you make-up men to throw away your kits and your tweezers? The public is so far ahead of you all and is so sick of your make-up that you are all managing to contribute to the destruction of stars.

DOS

To: Mr. Klune   October 6, 1939

Every time I try to cut down on my memos by giving verbal instructions, something happens which discourages me.

For months now I have been trying to tell everybody connected with *Rebecca* that what I wanted in the girl, especially in the first part, was an *un*glamorous creature, but one sufficiently pretty and appealing, in a simple girlish way, for it to be understandable why Maxim would marry her. But I was apparently unsuccessful with everybody for a long period of time.

The other day I sent verbal word to the set to be sure there was no misunderstanding that I wanted the girl to look as pretty and appealing as she could as long as she was *not* glamorous. The message was delivered to Miss Fontaine, to the cameraman, hairdresser, and everybody else that I wanted her to look "glamorous . . . more than at Manderley." This naturally threw everybody into confusion and obviously must have made everybody think I had suddenly gone mad. For the sake of whatever is left of my reputation for sanity, I should appreciate it if you would trace this error and explain what happened to those who received the message. And I should like to know, for my own sake, just who, stupidly or mischievously, delivered the message wrong.

DOS

To: Mr. Hitchcock   October 11, 1939

Dear Hitch:

In today's rushes I was a little disappointed in the reaction of the girl to Maxim's casual statement, "You little fool, I want to marry you." I think that the reason she is speechless is that she is completely flabbergasted and bowled over, and since I think that in any case this needs a close-up in order for it to be registered, I'd like to suggest that we pick this up.

Also, I think there is a wonderful chance for a cross between great humor and great poignancy in her line, "I do love you. I love you dreadfully, and I've been miserable and I've been crying all morning because I thought I should never see you again." . . . I think this should be a real cry from a young girl's heart, blurted out with great emotion and eagerness, since she has been far too modest to imagine that he loves her; and his interpretation of her seemingly not wanting to marry him as being because she does not love him would bring a spontaneous response from her that revealed her true feelings, for the first time without inhibition or modesty.

Also, I think this line would be easier to read with this in mind, if we copied it exactly from the book. (Please see page 62 of the book.) . . .

I think that Joan has been handled with great restraint, but I think we've got to be careful not to lose what little variety there is in the role by underplaying her in her emotional moments—whether these be the emotional moments of a young girl, or the emotional moments of the more mature woman, as particularly at the end of the "confession" scene. From this point on to the end I'd like to urge that you be a little more Yiddish Art Theater in these moments, a little less English Repertory Theater, which will make the restraint of the rest of the performance much more effective, in my opinion, and will not make it seem as though Joan is simply not capable of the big moments.

DOS

To: Mr. Alfred Hitchcock   October 13, 1939

Dear Hitch:

Today's rushes were, I thought, all right, but frightened me from the standpoint of tempo more than any we have had so far. . . .

Larry's silent action and reactions become slower as his dialogue becomes faster, each day. His pauses and spacing on the scene with the girl in which she tells him about the ball are the most ungodly slow and deliberate reactions I have ever seen. It is played as though he were deciding whether or not to run for President instead of whether or not to give a ball. I realize that he is not anxious to give the ball, and the reasons therefor, but even if the decision were a much more important one, for screen purposes the timing is impossible. For this reason I think you had better plan on picking up close-ups, as you discussed. . . . And for God's sake, speed up Larry not merely in these close-ups, but in the rest of the picture on his reactions, which are apparently the way he plays on the stage, where it could be satisfactory. But while you are at it, you will have to keep your ears open to make sure that we know what the hell he's talking about, because he still has the tendency to speed up his words and to read them in such a way that an American audience can't understand them. . . .

DOS

To: Mr. Hitchcock   October 23, 1939

Dear Hitch:

Don't you think it's awfully unfair, and damaging to performances as well, for the principals not to stand in and read the off-scene lines in important close-ups instead of having the script girl read these lines?

While Fontaine did very well in those of her confession-scene close-ups where Olivier had his lines read by the script girl, and vice versa with him, I should think that they'd both do even better if they were really played to; and most directors I know wouldn't permit such indifference of the actors to each other's performance.

Use your own judgment about this, and I don't mean it's necessary on unimportant things, but I do think it would help in important scenes.

Also, I have been meaning to speak to you for some time about Larry's habit of throwing away lines too much—for instance as he did in the dining room with his line in which he contradicts Frank's suggestion that he was ill at the time. I know that this is the modern style of acting, but it's also a modern style of losing points! He's been better lately, but I'd appreciate it if you would be on your guard about it in the remaining sequences.

DOS

To: Mr. Raymond A. Klune   November 14, 1939

With reference to the rushes:

I think the fire exterior of Manderley going through the front door is excellent; but I'm disappointed in the fire in Rebecca's room. It's satisfactory, but not nearly as good as it should be—and if we can fix it at little expense, I think we should do so.

My objections to the fire on the interior of Rebecca's room are as follows:

1. We don't know clearly enough that it's Rebecca's room. I don't

know quite why this is, except perhaps that there aren't enough distinguishing features such as the curtains (which I realize that we've seen Mrs. Danvers tear down). . . . The film of the early sequences in Rebecca's room should be looked at to study what it is that is most likely to remain in the audience's mind.

2. The lighting is extremely uninteresting. It should be lit weirdly with an effect as though entirely by firelight, with the shadow of the flames, etc. As it is now, the lighting is very unrealistic as well as being very undramatic, and clearly there are sources of light that should not be there—other than the firelight.

3. We're a trifle slow in getting up to the nightgown case; the nightgown case in a couple of takes is sloppily placed instead of being precisely placed, as was Mrs. Danvers's habit; when we get up to the case it's slow in taking fire; and we're a little slow in getting to the "R."

4. There's no photographic effect as there should be, if possible, of the flames rising as they devour the "R," to give us a natural curtain of flames as a background for our end title.

We don't seem to give to each unit that comes in the benefit of the lessons we've learned through previous pictures. In recent films we've finally been getting some really expert transparency photography, but the stuff in today's rushes on *Rebecca* is amateurish and goes back years, certainly for this studio. . . .

DOS

To: Mr. L. V. Calvert   December 2, 1939
cc: Mr. J. H. Whitney

I am afraid I might as well face the inevitable and toss in the sponge on the *Rebecca* [release] dates. I never for a minute dreamed that I would be unable even to look at a foot of *Rebecca,* as has occurred during the past week, due to the enormous amount of time I have had to spend on *Gone With the Wind,* particularly as to its dubbing and scoring, and the selecting of tracks to make the dialogue as audible as possible. (Incidentally, I know you will be glad to hear the sound on *Wind* is very advanced as to quality.)

Furthermore, the combination of my exhaustion, plus by natural nervousness about every detail connected with *Wind,* hardly leaves me in a mood to do the big editorial job that is necessary on *Rebecca* to make it as good a picture as we all hope, and as I know you and everyone else back East expect.

My procedure is therefore going to be as follows: I am going to try desperately between now and the time I leave for Atlanta to do some of the first editing on the picture, and to write some of such retakes as I may feel are necessary. The scoring will also proceed, instead of waiting for the final editing. But I don't think I will be able to complete even this process before I leave for the East.

On the off hope that I can complete it, and that some of this work can proceed while I am away as I have laid it out, I should like, if possible, to have an opening in Los Angeles on or before January 10 for two reasons: the first being to make it eligible with our other pictures for joint awards; . . . and second, and much more important, because I want to try out something I have been preaching for years —the editing of a picture through audience reactions under normal circumstances, instead of with a preview audience. *Rebecca* is a very tricky picture, with very peculiar moods and a very strange sort of construction and playing. I don't want to take the chance of finally editing it according to the reactions of an audience that has come in to see a Marx Brothers picture, or even a Joan Crawford picture, as might be the case at previews. I think the whole preview system is wrong, in that it is the equivalent of trying out a Eugene O'Neill play on the road by advertising to the public that they are going to see the *Ziegfeld Follies*, and then having the reactions of a *Follies* audience determine how the O'Neill play should be cut. I would like to have a period of days to study audience reactions at a theater such as the Four Star (or, less desirable, the State and Chinese) [all in Los Angeles], where we would have an audience that had bought tickets to see *Rebecca*, and that was therefore typical of the audience for whom the picture was made. I would then re-edit the picture and have it ready for perhaps a Lincoln's Birthday or a Washington's Birthday release, if it is desirable to hold it up a couple of weeks longer to get these holidays.

TO: MURRAY SILVERSTONE[28]   DECEMBER 28, 1939

DEAR MURRAY: WE HAD OUR FIRST SNEAK PREVIEW OF "REBECCA" TUESDAY NIGHT. I TOOK IT OUT WITH FEAR AND TREPIDATION

[28]United Artists executive.

BECAUSE THE PICTURE WAS IN THE ROUGHEST KIND OF ASSEMBLY
FORM AND WAS THOUSANDS OF FEET OVERLENGTH. BUT IT IS
WITH GREAT PLEASURE THAT I AM ABLE TO ADVISE YOU WE HAVE
SELDOM IF EVER HAD A MORE SPLENDID AUDIENCE REACTION,
AND THAT JUDGING BY THE ENTHUSIASM OF THIS PREVIEW
AUDIENCE WE HAVE WHAT MAY PROVE TO BE THE BEST AND MOST
SUCCESSFUL PICTURE WE HAVE MADE, WITH EXCEPTION OF "GONE
WITH THE WIND." I WAS ALSO ENORMOUSLY HEARTENED BY THE
TREMENDOUS AND EXTRAORDINARY APPLAUSE THAT GREETED THE
MAIN TITLE, WHICH WOULD SEEM TO INDICATE PUBLIC HAS BEEN
LOOKING FORWARD EAGERLY TO THIS PICTURE AND AWAITS IT IN
LARGE NUMBERS. . . .

To: Mr. Calvert   January 25, 1940
cc: Mr. Whitney

. . . You speak of *Wind* being a part of the *Rebecca* ads. It is my belief
that it is much too small a part of the *Rebecca* ads, as presently
planned. I think we have two major things to sell, and one of secondary
interest. The two major things are the great popularity of the book,
and the fact that the picture is the very next production of the maker
of *Gone With the Wind:* and the secondary selling point is Laurence
Olivier. . . .

To: Miss Katharine Brown   February 27, 1940

Dear Kay:

I suggest you drop a note to Daphne du Maurier telling her I have
tried to do the most faithful job possible on *Rebecca:* that early reports
are enthusiastic; that I hope she will like the picture and will be eager
for a reaction; that the press previews here were very successful,
particularly in the great number of people who commented on its
extreme faithfulness; that Van Schmus[29] of the Music Hall was not
simply enthusiastic, but particularly commented on what he termed
an even more faithful transcription than *Gone With the Wind;* and
that you will be glad to arrange for her to see it as soon as a print gets
to England. Also, please make such arrangements.

But the principal point that I would like you to make in the letter
is that there is one drastic change that was forced on us by the Hays

[29]W. G. Van Schmus, President and Managing Director of Radio City Music Hall.

office and that almost caused us to abandon the picture. I don't want her to think we are imbeciles when she sees this change, which is that Maxim actually did not kill Rebecca. Tell her that you are writing to forewarn her, but to please withhold any comment on this point until she sees the film, as even the readers of the book apparently are not aware of the change from the way in which we have handled it. Say that if she says anything publicly or privately about this it is going to hurt the picture, and we hope she will extend us the courtesy, in view of the courtesies we have extended her, of not mentioning this, especially as it would get us in wrong at the Hays office, etc.—that we simply wanted her to be forewarned and to know it was something forced upon us, and that I was heartbroken because of my desire for complete faithfulness. You might explain that Hays did what the censors would have done anyway—and that is, reject a story in which a murderer goes free.

You might say further that in spite of this change, the confession scene seems to be word for word her scene, and is not simply one of the best scenes in the film, but in my opinion one of the best and most unique scenes in any film.

DOS

To: Miss Katharine Brown March 3, 1941

Dear Kay:

Please determine Daphne du Maurier's present address and send her the following cable over my signature:

DEAR MISS DU MAURIER, YOUR SPLENDID NOVEL "REBECCA" MADE IT POSSIBLE FOR US TO WIN THE AWARD OF THE ACADEMY OF MOTION PICTURE ARTS AND SCIENCES FOR THE BEST PRODUCTION OF THE YEAR. PLEASE ACCEPT THE THANKS AND BEST WISHES OF OUR ENTIRE STUDIO. SINCERELY,

DAVID O. SELZNICK

PART

DAVID O. SELZNICK
PRODUCTIONS, INC.
(1940–1948)

"REBECCA" WON THE ACADEMY AWARD the year following the sweep-ing of the awards by Gone With the Wind. *It was the first time that an independent studio had won two awards in consecutive years. It also won the Critics' Award for the best picture of the year, and* Vari-ety's *Poll of the biggest box-office picture of the year, as well as awards all over the world, second only to* Gone With the Wind.

After Gone With the Wind *and* Rebecca, *to draw down our profits, which were substantial, the only way I could see of getting myself some money that I needed and could keep was to liquidate Selznick International. The other stockholders agreed; and we thus created one of our lesser contributions to Hollywood, the introduction of capital gains. We made an agreement with the government under which we would complete our liquidation within three years. When the three years were up, my tax lawyers insisted upon a course which turned out to be extremely costly for me (and which also turned out to have been unnecessary, as was determined in a Supreme Court decision of years later) to the tune of many millions of dollars: they said that either the Whitneys or myself had to dispose of our respective interests in* Gone With the Wind *(we had previously cut up and sold to each other the other assets), or the government would challenge the liquidation. So in a quite simple meeting with my old friend Jock Whitney as to who would buy the other one out, I sold to Jock—for the simple reason that he didn't want to sell. Subsequently, Mr. Whitney and Mrs. Payson sold their original interest and what they had acquired from me, to MGM, for a huge profit.*

I went back East to rest after Gone With the Wind *and* Rebecca *and the dissolution of Selznick International, and then formed my own company without outside partners. My only partners in David O. Selznick Productions, Inc. were executives who had been with me for years. In October of 1941 this company became twenty-five per cent owners of United Artists.*

I worked on various individual war causes, sold all the stories that I owned, and went to work on a story of the home front, Since You Went Away. *This was followed by* Spellbound.

The production of The Keys of the Kingdom *I had nothing whatever to do with; I simply bought the story and sold it to Twentieth Century-Fox. I had nothing whatsoever to do with* Claudia; *I simply bought the story, cast Dorothy McGuire in it, and sold the package to Twentieth. I also packaged* Jane Eyre *and sold it to Twentieth.*

Producer Dore Schary had just left MGM when I engaged him. Some of the MGM executives who heard I was dealing with him called me to caution me that I was buying a piece of manpower who was more interested in trying to sell his causes than in making pictures. Dore was a big message man; but I thought more of him as a picture man than apparently they did at that time. I made a contract with him which turned out extremely well for all concerned.

He made I'll Be Seeing You *for me. It sounded like a good idea, and I told him to buy it. After a few months, he sent me the script. I dictated all day long on it. (My criticism was as long as the script!) Dore came to see me and told me we had reached the crossroads, and this would prove whether or not it was possible for me to leave anybody alone. He said he felt about half of my comments were wonderful, and he thanked me for an education in screen construction. But he felt that he could not agree with the other half of the comments: that perhaps I was right, perhaps he was right, perhaps we were both right; and that each of us might make a good picture our own way, but that unless I was prepared to let him accept my advice on construction, and leave the details as to how the story would be told to him, it would be my picture and not his, and there was no hope of any kind of individuality for him. He was so reasonable and made such good sense that I told him to go ahead and make the picture.*

When I saw the picture, I requested him to let me re-edit it. Again, he was frightened. I then told him that if he did not like any part or all of what I did, he could put it back the way he wanted it. His fairness was demonstrated when he was enthusiastic with the editing and said he had never before realized how much could be done with a picture in re-editing. Thus, Dore and I arrived at a method of work giving him the autonomy he wanted, but giving me the basic controls I needed and letting him take my advice or leave it as to the details.

I assigned to Schary stories and casts of other pictures: The Spiral Staircase, The Bachelor and the Bobby-Soxer, *and* The Farmer's Daughter. *That was during one of my periods of retrenchment, and we sold the packages to RKO on a partnership basis. The pictures were produced by Schary and were all great successes. We did very well with them, RKO did very well with them and so did Schary, who had a percentage.*[1]

---

[1]Three other Schary films in which Selznick had an interest were *Till the End of Time* (1946), *Mr. Blandings Builds His Dream House* (1948) and *Walk Softly, Stranger* (1950).

Notorious *was entirely my conception. I did the script with Hitch-cock and Ben Hecht, prepared it for Ingrid Bergman and Cary Grant, and then sold the entire package to RKO, where Hitchcock not only continued with the direction, but took over from me as producer. So I have never included that in my productions, although I was responsi-ble for the whole project.*

Increasingly I learned to have great respect for Hitchcock. Thus, while I worked very closely with him on preparation, and while he left the editing to me, I left him entirely alone on the set. During Spell-bound, *I don't think I was on the set twice during the entire film.*

In 1946, when I formed my distributing company, the Selznick Releasing Organization, I was able to put into effect what I had long preached: that the whole method of distribution in the business was archaic, completely outmoded, and very wasteful. Within a matter of a few weeks, I arranged for physical distribution through existing nontheatrical channels on a per shipment basis. I was thus able, first, to cut costs of distribution by sixty per cent (and this with extremely few pictures) and got far more efficient distribution. Moreover, it proved that it was unnecessary to make pictures that nobody wanted to see in order to absorb production overheads, which are in most cases absurdly inflated, and in order to keep feeding an excessively expensive distribution method.

I made other moves in various countries of the world that effec-tuated similar savings, and in some cases greater savings, than in the United States. Duel in the Sun, *one of the highest-grossing pictures of all time, was thus distributed by my own sales department at a fraction of the distribution costs on other pictures. So were* The Paradine Case *and* Portrait of Jennie. *I have always felt that there was only one place to properly spend money in this business—and that is on what goes on the screen (plus advertising, in which I am a great believer in proper relationship to estimated gross). Incidentally, I was also able to effectu-ate a large saving on print costs.*

I had a plan which would have cut costs of distribution still more than what I had put into effect, but it was frustrated by the death of three men within a matter of a very, very short time. I made a deal with producer Mark Hellinger, who was in partnership with Hum-phrey Bogart, to make pictures for my distributing company (and also to absorb my production overhead) with the large number of stars that I had under contract—at the rate of three a year. Dore Schary was to produce three a year. I made a deal with veteran film executive M. J. Siegel to produce three smaller pictures to launch and further the careers of a group of younger players I had signed up. Hellinger and Siegel both died suddenly. And when Charles Koerner[2] died, his job at RKO was offered to Dore Schary, who begged me to let him take it. I intended to make one big picture a year myself. But with the combination of these three events, and after I had looked around for substitutes, I decided that the burden was altogether too great.

:: :: :: :: :: :: :: :: :: :: :: ::

July 13, 1940

Dear Vivien [Leigh]:

I am only in New York for the day, and hope to stay away from business for some time, getting that rest that I have been promising myself since long before we met while Atlanta was in flames. I am dictating this rapidly, just before leaving for Connecticut, and will not wait for it to get my signature.

Marie Adelaide is no stranger to me. I first read the play a long while ago when the Theatre Guild people and the authors expressed themselves as wanting Ingrid Bergman for it so badly that they just couldn't see anybody else in the part. . . .

I turned the Guild down on Ingrid for one of the reasons that I have to turn them down on you—a reason that would apply to anybody under contract to us. I say without fear of contradiction that there is no film producer in America that is more lenient about his people doing plays than I am, or that is more kindly disposed toward excursions into the legitimate theater. But I am neither tolerant enough, nor stupidly quixotic enough, to permit our players' pictures to become a side issue; and I cannot regard as anything but unmitigated gall the proposal of the Guild people that Ingrid or yourself should be available for a winter and spring season, a run-of-the-play contract, tryouts on the road, an extended engagement in New York, a summer given over to pictures, and an engagement the following fall for a further road tour. I am sure that they mean to be very generous in giving us the summer they can't use in which to make a picture, but I am afraid I don't appreciate this bone which they so graciously toss in our direc-

[2]Charles W. Koerner, General Manager of RKO Studio.

tion. I still choose to consider that a picture produced at a cost of twenty or thirty or forty times that of a play (without even going into such costs as that of *Gone With the Wind!*) is not something to be treated as an intermission between the efforts of a theatrical group, eager to capitalize on the following built up as a result of our initiative, our gamble, our success, and the opportunities we have extended. Where was their enthusiasm for our people when they were still in Sweden and in England—or, for that matter, when they were here and before we built them into attractions?

I am afraid, too, that I still consider a motion picture for which the finest talent in the world is engaged, in every department, a more important artistic endeavor than a theatrical production which is more often than not thrown together with comparatively second-rate talent, particularly when these productions are so obviously designed to cash in, on the road, with the "personal appearance" attraction value of film stars.

I am afraid that I still consider that from any standpoint it is more worthwhile to aim one's talents at an audience of between fifty and seventy-five million people the world over than it is to play to a tiny fraction of this audience. . . . It would be a very simple matter to prove that there are a hundred times as many people of adult intelligence and artistic appreciation in the audience of any film as there are in the audience of any play; the mathematics alone would prove it.

You may wonder why, if I feel this so keenly, I have permitted any ventures of our people behind the footlights. The answer is principally that I have done it to make the individual, such as yourself, happy, even when I have felt that I personally, and our company, had a great deal to lose financially through such ventures, to say nothing of the damage to a carefully nurtured investment. Forgive me, Vivien, if I call to your attention that we fought out the matter of your theatrical appearances at the time we made our contract, and that you secured certain important concessions in consideration of giving up the theater. Yet, in spite of this, I permitted you to do *Romeo and Juliet* [with Olivier] *solely* because of my desire to do something important toward your personal happiness. Everybody in the industry who heard about it thought I was absolutely insane to pass up the obvious value of Scarlett's time after *Gone With the Wind;* and the amazement was increased when it became known that another studio was backing *Romeo and Juliet,* and stood to profit therefrom. Since the unfortunate press on the production, I have had it thrown up to me that I have been foolish to permit your prestige to be placed in such jeopardy. But I can say in all honesty that nothing happened that I did not fear would happen, and that nothing happened that I was not prepared for; and that I recognized the danger to your career, and therefore to your value to us, of the production at the time that I gave consent. Even now I do not regret it, because I know that despite the heartache that you undoubtedly went through as a result of it, it made you happier at the time to do it. Frankly, though, Vivien, I didn't expect to get another request so soon. . . .

I have seen many cases of players who had achieved some success in the theater, entered films with the hope and the expectation that they would periodically, or at least eventually, go back to the theater, and had finally realized that the theater offered little or nothing by comparison with films. In fact, I can think of no single case where a player's film success exceeded his theatrical success in which the player did not eventually give up the stage entirely. . . .

We must be very careful in trying quickly to cement the enormous following that was so rapidly won by you and for you, before we take the chance of the New York critics giving you another black eye. You must get three or four more films under your belt: I don't expect that any of these will equal or even approach the success of *Gone With the Wind*, and I will be happy for you and for myself if they can duplicate the success of *Waterloo Bridge*[3]—for if they do, I will probably again be foolish enough to jeopardize an audience of countless millions through letting you aim at an audience of thousands. . . .

Please give Larry my affectionate regards.

> Devotedly,
> David

To: Miss Katharine Brown   January 31, 1941

To keep you up to date on the situation on Ingrid and *For Whom the Bell Tolls:*

I pinned [Ernest] Hemingway down today and he told me clearly and frankly that he would like to see her play the part. He also said this to the press today. However, he tells me also that at Paramount he was told that she was wooden, untalented, and various other things. Needless to say, I answered these various charges.

---

[3]The 1940 version featuring Miss Leigh and Robert Taylor.

Myron is working on it very hard.

I am also personally supervising a publicity campaign to try to jockey Paramount into a position where they will almost have to use her. You will be seeing items from time to time.

Incidentally, Ingrid wasn't in town today, or I could have brought her together with Hemingway. However, we are arranging for her to fly today to see Hemingway in San Francisco before he sails for China. If he likes her, I am asking him to go to town with Paramount on it.

If she doesn't get the part, it won't be because there hasn't been a systematic campaign to get it for her!

DOS

Mr. John Abbott[4]   February 19, 1941
Film Library; Museum of Modern Art
11 West 43rd Street
New York City, N.Y.

Dear Mr. Abbott:

I had a thought the other day about an extension to your Film Library's activities which I discussed with Mr. Whitney, and which he seemed to think was an excellent one. He agreed that I should write you concerning it.

As I think you will agree, the scoring of pictures is becoming increasingly important. The amount of time and effort devoted to these scores is increasing all the time; important musicians are finally coming to recognize their importance; and more and more, really fine musicians are recognizing that scoring is a new form of musical art. Why, then, would it not be a good idea to start to collect important scores, including those of real quality and those which have an effect upon the art as a whole?

You showed me some of the scores that were written for the early silent pictures, including cue sheets for some of the early short subjects, and I believe you also have the score of *The Birth of a Nation*. I think that without too much effort, you might accumulate scores of other important pictures up to the time that sound was introduced. From the time that sound came in, I would suggest inclusion of the score of *Tabu*,[5] which I believe was originally made as a silent picture;

[4] Director of the Museum of Modern Art Film Library.
[5] The score for *Tabu* (1931) was composed by Hugo Riesenfeld.

and the scores of early RKO pictures written by Max Steiner, such as *Bird of Paradise* and *Symphony of Six Million.*

I am under the impression, and I hope I'm not wrong, that it was I who was responsible for the first scoring under dialogue. I remember a discussion with Max Steiner in which he protested that the audience might ask where the music came from, for up to that time it was felt that scoring under dialogue was not possible unless it was first shown in action that a radio or Victrola had been turned on! I insisted there was no more reason for explaining scoring than there was for indicating the source of music that accompanied silent pictures.

More recent scores in the collection could include those for *The Informer, Gone With the Wind,* and Stokowski's adaptations for *Fantasia.*

I think that scores written since the inclusion of sound might be accumulated by the Library both in their written parts and in sound tracks, which I believe could be obtained with all dialogue and sound effects omitted.

I believe that it is high time that someone gave encouragement to the training of musicians for the express purpose of scoring; and that many musicians and musical students would be delighted to study the written scores, and to hear them played in your theater.

Sincerely yours,
David O. Selznick

To: Miss Katharine Brown,   March 11, 1941
     Mr. D. T. O'Shea

Commenting on the last group of tests: . . .

I am sorry to have to say that I don't see what we could do with Gregory Peck.[6] Maybe a big studio could use him, but we would have great difficulty in either using him ourselves or in getting other studios to use him that didn't have him under contract. He photographs like Abe Lincoln, but if he has a great personality, I don't think it comes through in these tests. He must be a fine legitimate actor, judging by your great interest in him, and while his performance in the scene from *This Above All* is satisfactory, considering how much work was done in the day, and considering the circumstances under which it was made, it is nothing to get excited about. As for his performance in [the

---

[6]Peck had never appeared in a film. His initial screen performance would come in *Days of Glory* (1944).

scene from] *The Young in Heart* [1938] my respect for Doug Fairbanks, Jr., goes up after seeing Peck play this scene. . . .[7]

DOS

Mrs. David O. Selznick   April 26, 1941
Waldorf Astoria Towers
New York, New York

Darling,

. . . Clare and Harry[8] leave tomorrow unless the Clipper is again postponed, God forbid. They have been wonderful and I have enjoyed them enormously, but I have had no time for my own work. Even as it is, I am taking on a tremendous amount of duties for the Chinese Relief. I cannot honestly say, though, that I am unhappy about it, and in fact I am rather enjoying accomplishing things which I am sure could not be put over by anyone else. Harry seems most enthusiastic about my help, and grateful for it—and still most keen about my ideas. . . .[9]

Incidentally, your father called me the other day and asked if I could bring "those people" over to lunch. But he wanted to be very sure that they didn't know he had called. I handled it in accordance with his wishes, and while Clare couldn't come because she hadn't known that Harry wanted her to make a good-sized speech (and accordingly had to prepare it at the last moment), I took Harry over, and your father made violent love to him. The luncheon was in the private dining room at the commissary, and I am glad to be able to report that there were just the three of us—no [producer] Arthur Freed, not even any [Mervyn] Le Roy. The luncheon was enlivened somewhat by a conception that your father apparently has that Harry is deaf. I don't know where he got this—unless he deduced it from Harry's curious habits of cutting in on people, driving through on his own points when they are trying to talk, etc. . . . Most of the time he got right up into Harry's ear, put his arm around him, and literally screamed at him. Curiously, Harry didn't seem to mind. I tried to find the opportunity for a signal to your father, but somehow couldn't. Later when I discussed it with Clare and Harry, they thought the reasons were probably those I have indicated above. . . . Furthermore, I learned to my

[7]Douglas Fairbanks, Jr., was a leading player in Selznick's *The Young in Heart.*
[8]Mr. and Mrs. Henry R. Luce (Clare Boothe Luce).
[9]Selznick was producing a spectacle at the Hollywood Bowl for the benefit of the China War Relief.

amazement that Harry *is* a little hard of hearing—"in one ear"—so once again your father is apparently smarter than he is sometimes given credit for. Clare made the revelation; Harry reluctantly admitted it, stating that "sometimes" he was a little hard of hearing, but that it always developed that "he knew what they had said." Clare translated this as follows: "Harry isn't hard of hearing, he just sometimes doesn't hear people!" . . .

After lunch your father insisted on driving us around all three lots [at MGM] until about three-forty-five, when I dragged Harry away because we were late for Disney. I am sure your father would have spent the whole day—and I must say Harry didn't mind in the least, and on the contrary seemed to enjoy it very much, and not even to mind the fact that during the hour or hour and a half we spent in the car your father had his arm wrapped around Harry's shoulder. . . .

I am exhausted and lonely—but for some mad reason, not at all depressed. . . .

I am now very late, and I like to think that you are waiting for a letter from me, so if you don't mind I will have this sent without waiting for my signature.

Devotedly,
David

To: Mr. Klune   May 8, 1941

For some time now I have been noticing that there is something about the recording of the music in Warner Brothers pictures that makes the music infinitely more effective than in our own, and in fact in the pictures of any other studio. I don't know whether it is the choice of instruments, and the manner of orchestrating, or whether it is the recording or the dubbing. But in any case, there is a richness to the music, and a volume to it, without the slightest loss to dialogue, that is not characteristic of other studios' scores.

I wish you could study just what it is that they do.[10]

DOS

---

[10]Ray Klune replied that for the most part the distinguishing factor of Warner Bros. music was the volume at which it was dubbed. Warner Bros. represented the extreme school of thought on this method of handling music. MGM represented the other extreme, with the score being only an incident of the film, and it was treated as such. It should be added that the orchestral coloring in Warner scores had a generally rich texture and style.

TO: MISS KATHARINE BROWN   JULY 22, 1941

REGARDING PHYLLIS THAXTER: I THINK DECISION ON WHETHER OR
NOT YOU SHOULD TEST SHOULD DEPEND ENTIRELY UPON
WHETHER OR NOT YOU THINK SHE IS GOOD BET FOR FUTURE
APART FROM "CLAUDIA." . . . IS THIS THE BIG-EYED GIRL WE SAW
IN THE OFFICE WHO HAD TWO CHILDREN? . . . INCIDENTALLY, IF
IT IS THE BIG-EYED GIRL I CERTAINLY THINK SHE IS WORTH
TESTING NO MATTER WHEN SHE WOULD BE AVAILABLE.[11]

DAVID

To: Mr. D. T. O'Shea,   July 25, 1941
       Miss Katharine Brown

I hate to let off another blast about the salaries of young girls that
we are considering signing and I do hope you will forgive me when
I say that the figures on Phylis Walker are in my opinion slightly
insane.

Here is a girl who has done nothing, or next to nothing, and we think
of starting her at $200. This isn't bad enough, but at the end of her
contract she gets up to $1500, $2000, and $3000. I think we are losing
all sense of proportion. At other studios girls in this position start at
absolutely minimum rate and get up to $300 or $400 or $500 top at the
end of seven years. . . . We certainly don't have to be held up in the
case of a Phylis Walker, and I think that Kay ought to immediately get
hold of the girl and tell her we wouldn't dream of paying her any such
figures. . . . We have been thrown way out of line by such exorbitant
figures as we paid to Vivien Leigh and Ingrid Bergman at the time we
signed them. Let's get down to earth.

DOS

To: Mr. Lowell V. Calvert   August 18, 1941

Thanks for your note about *Another Star Is Born*,[12] which is just
what I was after.

You might remind those people who have the notion that sequels
don't get anyplace about *After the Thin Man*, the title of which was
certainly just as similar to the original as would be the case here (if you

[11]Selznick was thinking of Phylis Walker (Jennifer Jones), whom he had seen the same
day for the first time.
[12]Contemplated but unproduced sequel to *A Star Is Born*.

will consult your memo you will see that some of them speak about the proposed title being too similar). *After the Thin Man* did much, much bigger business than the first one, and, in fact, the subsequent *Thin Man* pictures all did better than the first one. The same is true of all the Hardys.[13]

DOS

To: Miss Katharine Brown   August 19, 1941
cc: Mr. D. T. O'Shea

I finally had a chance to go over with Dan [O'Shea] your two memos concerning *Claudia,* Phylis Walker, etc.

Today I have chatted about the matter with Phylis Walker—for whom, incidentally, I have a great enthusiasm, in case you don't already know this. . . .

I have told Walker that I wouldn't want to give her a big opportunity, and make her a star at the expense of the insurance policy that we might have by giving these opportunities to established stars, only to find that we had difficulty later about her family being back East. She assured me that such would not be the case, and that if she is to move out here, her husband [Robert Walker] is quite prepared to move out with the two children and to settle here permanently, because they like California in any case.

Incidentally, what is the husband like? I wish you would interview him. And I wish you and Dan would discuss by mail, with copies to me, whether or not we shouldn't sign the husband as an element of protection, either now or at such time as we decide to give her *Claudia,* if this comes about. It might be better to do it now, if we could make a brief initial deal, so that it doesn't look as though we are buying him subsequently just because we are giving her *Claudia.* We ought to preserve his pride. But if he is a good actor—wouldn't it be wonderful if he turned out to be a good bet himself? . . . I think we have enough enthusiasm for her now to believe that we will give her an important lead and make her into a star, either with *Claudia,* or with the role I have discussed as a McGuire possibility in *Keys of the Kingdom,* or with something else; and it would be a very smart thing to have him in our employ too.[14]

DOS

[13]The MGM Hardy Family series.
[14]Walker eventually was signed by MGM.

To: Mr. Bolton[15]   September 10, 1941

I would like to get a new name for Phylis Walker. I had a talk with her and she is not averse to a change. Normally I don't think names very important, but I do think Phylis Walker a particularly undistinguished name, and it has the additional drawback of being awfully similar to Phyllis Thaxter, which is doubly bad because of Thaxter being in *Claudia* [on the stage], which Walker may do, and because of the fact that Thaxter may soon be in pictures.

I don't want anything too fancy, and I would like to get at least a first name that isn't also carried by a dozen other girls in Hollywood. I would appreciate suggestions.

                                                              DOS

To: Miss Katharine Brown   September 19, 1941
cc: Mr. D. T. O'Shea

. . . In view of Phylis Walker's impatience to get to work, and also because we want to arrive at our decisions on both *Claudia* and *The Keys of the Kingdom*, these tests ought to be made just as soon as we can get them organized.

Hopefully, we can get Dorothy McGuire to test for *The Keys of the Kingdom* as Nora after she finishes her other test.[16]

My present feeling is that I want Walker to do *Claudia* and McGuire to do Nora, but I would like these tests to confirm my present opinion. . . .

If the whole plan goes awry, I am not worried about getting opportunities for Walker. Once she is announced for either picture it is pretty sure that we will have all the opportunities for her we want, and I don't see what we are losing by passing up a play for her now by comparison with what we have to gain.

. . . Things have happened with the girl that were beyond her wildest dreams a few months ago, so she shouldn't be impatient. She has what may be her last opportunity for a long time to devote herself to her two kids, and she had better make the most of it. . . .

I am terribly afraid the girl is going to get spoiled. Already she has lost some of that eager, blushing quality that made her so enchanting when we first saw her and when she was just the girl from the tent

[15]Whitney Bolton, Director of Advertising and Publicity for Selznick.
[16]Selznick later sold *The Keys of the Kingdom* to Twentieth Century-Fox. Jane Ball (Mary Anderson) played Nora.

shows. I am terrified that by the time we get *Claudia* in work she will be wrong for it because the bloom will be off the peach. I hope she is not being made aware of the theatrical interest in her; I wish she would stay away from producers and agents and everything in connection with the theater until she comes to the Coast—unless we decide to let her do *Claudia* or something else on the stage after we see the tests. . . .

And incidentally, we ought to get a new name for her as soon as possible.

DOS

Mrs. William Brown Meloney[17]   September 30, 1941
c/o Miss Katharine Brown
David O. Selznick Productions, Inc.
630 Fifth Avenue
New York, New York

Dear Rose:

Thank you for your letter.

I appreciate more than I can say the help that you are giving us on *Claudia,* and your expressed eagerness to do everything you can to make the film a success. . . .

I am naturally very much disappointed by your feelings about Phylis Walker. I think the girl is a great natural picture success, and that whatever film she is launched in will be helped enormously by having her in it. So convinced have I been that she would make an excellent Claudia that I have kept her out of everything else until we could arrive at a final decision as to whether we wanted to use her in the role, after determining other possibilities—and, of course, the availability of Dorothy McGuire.

Everyone who has seen Phylis who is connected with either motion pictures or the stage, yourself excepted, has gone overboard about the girl. . . .

I say to you now that it is my sincere hope that Walker will overnight be a star . . . if we should cast her as Claudia. I am aware of the girl's shortcomings. I have seen her rehearse, I have seen her perform, I have seen her before audiences—and I know the excitement that she causes in audiences. And her tests for *Claudia* knocked everyone out here for a loop. Now I will concede that you have had a better oppor-

[17]Rose Franken, author of *Claudia.*

tunity to judge whether she can play *Claudia*, and have more familiarity with the requirements of the role, than anyone else; but all of us have at various times in our careers been led to change our minds about actresses after they have their opportunities; and in this case, the only opportunity that I feel we must give the girl is to test her thoroughly. The proof of the pudding will be in the testing: if she is wrong for *Claudia*, we can all see it with our own eyes, and we can judge whether she has inadequacies that would keep her from being able to sustain this role.

. . . We have seen the screen sometimes turn up startling surprises. I have seen player after player who seemed like nothing in rehearsal, but to whom the magic of the screen gave all sorts of new qualities, and who seemed quite a different person on the screen than in the office or the rehearsal room.

I should also like you to consider that playing on the screen is a good deal different from playing on the stage. The actress does not have to sustain a two-and-a-half hour performance, and has all the benefit of take after take of each individual scene—with no scene lasting more than a few seconds or a few minutes—until that individual scene is perfect, and I hope you know that I am notorious for not letting any scene leave my studio until it is right. I have carried this to such extremes that it has sometimes been considered ridiculous—but I like to feel that the finished result speaks for itself. Accordingly, Jane Doe might give an infinitely better performance than Phylis Walker in carrying *Claudia* through a full evening's performance on the stage; but an infinitely less exciting performance in a film, bearing in mind the result that we might get out of Walker through painstaking effort on each individual moment. . . .

We mustn't underestimate the value to any picture of an electric screen personality. That same personality on the stage might fail because it would have to sustain an entire performance; but great screen personalities are very rare things indeed, and when they are uncovered—as I believe we have uncovered one in the person of Walker— I for one am willing to go to great pains to supply them with what they may lack. . . .

I am disappointed to hear what you have to say about Dorothy McGuire being probably unavailable, for I still felt that she must be considered the odds-on favorite for the role on one basis, while we had considered Walker the odds-on favorite from another standpoint. . . .

Cordially and sincerely yours,

To: Mr. O'Shea   October 24, 1941

I am seriously worried about Phylis Walker's confession about her previous contract with Republic, about which Kay is writing you. . . . For all we know, she is either on suspension at Republic, or signed something that would prevent her from working for somebody else. I don't know how you will go about finding this out, but certainly we ought to find out somehow.[18]

DOS

TO: MISS KATHARINE BROWN   DECEMBER 11, 1941

IMMEDIATELY UPON YOUR RECEIPT OF THIS WIRE PLEASE DROP EVERYTHING AND RUSH OVER TO THE HAYS OFFICE TO REGISTER "MEIN KAMPF" AS WELL AS ANYTHING ELSE NECESSARY TO PROTECT IT, SUCH AS "LIFE OF ADOLF HITLER" AND "MY LIFE, BY ADOLF HITLER." I HOPE THAT THERE WILL BE NO NONSENSE ABOUT WHETHER THIS IS COPYRIGHTED OR NONCOPYRIGHTED WORK, AND I HOPE THE HAYS OFFICE HAS THE GOOD SENSE TO REALIZE THAT I CONSIDER IT NONCOPYRIGHTED AND HAVE NO INTENTION OF BUYING RIGHTS OR OF PAYING ROYALTIES, WHICH IN CIRCUMSTANCES WOULD OF COURSE BE RIDICULOUS. EVEN BEFORE WE WERE AT WAR, PUBLISHERS CONSIDERED IT IN THESE TERMS. . . . KEEP IT UTTERLY SECRET UNTIL I HAVE HAD OPPORTUNITY TO CHECK WITH WASHINGTON ON THE MAKING OF THIS FILM. . . . WILL AWAIT WIRED WORD FROM YOU, BUT BETTER ADDRESS ME TO MY HOME TO FURTHER GUARD SECRECY, AND PLEASE CAUTION NOT TO LEAVE ANY WIRES CONCERNING IT AROUND THE DESKS, AND NOT TO EVEN DISCUSS IT WITH PEOPLE IN OUR OWN ORGANIZATION. . . . FOR PURPOSE OF WIRES AND LETTERS SUGGEST YOU REFER TO IT AS "TALES FROM HISTORY." . . . TO POINT OUT IMPORTANCE OF TREATMENT I PLAN FOR SUBJECT, I AM THINKING ABOUT HECHT FOR SCRIPT AND HITCHCOCK FOR DIRECTION, BUT DON'T WANT ANYTHING SAID EVEN TO THESE TWO.[19]

DAVID

[18] In 1939 Phylis Walker had been under contract to Republic Pictures for six months and appeared in one John Wayne feature, *New Frontier* (1939), as well as a serial, *Dick Tracy's G-men* (1939), using her maiden name of Phylis Isley. The contractual arrangement was terminated with no impediments to subsequent dealings.

[19] This project, for unknown reasons, was not developed.

To: Miss Brown, Mr. Bolton   January 8, 1942

Where the hell is that new name for Phylis Walker?

Personally, I would like to decide on Jennifer and get a one-syllable last name that has some rhythm to it and that is easy to remember. I think the best synthetic name in pictures that has been recently created is Veronica Lake.

DOS

To: Miss Katharine Brown   January 24, 1942
cc: Mr. Whitney Bolton

As soon as you have set Jennifer Jones as Walker's name, would you please advise Whitney, as I have some notions about publicity which I would like Whitney to discuss with me.

DOS

Mr. Cary Grant   April 2, 1942
1038 Ocean Front   NOT SENT
Santa Monica, California

Dear Cary:

I am frankly very upset to learn that the plans for our collaboration on *Claudia* appear to be in jeopardy.

When you were gracious enough to tell me that you had always wanted to make a picture with me, and that you would gladly do any picture that I wanted you for, I was enormously flattered and excited. I was naïve enough to believe briefly that you might be one of that company of artists who had sufficient understanding of what I try to do with my films, and . . . to make a contribution toward this by working for somewhat less for me than you are willing to accept from the larger and more exclusively commercially minded producing companies. I am now disabused of this notion, but I am sure you will understand my assumption that the very most that would be demanded of me would be compensation equal to that which you had received for endeavors for others, where there was less value placed on perfection. Perhaps you can then be tolerant of my shock at learning that I was expected to pay a great deal more than anyone had ever paid you for a performance. . . .

I suppose it is unnecessary for me to point out to you how much of what you receive will go in taxes, and how little of the extra amount you would personally receive. However, perhaps it is in order for me to point out that production costs are increasing by leaps and bounds —and very curiously so, in view of the fact that world markets are decreasing [due to World War II] as costs are going up. . . .

I go to any extreme, and am willing to pay very dearly, for quality; but there is a point beyond which I simply cannot go, in all reason. And there is the further point that my pride cannot permit me to exceed the limits dictated by common sense. . . .

I do hope that you will consider the matter carefully, and shall look forward eagerly to some word from you.[20]

Cordially and sincerely yours,

To: Mr. O'Shea   August 15, 1942

Mindful of how valuable I expect Jennifer Jones to be, I think that when the next option is taken up or even before then, perhaps starting immediately, we should say we want a new seven-year contract starting immediately, so that the year or more that she has been on payroll without doing anything isn't time out of the contract. . . .

I saw her last night and she looked wonderful and most charming. . . .

DOS

Dear Coop:[21]   September 1, 1942
cc: Mrs. Selznick

I was delighted when Dorothy[22] told me over the phone the other day of this opportunity to reach you with a letter. I had often wanted to write you . . . but I had no notion of how to address you, and realized that it would probably take months for any correspondence to reach you. . . .

I am ashamed to say that I am practically in the same state of confusion that I was when you last saw me. I have a rather elaborate production program planned, but whether it will ever see the camera is dependent upon a large variety of factors, most of them dealing with just what I am going to do about the war effort. I have made a number of stabs and many trips to Washington since you and I talked to Hop-

---

[20]Robert Young played the role.
[21]Air Force Colonel Merian C. Cooper, General Claire Chennault's Chief of Staff.
[22]Mrs. Merian C. Cooper (Dorothy Jordan).

kins,[23] and since our meetings with the air staff, but so far as I can see
the government is convinced it can do very well without me. This
doesn't in the least either embitter or disappoint me, and my ego is
intact. I have sold myself on the idea that there must be hundreds like
me, perhaps thousands, eager and anxious to do their part, but who
haven't yet been fitted in. If all else fails, I have certain ideas as to what
I can do privately, because if we are going to have the organizational
drawbacks of a democracy, we certainly ought to have the benefits of
a democracy that go with private initiative; and it is obviously the job
of each of us to figure out how we can help privately if we can't help
officially.

I have refused several nibbles, and one definite bid, at a commission
because I didn't think the work that I was supposed to do under these
commissions represented what I could and should do, and this had
nothing whatsoever to do with rank, which is of course unimportant.
I was told I could have a majority, with an indication that maybe it
could be a little higher, particularly with a little training—and actually
the part that appealed to me most was the training; but the work they
wanted me to do—running a radio program—seemed to me ridiculous, and furthermore, I have very strong feelings against this sort of
commission. Rightly or wrongly, I feel that at least as far as I am
concerned, men in uniform should be fighting and shouldn't be doing
jobs that could be done just as well in civilian clothes. Furthermore,
I am not trying to be heroic about it and I am perfectly sincere in
saying I honestly think I can do better as a civilian than I can in some
of the jobs that many of the men in New York and Hollywood have
taken with army rank. I am not of course speaking of a man like John
Ford, who obviously is doing a tremendously important and very fine
and courageous job, or of men like him. I am not even speaking of a
man like Zanuck, who obviously has a great many Army men under
him, and must have rank to perform his function. (I suppose you know
that Darryl is now a full colonel—and there is some talk . . . that he
may be made a brigadier general.)

I did feel that commissions such as Darryl's and Jack Warner's would
be most justified if they gave up their studio jobs; and I did feel it was
a peculiar kind of a war when Spyros Skouras could announce that
Colonel Zanuck would be in charge of production for the next year.
I thought announcements concerning Colonel Zanuck's activities

---

[23]Harry Hopkins, President Franklin D. Roosevelt's special assistant.

ought to come from the War Department and not from the board room of Twentieth Century-Fox. But I daresay that other people must have felt the same way because a week after Skouras's announcement, just yesterday came the news that Colonel Zanuck has resigned from Twentieth Century-Fox and will be spending the war as a soldier, stationed in Washington and Hollywood as a member of General Olmstead's staff. I think this is fine, and I think Darryl will continue to do the perfectly splendid job that he has done so far. I can think of no better man in the entire industry to take charge of a program of training films and other army films than Darryl. There is no other man in the industry who combines his drive, his experience, his ability to get out great quantities of film, his gift for tempo and guts, his knowledge of the Army, and his gall. Certainly, if I had the choice of an appointment for this particular job, I wouldn't think twice about handing it to Darryl.

Perhaps you don't know that Jack Warner is a lieutenant colonel, in charge of films for the Air Force and for Warner Brothers. I am sure he is perfectly sincere and will probably do a good job for General Arnold, who appointed him, but I do wish that he would stop making commercial films while he is a member of the Armed Forces. However, I daresay time will straighten this out too, and it wouldn't surprise me if within a week or two Jack finds that, like Darryl, he is in the Army for the duration and that he will have to forget about box-office receipts. Actually, Darryl and Jack both have accomplished things that other people could not have accomplished for the Armed Forces, even when they were doing part-time jobs, because of the tremendous command they have of resources. . . .

Jack Ford's Midway film[24] is supposed to be superb, but I regard it as a great tragedy that it still isn't released, thanks to fumbling about how it should be distributed, which is as of this writing still not settled. . . .

Ford apparently has built a tremendous reputation for himself, and knowing something of the part you had in organizing this unit, I am sure you are very pleased. As you must know, he was wounded while filming the Midway pictures, and I understand displayed extraordinary heroism. . . .

I don't know how much you know about what Jock has been doing. He took an eight weeks' course, which I understand is a very tough one, at Harrisburg, as an intelligence officer for combat service, and

---

[24] *The Battle of Midway* (1942), a documentary short subject.

was shipped abroad ten days or two weeks after his graduation. He is thinner, in very fine shape, and seems very happy. God willing, we will see him back again, because so far as I can gather, he is really going to see active service. I must say I envy him. . . .

Before Jock left, we set the final obsequies for Selznick International, which you will recall has to complete its liquidation by August 31. Jock bought approximately half of the negatives and the unproduced stories, and I bought the others. I hope we are not stuck with them, but I don't think we will be. We offered them to the Lehmans and to Myron, who turned them down. We otherwise disposed of the other assets, except *Gone With the Wind* and *Rebecca*. Since the liquidation, I decided to sell my interest in *Rebecca*, and Jock's lawyers bought it on his behalf with advice from Altstock, etc. This leaves *Wind*, and within the next twenty-four or forty-eight hours, I will probably have sold my interest in this to Jock. This ends my part of the saga of SIP, which fortunately turned out so well for everyone. Your small interest has turned out to be worth more than I think you anticipated, and I daresay you will have a few checks coming to you. . . .

Things in Hollywood are not greatly changed outwardly, although the regulations are becoming more stringent every day. It has taken a war to force the companies to cut the unnecessary and ridiculous quantity of their product, which is presently being forced on them by an order limiting them—but not nearly enough—as to the number of films they can make. It seems that there is a great shortage of raw stock,[25] and I understand that the government already is using more film than the entire industry. There is now a very severe limitation on how much you can spend on sets—$5000 per picture for new materials unless you get a special dispensation; and the manpower situation is growing more serious daily. But somehow, I suppose pictures will be made despite the fact that they are going to have a terrible time finding leading men, much less directors, technicians, cameramen, etc. Gable is a private in the Army, [Tyrone] Power is a private in the Marines, [Henry] Fonda is a gob, [Van] Heflin has been drafted, and every day comes news of one or two more to add to the dozens who already are in. In the words of Adolphe Menjou, if the thing keeps up, the women stars in pictures will be willing to work with men of their own age. . . .

If you need any money in America, for Dorothy or for anything else,

[25]Unexposed film.

for God's sake whistle for it. To my own astonishment I am lousy with it, and I would certainly much rather use it for anything that you need than in the other ways, in which the odds are I would get rid of it. . . .

Irene isn't with me, but I am sure she would enthusiastically join me in sending you much love, and a fervently expressed desire to hear from you.

Sincerely,

Mr. James V. Forrestal   September 16, 1942
Undersecretary of the Navy
Washington, D.C.

Dear Jim:

You very flatteringly asked me the other day if I were available to take charge of the coordination of the Navy's motion-picture and other photographic activities, possibly through a new Bureau of Photography. I replied that I should be glad to serve if you thought me qualified for this work. . . .

You presented me to Secretary [of the Navy Frank] Knox as "an egotist," and to Admiral Horne you went further and termed me an "egomaniac." I didn't mind this in the least because your succeeding comments were so kind, and because I knew you wouldn't have sponsored me with your associates unless you had confidence that my virtues would outweigh my faults in accomplishing a job which obviously is crying to be done. Indeed, I am delighted that you seem to want me in spite of my advertised ego; but on the other hand, you are at this moment paying the penalty of this recognition, in that it has given me the courage to parade a bit of this ego for what I sincerely trust will be the last time with you—for if I go into the work, I am fully conscious of the responsibility to you to step on as few toes as possible, to offend as few people as possible, and to justify your confidence.

But I am worried as to whether you can set me up in such a way that I will not let you down. When I hinted at this point the other day, you were good enough to reassure me, and to say something to the effect that my reputation in motion pictures would insure for me the respect and attention of anyone with whom I worked in this branch. . . . But you must recognize, as I do, that Hollywood figures, however prominent and successful, are regarded with suspicion, and I am fearful that if I do not have the authority to do a job, under you and Secretary Knox, it is possible that I will be stymied—and give not merely myself a black eye, but give you one as well. . . .

Confidentially, and since talking to you, I have closed a deal to sell my entire business in order to clear the path. I haven't monkeyed around with price, and indeed cut several hundred thousands of dollars from what I thought it was worth, and what I would have insisted upon, if I hadn't wanted to free myself to do just such a job as you indicated might be mine, a job of the exact type for which this egotist is eminently well qualified. I estimate it will take me a couple of weeks to clean up the details; if you tell me that this is too long a delay, I will get started sooner. But I should like this much time not merely to say farewell to the picture business for the duration, and to do what I can for the principal people who have been dependent upon me, but also to make arrangements about Irene and the kids, to try to find living quarters, etc. . . .

In any case, my deepest gratitude for giving me such generous audience, and for the confidence you have already demonstrated.[26]

Respectfully and sincerely,

David

To: Mr. D. T. O'Shea   December 3, 1942

I called Bill Perlberg[27] today to ask him what the devil was going on about Jennifer.[28] He told me that he had made up his mind and so had Henry King[29] and, he believed also, Bill Goetz,[30] but that they had a situation under which they had promised Anne Baxter to make a test, and they felt they were obligated to do this before finally saying yes. He said the test should be made in the next couple of days with Anne Baxter, and I urged him to speed up, pointing out that we had kept our girl idle for a long time and that we were keeping her in Hollywood.

DOS

[26]Selznick followed up this letter the next day with a twelve-page tentative plan to establish a Bureau of Photography for the Navy Department (for purposes of extending combat intelligence as well as making recruiting, training, and promotional films). Neither this plan nor subsequent efforts by Selznick to involve himself personally in the war effort materialized. Nevertheless, he continued to send suggestions of various kinds to all the branches of the Armed Forces, the State Department, and the President.

[27]Producer at Twentieth Century-Fox.

[28]Regarding the decision to cast her in the leading role in Fox's *The Song of Bernadette* (1943).

[29]Director of *The Song of Bernadette.*

[30]William Goetz was now Vice-President in Charge of Studio Operations at Twentieth Century-Fox.

Mr. William Goetz   December 10, 1942
Twentieth Century-Fox Film Corp.
10201 West Pico Boulevard
Los Angeles, California

cc: Mr. Kenneth Macgowan[31]
      [Director and writer] Robert Stevenson
      Mr. Orson Welles

Dear Bill:

At luncheon today with Orson,[32] the conversation naturally turned to my deserted child, *Jane Eyre.*

Orson mentioned that he hoped you would have Bernard Herrmann on the score, and by coincidence, he is exactly the man I would have used, as Bob Stevenson knows. I do hope that you will consider this suggestion favorably; and I am sending a copy of this letter to Orson, with the suggestion that he send you a note about Herrmann's work. . . .[33]

I share wholeheartedly Orson's feeling, and have previously expressed my conviction, that you ought to try to get as many new character people in the picture as possible. In proof of this, I interviewed dozens of actors for the various roles in New York, and have many suggestions to make.

I would be glad to be present at a casting meeting on the subject, and do hope you will invite me to attend. I should also like to urge that you have Orson there, because I know few people in the history of the business who have shown such a talent for exact casting, and for digging up new people. One of the sure ways of aggravating any otherwise remote danger of staleness in *Jane Eyre* is to cast old, tired faces that people have seen in a hundred pictures, and that are fine for most subjects, but that are inclined to give to the picturization of a classic an atmosphere of a stock company production. . . .

I don't know what steps have been taken to bring down Vivien Leigh's child from Canada, who judging by her photographs, might be excellent for Jane the child. I was terribly excited when this idea first presented itself. I would also like to call to your attention the publicity value of such casting. The whole quality of the childhood sequences is going to be dependent to no small degree upon the charm and personality of the child playing Jane, and from what I hear of Vivien's

---

[31] Associate Producer at Twentieth Century-Fox.
[32] Cast as Edward Rochester in *Jane Eyre.*
[33] Herrmann did compose the score.

child, she is perfect for it. Further, as she has been living in British Columbia through most of her childhood, her accent probably will be greatly in her favor.[34] . . .

If there is anything at all I can do to be helpful, please be sure to call on me.

Cordially and sincerely yours,

MR. VAL LEWTON[35]   DECEMBER 14, 1942
RKO PICTURES, INC.
780 GOWER STREET
HOLLYWOOD, CALIFORNIA

DEAR VAL: I SAW "CAT PEOPLE" LAST NIGHT, AND I AM VERY
PROUD OF YOU. I THINK IT IS AN ALTOGETHER SUPERB PRODUCING
JOB, AND IS IN EVERY WAY A MUCH BETTER PICTURE THAN
NINETY PER CENT OF THE "A" PRODUCT THAT I HAVE SEEN IN
RECENT MONTHS. . . . INDEED, I THINK IT IS ONE OF THE MOST
CREDIBLE AND MOST SKILLFULLY WORKED OUT HORROR PIECES IN
MANY YEARS. . . . I AM SENDING A COPY OF THIS WIRE BY MAIL TO
MR. KOERNER,[36] WHO I AM SURE FEELS AS I DO, THAT RKO IS
FORTUNATE TO HAVE MADE SUCH A TEN STRIKE AS THE
ACQUISITION OF YOUR SERVICES AS A PRODUCER. OTHER STUDIOS
HOPEFULLY HAVE EXTENDED SUCH OPPORTUNITIES TO WOULD-BE
PRODUCERS BY THE SCORE WITHOUT GETTING A RESULT SUCH AS
YOU HAVE DELIVERED AT THE OUTSET.

SINCERELY,
DAVID O. SELZNICK

Mr. Samuel Goldwyn   January 6, 1943
1041 North Formosa
Hollywood, California

cc: Mr. O'Shea

Dear Sam:

Recently, you have had a couple of occasions to remind us forcibly that you are "a frank man," although God knows no reminder was

---

[34]Peggy Ann Garner eventually played the role.
[35]Formerly editorial assistant to Selznick and West Coast Story Editor. His first film as a producer was *Cat People* (1942.)
[36]Charles W. Koerner, General Manager of RKO Studio.

necessary. However, I do hope that you grant to others—such, for instance, as myself—the right to be equally frank:

Sometimes, Sam, I am frank to say that I don't understand you. You scream and yell about other people's ethics, and then behave in a fashion that makes my hair stand on end with a combination of anger and incredulity.

You recently have sent direct for one of my people, Alfred Hitchcock, and talked with him without so much as either asking us, or even letting us know after the fact. I wonder just how you would behave if I reciprocated in kind—or if any of the big companies did it with your people. I have always maintained that no one is in permanent bondage in this business, and that once a contract has expired, or is soon to expire, every individual in the business should be free to negotiate with anyone he sees fit, without giving offense to the studio to which he or she has been under contract, and regardless of the desire of the original contracting studio to make the bondage permanent. I am not talking about such a case: rather, I am referring to a man who you know full well is still under long-term contract to me. Or if you don't know it, everyone else in the business does, and you ought to know it. The very least you could have done was to find out. Ignorance is no more a defense in these matters, if that be your defense, than it is in the law.

Hitch has a minimum of two years to go with me, and longer if it takes him more time to finish four pictures, two of which I have sold to Twentieth Century-Fox. And not alone did you try to seduce him, but you tried something which I have never experienced before with any company or individual—you sought to make him unhappy with my management of him. When you told Hitch that he shouldn't be wasting his talents on stories like *Shadow of a Doubt* [Universal (1943)], and that this wouldn't be the case if he were working for you, what you didn't know was that Hitchcock personally chose the story and created the script—and moreover that he is very happy about the picture, which I think he has every right to be. Further, that in the years since I brought Hitchcock over here from England (at a time when nobody in the industry, including yourself, was willing to give him the same opportunity . . .) and established him as one of the most important directors in the world with the production and exploitation of *Rebecca*, he has never once had to do a story that he was not enthusiastic about. This has always been my attitude about directors, and I happen to know that it has not always been your attitude toward directors under contract to you. . . .

By contrast with your own behavior, I have for months met criticisms of you with praise for your work, and for your contributions to the business, and for your integrity of production. I have said to literally dozens of people in important positions that you have never received as much recognition in the industry as is your due. And just yesterday, and despite my growing rage with you, I went even further than this with an important magazine writer who is doing an article about you. I not alone sang your praises, but I painstakingly corrected some impressions he had gained elsewhere, taking half an hour out of a very busy day for the purpose. When I hear of you doing the same thing, instead of doing your best (which would appear to be synonymous with your worst) in the opposite direction, I will believe your fine statements, and not before. I regret that I have to write you in this vein, and I do so not because I have any reluctance about rebuking you verbally, for you know from our past relationship that I have never been hesitant about such matters when I felt you to be in the wrong. I write you now, first, because I want it a matter of record, in connection with my future dealings with you; and second, because I have learned from experience that it is impossible to get you to listen to this many words unless they are in writing.

With best wishes for a fine and reformed New Year,

Sincerely yours,

Mr. Franz Werfel   February 24, 1943
St. Moritz Hotel
50 Central Park South
New York City, New York

Dear Mr. Werfel:

As you may know, Jennifer Jones, who is to play the lead in *The Song of Bernadette*, is under contract to me and was loaned by me to Fox for this role. . . .

At the present time the picture is scheduled to start March 15 and I am very anxious to make a present to Jennifer, on her first day on the set, of a copy of your book, hopefully autographed by you. To this end I am taking the liberty of sending you the copy to which this letter is attached, which is a first edition and which I have had especially bound, in the hope that you will be so gracious as to autograph it to her for me. I should appreciate it enormously.

Cordially and sincerely yours,

Mr. William Goetz   April 17, 1943
Twentieth Century-Fox Film Corporation
10201 West Pico Boulevard
Los Angeles, California

bcc: Robert Stevenson

Dear Bill:

I have just heard that Orson is to receive producer, or associate-producer, credit for *Jane Eyre*. If this be true, I think I would be less than conscientious in my obligations to Bob Stevenson if I did not say that in my opinion such credit would be extremely unfair to Bob, who pretty clearly took up the responsibility of producer where I left off. . . .

You know as well as I do that Orson is such a personality that if he is credited as a producer, Stevenson's credit is likely to degenerate into something of a stooge status, as has occurred with [director] Norman Foster on *Journey Into Fear*—and, mind you, on *Journey Into Fear*, Orson chose not even to have his own name appear in connection with production, so you can imagine what would have happened, and what will happen in the case of *Jane Eyre*, with his name appearing. . . .

I want to make clear two things. First, I am not asking anything whatsoever for myself—and on the contrary, want to remind you that my contract with you specifically provides that my name cannot be used, for it is a phobia of mine that I should not receive any credit for anything on which I have not done one hundred per cent of the job from original conception to final dubbing. Second, Bob knows nothing whatsoever about this letter. . . .

I don't believe that Orson himself would any more think of taking this credit, once he had all the facts, and understood what he might be doing to Stevenson, than he would think of trying to take direction or codirection credit. . . .

Another reason why this comes as such a shock to me is my clear recollection of the circumstances surrounding Orson's agreement to [take the part.] . . . I did discuss it with Orson, one day at lunch at Romanoff's—as a matter of fact, we were at Romanoff's together when you reached me by telephone on the matter. Orson explained to me that one of the reasons why he had been reluctant to do the job was because it would "reduce" him from a producer-director-writer-actor to simply an actor, and that if he were reduced further to a costar with second billing, it would be too much of a comedown. I understood this viewpoint, and agreed that he could have first billing, above Joan

[Fontaine]—feeling that it was more important to her to have the right Rochester than for me to hold out for billing under the circumstances.

However, my agreement to this billing, with both Orson and yourself, was based solely upon his receiving only the acting credit. If Orson receives associate-producer credit, it will therefore be a double injustice—to Stevenson, and to Joan's status as a star of the first magnitude. Of these two injustices, I think the one to Joan is the lesser because I think much too much is made of stars' billing anyway, especially since exhibitors and the public will star whoever they see fit to star, and Joan and Orson are not in competition—whereas the unfairness to Stevenson is a very severe one, robbing him of much of the credit to which he so clearly is entitled. . . .

Please feel perfectly free to show this letter to Orson. I shall appreciate hearing from you.[37]

Cordially,

To: [Director] Edmund Goulding   April 21, 1943
cc: Mr. William Perlberg, Mr. William Goetz

Dear Eddie:

Bill Goetz and Bill Perlberg were kind enough to show me yesterday the tests of Dorothy McGuire. Mindful of the many things on which you have been flattering enough to seek my opinion, particularly on matters concerned with *Claudia,* and of your kind comments in connection with the high value you place on these opinions, I take the liberty of rushing to you some comments I have to make concerning those tests. It must be borne in mind that Dorothy's first picture is a matter of intense concern to me. It was I who signed her for the role, and who insisted that she be cast in the picture when I sold the property; and Twentieth shares her contract only to a fifty per cent extent. I am therefore of course most concerned that her screen debut should be as outstanding and successful as possible.

I think that both Dorothy and myself were fortunate to have a director not only of your capability and talents, but of your peculiar gifts for the presentation of feminine personalities. But, as you know, I have had considerable luck myself in this direction, and I am therefore most hopeful that you will consider what I have to say with more

---

[37]Welles received top billing, but no one was credited as producer or associate producer.

than the mere courtesy that I know I can count upon you to extend
out of friendship.

. . . Dorothy's personality caught the fancy of America, in this very
same role, to an extent that has had few parallels in the theater in
recent years. . . . Her personality became the personality of Claudia
—as though Claudia were an actual living person—with millions of
people; and her own *personality* enchanted audiences, whether cos-
mopolitan or provincial, wherever she played. And it is *this* personality that, terrifyingly, something has happened to in the tests.

It cannot be that there is a difference in the media, because whatever the weaknesses of the early tests, *the identical personality* registered on the screen. Nor can it even be traceable to the fact that
Dorothy is a couple of years older—for in life *today*, she has much the
same personality. I think it is rather that we are all at fault for trying
to change her too much, myself as much as anyone else. Frankly, I
didn't realize that in attempting to do a little gilding of this very odd,
funny kind of lily, we might be destroying it. . . .

I think that somebody must have told Dorothy that she was moving
about too much, that she should drop all the cute mannerisms that
made her appear so gay and buoyant and youthful and natural. In any
case, we have in the tests a comparatively sedate young woman who
has lost the bubbling vitality and the naïve, almost childish quality that
not alone was Dorothy McGuire but that also actually spelled Claudia.

I know that I was among those who criticized the lilt in her voice,
and her invariable tendency to an upbeat at the end of every sentence.
But without it, I am horrified to discover that her diction and voice
have lost their charm. . . .

Dorothy's values are, one, an extraordinary talent; two, a pixie kind
of personality that has never before been seen on the screen, and that
probably existed on the stage (maybe Maude Adams, from what I hear)
but certainly not in my time. . . .

Note too that in some of these photos, the odd shape and contour
of her face have not been too evened out. I noticed in the tests a
tendency to give her a more regular appearance—to smooth out her
features so, and to regularize her general physiognomy so, that once
again her personality was damaged. Objectively, the photography as
such was very good, and Dorothy looked prettier than she did in her
previous tests. I hope something of this superior prettiness can be
retained, but if it is at the expense of the *personality*, then Linda
Darnell and a hundred other Wampas starlets are prettier! . . .

The main thing I have said to Dorothy since seeing the tests is that

I wish she would try to forget any criticism she has ever heard from me or from anyone else. . . . I think she ought to be just as natural as possible. And for my money, I would hope that we could get back as far as we could to what she had originally, and not worry a damn if a few experts thought that this or that should be changed or cured. . . .

Cordially always,
DOS

To: Mr. Steele[38]   July 10, 1943
cc: Miss Flagg[39]

Referring to inquiries concerning the Bergman article:

Please be sure that these answers come from you and/or Harriett, and not from me.

Myron Selznick was the agent on the sale of the rights to *For Whom the Bell Tolls* [1943] to Paramount. . . .

I almost bought the book myself because of my conviction that it was so right for Bergman, but I was so exhausted after *Gone With the Wind* and *Rebecca* that I simply could not face a job of this size, and most reluctantly passed it up; yet I was determined that Bergman should play the part, regardless of who bought it. I planted all kinds of newspaper items to the effect that she was the only possible Maria; I widely publicized Hemingway's statement, after meeting her, that she was the only possible Maria. I propagandized with literally everybody I met in Hollywood so that it spread through the community, and this included everybody at Paramount, and also Gary Cooper, whom I assumed they would go after for the male lead. This campaign went on for the entire period from the time I read the book until she was finally cast in the picture. I don't know the exact time, but I believe it was well over two years. I think you should stress that I got exactly nowhere with Paramount, although I convinced everybody else. . . .

Finally the starting date became imminent; I had turned down several pictures for Bergman, but liked *Casablanca* when it was offered. Before closing *Casablanca* I called Paramount and warned them that if they finally decided they wanted Bergman, they might find that she was unavailable. They were uninterested. I closed for

---

[38]Joseph Henry Steele, Director of Advertising and Publicity for Selznick.
[39]Harriett Flagg, Selznick's East Coast Representative.

Casablanca, still telling Ingrid the whole time, as I had for two years, that she would play Maria in *For Whom the Bell Tolls*, and that she would win the Academy Award for it.

[Vera] Zorina was cast. Sam Wood insists this was at DeSylva's[40] insistence; DeSylva and Freeman[41] say it was at Wood's insistence. I told Ingrid that she would still play Maria, and continued these statements after Zorina started shooting, carefully watching the *Casablanca* schedule. . . .

The inevitable day came when Paramount called and wanted to know "if Ingrid were available, because they were thinking perhaps of making a change." By this time I had heard that they had destroyed Zorina's looks with a murderous haircut. . . . I called Ingrid and told her that she was Maria. She called me back the next day to beg me not to make demands that would keep her from getting the part. I replied that I had struggled for two years for the part, and that she need have no worries on this score.

Finally Paramount called to make the deal. I knew, as was subsequently confirmed by Dudley Nichols,[42] that the whole picture was in the balance; that Paramount was considering calling it off entirely despite their fabulous investment in it; that even Sam Wood had refused to proceed without the right Maria. I could have taken any advantage I wanted, but mindful of my own two-year campaign, my conviction of what it meant for Bergman (although, ironically, she was already established as a star), mindful of Ingrid's phone call, I made very modest demands, to which Paramount immediately acceded. . . .

Fortunately, *Casablanca* finished at this very time, having two days to go after the final phone call with Paramount. I wanted to demand a two-week hiatus in production to give Miss Bergman a rest, but she begged me to let her proceed at once, the day after she finished *Casablanca*. I devoted the next three days to supervision of her makeup tests, including particularly her haircut, which I insisted should be under my supervision, advising Paramount that I certainly would not take the chance that they would do to Miss Bergman what they had done to Zorina. I had a row with the union because of my insistence that Sydney Guilaroff, who was in wrong with the union because of an elaborate megillah, do the haircut, and finally settled with the union

[40]B. G. DeSylva, Paramount Executive Producer.
[41]Y. Frank Freeman, Paramount Pictures Vice-President in Charge of Studio Operations.
[42]Writer of the *For Whom the Bell Tolls* screenplay.

by agreeing that the haircut would be done at my home, where every lock was taken off under my eye.

Bergman's contract with me, which has been extended from time to time, still has three years to go with three pictures yearly. Miss Bergman has repeatedly advised interviewers, agents, and other companies that she hopes never to be under contract to anyone but myself as long as she is in pictures.

I must refuse to answer questions about salary either in Sweden or here. I will answer this question as soon as Harry Luce gives me the payroll of *Time* and *Life*. . . .

To: Mr. Myron Selznick   November 23, 1943

Dear Myron:

I have your note of November 18 about your dealings with me and with our studio. I never thought I'd have to go through this argument with you again, but since you ask for it, I suppose I'll have to take the time.

First, let me say that there is not a single instance . . . on which you ever favored me or us either on making a deal or on salary. I know you to be completely honest, so I will simply say what is an apparent fact, and has been increasingly so for a long time—that as your memory is getting worse, it is getting more and more convenient. . . .

You know perfectly well that Carole Lombard did not leave you because of anything to do with us, and that on the contrary, she took the position up to the day of her death that she would rather work for me than for any other producer in town, and she persisted in this attitude all through her difficulties with you and beyond these difficulties. You also know that you stuck me for the highest price ever paid for Carole Lombard on any deal you or anybody else ever made for her, either before the pictures she did for me, or after them. In fact, it was one of the laughs of your own staff and of everybody else in town as to the extent to which you stuck me on Carole Lombard and on others, including Freddie March, whom I also paid the highest price he has ever received in his career, either before or since. . . .

I will never again even answer a statement of this kind from you, either verbally or in writing, until and unless you can produce one single instance of any kind in which you ever showed the slightest favoritism toward me or toward the companies with which I have been connected. . . .

It is not my fault if people use a charge of favoritism toward me with you as an excuse to leave you—any more than it is your fault that the other agents use the claim that I allegedly favor your office when I want anything, and that I steer clients to you when I can, as an excuse for selling away from me people that I do want sometime. I have never made this an issue with you, and I think it outrageously unfair on your part to try to make the reverse an issue with me. And since I have not produced any pictures for years, and since I have built up my stock company through other agencies, thank goodness that I am in a position to say that there couldn't possibly be any basis for your statements of any kind whatsoever, true or false, for many years.

I am very glad indeed that you are not able to advance claims of "favoritism," and that you are not in a position to be able to try to disprove them, in connection with Ingrid Bergman, Joan Fontaine, Dorothy McGuire, Jennifer Jones, Joe Cotten, Alan Marshal, and all the others.

There is perhaps no better proof of the accuracy of my statements than Alfred Hitchcock, one of the cases you have tried to use in the past to prove the "trouble" you have been in with your clients as a result of us. Both Dan [O'Shea] and myself did everything possible to keep Hitch from signing with other agents, and to this day he has signed with none. Only the other day Dan took the occasion to point out to Hitchcock again, and as he has done often before, that your office sold Hitch to us at a price which we discovered to our horror subsequently was much higher than he had been quoted at, to every other studio in town, all of whom were not interested. Actually, we discovered that Metro had turned him down at *less than half* of what we signed him for.[43] . . .

Far from losing any clients from us, I am so sick and tired of hearing this completely unfair statement that some day I'd like to sit down with you and show you the long list of clients that you got through us, and others that you retain because of us. Actually, I have even had to do your agency work for you in the case of George Cukor, and this has extended over a period of ten years during which you have not done one solitary single thing for George while you have been collecting tens of thousands of dollars in commissions. . . .

In passing, contrast my relationship with the people who have advanced themselves as a result of the opportunities and the training they received with me, by comparison with your relationship with the people who have benefited from opportunities and training they have

---

[43]All of this was before Hitchcock came from England to do *Rebecca*.

received with you, and who have left you. You talk about slavery, but you consider it a personal affront if anybody leaves you to better themselves. As far as I am concerned, the people who have left me all have my blessing and my good will, and my continued friendship, and I am highly flattered that they got their greater opportunities as a result of having been with me. When people have served me for a period of years well and faithfully, I don't consider that they have any obligation to stay married to me if greater opportunities come along. You yourself have taken this position as to players, but you feel quite differently as regards people working for you. Why don't you be a little more consistent? . . .

I think one reason why you lose so many people is because you are such an extraordinarily bad judge of who are your friends and who are not. . . .

Also, nevertheless, and with love,[44]

David

Since You Went Away

MISS KATHARINE CORNELL   MAY 6, 1943
CARTER HOTEL
CLEVELAND OHIO

DEAR MISS CORNELL: I AM MOST SINCERELY GRATEFUL FOR YOUR CHARACTERISTICALLY GRACIOUS TELEGRAM. I HAVE TAKEN THE LIBERTY OF PASSING ON YOUR COMMENTS ABOUT THE BOOK[45] TO MRS. WILDER,[46] WHO WAS OF COURSE DELIGHTED BY THEM. WE ARE PLEASED AND FLATTERED BY YOUR INTEREST IN PLAYING ANNE. I DO HOPE YOU WILL NOT MISUNDERSTAND ME, AND THAT YOU WILL BEAR WITH ME, WHEN I REQUEST A LITTLE MORE TIME IN REPLYING TO YOUR SPECIFIC QUESTIONS. EXCITED AS WE ARE BY THE PROSPECT OF HAVING YOU FOR YOUR SCREEN DEBUT (AND I SHOULD CHOOSE TO REGARD IT AS THIS DESPITE YOUR APPEARANCE IN "STAGE DOOR CANTEEN" [1943]), I WANT TO BE VERY SURE THAT IT IS THE RIGHT THING FOR YOU TO DO. I AM OF

[44]Four months after this letter, Myron Selznick died of portal thrombosis at the age of forty-five.

[45]*Since You Went Away*, purchased by Selznick for production.

[46]Margaret Buell Wilder, author of *Since You Went Away*.

COURSE NOT ENTIRELY UNSELFISH IN THIS, EVEN THOUGH I AM
SINCERELY MOTIVATED IN MY CAUTION, PARTIALLY BY MY DESIRE
TO REPAY YOUR FAITH WITH THE MOST SINCERE AND CAREFUL
CONSIDERATION. . . . I AM SURE YOU RECOGNIZE THAT ALL THE
CHARACTERS IN THE BOOK WITH THE EXCEPTION OF ANNE ARE
SKETCHILY DRAWN; WE ARE ATTEMPTING TO GIVE THEM FLESH
AND BLOOD, INTERESTING CHARACTER RELATIONSHIPS, AND
CURRENT PROBLEMS OF THEIR OWN. . . . I AM ATTEMPTING TO
MAKE THE FAMILY SOMEWHAT MORE AVERAGE MIDDLE CLASS
THAN IS THE CASE IN THE BOOK. I WANT TO INDICATE THAT THEY
HAD SOME FEW OF THE LUXURIOUS AND SPECIAL THINGS IN THE
PAST, BUT ON THE OTHER HAND, I WANT THE FAMILY PROBLEMS
TO BE AS REPRESENTATIVE OF THOSE OF THE AVERAGE FAMILY AS
POSSIBLE. IN ORDER TO ACCOMPLISH THIS, AND AS PART OF THE
PROCESS OF MOVING THE STORY FORWARD TO THIS YEAR, WE ARE
INCLUDING EPISODES DEALING WITH FOOD RATIONING AND OTHER
TYPICAL, TIMELY PROBLEMS. . . . I THINK YOU SHOULD FRANKLY
KNOW THAT OUR EXCITEMENT ABOUT HAVING YOU PLAY ANNE IS
MITIGATED ONLY BY OUR WORRY OVER THE SEEMLINESS OF YOU
PLAYING SOME OF THE EARLIER COMEDY SEQUENCES . . . AND
ALSO BY A WORRY AS TO WHETHER KATHARINE CORNELL, WHO
REPRESENTS SOMETHING VERY SPECIAL AND ELEVATED,
SOMETHING PERHAPS UNTYPICAL AND THEREFORE REMOTE TO
AMERICAN AUDIENCES, SHOULD ESSAY THE AVERAGE AMERICAN
WIFE AND MOTHER. ON THESE POINTS YOUR OWN JUDGMENT AND
INSTINCTS ABOUT YOURSELF, WHICH YOU HAVE SO OFTEN
DEMONSTRATED TO BE SO ACCURATE, ARE UNDOUBTEDLY OF
SUPERIOR VALUE TO OUR OWN. WHAT IS RIGHT FOR ONE OF US IS
RIGHT FOR BOTH OF US. IT IS VERY TEMPTING INDEED TO GIVE
YOU A TYPICAL SALES TALK, AND ASSURE YOU THAT YOU ARE
RIGHT FOR ANYTHING, BUT I KNOW YOU GUARD JEALOUSLY EACH
STEP OF YOUR BRILLIANT AND DISTINGUISHED CAREER, AND
UNDER NO CIRCUMSTANCES COULD I BRING MYSELF TO DO ANY
LESS THAN REVEAL TO YOU ALL OF OUR FEELINGS IN DETAIL,
EVEN IF THIS MEANT THAT WE WOUND UP WITH A MUCH LESS
EXCITING PROSPECT THAN HAVING YOU PLAY ANNE. ON THE
OTHER SIDE, I HOPE YOU WILL NOT THINK ME TOO EGOTISTICAL IF
I SAY THAT I AM EQUALLY JEALOUS OF EACH OF MY OWN
PRODUCTIONS, AND THAT I AM AS CAREFUL ABOUT MY CASTING,
EVEN WHEN THIS MEANS LESS ATTRACTIVE "SHOWMANSHIP.". . . I
SHALL BE HAPPY TO TELEPHONE YOU OVER THE WEEKEND, IF YOU
WILL ADVISE ME WHEN AND WHERE YOU CAN BE REACHED. MY

Ingrid Bergman and Gary Cooper in *For Whom the Bell Tolls* (1943).

Jennifer Jones and Anne Revere in *The Song of Bernadette* (1943).

Rock Hudson, Jennifer Jones, Selznick, and Director John Huston discussing *A Farewell to Arms* (1957).

Writer Ben Hecht (right) and Selznick talking with John Huston on location during the making of *A Farewell to Arms*.

Jennifer Jones and Rock Hudson in *A Farewell to Arms.*

Jennifer Jones, Selznick, and Director Charles Vidor on location filming *A Farewell to Arms.*

Producer Selznick "overseeing every detail" of *A Farewell to Arms*.

Jennifer Jones and Jason Robards, Jr., in *Tender Is the Night* (1962).

WARMEST PERSONAL REGARDS TO YOU, AND AGAIN MY THANKS
FOR YOUR EXTREMELY KIND MESSAGE, AND MOST PARTICULARLY
FOR THE IMPLIED CONFIDENCE IN ME.

SINCERELY,
DAVID O. SELZNICK

To: Mr. Steele June 15, 1943

When we're ready, the story on *Since You Went Away* should be built on the following:

David O. Selznick today announced that . . . *Since You Went Away* will mark the return to production of Selznick, and be his first picture since *Gone With the Wind* and *Rebecca*. At the same time, Selznick confirmed previously published reports that Claudette Colbert will play the role of the young wife and mother in the film, which is based upon the Whittlesey House and *Ladies' Home Journal* story of the same title. . . .

With Claudette Colbert, Jennifer Jones, Monty Woolley, and Shirley Temple, the cast looms as one of the most important of recent years. Selznick also stated that there would be other important players cast shortly, to give the film a cast rivaling that of the producer's famous production of *Dinner at Eight*.

Rewrite the above as much as you want to, but please be careful to: (a) handle the mother and sister angles almost exactly as above; (b) use the casting in the recapitulation as stated above, i.e., Colbert first, Jones second, Woolley third, and Temple fourth; (c) I'm anxious to get the accent off this as a Temple vehicle and start hammering away at its tremendous cast; (d) the mention of *Dinner at Eight* is in line with my talk to you of the other day about getting in mentions of my other pictures as often as possible, as I'm getting tired of being referred to solely as the producer of *Gone With the Wind* and *Rebecca*, and would like to get some of the other pictures alluded to as often as possible (I can see my obituary now: "Producer of *Gone With the Wind* dies!") . . .

DOS

To: Mr. Klune October 28, 1943
bcc: Mr. O'Shea

I had a ridiculous telephone call this morning asking me whether a piece of lawn furniture could be borrowed from my home for the porch sequence. I brought a lot of props in from the house last time simply because we were getting such a wretched result in the house sets, but I certainly didn't think that the company was going to feel that I was running a prop house up on Summit Drive [Selznick's residence], and that I would be asked to bring in anything else.

DOS

To: Mr. Klune   November 8, 1943
cc: Mr. Cromwell, Mr. Kern

I think I have stumbled on something which is at the root of why Jennifer is so wonderful in readings in the dressing room or on the set, by comparison with what she is in the scenes—something which I wish to Heaven I had found out weeks ago, as we'd have had a much better performance to date, in my opinion, had I found it out sooner.

It seems to me Jennifer has been given the impression that she cannot play the scenes the way she reads them in the dressing room, or wherever there is a rehearsal, because the mixer [the sound-recording engineer] screams for more voice or more volume. I had to drag this out of Jennifer, and I am most anxious that you not quote her to the mixer or anyone else, because she is fanatically considerate—to her own harm—of everyone, and is panic-stricken to talk about anything in connection with the picture lest she should seem to be criticizing anybody. However, it develops that she learned the technique with [director] Henry King on *Bernadette* of talking in natural tones, and whenever the Sound Department squawked, he told the Sound Department where to head in, as he should have, and wound up getting the result that he required. On our picture [*Since You Went Away*] she has had to raise her voice, and throw it, and give more volume, and I needn't tell you the effect of this on her performance, for an actress who isn't used to using her voice as are those from the theater.

One of the great advantages of motion pictures over the stage is that microphones are able to pick up the thinnest whisper, or should be. If we have a mixer who is back in 1929, let's change him; if we have a Sound Department that insists upon actors using their voices as though they had to reach the last aisle in the Hippodrome, let's throw them out rather than let them ruin the performances of our players. . . .

DOS

To: Mr. Klune, Mr. O'Shea   December 3, 1943

I spent the morning on the set, and there are several observations I would like to make, most of which I have made repeatedly but in vain in the past, to which I should appreciate your immediate attention and a report from you:

After watching all morning spent on a two-shot of [Robert] Walker and [Jennifer] Jones, I learned to my horror at one o'clock that it was not the angle in which we are playing the bulk of the scene, but simply the matte shot[47] that will be used for the first twenty or thirty feet. Yet the company went on and on with take after take and rehearsal after rehearsal on a scene that will never be used. Please get together with Cromwell, Pereira,[48] and Kern and go over this immediately, so that we can avoid repetitions of this extremely costly and inexcusably inefficient procedure. The very first take would have been satisfactory for the purpose, and we could have been in the next angle two hours sooner. The loss of the two hours is a loss of about $3500, and I feel there is no excuse for it. . . .

Also, I lost my head this morning while in the middle of an excellent take when the sound man called "Cut." I learned, on inquiry, that the sound man had made a "deal" with Cromwell that if the plane noise was too loud, he would stop the scene. I don't want and won't have any of these deals between members of the staff at our expense. It is entirely possible that we could have gotten out of the scene a half hour earlier by using what promised to be the excellent take that was interrupted (and actually this take went beyond what we can use in any case, as noted above), by looping[49] it, even if the plane noise had interfered. This is the only studio in town that is still worrying about planes on exteriors, and although I have repeatedly asked that we stop worrying about them, and resort to wild lines[50] when necessary, we are still killing hours every day that we shoot on a back lot worrying about planes which inevitably are going to get worse until a directional mike or some other device is perfected. We will be in the railroad station for the next three days if this isn't corrected immediately.

[47]A shot that eventually combines live action with certain portions of the set or landscape painted in later by the matte-painting artist.

[48]William L. Pereira, Production Designer.

[49]Recording the dialogue at a later date to the projected picture, then combining the new track with the picture.

[50]Recording the dialogue alone between camera setups, or at the end of the day, in order to concentrate on sound only.

Nor can I ever understand the inordinate delay that goes on between takes. The camera is set, the actors are set, and the lighting is completely perfected; nevertheless, between takes there is a loss of five or ten or fifteen minutes fiddling and getting all lined up again, when they should be able to make the succeeding take immediately. . . . As a matter of fact, I feel that in many cases the cost of saving on lights and on laboratory work is nothing by comparison with the cost of the time lost killing the lights, slating the succeeding take, and going through all the other nonsense that is a carry-over from the days when electrical and film expense were a comparable item to time. . . .

DOS

DR. GEORGE GALLUP   FEBRUARY 1, 1944
AUDIENCE RESEARCH INSTITUTE
PRINCETON, NEW JERSEY

DEAR GEORGE, I HAVE BEEN TRYING FOR SOME TIME TO GET SOME HELP OUT OF THE AUDIENCE RESEARCH INSTITUTE, WHICH HAS BEEN MOST COOPERATIVE ON PRACTICALLY EVERYTHING ELSE, AND ABOUT WHOSE SERVICES IT IS THE FURTHEST THING FROM MY MIND TO COMPLAIN, ON ONE POINT WHICH IS OF CONSIDERABLE IMPORTANCE TO ME. UNTIL I RECEIVE SOME ADVICE ON THIS IT IS IMPOSSIBLE FOR ME TO SET UP THE ADVERTISING CAMPAIGN ON WHICH I AM NOW UP AGAINST DEADLINE.

I AM PERFECTLY AWARE THAT THE PUBLIC IS NOT INTERESTED, BY AND LARGE, IN PRODUCERS, DIRECTORS, ETC. HOWEVER, I RECALL YOUR TELLING ME A FEW YEARS BACK THAT I WAS ONE OF THE FOUR OR FIVE PRODUCERS AND/OR DIRECTORS WHO MEANT SOMETHING TO THE PUBLIC; AND ANY NUMBER OF SALES EXECUTIVES, EXHIBITORS, ADVERTISING MEN, ETC., AND SOME OF THE TOP EXECUTIVES OF OTHER COMPANIES . . . INSIST THAT THERE WILL BE GREAT INTEREST IN MY FIRST PRODUCTION SINCE "GONE WITH THE WIND" AND "REBECCA." SOME OF THIS I CHARGE OFF TO INSINCERITY, SOME OF IT TO THE PEOPLE BEING TOO CLOSE TO THE TRADE; BUT ON THE OTHER HAND, IT IS HARD TO DISMISS LIGHTLY THE OPINIONS OF A FEW OF THOSE WHO COULD HAVE NO SUCH MOTIVES OR ATTITUDES, AND WHO COULD BE PRESUMED TO KNOW WHAT THEY ARE TALKING ABOUT. I WANT TO BE COMPLETELY OBJECTIVE ABOUT THIS, AND MY DESIRE IS THAT THE PICTURE BE AS SUCCESSFUL AS POSSIBLE, NOT THAT I BUILD MYSELF UP.

I AM ACCORDINGLY AFTER EXPERT OPINION AND PROFESSIONAL
GUIDANCE AS TO HOW GREAT AN EXTENT I SHOULD ADVERTISE
MYSELF IN CONNECTION WITH THE FILM. ANY STUDY THAT YOU
MAKE ON THIS POINT SHOULD POSSIBLY BE MADE BOTH ON MY
NAME ITSELF, AND ON MY NAME WITH THE EXPLANATORY PHRASE
THAT THIS IS MY FIRST PICTURE SINCE "GONE WITH THE WIND"
AND "REBECCA," WITH THE NAMES OF THOSE TWO PICTURES
GIVEN VERY PROMINENT MENTION. I DO NOT WANT TO DISCOUNT
TOO MUCH THE EXTENSIVE PUBLICITY THAT I HAVE HAD AS WELL
AS THE MANY INDICATIONS I HAVE HAD FROM INDIVIDUALS
AMONG THE PUBLIC OF A KNOWLEDGE OF MY ACTIVITIES, AND OF
AN INTEREST IN MY NEXT PICTURE. I AM ALSO AWARE THAT ANY
NUMBER OF PEOPLE GO TO SEE A FILM BECAUSE IT IS A DE MILLE
PRODUCTION, OR A HITCHCOCK PICTURE, OR MADE BY CAPRA, AND
I THINK TO SOME EXTENT IN THE CASE OF A SAMUEL GOLDWYN
PICTURE. WHETHER I AM IN THIS CATEGORY AND TO WHAT
EXTENT ESPECIALLY AS A RESULT OF "WIND" AND "REBECCA" IS
THE POINT ON WHICH I HAVE BEEN ABLE TO GET NO REPLY FROM
YOUR ORGANIZATION.[51] WARMEST REGARDS.

DAVID O. SELZNICK

: : : : : :

To: Mr. King[52]   May 30, 1944

Dear Don:

I am sorry about the delay on the program,[53] but here it is 4 A.M.
and I have just tackled it. . . .

On the Jennifer Jones page . . . I would bring out the following facts:
I insisted Miss Jones stay in New York for a period of almost two years
while she received extensive training, on which she worked very hard,
and with dramatic coaches, voice coaches, on posture, diction, etc.,
and would not let her come to Hollywood until she was ready, except
for a few weeks to play the lead in the summer-stock company I had
established for the purpose of training my younger players in Santa
Barbara, where she played the leading role in the first production ever
given of William Saroyan's *Hello, Out There*. I made repeated tests to
demonstrate how much progress she had made and I refused to launch

[51]Gallup replied that his report showed sixty-six per cent of all moviegoers knew who
Selznick was. Other tests indicated that his name had a definite and substantial marquee
value, particularly with patrons in the upper-half income bracket.

[52]Don King, Selznick's Director of Advertising and Publicity.

[53]The *Since You Went Away* theater program.

her in Hollywood until exactly the right role came along.

When I read *The Song of Bernadette,* I personally and initially suggested her for the role and offered for the first time to let her test for another role,[54] so convinced was I that she would get it. . . . My enthusiasm was soon shared by Henry King, who credits her with the distinction and verity of the film. . . . All of these facts I have been trying to get our department to get over for many months, and I am amazed that they are not even in material that we print ourselves.

. . . I would wind up the story with a paragraph dealing with the fact that several important vehicles are in preparation for Miss Jones under Mr. Selznick's guidance, including Robert Nathan's unique story *Portrait of Jennie.*[55]

DOS

MISS JENIA REISSAR   OCTOBER 4, 1944
27 KNIGHTSBRIDGE COURT
SLOANE STREET SW 1
LONDON (ENGLAND)

I HAVE OF COURSE NOT YET RECEIVED BETTS'S[56] ATTACK AND SHOULD APPRECIATE YOUR MAILING ME A COPY. HOWEVER, UNITED ARTISTS INFORMS ME THAT BETTS IS PREPARED TO PUBLISH REPLY FROM ME AND HAVE GIVEN ME GIST OF HIS ARTICLE. . . . MY REPLY FOLLOWS:

DEAR MR. BETTS: I HAVE BEEN INFORMED BY CABLE OF YOUR ARTICLE ON THE SUBJECT OF THE LENGTH OF MOTION PICTURES AND PARTICULARLY OF "SINCE YOU WENT AWAY," AND ALSO OF YOUR GENEROUS WILLINGNESS TO GIVE ME SPACE FOR A REPLY. . . .

CRITICISM OF THE LENGTH OF PICTURES IS NOTHING NEW. IT DATES BACK TO THE FIRST TIME SOME COURAGEOUS PRODUCER OF THE PIONEERING DAYS DECIDED THAT PICTURES COULD BE LONGER THAN THE FIFTEEN- OR THIRTY-SECOND SUBJECTS OF THE PENNY ARCADES. I AM SURE THAT A LITTLE RESEARCH WOULD REVEAL THAT THERE WAS A GREAT OUTCRY WHEN SOMEBODY TOOK A CHANCE AND MADE A PICTURE THAT ACTUALLY RAN A FULL REEL IN LENGTH.[57] I MYSELF RECALL READING IN MY

[54] The first test was for *Claudia* (1943).
[55] Not produced until 1948.
[56] Edward William Betts, on the editorial staff of the *Daily Film Renter* in London.
[57] Approximately fifteen minutes, projected at silent speed.

CHILDHOOD OF THE COMMOTION THAT WAS CAUSED WHEN MY
FATHER, LEWIS J. SELZNICK, ANNOUNCED A REGULAR PROGRAM OF
THIRTY-MINUTE SUBJECTS, AND LATER HOW DARING HE WAS
CONSIDERED WHEN HE ANNOUNCED A REGULAR PROGRAM OF
ONE-HOUR FEATURES. I MYSELF HAVE NEVER BELIEVED IN
ARBITRARY LENGTHS FOR MOTION PICTURES. A FILM CAN BE TOO
LONG IN FIVE MINUTES AND TOO SHORT IN THREE HOURS. IT IS
ENTIRELY A MATTER OF THE SUBJECT, AND HOW LONG IT TAKES
TO TELL IT PROPERLY. . . .

I SHOULD LIKE TO EXPLAIN THAT MY PREVIEW SYSTEM IS
SOMEWHAT DIFFERENT FROM THAT OF THE BUSINESS AS A WHOLE.
I HAVE LONG SINCE ABANDONED THE SIMPLE PREVIEW CARD
WHICH IS STILL USED BY MOST STUDIOS, AND WHICH GIVES VERY
LITTLE INFORMATION THAT IS NOT OBTAINABLE FROM AN
EXPERIENCED, INTELLIGENT, AND SENSITIVE UNDERSTANDING OF
THE REACTION OF THE PREVIEW AUDIENCE DURING THE RUNNING
OF THE PICTURE. INSTEAD I USE A VERY ELABORATE
QUESTIONNAIRE FORM DESIGNED TO FORCE EVEN MORE
ANALYTICAL AND CRITICAL REACTIONS AND OPINIONS THAN
WOULD NORMALLY BE THE CASE WHEN A PICTURE IS RELEASED. I
HAVE FOUND THAT THERE IS A GOOD DEAL OF TRUTH TO THE
STATEMENT THAT EVERYONE HAS TWO BUSINESSES: THEIR OWN
AND THE MOTION-PICTURE BUSINESS. ALSO, AND CONTRARY TO
THE PREDICTIONS OF THE EXPERTS THAT THE MEMBERS OF THE
AUDIENCE WOULD NOT BE INTERESTED IN FILLING OUT SUCH A
FORM, I RECEIVE TWO TO THREE TIMES AS MANY ANSWERS AND
COMMENTS AS STUDIOS NORMALLY RECEIVE ON THE USUAL
PREVIEW-CARD FORM. THESE QUESTIONNAIRES CONTINUE TO COME
IN FILLED OUT IN THE GREATEST DETAIL FOR SEVERAL DAYS
AFTER PREVIEW. IT IS APPARENT THAT GREAT CARE IS TAKEN
WITH THE ANSWERS AND THAT MOST OF THE CARDS ARE NOT
SENT IN UNTIL THE RESPECTIVE QUESTIONS HAVE BEEN
CAREFULLY CONSIDERED, AND UNTIL THE REACTION TO THE FILM
HAS HAD TIME TO REALLY FORM. CERTAINLY, WHAT AN AUDIENCE
THINKS OF A PICTURE THREE HOURS OR THIRTY HOURS AFTER IT
HAS BEEN SEEN IS OF GREATER SIGNIFICANCE THAN THE SNAP
JUDGMENT FORMED IMMEDIATELY A FILM'S SCREENING IS ENDED.

TWO OF THE MANY QUESTIONS ON THIS PREVIEW FORM HAVE TO
DO WITH THE LENGTH. THE PUBLIC IS ASKED TO SAY WHETHER IT
HAS FOUND THE PICTURE TOO LONG, AND IT IS ALSO ASKED WHAT
SECTIONS OF THE PICTURE OR WHAT INDIVIDUAL SCENES IT

FOUND TOO LONG. ADDITIONALLY, IT IS ASKED WHAT SCENES IT LIKED LEAST. ALL OF THESE ANSWERS ARE CAREFULLY TABULATED AND ANALYZED. OF COURSE, THE OPINION OF AN INDIVIDUAL THAT IS CONTRARY TO THE OPINION OF ALL THE OTHERS IS DISCOUNTED. BUT IF IN A SINGLE AUDIENCE THERE SHOULD BE AS MANY AS A DOZEN PEOPLE WHO REACT UNFAVORABLY, THE PICTURE IS RE-EDITED TO MEET THIS NEGATIVE CRITICISM. I HAVE SOMETIMES PREVIEWED, OVER A PERIOD OF MONTHS, AS MANY AS A DOZEN TIMES UNTIL SUCH CRITICISMS ARE ELIMINATED. I CONTINUE TO EDIT AND CONTINUE TO RETAKE UNTIL THE PREVIEW REACTION IS UNANIMOUSLY NOT MERELY FAVORABLE BUT ENTHUSIASTIC, AND UNTIL ALL CRITICISMS INCLUDING IMPORTANTLY THOSE OF LENGTH ARE ELIMINATED. . . .

THERE ARE MANY EXHIBITORS WHO HAVE ALWAYS OBJECTED TO VERY LONG FILMS FOR THE SOUND BUSINESS REASON THAT THEY RESULT IN A FEWER NUMBER OF SHOWS PER DAY, BUT AS THESE EXHIBITORS HAVE REALIZED THAT THEY CAN DO AS MUCH BUSINESS OR MORE ON LONGER RUNS OF PICTURES FOR WHICH THERE IS A GREATER PUBLIC LIKING AND ON WHICH THERE IS GREAT "WORD-OF-MOUTH ADVERTISING," THESE CRITICISMS HAVE BEEN NATURALLY REDUCED. AN EXCEPTION FROM THE OUTSET HAS BEEN NICHOLAS M. SCHENCK, WHO AS PRESIDENT OF LOEW'S IS NOT ONLY THE HEAD OF ONE OF THE MOST IMPORTANT PRODUCING COMPANIES (MGM) BUT ALSO ONE OF THE PRINCIPAL EXHIBITORS OF THE UNITED STATES. AT THE TIME I PRODUCED "DAVID COPPERFIELD" THE AVERAGE PICTURE OF IMPORTANCE RAN SEVEN TO EIGHT THOUSAND FEET IN LENGTH. . . .[58] IN ITS FIRST CUT "COPPERFIELD" RAN OVER FOURTEEN THOUSAND FEET, OR ALMOST TWICE THE USUAL LENGTH OF FILMS AT THAT TIME. AS I WAS MADE SOMEWHAT NERVOUS BY THE OPINIONS OF THE EXPERTS, I ASKED MR. SCHENCK WHAT WAS THE MAXIMUM LENGTH IN WHICH HE THOUGHT WE COULD RELEASE "DAVID COPPERFIELD." MR. SCHENCK GAVE ME A REPLY WHICH I HAVE NEVER FORGOTTEN AND HAVE OFTEN QUOTED: "WHAT DO YOU MEAN, HOW LONG CAN YOU MAKE IT," ASKED MR. SCHENCK, "HOW LONG IS IT GOOD?" AFTER MANY PREVIEWS, I EDITED "DAVID COPPERFIELD" DOWN TO APPROXIMATELY ELEVEN THOUSAND FEET.[59] . . .

[58]Approximately one hour and twenty minutes to one hour and thirty minutes.
[59]The exact running time was two hours and nine minutes.

PERHAPS CONTRARY TO GENERAL BELIEF, I DO NOT TRY TO
MAKE PICTURES "LONG." IN OUR EDITING THEY ARE REDUCED TO
THE MINIMUM FOOTAGE NECESSARY TO THEIR EFFECTIVENESS AS
ENTERTAINMENT. "A STAR IS BORN" RAN ONE HOUR AND
FIFTY-TWO MINUTES. "NOTHING SACRED" AND "INTERMEZZO"
(RELEASED IN ENGLAND AS "ESCAPE TO HAPPINESS") RAN ONLY A
FEW MINUTES MORE THAN AN HOUR EACH. IN EACH CASE, THE
STORY WAS A SIMPLE ONE AND REQUIRED NO MORE THAN THIS
TIME TO TELL. IN "SINCE YOU WENT AWAY," I ATTEMPTED TO
TELL THE STORY OF AN AMERICAN FAMILY DURING WARTIME AND
OF THE ATTITUDES OF THE AMERICAN PEOPLE DURING THE
CRUCIAL YEAR 1943. ITS CONSTRUCTION WAS A JIGSAW PUZZLE.
THERE WERE LITERALLY MORE THAN A DOZEN MAJOR STORY
THREADS TO PURSUE TO SOME KIND OF A CONCLUSION; THERE
WERE THE CHANGING ATTITUDES OF A SCORE OF PRINCIPAL
CHARACTERS TO KEEP IN BALANCE. . . . WHETHER WE SUCCEEDED
FOR ENGLISH AUDIENCES REMAINS TO BE SEEN, ALTHOUGH I AM
HOPEFUL THAT THE PICTURE WILL HAVE THE SAME SENSATIONAL
SUCCESS ABROAD THAT IT HAS HAD IN THE UNITED STATES. . . .
THE GALLUP PEOPLE REPORT THAT THE MEMBERS OF THE
AUDIENCE OVERWHELMINGLY DO NOT FIND THE PICTURE TOO
LONG AND THAT ON THE CONTRARY, AS WITH THE PREVIEW
AUDIENCES, THERE IS A VERY LARGE PERCENTAGE THAT SAYS IT
WISHES THE PICTURE WERE LONGER. I HAD MY ORGANIZATION
STANDING BY ALL READY TO RE-EDIT AND RETAKE IF NECESSARY
HAD RESEARCH GIVEN US A DIFFERENT ANSWER OR EVEN AN
AMBIGUOUS ONE. . . .

I HAVE NEVER UNDERSTOOD WHY MOTION-PICTURE AUDIENCES,
MANY OF WHOM ARE ACCUSTOMED TO SEEING THREE OR FOUR
HOURS OF FILM ON A DOUBLE BILL, COULD BE EXPECTED TO
CRITICIZE A PICTURE THAT IT LIKES, SOLELY BECAUSE IT IS
LONGER THAN THE AVERAGE FILM. MANY AN EVENING'S FILM
FARE IS COMPOSED OF ONE PICTURE THAT IN QUALITY USUALLY
RANGES ALL THE WAY FROM POOR TO EXCELLENT, A SECOND
PICTURE THAT IN QUALITY USUALLY RANGES ALL THE WAY FROM
BAD TO MEDIOCRE, AND A FEW SHORT SUBJECTS. . . .

THERE WILL ALWAYS BE THOSE WHO WILL THINK PICTURES ARE
TOO LONG. . . . USUALLY THESE ARE PEOPLE WHO HAVE NO
COMPUNCTIONS ABOUT SPENDING AN ENTIRE AFTERNOON AT A
FOOTBALL GAME, WHO DO NOT OBJECT TO THOUSAND-PAGE
NOVELS, WHO SPEND SEVERAL HOURS LISTENING TO THEMSELVES

TALK AT A NIGHT CLUB, WHO SPEND THREE OR FOUR HOURS
PLAYING BRIDGE OR GIN RUMMY. TO NONE OF THESE AVOCATIONS
AND DIVERSIONS CAN THERE BE ANY CRITICISM (AND I HAVE
OFTEN SO INDULGED MYSELF), BUT IF SOMEWHERE BETWEEN
NINETY AND NINETY-NINE PER CENT OF THE PUBLIC IS WILLING
HAPPILY TO SPEND TWO AND A HALF OR THREE AND A HALF
HOURS AT A PICTURE WHICH IT FINDS TO ITS LIKING, I AM AFRAID
THAT I MUST QUOTE TO THE SMALL MINORITY THE WORDS OF
GEORGE BERNARD SHAW, WHOSE PLAYS INVARIABLY RUN LONGER
THAN THE AVERAGE. YOU WILL RECALL THAT SHAW, DURING
A CURTAIN SPEECH TO AN ENTHUSIASTIC AUDIENCE AT THE
OPENING OF ONE OF HIS PLAYS, WAS INTERRUPTED BY A
HECKLER WHO FOUND THE PLAY TOO LONG AND NOT TO HIS
LIKING. SHAW INTERRUPTED HIS SPEECH TO ADDRESS THE
HECKLER. "I AGREE WITH YOU, MY FRIEND," SAID SHAW, "BUT
WHAT IS THE OPINION OF JUST WE TWO AGAINST SO MANY?"
SINCERELY,

DAVID O. SELZNICK

: : : : : :

Mr. L. B. Mayer   January 24, 1944
Metro-Goldwyn-Mayer
10202 W. Washington Blvd.
Culver City, California

cc: Mr. E. J. Mannix
      Mr. Ben Thau
      Mr. Arthur Hornblow, Jr.
      Mr. George Cukor
      Miss Bergman

Dear L. B.:

Since you and Eddie and Benny have all been flattering enough to
ask for my detailed opinions on *Gaslight*,[60] I shall try to remember
everything I thought about the picture, and my reactions as I expressed them to [its producer] Arthur Hornblow and [its director]
George Cukor the night of the preview.

I'm very grateful to Arthur for his courtesy and kindness in inviting

[60]The 1944 version of Patrick Hamilton's extraordinarily successful English play, *Gaslight* (1938), presented in America as *Angel Street*.

me to the preview; and I am glad to have this opportunity to express my feelings, because I have been something of a kibitzer on the picture from the outset, because of my warm friendship and admiration for both Arthur and George and, of course, most of all because of my natural interest in the great success of a film in which both Ingrid Bergman and Joseph Cotten appear.[61]

I think the picture is an excellent one, beautifully produced and directed, and that it is something of which the studio may well be proud. Everything about it, including the settings and costumes, reflects the excellent taste of Arthur and of George, and the meticulous care for which both of them are so well known. If the picture goes out as it stands, it is worthy of success; but it is my firm belief that the difference between its being a sensational success, and perhaps only something less than that—a difference of perhaps half a million dollars or more in gross—depends upon the patience with which the picture is edited and the willingness of the studio to engage in a retake program which need not be extensive or even inordinately expensive, but to which a film of such sponsorship and of such potential importance is entitled. . . . A film of this type depends upon absolute perfection to achieve its maximum success, as we all know, and anything short of the ideal would in my opinion be a really great pity. . . .

My fear is that there may be a tendency to say that retakes are unnecessary, or that only a very few are necessary, either because of the natural reluctance of those responsible for the picture, who are both proud of the film and a little bored with it, to engage in such a program; or because your studio, which was once so famous for the brilliant things that it did with films through the polishing and retaking processes, has gotten out of the habit of making fine films just a little bit finer. In this case, I think the "little bit" will make an enormous difference, one that will well repay all the pains and effort that can and must be put into the final processes. Nor would I be thrown by excellent preview cards; a very good reaction is no reason for not aiming at a still better reaction.

After this long-winded preamble, I will get down to the specific things that I recall the film seemed to me to be in need of:

To begin with, I am sure that you will all agree that the very worst fault a picture can have is lack of clarity. If an audience doesn't know what is going on, and is worried by its own confusion, inevitably

---

[61]Selznick had loaned both players to MGM for the film.

dramatic values suffer greatly. This film suffers greatly from lack of clarity in at least three particulars:

(1)   The prologue and opening sequences. I defy any audience, or any individual, who is not thoroughly familiar with the story, to know what the devil is going on. . . .

(2)   The whole point of Boyer's search in the attic; his leaving the house and then coming around through the house next door; et cetera. I, of course, know this point and was able to figure it out, although even I was confused when I saw Boyer taking long walks down the street, which surely is contradictory with his going through the house next door.[62]. . .

(3)   The finding of the jewels. I couldn't tell what was going on— it looked to me as though Boyer was changing his pants in the scene which I was later told was supposed to be him shining his shoes and ironically finding at that moment what he had been looking for.[63] . . .

I think the picture's biggest single basic fault is in the early revelation that the husband is a villain. Once the character is tipped off as a heavy, an attempt must then be made to sustain the story through two hours of film without any second-act development. . . . If, for quite a while, the audience thinks that Boyer is playing a man who is deeply in love with his wife but is tied to a woman who is losing her mind, I think it will make for a much more horrifying and effective development as the audience becomes aware that she is being driven out of her mind by him. This is the twist that I think the story needs and should have, a twist which it is a very simple matter to obtain.[64]

I think the picture's second major fault is its lack of a love story, its short-changing of the audience on the sex story between the man and his wife. Presently, we have the one love scene at Como . . . and then nothing whatsoever to show why this woman is so tied to the man. She appears just a weakling and a fool, instead of what she should be—a woman so desperately in love, and so held by sex ties to the man, that she is unable to tear herself away despite his cruelties. . . . The picture is desperately in need of at least two more scenes . . . in which we see the husband as a lover, in which we see both his tenderness and also the Svengali-like sex hold that he has on her. Boyer is at his best in such scenes; Miss Bergman proved how superbly she can play scenes of

---

[62]This was clarified in the subsequent modifications to the film.
[63]This sequence was reshot and clarified considerably.
[64]This aspect of the film remained unchanged.

surrender in the Como sequences, and this type of scene is great showmanship, and what audiences will expect of Boyer and Bergman, quite apart from the story's great need of these scenes.[65] . . .

I'm sorry I have to say this, but I think the attempt to indicate a love story with the Cotten character[66] is impossible. I don't believe it, and there is no reason why I should believe it. I'd like to believe it, because I'd like to see Cotten's very weak part become as important as possible; but in the final analysis, it is the picture which is important, and the better the picture, the more even Cotten will benefit.

I don't understand why or when Cotten could possibly have fallen in love with the woman. And I certainly won't for a moment believe that she could have had the slightest opportunity or inclination to become interested in him. If the story is anything, it is that of a woman desperately, hopelessly, in love with a monster. I regard as absurd any attempt to tell me in the last couple of hundred feet of film that she could have had any interest in anybody else. . . . The audience has been rooting for two hours for her to be free of this man, and when she finally is freed of him, this is all the release and all the happy ending that is needed.[67] . . .

What the picture needs after she is free is very little—just something, as George Cukor suggested—such as there was in the English picture,[68] when she went to the windows of the house and threw them open, which was so played by Diana Wynyard and so directed [by Thorold Dickinson] as to give a great lift and a great sense of the woman's eventual freedom symbolically.[69] . . .

With further reference to the end of the picture, as a member of the audience I found myself seriously resenting the attempts to soften Boyer at the finish with his speech about always having loved her, and with the attempt to give him a kind of glamorous and gallant exit, *à la* Sydney Carton or Rupert of Hentzau. The character is that of a no-good son-of-a-bitch, a monster and a murderer, and as a member of the audience I didn't want him soft-pedaled at the end. He is getting his just deserts. . . . It is too clearly, and for too many reels, the story of a man who married a woman with the specific objective of getting at the jewels. I have seen him make a pass at the servant girl,[70] and

---

[65]One such scene was added.

[66]Cotten played a Scotland Yard detective.

[67]A slight indication of possible romantic interest between the characters portrayed by Bergman and Cotten remained in the final version of the film.

[68]*Gaslight* had been made as a film four years previously in England. MGM purchased the rights for this remake.

[69]This was accomplished in the additional filming.

[70]Played by Angela Lansbury.

presumably he has plenty of affairs with other women. . . . Having seen all this, I just won't swallow that he "loved her all the time."[71] . . .

I also urge, just as strongly as I can, that you rewrite and retake the final scene after Bergman is left alone in the room with her husband tied to the chair. . . . Indeed, I beg you, as a personal favor to me, to ask Arthur and George to redo this sequence, because I know what Bergman could do with it—and I think that a retake of this one sequence might very well mean great honors, and possibly even an Academy Award next year, as well as a much more effective finish.[72] . . .

I of course miss terribly the moment which, more than everything else in the play combined, made *Angel Street* such a sensational success in New York—that in which the detective has left his hat. This was perhaps the most widely discussed moment in the history of melodrama in this generation of theater. I saw the play in New York, and never before have I witnessed anything in the theater remotely approaching the effectiveness of this particular scene. The audience was so terrified that part of it literally stood to its feet and screamed, with at least a third of the audience screaming at the stage, "The hat! The hat!" When the detective returned for the hat, I cannot describe the audience's relief and pleasure. I think it would be worth almost anything to buy this particular moment from the owners of the play.[73] . . .

My congratulations to all of you on the film. It is not usually very pleasant to be in the role of a kibitzer on somebody else's film, and normally I shun the role. In this case, it is not so difficult because the picture is so superb, and my suggestions are only in the nature of gilding the lily; and also because Arthur has been so generous and so open-minded about seeking my opinions.

Sincerely yours,

To: Mr. O'Shea   March 4, 1944
cc: Mr. Scanlon   CONFIDENTIAL

With further reference to the subject of my note of yesterday concerning *Double Furlough* [*I'll Be Seeing You* (1944)], . . . I'll be very

---

[71] Boyer's speech about always having loved the woman portrayed by Miss Bergman was dropped, but the somewhat gallant exit remained.

[72] The scene was filmed again, and Miss Bergman won an Academy Award for her performance.

[73] For whatever reason, this suggestion was not followed; possibly because of the inability to negotiate successfully with the holder of the dramatic rights in America.

glad to discuss these matters with Dore [Schary]. . . .

Were I most sensitive, I would deeply resent a man who is working for us, and therefore for me, not accepting my opinions. The only thing I am sensitive about is Dore's yessing of me on the necessary changes, and then making them halfheartedly and superficially.

Arthur Hornblow is . . . a man who would have to be included in any list of the five outstanding producers in the business. Hornblow is not working for us, has no obligation to me, yet sought me out for advice on his script [*Gaslight*] (which I did not take the time to give him, although I took plenty of time on Dore's script), and sought my advice on the editing, which I gave him. He followed ninety per cent of my suggestions, spending a great deal of time and money along with Cukor and all the others in making these changes. He has thanked me repeatedly, as have Mr. Mannix and Mr. Mayer, who telephoned me to thank me at great length and to tell me that my suggestions were practically all being followed, both as to editing and as to retakes. I could get a huge fee from Metro just to read their scripts and give them the sort of analysis that I have given to *Double Furlough*. Yet we are faced with the ridiculous situation of a man working for us, with my money, rejecting these criticisms both as to operation (new writer, director, et cetera), and as to story and script changes. For me to put up with this is not alone being tolerant and patient, it is being Christlike—and I am not Christlike, in case you haven't found out. . . .

DOS

To: Mr. Johnston[74]   May 5, 1944
cc: Mr. O'Shea, Mr. Scanlon

. . . To get back to the question of retakes in advance of preview, this is a luxury which can and should be indulged in only on an extremely important picture, and I myself have done it very rarely. Only a very big picture can afford it, and it is folly on the face of it to retake scenes which may have to be retaken again after preview because of story changes, or which may be thrown out in their entirety after preview—thus having twice spent money on scenes which are unnecessary. This type of operation is one which is born only of nervousness or vanity or thoughtlessness in connection with what is only one showing for one audience. . . .

DOS

[74]Richard L. Johnston, Selznick's Production Manager.

To: Mr. Johnston, Miss Colby[75]   June 22, 1944

As I have advised Miss Bergman tonight, I am most dissatisfied with the [costume designer Howard] Greer sketches. I think they demonstrate a lack of understanding of the part[76] and/or a lack of interest in creating clothes to suit the role and our wishes concerning the dressing of the girl. . . .

I am hopeful that in the severity and utter simplicity of line and design we can aid the characterization of a woman of twenty-eight or twenty-nine or thirty who has deliberately disinterested herself in frivolity, kids herself that she is aloof from romantic interests, devotes herself entirely to science, and yet would have enough pride and fastidiousness and unaffected chic to look distinguished and smartly but severely groomed. It must also be borne in mind that the income of this woman in her first year as a member of the staff would unquestionably be not too great. Anita might check into what this would be, but I should be surprised if it were over $2500 or $3000 per year plus board. Certainly at the top it would be $5000. So let's not have her dressed as though she were a movie star, either as to the richness of the costumes, or as to the way in which hopefully they have been tailored. And please be sure that the clothes are reasonably aged before they are worn in the film. . . .

                                                    DOS

To: Mr. O'Shea   October 25, 1944

The more I look at the dream sequence in *Spellbound,* the worse I feel it to be. It is not Dali's[77] fault, for his work is much finer and much better for the purpose than I ever thought it would be. It is the photography, setups, lighting, et cetera, all of which are completely lacking in imagination and all of which are about what you would expect from Monogram.[78]

I think we need a whole new shake on this sequence, and I would like to get Bill Menzies to come over and lay it out and shoot it. . . .

We must bear in mind that [Gregory] Peck will be required for

[75]Anita Colby, consultant to Selznick regarding his feminine stars.
[76]The lady psychiatrist in *Spellbound* (1945).
[77]Salvador Dali, who had been commissioned to design the dream-sequence backgrounds for *Spellbound.*
[78]A studio specializing in low-budget films.

the day or two that will be required for shooting. Also Miss Bergman. . . .

DOS

To: Mr. Espy[79] November 3, 1944

. . . Shirley [Temple] is exceedingly hot at the moment. We can't
commence to fill demands for interviews and other press material on
her from newspapers and magazines; and this is, of course, an indication of the interest of the public. At the preview of *I'll Be Seeing You*,
costarring Ginger Rogers, Joseph Cotten, and Shirley Temple, Shirley's name was received with the biggest applause of all three, despite
the fact that the Gallup poll shows that Cotten is the great new romantic rage, and that Ginger is one of the top stars of the business. . . .

Shirley's publicity in the New York press, both in connection with
this appearance and in connection with her prior trip East to sell
bonds, received more publicity—including, astonishingly, big front-
page breaks in the middle of a war—than I think has been accorded
the visit of any motion-picture star to New York in many, many years.
Indeed, it is said (and I believe a check would confirm it) that her visit
received more space than that of General de Gaulle! She has made a
great hit in *Since You Went Away;* and in her first grown-up part, that
in *I'll Be Seeing You,* is a sensational success. Her fan mail is greater
than that of any other star on our list—actually exceeding by a wide
margin that of Ingrid Bergman, Jennifer Jones, and Joan Fontaine,
who are the next three, in that order. . . .

DOS

To: Mr. King February 7, 1945

. . . I want to remind you of what I reminded our Publicity Department at the time that they were being thoughtless concerning the
handling of Miss Bergman. At that time I warned them that all the
publicity troubles of Greta Garbo were directly traceable to the fact
that when she first arrived in this country she was handled by the
Publicity Department at Metro exactly as they handled any new stock
girl that had been signed up. When the day came that she became a
great star, she refused any kind of cooperation because she had lost all

[79]Reeves Espy, Selznick executive.

faith and confidence, and properly so, in the judgment and taste of the Publicity Department.

I am glad to be able to say that our department was not equally guilty with Miss Bergman, but they still didn't have the right attitude or right instincts about the handling of this great star, and her own judgment was infinitely superior to their own. The fact that she was right and that they were wrong was borne out by the invariably fine attitude on the part of the press toward Miss Bergman. But nevertheless the day came when Miss Bergman mistrusted everybody in the Publicity Department except Joe Steele. . . . The same thing will inevitably happen with Miss Jones—six months or a year or two years from now—if we don't exercise taste and handle her as expertly in publicity as I like to think I am handling her pictures and assignments. . . .

The color pages and black-and-white pages for *Modern Screen* are fine, and the other fan magazine photographs seem all right, provided that these photographs are not staged for either semi-cheesecake or for fashions or anything of that sort. They must have dignity and taste. In this connection, "Fun in Tucson" seems absurd for a star of this stature; and if "A Day with Jennifer" has anything to do with the usual tripe of this sort, with different costumes, etc., I think it should be canceled. . . .

I don't know what "Beauty 'Round the Clock" is, but if it is what it sounds like I urge that it be canceled immediately. It is exactly the opposite from what we are trying to do with her career, in which we are emphasizing neither beauty nor glamor, but talent. Obviously we want her to be as attractive and as beautiful as possible. But the emphasis should not be on this; and any publicity designed to take her 'round the clock in various costumes is idiotic from the standpoint of the handling of Miss Jones. . . .

DOS

To: Mr. O'Shea February 19, 1945
IMMEDIATE

. . . There should be entire review of our dealings with Vivien Leigh.[80]

---

[80]Selznick attempted to obtain an injunction to prevent Miss Leigh from appearing in a London theatrical presentation of *The Skin of Our Teeth*. However, the British courts ruled in favor of her, and the play opened three months after this memo was written.

. . . We consented to her stage appearance in *Romeo and Juliet* because of her and Olivier's urgings, although this meant passing up having Scarlett O'Hara in other films. This endeavor seriously damaged her career and reviews were terrible. This is one reason why we are so fearful of another theatrical engagement prompted and participated in by Olivier, with possibility of further serious damage to our property.

We heeded Leigh's urgings and pleas for a twelve-week leave of absence to go to England because we felt an Englishwoman should return to England during wartime and also because of her principal argument, which was that she might never see Olivier again, since he was planning on going into service.[81] We made this gesture in good faith and at a loss to ourselves, as we did subsequent gestures leading to extensions and further leaves of absence. . . .

Olivier is no longer in service, and there is no reason why she should not return to America or at least make an attempt to do so; and it might be stressed that she has consistently refused to even consider any such attempt, although we have stood ready and still stand ready to make pictures with her that could have enormously beneficial effect on British-American relations, with a potential audience of between fifty and one hundred million people throughout the world by comparison with the small number any play could reach.[82] . . .

DOS

Duel in the Sun

To: Messrs. [Director King] Vidor, Johnson,   February 28, 1945
       Kern, [Assistant Director Lowell] Farrell, Miss Keon

It has been my experience that the speed with which a picture is made, particularly a picture of this type [*Duel in the Sun*], is enormously affected by the success in getting speed at the outset. What we accomplish on the very first setup in the way of getting it with extraordinary dispatch; what we accomplish on the first day, what we accomplish during the first several days, is going to have a most enormous effect upon everybody, including the actors and everyone else, who

[81]Vivien Leigh and Laurence Olivier were married in 1940.
[82]Vivien Leigh never made another film for Selznick after *Gone With the Wind*. Their contract eventually was settled.

will [otherwise] slow down to a walk and lose valuable minutes that will cost one or two or more setups per day, and many days on the schedule. With this in mind, I will be grateful if Mr. Vidor will go to the most elaborate pains to be ready with his first setup each morning, especially the first setup the first morning, and if he can get this under his belt so fast that it startles everybody, even if it is not exactly what he wants and even if it isn't made as painstakingly as most of the things in the picture (although I hope I am not being foolishly optimistic in dreaming of meeting our original hopes on the shooting time of this picture). . . .

DOS

To: Mr. Kern　　　　　　　　　　　　　　　March 14, 1945

Dear Hal:

Please let King read this memo—but at a time when he won't say it held up production!!! . . .

The new take of Greg [Peck] making the flying mount is even better than the old one, and I am glad we did it over. I do wish we did not have his hat as far down on his head; and I wish you would tell both King and Greg that the hat has a tendency to make the material look like a double . . . and also I think he is so attractive without his hat that I think we should play more scenes without it. . . .

Please tell [second-unit director] Otto Brower that his stuff is almost all superb. The long shots of the gathering of the clan from all directions are enormously impressive. I do wish we had twice as many or three times as many horsemen, if they are obtainable; and I wish you would tell Brower that I want to shoot the works on numbers of horsemen, wild horses, cattle, etc. Also, Otto almost has a magnificent shot of the horsemen stretched across the screen, going from left to right on the road, with the rolling hills in the background; but I think it is potentially so good that I think he ought to redo it the next time he has a lot of horsemen, because I think he can get better photography, and also I think the shot will be much more impressive if he has enough horsemen so that we will see them enter, and be able to hold the shot long enough for the horsemen to completely cover the width of the screen from left to right. . . .

Please tell both King and Hal, and also Otto for their future guidance, that as I suspected and was willing to bet, the scene that was made too late [in the day] on a gamble, came through magnificently from a photographic angle and really gave us an effective sunset. . . .

And as to both units, I wish they would gamble more on their light at dawn, at sunset, and before and after dawn and sunset, for I am sure we will get our most stunning effects at times which would be normally considered too dark to shoot. Also I wish they would gamble more during the day, because I think we will get some wonderful effects even during very dark and overcast days if we will just take the gamble. Please get this over to everybody concerned. . . .

To: Mr. Johnston   April 6, 1945
cc: Mr. O'Shea

. . . I understand that [Josef] von Sternberg,[83] when asked about a setup by Mr. Vidor, replied that it would take him five hours to arrange the lighting and the setup. If this is true, you should personally bawl the hell out of von Sternberg, making clear to him that I will tolerate no such nonsense, that the second camera unit has been set up to save time, and that we don't propose that it be even slower than the first camera unit.

I also wish that at the same time you would tell Joe that so far, I have not gotten the contribution from him on angles and lighting that I had hoped for; and I have had many criticisms of what has been done, but criticisms after the fact are not what he is here for, and that I had hoped he would be able to supply the function of a Bill Menzies; that the lack of a production designer[84] has given him a terrific opportunity to fill this function but that he is not filling it; that he now has the opportunities to contribute to an improvement in lighting and in setups. If he would give me or Hal Kern his ideas on this before we get into a scene, we could eliminate confusion. He has the script, and there is no reason why he should not be able to come with a camera conception in advance just as Menzies does. I am convinced that a large part of our trouble is due to indecision on the set, and that this in turn is due in a large part to lack of a production designer. . . .

I have no objection if you read this memo in its entirety to Joe.

DOS

[83]Employed as a "special visual consultant" on *Duel in the Sun*.
[84]Joseph McMillan Johnson, head of Selznick's Art Department, later functioned as a production designer on the film and received sole credit as such.

To: Mr. Kern   April 9, 1945

I have the feeling that we are overdoing somewhat the use of huge close-ups. These are enormously effective for dramatic punctuation, but only if saved for this purpose. Even within a single sequence, I think it is much better to build from a waist figure or some other close angle, such as shooting across one profile into another face, handling the lines and reactions which we really want to punch with the larger close-ups. This is, of course, not intended as a generalization because there are cases—love scenes, etc.—where the very large close-up can be really effective, particularly if there is any kind of effective composition. But two occasions which I refer to are Pearl's[85] arrival at Spanish Bit and the scene in the dining room with Miss [Lillian] Gish. I think that the very large close-ups of Pearl are going to be very jarring in the assembly, and that there is no dramatic purpose served by having them this large in this scene. As to the dining room, the very large close-ups of Miss Gish are, in my opinion, only usable once or twice in the scene to get over her shock and transition. A large individual would have had a greater use for this, in my opinion. In any event, I would appreciate it if in the future you would bear my feelings in mind, and simply exercise some discretion as to when we go in for something really big.

I am aware that I have in the past stated that I thought some of our angles were much too distant; [and] this feeling still holds true. If there is any inconsistency in your mind between this and my attitude about the close-ups, please discuss it with me and I will explain further. But meanwhile, I wish you would arrange to get together with Mr. Vidor, Mr. von Sternberg, Mack [Joseph McMillan] Johnson, and Mr. [Harold] Rosson at lunch and have a thorough talk.

DOS

To: Mr. Agnew[86]   April 26, 1945
                                                           CONFIDENTIAL.

Dear Neil:

I need your immediate advice on a problem incident to *Duel in the Sun.* The picture's cost has mounted tremendously. It will be one of the most costly films ever made, probably close to $4,000,000, exclu-

[85]Played by Jennifer Jones.
[86]Neil Agnew, Vice-President of Selznick's new production company, Vanguard Films.

sive of prints and advertising.[87] This means that we will have to do pretty close to $6,000,000 before breaking even. . . .

I am under the impression that the combination of Jones, Peck, and [Joseph] Cotten is a tremendously powerful one. Gallup has reported that Van Johnson was the fastest rising male star in the country and Jennifer the fastest rising feminine star. She is absolutely sensational in *Love Letters,* as is Cotten—and Gallup also reports the tremendous rise in Cotten's popularity. Having had the foresight to benefit from *Duel in the Sun,* we specified that *Love Letters* had to be released not later than August. Peck we know to be the new rage, and if any further proof were needed, it was to be found in what happened at the previews of *Spellbound.* We could not keep the audience quiet from the time his name first came on the screen until we had shushed the audience through three or four sequences and stopped all the dames from "ohing" and "ahing" and gurgling. . . . By the time *Duel* is out, he will have been seen in *Spellbound* and *The Valley of Decision.* In other words, we have three really hot and really new personalities. How many more tickets we sell by costarring some [other] personalities I don't know, and whether the all-star-cast idea would work better than the three costars, I am not sure either.[88]

Do please consider this, discuss it with your men if you wish, even with one or two important buyers if you want, and either wire or telephone me. . . .

DOS

To: Mr. King Vidor   August 16, 1945

Dear King:

VJ-Day interfered with a more prompt reply to your very nice note.

I should hate to think that either of us is so juvenile as to let what happened interfere with a twenty-year friendship.[89]

I was much more mad at you in subsequent days than I was out on the Mesa[90] when I realized what there was left to shoot in the way of annoying bits and pieces. At least you might have left me one decent scene!

[87]The final cost, exclusive of prints and advertising, was $5,255,000.
[88]In addition to Jones, Peck, and Cotten, the cast included Lionel Barrymore, Herbert Marshall, Lillian Gish, Walter Huston, and Charles Bickford.
[89]Vidor had walked off *Duel in the Sun* after an altercation with Selznick on location.
[90]Lasky Mesa, west of the San Fernando Valley.

I do sincerely hope that in the next few days you will come over so that we can chat about the picture and what remains to be done. I like to think that it will be your biggest success in many years, and it will be something of which you can always be proud.

I am aware of what a nuisance I was on the set, but on the other hand I felt right along that you were happy with all my suggestions and even my interferences, because you seemed to always be so enthusiastic about my comments and changes.

In any event, we went through a terrible siege together, and it would be absurd if we didn't enjoy what I hope will be the fruits of a success in close friendship.

I went to the most elaborate pains to protect you with the press, and have not mentioned the contretemps to anybody. I have told every-one that the picture was finished and that only pickup shots remained, which certainly to all practical purposes was the exact truth—and that only second-unit shots remained to be made by [Chester] Franklin, Brower, and Menzies. Nothing was shot without one of these men being on the set, which confirms this story.

I will look forward to seeing you in the studio or perhaps over the weekend and hopefully we can get together for a little tennis. Mean-while, as always my warmest good wishes. . . .

Sincerely,
David

MR. NEIL AGNEW   OCTOBER 8, 1945
VANGUARD FILMS INC.
400 MADISON AVE
NEW YORK, N.Y.

. . . SKOURAS[91] IS AGREEABLE ANY TIME WE WISH TO BREAKING THROUGH PRESENT FIRST-RUN POLICY SYSTEM AND OPENING IN LOS ANGELES IN THREE OR FOUR THEATERS, PLUS SIX OR EIGHT OTHER NEARBY COMMUNITIES, INCLUDING BEVERLY HILLS, PASADENA, LONG BEACH, ETC., [concurrently] IN LINE WITH WHAT I HAVE SO LONG WANTED AND TRIED SO HARD TO GET ON "SINCE" [*You Went Away*]. . . . SKOURAS IS IN COMPLETE AGREEMENT WITH VERY BIG ADVERTISING, COVERING ALL THESE COMMUNITIES, WHICH WOULD OVERCOME THE PRESENT AND LONG-STANDING FOOLISH PRACTICE OF WASTING VERY EXPENSIVE ADVERTISING ON

[91]Charles Skouras, President of National Theatres Corporation and Fox West Coast Theatres.

ONE THEATER. IN FACT, I WISH WE COULD ON "DUEL" TRY TO
ESTABLISH A POLICY THAT WE WANT TO SPEND BIG MONEY IN
ADVERTISING IN A LOT OF THEATERS AT ONE TIME WITHIN A
METROPOLITAN AREA AND SUBURBS THAT ARE REACHED BY THE
IDENTICAL PRESS AND RADIO STATIONS. SINCE SKOURAS IS WILLING
TO GO FOR THIS, I THINK THIS PRESENTS THE IDEAL SITUATION TO
BREAK THROUGH THE FORMER POLICIES NATIONALLY. . . .
REGARDS

DAVID

To: Mr. Scanlon[92]   October 16, 1945
cc: Mr. O'Shea   CONFIDENTIAL

For what must be years, and certainly since we started on *Since You
Went Away,* I have been screaming that our costs are untenable; miles
above the cost of anybody else in town; and that this was quite apart
from the extra cost due to my method of operation. . . . This has been
consistently denied, or left unanswered, and there seems to be no
adequate answer as to why we had to pay so very much more for
comparable merchandise. Again and again I have pointed out that the
only thing that saved us was our reputation, permitting us to get the
highest possible terms; and the quality of our pictures, permitting us
to get grosses that would still give us big profits above costs that with
less quality, or less showmanship, would have ruined any other producing unit. . . .

It is no longer possible to deny that a picture such as *Duel in the Sun*
has cost us probably *at the very least* one million dollars more to make
than the same picture made by myself, in the same way, with the same
people would cost at a major studio.

It is no longer necessary to wonder why *The Yearling,* made in
Technicolor *twice* with all kinds of false starts, with expensive location
trips, back and forth to Florida, up to Arrowhead, with second units
working over the period of, I think, four years, with a shooting schedule greatly in excess of our own, with script and direction and supervision charges to dwarf our own, with Metro's huge overhead, the
biggest and most cumbersome tragedy of errors in MGM history,
winds up costing a million dollars less than *Duel.*

It is no longer possible to argue that a picture the size of *SYWA*
[*Since You Went Away*] and *IBSY* [*I'll Be Seeing You*] cost us hundreds
and thousands of dollars more than if they were made elsewhere. I

[92]E. L. Scanlon, Selznick's Executive Vice-President and Treasurer.

should estimate that on the four pictures made under this United Artists contract, our net profit is conservatively two million dollars less than if the pictures were produced under some other operating method. . . .

Directly we finish *Duel*, we must get down to deciding the basic problems of our future. The reason I am sending you this note now is that I feel that in the interim you should both be thinking about what other alternate methods of production are open to us. . . .

DOS

To: Mr. Glett,[93] Mr. Nelson[94]   October 29, 1945

I have never seen Miss Jones so exhausted as she was today after five hours of dancing—not even after the terrible beating she took in Arizona. . . .

Also, I think somebody had better warn Twentieth[95]. . . . It should be explained that she has been on this picture [*Duel in the Sun*] for almost a year off and on, during which she has played in every scene; has taken the most terrific physical beating ever administered to an actress because of the nature of the story, the work climbing the mountains, et cetera; that she had to get up at six o'clock in the morning to apply Indian make-up which also took her a couple of hours at night to get off, so in effect for the better part of a year she has had fifteen-hour days, and then has climaxed all of this by having to learn two new dance routines from scratch—one because we couldn't shoot it early in order to finish with Peck, and the other because we had to throw away a dance as a result of Breen, after she had spent months of arduous effort learning it. Also, that all of this was preceded immediately by work on another picture, *Love Letters*, and that she filled in her time by working as a Nurse's Aid. . . .

DOS

[Agent] George Volck   November 10, 1945
9441 Wilshire Boulevard
Beverly Hills, California

Dear George:

It is necessary that I immediately put into work the main title of *Duel in the Sun*, as well as the rather extensive advertising of the film.

---

[93]Charles Glett, Selznick's Studio Manager.
[94]Argyle Nelson, Selznick's Production Manager.
[95]Miss Jones was due to report to Twentieth Century-Fox for *Cluny Brown* (1946).

Before deciding what credit King Vidor should receive, I should appreciate it if you would discuss the matter with King and then come to see me about it. . . .

I think you are familiar with the circumstances of his resignation. . . . The straw that broke the camel's back, and caused me finally to lose the temper that I had had under control for so many months, was his behavior while on location at Lasky Mesa. . . .

I went out and moved with King up to the location. The camera was all set, ready to go. King rehearsed the actors in my presence. Repeatedly, I asked him whether the camera was all set and he assured me repeatedly and almost impatiently that I need have no worries on this score and that as soon as the actors were rehearsed, we would knock off the scene. When the rehearsal was finished, King moved over to shoot the scene and I went to a trailer to get caught up on some other work. Hours later, I went back to the set to see how it was progressing and, to my horror, discovered that once again King had completely changed the setup and had ordered tracks built.[96] It was perfectly obvious that by this one whim, arrived at so belatedly, he had thrown another twenty to twenty-five thousand dollars . . . down the drain, since clearly there was no possibility whatsoever any longer of finishing that day.

When I took King to task, he quit. . . . Fortunately, I am not a producer who ever has to crawl before . . . behavior of this type, and I was able to pick up on the setup. . . .

That I go way beyond my obligations as to directorial credit, both on the screen and in the advertising, has been often demonstrated. The latest case in point is that of *Spellbound*, where I have voluntarily, without any prompting whatsoever on Hitchcock's part, given to Hitchcock a double credit, calling my new picture Alfred Hitchcock's *Spellbound*, using "Hitchcock" half the size of the title, solely and simply because I think he is entitled to it. This is despite the fact that I produced the picture and that I worked for many months on both the script and editing, and is due to the fact that Hitchcock secured such remarkable quality with such prompt efficiency . . . and without the slightest set supervision on my part either as to quality or efficiency. . . .

[96]Dolly tracks to enable the camera to move while photographing a scene.

To: Mr. MacNamara[97]   February 6, 1946
cc: Mr. Scanlon   CONFIDENTIAL

With regard to the breakdown of the million-dollar budget on the prerelease advertising campaign of *Duel in the Sun*:

I think with a million-dollar budget before release, which is about what is spent by Universal or Columbia on their entire year's advertising for fifty pictures, we will have to be organized completely, which is a pretty big enterprise in itself. We have got to get into the heads of everyone associated with you that we are not trying to stage a new version of *Brewster's Millions*.[98] The money will go fast enough with organization.

DOS

To: Mr. Herzbrun[99]   April 1, 1946
cc: Mr. Vidor

I have received your letter of March 28.

It is quite true that some time has elapsed since my receipt of your "papal bull" dated February 8.

I have been extremely busy in the interim period. . . . I have been working in large part with the man who directed the film in all these later stages, William Dieterle; and I am still working with Mr. Dieterle on the preparation and shooting of additional film for this production. . . .

The only reason that I am troubling to reply to your . . . letter of February 8 is that it is now clear that the matter must go to [Screen Directors Guild] arbitration, and I wish the record to be complete . . . also because Mr. William Dieterle has advanced a claim for at least codirection credit. . . .

It was on the love scenes especially that, as Mr. Vidor will tell you, I was on the set morning, noon, and night, redirecting the actors, the camera, and even the lighting. This, too, is not a matter of opinion. The actors and many dozens of technicians will testify. . . . Please note that throughout these discussions I have not in any way attempted to take any directorial credit. . . .

I repeatedly asked King whether I was on the set too much and he repeatedly stated I was not. . . . I finance my pictures myself, and make

---

[97]Paul MacNamara, Selznick's Director of Advertising and Publicity.

[98]Referring to the novel, play, and film about a man who must spend a million dollars quickly in order to receive a major inheritance.

[99]Attorney Henry Herzbrun, now in private practice.

them myself, and I have been on the set constantly with only the finest directors in the business, and you are certainly not familiar with my operations if you think that anybody working for me could for one moment keep me away from my pictures in any of their stages. Furthermore, Mr. Vidor was thoroughly aware that . . . there were strict orders on the set that not a single scene was to be photographed, and not even a single angle of a single scene, until I was telephoned to come down on the set to check the lighting, the setup, and the rehearsal. Day after day, setup after setup, I was telephoned by the assistant director, who advised me that they would be ready in a few minutes for the next setup. I would then not merely check the exact direction of the scene, and ninety-nine times out of one hundred change it, but I would stay until I personally approved a take. Mr. Vidor made no complaints about this. . . .

I just received a tally of the present footage of the picture, broken down by directors. I am instructing my Publicity Department to issue a statement stating that Mr. Vidor is insisting on sole credit for the direction of the picture, of which he directed 6280', of which he did not direct 7739', at present writing. These figures will be further altered, against Mr. Vidor, with the retakes and additional scenes we are planning for this week and probably beyond. The story will state that Mr. Dieterle disputes this credit, and is receiving support from me; that I regard it as no more than just that Mr. Dieterle and the late Otto Brower should receive first-unit credit, with second-unit credit going to Reeves Eason; and that I have referred to the Screen Directors Guild for decision of the question as to how these four men should be credited. . . . There are several important scenes that were directed by a man who has not even been mentioned in these communications, Mr. von Sternberg, who, I shall propose to the Guild, will receive some kind of credit, if he will accept it. . . .[100]

Very truly yours,

To: Mr. Agnew   April 10, 1946
cc: Mr. O'Shea, Mr. Scanlon

The more I think about it, the more strongly entrenched I am in my conviction that *Duel in the Sun* simply cannot open in New York City.

I have finished my work on it, and I believe we have a really great

---

[100]The verdict of the Screen Directors Guild stipulated that King Vidor receive sole directorial credit. Otto Brower and B. Reeves Eason were listed in the credits as second-unit directors. William Dieterle received no official credit on the screen or in advertising. Neither did Josef von Sternberg, Chester Franklin, or William Cameron Menzies.

film. While I am aware that criticisms are not important to it and that it should do tremendous business, possibly unprecedented business, whatever the reviews, and while I feel that the reviews generally should be very fine, I am somewhat nervous about the New York notices it may receive. I think that the ballyhoo of the picture and a general negative attitude toward me on the part of the New York reviewers may lead to a patronizing type of review. And even though there may be only a small chance of this prediction coming true, I see no reason in the world for us to let ourselves in for it. Such a reception may depress everyone connected with the film no end, including myself, and might even affect their confidence in me. . . .[101]

My fears are not lessened by my recollection of the fact that although *Gone With the Wind* and *Rebecca* each won the Academy Award, and each won the poll with all the critics of America as the best picture of their respective years, the New York reactions were all the way from mild in some of the newspapers to downright panning in a couple of them. . . .

Do please think about this and discuss it with me when you see me.

DOS

To: Mr. MacNamara   June 26, 1946

. . . I would like you to consider, among other things, how much it would cost for what would be extraordinary in motion-picture advertising—a full page in the leading papers in perhaps fifty or seventy-five key cities, devoted to the announcement of the forthcoming *Duel.*

DOS

To: Mr. Agnew   July 22, 1946
cc: Mr. O'Shea, Mr. Scanlon

Dear Neil:

. . . I have been working on advertising plans with Mac [Paul MacNamara] based upon enormously and unprecedentedly heavy newspaper and radio advertising by territories in the eight or ten weeks before we go into each area, and during the first weeks that we are

---

[101] *Duel in the Sun* had a prerelease opening in Los Angeles in January 1947. In May 1948 the film opened in three hundred theaters simultaneously across the country. Most of the reviews were poor, but the picture was a financial success.

in each area. This plan can be revolutionary and productive of sensational results, in my opinion, if the multiple-booking plan will function; but on the other hand, it is perfectly ridiculous and we will be throwing away the larger part of many hundreds of thousands of dollars if this kind of big-gun campaigning is going to wind up in the bottleneck of single-theater booking. Another advantage of this advertising plan is that instead of spending our money nationally, with a staggered release, and thereby wasting a large part of the money, we will be able to flood an area just before we go into it. But this flooding is only good if there are an enormous number of seats available for the customers whom we will reach.

. . . Because *Gone With the Wind* was so heavily exploited naturally, both before and during release, it did not matter if the picture opened in one theater in each city and did not reach subsequent theaters for many weeks or months, whereas with *Duel* we cannot afford the tremendous advertising necessary to bring it up to the point of interest there was in *Wind*, or anything approaching it, unless our advertising is directed at whole groups of theaters by area. . . .

Warmest regards,
DOS

To: [Composer and conductor Dimitri] Tiomkin   August 28, 1946
cc: Mr. Stewart,[102] Mr. Kern

Dear Timmy:

. . . I should like you to understand that I have the most implicit confidence in the judgment of both Mr. Stewart and Mr. Kern as to how much music can go into dialogue. I have learned through long and bitter experience, as they have, that there is too often a tendency to throw away thousands upon thousands of dollars for musicians that cannot be heard because of the level at which this music must be played under intimate dialogue scenes. . . . The quality of music, as I am sure I needn't point out to you, is not wrapped up solely in the size of an orchestra, by any means; and the temptation to excessive orchestration and distracting tracks, in the scoring of pictures, is aggravated in many cases by the use of too large an orchestra, according to my observations. . . .

Cordially and sincerely,
DOS

[102]James G. Stewart, Selznick's Technical Supervisor.

PAUL MACNAMARA   MAY 2, 1947
VANGUARD FILMS, INC.
NEW YORK, N.Y.

. . . THE POINT OF THE WIRE IS MY GREAT FEAR THAT WE ARE
REACHING TOO FAR AND TRYING TOO HARD. . . . WHILE WE DID A
COMPLETE RIGHTABOUT-FACE, FROM THE TIME WE STARTED ON
"DUEL" ON EXPLOITATION, IN BREAKING ALL OUR RULES AS TO
DIGNITY THAT PREVAILED FOR MANY YEARS, THERE WAS AT LEAST
A CERTAIN AMOUNT OF FUN IN IT, AND I THINK IT WAS MOST
EFFECTIVE AND HAVE NO REGRETS ABOUT IT. BUT I THINK NOW
WE ARE IN DANGER OF GOING OVERBOARD, TURNING PEOPLE'S
STOMACHS AND MAKING OURSELVES AND THE PICTURE
RIDICULOUS, AS WELL AS ROBBING BOTH THE COMPANY AND THE
PICTURE OF ANY STATURE. . . . I WAS HORRIFIED AND
EMBARRASSED TO HEAR FOR THE FIRST TIME TODAY THAT ON
WEDNESDAY THERE IS TO BE SOME SORT OF BIG THING AT THE
WALDORF TO SELECT A "MISS DUEL IN THE SUN." ALSO, THEY
HAVE SOME KIND OF STUNT ABOUT DROPPING A THOUSAND OR
MORE BALLOONS ON TIMES SQUARE WITH GIFTS IN THEM. . . . I
CAN'T BELIEVE THAT A PICTURE OF THIS IMPORTANCE, COST, AND
EFFORT . . . REQUIRES THE TYPE OF STUNTS THAT . . . ARE
EMBARRASSING WITH THE PUBLIC AND THE PRESS AND THAT
CAUSE PEOPLE TO THINK WE HAVE A LEMON WE ARE TRYING TO
PALM OFF. . . . REGARDS

                                                    DAVID

PAUL MACNAMARA   MAY 7, 1947
VANGUARD FILMS, INC.
NEW YORK, N.Y.

PLEASE IMMEDIATELY ADVISE O'SHEA THAT I SPENT A COUPLE OF
HOURS OVER AT LOEW'S TODAY, AND THAT THEY ARE SIMPLY
INCREDULOUS OVER THE FABULOUS BUSINESS OF "DUEL." . . . THEY
ALL AGREE THE MULTIPLE-RUN PLAN IS PROVING OUT IN
CONNECTION WITH ALL THE OTHER THEATERS, AND IS
DEMONSTRATING WISDOM OF POLICY, EVEN IF IT IS AT THE
EXPENSE OF SOMEWHAT LESS BUSINESS AT DOWNTOWN HOUSE
THAN COULD OTHERWISE BE OBTAINED. . . . ENTIRE FILM TRADE
HERE REGARDS THIS AS TREMENDOUS MILESTONE IN

MOTION-PICTURE MERCHANDISING AND EXHIBITION, AND AS
MARKING REVOLUTION IN PICTURE BUSINESS FOR HANDLING BIG
PICTURES. . . . REGARDS.

DAVID

PAUL MACNAMARA   MAY 20, 1947
VANGUARD FILMS, INC.
NEW YORK, N.Y.

. . . I AM ONLY JUST COMMENCING TO SEE THE REVIEWS AND THE
FULL EXTENT TO WHICH WE HAVE BEEN PANNED, AND THESE
HAVE BEEN SO VIOLENT THAT I CANNOT BELIEVE THEY HAVEN'T
DONE SERIOUS DAMAGE. . . . REGARDS.

DAVID

To: Mr. MacNamara   August 13, 1947

I really think, Mac, that I have got to prepare to spend a great deal
of money . . . on the regaining of my personal position as it was before
Duel. Even the advertising and ballyhoo on *Duel* was damaging, and
was a complete contradiction of our former "Tiffany" standards. I am
not in the least criticizing what we did on *Duel*, for on the contrary,
and as I have often said, I think the campaign was tremendous, was
a great credit to you, and was what the picture needed. However,
there was a price, and a heavy one for it. . . . In view of the ballyhoo,
which became damaging, in view of what happened with the picture,
and in view of the consequent great loss and prestige with the trade
and press and public, I think the campaign on me is needed very
badly, if only from the standpoint of my own morale and my own
thinking—for even if I am wrong in exaggerating the extent of the loss
to my position, there is the matter of my family to think of, and it is
also a fact that if I think the damage has been done, it must affect my
state of mind and of my work, and therefore must be met exactly the
same as though I were not exaggerating the damage—and mind you,
I don't think I am exaggerating. . . .

DOS

: : : : : :

To: Mr. Hungate[103]   November 19, 1945
cc: Messrs. O'Shea, Scanlon

I am in despair about the delay on the new Peck deal. Won't you please, in God's name, tell me what is holding this up? . . .

Another year is about to end—another year in which we have carried on the same old negotiations without getting anywhere excepting only on Jennifer Jones. Bergman, Leigh, Hitchcock, Peck, Cotten, McGuire—it's the same old story—months and months of negotiations, endless conversations, yackety-yackety, and no deals; and if we do get anywhere near a deal, we spend enough time defining it and drawing contracts that the horse is stolen. Just give us enough time, and we will not have a single one of our personalities. Any other studio can negotiate, close, and get the contract signed in days or weeks, and they consider they are worn out if it takes months—but unless we spend two years, we don't think we have a deal, and some of our deals have gone much longer than two years.[104]

DOS

To: [Writer Mel] Dinelli   April 5, 1946
cc: Mr. O'Shea

Thank you for your note of the 30th about Miss Garbo.

I certainly share your enthusiasm for her as an actress and as a personality. Further, I thought her ideal for *The Paradine Case*, and have thought so ever since I bought the story for her when I was with MGM some thirteen or fourteen years ago.

Unfortunately, Miss Garbo has always had an aversion to the story and even today won't play it. My most sincere thanks for your interest.

DOS

To: Mr. Willson,[105] Mr. MacNamara   June 26, 1946
cc: Mr. O'Shea

. . . I want once again to stress a point I have tried to make, but I am afraid not too successfully. . . . What we have done with our players

---

[103]Richard Hungate, Secretary of Vanguard Films.

[104]The reluctance on the part of many of Selznick's personalities to sign new contracts was due to Selznick making very few films during this period and his not sharing the high loan-out fees he received from other studios with the personalities.

[105]Henry Willson, Selznick's Talent Department Head and assistant to President Daniel T. O'Shea.

has no parallel in recent years in any studio, large or small, and for the percentage of people that we launched as against the enormously high percentage of those we have developed successfully, there is no parallel in the entire picture industry. We have reason to be proud of it. It should be publicized, and in connection with this publicity, it is most important that we do nothing to lower the prestige of our stock company as a group, or its members as individuals. . . .

Furthermore, for years we had the pick of all the talented young artists as they appeared in the theater and elsewhere because they considered it such a mark of distinction to be with us, and this has given us a tremendous edge in being able to take away from the competition of the entire business almost any of the really great young new talent who came along. But now . . . we are losing our taste and our discretion and our respect for talent and experience and are going into fields that discount everything that should win our respect and encouragement. . . .

We must also recognize the fact that we are able to launch certain players with success but we are able to do little or nothing for another type of player. Betty Grable would not have gotten very far with us. On the other hand, Bergman and Fontaine and Leigh and Jones and McGuire and Cotten could have very likely become stars no place else, certainly not the great stars into which we made them. Even if I knew we had another Betty Grable, I should be very hesitant to sign her; first, because I don't think we could give or find her the right opportunities, and second, because we are known and should be known for players of a certain quality (without discounting the qualities which other studios exploit, or in any way running them down); we have a pride in this type of player; we know what to do with them; and I don't want to change what we stand for simply in the remote hope that somehow or in some way that isn't now apparent, we could put over a Betty Grable.

Let's continue to look at these young people, by all means; but let's sign them with more discretion. . . .

DOS

To: Messrs. O'Shea, Scanlon   August 20, 1946
                                   EXTREMELY CONFIDENTIAL

I have been studying our payroll as part of my own attempts to find out what's wrong with our operation.

. . . I think the first thing we have to do is to correct the organization of our own work, and I don't except myself. So long as I have to spend many hours worrying about such basic things as transportation, and so long as Dan has to sit for hours every day with Hitch, to a total of perhaps many weeks of sitting, all toward a new contract that is still not forthcoming, the place is going to continue to run with an ever greater overhead and with ever greater wastefulness. We simply must get someone in here who can do one of two things: either successfully carry through negotiations on his own, or successfully manage the place on his own with over-all executive supervision by the three of us.

I am going to have to stop being a producer otherwise in order to become an executive full time, because I am much too embarrassed by our present operation to let it go on uncorrected indefinitely. And the time I am having increasingly to spend on management, which is only a fraction of the time that is indicated, is robbing us of my services as a producer with a much greater cost than any saving I might effect, as I am well aware.

We have to have pictures made by other people because I haven't the time, nor am I in the state of mind to make more pictures, largely as a result of the increasing amount of deskwork that I have every day —which in turn is traceable to more and more of our people reporting to me directly, and which is of course due to our lack of proper organization—again with this vicious circle, all being traceable to the bottleneck in our whole operation, as I see it, of our negotiations, which are devouring us while at the same time they are not even successful in themselves.

If we are honest with ourselves, we will see clearly that the fault is in ourselves—in the three of us: that we're negotiators more and more, and with decreasing success, and taking more and more time about it while we are failing to do the job that is screaming to be done as executives. We keep adding more and more people in the hope that this will remedy the situation, when, in my opinion, the remedy is to be found simply in the reorganization of our own work. . . .

Maybe it wouldn't do us any harm to take one or two men from operations that we have been inclined rather ridiculously to look down upon, such as Universal, which can take one of our own scripts and make it for a million dollars less than we can with the very people that we would be using.

DOS

To: Mr. O'Shea   November 22, 1946
cc: Mr. Scanlon

Another endless day and night of work, and I still haven't had time to read a script, much less work on one. . . .

I am certain that *The Paradine Case* has tremendous flaws, and it looks to me as though it is going to have to go into work, willy-nilly. I simply will have to hope that somehow we will be able to get together the cast for what will inevitably be costly retakes—provided that even when the picture is finished, I have some time to do my job of producing.

In addition, we will have spent hundreds of thousands of dollars in film that will have to be cut out. . . .

DOS

MR. DANIEL T. O'SHEA   DECEMBER 6, 1946
SAVOY PLAZA HOTEL   CC: MR. SCANLON
NEW YORK CITY

. . . I AM ON THE VERGE OF COLLAPSE AND NOT THINKING CLEARLY, AND AM HAVING UNDER THESE CONDITIONS TO TRY TO PATCH UP AND REWRITE THE HITCHCOCK SCRIPT [*The Paradine Case* (1948)] (HECHT LEAVES US TOMORROW, WITH AN ENORMOUS AMOUNT OF WORK REMAINING TO BE DONE); AND THE BUSINESS PROBLEMS ARE MOUNTING DAILY. UNDER THE CIRCUMSTANCES, I SEE NO ALTERNATIVE TO PLANNING NO NEW PRODUCTION BY US WHATSOEVER BEYOND "PARADINE," AND UNTIL WE CAN GET ORGANIZED. . . . WE ARE GOING TO HAVE TO PACKAGE ALMOST EVERYTHING WE HAVE ON THE CALENDAR, IN VIEW OF WHAT WE ARE UP AGAINST, AND UNTIL THE DAY WHEN WE CAN GET PROPERLY ORGANIZED. THE INEVITABLE RESULT IS GOING TO BE A SERIES OF MEDIOCRE PICTURES AT THE HIGHEST COSTS IN THE BUSINESS, AND FOR RELEASE AT A TIME WHEN PROBABLY RECESSIONS AND POSSIBLE FREEZING OF CURRENCY IN ENGLAND WOULD MAKE EVEN RESPECTABLE COSTS DANGEROUS. . . . IT IS CLEAR THAT EVEN THOUGH I CONTINUE TO WORK EIGHTEEN HOURS AND TWENTY HOURS DAILY, "PARADINE CASE" WILL NOT BE WHAT IT SHOULD BE, AND MAY EVEN BE DANGEROUS AT ITS COST, WHICH I PREDICT RIGHT NOW WILL BE BETWEEN $3,200,000 AND $3,300,000, WITH ONLY ONE STAR OF IMPORTANCE, PECK. CLEARLY I WILL HAVE NEITHER THE TIME NOR THE ENERGY NOR

THE CLARITY OF MIND TO IMPROVE THE SITUATION, AND TO STRAIGHTEN OUT ITS PROBLEMS, WITHOUT WORRYING ABOUT ANY OTHER PICTURES. . . . REGARDS.

DAVID

To: Mr. O'Shea, Mr. Scanlon December 28, 1946

CONFIDENTIAL

I must advise you both that I am deeply concerned about progress on *The Paradine Case.*

In the first four days of shooting, we were two days behind schedule.

In addition, everything that was shot on Tuesday has to be redone, putting us at least three days behind.

In addition, we are going to have to wild-line a considerable part of what has been shot. I don't know what kind of a day we had on Thursday, but it is possible that we are more than three days behind in the first six days of shooting. . . .

Also, Hitch has slowed down unaccountably. . . . Further, I think that he has rather sensed our seeming indifference to cost, and the lack of the firm hand, which I at least once applied with him, and an indifference to costs and time, which disappoint me greatly, and which I think must be attributable to us, in view of what we have seen and what we know of his extraordinary efficiency when he wants to be efficient. This much I can assure you: you will see an entirely different result when he starts on his own picture; and you can also be sure that he will attribute this to efficiency in his own operation, against the gross inefficiency with which he charges us. He told me tonight that he thought it was disgraceful the way we went into this picture with the physical production—photography, sound, etc.—"twenty years behind the times." . . .

Even Metro, with all its wealth, has recognized that the rise in costs throughout the business has necessitated a tremendous shake-up in their organization and entirely different methods of operation. But we go blindly on our way, smug and secure in our own ignorance and in our own inefficiencies. . . .

DOS

Mr. David O. Selznick[106]   January 13, 1947
Selznick Studio
Culver City, California

Dear David:

I shall set forth herein a summary of the facts in my dispute with you. It is agreed that upon your receipt of my signature to these facts, you will pay me $60,000 in payment for the picture that I did not make for you under my contract, and for which I am claiming compensation.

These facts are as follows:

You brought me to this country when I was unknown to American- or English-speaking audiences. When I finished my contract with you, under your management, I had become one of the greatest stars in the world, this development taking place entirely while I was under your management.

It isn't true that you brought me to this country to do *Joan of Arc.* The idea of my doing *Joan of Arc* originated with you. You did not proceed with the idea for reasons which you have explained to me. Recently, after announcing Jennifer Jones as *Joan of Arc,* you offered me the role as a consequence of Miss Jones's insistence that it be offered to me before she would give any consideration to the idea of her playing it. . . .

During my initial years with you, you paid me for pictures I did not make rather than lend me for pictures which either you or I did not think worthy of me.

During the entire period of my many years with you, I was never directed to do a picture I did not want to do.

During the entire period of my many years with you, there was not a single picture in the entire industry that I wanted to make that you did not secure for me. I never lost a single role because of your demands, and I had the pick of the pictures of all studios.

I did my second picture, *Adam Had Four Sons,* despite your advice against it, and despite your statement that you would prefer to pay me for the picture and keep me idle rather than see me do it. I wanted to work, and since it was the best thing available, I chose to do it. . . .

During the time that Victor Fleming was working for you, you day after day ran scenes from *Intermezzo* with him and conducted a long

[106]This letter was written by Selznick to appear as though it had been drafted by Ingrid Bergman. He then sent it to Miss Bergman, rather than a more conventional letter, in order to make his point.

campaign to secure his interest in me, leading to my securing of the role in *Dr. Jekyll and Mr. Hyde* [the MGM 1941 version with Spencer Tracy].

You had conferences with [director] Michael Curtiz and with the Epstein brothers [writers Julius J. and Philip G. Epstein] concerning the loan of me for *Casablanca*, and decided jointly with me that this would be a good picture for me to do.

You assured me that I would play Maria in *For Whom the Bell Tolls*, after it was bought, for Paramount. . . .

You decided to lend me for *Gaslight* and I agreed. You personally conducted the negotiations with MGM, insisting upon Charles Boyer and Joseph Cotten, Arthur Hornblow, George Cukor to direct, and Joseph Ruttenberg as cameraman. You held conferences on the script. You worked on the cutting, sending a very lengthy and detailed report that took all day and all night to compose, giving cutting notes which were followed almost to the letter. You insisted upon a retake of the most important scene in the picture in order to give me the opportunity for . . . an Academy Award, which you had long promised me that I should win, and which you had conducted a very long publicity campaign toward my winning.

When my contract drew near to an end, our negotiations for a new contract bogged down upon your insistence on an exclusive contract for a period of seven years. Through these long negotiations, which had gone on for years, I repeatedly assured you that there could be not the slightest question about my continuing with you, but that I wanted to be free to do an occasional picture on the outside. I stated to you verbally and in writing, and repeatedly, that there could be not the slightest question but that I would continue with you. I made these statements right up to a few months before the expiration of my contract with you. . . .

As my contract drew near an end, and as I continued to negotiate without signing anything, although repeatedly assuring you that I intended to stay with you, you advised me that [director] Leo McCarey wanted to borrow me for *The Bells of St. Mary's*. You told me that you did not think I should do it because of your fears that it would be secondary to, and not as good as, *Going My Way*, but that since you had always checked with me before either accepting or rejecting a loan-out (exactly the contrary to what is done at every other studio) you did not want to turn it down without asking me. I met with Mr. McCarey, and thought I would like to do it. You then met with McCarey further, and laid down certain conditions of rewrite of the story before you would consider it further. You made various proposals for my character. McCarey, whether by coincidence or otherwise, used the scene of my confession which you had created when it was planned that I should do *The Keys of the Kingdom.* McCarey accepted other suggestions of yours, including the one that I should sing a Swedish song. . . .

You personally made *Spellbound* with me . . . and you completely re-edited the picture, following the first preview, taking out two reels, without any collaboration. You completely changed your plans about releasing the picture in order that it might be most beneficial to my career, after working with RKO and Warner Brothers, largely futilely, in order to get better time on the releases of three pictures that were coming out at approximately the same time [*Spellbound, Saratoga Trunk,* and *The Bells of St. Mary's*]. When you were unable to get these releases spaced as you desired, you arranged for the Sales Departments of the three companies to get together, all designed to protect my career. And when you realized that only a limited amount of spacing was possible, you went to work to turn this into an asset and to publicize it as "a Bergman year."

You worked for many months on the script of *Notorious,* through six or eight completely different drafts. When you turned it over to RKO, it was with the identical protection—in this case an insistence upon Alfred Hitchcock, Cary Grant, Claude Rains, and with all the approvals of cameraman, etc., which you had made a habit in my protection. . . .

Further, in connection with my second trip to entertain the troops, and with your loss of a picture, and with my statements that there were no pictures available for me anyway, you advised me that in addition to *Some Must Watch* [*The Spiral Staircase*], there were two other possibilities: a loan-out to Charles Brackett at Paramount for a picture called *To Each His Own,* and a script you and Dore Schary were preparing called *Katie for Congress* [*The Farmer's Daughter*]. . . . I read *To Each His Own,* and didn't care for it at all. I realize that it was produced with tremendous success by Paramount, and that Olivia de Havilland is now a leading contender for the Academy Award as a result of her performance in it. . . . I hear from you that you sold *Katie for Congress* to RKO when I refused it, and I also hear from you that it has been made by RKO with Loretta Young and Joseph Cotten, and that RKO considers it one of the best pictures it has had in many years.[107]

. . . When I went to Europe, I sent you a letter, a copy of which is attached hereto, in which among other things I said, "I think friendship and trust are of more worth than a piece of paper called contract. And if you never get that slip of paper you still will have, changed or unchanged, whatever you think, but still, your Ingrid."

You told me that you were continuing to take me on good faith, that you believed in me implicitly, and that you would continue to take me on faith until the end.

Unfortunately for you, when I returned from Europe, and had everything that I wanted, I forgot all about my promises and statements through the years. I forgot everything you had done for me. I forgot my promises, and even my letter. And I demanded payment for the picture which I asked you to give up, and which you had given up, and which could have been one of the subjects listed above, on which you would, of course, have made a great deal of money, as well as absorbed your overhead, which was idle, largely as a result of my not making a picture. It is true that I entertained the troops on my own insistent desire to do so, but I didn't see and still don't see why you shouldn't pay me $60,000 for having done so.

I complained that you did not make more pictures with me, both privately and in the press. I neglected to say to anybody that you wanted to buy *The Valley of Decision* and make it with me, but that I didn't want to do it; or that you wanted to make *The Spiral Staircase* with me . . . or that you wanted to do *Katie for Congress* with me; or that you wanted to buy *A Tree Grows in Brooklyn* and make it with me, making it more the story of the mother, but that I didn't care to do it, and that Twentieth Century-Fox thereupon bought it and made it into a great success for themselves and for your Dorothy McGuire; or that you wanted to make *Anna Christie* with me, but that I didn't want to do it because Garbo had done it; or that you wanted to make *Anna Karenina* with me but that I didn't want to do it, for the same reason; or that there were half a dozen other stories that you wanted to make with me, but that I didn't like; or that you took the unprecedented attitude that you would lend me to others for pictures I wanted to make rather than ask me to do pictures that you wanted to make, but in roles that I didn't care for.

Throughout the years, you devoted an enormous amount of time to

[107]Olivia de Havilland received an Academy Award for *To Each His Own* (1946), and Loretta Young received one for *The Farmer's Daughter* (1947). Miss Young created a Swedish dialect for her characterization.

going over material for me, and to reading scripts submitted from every studio in town, in order to be sure that I was the first actress in the history of the screen that had her pick of the best stories of *every* studio in town, plus the insistence of yourself as to how the picture should be set up and who should make them in each department. This insistence on your part meant that I had Fleming, Cukor, Curtiz, Wood, McCarey as my directors; that I had the best cameramen in the business, all selected and approved by you, since I didn't know any of them; that I had Spencer Tracy, Gary Cooper, Charles Boyer, Joseph Cotten, Bing Crosby, Gregory Peck, Cary Grant as my leading men, although any other rising young actress would have given her eye teeth for any one of these occasionally, and all of this through the formative period of my career. I am aware that I was the envy of every young actress in town, and even of every already established star, and that a great deal of trouble was caused at other studios by actresses who contrasted your handling of me with what they had to play in, whom they had to be directed by, and scripts, stories, leading men, publicity, etc. . . .

When everyone else in Hollywood disbelieved in me and wondered why you had brought me over, and through the long period when you couldn't lend me to anyone, and through the secondary period when you were lending me at cost and at less than cost, you insisted that I was the great actress of this generation, that I would be the greatest star in the industry, that I would be the Academy Award winner, that I would be universally acclaimed. . . .

And in consideration of the above, I herewith make demand upon you for $60,000 for the picture which I asked you not to make, and for the period that I was entertaining troops. Upon payment of this amount to me, you are free of the obligation which I feel that you owe me, having had the privilege and the glory of lifting me from obscurity to great stardom. . . .[108]

Ingrid Bergman

To: Mr. Hitchcock   February 18, 1947
bcc: Mr. O'Shea

Dear Hitch.

I had Lee Garmes[109] in tonight. . . .

When I discussed with him the multiple cameras on the cross-exami-

---

[108]The $60,000 was paid, and Bergman did not sign with Selznick again.
[109]Director of Photography on *The Paradine Case.*

nation scenes, he was quite excited, but stated that he understood this was only to be three cameras. I told him of your feeling that, properly planned, the whole cross-examination of Latour[110] (this also applies to the examination of Mrs. Paradine)[111] could be shot, not in three or four, as I felt it could be, but actually in one day, all twenty pages, with perhaps one additional day for additional reactions on angles not covered in the first day. Certainly I hope we will make this our goal because if we don't thoroughly organize such a plan, we are going to waste a fortune in Old Bailey on top of the inordinate amount of money already spent on the film.

DOS

To: Mr. O'Shea   February 28, 1947

After seeing tonight's tests and the previous day's work, I am more than ever disturbed about the enormous waste and overshooting. . . .

I think it would be most useful if for once we followed the efficient methods of the German studios, where there isn't an angle wasted, or even the methods of a competent craftsman like Milestone, who prepares for his staff and crew a complete blueprint of each day's shooting, showing exact angles to be made on each scene, and the exact portions of each scene to be used in these angles, and who has every part of a sequence or sequences that is necessary on each camera setup, instead of going back again and again to the same moving of the cameras with the enormous waste each time the camera is moved back to a position it has been in formerly, or something extremely close to it. . . .

DOS

DANIEL T. O'SHEA   APRIL 19, 1947
VANGUARD FILMS INC.

WILL YOU PLEASE CALL LELAND [Hayward] AND TELL HIM I
SHOULD LIKE TO HAVE ANOTHER CHAT WITH HIM ABOUT GARBO,
WITH A VIEW TO MEETING WHAT REMAINS OF HER ECCENTRIC
DEMANDS AND WORRIES BY OUR AGREEING TO A DEAL FOR THE
TWO THINGS ABOUT WHICH SHE WAS EXCITED, "BERNHARDT" AND

[110]Played by Louis Jourdan.
[111]Played by Alida Valli.

"THE SCARLET LILY," PLUS ONE MORE PICTURE . . . AND WITH MY
FURTHER TAKING HER WORD THAT SHE IS PLACING HERSELF IN
MY HANDS FOR A PERIOD OF AT LEAST SEVEN YEARS . . . THAT SHE
RECOGNIZES, FOR ITS INFLUENCE ON HER FUTURE ATTITUDES, THE
EXTREMES TO WHICH I AM GOING TO MEET HER PROBLEMS, TO
SHOW MY RESPECT FOR HER, AND TO DEMONSTRATE A
CONFIDENCE IN HER POSSESSED BY NO ONE ELSE, WHILE AT THE
SAME TIME TREATING HER AS THOUGH SHE WERE STILL A GREAT
DRAWING CARD, WHICH NO ONE IN THE INDUSTRY WILL CONCEDE
AND WHICH INDEED IS DENIED BY ALL THE SO-CALLED EXPERTS.
THE STIMULATION TO MY INTEREST, WHICH HAS NEVER FLAGGED,
HAS COME ABOUT FIRST BECAUSE I FEEL THAT THE GENERAL TONE
OF IMPROVED TASTE OF THE PUBLIC INDICATES THAT GARBO IN
THE RIGHT SUBJECTS WOULD BE ACCEPTED TODAY AS NEVER
BEFORE, AND COULD BE AN EVEN BIGGER STAR THAN EVER
BEFORE, AND THAT HER FIRST PICTURE ON RETURN COULD BE
MADE A GREATER BET, EQUIVALENT TO THE RETURN OF A
BERNHARDT OR A DUSE TO THE STAGE IN THIS COUNTRY AFTER
AN ABSENCE OF MANY YEARS; SECOND, BECAUSE OF MY
RELUCTANCE TO SURRENDER SO VALUABLE A SCRIPT ON
BERNHARDT, A SCRIPT OF QUALITY WHICH I AM NOT LIKELY TO BE
ABLE TO DUPLICATE VERY OFTEN IN THE NEXT FEW YEARS. . . .[112]
REGARDS

DAVID

Portrait of Jennie

To: Mr. O'Shea   May 1, 1947
cc: Mr. Scanlon   CONFIDENTIAL

. . . I can't find time for meetings on *Portrait of Jennie* more than
every few days, and these are when I'm exhausted, and when I am
harassed by all manner of other problems. Perforce, I have had to
spend a large part of my time on the sales and exploitation and censorship problems of *Duel*, and the new problems of organization of SRO
[Selznick Releasing Organization]. *The Paradine Case* sits waiting.[113]
Joan of Arc will, I suppose, go by the boards as another big write-

[112]Neither *Bernhardt* nor *The Scarlet Lily* was produced, with or without Garbo.
[113]Waiting for Selznick to find time to work on the editing.

off.[114] I can't get to any number of vitally important production problems, such as Garbo, and new stories . . . just to mention two, and not to go into *Portrait of Jennie*, to which Sidney Franklin or any other first-rate producer would be devoting one hundred per cent of his time and energy and thoughts. . . .

I finally faced the truth, like a big boy, and looked at the "cut film" of what was shot in Boston Harbor [for *Portrait of Jennie*]. It is fantastic beyond belief. There are some shots of Joe [Cotten] for a "montage" that can never be used at all. Then there are a couple of shots with doubles that probably can't be used—just a couple of shots, and that these were made after weeks of waiting for a particular kind of weather (which they finally got!) is incredible, because to all practical purposes they could have been made in any kind of weather, by a newsreel cameraman on assignment at so much per foot, and assuming that they will fit into the story at all, I suppose that this may be at the outside twenty-five or thirty feet of what amounts to second-unit film. And for this, we had a whole huge staff in Boston, and going out to the harbor, day after day, for weeks. . . .

We have spent over $15,000 for extra talent. I think the only extras visible in any of the film are skaters way in the background of two or three shots, skaters who for all practical purposes could have been the skaters that were in the park every day. Moreover, and equally incompetently, we spent tens of thousands of dollars on wardrobing these extras for merely specks in the distance! It is an absolute disgrace. . . .

My instincts tell me, and I repeatedly told you, that I was convinced that this whole *Portrait of Jennie* venture was doomed to be one of the most awful experiences any studio ever had. If I can only get free of some of these other burdens, I will somehow get in and try to salvage it. . . .

If I can get the time, I will see if we can't get a script that makes sense. . . .

Beyond *Portrait of Jennie*, I will not go. Whether we liquidate or not, whatever our future course may be, you may assume that we must lend out each and every one of our people until and unless we get a top general manager. Trying to function without one is too idiotic, and

---

[114]*Joan of Arc* (1948) was filmed by a company formed by Ingrid Bergman, Victor Fleming, and Walter Wanger.

it is a strain upon me which I will not longer endure—which indeed
I cannot longer endure, even if I were so foolish as to want to.

DOS

ERNEST SCANLON   MAY 17, 1947
VANGUARD FILMS, INC.
9336 WASHINGTON BOULEVARD
CULVER CITY, CALIFORNIA

. . . ONE OF THE MANY THINGS I HAVE DONE TO "PORTRAIT OF
JENNIE" IS TO PLAN A CONSIDERABLY CHANGED ENDING IN WHICH
I WANT TO BUILD UP THE HURRICANE AND ESPECIALLY THE TIDAL
WAVE AGAINST WHICH THE CHARACTERS FIGHT AT THE FINISH. I
HOPE TO GET A REAL D. W. GRIFFITH EFFECT OUT OF THIS THAT
WILL HAVE TREMENDOUS DRAMATIC POWER AND ENORMOUS
SPECTACULAR VALUE, THEREBY ADDING A BIG SHOWMANSHIP
ELEMENT TO THE PICTURE. I THINK THIS WILL HAVE A MATERIAL
EFFECT UPON PLANS FOR THE SPECIAL-EFFECTS DEPARTMENT.
OBVIOUSLY THEY WILL HAVE A TREMENDOUS JOB ON THEIR HANDS
IN MINIATURE AND MATTE WORK. THERE IS NO REASON WHY THIS
SHOULDN'T BE LAID OUT IN THE GREATEST DETAIL AT ONCE, AND
NO REASON WHY SHOOTING SHOULDN'T PROCEED
SIMULTANEOUSLY WITH THE PICTURE PROPER, AND JUST AS SOON
AS THE DEPARTMENT IS FREE FROM ITS WORK ON "THE PARADINE
CASE," WHICH PRESUMABLY WILL BE VERY SHORTLY. . . . I SHOULD
LIKE TO SEE A DETAILED CONTINUITY WORKED UP WITH
SKETCHES, IN THE MANNER OF THE ATLANTA FIRE IN "WIND," THE
GATHERING OF THE CLANS IN "DUEL," ETC. . . .

DAVID

Mr. Robert Nathan[115]   July 7, 1947
Truro, Massachusetts

Dear Mr. Nathan:

I send you herewith draft of the final script of *Portrait of Jennie* with
the thought that you might enjoy reading it. . . .

Although the picture is in production, I never consider it too late to
make improvements, right up to the time that a picture is released.
Therefore, if you feel that you could contribute anything to this script,

[115]Author of the novel *Portrait of Jennie*.

whether major or minor, I should be happy to have you do so; and I hope it is needless for me to add that I should be happy to pay you for this, and would anticipate no difficulties in arriving at an equitable arrangement.

. . . You will recall that in the book Adams[116] took Jennie on a picnic; and that other characters saw Jennie. This we changed because of my very strong feeling, although not true of the book, that Jennie should be seen by no one but Adams. . . .

I like to feel that we have uncovered and developed thematic values that were inherent in the original material, as well as an additional philosophy to give the story somewhat more uplift and a wider mass appeal. . . .

Many thanks for your kind invitation to us to visit you. We all regretted that we could not accept it because of the pressure of production, and because there were no scenes to be shot in your neighborhood.

With warmest regards,

Cordially and sincerely yours,
David O. Selznick

To: Messrs. O'Shea, Scanlon

July 22, 1947
CONFIDENTIAL

. . . I believe now that we are going to have to spend a great deal of money to make this picture [*Portrait of Jennie*] right, on top of what is already its absurdly high cost. . . .

When we have cleaned up our problems, I intend to set about building a new producing organization that can in some way compare with that which I built from scratch many years ago by rescuing Menzies from oblivion, giving Hal Kern authority, making Klune into a production manager, going miles and years ahead of the business through men like [Head of Special Effects] Jack Cosgrove and Mac Johnson, and getting a result that was hailed and acclaimed the world over as being way ahead of the industry. Presently, we have a tenth-rate production organization . . . wasting money at a prodigal rate that hasn't been equaled since the days of [silent-film director Erich] von Stroheim. . . .

I beg for your help. I assure you that I will do everything that I can. . . .

DOS

[116]Played by Joseph Cotten in the film.

To: Mr. [James G.] Stewart   July 24, 1947
cc: Messrs. O'Shea, Scanlon

. . . In connection with *Portrait of Jennie*, the suggestion has been made, which I think is a superb one, that the score could basically be from Debussy, utilizing in particular the sea nocturnes for the themes. It has exactly the right quality; doesn't need and couldn't use the absurd number of musicians that we let our people out here get away with, and couldn't be duplicated by even a Bernie Herrmann. . . .

Please think about this and let me know how you feel about it the next time we meet.[117]

DOS

MR. BEN HECHT   NOVEMBER 24, 1948
NYACK, NEW YORK

DEAR BEN: VERY MANY THANKS IN ADVANCE FOR COMING TO THE RESCUE AGAIN ON A FOREWORD.[118]. . . THE AUDIENCE WAS ENCHANTED WITH THE WHOLE IDEA OF THE FOREWORD, AND IT SET THE MOOD BEAUTIFULLY FOR THE PICTURE, ESPECIALLY WITH THE DEBUSSY MUSIC UNDER IT; BUT IT SEEMED TO ME TO FAIL IN THE FOLLOWING PARTICULARS: ONE. TOO MANY TITLES AND QUOTES. TWO. TOO ABSTRUSE AND HIGHFALUTIN' FOR COMPLETE AUDIENCE UNDERSTANDABILITY. IT NEEDS THE TYPE OF CINEMATIC FOREWORD JOURNALESE OF WHICH YOU ARE THE ONLY MASTER I KNOW, COMBINING A CERTAIN ARTISTIC TONE WITH OLD HEARST SUNDAY-SUPPLEMENT TYPE OF HOKEYPOKEY, PSEUDOSCIENTIFIC APPROACH, SO THAT THEY WILL BELIEVE IT WHILE AT THE SAME TIME THEY ARE ENTERTAINED BY IT.

MY PURPOSES ARE AS FOLLOWS: ONE. TO PREPARE THEM FOR AN ENTIRELY DIFFERENT KIND OF PICTURE THAN THEY HAVE EVER SEEN AND TO SET THE STAGE FOR THEIR ACCEPTANCE OF A DRAMATIC FANTASY, WHICH, AS YOU KNOW, IS FAR MORE DIFFICULT TO PUT OVER THAN A COMEDY FANTASY, AND IN WHICH THEY WILL ACCEPT ANYTHING. TWO. TO IMPLY THAT ANYONE THAT DOESN'T BELIEVE IT IS AN IGNORAMUS, AND TO FLATTER THE INTELLIGENCE OF THE AUDIENCE BY ASSUMING THAT THEY HAVE THE SAME KIND OF APPROACH TO THE GREAT

[117]Debussy themes were used as the basis of the film's score.
[118]For the opening sequence of *Portrait of Jennie*.

UNKNOWN QUESTIONS OF LIFE AND DEATH AS THE GREAT
PHILOSOPHERS AND POETS. THREE. TO PRESENT IT AS THOUGH IT
WERE THE TELLING OF AN ACTUAL TRUE STORY RATHER THAN AS
A PIECE OF FICTION, IN THE "BELIEVE IT OR NOT" SPIRIT, ON THE
BASIS OF "THIS IS WHAT IS KNOWN ABOUT IT AND WE DON'T
OFFER ANY EXPLANATION, MERELY THE FACTS AS KNOWN." FOUR.
TO TRY TO PREPARE THEM FOR THE BASIS OF THE FANTASY (A
MISPLACEMENT OF TWO PEOPLE IN TIME, WHICH INVOLVES THE
QUESTION OF ALMOST EINSTEINIAN RELATIVITY) AND THE THEME
OF THE PIECE (NO DEATH WHERE THERE IS LOVE AND FAITH).

THE ONLY GOOD FOREWORD TO A PICTURE I EVER SAW OUTSIDE
OF THOSE YOU HAVE WRITTEN FOR ME WAS THE ONE TO "THE
SONG OF BERNADETTE," WHICH WAS, I BELIEVE, FROM THE BOOK
AND WHICH, AS I RECALL IT, READ ABOUT AS FOLLOWS: "TO THOSE
WHO BELIEVE, NO EXPLANATION IS NECESSARY. TO THOSE WHO DO
NOT BELIEVE, NO EXPLANATION IS POSSIBLE." THIS WOULD HAVE
BEEN AN IDEAL TYPE OF THING FOR US TO WIND UP OUR
FOREWORD, AND I AM SURE YOU CAN FIND SOME SKILLFUL WAY
OF AT LEAST IMPLYING THIS CONTENT. I HAD MADE ANOTHER
ATTEMPT OF MY OWN, BUT I THINK IT MISSED FAR MORE EVEN
THAN THE FIRST. . . . IN ANY EVENT, I SHALL BE EAGERLY
AWAITING YOUR REDRAFT, WHICH CAN TAKE AN ENTIRELY
DIFFERENT FORM. . . . IT CAN HAVE QUOTES OR NOT . . . EITHER
ACTUAL OR HECHTIAN CREATIONS, WHICH WE MIGHT CREDIT TO
THE GREEKS OR THE PERSIANS IF IT IS NECESSARY TO INVENT A
FEW TO SAY PRECISELY WHAT WE WANT TO SAY. WARMEST
REGARDS. MOST GRATEFULLY.[119]

DAVID

: : : : : :

[119]The lengthy foreword by Hecht used in the film was spoken over a montage of
clouds and atmospheric effects, during which a quote from Euripides, and later Keats,
appeared on the screen. Excerpts from the foreword are as follows: "Since the beginning, Man has looked into the awesome reaches of infinity and asked the eternal questions: What is time? What is space? What is life? What is death? . . . Through a hundred
civilizations, philosophers and scientists have come with answers, but the bewilderment
remains. . . . Science tells us that nothing ever dies but only changes, that time itself
does not pass, but curves around us, and that the past and the future are together at
our side forever. Out of the shadows of knowledge, and out of a painting that hung on
a museum wall comes our story, the truth of which lies not on our screen, but in your
heart."

MRS. DAVID O. SELZNICK   DECEMBER 17, 1947
927 FIFTH AVENUE
NEW YORK CITY, N.Y.

DEAR IRENE: JUST READ BROOKS ATKINSON'S RAVE NOTICE IN
SUNDAY'S NEW YORK TIMES. . . .[120] ALSO, I AM IN RECEIPT OF THE
MOST WILDLY ENTHUSIASTIC TELEGRAM FROM BOB ROSS,[121] WHO
SAYS AMONG OTHER THINGS THAT YOU HAVE "ONE OF THE MOST
REWARDING, STIMULATING AND EXCITING PLAYS IN MANY A
SEASON," AND "A REAL AND DISTINGUISHED HIT." . . .
ACCORDINGLY, I FEEL JUSTIFIED IN SENDING YOU MOST EXCITED
AND DELIGHTED CONGRATULATIONS. IT IS A JOY TO KNOW THAT
ALL MY PREDICTIONS OF YOUR SUCCESS ARE COMMENCING TO
COME TRUE, AND IN A BIG WAY. I AM SURE YOU ARE WELL ON THE
ROAD TO RECOGNITION AS THE THEATER'S BEST AND MOST
DISTINGUISHED PRODUCER. LOVE

DAVID

To: Mr. O'Shea   December 1, 1947
cc: Mr. Scanlon

. . . I have been doing a great deal of thinking since I left the Coast
and am prepared to sacrifice staff and make other economies I dislike
making; but I am not prepared to sacrifice people who have been with
us for many years, and who have contributed importantly to my ability
to be in business independently. . . .

I have completely changed my mind about Elsa Neuberger.[122]
. . . I will not have her discharged. . . . She functioned perfectly under
Kay Brown, whom we also let go in one of these moments of aberra-
tion, when in a panic as a result of our costs and setbacks to the
business, we let a lot of good people go. . . . She is one of the two
remaining remnants of what was one of the finest independent producing organizations in the business. Step by step, these people have
been forced out and replaced with second-raters, and at least I intend

[120]Regarding Mrs. Selznick's première stage production of Tennessee Williams's *A
Streetcar Named Desire*, directed by Elia Kazan. The Selznicks separated in August
1945, and Mrs. Selznick subsequently went to New York, where she became a theatrical
producer. In addition to *Streetcar*, her successes were to include *Bell, Book and Candle*
and *The Chalk Garden*.
[121]Selznick's Eastern Production Representative.
[122]Now Selznick's Eastern Story Editor.

to save what is left and to try to get back the good people—such as Kay
—and in the alternate, with them not available, or where the appreciation of others for them has taken their salaries past a tenable point for
their jobs, with people of ability. . . .

When I think of what we were with Kay Brown and Val Lewton
. . . Bobbie Keon and Jimmie Newcom and Lyle Wheeler and all the
rest of the staff that took us up to the front of the business, I commence
to regain some perspective and some objectivity. . . .

It would appear that anybody who helped me make Selznick International Pictures has to go, whereas those who have helped dissipate
the direct and indirect profits of those pictures must stay. I just won't
have this any longer. . . .

DOS

To: Miss Reissar   June 19, 1948
cc: Messrs. O'Shea, Scanlon

Dear Jenia:

. . . I hope you will encourage [director Roberto] Rossellini to sign
up Bergman for one of our pictures, and will put this on your calendar
to also follow him up on it assiduously, since Bergman would be such
a tremendous asset to a picture that Rossellini would make for us. With
her great admiration for Rossellini, her desire to work with and for
him, and her lack of any pictures at all beyond the Hitchcock picture,
I think I would have an easy time in making a deal for him if you would
guide him and be the directing power behind the scenes in his
negotiations with her.

However, Bergman knows that Rossellini is tied exclusively to us.
Dietrich also knows it but insists that he has not signed a contract with
us; and between Dietrich and her pals among directors, such as Billy
Wilder, Bergman, and others, we are likely to have many people
urging Rossellini not to sign with us. I think you had better keep after
him, and in close touch with him; that you had better keep in daily
contact with him; and that you had better continue to advise him of
the enthusiasm of myself, our organization, yourself, Miss Jones,
etc. . . .[123]

---

[123]Rossellini did not make a film for Selznick.

To: Mr. Henigson[124]   August 23, 1948
cc: Messrs. O'Shea, Scanlon   CONFIDENTIAL

. . . I am sure that it is unnecessary for me to make the following statement, but I nevertheless feel that you will forgive me this word of caution, since so much is at stake: it is essential that you keep confidential any and all figures that you uncover here, which I know I can count upon you to do; not alone now but . . . in the future. I am not hiding anything from you, and on the contrary I not alone welcome but seek your investigation of our costs, since I feel that you can perform an invaluable service for us in relation to obviating any repetition of this wastefulness. . . . But the extent of our wastefulness and excessive costs could be very damaging to our future operations if it were made the subject of gossip or of industry knowledge, particularly bearing in mind that these things become exaggerated in the retelling. Accordingly, I should like to know that I may count upon the complete secrecy of you and of anyone to whom you relay the information. . . .

I am perfectly willing to plead guilty to this wastefulness *between ourselves,* since in the final analysis it is my fault for two reasons: (1) my production methods; (2) my tolerance through the years of the wastefulness. But I don't want to be guilty any longer, now that it is apparent that many millions of dollars of profits have been eaten up in this wastefulness, and that the most successful series of pictures ever made in the history of the business has produced profits which are perhaps not more than twenty per cent of what they should be. I have no fears about making pictures, and am most eager to make them; but I don't want to make any more until and unless I am properly organized, which very clearly we haven't been for years, in relation to matters of both overhead and physical costs. It is my hope that as part of the survey you are making, you will be able to present a thorough report on where we have gone wrong. . . .

DOS

---

[124]Henry Henigson, executive who functioned for a time as a consultant on cost control and reorganization.

PART

*EUROPEAN COPRODUCTION
AND MISCELLANY
(1948–1956)*

I STOPPED MAKING FILMS in 1948 because I was tired: I had been producing, at that time, for more than twenty years. I wanted to do some of the traveling that I had completely denied myself during my long concentration on work in Hollywood, and I felt I could combine business with pleasure by exploiting my backlog of films throughout the world.

Additionally, it was crystal clear that the motion-picture business was in for a terrible beating from television and other new forms of entertainment, and I thought it a good time to take stock and to study objectively the obviously changing public tastes. My company, as all picture companies, financed itself largely with bank loans; and these loans, with interest, had been extended to a total of about $12,000,000.

It seemed all too clear that if we continued to produce for a rapidly declining market the debt would grow, and that for the first time there might be a danger that we might not be able to repay it. I felt a particularly strong obligation in this connection because I was the sole owner of the stock of my company, and while I was not personally involved in the obligation this sole ownership imposed upon me— according to my lights—I had a personal moral obligation.

Certainly, I had no intention of staying away from production for nine years. I had originally estimated that it would take me four years to repay our loans, but the costs of operation mounted and my distributing company had to make millions more out of these films to sustain itself. Accordingly, it was something over five years before the obligations were repaid in full.

During those years I learned much about foreign distribution, about foreign production, and about the tastes of foreign audiences; and although I had always tried to make pictures for a world market, at last I fully realized the necessity for a world viewpoint in the making of Hollywood films.

I learned, too, something of foreign production methods, and came to have an even greater respect for the talents of motion-picture makers abroad. Consistent with this, and as part of the plans for the liquidation of my company and its debts, we devised what has since come to be known as coproduction; and since it was neither easy nor my desire to invest money in films in those times, we invested certain foreign rights of my pictures in acquiring Western Hemisphere rights to these coproductions.

The very first experiment along these lines was successful. It was The Third Man, which we produced jointly with Sir Alexander Korda and director Sir Carol Reed. The creation of the film was almost entirely Reed's. I did a little work on the script with Reed and Graham Greene, but nothing that contributed greatly to its success. I supplied the stars, and I re-edited the film for this hemisphere. It was a substantial contribution to making me financially healthy again and able to return to production, for I had promised myself that under no circumstances would I make another film—despite all sorts of tempting and even flattering offers—until we were free of debt.

During this period, I sold The Prisoner of Zenda to MGM. I did not see their remake, but I understand that they did an extraordinary thing: MGM used our script (which they had purchased from us) almost word for word, and they had a Moviola on the set to copy every single camera setup![1]

When the day finally came that I was able once again to produce personally, I found it difficult to go back: I was enjoying too much freedom from the intensive effort of production as I know it, and I still had no material about which I was enthusiastic.

:: :: :: :: :: :: :: :: :: :: :: ::

MISS BETTY GOLDSMITH[2]   OCTOBER 16, 1948
NEW YORK, N.Y.

. . . I HAVE READ COMPLETE SEPTEMBER 20 SCRIPT OF "THIRD MAN" VERY CAREFULLY AND HAVE MADE DETAILED NOTES ON IT. HOWEVER, NOT YET COMPARED SCRIPT WITH PRIOR DRAFT, ALSO WITH MY NOTES. BOBBY KEON WAS UP ALL NIGHT MAKING THIS COMPARISON AND IS NOT YET AVAILABLE. ALSO, AND AS YOU CAN IMAGINE, MY SCHEDULE IS SLIGHTLY CROWDED. HOWEVER, IN ADVANCE OF REFERRING TO THIS COMPARISON, I CAN TELL YOU THE FOLLOWING:

---

[1]This 1952 version, with Stewart Granger, Deborah Kerr, and James Mason, also utilized an adaptation of the Alfred Newman score from the 1937 Selznick production.
[2]Selznick's Foreign Coordinator.

(1) IT IS BASICALLY A VERY GOOD SCRIPT AND IN REED'S HANDS SHOULD MAKE A VERY GOOD PICTURE.

(2) IT IS, AS KORDA SAID, A GREAT IMPROVEMENT OVER THE PRIOR DRAFT; FOR THIS IN MODESTY, I CAN TAKE BOWS, BECAUSE MOST OF THESE IMPROVEMENTS ARE DUE TO THEIR FOLLOWING A LARGE PERCENTAGE OF MY CHANGES. . . .

(3) DESPITE THE IMPROVEMENTS, IT IS NOT SATISFACTORY FROM THE STANDPOINT OF THE PRICE OF THE PICTURE OR ITS ACCEPTABILITY TO AMERICAN AUDIENCES. . . .

(4) I AM CONVINCED THAT REED HAS NO FAMILIARITY WHATSOEVER WITH OUR RIGHTS IN THE MATTER; AND THEREFORE HAS SEEN FIT TO TAKE ONLY THOSE CHANGES WHICH SUIT HIM AND [author Graham] GREENE FROM THE STANDPOINTS OF ENGLISH STORYTELLERS, MAKING THE PICTURE FOR ENGLISH AUDIENCES. I THEREFORE URGENTLY REPEAT MY PRIOR SUGGESTION THAT YOU INSTRUCT JENIA [Reissar] TO MAKE REED PERSONALLY FAMILIAR, AND IN DETAIL, WITH OUR RIGHTS UNDER THE CONTRACT, WITHOUT FURTHER DELAY. . . .

(5) IT IS ABSOLUTELY ESSENTIAL THAT THERE BE AN AMERICAN WRITER ON THE JOB AT ONCE . . . WHO CAN MAKE THE DIALOGUE ACCEPTABLE FROM AN AMERICAN STANDPOINT, EVEN IF IT IS NOT AS GOOD AS IT SHOULD BE. PRESENTLY THE DIALOGUE IS IN MANY CASES SO LUDICROUS, FROM A STANDPOINT OF AMERICAN CHARACTERS BEING PRESENTED TO AMERICAN AUDIENCES, THAT THE PICTURE WOULD BE KIDDED TO DEATH BY OUR GALLERY AUDIENCES.[3] . . .

I CERTAINLY AM NOT GOING TO INSIST UPON LOTS OF LITTLE DETAILED THINGS WITH A MAN OF REED'S UNDERSTANDING AND ABILITY; BUT ON THE OTHER HAND, I CERTAINLY AM GOING TO INSIST UPON CERTAIN BASIC THINGS ON WHICH I SPENT MANY, MANY LONG HOURS OF WRANGLING IN ORDER TO GET REED'S AND GREENE'S AGREEMENT; THUS, FOR INSTANCE, THE SCRIPT IS WRITTEN AS THOUGH ENGLAND WERE THE SOLE OCCUPYING POWER OF VIENNA, WITH SOME RUSSIANS VAGUELY IN THE DISTANCE; WITH AN OCCASIONAL FRENCHMAN WANDERING AROUND; AND WITH, MOST IMPORTANT FROM THE STANDPOINT OF THIS CRITICISM, THE ONLY AMERICAN BEING AN OCCASIONAL SOLDIER WHO APPARENTLY IS MERELY PART OF THE BRITISH OCCUPYING FORCE, PLUS THE HEAVY (LIME), PLUS THE HERO (WHO

[3] Apparently, no other writers were assigned.

IS CANADIAN IN SOME SCENES AND AMERICAN IN OTHERS),[4] PLUS
ANOTHER AMERICAN HEAVY NAMED TYLER.[5] AND, JUST TO MAKE
MATTERS WORSE, THE AMERICAN HERO APPARENTLY IS
COMPLETELY SUBJECT TO THE ORDERS AND INSTRUCTIONS OF THE
BRITISH AUTHORITIES, AND BEHAVES AS THOUGH THERE WERE NO
AMERICAN WHATSOEVER AMONG THE OCCUPYING POWERS, NOR
ANY AMERICAN AUTHORITY, AND INDEED AS FAR AS THIS PICTURE
IS CONCERNED, THERE IS NONE. IT WOULD BE LITTLE SHORT OF
DISGRACEFUL ON OUR PART AS AMERICANS IF WE TOLERATED THIS
NONSENSICAL HANDLING OF THE FOUR-POWER OCCUPATION OF
VIENNA. . . . I WENT THROUGH THIS AT THE GREATEST LENGTH
AND IN THE GREATEST DETAIL WITH REED AND WITH GREENE,
AND COME HELL OR HIGH WATER, I SIMPLY WILL NOT STAND FOR
IT IN ITS PRESENT FORM. . . .

I AM SURE THAT KORDA TOLD THEM I KNEW MY BUSINESS, AND
THAT THEY COULD COUNT ON GETTING INTELLIGENT AND
HELPFUL SUGGESTIONS FROM ME; BUT TO FOLLOW ONLY WHAT
THEY SAW FIT TO FOLLOW. . . . I SPENT COUNTLESS HOURS GOING
THROUGH WITH REED AND GREENE, AND GETTING AGREEMENT
ON, THE TREATMENT OF THE WHOLE BACKGROUND OF VIENNA
TODAY, TO GIVE THE PICTURE SIZE, AND MORE IMPORTANTLY, TO
GIVE IT UNDERSTANDABILITY FROM THE STANDPOINT OF
AMERICAN AUDIENCES. WE LAID OUT IN THE GREATEST DETAIL
SCENES OF THE CHANGING OF AUTHORITY FROM ONE OCCUPYING
POWER TO ANOTHER, WITH THE FOUR POWERS IN TURN CHANGING
IN THE CHAIR; AND IN ORDER THAT THIS MIGHT NOT BE
EXTRANEOUS MATERIAL, WE WENT TO THE GREATEST PAINS TO
MAKE THIS MATERIAL BACKGROUND OF THE PERSONAL STORY,
AND TO TIE IT IN WITH THE PERSONAL STORY. WE FRANKLY MADE
THE RUSSIANS THE HEAVIES, IN PURSUIT OF THE GIRL. ALL OF THIS
HAS BEEN ELIMINATED, EVEN WHAT WAS IN THE ORIGINAL SCRIPT.
WE MUST INSIST UPON ITS RETURN, FOR PATRIOTIC REASONS, FOR
PURPOSES OF THE PICTURE'S IMPORTANCE AND SIZE . . . AND FOR
PURPOSES OF OUR UNDERSTANDING OF WHAT ON EARTH IS GOING
ON IN VIENNA THAT THESE THINGS CAN BE HAPPENING? AS IT IS,
THERE IS NOT ONE PERSON IN A THOUSAND AMONG OUR
AUDIENCES WHO WOULD EVEN BE ABLE TO FOLLOW THE
BACKGROUND OF THE PICTURE, THE KNOWLEDGE OF WHICH IS

[4]In the final version, he is American.
[5]This character was changed to a Rumanian called "Popescu."

ABSOLUTELY ESSENTIAL TO THE FILM'S ACCEPTABILITY AND EVEN
A LIMITED POPULAR SUCCESS.[6] (BETTY: MORE TO FOLLOW. PLEASE
WAIT. BELIEVE ME, DEEPLY SORRY TO BE MESSING UP YOUR
SATURDAY NIGHT IN THIS FASHION. WILL TRY TO MAKE IT UP TO
YOU IN SOME WAY. GRATEFULLY, DOS)

To: Mr. Hungate   September 23, 1949

I have just heard about our print order of *Fallen Idol*[7] from Pathé.
A laboratory should of course be chosen largely at this time especially
on basis of price. . . . But at this time, and hopefully always, quality
must be final determining factor, and this order is the first we have
placed since we started in business where we neither have a supervisor representing us watching prints nor a laboratory of such pride in
its work that such supervision is really unnecessary. We also have an
obligation to the producers, who have a huge investment in time and
effort and money on photographic results, to be sure that their work
and presentation of actors and contributions of other artists are not
destroyed or damaged by inferior printing. . . .

The assumption that the quality of printing is a matter of small
importance is of course far removed from the truth. Just use a lab that
puts features through the same as it would newsreels, and that does
not change its "soup" often enough, just to mention two things, and
the difference can be a picture which looks like a quickie, instead of
pictures that cost the fabulous sums that we've invested in; *Fallen Idol*
and *The Third Man*, respectively. So sensitive, indeed, is the quality
of the respective work turned out by different laboratories that in the
past, we have always consulted the cameraman, because often a cameraman has learned that for his type of lighting, one laboratory will
follow the printing indications from him better and more effectively
than another. To the best of my knowledge, we have never even asked
Reed or his cameraman or the English laboratory for any printing
instructions or advice or guidance in connection with the exquisite
photography of *Fallen Idol*. This we must do at once. At Metro we
wouldn't have to supply such protections, because the Metro lab

[6]A new opening, shot three months after the completion of the rest of the film, helped
to explain the location and situation in Vienna at the time. In the final version, the
Russians were "the heavies in pursuit of the girl [Alida Valli]," but the remainder of the
changes requested by Selznick—other than those already noted—are not apparent.
[7]The Selznick Releasing Organization distributed the Alexander Korda–Carol Reed
film in the Western Hemisphere.

would insist upon having this guidance if it was not thoroughly familiar with the work of the men involved. . . .

I also think you should know that one good print from a laboratory is no test. Almost any of them will, if watched, turn out one good print. What matters is the quality of the work they turn out when you are not checking them, particularly when you don't have a representative supervising their work and/or when the laboratory has such high standards itself that such supervision is unnecessary. This is just as true in black and white as it is in color; and, as I have stated so often, one reason why I shall be faithful to Technicolor, long after it has been demonstrated that other color processes can turn out a good initial print, is that Technicolor has demonstrated through the years its complete and absolute integrity and pride of craftsmanship about every single print that comes out of its laboratories in Hollywood and in England. . . .

DOS

Mr. Jack L. Warner   October 21, 1949
Warner Brothers Studios
4000 West Olive Avenue
Burbank, California

cc: Mr. O'Shea

Dear Jack:

On the personal side, we have had to content ourselves with just a few days of honeymoon[8] and with the hope that we would have one when *Gone to Earth*[9] was finished, not dreaming it would take this long. Additionally, Jennifer has been away from her children far longer than she anticipated and is much distressed about it. We both want a period of rest together, and a period of time with Jennifer's children. I have been begging Jennifer to take a rest for a year or more, but she has overruled me because of her desire to keep working and because of her reluctance to give up any role or new assignment for which she had great enthusiasm.

[8]Selznick and Jennifer Jones were married in July 1949. Selznick and Irene Selznick had received their final decree of divorce in January 1949. (Jennifer Jones and Robert Walker had been divorced in 1945.)

[9]The English title. The film was released in the United States as *The Wild Heart* (1952). Jennifer Jones played the leading role. Selznick took no credit on the film personally (which was written, produced, and directed by Michael Powell and Emeric Pressburger), although he worked on the American version extensively.

Also, Jennifer wants to work in Europe, and I want to work in Europe, which makes a fortunate coincidence. Accordingly, our present program is for me to go back to England a week or two hence to work on the editing and retakes of *Gone to Earth*, hopefully finishing them in time for us both to be back here for Christmas. We then hope to return to Europe with Jennifer's children, as early in the new year as possible, to stay for the greater part of the year, since I have a big production program over there and since neither of us wants any further separations from the other. Thus, Jennifer will be with me in Europe regardless of whether she does pictures there or not.

Now this whole program could be changed if, but only if, there were a picture here that was so outstanding for her as to again warrant our making our personal lives and plans secondary to our respective careers. Should this happen, Jennifer would at least first have some period of rest and time to be with her children, more than is possible if she is here but working; and I would rearrange my European productions until she had finished this job.[10] . . .

To: William Wyler   November 11, 1949

. . . I urge you, I hope not too egotistically, to run a picture I made once, called *A Star Is Born*. To a certain extent the construction was similar [to Wyler's *Carrie*], except that the construction was very carefully thought out and was complete. There was a definite form and pattern. An ambitious girl rises to the top while the man who has supported her and adores her goes to the bottom. She never ceases to love him, despite the fact that the relationship becomes more and more impossible. And in the great tragedy, her love survives.

We had a hell of a time getting the actual tag and audience satisfaction with the whole film—until we did get it. And you're going to need, *very importantly*, just such a moment. I don't mean the same comment, but something that says something and doesn't leave the audience way up in the air dissatisfied. I am sorry to have to say it, because I think *The Heiress*[11] must inevitably fail because of audience dissatisfaction with the ending despite its superb writing and direction and production. When I say "failure," I don't mean downright failure, but failure in achieving the reception you wanted. I think its reception must be somewhere between great disappointment commercially and

[10]Jennifer Jones's next film was to be *Carrie*, a film based on the Theodore Dreiser novel *Sister Carrie*, which was filmed in Hollywood in 1950, but not released until 1952.
[11]The William Wyler film, released a short while prior to the writing of this memo.

mediocre success, neither of them good enough for the effort. You got critical raves, and you'll no doubt get them on this if you don't make a single change. You may even get Academy Awards, but you've assured me that this isn't enough; and I point out to you that all the Academy Awards in the world aren't going to cause Paramount to let you get away with any more *Heiress* or *Sister Carrie* budgets if they don't pay off, so the result will be loss of opportunities beyond these if you don't bring it off commercially and from a mass-audience viewpoint. I beg you and the Goetzes [writers Ruth and Augustus Goetz] not to talk yourselves or each other into any specious or sophomoric intellectualism about what is "truer." You are making a drama, and a good drama has to have a good construction, certainly at these prices. You have to know what it is you're telling. . . .

I know I have been excessively emphatic in connection with some of these points, but it's part of the business of a script critic, invited or otherwise (and if you've been angry at some of these comments, I must remind you that you have invited them), to in turn dramatize his points in order to sell them.

Anyone reading these notes would think that my opinion of the script is a low one. It's nothing of the sort. I think it's an extraordinarily fine script, the tragedy from my standpoint being that it isn't really as good as it ought to be, and frankly, not by a considerable margin. I don't give a damn about making a bad script a little bit better. What I do care about is making a very good job into a great one. If you do nothing with this script, you will have a fine film, but only that— whereas if you really knock yourselves out to get the proper construction and character relationships you can have a truly memorable one, worthy to rank with [your direction of] *Wuthering Heights* and *Best Years of Our Lives.* If I may say so without offending the Goetzes, Brontë and Hecht and Sherwood—yes, and Goldwyn, too—are all superb constructionists. I think the Goetzes write brilliantly, but they start out with a Dreiser book that hasn't nearly the construction of a Brontë book, because Dreiser just wasn't as good as Brontë, and they haven't yet had the long years of motion-picture experience of Hecht or Sherwood. . . .

Warmest regards and the best of luck to you and to the Goetzes in your endeavors. I hope I haven't destroyed what seemed to be your genuine desire to have my comments.

. . . As to the casting of Hurstwood, I honestly don't know what to say. . . . I still am crazy about the idea of Olivier, and wish you would see it. I think he has every single thing the part requires. He not alone looks the exact age, he is the exact age. He can do a brilliant job of aging further before your eyes. He can have the spurious elegance. He would give to the picture the great distinction it should have. He would bring to it extraordinary freshness. If it were my picture, I would be breaking my neck to get him. . . . Saying "no" to Olivier is in my opinion exactly equivalent to having said "no" to Jack Barrymore for any role he could have played. In years to come it's likely to seem incredible to you that you turned down the suggestion.[12]

If you get a chance, please do give me a ring before I leave. I'll *still* be at the studio, no doubt. I'm dictating this at between three and four a.m. on Thursday night, having been here since early Wednesday morning. . . .

Sincerely,

DOS

TO: DANIEL T. O'SHEA   NOVEMBER 25, 1949

. . . CANNOT COMMENCE TO TELL YOU SENSATION CAUSED BY KARAS'S[13] ZITHER MUSIC IN "THIRD MAN." IT IS RAGE OF ENGLAND AND HAS ALREADY SOLD MORE RECORD COPIES THAN ANY OTHER RECORD IN ENTIRE HISTORY OF RECORD BUSINESS IN ENGLAND. IT IS WIDEST-PLAYED DANCE MUSIC IN ENGLAND. IT IS AD'S BIGGEST SINGLE SUCCESS OF FILM, AND ADS HERE USE "HEAR HARRY LIME THEME," ETC., IN TYPE DWARFING ALL OTHER BILLING. IT IS ONE OF THOSE UNPREDICTABLE, TREMENDOUS SENSATIONS THAT I CANNOT EXPECT ANY OF YOU TO UNDERSTAND WHO HAVE NOT BEEN HERE. ENTIRELY UNRELATED NEWSPAPER ARTICLES AND EDITORIALS, EVEN ON POLITICS, CONTINUALLY REFER TO IT. INEVITABLY, THIS SUCCESS WILL BE REPEATED AMERICA IF WE ARE PREPARED FOR IT. WE SHOULD BE ABLE TO MAKE FORTUNE OUT OF THIS MUSIC. REGARDS.

DAVID

To: Miss Jenia Reissar   June 13, 1950

Dear Jenia:

I somehow gathered from my talks with Ingrid in Rome that she has a very definite nostalgia for the protection of her contractual past with

[12]Olivier was cast in the role.
[13]Anton Karas, who composed and performed the zither score for *The Third Man.*

us, and I believe she would be greatly interested if we had anything for her. Certainly, it is quite definite that she wants to go back to work; that she is most kindly disposed toward us; that she feels her business troubles began with the days she started to free-lance, and she referred to this often; and that she has completely finished with Rossellini type of pictures, with a yearning for the company of professional actors and more conventional production methods (which I am glad to be able to say does not appear to be interfering in the least with her personal happiness with Rossellini).

I gathered also that she has been having conversations with Sam Goldwyn, although I am not too sure of this. In any event, it is my firm conviction that she would be sensationally successful if she had a good film. I think there has been, and will increasingly be, a strong sentiment that she has been persecuted to a ridiculous and untenable extent, and perhaps to a growing conscience that if Lindstrom had given her a divorce, when she wanted it, the whole situation would not have existed as a scandal.

In any event, I should be happy to welcome Ingrid back to the fold and actually, despite my present desire to avoid having people under contract, I'd like very much to have Ingrid under contract again, perhaps on the basis of one picture yearly, which is probably all that she would want to make and possibly all that she should make. . . .

Her downfall started with her very first picture after leaving us, *Arch of Triumph*, followed by *Joan of Arc*, which Rossellini persists in characterizing in her presence as a very bad picture, with which sentiment, I must say I agree. Then came Hitchcock's *Under Capricorn*, which hopefully demonstrated to her the difference in Hitchcock under our management and my supervision *(Spellbound;* and *Notorious)* and Hitchcock on his own . . . and then . . . *Stromboli.*[14] . . .

If her next picture is a fine one, I think she will be back as a top star; if, on the other hand, it is another turkey, coming on the heels of four very unpopular pictures, I think it may be curtains for her as a big star . . .

I said this before *Stromboli* was released—that I thought if the picture was a fine one, the notoriety would merely help, since it would get a far greater audience at the outset, and the public would be doubly receptive of it if it was a fine picture, but doubly critical if it was a bad one, or one they did not like. Rossellini may be right about

---

[14]Directed by Rossellini and filmed on the island of Stromboli off the northeast coast of Sicily in 1949, with Miss Bergman.

RKO butchering the picture in the recutting, but both she and Rossellini realize all too well the damage that has been done; and it is very clear that Rossellini is kindly disposed toward us. . . .

I believe Ingrid and Rossellini are either en route to Paris from Capri or already in Paris on their honeymoon. I am sure that she would leap at the chance to talk to you! I cannot commence to tell you how interested she is in talking over old times, the picture business generally, what to do about pictures, etc. And to be able to talk in English is in itself a joy for her! . . .

Regards,
DOS

Ruby Gentry[15]

To: Mr. King Vidor   April 11, 1952
      [Independent producer] Joseph Bernhard

Dear King and Joe:

I gather that Joe has been finding my memoranda on *Ruby Gentry* all rather lengthy. I am sorry. This is going to be lengthier. Those on *Gone With the Wind* were lengthier still. Those on *Rebecca* were considered worthy of rather lengthy publication in *The Saturday Evening Post.*[16] And those on *Tom Sawyer* were sent on tour, illustrated, by the Museum of Modern Art, where they were studied by thousands of people, after which people queued up for many months to read them in Paris, where they were exhibited as kind of a course in picture-making by one of the leading French museums.

. . . I would like to suggest that you immediately start to think about who is going to do the score. In this connection, I have a suggestion to make that might make you a great deal of money—*two* ways. . . . If we could come up with a good enough romantic title, I think it would be very smart to think about a theme melody that would be the basis of a popular song. . . . There are two ways of doing it: one, by adapting a theme from the film; the other, by buying the title of a hit tune that is already established. A third way is to try to get a song written to fit the title, which is the most difficult, and usually the least

---

[15]Selznick was not a partner in this production, but was involved on the side lines after Jennifer Jones had been signed for the lead.
[16]Not published.

successful. Examples of the second way are *I'll Be Seeing You* and *Till the End of Time,* both of which I purchased for films already made, the former of which I owned, and the latter of which I owned half of with RKO. I thought the latter a bad picture; but largely because of the song, it rolled up a very, very big gross. The former, not too great a picture, did approximately three-and-a-quarter million dollars domestically, traceable, in my opinion, largely to the song title. But the best plan is to follow the first way, as so many of us have done at various times, and as Sam Goldwyn did with *My Foolish Heart* and *Our Very Own* with great success. In each of these cases I believe Victor Young did the scores and also the songs. . . . He is an extremely practical and successful man in doing scores without chichi, and without tricks and without nonsense, and within economic boundaries. He operates to budget, and can do an inexpensive score very effectively.[17] . . .

Kindest regards,
DOS

To: Joseph Bernhard   April 23, 1952

. . . Let me get back for a moment to my general feelings about the script: in one of King [Vidor]'s script comments (page 20, point 99), I find this statement: "Motion pictures are an art form." Now it may very well be that the difference between King's approach to this subject and my own lies in the interpretation of this statement. *Of course,* motion pictures are an art form. But so is painting an art form. However, the audience that Picasso paints for is scarcely the audience of the poster "artist." Similarly, I was not under the impression that a commercial enterprise, such as *Ruby Gentry,* was an exercise in the use of motion pictures as an art form. Some films, by their nature and design, can be great pieces of artistry and still have a mass appeal. Some of the work connected with the commercial film, even the most blatant commercial film, can involve great artistry in some of its departments. But the great virtue of the motion-picture industry (and note the word "industry," for it is important to know what we are talking about) is also its greatest liability: the privilege on the one hand, the very clear obligation on the other, to plan things for *mass consumption.* Some writers find play-writing or novel-writing much

---

[17]Heinz Roemheld was engaged to write the score for *Ruby Gentry.* The main theme without lyrics became a hit as a single record.

more satisfactory, as do some producers and directors, than work in films for this very reason; and many gifted actors and actresses prefer the stage, one of their reasons for this preference being the ability to play to a limited and selective audience which does not have to have things "laid on the line."

I certainly agree that clarity need not be obvious; and I am even willing to concede that there can be a certain degree of artistry involved in finding ways and means of depending upon an audience's intelligence and imagination, as the British and European producers are doing increasingly, and with increasing success in competition with American films, even to some slight extent in this country, and increasingly, they are capturing foreign audiences.

Reliance upon the intelligence and knowledge of an audience, to the extent that King indicates it is his intention to do, makes no concession whatsoever to the immaturity of that section of the audience which can be disregarded with impunity only on rare subjects which are certainly outside the field of *Ruby Gentry*. This picture, if it is to get its costs back, not to speak of making a profit, must play not only to adult audiences but *also* to literally millions of people of the actual ages of between five and fifteen, and to still millions more of this mental age. I will grant that there are films of a high degree of intelligence and subtlety that appear to be successful, and that indeed are successful, but either (a) they have made things clear for the immature audience also, without insulting the intelligence of the adult audience, and/or (b) they are far afield in subject matter from *Ruby Gentry*.

I deny flatly, and can give countless cases to prove it, that commercial success and/or artistic success is abetted by, or indeed is anything but destroyed by, lack of clarity or other objectives of mine with which King disagrees in his notes on my comments. To put it more succinctly: if you make a picture as good or as successful, let us say, as *The Men* or *Cyrano de Bergerac*—and mind you, you don't have even the slimmest chance of getting the adult audience of these films to the same extent—you will still lose money. . . .

To: Mr. King Vidor   May 22, 1952

Dear King:

. . . In one of my previous memos, I spoke about my notion concerning the treatment of the music [for *Ruby Gentry*]. I learned to my pleasure that you had an exact or very similar idea!

The idea was that instead of having the type of musical score that in any case has become conventional and which, in this case, might become even worse than this because of your limited budget possibilities, you should score the picture entirely with *one* guitar.

Mixing this with more than one guitar and/or with other types of music would, in my opinion, only add expense, and at the same time destroy what conceivably could be an effectiveness equal to the effectiveness of the single zither in *The Third Man*.

But, if this is to be effective, I urge upon you three things:

1. That you start to work looking for an expert guitarist, who need not be an expensive one, *right now*. The beauty of what Reed did in *The Third Man* is that he conceived the zither scoring early in the game, had the music all selected and written before he started shooting, and was actually able to plan scenes for this zither underscoring.

2. That you not mix your scoring with any other type of music.[18]

3. That you not have anybody actually playing the guitar in the picture, any more than Reed had anybody actually playing the zither in *The Third Man*—because I feel, as I am sure you will feel on reflection if you do not feel this way already, if you mix the actual photographic use of the guitar being played by one character . . . with underscoring of the guitar, you throw the whole thing way off—because then it becomes one of the characters who is doing the underscoring, which of course would be all wrong, as well as leading to the danger that the audience might think that it was this character, out of camera line, who was playing this music. . . .

Incidentally but importantly, we made a fortune out of the publication and record rights of the theme from *The Third Man*. It may astonish you and Joe to learn that *our share* of the royalties to date has been very close to $100,000.

If you can start early enough and are equally lucky in getting a really good theme for *Ruby* or for the love scenes, you may come up with something that may produce a substantial fraction of this amount in revenue. But even the big royalties on *The Third Man* were nothing compared to the exploitation value of the song, which, in my opinion, did as much as any other factor of the ex-

[18]The score featured the harmonica.

ploitation, and as much as most of the things connected with the picture, to put *The Third Man* into the language and to make this the most successful picture ever produced in England from a grossing standpoint, other than, conceivably, such a road show as *The Red Shoes. . . .*

Warmest regards—and good luck!

Sincerely,
David

MR. AL LICHTMAN[19]   SEPTEMBER 26, 1952
BEVERLY WILSHIRE HOTEL
9441 WILSHIRE BOULEVARD
BEVERLY HILLS, CALIFORNIA

DEAR AL: I HAVE JUST FINISHED THIRTEEN UNINTERRUPTED HOURS DURING WHICH, JOINTLY WITH VIDOR, HIS CUTTER, AND MY CUTTERS, I DID A COMPLETE OVERHAUL AND RECUTTING JOB FROM BEGINNING TO END OF "RUBY GENTRY," ABOUT WHICH PERHAPS BEST COMMENT IS THAT VIDOR IS WILDLY ENTHUSIASTIC, NOT NINETY-NINE PER CENT, BUT ONE HUNDRED PER CENT. IT IS A JOB ON WHICH NORMALLY I WOULD HAVE SPENT A MONTH. I RESISTED ANY AND EVERY NOTION OF ANY KIND OF RETAKE WHATSOEVER, EVEN WHEN VIDOR SUGGESTED THEM, AND EXCEPTING ONLY FOR INSERTS. I AM CONTRIBUTING OUT OF MY OWN LIBRARY SEVERAL VITALLY IMPORTANT STOCK SHOTS[20] WITHOUT COST. THINK I HAVE COMBED ALMOST ALL OF THE JUNK OUT OF THE PICTURE AND THAT IT CAN NOW NOT ONLY GET MONEY, BUT EVEN ACTUALLY BE A RESPECTABLE PICTURE. I LAID OUT INNUMERABLE DUBBING, SOUND, AND MUSIC CHANGES AND ADDITIONS, NONE OF WHICH NEED COST ANYTHING WHATSOEVER BEYOND REDUBBING JOB, WHICH, IN ANY CASE, IS, OF COURSE, NECESSARY AFTER FIRST PREVIEW OF ANY PICTURE, PLUS MODEST SALARY FOR VERY BRIEF TIME OF MY FORMER MUSIC-CUTTER, AUDRAY GRANVILLE, WHO WILL BE ABLE TO DO MIRACLES WITH TRACK THEY ALREADY HAVE, IN ACCORDANCE WITH VIDOR'S AND MY OWN IDEAS. . . .[21]

DAVID

[19]Now Twentieth Century-Fox Vice-President.
[20]Scenes photographed for earlier films.
[21]*Ruby Gentry* was commercially successful.

:: :: :: :: :: :: :: :: :: :: :: ::

Mr. Roberto Rossellini   July 31, 1952
Via Bruno Buozzi 49
Rome, Italy

bcc: Miss Reissar

Dear Roberto:

... I do want very much one day in the not too distant future to do something with you; and I wish you would tell Ingrid that the same applies to her. I am just about finished with my long recovery program, and shall be returning to production this fall or winter. Nothing would give me greater pleasure than for Ingrid and myself to have a triumphant success in reunion. . . .

And I do want to emphasize that I don't want either you or Ingrid to feel under the slightest obligation to me for whatever very little I may have done in connection with the trial.[22] All the pleasure would be spoiled for me if I were to be rewarded with anything but your and Ingrid's continued and hopefully growing friendship. Jennifer and myself have such deep affection and respect and admiration for you both that I would be horrified if you let my testimony in any way be reflected in your business judgments. It is many years since Ingrid has been under contract to me, and you have never been, but permit me to take the liberty of giving you orders just the same: under no circumstances are you to let our personal feelings have any effect upon what you want to do about your careers or in business. It was a genuine joy for me to have the opportunity to say to Hollywood, in court, and to the entire world what I felt about the situation, and in particular what I felt about you and Ingrid. . . . It was heard by the court, by the spectators, by Lindstrom (he gave me his most ferocious glares!), and by the press. And I must have appeared very stubborn or persistent to the judge, because I took every opportunity to volunteer a great many comments, despite the judge's repeated cautions to me that I was to limit my answers! . . .

Jennifer's and my own fondest greetings to you both. We look forward to seeing you again. And if by any chance you plan on coming to Hollywood while we are here, we shall be very upset if you don't

---

[22]The Lindstroms divorced in 1950, and Bergman and Rossellini were married the same year. In 1952 Bergman unsuccessfully petitioned the California courts to allow her daughter, Pia, to visit her in Italy.

stay with us—either of you, or both of you, or the whole brood! We can't wait to see the twins. And by all means send us a cable in advance of your arrival.

Very sincerely,
David O. Selznick

To: Arthur Hornblow, Jr.   November 18, 1952

I should like to repeat my suggestion to you that the Screen Producers Guild seek as much authority, in connection with the Irving Thalberg award, as the various other guilds have, in connection with the awards, to members of their respective divisions. I feel privileged to make this suggestion because, as no doubt has been forgotten, it was I who originally suggested that there be an Irving Thalberg Memorial Award, and gave it its name; it was I who suggested, and even wrote, the phrasing of the award and its purposes; it was I who insisted that the award be given for *consistent* high quality of production *over the years*, rather than during any one particular year, or for any one picture—a condition which, I am afraid, has been honored more in the violation than in the observance.

My purposes were (a) to honor Irving's memory, (b) to give additional stature to the function of the producer, (c) to give recognition to the individual producer rather than to only the studio heads, who had always made it a practice of receiving the only producing award, that for best production, even though they personally may have had little to do with the production, and (d) most importantly, to encourage *consistent* high quality of production, rather than giving honor to the man who made an occasional fine picture while desecrating the screen with countless pieces of junk.

I had previously succeeded in selling the Academy on my other ideas on changes in the award rules, and I had personally initially suggested music awards, the documentary award, and others; but I was most pleased when I was able to put over the Irving Thalberg award.

Now I think it high time, with the producers organized, that they have the authority for setting up the rules for the Irving Thalberg award and for selecting its recipient, rather than making it a political football to be tossed around from one studio to another, and to be received principally by big studio heads, particularly in view of some of the disgraceful jockeying that has accompanied the selection of the winner in past years. . . .

To: [Director John] Huston   Rome, January 30, 1953

Dear John:

. . . Once again, if you feel you are at all stale, I do urge you to consider calling in Capote,[23] even if it is only for two or three weeks. . . . His is, in my opinion, one of the freshest and *most original* and most exciting writing talents of our time—and what he would say through these characters, and how he would have them say it, would be so completely different from anything that has been heard from a motion-picture theater's sound box as to also give you something completely fresh—or so at least I think. Moreover, I know you very well, and I know of very few writers other than Capote whose work is of the sort that I *know* would appeal to you. He can also be quite fast, but *only* if he is whipped every day. In this case, he can turn out *at least* one solid scene a day, and more if necessary, and certainly more in collaboration with you. Also, he is easy to work with, needing only to be stepped on good-naturedly, like the wonderful but bad little boy he is, when he starts to whine.

I would not presume to suggest that you get someone in under other circumstances, because I can honestly say to you, without flattery, and because I know you would never suspect me of engaging in flattery, what I have said to many others—that you are perhaps the most gifted screenwriter in the world, apart from your directorial talents. But I qualify this by saying that you are this good *only* (a) when you are not preoccupied with problems of getting a picture into work in fast time, as you are now; (b) when you are in the mood; (c) when you catch fire. But in this case I know that you are preoccupied; I sense that you are not in the mood; and I fear that you have not caught fire. I think therefore that you need the stimulus of a talent of sufficient size to merit your collaboration and respect; and as you are presently playing in luck to a degree that for the first time matches your talent, I think that this good fortune has also made Capote available at this present moment—for there is no one, *no one* in Hollywood, or Paris or New York, whom I feel could give you what Capote can give you

---

[23]Author Truman Capote, for work on *Beat the Devil* (1954). Selznick was not involved in this production, but Jennifer Jones had a leading role. Capote had previously written dialogue for *Indiscretion of an American Wife* (1954), a film starring Jennifer Jones and Montgomery Clift, produced and directed by Vittorio De Sica, and cosponsored by Selznick.

—for you to throw away or use, in part or in whole; and here he is in Rome, ready, eager, and willing to go to work with you. . . .[24]

Affectionately,
David

To: Mr. L. B. Mayer   September 16, 1953
[Screenwriter] John Lee Mahin

Dear L.B. and John:

I have been asked by you both to give you a critique of John's script of *Joseph and His Brethren.* You have told me that you wanted me to read and comment on this script for two reasons: first, because of your interest in having Jennifer play Potiphar's wife; and, second, because you want my comments on the script for purposes of possible improvement.

As to the former reason, let me say that Jennifer has also read the script, and I would like to have her play it, subject, of course, to other commitments interfering with your own presently uncertain date, and subject also to my belief that the character can be made more three-dimensional, and is probably too consistently villainous to be believable for present-day audiences, especially when one bears in mind that you have multiplied her villainies many times over those in the Biblical story.

As to my comments on the script, I must confess to you that I send these with great reluctance. It is at best both a difficult and a thankless task: difficult because, even with the not inconsiderable time I have devoted to a most careful reading and study of the script, distracting myself from pressing business matters of my own, including the editing of a picture I control,[25] a subject of this kind obviously cannot be accurately and intelligently diagnosed and dissected within a few days, and without knowing either the objectives of either the writer or the producer, or the style and intent of the producing director, if he is to collaborate on the next draft; and thankless because criticisms of another man's script normally and not unnaturally lead to resentment. But I shall do my best, despite the difficulties, and I shall chance the resentment, in view of L.B.'s repeated assurances to me that I could count on an appreciative audience not only in himself but in John, and that I need not fear any unfriendly reception or result. Since

---

[24]Capote collaborated with Huston on the screenplay.
[25]*Indiscretion of an American Wife.*

there is manifestly nothing whatsoever that I have to gain from this investment of time and energy (actually I have been forced to start to dictate this memorandum at one o'clock in the morning), I can only hope that these assurances are well grounded, and I am doing it only out of a desire to do any service to L.B. of which he thinks me capable.

. . . I gather from my talks with L.B. that he is of the opinion that the script is nearly ready for production, an opinion with which I regret I must disagree. I think that there is a great deal of work still to be done on it if it is to be worthy of the subject matter; if it is to be sufficiently better than the cinematic debauches which have been based upon careless and sloppy raids upon the Bible . . . and if it is to be the proper representation of the first work of Louis B. Mayer away from the MGM machine which he built.

One of the first things that I think must be decided in connection with this picture is its *style*.

Cecil B. De Mille is, of course, one of the most extraordinarily able showmen of modern times. However much I may dislike some of his pictures from an audience standpoint, it would be very silly of me, as a producer of commercial motion pictures, to demean for an instant his unparalleled skill as a maker of mass entertainment, or the knowing and sure hand with which he manufactures his successful assaults upon a world audience that is increasingly indifferent if not immune to the work of his inferiors. As both professionally and personally he has in many ways demonstrated himself to be a man of sensitivity and taste, it is impossible to believe that the blatancy of his style is due to anything but a most artful and deliberate and knowing technique of appeal to the common denominator of public taste. He must be saluted by any but hypocritical or envious members of the motion-picture *business*.

But there has appeared only one Cecil B. De Mille. Nothing is more appalling than second-rate De Mille: the result is the vulgarity without the showmanship which makes his work acceptable and even applauded by those of taste, albeit tongue-in-cheek; there is the size and spectacle without discrimination; there is the "big theater" without the rough but clever balance of characterization and character relationships; there is the indiscriminate use of resources to the ultimate extent, without any realization of why they are being used, but instead only the hope that the sheer weight and volume will produce a result; and there is the final resultant expense without the final resultant gross.

Thus, I must at the outset run the risk of offending you by saying that unless you have Cecil B. De Mille, or his equivalent—and I for one do not know his equivalent, as witness *Quo Vadis* [MGM (1951)], for one example (although Mervyn Le Roy is an extraordinarily able director on other types of subjects)—you must be on guard against assuming that you can deal with equal success in the broad strokes, the lack of subtlety, the clichés and convenient situations, in which he revels.

Actually, I should like to see this effort—which I of course know means a great deal to both of you, far more, I should think, than any other picture with which either of you has ever been connected—be something quite different from De Mille. The subject matter is such that it can be a picture that can live for many years, for decades, perhaps for even longer. I don't think either of you wants the quick type of money success that is represented, let us say, by so shoddy an effort as *David and Bathsheba*, so pretentious a successful failure as *Quo Vadis*, so corny a film as even *Samson and Delilah*, or De Mille's other lesser Biblical efforts. I have not seen *The Robe*, but it leans, to a large extent, upon a new device [CinemaScope], which may or may not still have tremendous values of exploitation by the time this film is out; as a motion picture it may be great, or good, or indifferent; but I am sure that in any event you have no intention of depending upon mechanical devices as a substitute for even showmanship, much less as a cinematic monument to what "L.B." stands for. . . .

I remember when L.B. called me in because his great intuitive gifts as a showman and his own taste told him that there was something drastically wrong with the completed production of *The Three Musketeers* [MGM (1948)]. I saw it at his request and recommended that he leave it alone: I told him that no little thing would cure it of its faults or make it into what he very accurately visualized it might have been; that it would gross a fortune as it stood; and that the opportunity to make it into something that was very much better *commercially*, and that could achieve a very much *bigger* gross than this version could and would achieve, however big this might be, was lost in every phase of its making, from its first approach; and that it could never be, in terms of memorability or in terms of grosses relative to the respective periods of manufacture, what Fairbanks's *The Three Musketeers* had been in the silent days, because Fairbanks had recognized and built upon the essence of Dumas's work—gallantry, chivalry, nobility—which were completely unrecognized from the outset by the makers of this new version.

You must forgive me if I extend the same warning in relation to *Joseph and His Brethren*. It was too late in the case of *The Three Musketeers*, for the picture had been finished—and it went out to achieve the ultimate gross that I predicted for it, without achieving the gigantic success that was not only its potential but its inherent right, unrecognized then—and I dare say unrecognized to this day— by its makers. I do not mean to indict this script to anything like the extent that I attacked the other film, for there is a world of difference in its approach and in its quality and in its conception and understanding of the subject matter, all in favor of your script, as well as a far greater realization on the mass-showmanship possibilities. Yet the fault is similar, lesser only in degree, however great the degree; and the fault, if I am correct in my appraisal, would be the more regrettable because the obligation is the greater. *Joseph and His Brethren* is one of the greatest, perhaps the greatest, heroic stories of the Old Testament, from a theatrical standpoint; the public is entitled to expect that it shall be treated with a respect and a reverence, and a sincerity, and an avoidance of easy theatrical tricks, to an extent far beyond even the considerable extent to which it is entitled to expect these things in the treatment of a classic. . . .

I am all too aware that you want a big show. There is nothing in what I have in mind that is to the slightest degree contradictory to this. You have working for you that greatest of all showmanship combinations —sex and religion. You have father love, mother love, brother love; you have lust and sentiment; you have a faithful husband and you have an unfaithful wife; you have complete blueprints for every conceivable production value, including spectacle, exterior scenes of great beauty, interiors of great pomp and circumstance, magnificent costumes, daring and revealing costumes, boudoir scenes, royalty and panoply, family life—indeed, the whole catalog of elements of mass appeal. *Not one of these needs to be lost:* they are all in the Biblical story, they are all in your script. Put them all together even in sloppy fashion, give them a good production, fairly good actors, fairly good direction, Technicolor or its equivalent, and good exploitation, and Louis B. Mayer will not fail to have a big-grossing, a very big-grossing, film. *But* add to these the ultimate in quality and integrity of approach, add to them idealism worthy of a Thomas Mann, and *there* will be a motion picture to be remembered for generations. . . .

Because of the deep sincerity with which I believe what I have said above, my comments are going to be based upon *this* kind of approach to the script . . . for what can be superb in a De Mille film can be disastrous in a film of more integrity; and what can be superb in a film of more integrity can be disastrous in a De Mille film. *You cannot and must not fall between the two schools,* for this would be the worst error of all. You cannot run away from clichés and artificial scenes and situations *partially:* you must go "whole hog" in one direction or another. So *beware* of my remarks; and do not buy my criticisms or suggestions *partially*—for then I would be doing you a disservice. You *must* decide upon the *style* and *type* of picture you want. . . .

It looks to me as though these notes are going to consume many pages and actually considerably more time than even I anticipated. Accordingly, I shall be grateful if you will each candidly tell me whether you wish me to go further . . . I know that neither of you would want me to go through this labor for no purpose, or small purpose.[26]

With warmest regards to you both, and my best for great success,

Sincerely,

DOS

[Writer-Producer-Director] Michael Powell   February 3, 1955
Flat 3
8 Melbury Rd.
London W1, England

Dear Mickey:

You were sweet to congratulate us on the arrival of our daughter, by name Mary Jennifer. Both Jennifer and I like to believe that your forecastings concerning a wonderful woman are going to be borne out, and that this is indicated by what everyone seems to think is her truly extraordinary beauty and talent and brightness for an infant her age.

I was rather startled by your warning against *War and Peace,* in view of the fact that in your previous letter you had included it as the sort of thing that you would like to see me make! Actually, it has been a long dream of mine, but I made the mistake of announcing it in anticipation of the completion of negotiations on financing—and what financing it would take to do it properly!—which are still not completed, but which I hope to conclude on an imminent trip East, probably in advance of the typing of this letter, so forgive me if it goes to you without my signature. In any event, a mad race started subsequent to my announcement, among all manner of producers, for productions of *War and Peace* in all sizes and shapes. Apparently, I made the motion-picture world aware of this obscure book by that obscure Russian novelist named Tolstoi, and there now appears to be a race on, with an entrepreneur named Mike Todd planning to do it in the new

---

[26] *Joseph and His Brethren* was not produced by Mayer.

(and quite wonderful) Todd-AO process, with Fred Zinnemann directing, and two Italian producers, [Carlo] Ponti and [Dino] De Laurentiis,
in collaboration with Paramount, preparing it for direction by King
Vidor.[27] What this will do to my plans for it remains to be seen.[28] It
is all very depressing, and the registration system has proven to be
something of a farce as far as protection goes.

Jennifer and I speak of you often, and always with great affection,
and with regret that it is so long since we have seen you. Jennifer had
a rather disastrous debut in the theater, I am sorry to have to report,
with an impossible adaptation of a book that was probably impossible
to adapt, *Portrait of a Lady.* How she got into it is a long saga of
promises of rewrite that were not fulfilled, of her eagerness to get to
the stage without further delay, of a semiprofessional setup of writing
and direction and production, and of all manner of other things. We
knew from its opening in Boston that it was headed for disaster, but
there was no alternative but to go through with it, with heavy hearts
for both Jennifer and myself.

I had pledged myself, with Jennifer's concurrence, not to interfere,
and I stayed away from it, other than to repeat the suggestion of
everyone else that they either close or go on the road long enough to
get it in shape, both of which suggestions went entirely unheeded.
Then after it opened, I was roundly denounced by all manner of
people for *not* interfering! *Variety* came out with an article headed
"Where Was David?"—the gist of which was that it was a great mystery as to why I had not interfered, including quotations from people
connected with the show that the result would have been entirely
different if I *had* interfered! Apparently I can't win, either by interfering or not interfering. . . .

Sincerely,
David

To: Mr. Buddy Adler[29]

March 12, 1955
URGENT & CONFIDENTIAL

Dear Buddy:

. . . Believe me, Buddy, I would not dream of making any suggestions
about *A Many-Splendored Thing*[30] were it not for both your repeat-

[27]The latter version eventually was completed in 1956.
[28]Selznick abandoned his version.
[29]Twentieth Century-Fox producer.
[30]*Love Is a Many-Splendored Thing* (1955), a Twentieth Century-Fox picture featuring William Holden and Jennifer Jones.

edly expressed eagerness and your solicitation in connection with anything I might have to say, which is most flattering, and for which I am most grateful—and your own suggestion, which I heartily echo, that these contacts between us should be kept strictly between ourselves. Going further, I would not make any suggestion but for my knowledge that you understand that there will not be the tiniest bit of resentment on my part if you disregard anything and everything that I have to say.

After this preamble, let me say that I am concerned about a few things of importance to Jennifer's performance (and therefore to the film). . . .

The first has to do with Jennifer's appearance. I am rather startled to hear that you and Henry King and your staff have decided to do nothing whatsoever with Jennifer's face to make her look Oriental. . . . I am all too aware that Jennifer is playing not a Chinese but a Eurasian; but on the other hand, *where* is the Chinese half of her to be seen, if her face is to be the same as that of the Jennifer Jones who has played so many American girls? It is all well and good to say that it is all in the hair, but surely that can't make the difference, or in the performance, which surely is putting an extraordinary burden on the actress visually. Certainly, it is difficult for me to be able to accept the fact that this is the one *half*-Chinese person in the world that looks American as Jennifer Jones. Surely there could be something in the eyes and/or in the color of the skin. . . .

My second worry has to do with what I gather is the additional and unnecessarily mature appearance that is given to Jennifer by the hairdo. If this makes her look much older, I think you will harm your love story, and that, instead of it being a good performance, the reaction will simply be "My, how old Jennifer Jones has gotten!" It is relatively easy for an actress to add twenty-five or thirty years to her appearance, and to play an old lady, but it is terribly dangerous to both the actress and to the love story to have her appear ten or twelve years older, for no reason. . . .

My third worry grows out of the point that you emphasize in the script, the doctor's English education and background. Clearly, she would speak English with a pronounced British accent, just as do all well-educated Chinese who have received their educations in England. . . .

I know that the Twentieth Century Studio customarily disregards these things, and that they have not the slightest compunctions about having Tyrone Power or any other actor play English roles—or for that matter even English nobility and royalty!—with the same accent that he plays Texans or Kansans. Obviously, or at least so it seems to me, this means a loss in both quality and reality, and it is one reason why so many pictures with an English background, made in Hollywood, don't do better in the very big English markets. It is also one reason why some generally good pictures don't get better receptions. But you are new at Twentieth, and are out to make pictures with the quality of *From Here to Eternity*.[31] And I am sure that you don't want to fall into these sloppy production habits, such as characterized not the best of Twentieth's product, not Darryl's personal pictures certainly, but at least some of the assembly-line films which are made even without any hope of approaching what I am sure are your dreams and expectations for this one. . . .

If you take any of these points up, please do so on your own, rather than as coming from me. Actually, the fact of the matter is that I am taking them up with you without even Jennifer's knowledge, and I would be grateful if you didn't even say anything to her about this letter or the source of its contents. I would appreciate it if you didn't show this letter to anybody, and would be grateful if you would tear it up after it has served your purposes.[32]

With warmest regards,
DOS

Mr. Nicholas M. Schenck   April 13, 1955
5369 Collins Ave.
Miami Beach, Miami

. . . It is a point of pride with me that I personally devised many of the clauses that have protected all the companies in the business against interference with their story rights of new and developing media. Long years before TV was anything but a dream from a practical standpoint, and in consequence of the development of radio, I believe that it was I who first caused to be inserted in contracts for such rights the phrase "media known and unknown." This was but one of many protections that I devised against encroachments upon the rights of picture companies by the still-uninvented creations of the scientists, and their effect upon the entertainment world. And I say now that I regard it as inevitable that the TV companies will in the

---

[31] Produced by Adler in 1953 at Columbia.

[32] In the completed film, the facial modifications on Miss Jones were very subtle; the hair styling imparted an Oriental flavor, and merely a suggestion of a British accent was used.

not too distant future overcome the present requirements of kine-scope for purposes of national broadcasting (in consequence of the difference in time), by means of visual tape, or of simultaneous na-tional broadcast, or of both.[33] . . .

Going further, I believe that pay-as-you-see television will some-day be a reality. Whatever the resistance, whatever the problems, there are very good reasons from the standpoint of the public in-terest why this should come about; and anything that is in the pub-lic interest must inevitably come about, whatever the resistance of those who control sponsored television or those who control mo-tion-picture exhibition. I am not now debating whether it is good for the motion-picture industry, or whether or not I am for it: parenthetically, it seems to me that if and when it comes, it will be a gigantic boon to those who own and those who produce motion pictures, while simultaneously it may be an unfortunate tragedy for many exhibitors. Perhaps it will not come, or more likely, it will not come for some years; but we who are concerned with long-range investments must necessarily deal with it as a potential men-ace. Accordingly, I strongly urge that you give instructions to your organization [Loew's, Inc.] that it is not to acquire story properties henceforth without every effort being made to clear all television rights of every kind, whether live or film, whether sponsored or pay-as-you-see. . . .

I am all too aware of the argument that picture companies are now buying properties that have appeared on television. However, I think a picture about the characters of *I Love Lucy,* for instance, with an entirely different story than those that have been televised, is quite a different matter from a particular single story appearing on television and then as a theatrical film. Unquestionably, there will be exceptions to the rule, but it does not seem to me logical to assume that forty or fifty millions of people who see a particular story on television are going to be breaking down doors to see it again. I do not even think the analogy of theatrical successes destroys the argument, for many reasons, including the relatively small size of the audience of even a hit play, by comparison with the television audience (the advertising value of a hit play is one thing that gives it value); the appeal of a live show, which does not exist with television or motion pictures; and the fact that whether a television show originates in live or in pictured form, it comes through on the television screen as a photographic

[33]This happened within two years.

image, and hence it is in direct competition with the motion picture for the interest of audiences.

June 10, 1955

Dear Irene [Selznick]:

. . . I am arriving at my decisions slowly and carefully; for my next moves, during the coming week or two, will determine the shape and course of most of what is left of my career. With some reluctance and some sadness, I have come to the conclusion that I might as well accept, without further resistance, my preference for continuing hard work and do whatever seems to offer the most exciting opportunities, rather than attempt leisure and semiretirement, for the enjoyment of which, other than briefly, my gifts are much more limited than I wish were the case.

. . . The time has been reached, certainly, when I must act according to my own judgment, for the vacillation is even more destructive than the wrong decision.[34]

With love,

Mr. Kenneth Macgowan   October 14, 1955
[Chairman of the Department of Theatre Arts]
University of California at Los Angeles
Department of Theater Arts
Los Angeles 24, California

Dear Ken:

Thank you for your letter. . . .[35]

I had long had the idea that a stunning effect might be achieved by utilizing the entire width of the proscenium arch for spectacle scenes. When working on *Gone With the Wind*, it seemed to me that we might do something particularly exciting by having the screen expand to the entire width of the stage, and perhaps up the side walls, accompanied by multiple sound effects, to give the audience the feeling that it was almost inside the Atlanta fire. . . .

Working with William Cameron Menzies, as both production designer and director of this Atlanta fire sequence (that portion of it without the principals), this is how we arranged to get the effect I was

[34]Selznick and his first wife maintained a close relationship for the remainder of his life.
[35]Macgowan was gathering material to be used in his posthumously published book on the history and techniques of the motion picture: *Behind the Screen* (1965).

after: using two cameras, we shot into two mirrors arranged to cover the area of the fire. The mirrors were used to overcome the difficulty of getting the two lenses close together. We planned to synchronize two projection machines and set them side by side so that the projected images joined together perfectly. We thought at first we would have to put in some object like a telephone pole to mask the joining of the two images but, in running it, found we had a perfect match.

We then rigged up a huge screen (about 20 feet by 90 feet, if I remember correctly), the entire width of the biggest stage here at Pathé,[36] to exhibit the result. . . . John Hay Whitney and Al Lichtman were invited by us to see the screening. It worked like a charm, and we were all enormously enthusiastic; but it was decided after discussion that the further delay that this would mean in the national release of the picture, plus the cost of equipping theaters, was not warranted for the one sequence and was unnecessary from an attraction standpoint. It should be remembered that we had whipped up an unprecedented public interest in the film, that the picture was still a year or more from completion and release, and that handling it on an individual theater basis would have meant a delay of at least another couple of years in getting the film to the public as a whole. So, with great regret, we dropped the idea. We had planned originally on handling the picture on a road-show basis in a limited number of theaters, but Lichtman's arguments that the picture must be released nationally simultaneously were obviously well founded, and we agreed to accept his opinion on this point, and regretfully abandoned this big-screen idea.

The situation on *Portrait of Jennie* was that I had argued with many people in the business that one answer to television was a very much larger-size screen in the theaters, and suggested a return to the previous "Grandeur" and "Magnascope" effects. When *Portrait of Jennie* was finished, I decided to put this into effect with the last reel, containing the hurricane sequence. We learned that there were a number of the large screens still in existence, and introduced the big screen to this era of exhibition with *Portrait of Jennie* at the Carthay Circle here and at the Rivoli Theatre, New York. The results were superb: *Jennie* did the best business that had been done at the Carthay Circle for well over a year, and had an extremely successful engagement at the Rivoli.

But I ran into all sorts of resistance from my own distributing heads, who felt that the expense of getting enough equipment for a national

[36]Otherwise known as "The Selznick Studio."

release was not warranted, and also from exhibitors. In consequence, we limited this treatment of *Jennie* to the handful of theaters that could be accommodated with equipment already in existence, and with a few additional pieces of equipment that we had made up at our own expense and routed through several theaters. Their judgment was wrong: the results on *Portrait of Jennie* without this big-screen effect were not remotely comparable with those in the theaters in which we conducted the experiments. What effect this experiment had upon the introduction of CinemaScope and the other big-screen processes, if any, I have no way of knowing.

It was good to see you again at the *Oklahoma!* screening.

With warmest regards,

Cordially,

To: Mr. Barry Brannen[37]   April 6, 1956
                                                                      CONFIDENTIAL

Dear Barry:

. . . Bill Paley has made it repeatedly clear through the years that he thinks I would be a fool to go into television—for Bill realizes, as I do, and as I am afraid you don't, that (a) the profits from fifty television shows do not equal the potential profit of one big film of the type I used to make, and (b) that my reputation is jeopardized, and therefore my position, both as to films and television, "every time I go to bat"—and that therefore it is as much work for me to do one big television show, literally as much work and perhaps even more, in view of having to get a comparable result with far less money and far inferior facilities, as it is to make a very big film. This danger is, of course, less if I did, as I would still like to do, one or more regular programs, so that it was crystal clear that with a hundred or two hundred shows a year on the air, I was not personally producing them. As Bill has stated repeatedly, any time I am "foolish enough" to go into television, I can make any kind of deal I want at CBS. My preference, as it took me literally years to convince David Sarnoff[38] (but I have already finally convinced him), is NBC, simply *because* of my very close friendship with Bill Paley—because dealing with Bill would be akin to dealing with my brother, and I would prefer to deal at arm's length with NBC.

I did one television show, and one only—*Light's Diamond Jubi-*

[37]Vice-President and General Counsel of The Selznick Company.
[38]Now Chairman of the Board, Radio Corporation of America.

lee[39] program, which had either the biggest or the second-biggest audience of any show that has ever played on television, estimated at between sixty and seventy million people. I did this show for the express purpose of learning what the medium was all about, and in preference to a *Selznick Theater of the Air* and various other proposals that had been made to me through the years for a continuing series, or for many continuing series, plus what had been offered to me by both NBC and CBS separately—a retainer for five or ten years, perhaps for much longer. . . .

This show was budgeted at $350,000, exclusive of the infinitely greater cost to the sponsors of time for all four networks (NBC, CBS, ABC, and Dumont, thereby pre-empting the full two hours of the entire television audience of America, to all practical purposes, excepting only local stations). Actually, the cost ran substantially over this. . . . Not only did we not make a cent on this: there was no fee to me, for we were supposed to make some money on the difference between what they paid us and the cost, which of course turned out to be nil; and all the time that I was engaged on it—many months of intensive day and night work—our overhead was rolling on, for which we received no reimbursement. . . . The cost of the stars was very low, because I found a great number of stars that wanted to be on it—and also because I got just under the wire before stars' salaries for television went skyrocketing . . . directorial costs were relatively low and writing costs were low, because that part of the script which I did not do myself was done by Ben Hecht in a few weeks, at a relatively low salary as a courtesy by Hecht to me. True enough, the cost was swollen greatly by the fact that I deliberately experimented, for purposes of my own education, in blending film and live, and of course, the film was very much more expensive; and also by the enormous amount of documentary material that I had to assemble, as well as the cost of going to Denver with a film unit to shoot a sequence with President Eisenhower. But nevertheless it was a lesson in the cost of a first-rate show.

The idea that *Gone With the Wind* could be produced [for television], even exclusive of fee and property, for $250,000, is too ridiculous even to contemplate. You must bear in mind that we would be competing with the memory of a film that cost $4,250,000 sixteen years ago, and the estimated cost of which to make today would be approxi-

[39] A two-hour telecast in the fall of 1954 celebrating the anniversary of Edison's discovery of the incandescent lamp. King Vidor, William Wellman, and Normal Taurog directed sequences.

mately what has been spent by De Mille on *The Ten Commandments* —somewhere between $10,000,000 and $12,000,000. Can you imagine what a $250,000 show of *Gone With the Wind* would look like? And where would be the equivalent of a Gable, Vivien Leigh, Leslie Howard, Olivia de Havilland, Hattie McDaniel, and all the rest? . . .

Everybody . . . recognizes that *Gone With the Wind* is a thing apart; and that if it is *ever* to be done on *sponsored* television—which I doubt, certainly until after paid television is exhausted either through theaters and/or via paid home television (if it goes in), it will have to be on a basis totally different from anything that has ever before been conceived for sponsored television. . . . In my opinion, the only way it can probably ever be done on sponsored television is if we have . . . a basis under which there would first be a weekly program for one year devoted solely to tests for the leading roles, followed by a one- or two- or three-year serial, depending upon the length of each show, at a price per show equal to the cost of the biggest dramatic shows now on the air—for a total running into many millions of dollars.

I have been paying now for some years—I think three or four— $15,000 per year just to *hold* the property. . . . I consider this a great bargain. I have made the investment looking toward the hope and expectation of profits of millions. Can you imagine squandering this on a single show that costs $250,000 and that, by nature of the appeal of the property, would exhaust its audience, or a very large part of it, with just this one show—which additionally could ruin my reputation, take a year of my time, and turn out to be the worst disappointment in the history of show business, by comparison with the film? . . .

Warmest regards,
DOS

June 25, 1956
London

Dear Spyros:[40]

I urge you not to listen to this nonsense about remakes.[41] You know as well as I do that exhibitors almost always fail to realize that generalities *never* apply in this business.

For many years, and although today it seems ludicrous, costume pictures were completely taboo, because of exhibitor insistence—fool-

---

[40]Spyros Skouras, now President of Twentieth Century-Fox.

[41]Selznick was negotiating with Skouras for Twentieth Century-Fox to finance and release his production of *A Farewell to Arms*, which would be a remake of the film (based on the Hemingway novel) produced by Paramount in 1932.

ishly listened to by distributors and producers—that costume pictures were not wanted by the public. When I scheduled the first *Little Women* for production, the heads of the RKO circuit (then affiliated with the RKO Studios) actually suggested that I should modernize it! The gigantic success of *Little Women* opened up costume pictures, after years of exhibitor-inspired prohibition of them.

Exhibitors were absolute death on what they called "Coonskin Westerns." They were referring, of course, to Westerns made with costumes that included the use of beaver hats. (They were influenced in this, of course, as they were in relation to costume pictures, by the fact that *bad* pictures, or pictures lacking showmanship, had failed.) Then along came Walt Disney—who, of course, has more showmanship than ninety-nine per cent of exhibitors—and set the world on its ear with *Davy Crockett*, a "Coonskin Western."

You will recall how, for many years, exhibitors put up signs reading "Not a musical"—because the public had had their fill of them, and because so many bad ones had been made. Then along came some good musicals, and once again the exhibitors were proven wrong.

Everyone shook his head—incredible as it seems today—over *Gone With the Wind*, because the public "didn't want Civil War pictures." They forgot about *The Birth of a Nation*, the all-time champion until *Gone With the Wind*: they remembered only the *bad* Civil War pictures that had failed.

Tragic endings were "absolute poison." Then along came some of the biggest pictures of all times with tragic endings, and it became apparent that this was just as much nonsense as the other negative generalizations—and that the making of successful tragedies required only proper construction and proper audience preparation; and also that to give an audience a happy ending that was incredible was *really* something to be avoided.

I could mention half a dozen other parallels to the present attitude toward remakes. There will be remakes that will be failures, many of them—precisely as there will be new stories that will be failures, many of them. There is no such thing as a generalization. If a picture is a good picture, and/or has showmanship, it will succeed; and if it is a bad picture, and/or lacks showmanship, it will fail. Of course, one doesn't want to be irrational, such as doing a remake too soon; and one must approach with trepidation the fighting of a memory that is both great and recent. But what rational reason is there for ruling out remakes *as such?*

Paramount has apparently spent *three times* as much on *The Ten Commandments* [the 1956 version] as was spent by that so-called "extravagant producer," Selznick, on *Gone With the Wind*. *The Ten Commandments* is a remake. Metro is planning on spending twice as much as was spent on *Gone With the Wind* on *Ben-Hur*—a remake.

A Place in the Sun was a remake [of *An American Tragedy* (1931)]; *Mogambo* was a remake [of *Red Dust* (1932)]; *The Prisoner of Zenda* was made by me after it had been made *two*, or I think maybe *three*, times previously. You will recall the great success of the Rex Ingram picture with Lewis Stone; you will recall the great success of my picture with Ronald Colman. Then MGM bought it back from me— and actually copied my previous production. . . . Arthur Loew will confirm to you that it was one of the most financially successful pictures on their program, indeed one of their few financial successes. You will recall Sam Goldwyn's original version and remake—both hugely successful—of *Stella Dallas*. MGM's vulgarized version of *The Three Musketeers* was a huge success, although it had been made by RKO only a few years previously, and although that in turn had been preceded by the famous Fairbanks version, and by other productions of it. *Robin Hood* was made again and again—by Fairbanks, by Warners with Errol Flynn, by Disney, always with great success. More recently: I do not think I need to tell you how successful Universal was with either its original version or its remake of *Magnificent Obsession*. In my own experience: *Little Lord Fauntleroy*, hugely successful, had been previously successfully made by Mary Pickford; *A Tale of Two Cities*, hugely successful, was a remake; and I actually remade *Anna Karenina* with huge success (the picture is still being reissued), with *the very same star* that it had been made with previously—Greta Garbo.[42] I made *The Four Feathers* in its first version;[43] Korda subsequently remade it, not once but *twice*.[44] All *three* versions were tremendous successes. *Tom Sawyer* had been made with great success *twice* by Paramount, prior to my hugely successful version of it.

If you want to challenge me, or if exhibitors want to challenge me, I will guarantee to give you at least twenty other examples, including some other very recent ones. What, for instance, about *Moby Dick*, made *twice* previously? What about the *The King and I* remake after the comparatively recent *Anna and the King of Siam?* Granted that music was added in this case, but this wasn't true of all the other examples. I don't know how *High Society* is going to do, but MGM has high hopes for it, and it's, of course, a remake of the well-remembered

[42]The first version with Garbo was *Love* (1927).
[43]Prior to the 1929 version, there was a 1921 silent British production.
[44]Korda's second version was retitled *Storm over the Nile* (1956).

The Philadelphia Story, which has been seen countless times on television, and the original production of which was reissued in New York about a year ago.

No, the answer is not in the avoidance of remakes. The plain fact is that remakes of very good original films sometimes fail because they have not been remade by people as talented as those who made the first versions.

There is a very good reason why a large percentage of that minority of films which are going to be successful will be remakes. The reason is that for forty years or more, the producers of the world have been combing the literature of literally *thousands of years* for good material. On the face of it, good new stories are not going to be written every year that are as good as the pick of the stories that have been written during many centuries. And this is doubly true in this barren age in literature.

David

Mr. William S. Paley   August 9, 1956
Columbia Broadcasting System, Inc.
485 Madison Avenue
New York, N.Y.

Dear Bill:

My people inform me that the deal is concluded with your company for our stock film, which should be of enormous value to CBS for many, many years to come and should add production values to both your live and your filmed shows that could not possibly be obtained in any other way. . . .

When we first formed the old Selznick International company, I started assembling a Trick (Special-Effects and Optical) Department. Forgive me if I say that one of the many fields in which the Selznick International pictures were way ahead of the rest of the business was in their enormous use of matte shots, optical effects, etc. Whereas other producers used these only when necessary, I made it part of my business, in the creation of scripts, to look for and to conceive opportunities for furthering the spectacular values and improve the production design of our films through the use of this equipment and the services of talented special-effects creators.

When *Gone With the Wind* came along, it became even more apparent to me that I could not even hope to put the picture on the screen properly without an even more extensive use of special effects than had ever before been attempted in the business; and, consistent with this, we made huge investments in this equipment. . . . There were substantially over one hundred shots in *Gone With the Wind*[45] which were so effective that to this day I would defy even the greatest experts in the picture business to spot more than half a dozen of them, and would welcome their comparison with present work in this field, even in the most pretentious of current films. . . . There were scenes achieved in *GWTW* that could not have been duplicated at any price, for they could not otherwise have been photographed at all. We multiplied small groups of extras into several times their number; we used miniatures plus glass shots on the wreckage of Twelve Oaks; the very longest shot with the wounded in the square (not the pull-back, of course) was in large part painted, even as to the wounded themselves. When, less than two weeks before the opening in Atlanta, I decided we needed something spectacular to symbolize the havoc wrought by Sherman, we went to the Trick Department and we took some odd pieces of film that we were not using in the picture otherwise and multiplied them into something startling, without shooting anything new. We never built the exterior of Twelve Oaks at all—only the doorway: the entire exterior, including the line of trees, was painted [and matted in] subsequently to achieve the effect.

I could go on and on with the most extraordinary array of special-effects shots in the history of the business, but I am sure the above is enough to make my point.

. . . Now there have been a few developments which have led me to the conclusion that I should sell this equipment complete. . . . There is the argument that sooner or later—and preferably sooner—you are going to have to expand the horizons of your creators to something more nearly approaching those of the makers of motion pictures for theatrical use. Granted that the small screen of the television boxes does not give the opportunity for pictorial size that theater screens have, it should not be assumed that increased spectacle is the only potential value of this equipment. I don't know if you remember *Rebecca*, but some of the most startling things in it were made possible by use of these devices. The entire exterior of Manderley, the English country mansion in which the story is laid, was done with this equipment—including one of the most effective shots of its kind ever made, that in which the house is gradually revealed through the windshield of the car as the young bride gets her first glimpse of it. (I even insisted upon the rain; and by means of miniature, plus painting, plus optical

[45]Involving matte paintings, optical effects, etc.

work, we were able to achieve this at an inconsequential cost.) The shots of the house and grounds were done with this equipment. The entire prologue of the picture, with the camera traveling through the underbrush, and finally coming to rest on the gutted ruins of Manderley, was done in miniature and with this equipment—and it would have been impossible to build or photograph such a setting in any other fashion.

. . . The second of what I like to think are opportunities for you lies in our enormous files of synopses.

. . . I don't think I need to labor the point that story material is increasingly going to constitute one of the very greatest problems of television entertainment. You yourself have paid gigantic salaries to executives simply because of their wide background and knowledge of story material, but even they have to get synopses made in order to have them available for discussion with their colleagues.

. . . I don't know what to ask you for these two extraordinary assets. . . . I should think something in the neighborhood of $100,000 for both items combined would not be exorbitant and would, in effect, constitute a bargain. But I would leave it entirely to you; you might think it should be more, you might think it should be slightly less. . . .[46]

With warmest regards,

Mr. Eliot Hyman[47]   December 27, 1960
Seven Arts Associated Corporation
270 Park Avenue
New York 17, New York

Dear Eliot:

. . . There are two subjects that I own that I think could make extremely important remakes.

One of these is *Rebecca*. . . . The other is *Intermezzo*. On this, my idea is to cast [composer and conductor] Leonard Bernstein in the role played by Leslie Howard in the original film, and to change it from simply a violinist to a pianist and orchestra leader. Any one of several feminine stars could be used in the Bergman role, possibly even Jennifer. It would be an infinitely more beautiful picture than the original, with actual foreign settings for their travels and for their romantic interlude on the Mediterranean. It would be in color, whereas the

[46]Paley purchased the files of synopses.
[47]President of Seven Arts Associated Corporation.

original was in black and white. Instead of having to fake the music, we would have the real music of Bernstein. And of course Leonard is as much of an actor as he is a musician, and a great personality with a big following. His fame is becoming worldwide. I have no way of knowing whether he will do it, since I have not spoken to him, but my hunch is that he would be delighted.[48]

. . . With warmest regards and best wishes for a fine holiday season to you and Betty,

Sincerely,

MR. JOHN HAY WHITNEY   MARCH 1, 1961
NEW YORK HERALD TRIBUNE
230 WEST 41ST STREET
NEW YORK, NEW YORK

DEAR JOCK: APPARENTLY ATLANTA IS GOING MAD ALL OVER AGAIN IN CONNECTION WITH THE REOPENING OF OUR OPUS [*Gone With the Wind*] AND IS HAVING THREE-DAY CELEBRATION CLIMAXING WITH A NEW "PREMIÈRE" ON MARCH 10. I TRIED TO PERSUADE MGM THAT IT WOULD BE MORE LIKE A WAKE, BUT THEY INSISTED THAT THE GEORGIANS WANTED THIS TO BE KEYSTONE OF THEIR CENTENNIAL, AND FINALLY—IF RELUCTANTLY—I AGREED TO BE PRESENT ALONG WITH OTHER PRINCIPAL SURVIVORS, VIVIEN AND OLIVIA. I WOULD FEEL MUCH BETTER ABOUT WHOLE THING IF YOU AND I COULD BE THERE TOGETHER, AND HAVE A FEW DRINKS OVER OUR RECOLLECTIONS. . . . EVEN IF YOU HAVE TO COME FROM NEW YORK, THIS TOO SHOULD BE FUN, SINCE THEY HAVE A SPECIAL PLANE FOR ALL OF US INCLUDING SCARLETT AND MELANIE. DO PLEASE WIRE ME THAT YOU CAN MAKE IT.[49]
AFFECTIONATELY,

DAVID

[48]To date, the films owned by Selznick which were sold to others for remake are: *Little Women* (1949), *The Prisoner of Zenda* (1952), *A Star Is Born* (1954), and *Nothing Sacred*, which was the basis for a 1953 Broadway musical, *Hazel Flagg*, and, in turn, became a considerably altered Dean Martin and Jerry Lewis film, *Living It Up* (1954).
[49]Whitney was unable to attend.

PART

THE LATER YEARS
(1956–1962)

FOR MANY YEARS *as a young producer, I had dreamed of making* A Farewell to Arms. *Warner Brothers owned the rights, having acquired them from Paramount in exchange for* A Connecticut Yankee in King Arthur's Court. *I tried to buy the property from Warners; they would not sell.*

There then developed a strange situation which made it at long last possible for me to acquire this magnificent property. Warners had bought the remake rights to A Star Is Born, *which had passed into other hands at the time of division with my fellow stockholders of the negatives produced by Selznick International. I still owned the foreign rights of* A Star Is Born, *and the negative had a unique value, both for reissue abroad and for initial release in some countries. I refused to sell Warners the negative, but suggested I would accept the rights to* A Farewell to Arms *in exchange. After considerable dickering, and with the addition of a substantial cash payment to Warners, the Selznick Company secured* A Farewell to Arms. *I had my choice of financing from several sources, and accepted a proposal from Spyros Skouras, President of Twentieth Century-Fox, to finance and distribute the film.*

I take credit for my pictures when they are good, so I must take the blame when they are disappointing. I frankly confess that while a lot of people thought extremely highly of A Farewell to Arms, *it is not one of the jobs of which I am most proud.*

It is one of the great regrets of my career that I did not make Tender Is the Night. *With Ivan Moffat I prepared what I thought, and still think, was a really outstanding script. Unfortunately, I sold the package, including Miss Jones, to Twentieth. I was supposed to have approvals of casting, and they were obliged not to change the script without my approval; but they ignored my advice, and, in my opinion, ruined the film.*

:: :: :: :: :: :: :: :: :: :: :: ::

A Farewell to Arms

JOHN HUSTON   OCTOBER 25, 1956
BLUE HAVEN HOTEL
TOBAGO, BRITISH WEST INDIES

DEAR JOHN: NEWS YOUR AVAILABILITY "FAREWELL" HAPPILY JUST
IN TIME TO KEEP ME FROM NECESSITY CLOSING WITH ONE OF
FOUR OTHER PROMINENT DIRECTORS. YOU WILL RECALL OFFERED
YOU ASSIGNMENT FIRST BEFORE EVEN OWNERSHIP PROPERTY
FINALIZED. HECHT, MYSELF HAVE FINISHED FIFTH DRAFT AND
HONESTLY THINK BEST SCRIPT MANY YEARS. VERY
CONFIDENTIALLY MALE LEAD ALMOST CERTAINLY ROCK HUDSON.
PLANNING MAKING ENTIRE PICTURE ITALY. . . . COULD YOU
CONCENTRATE WHOLLY ON "FAREWELL" UNTIL COMPLETION
PHOTOGRAPHY, AFTER WHICH BELIEVE YOU WOULD FEEL SAFE
LEAVING POST-PRODUCTION, INCLUDING EDITING, ENTIRELY MY
HANDS? SECONDLY, EXTREMELY SEVERE FINANCIAL PENALTIES,
WHICH I CANNOT AFFORD IF GO OVER BUDGET, PLUS
CONTRACTUAL ABILITY TWENTIETH CENTURY TAKE PICTURE OVER.
ESTIMATE CLEARLY INDICATES ABILITY STAY WITHIN BUDGET IF
MAKE PICTURE EVEN IN LOOSE SCHEDULE OF FOURTEEN WEEKS,
WHICH SEEMS EXTRAVAGANT TIME BECAUSE APART FROM
SPECTACLE SCENES, THREE QUARTERS OF FILM EXTREMELY
INTIMATE SCENES WITH SMALL NUMBERS PEOPLE. HOPEFUL YOUR
ASSURANCE EVERY EFFORT STAY AS MUCH UNDER ESTIMATE AS
POSSIBLE AND CERTAINLY NOT GO OVER. . . . BECAUSE OF YOUR
TIGHT SCHEDULE, AND ALSO BECAUSE EXTENT TO WHICH I
PERSONALLY PRODUCE IN EVERY SENSE OF WORD, I AM PERHAPS
NOT UNNATURALLY WORRIED LEST UNQUESTIONED EMINENCE OF
YOUR PRESENT POSITION WOULD CAUSE YOU TO RESIST AND
RESENT FUNCTIONING AS DIRECTOR RATHER THAN
PRODUCER-DIRECTOR. INCIDENTALLY, SHOULD ALSO MENTION THIS
NECESSARILY CREDITED AS SELZNICK RATHER THAN HUSTON
PRODUCTION. HOPEFUL YOU WILL FEEL THAT ALL MATTERS IN
THIS PARAGRAPH JUSTIFIED BY YOUR UNAVAILABILITY FOR BOTH

SCRIPT AND POST-PRODUCTION. HASTEN ASSURE YOU, HOWEVER,
OUR PERSONAL RESPECTIVE PRODUCTION, DIRECTION CREDITS
WOULD BE EQUAL. . . .

DAVID

Mr. Robert Chapman[1]   November 7, 1956
Eliot House C-31
Cambridge 38, Mass.

Dear Bob:

Thank you for your letter of November 3rd. . . .

Hemingway is not as easy to adapt as one might think. I recently
read a script of *The Sun Also Rises*, which my wife was originally
supposed to do, which was completely terrible, simply because they
had been so faithful to Hemingway, or at least thought they had. The
strange thing is just pulling scenes out of Hemingway and putting
them together results in a script that is not only unplayable, and
undramatizable, but just doesn't even tell the story Hemingway tells.
Hecht and myself went mad telling ourselves that Hemingway had
this or that scene, only to find that it was not there at all, at least in
words, but was somehow created by Hemingway's fantastic gift for
giving the impression of a scene without actually writing it. As Hecht
put it, "That S.O.B. writes in *water!*"

I discussed it at length with Aldous Huxley recently, and he told me
that it was a singular coincidence that we should have arrived at this
conclusion, because only a few weeks before he had stated to a group
that what Hemingway had to say was in the white spaces between the
lines. So if we have given to you the impression that we have "been
faithful to Hemingway" but for the points that you make, and if you
think we have been ninety per cent faithful in telling the story, it is
little short of a miracle and I am extremely pleased.

We actually did five drafts, complete, in six weeks! The first of these
was *completely* faithful: exactly what Hemingway wrote. It was worthless. Having then put on paper just what Hemingway wrote, we went
through to try to put on paper what Hemingway said, with his unique
magic, without his ever having put it into words. This was better. We
then proceeded to attack it as a motion picture, visualizing it as we
went along, and considering all our other problems besides—tempo,

---

[1]Playwright and Associate Professor of Playwriting and English at Harvard University, where Selznick's son, Daniel, was then attending.

logic, overcoming Hemingway's sloppy introduction of characters and careless handling of time elements, etc. We got closer. Then we had to grope with our Italian problems, and with censorship and Code problems. Each draft has been getting better and better, I think; and I believe that we will have a truly fine script in our final draft. . . .

If we have done violence in any particular to Hemingway, it has been with great reluctance and only after the most thorough discussion. I don't expect Hemingway to like it; there is ample evidence that if anybody changes a single word or scene or character, or even casts it any differently than Hemingway visualized the characters, he is very upset. But I must make a successful motion picture that appeals to audiences, readers of the book and nonreaders alike, and not just to Hemingway. . . .

With warmest regards,

Cordially and sincerely,

December 19, 1956

Dear Ben [Hecht]:

My present feeling is that eighty per cent of the script is eighty per cent right, and that twenty per cent of it is eighty per cent wrong. That's pretty damn good, considering the time we spent on it, even though it was twice as long as you normally spend. So let's really try to do a job that will be . . . something that we can be proud of for many years to come. . . .

Love,

To: Mr. John Huston   March 4, 1957

Dear John:

. . . I am forced to say that this torturing of the script has, I hope, come to an end—a belated end, for, whatever its gains or losses, it has played havoc with proper planning for the film. . . .

I went through with Ben every single point that we discussed during his absence. It was not just a case of mollifying Ben, who was very angry, but of listening very carefully to what he had to say about our hasty decisions on script to which he and I had devoted so many months. It is certainly not demeaning your talent to say that I don't think there is anybody alive who can come in on a job at the last minute and revise, *without serious danger*, work to which two old hands like Ben and myself have devoted many, many months of most careful work and devoted effort. . . .

It is true that this script was not done by Ben alone, but by the two of us, working as collaborators; but it is also true that I have never seen Ben or anyone else bring to a job more thorough analysis, more willingness to rewrite, than he has. He admired the book greatly, as I did; but, like me, he has been aware of the failures of others to bring Hemingway off on the screen, when they followed him slavishly. . . . The only Hemingway stories, without exception, that have been successfully adapted to the screen, were those which departed *widely* from Hemingway, notably the first *A Farewell to Arms* (a critics' pet) and *The Snows of Kilimanjaro* (a big commercial if not critical hit). Where faithfulness became the measure of the success of a Hemingway adaptation, disaster followed, as with *Francis Macomber,*[2] *The Old Man and the Sea,* and *The Sun Also Rises.* . . .

But to get back: it is not in the motion-picture scenes, original and outside Hemingway, that I think we may have made serious mistakes in recent days. Instead, it is within the dialogue scenes themselves, where we have made cuts of material, simply because it was not in the original Hemingway scenes, disregarding the vital fact that it had originally been added to the Hemingway scenes for very solid reasons. And I think we may also have gone wrong in adding material simply because it *was* in Hemingway, to these scenes, and otherwise. We approached the script, in these recent days, seemingly as though—which would of course be amateur— the sole measure of whether the scenes were good or bad was whether they were Hemingway. . . .

The obligation of adapters to the stage or the screen, respectively, is to do a play or a screenplay—not to regard the original as though it were Holy Writ. We have not only the privilege, but actually the obligation, to dramatize scenes, and to write such original material as may be necessary to fill in what the original author may have left out, for dramatic purposes, or for purposes of characterization, or for purposes of character relationships—and in this case, because of the necessary substitutions for narration and first-person telling. . . .

In any case, I have no alternative but to make—*now,* far too late for my obligations—the final decisions on the script and the dialogue, whether there are differences of opinion between the three of us, or between any two of us. . . .

Cordially,
DOS

[2] *The Macomber Affair* (1947), adapted from Hemingway's short story, "The Short Happy Life of Francis Macomber."

To: Mr. John Huston   March 19, 1957
cc: Mr. Arthur Fellows[3]

Dear John:

I should be less than candid with you if I didn't tell you that I am most desperately unhappy about the way things are going. It is an experience completely unique in my very long career. It is an experience that I feel is going to lead us, not to a better picture, as you and I discussed the other evening, but to a worse one—because it will represent neither what you think the picture should be, nor what I think it should be.

Going further than this, I feel that there is not one chance in hell of our meeting our schedule, or of our coming within the cost, if the shambles of these two days' "rehearsals" are any criterion. It is my opinion, and I think an experienced one, that a picture of this magnitude cannot possibly be made, for anything like our estimate—which, as you know, is already dangerously close to the outside figure—with the kind of "preparation" that we are having. Despite two days at the British Hospital, all that came out of it was the basic staging of two of the scenes—and forgive me if I say that it took all kinds of pressure to pin even this down; secondly, I had assumed, again based on un- varied experience, that far, far more than this had already been done, long before this trip, so that the time could be spent only in the rehearsals for which this trip was planned; thirdly, what was "accom- plished" on this trip represented what is normally not more than an hour's work—whereas we spent two days that were badly needed for the preparation of the advance, the retreat, and so many, many other things. . . .

You also threw me for a terrific loop yesterday and today with your discussions, which, mind you, took place only four days before the starting of the shooting of what is perhaps the most expensive spec- tacle sequences, foot for foot, in the recent history of the screen—the scenes of the advance. When I said to you, John, the other night, that I was prepared to work with you to improve the picture as we went along, I certainly didn't mean to include completely new concepts and new script at the last moment on such points as who goes on the advance. With thousands of troops involved, with fighting of the weather, with the monumental difficulties of shooting, with the lack of detailed preparation (particularly if it has not been figured out in

[3]Production executive on *A Farewell to Arms*.

advance any better than the British Hospital!), with our problems about the snows, it is literally unthinkable that we should even contemplate changes of this sort at this time. It is just plain too late—and we have too many other problems that should be occupying us, and that simply must be occupying us. . . .

Indeed, John, I hope it is clear to you—certainly I have made it clear over and over again—that I will not expect even any individual lines to be cut, altered, or transposed without my express approval; and this is one of the several purposes of my always being available. . . .

Additionally, these script points were very, very carefully thought out. I am terrified lest a casual and last-minute omission be made without reference to the solid reasons for its inclusion. . . . We are making a motion picture, we are not photographing Hemingway's book like slaves—at least I am not. Foot by foot, scene by scene, everything that I have learned in nine long months of study of this subject that is essential to make a good motion picture is being challenged. . . .

I have the greatest respect in the world for Hemingway, and my attitude toward his book is best demonstrated by what I have staked on it, but my ego—and also my record—doesn't permit me to think that Hemingway can prepare a better motion picture than I can. On the contrary, I know damn well that he can't; and I also know damn well that our script is infinitely better than a script resulting from any attempt, step by step, week by week, month by month, to go back to the few things, the bad or omitted things, based upon the book—which forgive me if I say that I know far better than you, which I have studied for nine months, and the qualities and faults of which for motion-picture purposes I know, and which book I am now finally prepared to throw away, having wrung it dry.

I am certain that there have been few books ever transcribed to the screen with the studied and loving care that Ben and I gave to this one through many weary months. . . . But the fidelity was not the kind of Papa-worshiping groveling that led to the transcription, scene by scene, in the script of *The Sun Also Rises* . . . by comparison with the scramble of every star of importance to do our script. Also, pardon me if I say that the trick was not achieved in *Moby Dick* [the Huston version of 1956], not only from the audience standpoint but even from the standpoint of novel lovers—demonstrated by the fact that lectures given at Harvard repeatedly attacked the complete failure to realize Melville in the film. I want the critics and I want the Hemingway fans,

I want the non-Hemingway fans and the nonreaders of Hemingway. . . . We are most definitely not going to get it if we start tearing apart the script and start searching the tiniest things of Hemingway that were left out by design because they were either unnecessary or bad dramatically. . . .

You have some strange phobia against short scenes. Short scenes are at the very essence of good motion-picture making, and one of the great values that we have in this medium, by comparison with the stage. I have had any number of wonderful scenes in many pictures that literally contained only one line—and for that matter, no line at all—and perhaps twenty of these in *Gone With the Wind,* some of them making very telling story points. You have a phobia against telling things en route to a scene, but this too is necessary to economical and sound motion-picture construction, and I can show you scores of examples to prove this point also. . . .

I am finishing this note the day after I started to dictate it. Since I started on it, I have made the trip up to Cortina [in northern Italy]. I think it shocking that the magnificent locations during the first part of the trip up from the plains to the mountains have not been thoroughly studied, with a view to far better locations than I think we have now. . . . There is not a location of the retreat—including even that with the cavalry—that doesn't exist on the way up to Cortina, or just before one gets into the mountains, with extraordinary atmosphere and settings of the type that alone warrant our shooting in this locality, at such cost. If I could spot these things on my first trip up, I think that our problems as to the bridge, and as to other sections of the retreat, should not only have long since been settled, but that actual camera setups should have been decided upon. I am forced to ask you, John, how many actual camera setups have you decided upon? Is it ten, twenty, fifty? Is it less, or more than that? Is it fair . . . for a director who has pledged himself to come within the costs, to, at this stage of the game, not be able to tell the Production Department, or the camera crew, or the art directors just what he has in mind on these extremely difficult locations?

Maybe this is the way you have worked, John. It is not the way I have worked. It is not the way I shall ever work. It is not the way I shall work on *A Farewell to Arms.* If you won't decide these things, then we have no alternative but to decide them ourselves. We can't spend hundreds of thousands of dollars of other people's money because of habits of procrastination or of creating things on the spur of the moment. Writ-

ers can do this for they have only their own time and their own paper
and pencils as an investment. Painters can do this and can stay telling
stories for hours, because they have only the investment of their own
time, paints, and easel. But a motion picture is a collaboration involving money that is owned and invested by thousands of stockholders.
I for one should hate to think that I had so little conscience that I could
spend the money of these people simply because I enjoyed creating
things at the last moment. This kind of self-indulgence simply won't
do, John. . . .

You are getting a fabulous amount of money—$250,000—to direct
a single motion picture. You are not entitled, therefore, to the privi-
leges of an artist with an investment. You are obliged to do a job, just
as I am obliged to do a job. The job is to make a picture which will
hopefully appeal to the critics, but which most importantly will appeal
to the tens of millions of people who will have to like it to pay its
cost. . . .

I urge you, John, and I have respect for you and your talent, not to
join the ranks of those critics' darlings of yesteryears, whose name is
legion—the La Cavas and the von Sternbergs, etc. Nor does it do any
good to point to a New York review, however desirable (and I like
them too). One can't cash it. . . .

I never concealed from you, John, that even your best friends
thought I was out of my mind to cast you on a romantic love story
of this kind. It was predicted over and over again that your interest would be in military matters, to the detriment of the love story.
I am sorry to have to say that unless I am very much on my guard,
and unless I hold you to the line on this as a love story, with the
war as a background to the extent—but only to the extent—that
Hemingway made it a background, the military emphasis is going
to throw the picture way off balance and to frustrate even readers
of the book. You *think* you are being faithful to the book—but you
are only being faithful to your concept of the book. The book is a
romance; the book is a love story; the book is almost a fantasy as a
love story, born out of some cockeyed concept of Hemingway's
about a girl and a boy that is far from being realistic, or even neo-
realistic. . . .

I don't want you to feel like a "prostitute," as you stated was your
feeling when we talked the other night, by doing a picture that you
don't believe in. I most certainly don't want you to be depressed by
any feeling that you are not honoring any pledges you may have made

to Hemingway. You can only do the job that is essential to this picture by fulfilling your promises to do what I decide, and I emphasize the "I," and to do it enthusiastically. Even in Rome, you repeated that you had "no requirements" in connection with your direction of this picture. Yet it would appear that the only way in which you will direct the picture, as I see it, is to direct it unenthusiastically. . . . I recognize *fully*, believe me, that if you dog it on the points that I make, I will be unable to use the scenes, so will have to retake them. Going beyond this, I recognize fully, believe me, that if you don't do them to the best of your ability, you can prove me wrong on my points. But I certainly would like to believe that you wouldn't be guilty of the former, and that you would fight scrupulously against the latter.

You made pledges to me—pledges that you would do the very best job you could, regardless of my decisions about script. Since that time, in all the months that have passed, you have not criticized things which you are criticizing at the last moment. Indeed, when Ben and I went through the lengthy process of going through the script with you, scene by scene, from beginning to end, in the tiniest detail—long weeks after we should have done it, and at great financial cost to the picture, and in my opinion at great cost to the quality of the picture too (because of the loss of both you and myself on its preparation)— you stated not once, but three or four times, that you had no further comments to make: "that's all," were your words. Yet not a day has passed that you have not revised this statement and brought up point after point. . . .

It is possible, John, that you have had a change of mind—or a change of stomach—since you accepted the assignment. Possibly in the back of your mind is the thought that you would, step by step, bring me round to your way of doing things. I must warn you, John, that I am not easily brought round. I am too old a horse for this. Maybe my way of making pictures is not your way, but it is the only way I know; and at this stage of my life and my career, I cannot change it. . . .

Let me say in conclusion, John, that fervently as I want you to direct the picture, I would rather face the awful consequence of your not directing it than go through what I am presently going through. I would rather have a worse picture, directed perhaps by someone who doesn't have your talent, a director who wouldn't have even the little preparation you have had, than sacrifice my health and my future to this kind of picture-making, which is totally unknown to me, and which, in my opinion, is no longer remotely tenable in the industry.

Also, my family and a long and happy life with it is even more important than *A Farewell to Arms.* . . .

I therefore ask you to let me know *at once* your reaction to these
comments. Frankly, I have not a remote idea as to how I will cope with
the situation if you resign from the picture. But I would rather face
this *right now* than face it later, or face it at an even more difficult
time. I am not asking you to resign; I am merely telling you the
circumstances, the only circumstances—and I think I am free, without
fear of contradiction by *anybody,* to say that I am both legally and
morally in the right about this—under which I think you can continue.
If this means that you are going to give me a bad directorial job
because of anger, or frustration, or disappointment, or because it is not
your custom to work this way, or because you cannot stand any longer
this kind of supervision, then I am sure you are an honest enough man
to prefer resignation. In this case you can be very, very sure that I
would inevitably be the heavy; that I would suffer severe consequences; and that I would be up against an even more serious situation
than when Cukor left *Gone With the Wind.* But I can only be true to
myself—and this is my show—and you yourself have repeatedly stated
that it is my show. I can only say what I said to Cukor: "If this picture
is going to fail, it must fail on *my* mistakes, not yours."

If you decide to resign, you may be sure that I would protect you
to the fullest, and that I would be perfectly prepared to emerge, with
your New York critical friends and with the entire industry, as the
tyrannical producer who didn't understand a gifted artist. I am used
to that role. I have coped with it before. I have learned that *nothing
matters but the final picture.* But whatever I have learned, I would
suggest that in the event that this should be your decision, it be based
on the statement that you and I could not see eye to eye on the script,
which obviously is true.

. . . This certainly doesn't mean that if you do decide to do
the picture, and to do it enthusiastically, that I don't want every tiny
bit of directorial talents and gifts that you can give to it: I would
be a fool—and I don't think you think I am that—to want anything
else.[4]

Very, very sincerely,
DOS

[4]The preceding memo has been edited from the original sixteen-page single-spaced
typewritten version.

Mr. John Huston   March 21, 1957
Grand Hotel
Misurina

bcc: Mr. Spyros Skouras
      Mr. Barry Brannen
      Mr. Earl Beaman[5]
      Mr. Arthur Fellows

Dear John:

Arthur Fellows has informed me that you received my memorandum dated March 19 (dictated partially on the 19th, partially on the 20th), and that you discussed its contents with him; that you said, in effect, that you could not only not agree with my decisions on the script, but could not see eye to eye with me on the other matters; and that under the circumstances, you could not possibly direct the picture.

Under the circumstances, we are proceeding accordingly to engage a substitute director, your services on the film having been terminated by you. . . .

Kindly immediately turn over to Mr. Fellows any and all material relating to *A Farewell to Arms* presently in your hands.

                              Very truly yours,
                              David O. Selznick

To: Charles Vidor[6]   May 6, 1957

. . . A strange thing has happened: with Huston, I was forever fighting against his slavishness to the book; with you, I have just the reverse problem because of your repeated statements that the book is not the Bible, and that we shouldn't feel obliged to follow it! I have had to go from the defender of changes from the book to the defender of the book! . . .

It is not that I have insufficient ego to change it when necessary; rather, it is that I don't want us to have so much ego as to think that we can cook up in a few days or weeks, the equivalent of the scenes and the characters and the character relationships that have given the book such gigantic stature. . . .

---

[5]Vice-President and Treasurer of The Selznick Company.
[6]Vidor (no relation to King Vidor) took over the direction of *A Farewell to Arms*.

To: Mr. Charles Vidor

May 14, 1957
Rome, Italy

Dear Charles:

I must say that Jennifer, in what is now my strong opinion, knew what she was doing when—for what was, believe me, the first time in all the pictures we have made together, or that she has made with anybody else—she asked for a "business appointment" with me today to discuss her deep disturbance concerning the change that we have made in her first scene with Henry[7] in the Milan Hospital. . . .

These were among Jennifer's arguments, which I am not phrasing nearly as well as she did. It is quite late, and I am dictating this merely as a synopsis of the high points. . . .

We have with the rewrite lost entirely the desperate hunger of these two for each other—in what Hemingway has called his "Romeo and Juliet," meaning partially and obviously the mad passion of two people for each other who scarcely know each other (which I think has been heightened rather than lessened by our moving up the first affair)— by investing this scene with all sorts of complicated psychology. . . .

Jennifer points out that in consequence of my long struggles with the Breen office,[8] over a long period of months, we were forced to drop many of the wonderful illicit love scenes of the book, and that we were fortunate in being able to retain this madly passionate first scene, plus the scene the following morning. She points out further that if we drop these, we have little left of the values of the love story that made the book such a sensational and lasting success. She points out further that in substitution we have given an argumentative, repetitious, psychological, and unpassionate scene that is inconsistent with Hemingway, inconsistent with our film, inconsistent with the passion of the scenes we have done in the British Hospital (about which, incidentally, she is enthusiastic). . . .

Jennifer had all sorts of other effective arguments, and I must say I was greatly impressed with her logic. Additionally, I am mindful of the fact that she has now studied the role—and I assure you, day and night—for months; and that she has figured out the playing of these scenes during all these weeks that she has been waiting. As I think you will discover, Jennifer is a very creative actress, who brings to a scene —that is, to a scene that she has had more than a few hours previously!

[7]The character played by Rock Hudson.
[8]The Motion Picture Producers and Distributors of America, Inc. was now headed by Joseph I. Breen.

—the benefits of intense study and her gifts as an actress. (Incidentally, please let me mention that I think you would be well advised always to let her play the scene for you first, of course then feeling free to redirect it as you see fit; but since she is so completely disciplined as an actress, if you direct her before getting her conceptions, I am fearful that you will lose the benefits of the intense and very lengthy study that she always gives, and has given particularly to this role, having had benefits in this connection that most regrettably you have not had, in connection with time to study. . . .)

DOS

To: Mr. Vidor   May 21, 1957

Dear Charles:

You once asked me why I didn't direct my pictures myself. . . .[9] Some day I may do one. If and when I do, I will have at my side, precisely as have a large percentage of the directors who have worked for me, my cutter.

This would not be because I did not feel secure about cutting, or about my angles. Having been cutting films for thirty years, I think I know this. But it would be for reassurance; to check the cutting of each sequence as I would have laid it out in advance; and to get the professional advice of a member of the staff who had nothing else to do than to think about the cutting, whereas I had so many other departments to watch.

This is a not very oblique way of suggesting that it would be no reflection upon your obviously great knowledge of cutting if you had one of our cutters available on the set to you at all times; if you talked over with him, before going into the scene, the cutting to the extent that you and I have not discussed it, and to the extent that it is not indicated by script; and if you encouraged him to have no fears of your being upset if he had alternate suggestions to make, or if he could save you setups, or if he had different concepts of his own to propose. . . .

I do hope that you won't take this suggestion amiss, or that you won't think it in any way a reflection on my opinion of how you have shot the stuff for cutting purposes so far (except as to excessive angles!).

[9]Columnist Art Buchwald quoted Selznick in 1957 as saying, "There is no mystery to directing. I don't have time. Frankly, it's easier to criticize another man's work than to direct myself. As a producer, I can maintain an editorial perspective that I wouldn't have as a director."

Rather, it is simply another attempt on my part to be helpful, and to supply you with all the tools and help I can, particularly on as trying a job as this one, on which you have had so little preparation. . . .

David

To: Messrs. Vidor and [Director of
    Photography Oswald] Morris

May 24, 1957
Rome, Italy
NOT SENT

Dear Charles and Ossie:

I have been spending the largest part of yesterday and today trying to figure out how to make up some substantial portion of the terrible situation in which we find ourselves on the budget . . . without the ultimate and most serious consequence of having to rush the scenes of the love story to such an extent that the picture will be destroyed.

Our cost problems break into two groups: (1) how to make up some part of the huge amount we have already gone over schedule and over budget; and (2) how to avoid repetitions of the troubles we have gotten into. . . .

Many of the finest pictures ever made have been achieved, even recently, with camera angles that have been so laid out in advance that their number, scene for scene, was a fraction of those that we are using. Precisely the same thing applies to the takes.[10] I have *heard* about this number of takes before, with some horror and disbelief; I have never before personally experienced it. The average on *Gone With the Wind* was less than four takes per setup (and, of course, with an infinitely smaller number of setups than we have on this film); we averaged on *A Star Is Born* (the first one) . . . actually 1.7 takes per setup. . . .

DOS

To: Mr. Vidor

May 27, 1957

Dear Charles:

. . . Time was when I would have reacted impetuously and violently to your telegram.[11] But the years have led me to examine the other

---

[10]A "take" refers to each time a scene, or portion of a scene, is photographed over again from the same camera position.

[11]In reply to one of Selznick's memos, Vidor had wired Selznick that the memo implied Vidor was inexperienced as a director, and that if he wasn't allowed to function, Selznick should direct the remaining scenes himself.

fellow's viewpoint. Also I have no intention of hurting myself *or* you. . . .

It is only two days since you were flattering enough to be enthusiastic about my memoranda, and to ask me to "keep them going." I am now confused: am I to keep sending them, but first to screen them through your sensibilities? And if so, how am I to know what these are, Charles? How am I to know what will give offense, and what not, when you react so strongly to mere review born of my longer preparation on and greater knowledge of the script?. . . .

Cordially,
David

To: Charles Vidor   May 31, 1957

A little while back, in a discussion with Ossie [Morris], I was telling him of a lesson I learned many, many years ago from Bill Menzies, who proved to me that ninety per cent of setups in all pictures are either not close enough or not far enough away, and who made it his business to persuade the directors with whom he worked, to their enormous benefit and indeed great gratitude, to always move their camera closer or very much further back. . . .

To: Mr. Vidor   May 31, 1957

Dear Charles:

. . . It is amazing how much value Hemingway gets out of the repetitions, in which he was admittedly influenced by Gertrude Stein. Like most picture-makers, during my entire career I have been afraid of repetitiousness and have edited scripts and pictures to avoid repetitiousness. But the curious thing about this book and this script is that, because it is essentially the story of a relationship rather than one of complicated plot, its very essence is its repetition as to scenes and even as to actual lines of dialogue; and I think we can get the same values out of these repetitions that Hemingway did in the book. The same phrases are repeated, sometimes in exactly the same words, sometimes in slightly different words. But I think that's the essence of its naturalistic quality—quality that has never been seen on the screen, and that most dramatists and scenarists and producers and directors would be afraid of. People *do* say the same things over and over again, in exactly the same language, and I think it will help the originality of the film, as it did the book. . . .

David

Mr. Ernest Hemingway   August 14, 1957
Finca Vigia   Rome, Italy
San Francisco de Paula, Cuba   NOT SENT

Dear Ernest:

. . . It may seem peculiar to you that I have waited to write you until the eve of my departure for home, and until the completion of the film. There are several reasons for this:

I gathered from various members of the "Papa" clique . . . that you were sore at Hollywood, and sore at me. I have been told that your rage at the movie world grows partially, or perhaps entirely, out of your resentment that you have made so little from your film rights. If true, this is understandable, although perhaps not too logical since you presumably made your sales twenty-five or thirty years ago at what then would seem to be good prices, and I don't think you have any more proper complaint than that of a man who sells a piece of farmland only to discover, decades later, that there is oil on it. In any event, I want you to know that, whatever price you got for *A Farewell to Arms,* I did not get it cheaply. I traded for it the foreign rights to my initial production of *A Star Is Born,* including reissue and initial release in certain territories, importantly including Germany; and the value of these rights has been variously estimated at between $150,000 and $200,000—and Warners (who, as perhaps you do not know, secured it from Paramount in exchange for *A Connecticut Yankee*) got an additional $25,000 out of me. I made this deal also with a certain rather grisly risk: if you had gone down on another plane between the time I acquired it and the time the copyright was renewed, I would have been out-of-pocket the full price! So if you are angry over what you got for *A Farewell to Arms* originally, please know that I didn't get the remake rights for any bargain.

Additionally, I want you to know that Jennifer has talked to me off and on for two years, since first she learned of the situation, to promise her that if the picture were a success, you would get something additional. Initially, I argued with her that she wasn't a businesswoman, and that she didn't understand these things, and that you had sold the property; but she persisted in her expressed conviction that it was somehow nevertheless wrong that you of all people shouldn't get anything out of it if it were successful. Finally, she persuaded me to her point of view. Obviously, Twentieth Century-Fox first has to get out its costs; and then I hope to get back the many hundreds of thousands of dollars that I have invested—frankly, going deeply into debt to do it—in order to make the picture as well as I could. But directly the costs are paid back, you are going to get something out of a share of the first profits. You can refuse it, or give it away, or do what you please with it, but you are going to get it anyway. And lest you think that hope of profit on the picture is just a dream, and that therefore this pledge means nothing, let me say that I don't think I would have taken my own big personal risk foolishly, or gone into debt for no purpose, or sweated through the toughest job of my entire life for the last year, without being pretty sure of profit; and those hard-headed movie businessmen who have seen even the roughest kind of first cut of the picture are very sure that it is going to be a gigantic success. . . .

I also remembered that the last time I saw you, at Leland Hayward's place on Long Island, after we had had a pleasant talk and as I said good-by to you, I asked you when I was going to see you again—and you replied with a smile, "When you need me." Frankly, this stayed with me to such an extent that I was frightened that if I got in touch with you at all, you would think it was because I needed something. Perhaps I do need something now: it is my desperate hope that you are going to like the film, and I don't want you to dislike it because allegedly you have taken a dislike to me.

I had flattered myself that, while I was never close to you, you had nothing against me. We have seen each other only off and on through the years, but ever since I first met you through Myron, you have always been cordial and friendly; and actually you went out of your way on one or two occasions to show Jennifer and me a pleasant time in Cuba. I therefore couldn't quite fathom the reasons for your antagonism toward me, as reported by some of my Hollywood "friends." Upon probing them, and from other sources, I received various conflicting explanations.

The first thing that was said was that you weren't sore at me, rather it was your lawyer. . . . He was apparently angry because some years back I had some kind of date with him—I think it was to discuss *Across the River and Into the Trees*—and I had to break the date, for reasons which I certainly don't remember. . . .

The second reason I received for your attitude toward me had also to do with alleged bad manners on my part. It is most unfortunate that there should be two such misunderstandings—because, while I have been accused of many things, I don't believe that I have been accused much, if ever, of being deliberately rude. Yet this second story has to do with what is supposed to be a case of deliberate rudeness on my part. When I was last in Cuba, a few years back, I told [author and screenwriter] Peter Viertel that I would love to see you if it was convenient to you, but that I didn't want to intrude or impose. Viertel called me a couple of times to say that we were going to get together, then that we weren't going to get together. He reported that you weren't feeling well; but the plain fact of the matter was that for your own reasons, which I of course didn't and don't have the privilege of challenging, you either didn't want to see me or couldn't see me. I accepted it. Then Peter showed up, and to my surprise, your wife was with him. She couldn't have been more charming. I am told that you were miffed because I didn't stand up. I remember the occasion very well: I was being taught some Mexican version of canasta by a man named Santiago Reachi. I certainly did not expect a lady to call. It was hot as hell, and I was sitting in a sport shirt and my underpants. I tried to figure out which would be the ruder thing to do: to get up or to stay seated. I decided that in the latter was the lesser rudeness! Now for me to be charged with deliberate bad manners to your wife is fantastic. Whatever you think of me, you have always been exceedingly gracious to Jennifer, and what on earth would prompt me to be rude to your wife, even if you hadn't been so gracious to my own?

The final story I got was that I had not contacted you when I acquired *A Farewell to Arms.* All I can say to this is that if this story is true, there is something wrong with the cable deliveries in Cuba, because I actually and literally cabled you not five minutes after I acquired the rights. It was the very first thing that I did. I had naïvely and egotistically hoped that you would be glad that I had acquired them, after the botch they had made of the first picture and after having heard from you personally of what you thought of *The Snows of Kilimanjaro* and other movie versions of Hemingway. . . .

I had wanted to make *A Farewell to Arms* since it was first published. It broke my heart that I was still too young as a producer to be given the privilege of making it when it was first filmed. Through many long years I tried to acquire it. I was bitterly disappointed that you did not reply to my cable. I wanted to pour out my heart to you as to what I wanted to do with the film and as to what I saw in it. But the lack of even an acknowledgment, plus the stories concerning your attitude toward me, plus your avowed and even published statements that you were through with Hollywood once and for all, left me with the feeling that any attempt to get in touch with you would meet with silence, if not actual rebuff. Finally I decided to make the film, and to hope that you would be happy with it.

You may have become disillusioned with the realization that no book can be put on the screen word for word and scene for scene as written. . . .

Jennifer and I read the script on *The Sun Also Rises.* She had always wanted to play Lady Brett, and she actually had a contract to do it. We thought the script appalling. We read subsequent scripts. . . . Heartbroken at losing a role she had always wanted to do (and actually had made very great sacrifices to do: she had played a bad role in a bad film on condition that she would do Lady Brett), Jennifer refused to do the film, and was able to get out of it because they weren't ready to go. . . .

I hope you will be seeing the film. I hope most fervently that you will like it. You have only to say the word, and as soon as the thing is assembled in some kind of shape, I'll send a cutter and a print of it down to Cuba to have a special screening for you, so that you can see it as long before it is released as possible. And lest your suspicions prompt you to think that I am suggesting this for publicity purposes, let me hasten to add that if you want us to do this, I shall pledge you that it will be kept as completely secret as whatever arrangements you want to make for screening it will permit.

And now I am leaving for Hollywood, having spent twelve of the last eighteen months in Italy on this job, including the last five months of the most agonizing combination of problems I have ever been up against, starting with the bitter resentment of the Italian Communists on the one side, and the Fascists on the other, against the picture being made at all. I shall be devoting the next several months to editing it, and the months after that to exploiting it and getting it launched. I feel years older for the effort.

Do please give my apologies and my explanation to your wife.

Sincerely,

David O. Selznick

To: Charles Vidor   December 28, 1957

. . . It is still not too late to recut the picture. I invite you once again, as I have repeatedly, to come in with Jim Newcom[12] and present to me your version of how you would recut any of the scenes referred to.[13] If you are unwilling to do this, or if you attempt it and find yourself unable to do it, then I think you ought to retract these state-

[12]Film Editor on *A Farewell to Arms.*
[13]*A Farewell to Arms* had just opened in some theaters.

ments; and meanwhile, whether true or not, I don't think you ought to foul your own nest by making them.

As to the comments of your "friends," I am bored to death with the cutting suggestions of these "friends," whom I have seen destroy many films with their gratuitous and unknowing advice. Of those who have seen the film, and I think I know to whom you are referring, I know of none of them whose career has not been characterized by outstanding and successive failures. It may interest them, as I know it will you, to hear that the picture is doing simply extraordinary business, and will outgross any two—*any* two—of its competitors combined. And they could have a bet on this.[14]

Sincerely yours,

Tender Is the Night

To: Mr. Stone[15]   January 28, 1951

Dear Lou:

This is the first opportunity I have had to reply to your memo of January 17 on the subject of the Fitzgerald biography.[16]

I regret this because I am really more eager than I can say about this biography, because I am fearful there will be competition because of the growing interest in Fitzgerald. . . .

Dealing with Mrs. Lanahan's[17] sensibilities, these do not seem to me to present any insuperable obstacles. . . .

Certainly there would be no intention to portray Zelda Fitzgerald[18] as "mad" or "insane," and, on the contrary, it would be my intention to present her as a psychiatric case—with very advanced neuroses, rather than psychoses. I quite agree that she should be treated as an "ill" person, instead of an insane one. And now that the family has had the facts of Zelda's death revealed to them, what further damage can there be in having them revealed again? . . .

You might find the occasion to dwell on these points: I knew Fitzgerald very well in person. When I was still in my teens, I persuaded

[14]*A Farewell to Arms* did well at the box office, but relative to its cost, it made only a minor profit.
[15]Louis Stone, assistant to Selznick.
[16]*The Far Side of Paradise*, by Arthur Mizener (1951).
[17]Frances Lanahan, Fitzgerald's daughter.
[18]Fitzgerald's wife.

my brother Myron to engage him—Fitzgerald was in his early twenties at the time, and in the first flush of his success—to write some originals, and while the originals were never made (they were awful!), the relationship with Fitzgerald was a good one. I kept up contact with him, and—unsolicited—he made it a practice to send me an autographed copy, with a personal sentiment, of each of his books as it appeared, and I of course value them highly for my library. Not too long before his death, Fitzgerald again worked for me, this time in connection with some episodes of *Gone With the Wind,* into the writing of which I called him (for your information only, he was able to contribute nothing—but here again the relationship was a good one despite this). . . .

Throughout a period of some twenty or twenty-five years I saw him only rarely, . . . but we never had the slightest misunderstanding about anything, and we always got along very well, both personally and professionally. . . .

Warmest regards.

DOS

To: Miss Reissar   June 22, 1951
                                  URGENT & CONFIDENTIAL

Dear Jenia:

I hasten to reply to your letter of June 18 on the subject of *Tender Is the Night,* because of the urgency which you attach to it.

There can be no question that *Tender Is the Night*—or the story based upon the life of Scott Fitzgerald . . . would make a superb setup with either Vivien or Jennifer.

. . . I would certainly be delighted if Larry [Olivier] would do the picture in almost any capacity or combination of capacities he wishes, but particularly playing the male lead.

I continue to have the greatest admiration for Vivien and pride in her success; but Jennifer and I have both had our hearts set on her playing this role for several years now, and under the circumstances, I deeply regret that this is one story that I cannot offer them as a team. . . .

For many, many months prior to Larry's letter, I tried to persuade Scott Fitzgerald's daughter to let me do a story based on the lives of her parents. She listened attentively, knowing of my long personal friendship and professional associations with Fitzgerald. But she is bitter about articles and books that have appeared about her parents, and even about *The Disenchanted*,[19] and is thus far adamant about any biographical material portraying them. . . .

Kindest regards.

DOS

[Producer Jerry] Wald   July 24, 1951
and [Coproducer Norman] Krasna

Dear Jerry and Norman:

Pursuant to our conversation on *Tender Is the Night*: . . . It is, in my opinion, Fitzgerald's best—and inevitably so, since it came out of his maturity, his disillusionments, and his own personal heartbreaks. I think its title is one of the best I have ever heard; its characters the truest and deepest and most fully rounded that he ever created; and its background and period exciting beyond words. . . .

There are only a few directors who actually have the feeling of the period, and who know it and the type of characters the story portrays. George Cukor is one of them. I have discussed this story with him many times, and he would love to do it. . . . He directed *The Great Gatsby* on the stage.

Cary Grant, Jennifer Jones, Scott Fitzgerald, George Cukor, *Tender Is the Night*: how could you resist it? Add to this the team of Belasco and Frohman[20]—I beg your pardon, Wald and Krasna. . . .

I hope you will give me some fast action on it.

Warmest regards to you both.

David

To: Mr. Robert Chapman   August 7, 1956
       [Writer] Sidney Carroll

Dear Bob and Sid:

. . . *Tender is the Night* has frustrated the attempts at adaptation of some very able men. It has attracted great film-makers like Willy Wyler and Fred Zinnemann, but each of them has recognized the enormous problems of getting it into screenplay form, precisely as I do. I mention this now to keep you from being discouraged. . . .

This is not a story of a few dramatic climaxes; rather it is, like

[19]Budd Schulberg's 1950 novel, later dramatized, which drew heavily from Fitzgerald's life.
[20]David Belasco and Daniel Frohman, noted theatrical producers of the late nineteenth and early twentieth century.

Maugham's *Of Human Bondage*, a story of intimate and subtle human relationships, and of the processes by which people become enslaved to each other. Discerning critics and a limited audience read into this book, perhaps Fitzgerald's masterpiece because he felt it more keenly than anything else he ever wrote, what he did not put on paper—and perhaps even partially because they, this limited group, read into it what they knew of the relationship between Fitzgerald and Zelda. We too are among this small company that read into it what we know of this relationship. But ninety-nine per cent and more of the reading public did not "get" it, and the book failed. . . . I think it would be self-deceptive to argue that it failed solely because readers of that period looked down their noses at stories about the idle rich. Just so, ninety-nine per cent and more of our picture audience will not "get" it unless they see and hear what Fitzgerald knew and lived through, in this kind of enslavement, instead of seeing only the results, and only hints at the full revelation of the truth. . . .

I have learned the folly of being faithful to a book that had failed, however much I might personally be in love with that book. . . .

Our problem is more complicated than that of Maugham's *Of Human Bondage*, because he was dealing with the destruction of a sympathetic and sensitive character by a monstrous trollop—whereas in *Tender Is the Night* it is essential that we have not one but two sympathetic characters, each lovable, each pitiable. Our problem is more difficult because the paths must cross; one must be destroyed while the other gets well. And it is of the essence of the tragedy of the story that it is their *love* for each other that results in this paradoxical conclusion.

It is Nicole's romantic and sexual attraction for Dick[21]—romantic appeal even more than the sexual attraction, perhaps—that enslaves him and leads to his destruction; it is Nicole's mad and passionate love for Dick that leads her to jealously possess and destroy him, as effectively as if it were deliberate, which of course it is not. We must see the love scenes, the arguments, the ambivalence, that lead to the destruction of Dick; we must see the processes by which Dick, at the price of his own destruction, treats her and treats with her—as a psychiatrist and as a lover and as a husband. We must see that Nicole, while adoring him, resents him and has a fanatic and unreasonable jealousy of his attractiveness to other women, although reasonably she should understand that he is innocent (until late in the story), and that

[21]The protagonist of *Tender is the Night.*

his attraction for other women is no different from what has attracted her, and is as much a part of him as a human being as his eyes or legs. We must see that Dick's worship of Nicole is such that even though he is aware of what she is doing to him, even though there are times when he loathes and despises her and could almost do violence to her, his conscience as a doctor and as a husband and his adoration of her are such that there is no release for him, and that he must go her way, that he must propitiate her and quiet her and treat her, that he must surrender to her, even though he knows (and the audience must see this and agonizingly go along with it) that it is leading to his destruction as a doctor and as a person. It is out of this, as I see it, that he succumbs to Rosemary; if Rosemary hadn't come along, some other girl would have. Rosemary in one form or another is inevitable: she is escape from the horrific problems of Nicole and his relationship with Nicole. . . .

I do want to stress that I want to keep as much of Fitzgerald as possible; I am not quarreling with what he wrote, I am quarreling with what he did *not* write—or perhaps with what he deleted because it was too close to him and/or what consciously or subconsciously he could not bring himself to write. The tragedy of *Tender Is the Night,* and the greater tragedy of what the failure of the book did to Fitzgerald (for it is my conviction that it was the failure of this book that broke his heart and his spirit more than any other single factor, excepting only his relationship with Zelda), is that Fitzgerald had a great story to tell, but told only its superficial aspects, omitting each and every one of those scenes that really constituted what he had to say. . . .

It is universally true that in each partnership between a man and a woman, there is an amount of give and take: the very meaning of marriage is the abandonment of the individual to the couple and to the family. Sometimes this is mutually constructive, to a greater or lesser extent; sometimes it is mutually destructive, to a greater or lesser extent; sometimes one benefits and the other is damaged. But no two people in a lasting marriage are ever the same as they were as individuals. The consequences of the effect of two people upon each other in a marriage thus have a universal applicability, and an audience identity, to at least some extent, differing of course with each couple among the countless millions of couples in our audience. . . .

DOS

To: Mr. Romain Gary[22]   June 2, 1958

Dear Romain:

... I should like urgently to recommend that you see an extraordinary film I viewed the other night—*The Goddess*. It has many things wrong with it, particularly from a standpoint of wide popularity. But it has many things in it that are brilliant too, and [Paddy] Chayefsky has again proved that he is one of the most original and gifted modern dramatists.

In particular, I should like you to see his portrayal of the origins of the impossible and volatile creature who is the "heroine"—an idol of the world who is completely impossible, and who cannot be wife, mother, or human being, and who is completely worthless to be anything but a movie star. It is a ruthless but brilliant and amazing portrait; it is savage, but it rings true in the destruction of other people by this woman; and, most apropos of this point, it is heartbreaking in its early revelation of what caused this woman to be as she is. There is a sequence in which the lonely child can find no one to tell that she has been promoted at school, finally winding up telling it to her kitten, that gives completely all that we need to know as to the origins of this monstrous woman. We are dealing in different materials, but certainly we must have something at least as good. ...

I always felt that Daphne du Maurier must have been greatly influenced by *Tender Is the Night*—for if you know *Rebecca*, it dealt in retrospect with "the most glamorous couple in Europe," Max de Winter and his wife Rebecca, who were the envy of the whole world. This is what was true of Nicole and Dick. It is true of many couples that you and I know—brilliantly talented, beautiful to look at, the envy of the world—but with something rotten underneath that only they know, precisely as is true of Dick and Nicole. Or perhaps I should say that there are a few intimates who know that there is something wrong underneath. ...

Tender Is the Night is a very difficult assignment. Able writers have come a cropper on it. It would be just too miraculous to believe that you could lick it in a week or two weeks, or even in more time than this. I am sure that you can lick it faster than any writer I know, but I hope that you have the patience to probe its every relationship, to preserve every Fitzgerald value. ...

Warmest regards.

DOS

[22]French novelist engaged by Selznick to do an adaptation of *Tender Is the Night.*

To: Mrs. David Selznick   January 27, 1959

Darling:

Have received your wire about Bill Holden and *Tender Is the Night*, to which I hasten to reply, because it affects so many things about the preparation and planning of the film. . . .

Firstly, let me say, as emphatically as I can, that despite your own insistence that I should do what I think best, I want to at least try to effectuate what *you* want, in this above all cases. . . . *Tender Is the Night* has long been your dream. I have seen too many other dreams of yours come very close to realization, only to be spoiled by one thing and another, to be unaware of, or insensitive to, what it would mean to you to have *Tender* finally prepared and finally go into work, but with the wrong director, or with the wrong costar from your standpoint. I shall always feel sad that, despite the very substantial success of *Farewell*, it was not what you wanted. . . .

We are partners in everything, and doubly so, certainly, in your own films with me, or prepared by me. So, for these reasons, I want you to keep arguing with me whenever you think you are right, as in this case concerning Bill.

I also want to say that I am in complete agreement that Bill is the best man for the role, from a performance standpoint, from a box-office standpoint, and also as to proper casting. I might say that he is not one hundred per cent casting, since I think there is something in Bill's "squareness" that keeps him from being slightly less than ideal for the role of an artist or a scientist, or—despite his own neuroses—anything so neurotic as Scott Fitzgerald turned into Dick Diver. Yet I cannot deny that among the stars, he comes closest to being ideal. Nor could anybody have the slightest quarrel with your viewpoint that the combination was proven by *Love Is a Many-Splendored Thing* to be a successful one. . . .

Yet the longer we delay in coming to grips with the availability of our second or third choice, the more *certain* it becomes that we shall have to face a choice of evils: either a further delay in making the picture, or taking somebody that is far less desirable than the man we might get if we moved as quickly as possible, instead of waiting for Bill. . . .

Thus we must come to a conclusion, and very, very fast. . . . There are certain actors whom I believe we could get today . . . :

I don't know whether Twentieth[23] would approve [Henry] Fonda,

[23]Selznick had sold the property to Twentieth Century-Fox, retaining certain approvals.

since he is not in the list in the contract, but since he is the sole star of Nunnally Johnson's *The Man Who Understood Women* (playing a character that was described by someone to a group of people as "a combination of Hitler, Jed Harris,[24] and David Selznick"), Skouras would be hard put to say no, and indeed I think he would say yes. . . . I think that Fonda has certain things in his favor that Bill does not: firstly, I could believe that he is a gifted psychiatrist more than I could believe it about Bill; there is about him a trace, or at least a hint, of weakness that doesn't exist in Bill, and that is desirable for the character; and I think he is actually a somewhat better and more experienced and more sensitive actor than Bill. . . .

Then there is [Robert] Mitchum, although I think Fonda has considerably more standing and prestige. . . .

Greg Peck would be excellent. And I think that we could get him, and that Skouras and Adler[25] would be enthusiastic. (As against this, Peck hated the book and could not understand why anybody was making it, and thought there was "no point in making a picture about people who contributed nothing to the American scene"!) . . .

Monty Clift has I think become so impossible to work with that I am afraid he would throw you higher than a kite, although there are many things to recommend him for the role—as against which he seems a little lightweight, and perhaps has become too peculiar in appearance and in personality for the part. . . .

The others on Twentieth's list—and, believe me, they would take any of them, however foolish the casting might be—are obviously impossible for the role. I refer to Clark Gable, Gary Cooper, and Bing Crosby, all of whom I think too old . . . John Wayne, who I think would be awful in this role; and a few other remote possibilities that they might suggest but whom I think are completely out of the question, such as Bob Taylor.

There is one other outstanding possibility, and that is Christopher Plummer. . . . I must say that he again impressed me, as he has never failed to impress me, in *J.B.* There is something electric in Chris when he is on the stage, and my only doubt is as to whether this could also be communicated through the camera. . . . I am again convinced that he is the best young actor in the English-speaking theater. He is right in age for *Tender Is the Night*, since he could bring off very effectively

---

[24]Noted theatrical producer and director.
[25]Buddy Adler, now Executive in Charge of Production at Twentieth Century-Fox.

the thirty-five- to forty- or forty-five-year age span that are outside
elements of the age of the character. . . . He has the intellectual
stature. He has the talent. . . . He is very eager to play the role,
and this is after mature consideration. (He realizes the great mistakes he made; it is clear that he wishes he had done *A Farewell to
Arms.*)

. . . Any number of people have suggested Jason Robards, Jr., the
lead in *The Disenchanted.*[26] But I must say that I find him un-
prepossessing physically for Dick Diver.[27]. . .

Olivier's name has also come up. But, firstly, and strange as it
may seem to you, I don't think Twentieth would regard him as a
big enough star, even though I think I could sell him; and, secondly, and more importantly, I think he . . . is altogether too old-
looking for it to be believed that his life could be destroyed by a
woman. . . .

Please read this letter very, very carefully, not once but twice.
Don't give me your reactions at once, brood about them for a couple of days at least. Then make your notes on a separate piece of
paper. . . .

Devotedly,
David

To: [Attorney] Arnold M. Grant November 9, 1960

Dear Arnold:

. . . When it became apparent that I could no longer produce the
picture [*Tender Is the Night*], because of the British boycott situation[28]
(and, as I recognize, also because of the guarantee question), I was
nervous about [director John] Frankenheimer doing it, as I must confess to you. I nevertheless proceeded with him because I felt a moral
obligation to him, and because of his eagerness to check with me daily
on the handling of each individual scene, each piece of casting, lighting effects and tempo, etc., etc. . . .

Sincerely,
David

---

[26]The theatrical version of Budd Schulberg's novel.
[27]Robards played the role.
[28]When Selznick sold his feature pictures to television, British theatrical film-distribu-
tors and theater-owners threatened to boycott his future productions.

Mr. Henry King[29]   December 11, 1960
Twentieth Century-Fox Film Corporation
Beverly Hills, California

Dear Henry:

Are you really sure that you want to give up the struggle to get *Tender is the Night* made entirely abroad, with studio work in Paris? . . .

The savings on the actors is in itself tremendous on pictures made in Paris, because of the six-day working schedule, as against the five-day week in Hollywood. . . . The savings on sets and costumes runs into hundreds of thousands of dollars. Also, there are many actual interiors and exteriors that can be shot in Europe that will have to be reproduced on the back lot or elsewhere in this neighborhood, and this represents a further saving of a huge amount of money.

I am normally opposed to European production, particularly when its sole purpose is either the whim or the working habits or the tax savings of directors and actors; but when we have, as in this case, a director and actors who actually would be greatly inconvenienced by working abroad and who would have no tax saving in consequence of it, it seems a pity that all the arguments of good picture-making should be brushed off—by contrast with what is granted to other units and other directors and other actors who have nothing but selfish motives for working abroad. . . .

[Spyros] Skouras has been burned by producing in odd places and because of such insanities of making the exteriors of *Cleopatra* in the winter in England,[30] as well as by experiences in Italy and in Greece. But all of his experiences of working in Paris have been excellent, as for instance on *Anastasia* [1956]. And I gather from [director] Billy Wilder and others that, by contrast with the delays and problems of working in other European countries, shooting in Paris is extraordinarily efficient—according to Billy Wilder, at least as efficient as Hollywood. And of course Paris is the ideal headquarters for this film.

I am also concerned for you, and therefore for the quality of the film, that if you make only the location scenes in Europe, you will be up against the pressure of the studio to work there for only twelve days, which is what Skouras said when we met with him, when obviously this is hopelessly inadequate for the amount of work that should be done there.

[29]Twentieth Century-Fox director who was assigned to *Tender Is the Night.* John Frankenheimer had done some preliminary work on the project before King was set.
[30]The false-start filming of the 1963 film, which was later discarded.

Also, it seems to me inevitable that in addition to the shooting you will do abroad yourself, this kind of pressure will result in the necessity of setting up a second unit to do other things, with a tremendous loss in quality. . . .

Whether or not an actual villa is used for the interiors as well as the exteriors (which of course would have the further great advantage of our being able to have the actual backgrounds from the terrace, through the windows, etc.), you may wish to consider utilizing the old studio in Nice, which I gather has been brought up to date, for cover sets.[31] (Interestingly, there is a chapter in the book, which we have not used in the script of course, that is written against the background of this very studio, which as you will recall was built by [silent-film director] Rex Ingram—who was the original of the character of the film director in the book.) . . .

Zinnemann and [director Otto] Preminger and Wyler and Wilder and the other small company of men who are getting fine results in the industry as it is constituted today have been able to achieve these results largely because they were free to make their pictures where they should be made—whether in Israel, or Rome, or Australia, or Paris, or any place else in the world. The junk that is being ground out in the big studios today is as bad as it is, and rolls up such huge losses, because other picture-makers do not have the same freedom in this and in other respects that is given to the independent units functioning for other companies, and particularly for United Artists. Your own position and prestige and enviable record are such that one would think you would also be able to make pictures the way they should be made, if the industry is to survive at all in anything resembling its present form.

In the hope that you will be able to achieve modern opportunities equal to those secured by these men and by their agents for them, I am going to take the liberty of throwing at you every thought I have had about the picture, and how it should be made, over a long period of years. I know you well enough to be sure that you will not be offended by these thoughts, and will understand the spirit in which they are advanced—which is based upon the hope that *Tender Is the Night* will come as close to achieving its full potential as is possible under your skillful hand. You can then, as they used to say at Dinty Moore's, "Eat what you want and leave the rest."

Cordially,

---

[31]Stand-by interior sets to be used in case of bad weather.

Mr. Henry Weinstein[32]   January 18, 1961
Twentieth Century-Fox Film Corporation
Beverly Hills, California

cc: Mr. Henry King
bcc: Miss Jones

Dear Henry:

. . . Let us hope that the stage-space shortage at Twentieth will drive
the picture to where it should be made! It doesn't matter whether the
picture is moved to Europe for good or for bad reasons—I am glad to
know that you are also eager to have it moved to Europe.

In this connection, let me strongly urge you to fight to the end for
Paris instead of Rome or London. Firstly, this would permit you to pick
up some scenes in Paris that would otherwise have to be simulated,
with a loss of both quality and of cost. Secondly, there is no question
whatsoever but that film-making in Paris is infinitely more efficient
than in Rome, or in London, and with a far higher standard of quality
than in Rome. . . .[33]

Another advantage I might mention is that the studios are very
convenient to the heart of Paris, whereas there is an enormous loss of
time in getting to and from studios in both London and Rome. . . .

With warmest regards,

Cordially,
DOS

To: Mr. Brannen (Office, Home)   February 9, 1961
                                        Cuernavaca, Mor., Mexico
                                        URGENT

Dear Barry:

. . . Henry King has already demonstrated, in a wire to me, his
resentments of my comments. I have tried, in a wire reply to him, to
minimize the risks of this antagonism growing to a point where he
might retire from the film with the whole can of beans opened up
again. . . . I have fought for him on the picture . . . because (1) he is
wonderful with Jennifer and gets a better result with her than any
other director she has ever worked with . . . (2) he is *the* senior piece
of talent on the Twentieth Century lot, and they don't push him

---

[32]The producer Twentieth Century-Fox selected for *Tender is the Night*.
[33]Exteriors were filmed on the French Riviera and in Zurich, Switzerland. The interiors were filmed at the Twentieth Century-Fox studios in Beverly Hills.

around the way they do newcomers there, and thus will not be subject equally, in my opinion and hope, to pressures as to length and schedule, etc., that could be most damaging to the film. . . .

So my struggle is to keep King on the picture rather than winding up with some director who would not have these advantages, and who would be pushed around by the studio, while at the same time try to cope with King to make him understand the picture and to leave the script as close to the form in which we delivered it as I can manage. This is no small task, particularly from Mexico! . . .

Now there are very suspicious circumstances in relation to the casting of the film. There is endless stalling about closing with actors that we have all agreed upon. I think there is good reason to suspect that they are deliberately stalling on making commitments until they are sure that they have their own way about the script, particularly since they of course understand and know—even though I am sure they will try to violate their agreement—that all of our contracts with them, including the last one, provide that no changes or cuts can be made without my approval, and the last one even states that the script we submitted is "accepted." . . .

I am now fearful that Frankenheimer, who would certainly be my first choice for the film, as he has always been, will no longer be available, even though he is still desperate to do the picture. . . .

Obviously, there is great urgency about this matter because I cannot stall more than a couple of days at the most in regard to my comments on the script, now that I have received it.

Warmest regards.

DOS

Mr. Henry Weinstein   February 14, 1961
Twentieth Century-Fox Film Corporation
Box 900
Beverly Hills, California

Dear Henry:

. . . Concerning the incidental music, let me call to your attention that the script contains an extraordinary number of both opportunities and requirements for songs of the period. This was also true of the book, which as you know was loaded by Fitzgerald with references to, and even quotations from, the lyrics of the popular songs of the period —both romantic songs and hot numbers of the Jazz Age. This is as it should be, because if anyone were asked to list the most salient thing about the twenties, the age of the Charleston, for instance (and the famous original "Charleston" song is surely a *must*), they would have to place the obsession of the people of the period with music high on the list.

It is my hope, as I am sure it is that of Henry and yourself, that *Tender Is the Night* will be *the* definitive picture about the twenties. This is why I have written you so repeatedly about the research, and about such details—to mention but two of what should be countless details—as the chopped ice instead of the ice cubes (for this was of course before refrigerators as we know them today) and electric fans —lots of them—for this was, of course, before air conditioning, and wealthy people of this sort would have the best fans of the period available in every room, and this would be true of hotel rooms, night clubs, etc.

Every other film about the twenties, without exception, has failed to capture the period—in its costuming, in its detail, in its *music*. If Scott Fitzgerald, the great symbol of the twenties, and Scott Fitzgerald's semiautobiographical masterpiece, are to be realized on the screen in such a manner as to really capture the mood that one can see in the documentaries of that time, the music is of course essential.

You must forgive my telling you many things about production that are of course known to Henry King, but on which presumably it will be your job to follow up and to do also creative work—and I do so only because I realize that you are not yet aware of the indifference of big studio machines to getting the best results in these departments, and of the stumbling blocks that you may encounter, and will, I know, want to fight to overcome, all of which constitute one of the more unfortunate aspects of assembly-line, big-studio production. An independent producer such as myself would have had these matters long since in work, and would be giving them daily attention; and I fervently hope that you will be able to achieve something approaching the results that would be obtained by a conscientious and knowledgeable independent producer.

The requirements of this particular picture in the way of incidental music are greater than those of any picture I have ever previously known. Normally, most of these things can await the finish of the picture, even though of course it is folly to do so—folly because it always costs a great deal more to clear rights, for instance, under pressure, and folly because the director then has to worry about these things during production, as does the producer, when all of this work could and should be done in advance. . . .

As to the choice of the songs, I long since did considerable research, and this research is available to you if you wish me to send it to you. Please let me know. But I would strongly recommend that we follow Fitzgerald. We may be certain that he gave most careful thought to the selections of the many songs that he mentions. . . .

Fitzgerald stated, accurately, although he was not a vain man, that "no one knows better than I the *sound* of my generation"—and of course he was referring both to dialogue, and in this connection Ivan [Moffat] and I struggled constantly to match the flavor of Fitzgerald (and even had [playwright] Lillian Hellman give us detailed criticisms of our new lines, criticisms we studied very carefully)—and, at least equally, to the music and to the songs. . . .

Now as to the title song:

There is nothing new about title songs. Indeed, they have been overdone. Actually, I believe I may have been the originator of title songs, for I personally made arrangements literally forty-two years ago, when I was still at school, with the leading music-publishing company of the period, to get out a title song for each of the fifty-two pictures yearly that my father's company was making. Most of these songs, as indeed the vast percentage of title songs that are gotten out today, were so much junk, because they were written by second-rate people, and hastily. Yet when the songs are composed by expert tune-smiths and lyricists, and when the demand is for something really good, they can be of enormous value to both the quality and the success of the films for which they are written, despite the overuse of title songs.

An outstanding case of a successful song, one of the most outstanding, was "Love Is a Many-Splendored Thing," from Mr. King's production of that name. . . .

I am certainly not for one minute suggesting that *Tender Is the Night* use a title song in the manner that was used at the end of *Love Is a Many-Splendored Thing*, with the voices driving the audiences out of the theaters, for while such use was undoubtedly effective in that picture, it has since become a cliché treatment that has justifiably, in connection with its excessive use in other films, become a source of ridicule. . . .

The difficulty is that most of the better composers of scores are not necessarily equally talented at composing popular songs. A notable exception is Dimitri Tiomkin, who of course has done many of the great scores of the better pictures for many years, and whose principal themes for these pictures have been converted by him into hugely successful songs in a great many cases. I think Tiomkin should be seriously considered by the studio and by Henry King and yourself, not only for these reasons, but also because he is so thoroughly knowledge-able about music of the twenties, and of course, it is *essential* that whoever does both the score and the song should be steeped in the rhythms and moods and tempos of the twenties.

If you want Tiomkin, you are undoubtedly going to have to move fast, because he is always booked up well ahead; but I should like to caution you that if you do engage him, you insist upon limiting him as to the number of jobs that he can even touch until *Tender Is the Night* is completely scored. . . .

Failing Tiomkin, you should immediately find out who are the others who might be available, including Alfred Newman—for if the choice of whoever is going to do the score is not a man who is good at songs, then a part of the deal should be that you are free to bring in somebody else to do the song, and if you are going to have difficulties about this, you had better know it at once. . . .

In my opinion, one of the great mistakes that is made by the big studios is that they don't even bother thinking about the underscoring until after the picture is finished. Obviously, this means a hasty and bad job. This is another reason why the scores of the better independent pictures are so much better than the scores of the big studios. . . .

At Twentieth the situation and the danger is aggravated because of its policy of hasty editing and hasty releasing. . . .

To: Mr. Weinstein   June 23, 1961

Dear Henry:

. . . Research is one of the most usual things in motion pictures. There are absolutely wonderful people available, who could have been feeding details of the most wonderful and attractive type to all of you, scene by scene. Frankenheimer and I had discussed this in detail, and we had a million notions as to what should be done, and all sorts of notes on it. Johnny and I had each gone through hundreds of magazines, and many books, most of which we sent to you. But it is all precisely as though nothing ever happened, and nobody ever suggested it, whereas every single scene should have some reminder of the twenties, and you should not be relying on the costumes and the music solely. Isn't this really a great pity and a great shame, Henry?

If I were producing this picture, I would be thinking about this in connection with every single scene, every single setup. . . .

I keep hoping that you won't fall into the do-nothing trap of the vast majority of big studio producers. Look at the better pictures of the old days that are on television, and you will see how much loving care was put into these things. It is one of the many reasons why pictures today are so *lousy*, and it is one of the many reasons why pictures made abroad and even in New York are so much better. You simply must show your producing abilities and interest and conscientiousness and thoroughness and perfectionism in this type of manner, Henry, if you are going to raise your head above the common or garden variety of so-called producers in this town, who don't do a damn thing about any of these departments. . . .

It just makes me sick at my stomach, and angers me, to see the sloppiness with which pictures are made today, including, I'm sorry to say, *Tender Is the Night.* In this, as in all other departments, these are the functions of the *producer.*

You don't know how hard it is, Henry, to produce independently. You don't know how easy it is, by comparison, to produce in a big studio. You don't have to worry about financing, and distribution, and studio management, and space, and a hundred other things. *All* you have to worry about is the quality of the picture. . . .

Ivan and I spent a very long time going through every detail of sanitarium life, and of the settings, and the decoration. But all of this was to no purpose, because apparently nobody connected with the making of the picture gives a damn about such matters.

The home in which Nicole and Dick live (in Zurich, after they are married) really needs the most careful and detailed study. It would be a house dating back maybe six or eight hundred years, that had gone through rebuilding maybe in the 1880s or 1890s. It would be heavy and somber and depressing, as it must be for the story, despite its original "magnificence." But, and this is important, Nicole would have tried mightily to make it more livable. . . .

Also, the *mood* of these scenes, photographically, and their lighting, must be different from the rest of the picture. I discussed with Frankenheimer and with [Director of Photography Leon] Shamroy getting either the black-and-white effect that was achieved so brilliantly in the opening reels of *Moby Dick,* or its equivalent. Shamroy was positive he could do it. . . . Frankenheimer was doubtful. But the point is, that we were *trying.* . . .

All of the rooms of these Swiss homes, dating back as they do eight hundred or a thousand years, have altogether too few and too small windows. They were grim and forbidding. I made it my business to see many of them. There should be a *minimum of sunlight*—to get the values of the glaring sun of the Riviera, and the importance of this contrast in the story. . . .

I worked hard on Jennifer's costumes with [clothes designer Pierre] Balmain and with Jennifer, and I think it is paying off, and it is perhaps significant that the only costume that has thus far turned out to be a bad one, that on the yacht, was never seen in advance and that no sketch of it even was approved. I worked hard also on Jennifer's hairdressing with George Masters, and while obviously a sensational job is being done, it is mostly Masters (and secondarily, Jennifer), at least I fought this battle successfully—and, thanks to your support, won it. . . .

But as for the other things on which I would have been working equally hard, *nobody* is doing anything worth mentioning. There is relatively ineffectual repair work after the damage is done, on the sets and the set-dressing—in consequence of the wrong people, lack of discussion, lack of sketches, lack of *interest* even. And so it goes, down the line.

Further apropos of the set-decorating, the sets ought to be as chic and as famous, and have the same effect upon interior decorating all over the world, as my sets in *Dinner at Eight* [1933], or as Thalberg's sets in *When Ladies Meet* [1933]—both of which revolutionized people's concepts of interior decorating throughout the world, and both of which achieved gigantic publicity, just on the sets alone. . . .

You can't make a great picture in union hours. If this were my picture, I would be having meetings every night of the week with different department heads, and I would be raising hell to raise their own sights and to lift them out of the rut to which they have been sent by past administrations at Twentieth.

I note that George Cukor is going to do a picture at Twentieth. I hope you will have an opportunity to observe how he works on sets and set-dressing. Also, George has recognized that he doesn't understand cinematics and lighting as well as he would like to, so he has had the great intelligence to employ [art director] Gene Allen and [color consultant] George Hoyningen-Huene to give his pictures great distinction in all the production-design departments. Twentieth will not argue with this, any more than any other studio for which George directs would. His picture will accordingly have quality in all these departments, even though the subject is not that of *Tender Is the Night* and thus does not have these opportunities. I could cry when

I think of what this picture would *look like,* apart from the more important things of script and performance and direction (all of which would also have been excellent) if it had been done by George Cukor. This is to take nothing away from Henry King, who is a superb director, but who is not supposed to be responsible for these things, particularly if he has no taste for them or no flair for them. This is where the producer comes in—provided he does come in. . . .

There are scenes that are of relatively secondary importance which should be speeded up to the maximum, consistent with the wise observation of George Abbott that "if you have a bad few minutes in a play, the thing to do is to race through them so that the audience doesn't recognize how bad they are, or how boring they are." . . .

You are the last of a long line who have felt that the working hours in production are irrational, and I hope that you are young enough to try to fight it out. . . . I urge you to point out how much could be gained, in shooting time and in quality, and in time for proper discussion, if the company started shooting at 11:00 and worked until 8:00—with a lunch break—or alternately followed the French system, which I believe is from 12:00 to 7:00, with no break at all, except for sandwiches and refreshments on the set. (But you might check this, since I believe it varies from one French producer to another.)

Instead of actors coming in exhausted, with too little sleep, they would come in fresh. (The first setups would be ready, working with the stand-ins, so that all this time that is lost the first thing in the morning would be largely saved.)

The people would have a better morale, because they could have at least some kind of personal life, and at least be able to have dinner with their families, or boy or girl friend or whatever, and still get in bed in time to be made up at 11:00.

The producer, the director, the cameraman, the production designer, etc., would have some time to discuss the problems of the day's work, and to improve its quality, and to see the rushes of the previous day's work if they haven't seen them the day before.

These are only *some* of the benefits.[34]

It is one of my great regrets that I did not push this through in the days when I was making forty pictures a year—yes, forty!—and the later days when I had my own company, and was making three pictures a year. I have no alibi to offer. I was as stubborn as my colleagues

[34]The picture was made during traditional working hours—from early morning to 6:00 or 7:00 P.M.

in the business, and as much a creature of habit as they were. . . .

Please don't *compromise*, Henry. . . . They expect great things of this picture, and they are not going to thank you for saving one per cent of its cost, or even five per cent of its cost, if the price of this is the difference in quality that would make it into a fine picture. They are not even going to credit you if you save ten per cent of the cost. You have a great opportunity, still, Henry, but you are going to muff it if you compromise, compromise, *compromise*, and if you rationalize bad things. . . .

DOS

To: Mr. Weinstein   August 7, 1961

Dear Henry:

. . . You spoke of the "tendency of Henry King's letting scenes play at a slower pace." I warned you of this danger over and over again. . . .

[You] talk about what can be done in the cutting "to use different rhythms" and "to bring about the sense of pace and urgency where they may not now exist" and "develop a rhythm in the use of visual pace.". . . These are not the silent days, when far more could be done with film and cutting than with talking pictures—and even then, the limitations as to what could be done with cutting were obviously proscribed by the tempo at which scenes had been photographed. As things are today, manifestly such things as rhythm and pace and tempo are determined by what has been done with the recording. I know of no one who has yet come up with a way of achieving what you are talking about in the cutting room—and most particularly with the type of shooting that Henry King does, with scenes limited to one or two or three standard angles which must be used as photographed, if at all, and on which the only thing that can be accomplished is the use of whatever angles have been shot to possibly shorten dialogue in some scenes; to improve the selection of readings and performances by intercutting more desirable takes of portions of scenes; to a very minor extent, to eliminate certain pauses if they exist; and otherwise to achieve those things with which expert cutting can improve a film —but which most certainly does not include any possibility of improving by changing the pace or tempo of the individual scenes from that of the original photographing and recording. . . .

Often a picture looks terrible in rushes, and wonderful when put together; often the reverse is true. . . .

Mr. Henry Weinstein   November 14, 1961
Twentieth Century-Fox Film Corp.   NOT SENT
Beverly Hills, California

Dear Henry:

. . . I am all too aware of the present "system": it has practically emptied the theaters of the world, or at least those that show Hollywood product. . . .

You say that Henry King has full authority, as I must know by now, to exercise his prerogative; and that that includes dubbing, music underscoring, rerecording, editing, etc. With all due respect to directors, and I have worked with a very large percentage of the best of them, if this be true . . . why on earth does the picture need a producer at all? . . .

The best servant of a company and its stockholders is not the one who clicks his heels, salutes, and accepts all decisions as though they came from Mount Sinai, engraved on tablets. No executive who has had enough on the ball to achieve a high position wants this kind of servility, and this type of company servant speedily becomes an ex-servant. I have seen hundreds of executives and producers, and scores of production heads of major studios, go into the discard—and some of them even into the Motion Picture Relief Fund home—in consequence of lack of guts and an unwillingness to fight for what they believed would be right. You have even seen it at Twentieth Century-Fox, in the short time you have been there. *Tender Is the Night* has run the gamut of three or four administrations. . . .

. . . You told me, after a yessing session with Bob Goldstein,[35] that the picture would have its locations made here—and, having never been in Europe, you went about the business of finding the Riviera at Malibu, and Zurich on the *Bernadette* back-lot streets; it became my job to persuade twelve assembled Twentieth Century-Fox executives, who had made up their minds that the picture was going to be shot here, to send a company abroad. . . .

As to Bernie Herrmann,[36] you are quite correct in your statement that I had and still have enormous respect for him as being very considerably talented. . . .

Of course Bernie Herrmann should be heard before any underscoring is taken out; but . . . musicians notoriously hear only their music, which is as it should be; but that it is the *producer's* function, assuming

---

[35]Robert Goldstein, Executive in Charge of Production, Twentieth Century-Fox.
[36]Composer and conductor of the score for *Tender Is the Night.*

there is a producer, to decide when the underscoring is damaging to the total effect, either because it is the wrong music, or because of any one of a dozen other reasons, including perhaps that it should not be in at all. You also have not yet learned, as believe me you will, not to judge music by what it sounds like separately, on the scoring stage or in the projection room. You are not releasing a score; you are releasing a *picture*. And if the audience is even conscious of the score, it defeats its own purpose—except when used to disguise bad or inadequate scenes, precisely as an architect uses vines to cover bad design. . . .

I am trying desperately, still, to keep up the high hopes for the film, and to try to preserve as much of what was conceived as is possible, even at this late date. We both know—indeed you have expressed it, and repeatedly—that whether it is successful, as we all hope, or not, it will never be what it might have been. . . .

I suppose that the next thing I will hear will be the voices of a big chorus singing those corny lyrics of the song under the main title and at the end.[37] This, too, will sell more copies of the song; this, too, will help Twentieth Century toward a loss on the unnecessarily high production cost.

Sincerely,
DOS

Mr. Spyros P. Skouras December 8, 1961
Twentieth Century-Fox Film Corporation St. Regis
444 West 56th Street New York, New York

New York, New York

cc: Mr. Levathes[38]

Dear Spyros:

You are not going to hear much more from me about *Tender Is the Night*, as I'm sure you will be glad to know. As always happens, even experienced advice is disregarded when it is free. . . .

I am afraid I find it rather depressing to have so new an administrator as Pete fall back on such a cliché as "we are interested in dollars, not honors.". . .

---

[37]The title song was written by Sammy Fain and Paul Francis Webster.
[38]Peter G. Levathes, Vice-President in Charge of Production at Twentieth Century-Fox.

I have never gone after "honors instead of dollars." But I have understood the relationship between the two. No pictures in the history of the industry ever received, picture for picture, as many honors as my own; no pictures in the history of the industry, picture for picture, have ever achieved comparable grosses or comparable profits.

I first started hearing these statements about "dollars instead of honors" from Ben Schulberg, and quit Paramount rather than be even partially blamed for the debacle that was the inevitable consequence of this philosophy. Since that time, I have seen studio administration after administration go under, because of the failure to realize that honors in the picture business are not only a satisfaction to the recipients, and proper rewards for work well done, but (a) worth millions in gross; (b) an incentive to better work; (c) invaluable to a studio's morale, and to its *commercial*—that is, "dollars," not "honors"—results on an over-all basis.

I am convinced that you will suffer in consequence of this decision—and I am not referring to anything connected with me—in many ways, seen and unseen, with the top people in the business. Studio administration cannot be calloused and cynical toward the ambitions of, and the promises made to, the creators, without paying dearly for so hard-shelled an attitude. As things stand, already too many of the top stars and directors and writers and producers in the business have contempt and hatred for their employers. And this contempt and hatred can cost all of the companies, certainly by no means excepting your own, countless millions of dollars. This particular incident is simply typical of what has prompted an attitude on the part of employees that has no parallel in any other business—because in other businesses, there is gratitude for the work of those who knock themselves out for their employers, and understanding of the temperaments and ambitions of the individual, even in those industries where they are not dealing every day of the year with sensitive creative artists. . . .

I regret this new evidence of the complete passing of showmanship from the industry, and of the complete evaporation of any feeling for the work of its creators, as well as the new attitude of indifference to promises. I can only look back nostalgically on different days that produced different results.

I think this is where the bus stops.

Sincerely and regretfully,
David

Mr. Spyros P. Skouras   January 3, 1962
Twentieth Century-Fox Film Corp.   DON'T SEND
444 West 56th Street
New York, New York

cc: Mr. Peter Levathes

Dear Spyros:

I hope that, like myself, you and Pete are hopeful for the best on *Tender Is the Night*, but are prepared for the worst. I have steeled myself, I have attempted to steel Jennifer, and I now would like to try to steel you against what may be an onslaught by the critics against what they may conceive to be a mutilation of their favorite author's most beloved work. . . .

I hope you will remember what the picture might have been, had I been listened to—and this regardless of whether or not it delivers satisfactorily or better. . . .

I just think of what the picture might have been had it been made the way I visualized it: Jane Fonda as Rosemary—and she was desperate to play the role, and even volunteered to make a test for it, before the moles at the studio destroyed the character of Rosemary with unauthorized script cuts (and you would have had enormously valuable options on Jane Fonda for the future). . . . Imagine Fred Astaire, or Monty Clift, or any one of the dozen other actors that I tried to sell the studio on for the role of Abe—instead of Tom Ewell. Imagine my suggestions of Peter Ustinov or Joseph Schildkraut in the role in which they cast [Sanford] Meisner . . . not that Meisner is not a good actor, but obviously he does not have the personality. And so it went through all the casting, right down to the minor roles, which destroyed utterly the party sequence—thus resulting in its having to be cut to ribbons. And most of all, I hope you remember my urgings of Richard Burton or Peter O'Toole for Dick, only to be told that Burton was "poison," and that nobody knew O'Toole; and what could have been done with the role of Tommy, with someone like my first choice, Louis Jourdan, or my final attempt, Marcello Mastroianni.[39] . . .

Of course the script cuts made the whole difference in more ways than the casting. These cuts included all of the showmanship with which I had loaded the picture. . . . Even promises that were made during the shooting were not kept—none of them. . . .

Even on the music, I failed. . . . The score is completely unnostalgic,

[39]The role of Tommy Barban was played by Cesare Danova.

and hence another great element of showmanship was thrown away. On the underscoring, further errors were made: actually some of the best scenes in the picture were infinitely better in the picture's rough cut, because they did not suffer the destructive underscoring—notably in the film's best scenes. . . .

The damage was further compounded with one of the worst and most wasteful habits of Hollywood studios—the dubbing of scenes that were perfect in their original recording. Scene after scene is about half as good as it was originally, because the Sound Department has to justify itself, and its needlessly and foolishly expensive attempts to "perfect" sound, without regard to the quality of the original performances. This is one of the various fields in which European productions are getting better and better, by comparison with Hollywood's output, because they do not have the money to squander on these alleged "improvements," which actually break the hearts of the performers and the director, and damage scenes immeasurably, even when they are good. . . .

Even the main title is a disgrace—and the danger with the critics has been aggravated by the insult of giving Fitzgerald a credit . . . equivalent to that given to the hairdressers and the makers of the main title! And the foreword which I had written, out of Fitzgerald's own language and best-known phrasing, to at least get the picture started on the right note, was also disregarded. . . .

All of this is water over the dam. It is literally true that I worked harder and longer on this film than I did on *Gone With the Wind*—the difference being that it took five times as much time and effort to have only a fraction of my ideas listened to than it did to actually do them, down to the last detail, in *Gone With the Wind*, and in all the other pictures that I have made. To me, it is heartbreaking. . . .

Very sincerely,

Mr. Spyros P. Skouras   January 16, 1962
Twentieth Century-Fox Film Corporation
444 West 56th Street
New York, New York

cc: Mr. P. Levathes

Dear Spyros:
   . . . If, by any chance, we are all disappointed, and the picture dies, there is still a chance of saving it with courageous action for the bulk

of the country and for what could have been, and could still be, its big foreign gross. I urge you to give *immediate* instructions, before it is too late, to save for a while all of the trims, all of the outtakes, all of the sound tracks, and everything else connected with the editing. This will cost you nothing, but it may be worth a fortune to you. I say this because, however absurd and impractical you may think it at the moment, I continue to think that you may want to pull back the picture, including all the prints, for a little reshooting and re-editing —including not only cuts but restorations to make the picture somewhat closer to what it could be. I would still like to do the job, and I know what can be done, but only if I am given a chance to function in the way that I have throughout my career. . . .[40]

Great films, successful films, are made in their *every detail* according to the vision of one man, and through supporting that one man, not in buying part of what he has done. Often, using a portion of his concept is worse than if you had used none at all. . . .

This is not the way to make pictures, Spyros, believe me; and I don't know how many more disappointments you are going to have to suffer before you realize this. . . . You continue to believe that if you hire a good director, and get a good title, and put down a couple of casting names on paper, the picture is made. You fail to realize, apparently, that this is a two-edged sword; that this is merely an invitation to trouble and disaster; that great producers have not achieved their reputations in this fashion; that picture after picture is a failure *despite* these elements, because they have not been *produced* (whether by producer/director or by producer) with the skill and the experience and the showmanship to know what pays off, dramatically and commercially.

. . . You cannot simply nominate people to be producers, or to make creative production decisions, regardless of whether they have proven their qualifications or not. It takes endless years of training and experience, as well as talent and insight and knowledge of human behavior and of audience reactions, to qualify for the role. . . .

Sincerely,

---

[40]The film went into release without any further revisions, and was not a notable success.

During the years 1962 to 1965, Selznick made frequent but unsuccessful attempts to secure a commitment from a motion-picture company to make another film.

In April 1964, he suffered the first of five heart attacks to occur over a fifteen-month period. On June 22, 1965, Selznick was stricken in the Beverly Hills office of his attorney, Barry Brannen, and died shortly afterward from an acute coronary at the age of sixty-three.

There were three eulogies given at the services. They were written by Joseph Cotten, William S. Paley, and Truman Capote, respectively. In the latter's tribute, delivered by George Cukor, Capote reported that Selznick had even dictated a memo covering his funeral. It requested that the services be kept simple and brief, so that no one would be bored.

Appendix
Cast of Characters
The Films of
David O. Selznick
Index

Appendix: The Functions of the Producer and the Making of Feature Films

(Excerpts from a lecture given by Selznick to a Columbia University extension film-study group, in conjunction with the Museum of Modern Art, on November 1, 1937.)

. . . There are producers and producers. One man is an office producer, another is a directing producer, and still another is an executive producer. All these terms you have probably seen, as well as others—fancy names that fit a man's fancy, or that are tacked on to him by the head of the studio. . . .

I will refer primarily to how I operate. It wouldn't be fair about how another man operates, because no one knows about what a producer does behind the closed doors of his office. . . .

I think it is high time that people started out in life taking up pictures as a career. While courses have been in existence for some years on writing and direction and photography, I am hopeful that the day will come when there will be courses leading to production. I think it would be an exaggeration to say that there are even a handful of people who study to be producers. I don't know why this is, whether it is because the functions of the producer are so mythical or so overexploited or overmaligned, or whether it is because it is a mysterious job that people can't reach. But I do know that it is a fact that of all the people who come to Hollywood, I have yet to have a person come to me and say, "I am anxious to be a producer." They want to write, direct, be cameramen or actors—mostly actors—but for some mysterious reason they don't want to be producers. . . .

The reason for this, I suppose, is that producing involves the knowledge of so many departments. If you find a man who is trained in one creative end of the business, he has no knowledge of the other creative ends of the business. Or, if he has knowledge of all the creative ends, he has no knowledge of distribution, exhibition, the commercial end of the business, which should and must go into the make-up of a producer if he is to make more than one picture. So that I would like to see, looking ahead ten or fifteen years, people who were trained for production, which would involve a schooling in every single branch of the business—distribution, exhibition, and production. If he is a properly trained man he will have to go through all those branches. And with that in mind, it is a pleasure to be able to give one of the first talks on the functions of the producer.

To begin with, let me say that different studios are organized differently. A studio such as the Goldwyn studio and our own [Selznick International] have at their head an executive who is, usually, also the producer of the pictures. By the producer of the pictures I mean the man who is most of the time responsible for the creation of those pictures, which is a fact not generally known. . . . At some studios the producer is purely a creative producer, and has nothing to do with the business end. Many of these producers would be helpless without a big studio behind them. On the other hand, a producer like Goldwyn is in charge of the creative and business end. . . . Then, there is the very able factory head who is a mass-production expert, able to keep the wheels turning and boss a great number of projects effectively by dividing his time among them. In that field I suppose the best examples are Zanuck[1] and Wallis.[2]

Film critics and writers constantly, repeatedly, almost invariably mistake the functions of the director and the producer. You see the producer credited with something for which the director should be credited, and vice versa. . . . But those things are traceable to the vanity that most of us in the business have. We like to see our names associated with our efforts, and it is perhaps worth a minute or two to clarify just where the directing producer is different from the producer.

There are in Hollywood today, and I dare say in London and other places where pictures are produced, men who perform both functions. I might mention Frank Capra, who is both a producer and a director. A person, in order to achieve that dual post, must demonstrate that he is not merely a capable director but that he is able to sense the commercial aspects of a picture, to determine the elements that go to make up a picture, and to keep an editorial perspective on a picture. The great danger in a producing setup is that the director, being close to the picture, on the set day by day and in the cutting room day by day, has no perspective on the picture as a whole, on its story values, entertainment values, or, least of all, its commercial values. Frank Capra told me recently that he was dissatisfied with *Lost Horizon.* I don't know how many of you saw it, but he felt that if he had had someone to lean on or someone to guide him, someone he could have respected, many of the faults of the picture would have been remedied and the picture would have been much better. . . .

The director, on the other hand, operates differently in different studios. At MGM for instance, the director, nine times out of ten, is strictly a director, in the same sense that the stage director is the director of the play. His job is solely to get out on the stage and direct the actors, put them through the paces that are called for in the script. At Warner Brothers the director is purely a cog in the machine. It is true with ninety per cent of the Warner films: the director is handed a script, usually just a few days before he goes into production. Otherwise it would obviously be impossible for a man to produce and direct five or six pictures a year. . . .

Another case would be Lewis Milestone, who would be in on everything, every phase of production, from the first step to the last, and who actually, with his own hands, cuts the film. . . .

At other studios the director—as, for instance, with me—is in on the script

---

[1]Then Vice-President in Charge of Production, Twentieth Century-Fox.
[2]Hal B. Wallis, then Associate Executive in Charge of Production, Warner Bros.-First National.

as far in advance as it is possible for me to have him. He is in the story conferences with me and the writers, in the development of the script, and I always have my director in on the cutting right up to the time the picture is finished. That is not obligatory with me, nor is it the custom in most of the larger studios, although there is a great movement at the moment, on the part of directors who have organized themselves into a guild, to insist upon the privilege of at least presenting to the producer a first cut of what they shot, which I think is perfectly reasonable. The director at least should have the opportunity of presenting to the producer his direction as he has directed it, and not as some cutter has assembled it. . . .

The director is, as often as not, called in after the script is finished. He is handed a script, sets, staff, everything else, all the tools, and he goes out and directs. I don't think it is a very sound process because, after all, the man who is directing the individual scenes should have some conception of what was intended in the preparation of the picture as a whole. But since we are not talking about the functions of the director but the functions of the producer, I should like to clarify the practice of producers as opposed to executives, who do not actually produce. The producer today, in order to be able to produce properly, must be able not merely to criticize, but be able to answer the old question "what" or "why." He must be able, if necessary, to sit down and write the scene, and if he is criticizing a director, he must be able—not merely to say "I don't like it," but tell him how he would direct it himself. He must be able to go into a cutting room, and if he doesn't like the cutting of the sequence, which is more often true than not, he must be able to recut the sequence. Now by recutting I don't mean the actual physical handling of the film, but to sit in a projection room, where most cutting is done today, and say, "Take two feet off there"—"Get me this angle of that scene"—"Play this in close-up," etc.

Cutting today, I may say in passing, is quite different from what it was in the silent days. In the silent days the cutter had a much more important post than he has today. A good cutter could ruin a picture in the silent days, or he could help it enormously, because you were able to take your film and juggle it around any way you saw fit. Scenes that were intended for reel four could be put in reel one; maybe the middle of the scene was taken out and a close-up from some other scene inserted, and even though the lips moved, the film could be matched with no one being aware of the change.

But in talking pictures you are limited by dialogue. Cutting today hasn't nearly the range of possibilities in the changing of the film that it had in the silent days. And that means, of course, that you have to be much more right with your script than you were in the silent days. In the silent days you could save a bad film simply with cutting and clever title writing. Those days, as I say, are gone. Your film is in sound, basically, and if it isn't written and directed properly, no cutting will save it. You can improve a picture, to be sure, and substantially you can improve it, even [to] the illusion of tempo, by cutting out slow spots, trimming out dull lines, which is done after previews. But if the tempo is slow in the playing, it is going to be slow in the finished picture. If the writing is bad, basically, it is going to be in the finished picture, and only retakes can save you.

A picture is usually born in two or three different ways. Either the producer gets a conception that he would like to make such and such a picture, would like to buy such and such a play, or create such and such an original. He determines what is known as his setup, which means his stars, director, his writers, who, up until recently, were considered a very minor element in the production of a picture. But as time goes on, producers come to realize more and more that writing is, after all, the basic and most important quality of a picture. Or the idea comes, perhaps, from one of the staff, or a director may come in with tremendous enthusiasm for a story, or a star may come in and will sign a contract provided you do such and such a story. But more often than not, the story idea is born in either the Story Department or in the producer's mind.

He starts, from that, to select the people who are going to make the picture with him. Now the casting of the people who are going to make the picture is today an even more important factor than the casting of the actors, because you can take the best writer in the world, and if he is misassigned, you will get a bad job. Take the best director in the world, and if it does not happen to be his particular type of picture, you are also defeated. . . . More pictures go wrong in the selection of the director and the writer than at any other time, except perhaps in the selection of the story. Today in pictures, hours, weeks, months, and even sometimes years are devoted to making a picture right, on which only a few hours have been spent in deciding the basic elements of the picture; whereas had the weeks been spent, just a small fraction of the time, in carefully weighing the showmanship elements, the entertainment elements, novelty elements of the basic material—and beyond that, the selection of the writer and director, perhaps many pictures would never be made that are made today which cause hours of misery and red ink on the books, because people have tried to figure out how to make the picture right, and it couldn't be right, no matter what they did with it. . . .

But the first step in either the creation of an original story or the adaptation of a book or play is usually—with most producers—the preparation of what is known as an adaptation, which is simply a narrative outline told as a short story would be told, in synopsis form. That adaptation could be three pages in length or very full. Again, speaking of my own method of working, our first days of discussion are what lines the story will take, resulting in a simple breakdown by sequences or chapters. I like to be able to look at the outline in sequence form and analyze where it seems weak, dull, or slow. Or where it misses its climax, its opportunities for showmanship, for only in such naked form are you able—at least, am I able—to determine what the picture will be like, what the bones of the picture are—stripped of the charm of its teller— because, as often as not, in buying basic material or taking basic material under option, you are fooled by some trick of the storyteller, some narrative style, perhaps, that does not come through in the finished picture. So that basically, I find it terribly important to get it down to what I call the bones of the story, before we start putting the flesh on it in the way of scenes, business, dialogue, and the dressing.

There are many pictures in which the skeleton is very sickly, but which are made into delightful entertainment by the charm of their treatment. I will even concede that today the treatment is more important than the skeleton, but I do feel that if basically you are sound, if basically your story has elements of showmanship and popular appeal, that even if the treatment is disappointing, enough will come through so the picture won't be an out-and-out disappointment to its makers or audiences.

Once you have gotten by the stage of that original outline, then the work begins. As I say, you can't standardize it. Sometimes you go through as many as six, nine, ten, or fifteen treatments before you get the treatment or the outline that satisfies you in its basic elements. That process may see the demise of half a dozen writers or more before you get to the point that satisfies you. . . . More often than not, you are unfortunately forced by the exigencies of contracts and dates to start a picture before you are ready, or to rush your preparation. It is one of the most unfortunate things about the business that there is such a shortage of talent, and that the talent is so high-priced, that you can't go on carrying it indefinitely, and unless you do start on a given date, you will find those people are no longer available.

Therefore, as often as not, you may have to start the actual script before your outline is satisfactory, and you may have to start the actual picture before your script is complete. For that reason alone, it is a great satisfaction to have your treatment sound, because if you know the direction that your story is taking, you are not worried so much about writing the script as the picture is in progress as you would be if you didn't have that outline and just hoped, somehow, to stumble through on a script and outline without perspective. . . .

. . . The other functions of the producer include the costuming. . . . It starts with a conference with the head of the Costume Department, an explanation of your needs, an indication of what point, dramatically, you want to make with each costume, and subsequent acceptance or rejection, in whole or part, of sketches.

With the sets you go through the same process: meetings with the designer of the sets, the head of the Art Department, and with the head of the Trick [Special-Effects] Department, because today, a large part of the business of making sets is in trick work. In almost all pictures of importance that you see today, there are from ten to a hundred shots that are either glass shots or matte shots, which means that some part of them is painted in by one process or another, with only part of the set being built. The decision as to which part of the set is to be built and where the money can be saved on painting is only one of the many problems connected with the building of sets.

I won't bore you with the other problems such as stage space, scheduling of when sets should be built, rescheduling of the picture to avoid overtime charges on building, and all the other aspects. . . . Sometimes there is the necessity of digging through research yourself to find out something that parallels what it is you are trying to get over to an art director who either pretends, or does not know what you are talking about.

And then you get into the set-dressing, which means after the set is constructed, after the walls are up and the set generally is laid out, going out, looking at it, making such changes as you think advisable; the director going out, mapping out his action, saying "I would rather have a door there than here"—avoiding a long walk. Then, if you are smart, you also approve the actual interior decoration, indicate whether you think it is what you want, because the mood of a picture is made up of all those details. A story can be thrown off if a set is dressed wrong—at least I feel that way. Perhaps I am too much of a fuss-budget, but all those processes are, of course, a great deal more complicated in color production than in black-and-white production.

During all this time that all these processes are going on about locations, sets, costumes, and whatnot, the script, if it has been finished before the picture is started, is sometimes faithfully adhered to. Sometimes changes are necessary as you go along, possibly because you find the picture is getting overlength and shortening is necessary. Possibly because you are considerably overbudgeted and tightening is necessary. Possibly because the scenes just don't come out right and you realize that you are on the wrong track in the writing or characterizations.

Now in the making of the important pictures today, for one reason or another—which all efficiency experts have tried to cure but none have solved —you usually find yourself writing the script itself during production.

Then there are, of course, the conferences on the set with the director and actors, when the director is in a jam and doesn't feel that the scene plays properly, and when you go down alone or with the writer and rewrite it on the set. Then, similar conferences when the actors feel that the scene isn't right, that they can't play it or just don't like it. . . . According to the importance of the actor and the firmness of the director depends the amount of work that you have to do of that kind. . . .

Now, the day finally comes when your picture starts and you get that first-day nervousness, waiting impatiently for the first rushes. Rushes is a term for the film as it comes straight from the laboratory. Another term that is used as often as rushes is dailies. In each case, rushes means that the film is rushed back from the laboratory, and dailies means the daily takes. That means, naturally, what has been photographed. Now, in the old days, a director was permitted to print up as many takes of each scene as he saw fit, so that you had the spectacle of producers going into a projection room and sitting through eighteen to twenty-five and thirty takes of a single scene. It was so overdone on the part of directors that the studios, almost simultaneously, arrived at a control system. . . . It depends upon how meticulous a director is about the red ink, or how much executive ability and judgment he has; and on deciding on the spot whether or not he has the scene, or having to wait until he gets into the projection room to see it. Of course, there are directors of sufficient importance, such as the producing directors, who refuse to subscribe to any such plan, but they are in the great minority.

Now the rushes come through. Each scene is photographed from several angles, varying all the way from one angle to, let's say, ten. The angles include long shots, pan shots, close-ups of the individual actors, medium shots, and so on, all of which come through in the rushes. You then make what are known as the selections, which means that the producer and the director jointly select which of these takes is the best take, after seeing it on the screen. That, then, gives you your selections, from which the film editor roughly assembles the sequence, using his judgment or not, according to the faith and willingness of the individual producer and the individual director in trusting the judgment of his cutter. But after all, it doesn't involve a great deal of trust, because you can, and always do, recut the sequence. . . . Usually the producers and directors have with them cutters who have been with them for many years and know how they like a scene assembled.

Then, the assembled sequence is shown to the producer and the director for corrections in editing the assembly, or what lines or action should be placed in close-up, medium, or whatnot. And, of course, the putting together of all those rough sequences means your rough picture. That is, the first rough assembly of your picture, which you see, as a rule, not more than two days after the last day's shooting, because the assembling is kept right up to date. The only things that will be missing when you see that rough assembly will be the trick shots, which, of course, take longer, and the sound effects, which are a separate process. Music, of course, doesn't come in until the final step. You then start your cutting conferences, far into the night, on getting the picture into shape for preview.

. . . Of course, when your picture is edited, you usually preview with what is known as stock music. That is a music track that has been used in other pictures and which you dub behind the dialogue for your previews, because it would obviously be a costly process to make music—final music—for the previews. Then you would have to cut the film and have to do the music all over, so you use stock music for previews. In the vast majority of films, that is, the cheaper films, and even some of the more costly and pretentious films, that stock music is sometimes used over and over.

Then, after you have completed your final editing, while the negative is being cut and the sound effects are being put in, the score, which has been in the process of composition in the weeks preceding, is then recorded by a thirty-, forty-, or sixty-piece orchestra, which process is very simple. It is simply the projection of the film on a large stage, with the orchestra in front of the recording booth. The music is timed down to the last foot of film by the man in charge of the music, before it is actually recorded. But there is the process that precedes that, which is a series of conferences with the composer, the exact laying out of where music is required, what type of music, etc.

Of course the picture comes through with the image on one film and the dialogue on another—separate track and film—and they are previewed on two films—separate track and film—with the use of what are known as "dummy heads," which is a device put on the projection machines in the theaters in which you preview, to permit you to run the sound and the film separately. The picture is kept on separate sound and film right up through your final stage, when you are all finished with the picture. You then cut negative, because you don't dare cut negative until you are absolutely sure that your editing is final.

Cast of Characters

COMPILED BY RUDY BEHLMER AND CLIFFORD McCARTY

The following listing includes people to whom Selznick wrote or referred throughout the book. Actors and actresses have been excluded because of the considerable number mentioned, and because of their relative familiarity; the only exceptions are performers who are also the wives or husbands of prominent persons appearing in the book. Credits, when given, are meant as a cross-section or, in certain instances, as highlights of a career to date with the emphasis on Selznick films. Death dates, where applicable, appear following names.

Abbott, George
Theatrical director, playwright, and producer (*Chicago*, 1926; *Boy Meets Girl*, 1935; *On the Town*, 1944; *The Pajama Game*, 1954).

Abbott, John E.
Director of the Museum of Modern Art Film Library, 1935–1947.

Adler, Buddy (d. 1960)
Columbia Pictures producer, 1947–1954 (*From Here to Eternity*, 1954), Twentieth Century-Fox producer, 1954–1956 (*Love Is a Many-Splendored Thing*, 1955), Executive in Charge of Production at Twentieth Century-Fox, 1956–1960.

Adrian, Gilbert (d. 1959)
Costume designer.

Agnew, Neil (d. 1958)
President of Selznick Releasing Organization; Vice-President of Selznick's Vanguard Films, 1944–1947.

Allen, Gene
Art director (*My Fair Lady*, 1964).

Altstock, L. Francis
Selznick International Comptroller during the late 1930s.

Ashton, Winifred (*See* Clemence Dane)

Aylesworth, Merlin Hall (d. 1952)
President of Radio-Keith-Orpheum Corporation, 1932–1935.

Balderston, John L. (d. 1954)
Playwright (*Berkeley Square*, 1926) and screenwriter (*The Prisoner of Zenda*, 1937; *Gaslight*, 1944).

Balmain, Pierre
French clothes designer (*Tender Is the Night*, 1962).

Barnes, George (d. 1953)
Director of photography (*Rebecca*, 1940; *Jane Eyre*, 1944; *Spellbound*, 1945).

Barry, Philip (d. 1949)
Playwright (*Holiday*, 1929; *The Animal Kingdom*, 1932; *The Philadelphia Story*, 1939).

Beaman, Earl (d. 1967)
Assistant Treasurer of The Selznick Company, 1945–1949; Vice-President and Treasurer, 1949–1966.

Beaton, Welford (d. 1951)
Editor and publisher of *Hollywood Spectator*.

Behrman, S. N.
Playwright (*Biography*, 1932; *No Time for Comedy*, 1939; *Fanny*, 1954), screenwriter (*Anna Karenina*, 1935; *A Tale of Two Cities*, 1935; *Waterloo Bridge*, 1940; *Quo Vadis*, 1951), and biographer (*Duveen*, 1952; *Portrait of Max*, 1960).

Belasco, David (d. 1931)
Theatrical producer and playwright of the late nineteenth and early twentieth century.

Berman, Pandro S.
Assistant to Selznick at RKO, 1931–1933; RKO Radio producer, 1933–1938 (*Of Human Bondage*, 1934); RKO Radio Vice-President in Charge of Production, 1938–1940; MGM producer, 1940–1966 (*National Velvet*, 1944; *Father of the Bride*, 1950; *The Blackboard Jungle*, 1955).

Bern, Paul (d. 1932)
MGM production executive, 1926–1928, 1930–1932. Husband of Jean Harlow.

Bernhard, Joseph (d. 1954)
Motion-picture executive, 1930–1950, and independent producer (*Journey into Light*, 1951; *Ruby Gentry*, 1953).

Bernstein, David (d. 1945)
Vice-President and Treasurer of Loew's, Inc. and MGM.

Betts, Edward William
Editorial staff member of the *Daily Film Renter* in London.

Birdwell, Russell
Director of Advertising and Publicity, Selznick International, 1935–1939.

Blaker, Richard
Writer.

Boleslawski, Richard (d. 1937)
Director (*Rasputin and the Empress*, 1932; *Men in White*, 1934; *Clive of India*, 1935; *The Garden of Allah*, 1936).

Bolton, Whitney (d. 1969)
Selznick's Director of Advertising and Publicity, 1941–1942.

Borzage, Frank (d. 1962)
Director (*Humoresque*, 1920; *Seventh Heaven*, 1927; *Three Comrades*, 1938).

Boyle, Edward G.
Set decorator (*Made for Each Other; Gone With the Wind*, 1939).

Brackett, Charles (d. 1969)
  Screenwriter and producer (*The Lost Weekend*, 1945; *Sunset Boulevard*, 1950), producer (*Titanic*, 1953; *The King and I*, 1956).
Brackman, Robert
  Artist; teacher at the Art Students League, New York; painter of the "Portrait of Jennie."
Brannen, Barry
  Vice-President and General Counsel of The Selznick Company during the late 1940s, 1950s, and 1960s.
Breen, Joseph I. (d. 1965)
  West Coast assistant to Will Hays, President of the Motion Picture Producers and Distributors of America, Inc.; later, President of that organization. Director, Production Code Administration, Association of Motion Picture Producers, Inc., 1934–1954.
Brock, Louis (d. 1971)
  Associate producer, RKO, 1933–1935.
Brower, Otto
  Director (*Fighting Caravans*, 1930) and second-unit director (*Suez*, 1938; *Duel in the Sun*, 1946).
Brown, Clarence
  Director (*Flesh and the Devil*, 1927; *Anna Karenina*, 1935; *National Velvet*, 1944; *The Yearling*, 1946).
Brown, Hiram S. (d. 1950)
  President, Radio-Keith-Orpheum Corporation, 1929–1933.
Brown, Katharine (Kay)
  Eastern Story Editor, FBO, 1925–1929; Eastern Story Editor, RKO, 1929–1935; Selznick's Eastern Story Editor, 1935–1938; Selznick's Eastern Representative, 1938–1942. Left to join Hunt Stromberg Productions as Executive Vice-President. Currently with International Famous Agency.
Buchwald, Art
  Internationally syndicated newspaper columnist.
Butcher, Edward W. (d. 1960)
  Production Manager, Selznick International, in the late 1930s.
Calvert, Lowell V.
  General Manager in Charge of Sales and Distribution for Selznick International, 1935–1940, and Pioneer Pictures, 1933–1938.
Campbell, Alan (d. 1963)
  Screenwriter (*A Star Is Born*, 1937; *The Little Foxes*, 1941), and husband of Dorothy Parker.
Canutt, Yakima
  Stunt man, actor, director, and second-unit director.
Capote, Truman
  Author (*Breakfast at Tiffany's*, 1958; *In Cold Blood*, 1965) and screenwriter (*Beat the Devil, Indiscretion of an American Wife*, 1954; *The Innocents*, 1961).
Capra, Frank
  Producer-director (*It Happened One Night*, 1934; *Mr. Deeds Goes to Town*, 1936; *Lost Horizon*, 1937; *Mr. Smith Goes to Washington*, 1939). Past President of the Screen Directors Guild (1938–1941, 1959–1961).

Carroll, Sidney
  Screenwriter (*The Hustler*, 1961; *A Big Hand for the Little Lady*, 1966).
Carson, Robert
  Novelist (*The Magic Lantern*, 1952) and screenwriter (*A Star Is Born*, 1937; *Beau Geste*, 1939).
Chapman, Robert
  Playwright (*Billy Budd*, 1951) and Associate Professor of Playwriting and English at Harvard University.
Chayefsky, Paddy
  Television writer, playwright (*Middle of the Night*, 1956) and screenwriter (*Marty*, 1955; *The Goddess*, 1958; *The Hospital*, 1971).
Cline, Wilfrid M.
  Technicolor cinematographer (*Gone With the Wind*, 1939).
Colby, Anita
  Former actress; consultant to Selznick regarding his feminine stars during the 1940s.
Conway, Jack (d. 1952)
  Director (*Viva Villa!*, 1934; *A Tale of Two Cities*, 1935; *Boom Town*, 1940).
Cooper, Merian C.
  Producer-director (*Chang*, 1927; *The Four Feathers*, 1929; *King Kong*, 1933); Executive Assistant to Selznick, RKO Radio Pictures, 1931–1933; Vice-President in Charge of Production, RKO Radio Pictures, 1933–1934; producer (*The Last Days of Pompeii*, 1935; *The Quiet Man*, 1952; *This Is Cinerama*, 1952). Executive Producer, Pioneer Pictures, 1935–1937; Vice-President, Selznick International, 1935–1937.
Corbaley, Kate
  Assistant Story Editor, MGM.
Cormack, Bartlett (d. 1942)
  Playwright (*The Racket*, 1927) and screenwriter (*The Front Page*, 1931; *Fury*, 1936).
Cosgrove, Jack (d. 1965)
  Head of Selznick International's Special-Effects Department, 1936–1940.
Cromwell, John
  Director (*Of Human Bondage*, 1934; *Little Lord Fauntleroy*, 1936; *The Prisoner of Zenda*, 1937; *Since You Went Away*, 1944; *Anna and the King of Siam*, 1946).
Cukor, George
  Director (*Dinner at Eight, Little Women*, 1933; *David Copperfield*, 1935; *Camille*, 1936; *The Philadelphia Story*, 1940; *Gaslight*, 1944; *Born Yesterday*, 1950; *My Fair Lady*, 1964). The original director of *Gone With the Wind*, 1939.
Curtis, Edward P.
  Sales Manager, Motion Picture Film Department, Eastman Kodak Company.
Curtiz, Michael (d. 1962)
  Director (*The Sea Hawk*, 1940; *Yankee Doodle Dandy*, 1942; *Casablanca*, 1943).

Dali, Salvador
Spanish surrealist artist who designed the dream sequence for *Spellbound*, 1945.

Dane, Clemence (d. 1965)
Pen name of Winifred Ashton, English novelist (*Broome Stages*, 1931), playwright (*A Bill of Divorcement*, 1921), and screenwriter (*Vacation from Marriage*, 1946).

Daniels, William (d. 1970)
Director of photography (*Greed*, 1923; *Dinner at Eight*, 1933; *Anna Karenina*, 1935; *The Naked City*, 1948; *Cat on a Hot Tin Roof*, 1958).

De Laurentiis, Dino
Italian producer (*Bitter Rice*, 1948; *La Strada*, 1954; *The Bible*, 1965).

De Mille, Cecil B. (d. 1959)
Pioneer producer-director (*The Squaw Man*, 1913; *The King of Kings*, 1927; *The Ten Commandments*, 1956).

De Sica, Vittorio
Italian director (*Shoeshine*, 1946; *The Bicycle Thief*, 1947; *The Garden of the Finzi-Continis*, 1971) and actor (*A Farewell to Arms*, 1957; *General Della Rovere*, 1959).

DeSylva, B. G. ("Buddy") (d. 1950)
Paramount Executive Producer, 1941–1944. Previously a songwriter ("The Best Things in Life Are Free," 1927).

Dickinson, Thorold
English director of the first *Gaslight*, 1940, and *The Queen of Spades*, 1950.

Dieterle, William
Director (*The Story of Louis Pasteur*, 1935; *I'll Be Seeing You*, 1945; *Portrait of Jennie*, 1948).

Dietz, Howard
Director of Advertising and Publicity for MGM, 1924–1959, lyricist (*The Band Wagon*, 1931), and screenwriter (*Hollywood Party*, 1934). Also wrote sketches, verse, and magazine articles.

Dinelli, Mel
Screenwriter (*The Spiral Staircase*, 1946; *The Window*, 1949).

Disney, Roy (d. 1972)
Brother of Walt Disney; in charge of financial matters for Disney Enterprises.

Dreiser, Theodore (d. 1945)
Novelist (*Sister Carrie*, 1900; *Jennie Gerhardt*, 1911; *An American Tragedy*, 1925).

Dryden, Ernest
Wardrobe designer (*The Garden of Allah*, 1936; *Lost Horizon*, 1937).

du Maurier, Daphne
English novelist (*Jamaica Inn*, 1936; *Rebecca*, 1938; *My Cousin Rachel*, 1951; *The House on the Strand*, 1969).

Eason, B. Reeves (d. 1956)
Second-unit director (chariot race in *Ben-Hur*, 1925; *Duel in the Sun*, 1946); also directed many low-budget pictures and serials.

Eckman, Sam, Jr.
  Managing Director of MGM Pictures, Ltd., London.
Eisenstein, Sergei (d. 1948)
  Russian director (*Potemkin,* 1925). Came to the United States in 1930
  and worked on *An American Tragedy,* but his version was not produced.
  Later returned to Russia (*Alexander Nevsky,* 1938; *Ivan the Terrible,* 1944–
  1946).
Eliot, Charles William (d. 1926)
  President of Harvard University, 1869–1909, and Editor of the Harvard
  Classics.
Epstein, Julius J. and Philip G. (d. 1952)
  Screenwriters (*The Man Who Came to Dinner,* 1941; *Casablanca,* 1943; *My
  Foolish Heart,* 1949).
Esmond, Jill
  Actress and first wife, 1930–1940, of Laurence Olivier.
Espy, Reeves
  Selznick executive in the mid-1940s.
Fain, Sammy
  Songwriter ("I'll Be Seeing You," 1938; "Love Is a Many-Splendored Thing,"
  1955; "Tender Is the Night," 1962).
Farrell, Lowell
  Assistant director (*Spellbound,* 1945; *Duel in the Sun,* 1946).
Faulkner, Ralph
  Fencer, fencing instructor, actor (*The Three Musketeers,* 1935; *The Prisoner
  of Zenda,* 1937).
Feist, Felix (d. 1965)
  In Charge of Sales, MGM.
Fellows, Arthur
  Production executive (*A Farewell to Arms,* 1957).
Fineman, B. P. (d. 1971)
  Paramount Production Supervisor, 1926–1930; MGM Associate Producer,
  1930–1933.
Firpo, Luis Angel (d. 1960)
  Prizefighter; called "The Wild Bull of the Pampas." Defeated in 1923 by Jack
  Dempsey in bid for heavyweight championship of the world.
Fitzgerald, F. Scott (d. 1940)
  Author (*This Side of Paradise,* 1920; *The Great Gatsby,* 1925; *Tender Is the
  Night,* 1934) and screenwriter (*Three Comrades,* 1938). Worked briefly on
  Gone With the Wind, 1939.
Fitzgerald, Zelda (d. 1948)
  Wife of F. Scott Fitzgerald.
FitzPatrick, James A.
  Producer of the *FitzPatrick Traveltalks* and other short subjects.
Flagg, Harriett
  Selznick's East Coast Representative during the 1940s.
Flaherty, Robert J. (d. 1951)
  Director (*Nanook of the North,* 1922; *Man of Aran,* 1934; *Louisiana Story,*
  1948).

Fleming, Victor (d. 1949)
Director (*The Virginian*, 1929; *Red Dust*, 1932; *Captains Courageous*, 1937; *The Wizard of Oz, Gone With the Wind*, 1939; *Joan of Arc*, 1948).

Forbes, Lou
Music Director of Selznick International. Brother of Leo F. Forbstein.

Forbstein, Leo F. (d. 1948)
Head of Music Department, Warner Bros.-First National. Brother of Lou Forbes.

Ford, John
Director (*The Iron Horse*, 1924; *The Informer*, 1935; *Stagecoach*, 1939; *The Grapes of Wrath*, 1940; *My Darling Clementine*, 1946; *She Wore a Yellow Ribbon*, 1949; *The Quiet Man*, 1952).

Forrestal, James (d. 1949)
Undersecretary of the Navy, 1940; Secretary of the Navy, 1945; Secretary of Defense, 1947.

Foster, Norman
Director (*Journey Into Fear*, 1942; *Rachel and the Stranger*, 1947). Previously an actor.

Franken, Rose (Mrs. William Brown Meloney)
Novelist (*Claudia*, 1939, and five sequels), playwright (*Claudia*, 1941), screenwriter (*Beloved Enemy*, 1936; *Claudia and David*, 1946).

Frankenheimer, John
Director (*The Manchurian Candidate*, 1962; *Seven Days in May*, 1964; *Grand Prix*, 1967).

Franklin, Chester M. (d. 1954)
Director (*Sequoia*, 1935) and second-unit director (*Gone With the Wind*, 1939).

Franklin, Sidney
Director (*The Good Earth*, 1937) and producer (*Mrs. Miniver*, 1942).

Freed, Arthur
Producer (*Meet Me in St. Louis*, 1944; *An American in Paris*, 1951; *Singin' in the Rain*, 1952) and lyricist ("You Were Meant for Me", 1929).

Freeman, Y. Frank (d. 1969)
Vice-President in Charge of Studio Operations, Paramount, 1938–1959.

Frohman, Daniel (d. 1940)
Theatrical producer of the late nineteenth and early twentieth century.

Furthman, Jules (d. 1966)
Screenwriter (*Shanghai Express*, 1932; *The Big Sleep*, 1946; *Rio Bravo*, 1959).

Gallup, George
Founder, Institute of Public Opinion, 1935; head of the Audience Research Institute.

Garmes, Lee
Director of photography (*Shanghai Express*, 1932; *Duel in the Sun*, 1946; *The Paradine Case*, 1948). The original cameraman on *Gone With the Wind*, 1939.

Garrett, Oliver H. P. (d. 1952)
Screenwriter (*City Streets*, 1931; *Manhattan Melodrama*, 1934; *The Hurricane*, 1937; *Duel in the Sun*, 1946). Also worked on *Gone With the Wind*, 1939.

Gary, Romain
  French novelist (*The Roots of Heaven*, 1958; *Lady L*, 1959).
Gilliat, Sidney
  English screenwriter (*The Lady Vanishes*, 1938); later, a producer and director.
Ginsberg, Henry
  Vice-President and General Manager of Selznick International, 1936–1939.
Glett, Charles
  Selznick's Studio Manager during the mid-1940s.
Goetz, Ruth and Augustus (d. 1957)
  Playwrights (*The Heiress*, 1947) and screenwriters (*Carrie*, 1952; *Rhapsody*, 1954).
Goetz, William (d. 1969)
  Vice-President in Charge of Studio Operations, Twentieth Century-Fox, 1942–1943; Vice-President in Charge of Production, Universal-International, 1946–1954; then an independent producer (*Sayonara*, 1957).
Goetz, Mrs. William (*see* Edith Mayer)
Goldsmith, Betty
  Selznick's foreign coordinator during the 1940s and 1950s.
Goldstein, Robert
  Executive in Charge of Production, Twentieth Century-Fox, 1961.
Goldwyn, Samuel
  Pioneer film producer, 1913; independent producer (*Stella Dallas*, 1925; *Bulldog Drummond*, 1929; *Dodsworth*, 1936; *Dead End*, 1937; *Wuthering Heights*, 1939; *The Little Foxes*, 1941; *The Best Years of Our Lives*, 1946).
Goulding, Edmund (d. 1959)
  Director (*Grand Hotel*, 1932; *Dark Victory*, 1939; *Claudia*, 1943). Also a screenwriter (*Tol'able David*, 1921).
Grant, Arnold M.
  Attorney.
Granville, Audray
  Music editor.
Greene, Graham
  English author (*Stamboul Train*, 1932; *The Power and the Glory*, 1940; *The Ministry of Fear*, 1943; *The Heart of the Matter*, 1948), screenwriter (*The Fallen Idol*, 1949; *The Third Man*, 1950), and playwright (*The Potting Shed*, 1956).
Greene, W. Howard (d. 1956)
  Technicolor cinematographer (*The Garden of Allah*, 1936; *A Star Is Born*, 1937; *The Adventures of Robin Hood*, 1938).
Greer, Howard
  Costume designer (*Bringing Up Baby*, 1938).
Griffith, D. W. (d. 1948)
  Pioneer film director (*The Birth of a Nation*, 1915; *Intolerance*, 1916; *Orphans of the Storm*, 1922).
Griffith, Edward H.
  Director (*The Animal Kingdom*, 1932; *Bahama Passage*, 1941).
Guilaroff, Sydney
  Hair stylist.

Guinzburg, Harold (d. 1961)
Cofounder and Director of The Viking Press, 1925–1961; founder of the Literary Guild, 1925.

Haller, Ernest (d. 1970)
Director of photography (*Jezebel*, 1938; *Gone With the Wind*, 1939; *Dark Victory*, 1939; *Rebel without a Cause*, 1955).

Ham, L. C.
London Representative for the Selznick-Joyce talent agency.

Hamilton, Patrick (d. 1962)
English playwright (*Rope [Rope's End]*, 1933; *Gaslight*, 1938) and novelist (*Hangover Square*, 1942).

Hammett, Dashiell (d. 1961)
Novelist (*The Maltese Falcon*, 1930; *The Thin Man*, 1934) and screenwriter (*City Streets*, 1931; *After the Thin Man*, 1936; *Watch on the Rhine*, 1943).

Harris, Jed
Theatrical producer (*Broadway*, 1926; *Our Town*, 1938; *The Heiress*, 1947).

Harrison, Joan
English screenwriter (*Rebecca*, 1940; *Suspicion*, 1941), producer (*Ride the Pink Horse*, 1948), and assistant for many years to Alfred Hitchcock. Produced TV series, *Alfred Hitchcock Presents*, 1955–1965.

Hartsfield, William B.
Mayor of Atlanta, Georgia, 1937–1961.

Hawks, Howard
Director and producer-director (*Dawn Patrol*, 1930; *Scarface*, 1932; *Twentieth Century*, 1934; *The Big Sleep*, 1946; *Red River*, 1948; *Hatari*, 1962). Was the original director on *Viva Villa!*, 1934.

Hays, Will H. (d. 1954)
President of Motion Picture Producers and Distributors of America, Inc., 1922–1945.

Hayward, Leland (d. 1971)
Literary and talent agent, 1937–1944; theatrical producer (*Mister Roberts*, 1948; *Call Me Madam*, 1950) and film producer (*The Old Man and the Sea*, 1958).

Hebert, William (d. 1962)
Director of Advertising and Publicity, Selznick International, 1939–1940.

Hecht, Ben (d. 1964)
Journalist, novelist (*Count Bruga*, 1926), playwright (*The Front Page*, 1928), short-story writer, screenwriter (*Underworld*, 1927; *Viva Villa!*, 1934; *The Scoundrel*, 1935; *Nothing Sacred*, 1938; *Wuthering Heights*, 1939; *Spellbound*, 1945; *Notorious*, 1946; *A Farewell to Arms*, 1957), producer-director (*Specter of the Rose*, 1946). Worked briefly on *Gone With the Wind*.

Hellinger, Mark (d. 1947)
Producer (*The Naked City*, 1948); formerly a journalist and screenwriter.

Hellman, Lillian
Playwright (*The Children's Hour*, 1935; *Watch on the Rhine*, 1941) and screenwriter (*The Little Foxes*, 1941; *The North Star*, 1943).

Henigson, Henry
Producer (*Imitation of Life*, 1934) and executive.

Herrmann, Bernard
Composer and conductor (*Citizen Kane,* 1941; *Jane Eyre,* 1944; *Psycho,* 1960; *Tender Is the Night,* 1962).
Hertz, John Daniel
One of the original backers of Selznick International.
Herzbrun, Henry (d. 1953)
Resident Attorney, Paramount Studios in Hollywood, 1926–1935. Vice-President and General Manager of Production at Paramount, 1935–1937; resumed general practice of law, 1938.
Hitchcock, Alfred
Director (*The Lodger,* 1926; *The 39 Steps,* 1935; *The Lady Vanishes,* 1938; *Rebecca,* 1940; *Spellbound,* 1945; *The Paradine Case,* 1947; *Strangers on a Train,* 1951; *Vertigo,* 1958; *Psycho,* 1960).
Hoffenstein, Samuel (d. 1947)
Poet (*Poems in Praise of Practically Nothing,* 1928) and screenwriter (*An American Tragedy,* 1931; *Dr. Jekyll and Mr. Hyde,* 1932; *Cluny Brown,* 1946).
Hogan, Michael
English screenwriter (*Rebecca,* 1940; *Forever and a Day,* 1944).
Holman, Leigh
First husband (1932–1940) of Vivien Leigh, who adopted his first name professionally.
Hopkins, Harry L. (d. 1946)
Special Assistant to President Franklin D. Roosevelt.
Hornblow, Arthur, Jr.
Producer (*Ruggles of Red Gap,* 1935; *Gaslight,* 1944; *The Asphalt Jungle,* 1950).
Horne, Frederick Joseph
Vice-Chief of Naval Operations, 1942–1945.
Howard, Sidney (d. 1939)
Playwright (*They Knew What They Wanted,* 1924; *The Silver Cord,* 1926; *Yellow Jack,* 1934) and screenwriter (*Arrowsmith,* 1932; *Dodsworth,* 1936; *Gone With the Wind,* 1939).
Howard, William K. (d. 1954)
Director (*The Power and the Glory,* 1933; *Fire over England,* 1936).
Howe, James Wong
Director of photography (*Peter Pan,* 1924; *Viva Villa!,* 1934; *The Thin Man,* 1934; *The Prisoner of Zenda,* 1937; *The Adventures of Tom Sawyer,* 1938; *Body and Soul,* 1947; *Hud,* 1962).
Hoyningen-Huene, George (d. 1968)
Fashion photographer and color consultant for films (*A Star Is Born,* 1954).
Hulburd, Merritt
Production executive.
Hungate, Richard
Secretary of Selznick's Vanguard Films during the late 1940s.
Huston, John
Director (*The Maltese Falcon,* 1941; *The Treasure of the Sierra Madre,* 1948; *The African Queen,* 1951; *The Misfits,* 1961) and actor (*The Cardinal,* 1964). The original director of *A Farewell to Arms,* 1957.

Huxley, Aldous (d. 1963)
English author (*Point Counter Point*, 1928; *Brave New World*, 1932; *The Doors of Perception*, 1954) and screenwriter (*Pride and Prejudice*, 1940; *Jane Eyre*, 1944).

Hyman, Bernard H. (d. 1942)
MGM producer (*Rasputin and the Empress*, 1933; *Tarzan and His Mate*, 1934; *Conquest*, 1937).

Hyman, Eliot
President of Seven Arts Associated Corporation, 1960–1967.

Ingram, Rex (d. 1950)
Director (*The Four Horsemen of the Apocalypse*, 1921; *The Prisoner of Zenda*, 1922; *The Garden of Allah*, 1927).

Isley, Phylis
Maiden name of Phylis Walker (*see* Jennifer Jones).

Johnson, Joseph McMillan
Production designer; head of Selznick's Art Department in the mid-1940s.

Johnson, Nunnally
Producer (*The Gunfighter*, 1950), director (*The Three Faces of Eve*, 1957), and screenwriter (*The Grapes of Wrath*, 1940).

Johnston, Richard L. (d. 1961)
Selznick's Production Manager during the 1940s.

Jones, F. Richard
Director (*The Gaucho*, 1928; *Bulldog Drummond*, 1929).

Jones, Jennifer
Actress (*The Song of Bernadette*, 1943; *Since You Went Away*, 1944; *Love Letters*, 1945; *Duel in the Sun*, 1946; *Portrait of Jennie*, 1948; *Carrie*, 1951; *Ruby Gentry*, 1952; *Indiscretion of an American Wife*, 1954; *Love Is a Many-Splendored Thing*, 1955; *A Farewell to Arms*, 1957; *Tender Is the Night*, 1962). Professional name of Phylis Isley. Wife of Robert Walker, 1939–1945. Wife of David O. Selznick, 1949–1965.

Jones, Robert Edmond (d. 1954)
Designer for stage (*Hamlet*, 1922) and screen (*La Cucaracha*, 1934; *Becky Sharp*, 1935).

Jordan, Dorothy
Actress and wife of Merian C. Cooper.

Kahane, Benjamin B. (d. 1960)
President of RKO Radio Studios and RKO Pathé Studios, and Vice-President of the parent corporation, Radio-Keith-Orpheum, 1932–1936.

Kalmus, Herbert T. (d. 1963)
President and General Manager, Technicolor Motion Picture Corporation, 1915–1960.

Kanin, Garson
Director (*Bachelor Mother*, 1939), screenwriter (*A Double Life*, 1947; *Pat and Mike*, 1952), playwright (*Born Yesterday*, 1946), novelist (*Blow Up a Storm*, 1959), and biographer (*Tracy and Hepburn*, 1971).

Karas, Anton
Composer and zither-player (*The Third Man*, 1950).

Katz, Sam (d. 1961)
 Vice-President, MGM and Loew's, Inc., 1936–1949.
Kaufman, Albert A. (d. 1957)
 Executive Assistant to Jesse L. Lasky.
Keon, Barbara (d. circa 1955)
 Selznick's scenario assistant and production secretary in the 1930s and 1940s.
 Formerly with MGM.
Kern, Hal C.
 Selznick's Supervising Film Editor during the 1930s and 1940s.
King, Don
 Selznick's Director of Advertising and Publicity, 1944.
King, Henry
 Director (*Tol'able David,* 1921; *State Fair,* 1933; *The Song of Bernadette,*
 1943; *Twelve O'Clock High,* 1949; *Love Is a Many-Splendored Thing,* 1955;
 Tender Is the Night, 1962).
Klune, Raymond A.
 Production Manager, Selznick International, 1935–1942.
Knox, Frank (d. 1944)
 Secretary of the Navy, 1940–1944.
Koerner, Charles W. (d. 1946)
 General Manager of RKO Studios, 1942–1946.
Korda, Alexander (d. 1956)
 Independent producer (*Things to Come,* 1935; *The Thief of Bagdad,* 1940;
 The Third Man, 1950) and director (*The Private Life of Henry VIII,* 1933;
 Rembrandt, 1936).
Krasna, Norman
 Playwright (*Dear Ruth,* 1944; *John Loves Mary,* 1947) and screenwriter
 (*Fury,* 1936; *The Devil and Miss Jones,* 1940; *Let's Make Love,* 1960).
Kurtz, Wilbur G. (d. 1967)
 Historian and technical advisor for *Gone With the Wind.*
La Cava, Gregory (d. 1952)
 Director (*Symphony of Six Million,* 1932; *My Man Godfrey,* 1936; *Stage
 Door,* 1937).
Lambert, Edward P.
 In charge of wardrobe (*Gone With the Wind,* 1939).
Lanahan, Mrs. Frances
 Daughter of F. Scott Fitzgerald.
Lardner, Ring, Jr.
 Worked for Selznick as a junior writer (*A Star Is Born,* 1937). Screenwriter
 (*Woman of the Year,* 1942; *Forever Amber,* 1947; *M*A*S*H,* 1969).
Lasky, Jesse L. (d. 1958)
 Pioneer executive and producer. Vice-President in Charge of Production,
 Paramount Pictures, 1916–1932.
Le Baron, William (d. 1958)
 Vice-President in Charge of Production at RKO Studios, 1929–1931.
Lehman, Arthur (d. 1954)
 One of the original backers of Selznick International.
Lehman, Robert (d. 1969)
 Board member of Selznick International.

Lehmann, Rosamond
  English novelist (*Invitation to the Waltz*, 1932).
Leonard, Robert Z. (d. 1968)
  Director (*Strange Interlude*, 1932; *Dancing Lady*, 1933; *Pride and Prejudice*, 1940).
Le Roy, Mervyn
  Director (*Little Caesar*, 1930; *Waterloo Bridge*, 1940; *Quo Vadis*, 1951); producer (*The Wizard of Oz*, 1939).
Levathes, Peter G.
  Executive Vice-President in Charge of Production, Twentieth Century-Fox, 1961–1962.
Levec, M. C.
  Talent manager.
Lewin, Albert (d. 1968)
  MGM associate producer (*Mutiny on the Bounty*, 1936; *The Good Earth*, 1937). Later, director (*The Moon and Sixpence*, 1942).
Lewton, Val (d. 1951)
  Selznick International West Coast Story Editor and editorial assistant to Selznick. Later, producer (*Cat People*, 1942; *The Body Snatcher*, 1945).
Lichtman, Al (d. 1958)
  MGM executive and Loew's, Inc. Vice-President, 1935–1949; Twentieth Century-Fox Vice-President, 1949–1956.
Lighton, Louis D. (d. 1963)
  Associate producer, Paramount, 1928–1935; producer, Metro-Goldwyn-Mayer, 1936–1940, and Twentieth Century-Fox, 1944–1955.
Lindstrom, Petter (Peter)
  Swedish physician; first husband (1937–1950) of Ingrid Bergman.
Loew, Arthur M.
  First Vice-President of Loew's, Inc. (son of the founder, Marcus Loew).
Logan, Joshua
  Dialogue director on *The Garden of Allah*, 1936. Later, a playwright and stage director (*Mister Roberts*, 1948; *South Pacific*, 1949), also film director (*Picnic*, 1956; *Paint Your Wagon*, 1969).
Lombard, Carole (d. 1942)
  Actress and third wife (1939–1942) of Clark Gable.
Lubitsch, Ernst (d. 1947)
  Producer and director (*The Marriage Circle*, 1924; *The Love Parade*, 1929; *Ninotchka*, 1939).
Luce, Clare Boothe
  Playwright (*The Women*, 1936; *Kiss the Boys Goodbye*, 1938); Congresswoman from Connecticut, 1942–1946; U.S. Ambassador to Italy, 1953–1957.
Luce, Henry R. (d. 1967)
  Founder and Editor of *Time, Life,* and *Fortune* magazines.
Macconnell, Franclien
  Selznick International Assistant Story Editor in the late 1930s.
MacDonald, Philip
  Scottish novelist (*The Rasp*, 1924; *Warrant for X*, 1938; *The List of Adrian Messenger,* 1959) and screenwriter (*The Lost Patrol*, 1934; *Rebecca*, 1940; *Sahara*, 1943).

Macgowan, Kenneth (d. 1963)
  Associate producer at RKO Radio (*Little Women*, 1933) and Twentieth Century-Fox (*Stanley and Livingstone*, 1939); later, Chairman of the Department of Theatre Arts, U.C.L.A., 1946–1958.

MacNamara, Paul
  Selznick's Director of Advertising and Publicity, 1945–1949.

Mahin, John Lee
  Screenwriter (*Red Dust*, 1932; *Captains Courageous*, 1937; *Dr. Jekyll and Mr. Hyde*, 1941; *Heaven Knows, Mr. Allison*, 1957).

Mamoulian, Rouben
  Director (*Love Me Tonight*, 1932; *Queen Christina*, 1933; *Becky Sharp*, 1935; *Blood and Sand*, 1941).

Mankiewicz, Joseph L.
  Screenwriter (*Skippy*, 1931; *Manhattan Medodrama*, 1934); later producer and writer-director (*A Letter to Three Wives*, 1949; *All About Eve*, 1950; *Cleopatra*, 1963).

Mannix, Edgar J. (d. 1963)
  MGM Vice-President; later, General Manager of MGM Studios.

Marsh, Mrs. John R. (*see* Margaret Mitchell)

Marx, Samuel
  Screenwriter and MGM Story Editor.

Masters, George
  Hair stylist.

Mayer, Edith
  Older daughter of Louis B. Mayer and wife of William Goetz.

Mayer, Irene (*see* Irene Mayer Selznick)

Mayer, Louis B. (d. 1957)
  Vice-President in Charge of Production, Metro-Goldwyn-Mayer, 1924–1951.

McCarey, Leo (d. 1969)
  Director (*Duck Soup*, 1933; *The Awful Truth*, 1937; *Going My Way*, 1944).

Meloney, Mrs. William Brown (*see* Rose Franken)

Menzies, William Cameron (d. 1957)
  Production designer and art director (*The Thief of Bagdad*, 1924; *The Beloved Rogue*, 1927; *The Adventures of Tom Sawyer*, 1938; *Gone With the Wind*, 1939; *Around the World in 80 Days*, 1956) and occasional director (*Chandu the Magician*, 1932; *Things to Come*, 1936).

Milestone, Lewis
  Director (*All Quiet on the Western Front*, 1930; *The Front Page*, 1931; *A Walk in the Sun*, 1946).

Mitchell, Margaret (Mrs. John R. Marsh) (d. 1949)
  Author of the novel *Gone With the Wind* (1936), her only book.

Moffat, Ivan
  Screenwriter (*Giant*, 1956; *Bhowani Junction*, 1956; *Tender Is the Night*, 1962).

Molander, Gustaf
  Swedish director and cowriter of the first *Intermezzo* (1936).

Morris, Oswald
  British director of photography (*Moulin Rouge*, 1952; *Beat the Devil*, 1954; *A Farewell to Arms*, 1957; *Lolita*, 1962; *Oliver!*, 1968).

Morrison, Charles (d. 1957)
Restaurateur; employed by Selznick as a talent scout.
Moskowitz, Charles C.
Vice-President of Loew's, Inc., 1942–1957.
Murnau, F. W. (d. 1931)
German director (*The Last Laugh*, 1924; *Sunrise*, 1927; *Tabu*, 1931).
Myers, Zion (d. 1948)
Director, producer, writer.
Nathan, Robert
Novelist (*One More Spring*, 1933; *Portrait of Jennie*, 1940; *A Star in the Wind*, 1962).
Nelson, Argyle (d. 1970)
Selznick's Production Manager and Studio Manager during the mid-1940s.
Neuberger, Elsa
Selznick's Assistant Eastern Story Editor, 1935–1939; Eastern Story Editor, 1939–1949.
Newcom, James E.
Film editor (*Nothing Sacred*, 1937; *Made for Each Other*, 1939; *Gone With the Wind*, 1939; *A Farewell to Arms*, 1957).
Newman, Alfred (d. 1970)
Composer and conductor (*Street Scene*, 1931; *The Prisoner of Zenda*, 1937; *The Song of Bernadette*, 1943; *Love Is a Many-Splendored Thing*, 1955; *Airport*, 1970).
Nichols, Dudley (d. 1960)
Screenwriter (*The Informer*, 1935; *For Whom the Bell Tolls*, 1943).
O'Brien, Willis (d. 1962)
Special-effects creator and technician (*The Lost World*, 1925; *King Kong*, 1933; *The Last Days of Pompeii*, 1935).
Osborn, Paul
Playwright (*On Borrowed Time*, 1938) and screenwriter (*The Young in Heart*, 1938; *Portrait of Jennie*, 1948).
O'Shea, Daniel T.
Resident Counsel, RKO Studio, Hollywood, 1932–1936; Secretary of Selznick International Corporation, 1936–1939; Vice-President, Selznick International, 1939–1941; Executive Vice-President and General Manager, David O. Selznick Productions, Inc., 1941–1949; President of Vanguard Films, 1942–1949.
Paley, William S.
President of the Columbia Broadcasting System, 1928–1946; Chairman of the Board, CBS, 1946–date.
Parker, Dorothy (d. 1967)
Poet, short-story writer, and screenwriter (*A Star Is Born*, 1937; *Smash-Up —The Story of a Woman*, 1947).
Payson, Mrs. Charles S.
One of the original backers of Selznick International and sister of John Hay Whitney.
Pereira, William L.
Production designer (*Since You Went Away*, 1944), producer (*From This Day Forward*, 1946), and architect.

Perlberg, William (d. 1968)
Producer (*Golden Boy*, 1938; *The Song of Bernadette*, 1943; *The Country Girl*, 1954).

Plunkett, Walter
Costume designer (*Little Women*, 1933; *Gone With the Wind*, 1939).

Ponti, Carlo
Italian producer (*War and Peace*, 1956).

Potter, H. C.
Director (*The Story of Vernon and Irene Castle*, 1939; *Mr. Blandings Builds His Dream House*, 1948).

Powell, Michael
British writer, producer, director (*Black Narcissus*, 1946; *The Red Shoes*, 1948; *Gone to Earth* [*The Wild Heart*], 1952).

Powers, Patrick A. ("Pat") (d. 1948)
Pioneer motion-picture executive.

Preminger, Otto
Director, producer (*Laura*, 1944; *The Moon Is Blue*, 1953; *Anatomy of a Murder*, 1959).

Pressburger, Emeric
British writer, producer, director (*Black Narcissus*, 1946; *The Red Shoes*, 1948; *Gone to Earth* [*The Wild Heart*], 1952).

Price, Will (d. 1962)
Southern dialect coach on *Gone With the Wind*.

Provost, Heinz
Swedish composer of the score for the first *Intermezzo* (1936).

Rabwin, Marcella
Selznick's executive secretary during the 1930s; then Executive Assistant to Selznick, 1939–1940.

Ramsaye, Terry (d. 1954)
Author of *A Million and One Nights* (1926) and editor of *Motion Picture Herald*, 1931–1949.

Rapf, Harry (d. 1949)
MGM associate producer, then producer (*The Champ*, 1931; *Tugboat Annie*, 1933; *Stablemates*, 1938).

Rathvon, N. Peter
President of RKO Radio Pictures, 1942–1948.

Ratoff, Gregory (d. 1961)
Actor (*What Price Hollywood?*, 1932; *All About Eve*, 1950), director (*Intermezzo*, 1939; *The Corsican Brothers*, 1941), and screenwriter (*You Can't Have Everything*, 1937).

Reed, Carol
English director (*Odd Man Out*, 1947; *The Third Man*, 1949; *The Outcast of the Islands*, 1952; *Oliver!*, 1968).

Reissar, Jenia
Selznick's London Representative in the late 1930s, during the 1940s, and into the 1950s.

Rennahan, Ray
Technicolor cinematographer (*Becky Sharp*, 1935; *Gone With the Wind*, 1939; *For Whom the Bell Tolls*, 1943; *Duel in the Sun*, 1946).

Riesenfeld, Hugo (d. 1936)
  Composer and conductor (*Beau Geste*, 1926; *Tabu*, 1931).
Roberts, Oren W.
  Head of Paramount's Special-Effects Department.
Rodgers, William F.
  General Sales Manager, Loew's, Inc., 1936–1951.
Roemheld, Heinz
  Composer and conductor (*Yankee Doodle Dandy*, 1942; *Ruby Gentry*, 1953).
Rogers, Hazel
  Hairdresser (*Gone With the Wind*, 1939).
Rosenblatt, Sol A.
  Attorney; appointed (1933) Division Administrator under NRA, in Charge of Codes for the Motion Picture.
Ross, Robert
  Selznick's Eastern Production Representative in the late 1940s.
Rossellini, Roberto
  Italian director (*Open City*, 1945; *Paisan*, 1946; *Stromboli*, 1949; *General Della Rovere*, 1959), and second husband (1950–1957) of Ingrid Bergman.
Rosson, Harold
  Director of photography (*The Garden of Allah*, 1936; *The Wizard of Oz*, 1939; *Duel in the Sun*, 1946).
Rothafel, Samuel L. ("Roxy") (d. 1936)
  Managing director of various showcase theaters.
Rozsa, Miklos
  Composer and conductor (*The Thief of Bagdad*, 1940; *Spellbound*, 1945; *Ben-Hur*, 1959).
Rubin, J. Robert (d. 1958)
  Vice-President and Secretary, MGM, and a Director of Loew's, Inc.
St. Johns, Adela Rogers
  Journalist, novelist (*A Free Soul*, 1924), autobiographer (*The Honeycomb*, 1969), and screenwriter (*What Price Hollywood?*, 1932).
Sandrich, Mark (d. 1945)
  Director (*Melody Cruise*, 1933; *The Gay Divorcee*, 1934; *Holiday Inn*, 1942).
Sarnoff, David (d. 1971)
  President of Radio Corporation of America and Chairman of the Board of Radio-Keith-Orpheum Corporation, 1930–1947; Chairman of the Board of RCA., 1947–1971.
Saroyan, William
  Playwright (*The Time of Your Life*, 1940; *Hello, Out There*, 1942) and novelist (*The Human Comedy*, 1942).
Scanlon, Ernest L.
  Treasurer, Selznick International Pictures, Inc., 1936–1942; Executive Vice-President and Treasurer, Selznick's Vanguard Films, Inc., 1942–1949; Vice-President, Selznick Releasing Organization, 1945–1949.
Schaefer, George J.
  Vice-President and General Manager in Charge of Sales for United Artists, 1936–1938.

Schary, Dore
  Screenwriter (*Boys Town*, 1938), playwright (*Sunrise at Campobello*, 1958), producer (*I'll Be Seeing You*, 1944; *The Spiral Staircase*, 1946; *The Farmer's Daughter*, 1947); Vice-President in Charge of Production at RKO, 1947–1948, and at MGM, 1948–1956; later, independent writer-producer.
Schenck, Joseph M. (d. 1961)
  President of United Artists, 1927–1935; Chairman of the Board, Twentieth Century-Fox, 1935–1941. Brother of Nicholas M. Schenck.
Schenck, Nicholas M. (d. 1969)
  President of Loew's, Inc. and Metro-Goldwyn-Mayer, 1927–1955. Brother of Joseph M. Schenck.
Schnitzer, Joseph I. (d. 1944)
  President of RKO Radio Pictures, 1929–1932.
Schoedsack, Ernest B.
  Director and cinematographer (*Chang*, 1927; *The Four Feathers*, 1929; *King Kong*, 1933).
Schulberg, B. P. (d. 1957)
  General Manager of Paramount's West Coast Production, 1925–1932; later, an independent producer.
Schulberg, Budd
  Novelist (*What Makes Sammy Run?*, 1941; *The Disenchanted*, 1950) and screenwriter (*On the Waterfront*, 1954). Worked as a junior writer on Selznick's *A Star Is Born*, 1937. Son of B. P. Schulberg.
Schuster, M. Lincoln
  Publisher; cofounder (1924) of Simon and Schuster.
Selznick, Daniel Mayer
  Younger son of David O. Selznick and Irene Mayer Selznick. Motion-picture production executive.
Selznick, Florence (d. 1959)
  Mother of David; wife of Lewis J. Selznick.
Selznick, Irene Mayer
  Younger daughter of Louis B. Mayer and first wife (1930–1948) of David O. Selznick. Subsequently a New York theatrical producer (*A Streetcar Named Desire*, 1947; *Bell, Book and Candle*, 1949; *The Chalk Garden*, 1955).
Selznick, Lewis J. (d. 1933)
  Pioneer film producer and father of David O. Selznick. He appointed himself General Manager of Universal Pictures in 1912; coorganized World Films, 1915; founded Lewis J. Selznick Enterprises, Inc., 1916–1923.
Selznick, Lewis Jeffrey
  Older son of David O. Selznick and Irene Mayer Selznick. Production associate on *A Farewell to Arms*, 1957; subsequently, a film producer in Europe.
Selznick, Mary Jennifer
  Daughter of David O. Selznick and Jennifer Jones.
Selznick, Myron (d. 1944)
  David's older brother, who eventually headed the leading talent agency in Hollywood (1929–1944). Previously was General Manager in Charge of Production for Lewis J. Selznick Films in the early 1920s.

Sennett, Mack (d. 1960)
  Pioneer comedy producer, director, and actor.
Serlin, Oscar (d. 1971)
  Theatrical producer *(Life with Father)*; talent scout and assistant to Selznick, 1938–1939.
Shamroy, Leon
  Director of photography *(The Young in Heart*, 1938; *The King and I*, 1956; *Tender Is the Night*, 1962).
Shapiro, Victor M. (d. 1967)
  Director of Advertising and Publicity for Selznick International during a short period in 1939.
Shearer, Norma
  Actress and wife of Irving Thalberg.
Sheldon, E. Lloyd
  Paramount Production Supervisor, 1926–1936.
Sherwood, Robert E. (d. 1955)
  Playwright (*Waterloo Bridge*, 1930; *The Petrified Forest*, 1935; *Abe Lincoln in Illinois*, 1938), screenwriter (*Rebecca*, 1940; *The Best Years of Our Lives*, 1946), and biographer (*Roosevelt and Hopkins*, 1948).
Siegel, M. J. (d. 1948)
  President of Republic Pictures, 1937–1944.
Siff, Philip
  Assistant to Selznick, 1931–1934.
Silverstone, Murray (d. 1969)
  United Artists executive.
Skouras, Charles P. (d. 1954)
  President of National Theatres Corporation and Fox West Coast Theatres.
Skouras, Spyros (d. 1971)
  Fox West Coast theater executive; later, President of Twentieth Century-Fox, 1942–1962.
Stacey, Eric (d. 1969)
  Assistant director of several Selznick International films, 1936–1939.
Stahl, John M. (d. 1950)
  Director (*Imitation of Life*, 1934; *The Keys of the Kingdom*, 1944).
Stanhope, Paul (d. 1960)
  Make-up artist.
Steele, Joseph Henry
  Selznick Director of Advertising and Publicity, 1943.
Steiner, Max (d. 1971)
  Composer and conductor (*Symphony of Six Million*, 1932; *King Kong*, 1933; *The Informer*, 1935; *Little Lord Fauntleroy, The Garden of Allah*, 1936; *A Star Is Born*, 1937; *Gone With the Wind*, 1939; *Casablanca*, 1943; *Since You Went Away*, 1944; *The Caine Mutiny*, 1954).
Sternberg, Josef von (d. 1969)
  Director (*Docks of New York*, 1928; *The Blue Angel*, 1930; *An American Tragedy*, 1931; *Shanghai Express*, 1932). Special visual consultant, *Duel in the Sun*, 1946.

Stevens, Gosta
Swedish cowriter of the original Swedish version of *Intermezzo* (1936).
Stevenson, Robert
Director (*Tom Brown's School Days*, 1940; *Jane Eyre*, 1944; *Mary Poppins*, 1964).
Stewart, James G.
Sound engineer; Selznick's Technical Supervisor, 1945–1948.
Stone, Louis
Assistant to Selznick in New York during the late 1940s and early 1950s.
Stothart, Herbert (d. 1949)
MGM Musical Director; composer and conductor (*David Copperfield, Anna Karenina*, 1935; *The Wizard of Oz*, 1939; *Northwest Passage*, 1940; *National Velvet*, 1945).
Stradling, Harry (d. 1970)
Director of photography (*Pygmalion*, 1938; *The Picture of Dorian Gray*, 1945; *My Fair Lady*, 1964). The original cameraman on *Intermezzo*, 1939.
Strickling, Howard
Director of Publicity for MGM on the West Coast, 1926–1969.
Stroheim, Erich von (d. 1957)
Director (*Greed*, 1924; *The Merry Widow*, 1925) and actor (*Grand Illusion*, 1937; *Sunset Boulevard*, 1950).
Stromberg, Hunt (d. 1968)
MGM producer (*White Shadows in the South Seas*, 1928; *Red Dust*, 1932; *The Thin Man*, 1934; *The Great Ziegfeld*, 1936; *Northwest Passage*, 1940).
Sullivan, Ed
Hollywood columnist for the *New York Daily News;* later, TV master of ceremonies.
Sutherland, A. Edward
Director (*The Dance of Life*, 1929).
Swerling, Jo
Screenwriter (*Made for Each Other*, 1939; *The Pride of the Yankees*, 1942; *Guys and Dolls*, 1955). Worked on *Gone With the Wind*, 1939.
Taurog, Norman
Director (*Skippy*, 1931; *The Adventures of Tom Sawyer*, 1938; *Boys Town*, 1938).
Thalberg, Irving (d. 1936)
MGM Production Manager, 1924–1933, and later Vice-President and Executive Producer, 1933–1936 (*The Big Parade*, 1925; *Ben-Hur*, 1925; *Trader Horn*, 1931; *Grand Hotel*, 1932; *Mutiny on the Bounty*, 1935; *A Night at the Opera*, 1935; *Camille*, 1936).
Thau, Benjamin
Assistant to Louis B. Mayer; later, MGM Executive Producer.
Tiomkin, Dimitri
Composer and conductor (*Lost Horizon*, 1937; *Duel in the Sun*, 1946; *Portrait of Jennie*, 1949; *High Noon*, 1952).
Toland, Gregg (d. 1948)
Director of photography (*Dead End*, 1937; *Intermezzo, Wuthering Heights*, 1939; *The Grapes of Wrath*, 1940; *Citizen Kane*, 1941; *The Best Years of Our Lives*, 1946).

Van Dine, S. S. (Willard Huntington Wright) (d. 1939)
Author of the Philo Vance mystery novels (*The Bishop Murder Case,* 1929).

Van Druten, John (d. 1957)
Playwright (*The Voice of the Turtle,* 1944; *I Remember Mama,* 1945; *Bell, Book and Candle,* 1950) and screenwriter (*Johnny Come Lately,* 1943; *Gaslight,* 1944). Worked briefly on *Gone With the Wind,* 1939.

Van Dyke, W. S., II (d. 1944)
Director (*White Shadows in the South Seas,* 1928; *Trader Horn,* 1930; *Manhattan Melodrama,* 1934; *San Francisco,* 1936).

Van Schmus, W. G.
President and Managing Director of Radio City Music Hall.

Vidor, Charles (d. 1959)
Director (*Cover Girl,* 1944; *Gilda,* 1946; *Hans Christian Andersen,* 1952; *A Farewell to Arms,* 1957).

Vidor, King
Director (*The Big Parade,* 1926; *The Crowd,* 1928; *Bird of Paradise,* 1932; *The Citadel,* 1938; *Northwest Passage,* 1940; *Duel in the Sun,* 1946; *Ruby Gentry,* 1953; *War and Peace,* 1956).

Viertel, Peter
Screenwriter (*We Were Strangers,* 1949; *The Sun Also Rises,* 1957) and novelist (*White Hunter, Black Heart,* 1953). Son of Salka Viertel.

Viertel, Salka
Screenwriter (*The Painted Veil,* 1934; *Anna Karenina,* 1935). Mother of Peter Viertel.

Vogel, Joseph (d. 1969)
Loew's, Inc. executive; President of MGM, 1956–1963.

Volck, George
Agent.

Wald, Jerry (d. 1962)
Producer (*Mildred Pierce,* 1945; *Johnny Belinda,* 1948; *Peyton Place,* 1957). Previously a screenwriter.

Walker, Robert (d. 1951)
Actor and first husband of Jennifer Jones.

Wallace, Edgar (d. 1932)
English author (*The Four Just Men,* 1905; *Sanders of the River,* 1930).

Wallace, Richard (d. 1951)
Director (*The Shopworn Angel,* 1929; *The Young in Heart,* 1938).

Wallis, Hal B.
Associate Executive in Charge of Production, Warner Bros.-First National (1933–1944); later, independent producer (*Love Letters,* 1945; *The Rose Tattoo,* 1955; *Anne of the Thousand Days,* 1969).

Walpole, Hugh (d. 1941)
English author (*Mr. Perrin and Mr. Traill,* 1911; *Rogue Herries,* 1930) and screenwriter (*David Copperfield,* 1935; *Little Lord Fauntleroy,* 1936).

Wanger, Walter (d. 1968)
Paramount General Manager of Production in the late 1920s and early 1930s; MGM producer (*Queen Christina,* 1933); later, independent producer (*Stagecoach,* 1939; *Joan of Arc,* 1948).

Warner, Harry M. (d. 1958)
   President of Warner Bros. Pictures, 1923–1958.
Warner, Jack L.
   Vice-President in Charge of Production, Warner Bros. Studios, 1923–1967.
Waxman, Franz (d. 1967)
   Composer and conductor (*The Young in Heart*, 1938; *Rebecca*, 1940; *The Paradine Case*, 1947; *The Nun's Story*, 1959).
Webster, Paul Francis
   Lyricist ("The Loveliest Night of the Year," 1951; "Love Is a Many-Splendored Thing," 1955; "Tender Is the Night," 1962).
Weingarten, Lawrence
   MGM associate producer and later producer (*Libeled Lady*, 1936; *Pat and Mike*, 1952).
Weinstein, Henry T.
   Theatrical producer and television producer (*The Play of the Week*, 1959); film producer (*Tender Is the Night*, 1962; *Joy in the Morning*, 1965; *The Madwoman of Chaillot*, 1969).
Welles, Orson
   Producer, director, actor, writer (*Citizen Kane*, 1941); producer, director, writer (*The Magnificent Ambersons*, 1942); actor (*Jane Eyre*, 1944; *The Third Man*, 1950); also theatrical and radio producer, director, actor, writer.
Wellman, William A.
   Director (*Wings*, 1927; *The Public Enemy*, 1931; *A Star Is Born*, 1937; *Nothing Sacred*, 1938; *The Ox-Bow Incident*, 1943; *The High and the Mighty*, 1954).
Werfel, Franz (d. 1945)
   Austrian author of the novel *The Song of Bernadette* (1941).
Westmore, Monty
   Make-up artist (*Intermezzo; Gone With the Wind*, 1939).
Wharton, John
   Treasurer of Selznick International, 1935–1940, and Comptroller of Pioneer Pictures, 1933–1938.
Wheeler, Lyle
   Art director for Selznick International (*The Garden of Allah*, 1936; *Gone With the Wind*, 1939; *Rebecca*, 1940); in 1944 appointed Supervising Art Director at Twentieth Century-Fox.
Whitney, C. V. ("Sonny")
   Board member of Selznick International and cousin of John Hay Whitney.
Whitney, John Hay ("Jock")
   Chairman of the Board, Selznick International Pictures, and President of Pioneer Pictures. United States Ambassador to Great Britain, 1956–1961; Publisher, President, and Editor-in-Chief of the *New York Herald Tribune*, 1957–1966; Chairman, international *Herald-Tribune*.
Wilder, Billy
   Director and writer (*Double Indemnity*, 1944; *The Lost Weekend*, 1945; *Sunset Boulevard*, 1950; *Some Like It Hot*, 1959).
Wilder, Margaret Buell
   Author of the book *Since You Went Away* and screenwriter (*A Stolen Life*, 1945).

Wilkerson, William R. ("Billy") (d. 1962)
    Editor and Publisher of the *Hollywood Reporter*.
Willson, Henry
    Head of Selznick's Talent Department and assistant to President Daniel T.
    O'Shea.
Wood, Sam (d. 1949)
    Director (*A Night at the Opera*, 1935; *Goodbye Mr. Chips*, 1939; *Kings Row*,
    1942; *For Whom the Bell Tolls*, 1943). Worked on *Gone With the Wind*, 1939.
Wright, Geraldine
    Script clerk.
Wright, Willard Huntington (*see* S. S. Van Dine)
Wright, William H.
    Selznick International Production Associate in the late 1930s. Previously an
    assistant to Selznick at Paramount and MGM.
Wurtzel, Sol M. (d. 1958)
    Twentieth Century-Fox Executive Producer.
Wyler, William
    Director (*Counsellor at Law*, 1933; *Dodsworth*, 1936; *Wuthering Heights*,
    1939; *The Little Foxes*, 1941; *The Best Years of Our Lives*, 1946; *Carrie*, 1952;
    Ben-Hur, 1959).
Young, Felix
    Paramount production executive in the early 1930s.
Young, Victor (d. 1956)
    Composer and conductor (*For Whom the Bell Tolls*, 1943; *Shane*, 1953;
    Around the World in 80 Days, 1956).
Zanuck, Darryl F.
    Head of Production (in association with Jack L. Warner) at Warner Bros.-
    First National, 1929–1933; Vice-President in Charge of Production, Twen-
    tieth Century-Fox, 1935–1956; independent producer, 1956–1962; President,
    Twentieth Century-Fox, 1962–1971.
Zeidman, Bennie F. (d. 1970)
    Paramount Production Supervisor in the late 1920s.
Zinnemann, Fred
    Director (*From Here to Eternity*, 1953; *The Nun's Story*, 1959; *A Man for All
    Seasons*, 1965).
Zukor, Adolph
    Motion-picture pioneer; President, 1916–1935, and later Chairman of the
    Board, of Paramount Pictures, 1935–date.

The Films of David O. Selznick

COMPILED BY RUDY BEHLMER

The listing is in chronological order, with the year shown representing the United States release date. The production company and distributor precede the credited director's name and featured players.

The Paramount films were produced over a period of time when Selznick was functioning in different capacities at the studio. The list was determined by examining credits (official and otherwise), referring to correspondence written at the time, and noting later references made by Selznick to this compiler and others regarding the films on which he was either "supervisor," "producer," "associate producer," "executive producer," or a substantial contributor.

The RKO list does not include all the films the studio released during that period, but consists of productions with which Selznick was heavily involved as Vice-President in Charge of Production.

The MGM, Selznick International, and David O. Selznick Productions were, of course, personally produced by Selznick, unless otherwise noted.

SHORT SUBJECTS

1. *Will He Conquer Dempsey?* (1923), Selznick Distributing Corporation. Silent. No director credit. Luis Angel Firpo.
2. *Rudolph Valentino and His 88 American Beauties* (1923) Silent. No director credit. Rudolph Valentino.
3. *Reward Unlimited* (1944), U. S. Public Health Service. Sound. No director credit. Dorothy McGuire, Aline McMahon, and James Brown.

FEATURE PRODUCTIONS

1. *Roulette* (1924), Aetna-Selznick Distributing Corporation. Directed by S. E. V. Taylor. Silent. Montagu Love, Norman Trevor, Maurice Costello, Edith Roberts.
2. *Spoilers of the West* (1927), MGM. Directed by W. S. Van Dyke II. Silent. Tim McCoy, Marjorie Daw, William Fairbanks, Chief Big Tree.
3. *Wyoming* (1928), MGM. Directed by W. S. Van Dyke II. Silent. Tim McCoy, Dorothy Sebastian, Charles Bell, William Fairbanks.

PARAMOUNT

4. *Forgotten Faces* (1928), Paramount. Directed by Victor Schertzinger. Silent. Clive Brook, Mary Brian, William Powell, Olga Baclanova.
5. *Chinatown Nights* (1929), Paramount. Directed by William A. Wellman. Sixty-five per cent dialogue. Wallace Beery, Florence Vidor, Warner Oland, Jack Oakie.
6. *The Man I Love* (1929), Paramount. Directed by William A. Wellman. Sound. Richard Arlen, Mary Brian, Olga Baclanova, Jack Oakie.
7. *The Four Feathers* (1929), Paramount. Directed by Merian C. Cooper, Ernest B. Schoedsack, and Lothar Mendes. Silent, with synchronized music and sound effects. Richard Arlen, Fay Wray, Clive Brook, William Powell.

All subsequent productions are sound films.

8. *The Dance of Life* (1929), Paramount. Directed by John Cromwell and A. Edward Sutherland. Two-color Technicolor sequences. Hal Skelly, Nancy Carroll, Dorothy Revier, Ralph Theodore.

9. *Fast Company* (1929), Paramount. Directed by A. Edward Sutherland. Evelyn Brent, Jack Oakie, Richard "Skeets" Gallagher, Sam Hardy.

10. *Street of Chance* (1930), Paramount. Directed by John Cromwell. William Powell, Jean Arthur, Kay Francis, Regis Toomey.

11. *Sarah and Son* (1930), Paramount. Directed by Dorothy Arzner. Ruth Chatterton, Fredric March, Fuller Melish, Jr., Gilbert Emery.

12. *Honey* (1930), Paramount. Directed by Wesley Ruggles. Nancy Carroll, Stanley Smith, "Skeets" Gallagher, Lillian Roth.

13. *The Texan* (1930), Paramount. Directed by John Cromwell. Gary Cooper, Fay Wray, Emma Dunn, Oscar Apfel.

14. *For the Defense* (1930), Paramount. Directed by John Cromwell. William Powell, Kay Francis, Scott Kolk, William B. Davidson.

15. *Manslaughter* (1930), Paramount. Directed by George Abbott. Claudette Colbert, Fredric March, Emma Dunn, Natalie Moorhead.

RKO

16. *The Lost Squadron* (1932), RKO Radio. Directed by George Archainbaud. Richard Dix, Mary Astor, Erich von Stroheim, Joel McCrea.

17. *Symphony of Six Million* (1932). RKO Radio. Directed by Gregory La Cava. Ricardo Cortez, Irene Dunne, Anna Appell, Gregory Ratoff.

18. *State's Attorney* (1932), RKO Radio. Directed by George Archainbaud. John Barrymore, Helen Twelvetrees, Jill Esmond, William Boyd.

19. *Westward Passage* (1932), RKO Radio. Directed by Robert Milton. Ann Harding, Laurence Olivier, Irving Pichel, ZaSu Pitts.

20. *What Price Hollywood?* (1932), RKO Radio. Directed by George Cukor. Constance Bennett, Lowell Sherman, Neil Hamilton, Gregory Ratoff.

21. *Roar of the Dragon* (1932). RKO Radio. Directed by Wesley Ruggles. Richard Dix, Gwili Andre, Edward Everett Horton, Arline Judge.

22. *Bird of Paradise* (1932). RKO Radio. Directed by King Vidor. Dolores Del Rio, Joel McCrea, John Halliday, Creighton Chaney (Lon Chaney, Jr.).

23. *The Age of Consent* (1932), RKO Radio. Directed by Gregory La Cava. Dorothy Wilson, Richard Cromwell, Eric Linden, Arlene Judge.

24. *A Bill of Divorcement* (1932), RKO Radio. Directed by George Cukor. John Barrymore, Katharine Hepburn, Billie Burke, David Manners.

25. *The Conquerors* (1932), RKO Radio. Directed by William A. Wellman. Richard Dix, Ann Harding, Edna May Oliver, Guy Kibbee.

26. *Rockabye* (1932), RKO Radio. Directed by George Cukor. Constance Bennett, Joel McCrea, Paul Lukas, Walter Pidgeon.

27. *The Animal Kingdom* (1932), RKO Radio. Directed by Edward H. Griffith. Ann Harding, Leslie Howard, Myrna Loy, Neil Hamilton.

28. *The Half-Naked Truth* (1932), RKO Radio. Directed by Gregory La Cava. Lupe Velez, Lee Tracy, Eugene Pallette, Frank Morgan.

29. *Topaze* (1933), RKO Radio. Directed by Harry D'Arrast. John Barrymore, Myrna Loy, Albert Conti, Luis Alberni.

30. *The Great Jasper* (1933). Directed by J. Walter Ruben. Richard Dix, Florence Eldridge, Wera Engels, Edna May Oliver.

31. *Our Betters* (1933), RKO Radio. Directed by George Cukor. Constance Bennett, Gilbert Roland, Charles Starrett, Anita Louise.

32. *Christopher Strong* (1933). Directed by Dorothy Arzner. Katharine Hepburn, Colin Clive, Billie Burke, Helen Chandler.

33. *Sweepings* (1933), RKO Radio. Directed by John Cromwell. Lionel Barrymore, Alan Dinehart, Eric Linden, William Gargan.

34. *The Monkey's Paw* (1933). RKO Radio. Directed by Wesley Ruggles. C. Aubrey Smith, Ivan Simpson, Louise Carter, Bramwell Fletcher.

MGM

35. *Dinner at Eight* (1933), MGM. Directed by George Cukor. Marie Dressler, John Barrymore, Wallace Beery, Jean Harlow, Lionel Barrymore, Billie Burke, Edmund Lowe.

36. *Night Flight* (1933), MGM. Directed by Clarence Brown. John Barrymore, Lionel Barrymore, Helen Hayes, Clark Gable.

37. *Meet the Baron* (1933), MGM. Directed by Walter Lang. Jack Pearl, Jimmy Durante, ZaSu Pitts, Ted Healy and The Three Stooges.

38. *Dancing Lady* (1933), MGM. Directed by Robert Z. Leonard. Joan Crawford, Clark Gable, Franchot Tone, Winnie Lightner.

39. *Viva Villa!* (1934), MGM. Directed by Jack Conway. Wallace Beery, Leo Carrillo, Fay Wray, Stuart Erwin.

40. *Manhattan Melodrama* (1934), MGM. Directed by W. S. Van Dyke II. Clark Gable, William Powell, Myrna Loy, Mickey Rooney.

41. *David Copperfield* (1935), MGM. Directed by George Cukor. W. C. Fields, Freddie Bartholomew, Frank Lawton, Basil Rathbone.

42. *Vanessa: Her Love Story* (1935), MGM. Directed by William K. Howard. Helen Hayes, Robert Montgomery, Otto Kruger, May Robson.

43. *Reckless* (1935), MGM. Directed by Victor Fleming. Jean Harlow, William Powell, Franchot Tone, May Robson.

44. *Anna Karenina* (1935), MGM. Directed by Clarence Brown. Greta Garbo, Fredric March, Basil Rathbone, Freddie Bartholomew.

45. *A Tale of Two Cities* (1935), MGM. Directed by Jack Conway. Ronald Colman, Elizabeth Allan, Blanche Yurka, Basil Rathbone.

SELZNICK INTERNATIONAL

46. *Little Lord Fauntleroy* (1936), Selznick International–United Artists. Directed by John Cromwell. Freddie Bartholomew, Dolores Costello, C. Aubrey Smith, Guy Kibbee.

47. *The Garden of Allah* (1936), Selznick–UA. Directed by Richard Boleslawski. Technicolor. Marlene Dietrich, Charles Boyer, Basil Rathbone, C. Aubrey Smith.

48. *A Star Is Born* (1937), Selznick–UA. Directed by William A. Wellman. Technicolor. Janet Gaynor, Fredric March, Adolphe Menjou, May Robson.

49. *The Prisoner of Zenda* (1937), Selznick–UA. Directed by John Cromwell. Ronald Colman, Madeleine Carroll, Douglas Fairbanks, Jr., C. Aubrey Smith.

50. *Nothing Sacred* (1937), Selznick–UA. Directed by William A. Wellman. Technicolor. Carole Lombard, Fredric March, Charles Winninger, Walter Connolly.

51. *The Adventures of Tom Sawyer* (1938), Selznick–UA. Directed by Norman Taurog. Technicolor. Tommy Kelly, Ann Gillis, May Robson, Walter Brennan.

52. *The Young in Heart* (1938), Selznick–UA. Directed by Richard Wallace. Janet Gaynor, Douglas Fairbanks, Jr., Roland Young, Billie Burke.

53. *Made for Each Other* (1939), Selznick–UA. Directed by John Cromwell. Carole Lombard, James Stewart, Charles Coburn, Lucile Watson.

54. *Intermezzo: A Love Story* (1939), Selznick–UA. Directed by Gregory Ratoff. Leslie Howard, Ingrid Bergman, Edna Best, John Halliday.

55. *Gone With the Wind* (1939), Selznick–MGM. Directed by Victor Fleming. Technicolor. Clark Gable, Vivien Leigh, Leslie Howard, Olivia de Havilland.

56. *Rebecca* (1940), Selznick–UA. Directed by Alfred Hitchcock. Laurence Olivier, Joan Fontaine, Judith Anderson, George Sanders.

DAVID O. SELZNICK PRODUCTIONS, INC.

57. *Since You Went Away* (1944), Selznick–UA. Directed by John Cromwell. Claudette Colbert, Jennifer Jones, Joseph Cotten, Shirley Temple.

58. *I'll Be Seeing You* (1944), Selznick–UA. Directed by William Dieterle. Selznick was executive producer over producer Dore Schary. Ginger Rogers, Joseph Cotten, Shirley Temple, Spring Byington.

59. *Spellbound* (1945), Selznick–UA. Directed by Alfred Hitchcock. Ingrid Bergman, Gregory Peck, Leo G. Carroll, Rhonda Fleming.

60. *Duel in the Sun* (1946), Selznick Releasing Organization. Directed by King Vidor. Technicolor. Jennifer Jones, Gregory Peck, Joseph Cotten, Lionel Barrymore, Lillian Gish.
61. *The Paradine Case* (1948), SRO. Directed by Alfred Hitchcock. Gregory Peck, Charles Laughton, Ann Todd, Alida Valli, Louis Jourdan.
62. *Portrait of Jennie* (1948), SRO. Directed by William Dieterle. Jennifer Jones, Joseph Cotten, Ethel Barrymore, Cecil Kellaway.

COPRODUCTIONS, ETC.

63. *The Third Man* (1950), SRO. Directed by Carol Reed. Selznick cosponsored and cofinanced with Alexander Korda. Joseph Cotten, Orson Welles, Trevor Howard, Alida Valli.
64. *The Wild Heart* (1952), RKO Radio Pictures. Directed by Michael Powell and Emeric Pressburger. Released in Europe as *Gone to Earth*. Technicolor. A coproduction. Rouben Mamoulian reshot almost one third for U.S. release under Selznick's supervision. Jennifer Jones, David Farrar, Cyril Cusack, Esmond Knight.
65. *Indiscretion of an American Wife* (1954), Selznick–Columbia. Directed by Vittorio De Sica. Released in Europe as *Terminal Station*. Selznick cosponsored and coowned. Approximately one third cut for U.S. release by Selznick. Jennifer Jones, Montgomery Clift, Gino Cervi, Richard Beymer.
66. *A Farewell to Arms* (1957), Selznick–Twentieth Century-Fox. Directed by Charles Vidor. Color by De Luxe (Eastman). Jennifer Jones, Rock Hudson, Vittorio De Sica, Alberto Sordi.

TELEVISION PRODUCTION

Light's Diamond Jubilee (1954), Telecast on all networks. Various directors. Judith Anderson, Lauren Bacall, Walter Brennan, Joseph Cotten, Dorothy Dandridge, George Gobel, Helen Hayes, Thomas Mitchell, David Niven, May Robson, and others.

Index